Awaiting
the Fire

Donna Lea Simpson

BERKLEY SENSATION, NEW YORK

THE BERKLEY PUBLISHING GROUP
Published by the Penguin Group
Penguin Group (USA) Inc.
375 Hudson Street, New York, New York 10014, USA
Penguin Group (Canada), 90 Eglinton Avenue East, Suite 700, Toronto, Ontario M4P 2Y3, Canada
(a division of Pearson Penguin Canada Inc.)
Penguin Books Ltd., 80 Strand, London WC2R 0RL, England
Penguin Group Ireland, 25 St. Stephen's Green, Dublin 2, Ireland (a division of Penguin Books Ltd.)
Penguin Group (Australia), 250 Camberwell Road, Camberwell, Victoria 3124, Australia
(a division of Pearson Australia Group Pty. Ltd.)
Penguin Books India Pvt. Ltd., 11 Community Centre, Panchsheel Park, New Delhi—110 017, India
Penguin Group (NZ), 67 Apollo Drive, Mairangi Bay, Auckland 1311, New Zealand
(a division of Pearson New Zealand Ltd.)
Penguin Books (South Africa) (Pty.) Ltd., 24 Sturdee Avenue, Rosebank, Johannesburg 2196,
South Africa

Penguin Books Ltd., Registered Offices: 80 Strand, London WC2R 0RL, England

This is a work of fiction. Names, characters, places, and incidents either are the product of the author's imagination or are used fictitiously, and any resemblance to actual persons, living or dead, business establishments, events, or locales is entirely coincidental. The publisher does not have any control over and does not assume any responsibility for author or third-party websites or their content.

AWAITING THE FIRE

A Berkley Sensation Book / published by arrangement with the author

PRINTING HISTORY
Berkley Sensation mass-market edition / September 2007

Copyright © 2007 by Donna Simpson.
Cover art by Phil Heffernan.
Cover design by George Long.
Interior text design by Stacy Irwin.

ISBN: 978-0-425-21761-0

BERKLEY SENSATION®
Berkley Sensation Books are published by The Berkley Publishing Group,
a division of Penguin Group (USA) Inc.,
375 Hudson Street, New York, New York 10014.
BERKLEY SENSATION and the "B" design are trademarks belonging to Penguin Group (USA) Inc.

PRINTED IN THE UNITED STATES OF AMERICA

10 9 8 7 6 5 4 3 2 1

Chapter 1

London, 1795

"WES, I'M frightened."

Simeon St. Ange, the Earl of Wesmorlyn, waited for his valet to finish the last detail, the positioning of his jacket cuff to properly display the elegance of his pearl gray gloves, then turned to face his much younger half sister, Hannah, as his valet retreated. Her gentle voice, so quiet it was almost a whisper, had hardly echoed in the grand front hall of his London townhome. He moved to stand in front of her and gazed down at the pale oval face trustingly turned up to his. "Hannah, you have more courage than you know. Think of our family, stiffen your spine, and stand up straight."

She did as she was told, but the paleness of her face gave away her continuing terror.

"It is a ballroom, not a torture chamber," he chided.

"B-but there will be so many people, and they will all be looking at me."

"You must not be so morbidly vain. Some will look, but you will only suffer that for a moment, and then it will pass.

Once Countess Charlotte von Wolfram and her brother arrive, all eyes will be on them."

"That frightens me too," she said, staring up at him, her almond-shaped eyes wide with anxiety. "Aren't you the least bit anxious, Wes? Countess Charlotte is your future bride. What if you dislike her, or what if she is rude? What if . . . what if she doesn't like *me*?"

He smiled, finally understanding her fear. His own anxiety about meeting his German-born fiancée for the first time was well controlled and no one else would ever know his inner turmoil. The Wesmorlyn heir always married a lady from outside of England; he was following family tradition. Honor your father and your mother, the rules said, and he had always done so, even to following their last wishes by choosing a bride from another land. He would not allow a trembling uncertainty in his gut to undermine this first meeting. He framed Hannah's delicate face with both of his hands, noting that her usually flyaway hair was ruthlessly tamed into a perfectly modest hairstyle befitting her status as a young lady about to enter her first season the next spring. This ball to welcome his bride and her brother would be a modest practice for his sister, with the excuse that she was to meet her sister-in-law-to-be; perhaps in the spring she would not be as nervous and green as the other sixteen-year-old girls.

"Hannah," he said, patting her cheek. "You are a sweet angel from heaven. How could the countess not like you?"

"I've never had a sister," she said, brightening. "Perhaps she will like me a little, and we'll become friends."

"How could she help but love you?"

Hannah smiled, radiantly, her pale skin glowing like nacre. "Will Lyulph be there?" she said, casually, of their old family friend and neighbor from Cornwall.

"Of course," Wes said, frowning and noting that she turned away into the shadows as she spoke of him. "He is in London, as you too well know, and did hint for an invitation. How could I refuse?"

"I thought you might say no," Hannah said, softly, fiddling with her fan. "You are not so close to him now as you once were."

"Things are different in London, Hannah. In the country

our various stations in life do not matter so much, but in town the boundaries must be observed." He was silent for a moment, observing her, the peachy perfection of her skin, the exquisite flawlessness of the matched pearls around her slender neck. Coupled with her naïveté, her beauty and wealth could draw the wrong kind of attention from predatory males. But had he been unwise to keep her so cloistered from the outside world? Is that why she had such a fixation on Lyulph Randell? He had done what he thought right, and her mother had never objected. Perhaps he should have reversed things . . . introduced her more to the world and kept her from Lyulph Randell's company. If there was one man in the world she must not marry, it was him.

"I hope," he said, watching her open and shut her fan, "that you don't spend all of your time talking to Lyulph this evening. I would not have even invited him except that I give him no excuse for feeling slighted. But still, you must not be seen doing any more than briefly acknowledging his presence; you may be polite, say hello, and inquire after his well-being, but little else. This ball is for Countess Charlotte and her brother, Count Christoph. Please be polite to them both and do not hide away. I know it's difficult, but not much will be expected of you; it's your first appearance at a ball, after all, and you are just now out of full mourning for your poor mother, and so you should be a little reticent. Your modesty and shyness will be seen as becoming in a girl your age. But do not let the ease of Lyulph's familiarity lead you to spend an inordinate amount of time with him," he finished, shaking his finger at her.

"I will be correct, Wes, I promise," she said, her tone satisfactorily submissive. She folded the fan, prettily painted with biblical scenes, and held it still in her gloved hands.

"See that you are. As a St. Ange, much is expected of you. It is especially important to make a good impression on our cousin the marchioness, Lady Harroway, for if she likes you she will sponsor your coming out next spring." He stopped himself from fussing too much, afraid he would make her more nervous than she already was.

She stood away from him. "Am I presentable?"

"Turn," he said, and examined her as she slowly turned in

a complete circle. Her gown was gray and delicate, with little ornamentation, but had a tiny cape of gauzy silk falling from her shoulders to below her waist in an unusual style those females born to the St. Ange family had always affected. Her hands were gloved in gray silk that stretched up her slender white arms to above her elbows.

"Nothing is showing?" she asked.

"You look perfectly lovely," he said.

"I wish mama was here." She bit her lip, but tears welled in her eyes.

"I know," he said, and stepped over to her, taking her in his arms and hugging her, the briefest of gestures before turning away to accept his walking stick from the butler. "Your mother would be proud. She loved you very much. I'm sure she can see you tonight, Hannah."

As she turned away and applied a delicate scrap of lace to her welling eyes, he felt a pang of pity. Hannah's mother, his father's second wife, had outlived her husband by many years, but in the autumn of the previous year she had succumbed to a fever. It was then, forced to acknowledge mortality anew, that he accepted what he had known for some time. He must marry and start a family. He was twenty-nine, and life did not last forever. It was up to him to bring to earth the next Earl of Wesmorlyn.

When the Prince of Wales had condescended so far as to suggest he consider marrying a cousin of his new wife, Caroline, Wesmorlyn had cautiously agreed to hear more. Countess Charlotte von Wolfram, suggested to him as an appropriate bride, was a young lady of impeccable lineage and related by birth to many kings and princes. She was intelligent, could speak at least three languages, and had been under the tutelage of an Englishwoman to learn British ways and manners, for her family was looking for an English husband for her. That fact alone, that she had made a study of English ways, appealed to him; she seemed the ideal bride for a man like him, and so he had acquiesced.

He had eschewed the need for a likeness before the engagement. Beauty was not necessary nor even particularly wanted. Modesty, chastity, obedience, and good birth were all far more important, and attested to by the girl's uncle, Count

Nikolas von Wolfram. The betrothal, which was firm on his side but conditional on hers, served the purpose of finding him a wife of excellent heritage and foreign birth, and ingratiated the prince to him. He had made the contract, but had specified that the young lady had the right to refuse if she came to England but found she could not go through with it. He would force no woman to uphold a contract in which she had little say, though friends thought him odd and overly nice in his notions of consideration toward the fairer sex.

Of course, now that the prince's marriage was turning out as it was—unhappy and combative, even though the princess was successfully with child—it would not serve Wesmorlyn politically to wed the Countess von Wolfram, but he was never one to evade a commitment once it was made. If she wished the marriage to proceed, he was obligated in every way. He took in a deep breath. He just hoped his future wife would not be the embarrassment to his reputation that Princess Caroline had become to the prince. Raw, bawdy and jocose, forward and disobedient, Caroline was distasteful to Wesmorlyn and even more so to the poor prince, who must nonetheless support his wife until the birth of his heir freed them to live separate lives.

"You look very pleasant, and exactly as you should," he said to his sister, and patted her shoulder. "But you mustn't cry; you don't want to have red, swollen eyes, or people will talk."

"Thank you, Wes. You are always so kind to me," Hannah said with a sniff, stiffening her spine and defeating with a great effort the tears that threatened to spill over onto her cheeks.

"And so we are ready to go," he said. "Will we do, Sam?" he asked, raising his voice.

Semyaza, commonly called Sam, who had appeared while they spoke and stood waiting by the door, nodded solemnly. "It is raining. Be sure that your sister does not get cold."

"Of course. Her cape, please."

The tall, solemn-visaged Semyaza picked a dove gray cape up from a seat near the door and helped Hannah into it. She looked up at him and he nodded.

"Thank you, Sam," she said, her voice once again quiet and restrained.

"Shall we go?" Wesmorlyn said, as he took his sister's arm.

LYULPH Randell arrived back at his London townhome just a moment before the rain began to sheet down, changing from the sprinkle of late summer drizzle it had been, to a torrent from above. He had timed it well, but then, he had a sense about such things. Nature was no mystery to him, and the change in the air that preceded the downpour was like a beacon shining through the mist.

He shook the dampness from him, droplets flying from his unruly, dark hair, and raced up the stairs to where his faithful serving man, Diggory, waited patiently with his evening clothes laid out. This ball at Lady Harroway's would be a dreadful bore, but he had two objectives in mind, and so would find interest enough. First, he must at any cost make sure Wesmorlyn and his foreign fiancée did not get along, and then, he must continue his campaign of winning little Lady Hannah's heart so thoroughly she would never dream of marrying anyone but him.

Given his peculiar talents and attractions, he did not see that as a problem. No, it was Wesmorlyn who would prove to be the thorn. And so he must think of how best to detach the young lady to whom the earl was engaged. Again, he had talents that would make it simple enough, but still, he would not risk offending Hannah. She was the ultimate prize.

As the wordless Diggory assisted him, Lyulph hummed a merry tune. Tonight would see many of his schemes advance. Wesmorlyn, stultifyingly boring and priggish, had no chance against him in the end. Too polite to cut him out of his life completely, the earl would one day regret that softness.

SHEETS of rain obscured the view outside of the carriage, but Countess Charlotte von Wolfram was not looking out anyway. She was glaring resolutely ahead, to the seat opposite her where her half sister Fanny sat, her mild blue eyes filled with tears. But Charlotte hardened her heart. "Take me home, Christoph," she said to her older brother, who sat beside Fanny, "or at least to that moldy, damp, disgusting pretence of a home we are forced to live in while we stay on this godforsaken island in this disgraceful city. London! Pah! Nothing better than an open sewer."

"We must attend this ball!"

Charlotte glared at her older brother, almost as blond as she, but without the dimple in the chin and bow mouth. In a measured and calm fashion that belied the way her insides were quivering with nerves she said, "I don't want to."

Fanny wept openly, but Christoph spoke from the gloom, his tone resolute. "We are going to Lady Harroway's ball, Charlotte, even if I have to carry you kicking and screaming. I will not have you insult the Earl of Wesmorlyn, your future husband, for God's sake, by running away."

If only he had offered one scrap of sympathy, said one kind word, she would have broken down and confessed all her fears, her exhaustion, the way her stomach wrung like a washcloth in her belly. Instead all he did was bark orders, and she couldn't bear to tell the truth about being afraid with him so remote and frigid. She tensed. Her stubbornness was his own fault. He should never have told her to mind her manners, to curtsey properly, to speak only when spoken to, and all of the other bits of "advice" he had seen fit to impart. Any anticipation she may have had for the ball was now dead, stomped out by his fussing, and her nerves were wrought up to a fine, high, feverish pitch. "I wouldn't be running away," she said, through gritted teeth. She took a deep breath, trying to calm the wave of hysteria that threatened to overwhelm her. "I would merely be delaying the meeting until I have rested. And I haven't agreed to marry him. I just said I'd look him over." She clutched her hands together in her lap to keep them from shaking.

"We came all the way from Germany to do so!" Christoph said, his normally quiet voice holding a note of tension. "I will not have you insult the earl by not attending the ball put on in our honor!"

Fanny, choking back her tears, said, "We *did* just arrive

this morning, Count Christoph, and I think Charlotte is weary."

"Stop calling him 'count'! Call him Christoph!" Charlotte barked at her half sister. "He's your brother, almost as much as he is mine!"

"It will take more time than I have yet had to learn to call him brother, I'm afraid," the girl demurred, with quiet dignity.

"Get out of the carriage, Charlotte," Christoph muttered, "or I swear—"

"Don't threaten me," she replied, lowering her head and glaring at him through her fringe of blonde hair, "or you *will* have to carry me in, and I will make a scene such as you have never imagined." He should know how she felt, she thought, desperately, peering through the shadowy gloom, without her having to say a thing. Couldn't her brother tell that she was walking the precipice above a deep, dark pit of anxiety? This was no great moment for him or for Fanny, but this was supposed to be the night she met her future husband. She was tired, she was scared, and Christoph should know that. They had always known what the other was thinking and feeling.

Back home, when she had agreed to come and meet the earl, it had seemed a far-off hazy event; and she had agreed because she had a more important reason for wanting to come to England—one that did not include her potential husband. She was supposed to meet Lord Wesmorlyn in a private fashion, find out if she liked him, and if she didn't, she would never have to face any public exposure. But there had been delays along the way to England, and now, to see him immediately at almost the very hour of their arrival in London and be forced to meet for the very first time in public . . . it was all too much.

"Please, Charlotte," Fanny said, putting one hand on her half sister's arm. She glanced out the carriage window. "Look, the rain has stopped now, and the house is alight with candles, and there are lovely ladies dressed so prettily going in!"

"Charlotte, so help me, if you do not go in . . ." Christoph's words trailed off, for he had no threats that could command his sister if she had truly decided against going in.

"Charlotte," Fanny said softly, "we have such pretty gowns

on, and it really would be a shame to not go in after all the time it took to dress."

Charlotte sighed and looked down at her gloved hands, pulling at the end of one finger, a loose silk thread unraveling as she did so. She knew Fanny, though frightened, was looking forward to this ball more than she would ever admit. Her sister had a new gown of lovely pale blue with silver stars embroidered on the skirt; it had been made for this night, this grand occasion. Taking in a deep breath, Charlotte summoned up her courage, willing her exhaustion and nervousness to subside. She was a von Wolfram. No mere lot of English lords and ladies could intimidate her. She supposed since she had made an agreement, she would fulfill her part of it, which was just to look at the Earl of Wesmorlyn and say yea or nay to marrying him. She had already decided what her answer would be, but she must go through the forms.

And after all, she thought, working herself up to what must be done, it was not the earl's fault that their journey through Europe and over the Channel had been difficult and arduous, their arrival delayed, their house in London a disgrace, and their hired serving staff barbarians. She admitted to herself that none of that would ever stop her from doing something she wanted to do. She had great personal courage, had displayed it in the past, and so would not let her nerves and a fluttering stomach keep her from doing what was right.

Decision made, she said, "All right. I'm ready. Let us go in."

Christoph rolled his eyes. "Finally!" But as the two young ladies got ready to get out of the carriage, he put one quelling hand on his sister's arm. "Charlotte, you must promise to behave once we are inside."

"Do *not* begin in that fashion again," she said, "or I vow I will sit here and let you go without me."

They all descended to the wet pavement, and Christoph took one lady on each side of him. Together they climbed the stone steps and entered the doors being held open by silver-liveried servants in powdered wigs. As their names were announced by yet another liveried servant, an elderly lady, dressed in a dark purple velvet gown and wearing a turban decorated with tall gray feathers glided forward and accosted them.

"Count von Wolfram," she said, in dulcet, cultured tones, "I am Lady Harroway."

Charlotte examined her as Christoph acknowledged her greeting. This, she knew, was Marchioness Harroway, elder cousin of some sort to the Earl of Wesmorlyn, her fiancé. This was her London home and she was hostess of this ball, held in honor of Charlotte and Christoph's arrival in England after an arduous and at times unnerving trip from their home in Germany through the Low Countries.

"And this," Christoph said, stepping back, "is my sister, Countess Charlotte von Wolfram and . . . and my younger half sister Miss Fanny, uh, Sanderson."

Fanny colored at his stumble over her name. Being their illegitimate half sister, a fact she did not even know until mere months before, she was sensitive about the relationship and unsure of herself, Charlotte knew. It had not been her choice to acknowledge the relationship in public; it had been Charlotte and Christoph's joint decision. Fanny was still not sure it was a wise one, she had said just that afternoon, and even as excited about it as she was, and as enthralled with her new gown, that it might even be considered an insult to the hostess to bring someone of her birth to such an affair. She was willing to go only as Charlotte's attendant, but Charlotte felt strongly that their little sister deserved consideration. It was not Fanny's fault that their father, Johannes von Wolfram, was a philanderer and adulterer who had seduced her mother, a young English girl visiting Wolfram Castle. As the daughter of their father, she had every bit as much right as they to enjoy the privileges of their station. That may not be the way of the world or of the law, but it was Charlotte's way.

Charlotte curtsied perfunctorily and gave her hand to the woman, watching for any insult at all to Fanny, but the slight did not come and the woman was perfectly polite, if a shade condescending for Charlotte's taste. She offered to introduce them to the Earl of Wesmorlyn and his younger half sister, Lady Hannah St. Ange.

Charlotte's heart rate accelerated as they followed the serene woman through the crowd, and she was alive to a thousand sensations. The ballroom, really a series of rooms thrown together, was large enough, but overcrowded and hot, with the humidity of the air barely dispelled by the candles flaming brilliantly in wall sconces and a row of enormous chandeliers that hung above them. Crowds of young people, more than she had ever seen in all her sheltered years, stood in groups conversing, and older gentlemen and ladies sat in chairs that rimmed the ballroom. She clutched Fanny's arm close and whispered, "It's dreadfully warm in here, don't you think?"

"Yes," Fanny murmured back, her voice faint and tremulous.

Charlotte at first kept her eyes firmly on a prominent mole on the broad back of the dowager marchioness, who sailed along on Christoph's arm. Her brother, as always, was perfectly upright, ramrod straight, his sandy blond hair glittering in the flickering light. But gradually, as they made their way slowly through the crowd, Charlotte became aware of the voices of those around them.

"What an odd dress she is wearing. And who is that naïve-looking girl on her arm?"

"I know! It looks for all the world like she has brought her maid with her to the ball!"

Some giggling followed, but when Charlotte turned, wrath in her eyes, she could not tell among the half dozen young ladies nearby who had made the unkind remarks, and they had to move on to follow the marchioness and Christoph.

"How outré her hairstyle!" another cutting voice, this one male, proclaimed. "Not even *last* year's fashion, nor the year before that!"

Charlotte turned again, but saw only perfectly polite faces of young women and men. There was some delay, and the crowd surged around them. Young men, their pale faces set in blank expressions, gazed back at her as she stared. She couldn't breathe. She was suffocating and felt faint.

Fanny squirmed, and whispered, "Charlotte, you are squeezing my hand so tight it hurts!"

"I'm sorry." She let go of Fanny then, trying to ignore the trickle of perspiration that trailed down her back. The anxiety had returned and was stifling her, choking her. Her lungs would not fill, and her breath came in short gasps. The edges of her vision became hazy and pinpoints of light prickled before her. Finally Lady Harroway and Christoph ahead of them moved on, and Charlotte followed on numb legs, placing one foot in front of the other and trying to overcome the panicked sense of the crowd closing in around her.

They were almost to the far end of the ballroom, and she could see a few sets of large glass doors, beyond that the darkness of outdoors, torchlight flickering in the twilit dimness. Instantly her mind went there: the night air, cool dampness, being able to breathe without the scent of a hundred or so bodies overwhelming her. Her longing for the outdoors was like the memory of a flavor, something she could almost taste in recollection, but with her attention focused, she could almost breathe again.

Christoph and Lady Harroway stopped, then Christoph, still in front of Charlotte, bowed low. The two parted, and before her was standing a tall man with broad shoulders; he was slender, russet-haired and very handsome, with even, stern features, a beaky nose and a broad forehead. No smile was on his well-shaped lips. On his arm was a very slight, dainty girl who looked no more than a child next to him.

"Charlotte," Christoph said, taking her arm and drawing her forward, "this is his lordship, the Earl of Wesmorlyn, and his younger sister, Lady Hannah St. Ange. My lord, this is my sister, Countess Charlotte von Wolfram."

Charlotte curtsied, then looked up into his brown eyes. With a jolt she read his expression. He was disappointed! He bowed, the frown swiftly erased as his expression became a polite, smooth social mask. Trembling, she turned to the young lady, who almost hid behind her larger brother. But the girl, at a muttered order from her brother, stuck out her hand and murmured something too softly to be heard. Charlotte took her hand and they exchanged the merest light pressure before the girl released her.

Turning and pulling Fanny forward, Charlotte said, "This is our sister, Fanny."

Fanny, pale and quivering, curtsied but would not raise her head.

"Sister?" the earl said, his voice quiet but penetrating. "I had not understood you to have any other siblings but each other."

"She is our half sister, newly discovered, in one sense," Christoph said.

"I am Wes's half s-sister," Lady St. Ange said, the last word coming out with a nervous stutter. "Just like Miss Fanny is yours."

Charlotte warmed toward the delicate and fragile beauty, the earl's half sister. The girl looked terrified, but then her expression calmed as she looked behind Charlotte.

"Lyulph," she cried, affection in her voice.

Charlotte turned to see another gentleman, not quite as tall as the earl and darker, with olive skin, startling green eyes, and dark thick hair that curled deliciously on his forehead. He gazed down at her and his smile turned up one corner of his full mouth in a delighted grin.

Lady Hannah looked up at her brother, but he made no move to introduce anyone, so she stuttered, "C-Countess von Wolfram, this is Mr. Lyulph Randell, a neighbor and *very* good friend of ours from Cornwall. Mr. Randell, this is Countess Charlotte and her brother, Count Christoph von Wolfram. Oh! And M-Miss Fanny, their sister," she said, the last introduction coming out in a jumble.

The earl cleared his throat, and Charlotte caught a look between him and his sister, who turned pink, her doe eyes widening. Familiar with the ways of brothers, she immediately knew the earl was correcting his sister on something she had done or said. She fumed. How priggish he seemed, and so tightly controlled. The man had not a natural bone in his body, judging from the rigid way he held himself. She looked back to Mr. Randell. He was relaxed and smiling, bowing.

"How charming to meet you, Countess. You light up this drab occasion with your golden beauty."

"You are a friend of the family, then?"

"More than just a friend," Lady Hannah blurted, and then clapped her mouth shut and looked up at her brother again with alarm.

Lady Harroway, who had been drawn away immediately after introductions were made, returned and glanced around at the various expressions. "The dancing is about to begin," she said, with a wave of her gloved hand toward the ballroom floor.

"May I solicit the exquisite pleasure of the first dance with you, Countess?" Mr. Randell said, with a hopeful smile.

"I would be absolutely delighted, sir," Charlotte said with a happy sigh, relief flooding her. Dancing would dissipate the nerves; all of her fearful anxiety would have an outlet.

"Charlotte, the earl should have your first dance," Christoph said in her ear, though his voice was loud enough to carry to the others even over the sound of the orchestra tuning up.

"But Mr. Randell asked first," she whispered back at him. "I could hardly refuse."

"That is quite all right, Count von Wolfram," the earl said, with a stiff bow. "Since Randell has been so forward and quick, he must, I suppose, be rewarded, but I will solicit the second dance and the supper dance."

Charlotte curtsied. "Perhaps, as Fanny is not engaged for this dance—" she began.

"Since this is my sister's first ball," Wesmorlyn said over her words, "and she really cannot dance with anyone else, I will dance with her for the first set."

How rude, Charlotte thought, turning to take Mr. Randell's arm as he led her to the dance floor. She glanced back at Fanny, trying to encourage her to smile with a look, but it was no use. The poor girl was mortified. Charlotte felt in that moment that she would never forgive the earl for that rudeness. But then her attention was commanded by her partner and the exigencies of the dance.

She glanced around the room as the couples lined up. *Good.* Christoph had taken poor little Fanny into the dance. How rude the earl had been, snubbing their sister like that, but strangely, it had eased the rest of her nerves. She could not care what he thought of her, not when he was clearly not the picture of perfect English gentility. While she had imagined him to be the epitome of good breeding and refinement, she had worried about hurting his feelings when she had to tell him she had no intention of marrying him, but now she had no such compunction. She caught sight of Fanny and smiled. She would certainly not worry about the Earl of Wesmorlyn any more, and would just enjoy her very first public ball.

• • •

"I'M very nervous, Wes," Hannah whispered across the form to her brother. "I'm so grateful you are my first partner. I feel sure I should faint if it was anyone but you or Lyulph."

"Though I do not like Lyulph putting himself forward like that to the countess," he said, smiling over at her, "I was happy that it worked out this way, for I did not quite know how to tell my fiancée that I really wanted to give you your very first dance. And you know, because you are not truly out yet, you may not dance with any other young man this time."

"I hope that Miss Fanny was not hurt. She looked for a moment a little—"

"Now Hannah, you are just inferring how you would feel, with your own overly tender feelings, in such a situation. I'm sure Miss Fanny has no wish to dance with me."

"How could any young lady not? You are so much the handsomest man here," Hannah said. "You, and Lyulph, too."

There was that mention of Lyulph again! How could he expunge the man from his sister's tender heart? They could never marry—nature forbade it—and yet it was not something Wes could explain to her yet. Though perhaps he would have to, as indelicate and earthy as the subject would become when it approached the impossibility of them having a child together. "You are just prejudiced in my favor, my dearest little sister. And it is all the easier to say since this ball is so very thin of society, barely enough people here to call it a ball. Of course, it *is* August, and all the best company will have retreated to their homes in the country. Indeed, Lady Harroway only kept her home open and held this ball for my sake." He gave her a nod to let her know when their pattern was about to begin, and as they came together, he whispered, "Keep your chin up, Hannah, and a smile on your face. No matter if you make a slight error in the figures, just keep smiling. You are young, and not expected to be perfect."

As the dance progressed and Hannah appeared to be doing well, he had leisure to look about him, and he gazed down the line at Countess Charlotte von Wolfram. It had been a severe jolt to find her so absolutely breathtaking. After meeting the prince's German wife, Caroline, he supposed he had expected someone along her lines, short, stout, and ruddy. That had not

concerned him at all. The lady's behavior was far more important than her appearance, and he had been prepared to censure
her if she was loud, crude, bawdy, or forward.

But finding the young countess lovely of face and form—
wide blue eyes, skin like pearls, pink bow lips with a faint
dimple in her chin and possessed of a slim, lively figure—he
had experienced a rush of something like disappointment.
Why was that? Had he really preferred a dowdy woman? Was
this tug of attraction he felt something to be dreaded? Did he
fear he would not keep strictly to a morally perfect path if he
wished to marry her for other reasons than good bloodlines,
excellent lineage, and the hope of children to carry on his
title?

She was laughing at something Lyulph Randell said as
they came together in the figures. What a contrast she was to
the languid beauties who stepped through the paces of the
dance as if they suffered permanent fatigue. Her step was too
lively; she bounced too high and laughed too loud. She also
held Lyulph's hand too long and let her gaze linger on his
face.

It hit him like a blow to the stomach. She was flirting!

"Wes, what is wrong? You look most fierce," Hannah whispered as they joined to do a step together.

He calmed his expression. "Nothing is wrong."

"But it is, for—"

"Hannah!"

The dance ended and Randell behaved correctly, Wes was
relieved to see, and returned Charlotte to her brother, who had
been dancing with his half sister. Taking Hannah's arm, he escorted her back through the crowd.

Charlotte, happily out of breath, was whispering to Fanny
about how unexpectedly enjoyable dancing had been, when
Christoph drew her away.

"What is it?" she asked, looking up into his eyes.

"I felt something the minute we came into the ballroom,"
he said in a hushed voice. "And now I know what it is."

"What, Christoph? What is it?"

"There is, in this ballroom, another werewolf."

Chapter 2

"ANOTHER WEREWOLF?" Charlotte asked, studying Christoph's face. Personal knowledge of her family's inheritance, the predisposition to become werewolves, was still new enough that she found it exciting and thrilling. Stretching back hundreds of years, the unique legacy made them different and gave her the sense, in walking through a crowded room, of being something more than the others, even though as a woman she could not share in the most exciting of gifts, the ability to transform.

"Yes, another werewolf." Christoph stared across the distance.

"Who is it?" she asked, breathless with anticipation. She followed his gaze back to the knot of people, Lady Harroway, Fanny, Hannah, the earl, and Lyulph Randell. A faint prickle of presentiment trilled up her spine like fingers on piano keys. *Could it be?* She grasped Christoph's sleeve and gave it an impatient tug. "Who? Who is it?"

"Lyulph Randell; he's the werewolf," Christoph said, his voice tight with tension. "And he knows I'm one, too. I can see it in his eyes."

"How exciting!" Charlotte said, watching the man, remembering the magical green eyes and quirky smile. She had danced with him, touched him, and yet had not known his secret. To her chagrin, that once again pointed out the gulf between herself and her brother. She was destined to merely pass on the transformational ability, and never experience it for herself.

Christoph wasn't so sure it was exciting. He would need to approach this delicately, for his uncle, Nikolas von Wolfram, leader of their family and a werewolf himself, hadn't prepared him for this eventuality. Werewolves were not so common that one would expect to meet one in every ballroom in London. In fact, he had never even considered that he would encounter another one, though the extended clan of lupine humans seemed to draw and repel each other simultaneously in some odd brotherhood. Like attracted like, and yet two adult males of the wolf blood could not coexist in the same house without quarreling and jousting for dominance, which was why he had had to leave Wolfram Castle. He and his uncle, as much as they now respected each other, were constantly butting heads since he had experienced his first transformation just that spring, and in fact for years, even before he had been told the family secret.

"We must go back," he said, taking her arm. "I suppose I should ask the earl's sister to dance. I wish I had paid more attention to Elizabeth's lessons. Or our dancing master's tutelage. Remember him, Charlotte? Nice enough young fellow, but mousy and easily cowed. I don't even remember why he left."

"Never mind that," Charlotte said, sharply, pulling her elbow from his grip. "If you dance with Lady Hannah, I suppose I will have to dance with the earl."

He frowned down at her, a puzzled grimace twisting his mouth. "Of course you must dance with him! He is your betrothed husband, no matter what you think this moment. Why do you dislike him so already?"

"He was rude to Fanny. Didn't you see it?"

Christoph sighed, glancing around at the crowd, waiting for an opportunity to head back to their group through the crush. "If you remember, it was not my idea for her to come.

I thought it would be awkward for the poor girl, and I don't think she really wanted to attend."

"Yes she did!" Charlotte said, with an exasperated sigh. This was a topic they had canvassed already, and it wearied her to have to defend her certainty yet again. "She had a new gown for it, and was very excited, more so than I. You're not a lady, Christoph, and you will never understand how important balls and gowns and dancing are to girls."

"Well, still, it's a delicate position for poor Fanny."

"She's our sister, Christoph."

"Our illegitimate half sister, Charlotte!"

She dragged in a sharp breath. "How can you be so cruel?"

"I'm not," he replied, putting his hand to her back and firmly guiding her toward their party. "I feel sorry for her, too. I just think it was more your idea than hers for her to come, and you got her excited about it."

Charlotte shrugged away from his guiding hand and sped ahead to where the earl, Mr. Randell, Fanny, and Lady Hannah stood in an uncomfortable knot. Christoph, following more slowly, observed Lyulph Randell, wondering how to approach the man with their unacknowledged shared identity. Or even if he should approach him. What was the protocol? And did the earl know his friend's secret, Christoph wondered? Perhaps he would find out in time, if he became friendly with Mr. Randell.

Though that did not seem likely. Even at this distance he could feel his wolf sense, hackles rising, at the challenge of another wolf. Perhaps he was intruding on Randell's territory, or perhaps this was *his* territory now. Among men there were etiquette, established rules of conduct, and precedence by rank or title. Among wolves, only challenges met, acknowledged, and fought or withdrawn from. But what was there between men who were also wolves?

The dance lines were forming again, and Charlotte, with an unhappy expression, was being led into the dance by the earl. Lyulph Randell led Lady Hannah out, so that left Christoph along the side. He talked quietly with Fanny and watched, letting her in on the secret of his discovery of Lyulph's werewolf identity, which she heard with wide eyes. But she accepted it readily enough, and went back to avidly watching the dancing, breathlessly commenting occasionally on different ladies' dresses and appearance. Perhaps Charlotte was right about bringing her, he thought, looking down at Fanny's pretty, happy face. Perhaps he worried too much about the implications of every little action, but he had learned the hard way never to take anything for granted in his life.

Charlotte, coming together with the earl in the figures of the dance, was trying to decide if she truly did not like him, or if she had just allowed her first impulsive impression to rule her. She had no wish to be unfair.

"Is Miss Fanny your younger sister, Countess?" Wesmorlyn asked, as they promenaded in the middle of the dance.

"Yes. I am twenty-two; she is just nineteen."

"Is she your father's child or your mother's?"

Though he knew all about her antecedents from her Uncle Nikolas, but Fanny would not have been mentioned. His curiosity was natural, but awkward. "May I ask the same of Lady St. Ange first?" she replied, stalling the inevitable while she tried to figure out a delicate way of explaining.

"My mother died very young, and my father remarried a few years later. Hannah was their only child. My father died ten years ago when she was just six. We are in the last months of mourning for my stepmother, who passed from this earth last autumn."

"Oh, how sad for you both." Now, how could she acknowledge Fanny's illegitimacy? What was a delicate way to put it? "My father had . . . outside interests. Fanny's mother was an Englishwoman staying at our castle for the summer." His hand tightened around hers.

"Then she's . . ." He didn't finish.

She could feel his rigidity. "Yes, she's illegitimate," Charlotte murmured, her voice tight. She waited; what he said that moment would tell her much about him.

"Baseborn, and yet you brought her here, to this ball?"

The room swirled around her and she felt the heat rise to her face, her cheeks no doubt blazing red. Exhaustion reclaimed her. She was hot and miserable, and sure she looked a fright compared to all the other languid, pale young ladies who drifted by, stepping through the dance as if every movement was an effort. "Surely, my lord, the misbehavior of my father and her mother is not her fault?"

He frowned over at her, his brows slanting over brown eyes in a disapproving expression. "Did you not think," he said, quietly, as they came together again and clasped hands across the line, "that it may have been impolite to bring her to this ball, to Lady Harroway's home?"

A violin in the string section screeched, and she clenched her teeth against the discordant sound. "Impolite?"

"*Worse* than impolite," he muttered, as he turned her in the figure of the dance. "Surely you can see what a grave insult you have offered?" He shook his head. "What have you done? How can we explain this to poor Lady Harroway?"

Mercifully the dance parted them at that moment; another second and she would have replied rudely. She watched him make his way down the line of ladies, weaving in and out, as she did the same down the line of gentlemen. Her first impression was confirmed; he was a cold, priggish fish. She was relieved, in a way, for now she need not feel another moment of guilt about deserting their engagement!

"There is no need for explanation," she muttered to him, when the figures brought them back together again. "No one else need ever know, and I will not be the one to tell Lady Harroway, if that is your concern. I only told you because you asked!"

The dance ended and she rejoined their group, her chin up in what she hoped was clearly haughty disdain of his lordship's precious opinion. Mr. Lyulph Randell introduced a few friends, and in minutes Charlotte's weariness was swept aside by the group of admiring gentlemen, who chatted with her and complimented her, kindly bringing Fanny into the circle and plying her with attention, too. Just as she had told Wesmorlyn, there was no need to explain Fanny's birth. She was accepted as Charlotte and Christoph's younger sister. Other young ladies watched, and Charlotte could feel their jealousy at the attention they were receiving from the men. After the rude remarks she had overheard about her looks as she entered, she experienced a heady rush of triumph.

"How fortunate we are that you made the arduous journey from your homeland to ours," one young gentleman said after one of her stories about their trip. He cast a languishing look in Charlotte's direction.

"Are you truly already affianced to that old sobersides, Wesmorlyn?" another fellow, a shorter man with a bulky frame, said. He made a gesture at the other young gentlemen, and added, "Any one of us here would make a more entertaining husband for such a lovely young lady!"

She laughed and tapped him with her folded fan. "How impertinent English gentlemen are!" she cried.

"And how delightful German ladies!" he replied with a saucy wink.

Mr. Randell held up one hand. "Gentlemen, I am going to steal the countess away for a stroll about the ballroom, for I am jealous of dividing her attention." He took her arm and led her away.

"Are you really so jealous, sir?" she said, looking up at him through her lashes. She felt a quivering sense of her own power; she had captured so much attention, when there were many girls left languishing with the spinsters along the side of the ballroom floor. Whichever ones had made the cutting remarks when she first entered were getting their just punishment, she was happy to conclude, for her companion most certainly was a fine figure. The earl was perhaps better-looking in the strictest sense, but Mr. Randell had a liveliness of expression Wesmorlyn did not possess.

"Am I jealous? I shall choose not to answer that, for you will think poorly of me if I say yes. Instead I will say that you have the most enchanting eyes and a delightful laugh, and I wanted both for myself."

She chuckled, and glanced back at the earl and Christoph, standing with Lady Hannah. The Earl of Wesmorlyn watched her, and then he turned to Christoph and said something. Christoph eyed her for a moment, and Charlotte remembered what he had said about Lyulph Randell being another such as he. She looked up at her companion. His sparkling green eyes met hers and he smiled, white teeth showing in his grin.

"I think we have much in common, sir," she said, shutting out the voices and hubbub swirling around them.

"Do you? I am captivated by the idea, Countess." He pulled her closer to his side, ostensibly away from the crowd.

"I think you know of what I speak, sir," she said, feeling the power of his body beneath his jacket, her breath coming a little faster.

"I hope I do," he replied. "May we retreat to the privacy of the terrace and speak of this?"

She opened her mouth to say yes, but stopped. It was hardly fair to the earl to flirt like this and then go outside with another man at the ball meant to introduce her to London as the earl's nominal fiancée. It wouldn't be right, she decided, with regret. "I don't think I can, sir," she said, even as the gentleman's astounding green eyes drew her in. It was tempting, but no, she must be firm. "Shall we meet again while I am in London? I'm afraid this is not the time nor the place to further our acquaintance."

He glanced around. "Why ever not? No one would notice, I assure you, in this odd crowd. Lady Harroway always invites too many people, and since all the best have left London for the country, this is a motley assortment indeed. Come, do not be coy." He touched her hair and stroked her neck with one finger.

Breathless and feeling a thrill of consciousness at his touch, she was still master of herself enough that she was shocked at his forwardness, and was about to draw away from him, when her elbow was grabbed and she was *pulled* away. She turned to find her brother glaring down at her. "What is it, Christoph?" she asked, alarmed by his expression.

"You are acting like a common flirt, and making a fool out of the earl and of me with your behavior," he said, his tone a growl.

She gasped. "I beg your pardon?"

"You will behave yourself and show some restraint, Charlotte."

"What exactly have I been doing that is so wrong?"

"You laugh too loudly, and look too much at Randell, and—"

"This is what the earl has said?"

"He is concerned only for your reputation, Charlotte. He would not have you become ridiculous, as our cousin Caroline apparently became upon her arrival to wed the prince."

In a furious but restrained tone, Charlotte retorted, "Caroline always was thoughtless, forward, and heedless. You know that's true. Do you dare compare me to her?" Though even as she said the words, she felt a blush of shame for past indiscretions that would make her perhaps worse than her cousin. Still, he should not be reprimanding her in public.

"Of course not, but I will not have you become the center of gossip, nor will I have you disgrace the earl in this manner. You have everyone looking at you, and next they will be gossiping. Would you have them call you common? Or hoydenish?"

She stared at her brother for a long minute, thinking how out of character this was for him. She glanced across the ballroom and caught the earl watching the scene intently. "So, the earl sent you to do his bidding, did he, to reprimand me?" she muttered. The babble of whispering voices threaded through the music, filling the pauses with a sound like dry leaves blowing in the wind.

"He merely mentioned his concern."

"How kind of him. What exactly did he say?" Their little contretemps was now drawing attention, just what Christoph and the earl said they wished to avoid.

"He said you were being common and courting scandal by standing too close to Mr. Randell." Christoph's blue eyes narrowed. "I have to say, I have never seen you behave like this."

Astonished, Charlotte glanced around the ballroom. Everywhere groups of young men and women gathered, flirting, talking, strolling. She had done nothing out of the ordinary, if she was to judge by every other young lady at the ball's behavior. It was only now, with Christoph standing at her elbow, his pale face turning ruddy with emotion, that they were drawing unwanted attention. "Well, perhaps I have not been in company enough to expose how heedless and hoydenish I can be," she said, her tone laden with sarcasm. "Really, Christoph, I can't believe what you are saying to me! I've done nothing wrong."

"May I be of assistance?" Mr. Randell said, approaching.

"Keep your distance, Randell," Christoph said, leveling a glare at the man. "This has nothing to do with you."

"On the contrary, I think it does. Has Wesmorlyn complained to you about my attentions to your sister?"

"Leave us alone, Randell," Christoph said, taking Charlotte's arm and hustling her back around the ballroom to rejoin Fanny, Lady Hannah, and Wesmorlyn.

She pulled her elbow from his grasp and stalked the rest of the way alone, but just before they rejoined their party, she turned to him, glanced around to be sure they were out of hearing distance from others, and then said in a low voice, "You have embarrassed and humiliated me, Christoph; surely if you had a concern you could have voiced it in a manner not so public, nor so graceless. Do not come near me for the rest of the evening, or I shall have no compunction against setting you right in front of everyone. So the earl sent you to do his bidding and you trotted along like a good little puppy; well, you are no wolf, sir, nor even a good brother." She whirled and stalked to Fanny, took her arm, and whispered to her that she needed a breath of fresh air. With a frosty glare at Wesmorlyn, she left the ballroom through the huge glass doors that stood open just beyond some potted plants.

"How *dare* he behave that way?" Charlotte fumed sotto voce to Fanny as they walked the length of the flagstone terrace, which was peopled by couples and pairs of ladies and gentlemen escaping the heat of the ballroom in favor of the cooler night air. Potted plants and stone benches provided refreshing and yet semiprivate spots to talk, and three steps led down to the grassy and inviting lawn, beyond which extensive gardens stretched.

"What happened?" Fanny asked.

Charlotte briefly acquainted her with what had gone on between her and their brother. Fanny was silent after the recitation of grievous ills.

"You do not think him right, do you?"

"No, of course not, Charlotte, but . . ."

"But what?"

"I suppose he was just doing what he thought correct. Gentlemen usually do."

"That doesn't mean he was right to chastise me publicly!"

Mr. Randell approached them diffidently. "Countess, Miss Fanny," he said with a nod. "I hope you are enjoying the night air?"

Out of charity with everyone in that moment, Charlotte snapped, "As much as I can enjoy any air in this stifling city."

He nodded. "It is as I feared. You are out of sorts now because your brother, sent by the earl, chastised you for walking with me, was that right?"

Charlotte observed him for a moment, then sighed and said, "But it was my behavior and not yours that incited the reprimand."

Randell sighed. "Wesmorlyn always was a stiff fellow. He means well enough, I suppose."

"And yet you are good friends?"

"We were at one time the best of friends, as close as brothers and raised almost together. We went to the same school at the same time. I fear our difference in position has parted us. He is a little too aware of his consequence as an earl."

"How revolting," Charlotte said. "I could never bear to be married to a prig such as he."

Fanny whispered in her ear that she was perhaps being a little too open, and Charlotte sighed. It was her constant failing, and one that she fought to correct, an impulsive and hasty nature. No matter the extreme provocation, it was not fair to expose the earl to gossip, and she had no wish to be the genesis of any ill-natured talk.

"Please don't say anything to anyone of what I just said, sir. It was ill-mannered of me." She paused, but then continued. "I would ask that you keep this in the utmost confidentiality, for I am committed to at least consider this engagement with the earl, and I'll not let myself judge him too harshly before we even have an opportunity to speak privately."

"How gracious you are," he said, admiration shining in his eyes. "In truth, I think you the wisest and most beautiful young lady I have met in many a long year. How fortunate Wesmorlyn is."

She smiled up at him, her ire beginning to cool in the face of his warm admiration. There was something very attractive about him, so open and manly and yet gracious and diffident, and she felt the attraction like a tonic surging through her veins, making her tremble. "And how pleasant *you* are sir!"

"In truth," he said, gently, approaching more closely, "I think all you need is a short walk in the coolness of the night air, and you'll feel refreshed. May I escort you?" He gestured to the lawn. "There are many others enjoying the stroll about the grounds, after which the ballroom will not seem so confining, I promise you."

She gazed longingly into the dimness of the treed lawn, where couples, arm in arm, strolled and chatted. Lanterns twinkled in the branches overhead, throwing dancing pools of light over grassy pathways that wove among the gardens, and night flowers bloomed, giving off a delicious scent. She longed to walk among them. She glanced quickly back at the ballroom, and in that moment saw her fiancé dancing with another young lady, swirling past the window, his stony gaze fixed on her upturned face.

"You must not, Charlotte," Fanny whispered, her tone frantic. She wrung her hands, her gloves bunching and twisting. "Oh, please don't! Christoph will be so angry! And the earl!"

"Let us walk, sir," she said immediately, exasperated by Fanny's frightened voice in her ear. She took his arm and allowed him to lead her down the three steps to the mossy walkway that led to the trees. She heard Fanny's quick, tapping footsteps on the flagstone behind her. Turning, she said, "You don't need to accompany me, Fanny. I shall be quite all right with Mr. Randell."

"I'm too frightened to stay alone."

"Then go back to Christoph," she said.

Mutely, Fanny shook her head, and Charlotte, relenting, held out her gloved hand. "Then come walk with us. I don't mean to be a bear, Fanny, you know I don't, but I do so want to see the gardens, and look how many others are doing the same thing. With your company it will be even more acceptable." She took her sister's hand in her free one and they walked. She needed this respite, this moment of peace and calm. "Have you ever seen anything so delicious?" she asked, noting the clustered plantings of night-blooming stocks, their scent like fine perfume in the air.

"It's beautiful," Fanny said, meekly.

"You must be terribly weary," Randell murmured in Charlotte's ear. "For I understand you only this afternoon got to London after your long journey."

"I *am* weary," Charlotte said. "This whole day and evening

feels unreal, as if it is a pantomime I am watching, with actors playing out their roles, though it is really me!" It was a relief to have someone so sympathetic to talk to, and she felt his concern for her radiate. When the damp night breeze felt a little chilly, he pulled her closer to his side, and she could feel his warm solidity. It was comforting and yet discomforting at the same time.

"We have been walking too long," Fanny finally said. "We must go back!"

Charlotte sighed. "I suppose you're right." She turned to her companion, looking up into his face. "We should return to the ballroom, sir."

In profile, his face was a study in agitation, his dark brows furrowed, his mouth twisted. He turned to gaze down at her. "Please, Countess, tell me you will not rush into anything with Wesmorlyn. He's a good man, but I just don't know if he can appreciate what a precious flower he has in you! If it were anyone else but a good friend like Wes I would . . . but never mind."

"What?" she asked, breathless, noting the pain in his grimace. "What were you about to say?"

"We have to go, Charlotte!" Fanny said. She dropped Charlotte's hand and edged toward the pathway, from which they had wandered away.

"I truly can go no further, as a gentleman of honor," Randell said. "There are things about the earl . . . but no, I must not go on."

"Do you know something to Wesmorlyn's discredit?" Charlotte asked, intrigued. Why did he stop just as he was about to relate some interesting tidbit?

"Charlotte!" Fanny said, with more urgency.

"Please don't ask me that," Randell said, softly. He touched her cheek with one long finger, and drew it down to cradle in the dimple in her chin. "You are so lovely, in looks, of course, but in heart and soul more. If I could but fight for you myself, but I suppose it can never be." He looked away.

Her breath catching in her throat, Charlotte said, "Sir, if I have said anything to lead you to believe—"

"No!" he cried. "No one as perfect as you could ever do anything like that. It is all me, all my own heart, my own senses." He turned and stared down at her. "I've never met anyone like you. I know there can be nothing between us, but oh! My poor heart would rest easier if I had but one sweet memory to look back on."

"What do you mean?"

"One precious, chaste kiss." He lowered his face to hers, but hesitated.

She felt his warmth, and trembled, her heart pounding. What was he asking but what she wanted, too? And yet— "I can't, sir," she murmured.

"You can," he whispered. He touched her lips with his, his warm breath mingling with hers. "You can," he whispered against her lips, and deepened the caress.

Caught in confusion, she did nothing, neither responding, nor pulling away. Her weariness numbed her and the day's confusion washed through her in the seconds as he deepened the kiss. She was irresolute, unsure, and so quiescent. When he paused in the caress, she said, "I don't think that was proper at all, sir, and I think—"

But he kissed her again.

Chapter 3

THE EVENING had not begun nor progressed as Wesmorlyn expected. Some odd sense of being usurped had overcome him as he watched Countess Charlotte and Randell stroll around the room, comfortably laughing and chatting as if they were the engaged couple. He had expected the young lady to be awed into silence by his rank and bearing, but instead she had appeared to appraise him and find him wanting, preferring an untitled nobody with whom to spend her precious time. It was unconscionable and humiliating, and he had put an end to it by alerting her brother to her behavior. He may have been precipitate, and it had, perhaps, caused a rift between the Count and Countess von Wolfram, but it was too late to take it back.

After dancing with yet another intimidated young miss at the marchioness's express request, he looked everywhere for his fiancée, but could not find her in the crowd. The count was also covertly searching the ballroom for his sisters. Wesmorlyn started toward the terrace doors, but just then their younger half sister, Fanny, bolted in through them, went directly to the count, and whispered something in his ear. Immediately he loped out the doors ahead of her.

Wesmorlyn followed. Had the countess fainted, or been attacked? Alarmed, he raced after them, through the dimly lit garden, over the damp grass, through the misty night air, and circled a clump of bushes just behind Christoph and Fanny. There, entwined in the shadows in an ardent embrace, was his fiancée and Randell. She was being thoroughly kissed, bent almost backward in the fellow's grip.

"Let her go, Randell," Wesmorlyn shouted, elbowing past the shocked and silent Count von Wolfram.

Randell did release her, and she, her cheeks ruddy and her hair ruffled, backed away from the angry confrontation.

"What were you thinking, Charlotte?" Count von Wolfram said to his sister, in a harsh and guttural tone.

"More to the point," Wesmorlyn said, stalking toward Lyulph, "is what were *you* thinking? How dare you take my fiancée out to the garden and molest her in that insane manner?"

"He didn't molest me," Charlotte protested, patting her hair back, tucking a stray strand behind her ear. Fanny had retreated to her side and clung to her sister.

"I promise you Wes," Randell said, his green eyes glinting in the light from a single lantern hung in the branches of the linden tree nearby. "If she had protested, I would have released her immediately."

That could not be allowed to pass without comment and reaction. A breeze came up and the leaves rustled, the light shifting and bobbing, shadows dancing. Controlling his fury as best he could, he muttered, "Lyulph Randell, you have trespassed on my kindness long enough and have impugned this young lady's character. As her fiancé and protector, I demand satisfaction!" He stopped, hardly believing the words that were coming out of his own mouth. A challenge? From him? But he continued, compelled by some inner force he had never experienced. "Tomorrow morning you will meet me at dawn on Battersea Fields. Swords, not pistols. First blood only will suffice, sir!"

Christoph, his mouth open in surprise, stared at him.

"You are challenging him?" Charlotte cried, shaking off

her sister's arm and stepping forward. "How *dare* you take this as a slight to you?"

"A duel?" Randell said, his dark brows diagonal slashes over his green eyes. He lounged against the trunk of the tree, the very picture of ease. "Really, Wes, are you not taking this all too far?"

"I'm not taking this as a slight to me," Wesmorlyn said to Charlotte, ignoring the other man, "but to you! Did you not hear him? He impugned your character, and yet you can defend the scoundrel?" He stared at her in puzzlement, as a breeze wafted through the shadowy, moonlit garden and lifted her ruffled curls. Her pale face had two dark spots of red high on her cheeks, and her hands were balled into fists at her sides. He was mystified by her, and yet entranced.

"I heard no impugning of my character, but just your own precious sense of outrage that he has interfered with what you deem your prerogative!"

"Charlotte, be quiet . . . *now*!" Christoph said, his face brick red down to his collar. "You have done enough damage for one evening. I'm ashamed to call you sister. And you, Randell," he went on, turning to Lyulph, "you are fortunate indeed that it is the earl who has challenged you," he said, jabbing his finger in the other man's face. "I think you know exactly what I mean when I say you had better stay away from my sister." With that he turned and stalked away, clearly struggling for self-control.

Wesmorlyn glanced back at Charlotte and his heart constricted, seeing her beautiful blue eyes fill with tears as she watched her brother stalk away. Her lips trembled, and the tears spilled over and rolled down her smooth cheeks, dripping off her dimpled chin. Fanny put her arm over her shoulder, gave both men a look of disgust, and pulled her elder sister away. Charlotte's sobs echoed.

"You have such a way with ladies, Wes," Randell said with a cynical smile, "that I'm not surprised you had to gain a wife by mail." He, too, turned and walked away, back toward the brilliantly lit house.

"Tomorrow morning, Randell," Wesmorlyn called after him. "Dawn, at Battersea Fields; I shall provide the surgeon. Choose a second and come prepared!" He whirled and stomped back toward the ballroom, by a different route than his adversary.

Charlotte sat on a bench in a quiet corner of the terrace overhung with the branches of potted ornamental trees and tried to regain her composure. The night air was damp and misty, muffling nearby murmured conversations of people who strolled the long flagstone terrace in the far shadowed reaches beyond the torchlight. She smiled tremulously at Fanny in the dim light that trailed out of the many glass terrace doors and windows that lined the flagged veranda. "I've made a terrible mess of everything, haven't I? One day in London and I've become an example of how not to behave at a ball."

Fanny sighed. "Why did you allow Mr. Randell to kiss you?"

Shrugging, Charlotte tried to untangle her emotions, but the knotted mess had an enigma at the heart. "I don't know. I really don't. It sounds absurd to say, but I felt as if I was in a fog and was not really thinking about anything. I don't know if I was weary, or just numb, but when he gazed into my eyes, I felt as if I were experiencing Herr Mesmer's infamous animal magnetism and was in a trance." She shook her head and shrugged again.

"Do you like him?"

"He's very handsome and very flattering," she admitted. "And he has the most beautiful green eyes. I must admit, I find it fascinating that he is a werewolf. Who would have thought we would meet another werewolf almost the moment we land in this country? But I don't know why I let him kiss me." The moonlight had played a part, she was suddenly convinced. He had stared down at her, and the moon had sparked in the green depths of his eyes. She had leaned forward, drawn to him; she shook herself, trying to rid herself of that sensation, the feeling of being drawn in, but the effects lingered.

There was a ready explanation, though, and given her contrary character, it was the likeliest answer. "He is very handsome and sympathetic," she mused, "but I think it more likely that it was in retaliation for how the earl and Christoph made me feel earlier in the ballroom, like I was some silly little horrible child who couldn't make her own decisions." She sighed and slumped. Impetuosity, her fatal flaw. "And now I've just confirmed every awful fear Christoph had of my ability to behave in a ladylike manner and have truly made a fool of myself in front of the earl."

"I'm so sorry I ran to Count Christoph, but Mr. Randell frightens me, and I was worried."

"Don't apologize Fanny. I would have done the same thing, perhaps, though you must know I was in no danger. Mr. Randell, after all, would have stopped immediately if I had protested. Even as he kissed me I could feel that. He's just a very nice gentleman who was overcome by his attraction to me."

"Do you really think they'll fight a duel over you?" Fanny said, her blue eyes wide. "It's so romantic!"

"It's not romantic in the slightest," Charlotte retorted, astonished by her half sister's hitherto unrevealed romanticism. "Wesmorlyn had no right to do such a melodramatic thing. No one saw us, nor did anyone hear the words that passed between the two men. A duel is completely unnecessary and farcical. Mr. Randell was perfectly right in his disbelief. Wesmorlyn only offered the challenge because of his own injured sensibilities; it had absolutely nothing to do with any care for my reputation, which will surely be more damaged by two gentlemen having a duel over me than from a confrontation no one else saw."

She stopped and looked off into the darkness. The night had lost all of its charm, and she was back to thinking of London as dreary and dull. She faced her pain and admitted it. "The worst of it is, I never thought Christoph would treat me the way he did tonight. I know I disappointed him, but still, he shouldn't have said what he did."

"He had no right to speak to you like that," Fanny agreed, crouching down and hugging Charlotte. "He said horrible things!"

Charlotte was deeply wounded by Christoph's words. The bond between them had always been strong, but from the very moment of their arrival in London, it felt strained and tenuous. She could not think of that or she would cry. Instead she pondered what the earl had said about her poor judgment in bringing Fanny to the ball. It was an echo of what Christoph had said to her, though the two men were saying much the same thing for different reasons. She still didn't regret her decision; she couldn't blithely rush off to a ball and leave poor Fanny alone in a strange house on her first night in England. Their younger sister was her responsibility, she felt, much more so than she was Christoph's. And if Fanny was coming to this ball, she was coming as their sister.

She took a deep breath and let it out slowly. This was not what she had come to England for: going to balls, dancing, being kissed in the dark. She had come, in truth, solely to find her half sister's mother, and to unite the two of them so they could have a chance at a mother and daughter bond, the chance that had been denied to Charlotte by her mother's early death. And that was what they would do.

"Fanny," she said, rising and holding her hand out to help her sister up, "I think tomorrow we shall embark on a little adventure."

"What do you mean?"

"I brought you all this way to find your mother. Eleanor Dancey is out there somewhere, and I intend to find her."

"*You* intend to find her? H-how?" Fanny stammered. "I don't understand. What will you do about the earl and Christoph?"

"What of them?" Charlotte said, resentment of the two men bubbling up within her. She took in a deep breath and stiffened her spine. "I may have behaved imperfectly this night, but they both have acted worse. If they get along so splendidly, having found a common enemy in Mr. Randell, they can have each other and their duels at dawn and their violent ways. Men!"

"Charlotte," Fanny said. "Though we may not understand, gentlemen have their own notions of honor, and are merely doing what they feel necessary."

"The earl seems to be satisfying his own sense of injury rather than any perceived slight to my honor."

Fanny abandoned the topic, and returned to the subject of their search for her mother. "But what about the inquiry agent your . . . our uncle Nikolas hired to find my mother?" she said, wringing her hands together, but stopping as her gloves twisted. "Should we not wait to see what he finds out?"

"I have little confidence in him; he will surely draw the search out just to earn a higher fee." Charlotte frowned and paced a few steps. "We can figure this out for ourselves. Frau Liebner told me that when she last visited Miss Eleanor Dancey, the woman was happy to hear that you were a good girl and settled at Wolfram Castle. She also said that she had to travel all the way to Plymouth to find her. Therefore," she said, returning to her sister's side and linking Fanny's arm through hers, "we shall set off for Plymouth and make our own inquiries. There's nothing wrong with two young ladies traveling together in such a manner. I have money; we'll hire a carriage and driver and stay at a respectable coaching inn. It will all be quite upright."

"Excuse me for interrupting your conversation," a voice said out of the dimness created by the potted trees.

Fanny jumped and gasped; Charlotte steadied her with a calming hand. "You startled us, Mr. Randell."

"I'm so sorry, ladies," he said, as he walked up the three steps toward them and bowed. He appeared ill at ease, glancing up and down the long flagstone terrace and at the windows that showed the ballroom inside like a series of paintings of elegant London life.

"Sir," Charlotte said, eyeing him warily. "I think it would be best if we are not seen talking right now."

He retreated slightly, until he was concealed by the shadow of a potted tree that overhung the terrace, its leafy branches extending to create welcome privacy. "I agree, and I promise not to detain you. I only approached you to apologize most sincerely." He cast his gaze down at the terrace. "I am abominable. Never have I let my feelings carry me away like that, but your beauty and sweetness . . ." He broke off and shook his head. "I'll not meet your like again," he whispered.

"How romantic," Fanny sighed, some of her prejudice against the man apparently tempered by his heartfelt admission of preference and apology for causing Charlotte trouble.

Pity for his obvious discomfiture moved Charlotte to say, "Perhaps you should not have behaved so, sir, but I am equally to blame. I should not have walked with you in the garden like that. But it matters not, as I doubt we shall meet again, for I'm leaving London tomorrow. I pray that you and the earl can settle your differences without resorting to violence, which I abhor most severely."

He gazed into her eyes with a feverish expression on his darkly handsome face and struck his chest with the flat of one hand. "For you, countess, I would even desert honor and delope rather than let you suffer a moment of worry for the earl's health."

"I'm not concerned for him," she said, sharply.

"Oh. Well, good. Wesmorlyn can take care of himself. But where are you going? I had understood you to be settled in London for the time being?"

"My sister and I are going . . . uh . . ." She hesitated, exchanged a look with Fanny, and continued, saying, "We are going to seek an old acquaintance down Plymouth way." The evasion came easily. She had never thought herself such a practiced liar.

"Plymouth! Why, you will be going almost all the way to my own estate in Cornwall. Who is it you seek, if I may be so bold?"

"Well . . ." She hesitated, but what did it matter really if she said something to him? "Fanny was raised with us, but her mother returned to her homeland. It is my half sister's mother, in fact, whom we seek, a Miss Dancey."

"Miss Dancey?" he said, staggering back a step. "Could it possibly be a Miss *Eleanor* Dancey, formerly of Plymouth? Oh, this is too much of a coincidence!"

"Whatever do you mean?" Charlotte asked, clutching Fanny's cold hands in hers. "Do you know the woman?"

"I have just in the last few months rented one of my houses to a Miss Eleanor Dancey, once of Plymouth but now settled in Cornwall for a short while, before she leaves the country forever!"

"Miss Eleanor Dancey?" Fanny whispered, her voice trembling with emotion. "Can it be true?"

"How many ladies of that name can there be?" Mr. Randell said, earnestly. "Truly, Dancey is not an uncommon name, but putting everything together, I think we must take it as a certainty that this is the lady you seek."

"But you said she leaves the country?" Charlotte said. "Why would she leave the country?"

"Well, it is not my place to say." He moved slightly out of the shadows and lowered his voice even more. "She confided her situation only as a great secret, you know, but she alluded to an indiscretion in her background and that someone was using it to make her feel uncomfortable." He looked both ways, up and down the terrace. "I dare not say another thing to protect the poor woman's confidence. But she did mention in her letter leaving her past behind and moving to . . . to Ireland."

"Ireland?"

"Or perhaps she said Upper Canada, the colonies."

"Oh, *no*! So far?" Charlotte staggered back a step, alarmed at this news.

"Yes, I'm sure it was Upper Canada," he said, earnestly. The terrace was now deserted, and he moved from the shadows, lounging against a low wall that bounded one part of the veranda. "She came to my attention through a mutual acquaintance, and I only remember some of the letter. I wrote back that she could have Moor Cottage for as long as she wished."

"Upper Canada?" Fanny said, looking up at Charlotte. "Is that not a great distance away, across the ocean? How could we ever follow so far?"

"That decides it," Charlotte said, brushing her skirts down with swift movements. "We must go immediately." She paced a few steps. "I will go now to Christoph and—" She stopped abruptly, remembering that she and her brother were not on good terms that moment.

"What is it?" Randell said.

She chewed her lip. Would she be able to convince Christoph? And how could she tell him what Mr. Randell had said when she could not even say his name at the moment?

"I will give you the directions," Mr. Randell said, watching her, "and you ladies and your brother may set out on a little jaunt down to Cornwall. I'm sure the earl will understand once you tell him your mission."

Would the earl really understand a trip out of London to find her illegitimate sister's disgraced mother? And that was not the sticking point; it was Christoph's opinion about which she cared.

"What is it, Countess?" Mr. Randell asked.

She turned back to him. "It's complicated. But after that little scene in the garden I'm sure you understand that offering my brother your information will not be a simple matter."

He paused and nodded. "I hadn't thought of that. How clever you are! What shall we do about that?"

"It will have to wait," Charlotte said reluctantly. She turned to Fanny. "I don't see any other way. You know I would do anything to find Eleanor Dancey, but we may have to wait until I can convince Christoph. Perhaps we may get her direction and write to her," she said, turning back to Randell.

"Of course, Charlotte," Fanny said, putting one small, gloved hand on Charlotte's arm. "We shall write her a letter."

"I'm sure you're being very wise," Randell said, nodding. "If Miss Dancey should leave Cornwall this week, as she mentioned—"

"This week?" Charlotte cried.

"Did I not say that? I believe this week or next was her projected time for sailing."

Charlotte stared at Mr. Randell for a long moment, searching his eyes, trying to see into his heart. Was this true? It had to be; try as she might she could think of no reason why he would mislead them. He barely knew her, and even if there was some absurd plotting behind all of this, if he had become swiftly enamored of her and wanted to part her from the earl, he knew enough already to know that she had no intention of marrying the man, so there would be no reason to hasten her departure from London. No, this must be legitimate, as coincidental as it seemed.

"I wish I could rely on Christoph to be reasonable!" she mused. "But he seems irritable, and the earl! I will not abuse him in front of an old friend, though it seems to me he has not acted like any friend, but he is so completely unreasonable that actually, it matters not that I make him even angrier, for I have already made my decision."

"Your decision?"

"You must know I have no intention of marrying such a loutish prig!" She clapped her hand over her mouth, but her incautious tongue had already led her so far, and really, what harm had it done? He must already know that was true. "I should not have said it so, but it's true."

"Then . . ." The gentleman paused.

"What is it, sir?"

"It seems to me that what matters most is that this young lady find her mother and be united with her," he said, waving his hand toward Fanny. "At least they can meet before Miss Dancey departs these shores forever. I suppose you could hire a carriage driver, stay at inns along the way, and then follow my directions to Moor Cottage on the Little Honet road near Bodmin in the Eastern District of Cornwall."

She glanced over at a speechless Fanny, who listened with wide eyes. "It seems such a daunting journey," she said, imagining the difficulties inherent in such an expedition. When she had impulsively suggested it to Fanny, she had clearly not thought of all the details. "I'm not a coward, but it does seem arduous, as we don't know England at all. And with the pressure of time, I would not wish to become lost along the way."

"I have never in my entire life met a lady with such courage and brilliance," he said, with a low bow. "If it would not be too forward, it would be my great honor to give you the use of my closed carriage and driver; my man knows the way intimately, and you will have nothing to do but unite this sweet young lady with her mother."

It was becomingly said, and Charlotte clapped her hands. "Spoken like a true gentleman!" His altruistic kindness pleased her after the treatment she had received at the hands of the earl and her own brother that evening, but she paused, and then shook her head, reluctantly acknowledging that she could not take him up on his kind offer. For once in her life she would be prudent. "However, I don't think that would be wise. How would it look, sir, if we accepted your generous offer? And truly, I should stay in London long enough to consult with my brother. And, as little as I wish it, the earl. Until I inform him of my decision, I am still his betrothed."

He gazed at her for a moment, in the moonlight, and then said, "I must, of course, bow to your concerns, but pardon me if I express my innermost fears. I'm afraid if Wesmorlyn is informed of your intentions before you go, he will stop at nothing to detain you."

"Why would he do that?"

Mr. Randell hesitated. "There may be reasons I cannot and will not canvass at this moment. But even beyond the reasons I cannot tell you, you saw how he was in the garden. Just so is he with everything in his life; whatever he feels he possesses he jealousy guards like a dog with a bone. For example, his younger sister Hannah has a great affection for me, almost like another brother. You saw how she greeted me in the ballroom! She is truly the sweetest child in the world. Our estates are very close, and I have been in the habit of giving the poor girl a few happy hours of riding about the countryside in my open gig. But when Wesmorlyn heard of our jaunts, he put a stop to it. She is not allowed such treats anymore."

"How sad," Fanny said.

"How intolerably mean-spirited," Charlotte said, indignantly. "But why would he do such a thing if his sister enjoyed the treat so? Does he not love her?"

"Yes, he does. He's a good brother, truly he is. But I fear poor little Hannah expressed her joy in such a way as to make him believe I had usurped his position as a favored brother might."

"You do him honor by imagining him with motives inspired by affection rather than resentment." She observed the man for a moment in the shadowy light from the torches. Everything he said, everything he did, showed him to be the more truly honorable of the two men. If things were only different, she could imagine falling in love with just such a man as this. "We so appreciate your kindness, sir. My brother said something to me about you." How could she raise their shared bond, the werewolf heritage that linked them irrevocably? She had never spoken of it to anyone outside of their family, but she felt it strongly in his presence, and perhaps that was what he felt for her, too. Maybe what she was feeling was the kinship of their blood, and so perhaps it was natural that she was drawn so to him. Christoph had claimed that Lyulph Randell was aware of him as another of the wolf blood, but it was still an awkward topic. "He told me that you are very much alike, that you both . . ." She paused, confused about how to go on.

"Yes, well, it is not something to discuss in a ballroom set-

ting," he said, with a smile and a hasty glance at a couple a
ways down the terrace who had just exited the ballroom. "Let
me just say," he murmured, melting back into the shadows
thrown by tree branches, "that I truly hope that the count and
I can someday be as close as brothers, perhaps in more ways
than one."

"You're very kind," she said, feeling her cheeks warm at
his implied interest in her.

"Will you *please* take my offer of my carriage and driver?"
he said, his hands clasped together in a gesture of supplication. "I would only feel secure that way, knowing that the
driver will take you directly to the country home I have rented
to Miss Dancey."

Charlotte glanced back into the ballroom, the swirling couples, the haughty ladies. As much as she had thought this
might be entertaining, it had turned into a debacle, mostly due
to her own behavior. This was not her life. She had never
really cared for gowns and dancing and gossip beyond a passing interest, and she was too old to start now like some green
girl in her first year. She had no intention of marrying Wesmorlyn, nor did she even intend to stay in England. She
glanced over at Fanny; they had one chance, perhaps, to find
Eleanor Dancey. How could she live with herself if she waited
for Christoph's approval, only to find that Miss Dancey had
already sailed out of Fanny's life forever?

And to be honest with herself, did she have the slightest
idea of how to go about hiring a carriage and directing the
driver to go down to Cornwall to find this cottage? If she had
paid attention to her Uncle Nikolas's hasty lessons on English
geography she might be able to point out Cornwall, but the
sad truth was she couldn't. She was being given the opportunity to get what she had, after all, come to England for. Making a sudden decision, Charlotte impulsively said, "Yes! Yes,
Fanny and I would be delighted to accept your kind offer." Beside her Fanny gasped and started, but she put out one staying
hand to silence any exclamation.

"But you must go tonight! I would not want you to be disappointed after going all that way, only to find her already
gone. It will take a few days to get there, you know."

"How are we to arrange it?"

"I will have my driver by your door at two in the morning, awaiting your pleasure. I shall leave a note with him telling you what inns you should stay at along the way, and where he is taking you. If I can get away after this ridiculous challenge of Wesmorlyn's, then I will meet you in Salisbury and accompany you on horseback the rest of the way. If your brother is with you, so much the better, but if he is not, then you will at least be safe."

"Christoph *must* come!" Charlotte paused and gazed at him steadily for a long moment. "I'm not sure how to proceed if we cannot convince my brother. To go alone in your carriage, and accompanied by you—"

"Oh!" he exclaimed, hand over his heart. "It shall all be completely proper, I promise you. I would not dream of traveling in a closed carriage with you, I swear."

Charlotte nodded sharply, taking Fanny's hand in her own. "We'll do it; I'll convince Christoph somehow. If I don't do another thing while I'm in England, uniting Fanny with her mother will be enough." She gave him their address, and indicated that there was a tiny, grim park opposite, in front of which a carriage could park at that time of night without being noticed.

"Burgess is one of my drivers, a little surly and quite the West Country character, but perfectly reliable. He'll be waiting outside your townhome at two in the morning, at your disposal." Randell bowed and disappeared back into the shadows.

Fanny and Charlotte returned to the ballroom. Christoph and Wesmorlyn stood on either side of Lady Hannah St. Ange like two grim sentinels, and the poor girl appeared extremely uneasy. Charlotte would have offered the young lady her arm to stroll about the room, but knew the earl would consider her an unfit companion for the innocent child. The notion made her burn, but she joined the unhappy group. All she wanted was to leave and get on with their plan.

"I saw you sitting with Fanny on the terrace and thought the cool night air might calm your temper," Christoph muttered, without meeting her eyes. "Have you recovered sufficiently to behave as a lady would, for a while, at least?"

"How beastly you're being," she replied, through gritted teeth. "I wish we'd never come to this miserable island."

"After tonight, I'm sure that will not be a problem."

"What do you mean?"

"We'll speak of it later!" he hissed. "Smile as if you are having a lovely time!"

She blinked, trying to hold back the tears brought on by his continuing anger at her. She was homesick for Germany: dear, dismal Wolfram Castle, the dark forests, and even little Wolfbeck, their village. And yet she was wholly committed to helping Fanny find her mother before she left this wretched country. Caught up in her misery, she was unaware of anything more until Fanny tugged her sleeve. She looked up to find everyone's eyes on her.

"The earl asked you a question, Charlotte," Christoph said, impatiently.

"I beg your pardon. What was the question?"

"Would you do me the honor of promenading to the conservatory with me?"

Her first thought was to say no, but almost anything would be a relief from standing in this frozen unhappy group saying nothing. She took his arm.

Wesmorlyn had never felt such a conflict of emotions all at once in his whole steady, quiet, safe life. The fury he had felt upon witnessing Randell kissing the countess, his betrothed bride, was an amalgam of frustration, possessiveness, jealousy, and pique, he had concluded. And yet jealousy implied attraction. He *was* attracted to her, he admitted to himself, but it was surely the passing interest one would have in any lovely lady. He would not allow it to go beyond that.

She was unsuitable in so many other ways: forthright, outspoken, bold, haughty, and brash. It would be the best thing for him if she would reject their engagement and go home. Even as he told himself that, though, he fumed, for as much as he had intentionally left the engagement open on her end so that she could do so, he had never considered until now that she might reject him. How dare this girl throw away his hand in such a bold manner? For surely kissing another man at the ball intended to introduce her to London society as his fiancée must be considered a rejection of his hand in marriage. His thoughts were a tangle of contradictory and confusing responses.

He glanced down at her strolling beside him, her figure stiff, her expression unhappy, her sweet bow lips turned down in a scowl. Curious glances followed them, and whispered words passed from lips to ears. What a sight for the gossips they must be. He shuddered to think what the society column in the newspapers would hint; never before had he been fodder for them, but he feared that he was about to learn how scathing they could be, especially if word got around about his duel with Lyulph Randell the next morning. He still wasn't sure that he had taken the right action, but the man's words had provoked his seldom-roused temper.

He must transcend his anger and triumph. He *must* condescend and speak with her, for though his sense of rectitude was outraged at her conduct, he would not leave her with anything of which to complain. "Countess Charlotte," he said, stiffly, "I'm sorry your first evening in London has been so difficult." Even though she had brought it all on herself.

"And so you should," she said, not looking up at him, but only straight forward. "I have never been so humiliated in all my life."

Staggered by her words, he restrained a quick retort, and instead managed a tolerably restrained reply. "And how would you say *my* conduct was lacking?"

Now she did look up at him, her blue eyes wide with incredulity. "You don't know? How is that even possible? You insult my poor sister—"

"I did no such thing!"

"By insinuating to me that she is not a fit guest in this house, and then . . . and then . . ."

"And then what? I am agog to hear what next you consider my failing."

"And then you blunder in to what is clearly a private moment and issue that idiotic challenge," she said, her voice cracking with fury. Her cheeks were pink, glowing with emotion, and the delicate draped curls that caressed her neck danced from her trembling.

He felt her quiver and steadied her by tightening his grip on her arm. "I certainly did issue a challenge," he growled, but then clamped his lips shut. They passed through a crowded spot near the door to the card room, where a group of men were clustered, some of them fellows with whom she had been speaking earlier. Once they were out of earshot, he said, "That challenge was the only honorable response I could make to the man who was kissing my fiancée, and who then deepened his discreditable conduct by implying that he was only doing that which she had invited!"

She gasped. "He said no such thing!"

"He may as well have."

"But he didn't! And anyway, another moment and I would have parted from him. I was merely taken off guard."

"Off guard?" He jerked her closer to him and guided her past another cluster of ladies. "You shouldn't have been out there with him in the first place. That is the behavior of a trollop. Have you no restraint, no idea of what proper conduct for a young lady is?"

She dropped his arm and stepped away from him. Her contemptuous gaze swept around the room at the knots of young men and women. "Oh, I have heard and seen enough to know what is considered fit conduct in London society," she said, her voice low but trembling with anger. "It is fit conduct, apparently, to insult a stranger to your shores, her mode of dress and hairstyle, even her choice of companion, as some of these fine young ladies and gentlemen did tonight," she said, waving a hand to indicate the room at large. "It is fit conduct to be so insipid that one barely has a pulse, judging by these simpering ladies." She glared up at him. "And it is fit conduct to make a lady feel that nothing she could ever do would be good enough and that she is despoiled by the merest impromptu kiss in the garden." She whirled and began to walk away.

His temper ready to burst, a pounding headache accompanying it, he grabbed her arm and pulled her back, twisting her around to face him. "Merest impromptu kiss? You were entwined around him like the serpent in the garden, young lady, and I know Lyulph Randell well. I have *never* seen him act thus, so without some extreme provocation on your part, for I must believe you threw yourself at him shamelessly—"

She slapped him hard; it resounded like a clap in the ballroom, and even the orchestra did not drown it out. Horrified,

Charlotte stared at the earl, who, thunderstruck, nursed his reddening cheek. "I . . . I'm sorry," she cried, then whirled and ran out of the ballroom.

Stumbling toward the lady's withdrawing room, Charlotte found the door and bolted to a dark corner where she huddled on a stool and sobbed. A few moments later Fanny, pale and frightened looking, slipped over and crouched down by her. "Charlotte, Count Christoph says if you know what is good for you, you will this minute accompany me outside where our carriage will be waiting," she said, her voice trembling on the edge of tears. "He has made his apologies to the earl for your behavior, he says, and we will sort out the rest tomorrow in a place not so public, since, he said, he cannot trust you."

"Enough. I've heard enough," Charlotte said, rising, her wretchedness turned to cold anger and her tears drying on her cheeks. "And did my brother even ask the earl what he said to occasion such an outburst on my part? No, he wouldn't. I don't know what's wrong with Christoph, but since the moment we landed on the shores of this dreadful nation, he has not been the brother upon whom I have my whole life been able to rely."

Fanny was silent, her blue eyes filled with tears and misery.

"There, there, Fanny," Charlotte said, patting her sister's shoulder, ignoring as best she could the curious knot of ladies who lingered nearby and rudely listened in on their conversation. "It is nothing to do with you, you know. Come, let us leave. If anything could have stayed me in my plan, it is clear now that there is not one reason to remain in this filthy city." Raising her voice, she said, with a proud look around, "German manners are to make a stranger feel comfortable and welcome, but apparently the English do not subscribe to such a code of conduct." She lifted her skirts and swept from the room.

The carriage ride back to their townhome was silent; Christoph was rigid with anger and Charlotte much the same. They had not quarreled so since they were children, and she felt alone, suddenly, bereft. She knew she had behaved badly, but strongly felt that each one of them had: she, Christoph, and the earl. Fanny only was innocent of any wrongdoing.

The moment they arrived she stalked upstairs, deigning to

say not a word to her brother. He didn't deserve her forgiveness and wouldn't get it even if he asked. But a half hour's pacing and calm reflection cooled her somewhat. Her plans swirled in her mind, but the old habits of reliance on her brother would not allow her to abandon him without at least trying to draw him into her scheme. She tapped on his door and he called out "come." When she entered, it was to find him at the desk in his sitting room. He was writing a letter.

"Christoph," she said.

"What is it?"

"To whom do you write?"

"To Frau Liebner, to tell her we will be going home as soon as I can arrange passage."

"What?"

He turned, his blue eyes blazing with fury. "Isn't that what you want, Charlotte? Isn't that what all of this evening's antics were about?"

"Never mind about me, what about Fanny? We are to find her mother—"

"She doesn't care about that! She never has. I asked her after you stormed upstairs to pout and she says it doesn't matter."

"Of course she would say that to you, idiot! She's *terrified* of you. And especially since you probably bellowed at the poor girl, and—"

"No, Charlotte, not another word!" he roared, interrupting her. His face was scarlet and a vein pulsed blue at his temple. "It has always been your scheme, not hers. The girl was completely content at Wolfram Castle until you filled her head with some idiotic idea that to feel whole she must meet her mother."

"Perhaps that was true in the beginning, but Christoph, now we have an idea of where to find—"

"Enough, Charlotte! I've heard enough from you for one night," he said, his voice holding a harsh tone of cold fury she had never heard before. The color had ebbed from his face, but the vein still throbbed along his hairline. "We're going home so I can deposit you in our uncle's care, and not a single word you can say will change my mind. I will break your engagement to the earl so he doesn't have to suffer your hideous behavior, and we will leave directly."

"What is wrong with you?" she cried. She was the impetuous one, not he. He was always so reasonable, so thoughtful, but now he was acting as if . . . a thought occurred to her. "You don't know how to handle meeting another werewolf. Is that it? Is Lyulph Randell behind your sudden decision to leave?"

"Don't be absurd! Shut the door on your way out, please. Good night, Charlotte." He turned away from her, hunching his shoulders and scribbling, dipping his quill rapidly and spilling blotches of dark ink over the page in front of him.

So that was it. She stared at his back for a long minute, and then left, closing the door quietly behind her. She went down the hall and tapped on Fanny's door. Entering, she went to the wardrobe that the hired-in serving staff had filled with Fanny's clothes and dragged out one bag.

"What is it?" Fanny said.

Charlotte looked up. "Christoph is being completely unreasonable. He is arranging for us to go back to Wolfram Castle, and will not listen to reason. So if we are to find Eleanor Dancey, we have no other choice but to take Mr. Randell up on his kind offer and meet his carriage at two. That gives us one hour to prepare."

Chapter 4

LYULPH RANDELL pelted into his townhome and hastily called for his most trusted servant, bound to him by a magic so old and deep most had forgotten it ever existed. Diggory attended him in the library, where Lyulph sat at a desk, a pool of lamplight cast over the leather surface.

"Master?" Diggory said, gently.

Scribbling a hasty letter, Lyulph gestured and his servant fell silent, simply waiting in stasis for what should be required of him. Everything had changed, Lyulph thought, as he paused, in ways he had not foreseen. The moment the young German count had entered the ballroom he had felt the surge of energy from him, the threat to his power, the challenge to his dominion. No other werewolf existed in all of England, and he intended it should stay that way, thus the male of their line must be eliminated or chased from the island and the female . . . he closed his eyes, remembering his first sight of Countess Charlotte von Wolfram, sweetly rounded and elegant of figure, lovely of face and form, but intelligent, and yet with a naïveté that was deeply appealing. Ruined or subjugated? Which was most logical? Perhaps ruining her and letting her fall into disgrace in Wesmorlyn's priggish and haughty glare would be most entertaining, but there was an attraction in considering taking her as his woman, and mother to his brood.

His plans, formulated during many late-night runs in the forest near Randellwood, had been overturned in just one night. He had always intended that Wesmorlyn's chosen bride would be disgraced, and Wesmorlyn himself should die childless. Then he, Lyulph Randell, would marry Lady Hannah St. Ange, righting the wrong that had been done to his family four hundred years ago or more when the earldom of Wesmorlyn, promised to his ancestor, was instead handed to Wes's ancestor in a breathtaking betrayal. Thus he had always maintained a careful friendship with Wesmorlyn, never allowing any hint of his deeper plot to peek through his veneer of casual amity. The conflict this night over the countess was a hasty concoction to thrust a wedge between them. Had he taken the right course? He must think. He stopped scribbling and put his head in his hands. Careful planning, using every bit of his considerable charm, the attraction of the wolf, on the impressionable Lady Hannah St. Ange, all would be for naught if he diverged from his careful plan now and instead decided to make Charlotte von Wolfram his bride and mother to his children, the future heirs of a dynasty.

He must not be rash. Each lady had her charms. In Lady Hannah he would gain the Wesmorlyn estate, eventually, though it would require more in the way of devious scheming to find a way to eliminate Wesmorlyn without shedding blood. He did wish to avoid that if possible. Also, with her as his bride his offspring would have the most unique heritage of any child ever born on earth. No one even knew what one would be like, a child born with the combined talents of his and the Earl of Wesmorlyn's lines. There was a risk, though, in that Wesmorlyn was absolutely resolute that the Randell and St. Ange families would never mingle their bloodlines. Unless he could find a way to change the earl's mind, he must either wait until Hannah was of age to marry without her brother's permission—that was years away—or escape with her to Gretna.

If he changed courses now and took Countess Charlotte

von Wolfram as his bride, with her fresh, vigorous, and untainted line of werewolf blood, he could be assured that his children borne of her would be powerful and fast, strong and pure. It was an intriguing thought, and he had made a promising start in attracting her sufficiently to break with Wesmorlyn and take him as a mate instead. She appeared to be vulnerable to his wolfish glamour.

But there was one more option. What if he simply told Wes about the von Wolframs' werewolfism? With the earl's poorly concealed disgust of the breed he would immediately repudiate the countess, and that would no doubt force the Germans to leave England or suffer humiliation. But *would* he reject her? The earl's intent that Hannah not mingle her offspring's blood with the Randell werewolf strain did not indicate that he would be so delicate himself. No, Lyulph reluctantly decided, it was far too dangerous to take that path. If he told Wes the truth, and the earl then decided that there was an attraction in the thought of the power, strength, and possibly unusual talents their children might have, bloodshed would be the inevitable result.

Lyulph sighed deeply. What to do? His control over Hannah had borne interesting fruit. At his command she had spent some time talking to Fanny, Countess Charlotte's sister, and had winkled the story of the countess's plan to find Fanny's mother, now that they were in England, out of the girl. Was it happenstance that he then overheard Countess Charlotte and her illegitimate sister talking about their plan to leave London and find the younger girl's natural mother? Or was destiny conspiring to bring him everything he needed to become undefeatable? It was as if the maidens were thrust into his control, so perhaps fate was giving him the opportunity to build a future beyond what he had even imagined. Or the chance to make a huge mistake by not staying with his plan.

Perhaps he could go on with his current project without making a final decision. He finished the letter, scrawled his signature, sanded and sealed it. "Diggory," he said, and his servant snapped to attention. "Take this letter to Moor Cottage in Cornwall," he said, handing him the note. "You must start immediately and on horseback."

The man blanched and began to shake. "Moor Cottage. To Madam Morwenna?"

"Yes, to Morwenna." The man hadn't touched the letter. "Diggory!" he said, waving it. "Take it and do as I say."

Quivering still, the pale fellow took it and began to sob.

"What's wrong with you? Are you afraid of her?"

He nodded.

"She won't hurt you; she won't even touch you!"

"But she doesn't have to, sir. Touch me, I mean. She was inside of me last time, and I couldn't do a thing!" He shuddered convulsively. "She began to seek my thoughts, and when she found things she did not like, she tossed them out. It was like I was a room, and she began to move the furniture around inside my head! I thought I was going mad." He touched his forehead with one shaking hand, terror in his eyes, which had gone black and empty.

Diggory perhaps had reason to fear Morwenna simply because of his susceptibility to magic, and she did like to amuse herself on occasion with simpletons and the vulnerable. Lyulph drew an amulet out from under his shirt and pulled it off over his head. It was a sharp canine tooth strung on a leather thong, and he held it out to Diggory. "Take this and wear it. It is mine and will protect you from her. Do not let her see it, and you must never take it off. Don't let her charm you into taking it off, for she has her ways, does Morwenna, and none know that better than I. It amuses her to practice her wiles on the unwary. I have her under my control right now, but how long that will last I cannot say. Do this and you will be safe."

Reminded of his distrust of Morwenna's complete commitment to him, he quickly scrawled another letter in a language far different from English, and sealed it as well. "This also must be delivered," he said, handing him the other letter as well and giving him the direction of how to find the recipient. "Now, take them both and fly like the wind, Diggory."

The servant slipped the amulet over his head and tucked it under his shirt. An expression of peace covered his face and he sighed. "Thank you dear sir, and bless you." He ducked his head and bowed, taking the letters. "I will do your bidding."

"Send Burgess to me, even if you have to waken him from

a drunken stupor. And then leave immediately, but come directly back from Cornwall after delivering the letters, for I have some tasks here in London for you."

THE street was wet from another brief shower, but the moon had come back out from behind the clouds, casting a faint glimmer of silver across the wet paving. As Charlotte tugged Fanny after her, lugging their bags over her other arm, she felt more afraid than she ever had in her life, even though she had faced grave, deadly danger in the past and seen things no young lady should ever witness. But this step was her own responsibility, and thus, the consequences. Fanny was depending on her.

"There is the carriage, just as Mr. Randell promised!" she exclaimed, as a distant church bell pealed the time. Two bells. The carriage stood waiting across the street by the little park, a dark blot in the misty shadows. Pulling Fanny behind her, she hurried across the wet street, looking back at the tall, narrow row house and hoping no one in their own abode or the attached ones to the left or right had seen or heard them leave.

The driver leaped down and approached. "Bist you th'forrin lasses?" he grunted, his eyes just shadowy hollows in his seamed face.

"Yes," Charlotte said, relieved that he had made it easy to know he was the right man. "You are Mr. Randell's driver?"

"Ar, that'd be me. Burgess I be by name." He grabbed the bags from her and tossed them into a trunk on the back of the carriage and opened the door. "Letter for 'ee frum Maister Randell on th' seat o' the carriage."

"Come, Fanny," Charlotte said, taking her sister's arm, but Fanny hung back. "What is it?"

"Are you sure we're doing the right thing?" she said, her light-timbered voice trembling.

Charlotte stopped for one moment and thought. Were they? If the objective was to find Fanny's mother, then this seemed not only the correct thing, but the *only* thing to do, and since Christoph would not help them, they must do it alone. She had tried to be prudent, but now she must be decisive. "We have to do it this way. Christoph is being completely unreasonable right now and I have no confidence that I could convince him to help us. He has never, through all the turmoil and horror of the last years, treated me so abominably."

She took her sister's hands and stared at her, then touched her cold cheek. "Fanny, if it were not a matter that Eleanor Dancey is about to leave England forever, I would not be so hasty, but time is against us. Come. It's not so far; we've come much further already, all the way to England. We can't leave this vile land without finding your mother."

"But I'm afraid to leave without Christoph."

"I'm not afraid, Fanny. Trust me, and come. It will be an adventure."

"I don't think I like adventures."

"I'll take care of you, I promise."

In the light of the street lantern Fanny gazed up into Charlotte's eyes, and then she nodded once. "All right," she said, and climbed in ahead of Charlotte and took a seat.

Charlotte climbed in behind her and rapped on the roof of the carriage. It began to pull away. As confident as she was of doing the right thing, when she gazed through the carriage window up at the townhome and saw a dim, flickering light in Christoph's window, still she felt a pang of heartbreak. Her brother had always been her rock in an uncertain world. When their parents had died tragically weeks apart from each other, Christoph, then just nine years old, had been stoic and steadfast, comforting his little sister and helping her through it with an amazing maturity. Though life since then had been difficult in many ways, and he had been through his own share of troubles, she had always been able to talk to him. Now she couldn't.

She turned away from the window and hung her head. Fanny's small hand on her arm brought her back to reality and she forced a smile to her lips. She had leaned on Christoph often enough in her life, but now it was her turn to be the strong one for someone else. "Let's open Mr. Randell's note, shall we?" she said, brightly, shedding her Brunswick cape and turning up the coach lamp. She broke the wax seal as the carriage jolted.

She could not look back, and refused to even glance

through the window, instead scanning through the letter. She nodded. "That's good. Mr. Randell says that in the morning when he meets Wesmorlyn he will do his best to talk reason to him. He has no desire to duel with such a good friend and sees no need of it; he hopes that after a break the earl will be more agreeable. At that time Mr. Randell will also let him know that you and I are safely on our way to Cornwall to meet Eleanor Dancey. He says not to worry, he will take care of everything. We are just to concentrate on meeting your mother."

She folded the letter and stowed it in her reticule, feeling heat rise to her cheeks at some other nonsense in the note, his professions of undying fidelity, and his hopes that he did not shock her too much with his ardor. "The rest is just directions of where to stay, and his hopes of meeting up in Salisbury, which is on the way, so he can guide us and introduce us to Miss Dancey. Isn't this exciting?"

"Certainly, Charlotte," Fanny said, but her voice was tremulous.

"Now, Fanny, you must be brave!"

"I will try to be, but it is not so natural to me as it is to you. You're so courageous, and have even faced werewolves!"

Werewolves! Fanny knew about Christoph, but persisted in her odd belief that werewolves were terrible, deadly creatures; Christoph was an exception in her mind, an aberration from the general run of things. No amount of reasoning about their Uncle Nikolas being one, too, and others in the family, would shake her irrational fear. Charlotte sighed.

"Why is it," Fanny asked, her expression one of puzzlement, "that men of the family transform but ladies don't?"

"I don't know. Frau Liebner says that Uta told her much before passing on last spring." Countess Uta von Wolfram, Charlotte's great aunt and the holder of many family secrets, had died in the spring, but had used every bit of time she had left on earth sharing that lore so the next generation in their family would have all they needed to deal with their unusual and difficult heritage. "But no one can explain to me why men transform and women do not. They just say that is how it is. How I wish I could become a wolf! I would run with Christoph."

"I don't wish such a horrid thing," Fanny said, shuddering. "I'm afraid enough of the power we ladies *do* have!"

She spoke of the women of the family's ability to pass on werewolfism to a man they bonded with. It was a poor exchange, Charlotte thought, for the power to *become* a werewolf, faster and more powerful than a true wolf, and with lingering abilities even in human form that gave Christoph better sight, hearing, and smell than she could imagine. "It's not enough. I will always think that we, as women, received the poorer end of the bargain."

"What do you mean, Charlotte?" Fanny asked, her voice small.

"I was just wondering if any woman has ever really *tried* to transform. Is it just a story that we are unable? Is there more beyond our abilities than simply passing on the gift to a man? I wonder."

"Best not to try," Fanny said, clasping her hands together in her lap. "I wouldn't want to become a beast. I'm very happy as a lady."

Charlotte started laughing and could not stop, hugging Fanny close, tears streaming down her cheeks as her laughter turned to weeping. "Oh, Fanny, I'm so happy I have you."

A mist as thick as blanc mange rolled up from the river and clung to the dips and hollows of Battersea Fields. Wesmorlyn paced, his sword swinging at his side. Semyaza stood nearby, ramrod straight and impassive. In the distance, on a rise, was the carriage holding the surgeon. Not having slept or eaten at all, the earl was strung as taut as a bow. His back itched between his shoulder blades, and that was not a good sign. Since he was a child he had always thought of that as a portent that he was on the wrong path.

He strode up to Semyaza. "Do I have it wrong, Sam? Have I doomed us, my whole family? Good heavens, I pray that I have not wasted the efforts of a lifetime, for I couldn't bear it if I destroyed poor Hannah's chance of redemption just on this foolishness."

Semyaza merely bowed his head.

"I know. You cannot say." Wesmorlyn strode away and

gazed out over the amorphous landscape, fretting. Was it right? Was it wrong? In the moment Randell had said the words implying that the countess had invited his kiss it had seemed there was only one choice, and that was to preserve her honor by dueling, though he had never done such a rash thing in his entire careful life. Now it seemed not so certain an answer. Perhaps it was hubris, pitiful vanity, one of the deadly sins, to think that her honor could only be preserved by an action of his own.

Another hour passed, and still Lyulph did not arrive.

It gave him too much time to think as he paced. The mist began to burn off, and the river became visible down the slope, and beyond it, on the other side, Chelsea. What was he doing? Why had he reacted so impulsively as to challenge Lyulph Randell, long his friend and Cornwall neighbor? Perhaps when the man showed up, both would offer a nick of the sword tip to each other, to satisfy honor and the challenge of first blood, and then talk out their differences, he thought, glancing toward Semyaza, still impassive but watching him with burning interest. Yes, that was the right thing to do; he felt it, and the itching between his shoulder blades eased as he considered that course of action.

But where *was* the man? He took out his watch and read the time. It was almost nine. Wesmorlyn was anxious now for the meeting, for he wished to explain to Randell why he had felt honor bound to issue the challenge, and to ask what had been in his heart when he took the lovely countess in his arms to kiss her. Had the young lady really done something to invite the kiss? He knew so little of her, and could not determine if she had lured Lyulph to such an uncharacteristic gaffe. Lyulph Randell had always had some kind of special charm that attracted women to him in droves. He had never been celibate, but Wesmorlyn refused to judge him for only doing what most other men their age did. Most of his friends took lovers and mistresses, happily indulging in sexual excess as much as alcoholic and prandial excess.

The intertwined histories of their families and the proximity of their estates in Cornwall had forced Wesmorlyn and Lyulph into a kind of friendship over the years. The Randells could not help being what they were, and in truth, Lyulph more than any other Randell male seemed to the earl to exhibit the most positive attributes of humility, hard work, and fortitude. It was not enough to make Lyulph a safe companion for Hannah, and Wesmorlyn had been forced to step in to keep the two from spending too much time together over the last year, while Hannah was in mourning for her mother, but Randell was a vast improvement over his father, who had been dissolute and dangerous. Most importantly, Lyulph Randell had never tasted human blood, and that, for a werewolf, was a feat of great self-restraint.

A werewolf. An *animal*. Wesmorlyn had never been able to conquer the disgust he felt knowing Lyulph for what he was, though the man could not help his heritage. It comforted him that he had never shown the other man his repulsion. That would be cruel and impolite. He paced along the hillside and gazed into the distance. Where was Lyulph Randell?

CHRISTOPH swung his legs over the side of the bed and sat staring at the triangle of faint dawn light left by the partially open draperies. His first morning in London. He scrubbed his eyes with his fingers and yawned, stretching out his shoulders and trying to push away the last shadows of the awful dreams he had experienced all night, dreams of running as a wolf and being netted, then speared. He couldn't imagine from whence such thoughts came.

However, it was true that the urge to transform and run as a wolf had overcome him in the ballroom, and he had longed for open space and freedom with a fierce, ripping need in his gut. The confinement of the ballroom, so stifling hot it was like being smothered, the tension, his uncertainty about how to behave toward Lyulph Randell, Charlotte's unusual behavior, the roomful of ladies and gentlemen staring at them: it had all felt like a weight on his shoulders. The cool, green, fragrant forests of Wolfram Castle had never seemed so distant as in that crowded ballroom. The nightmare of being netted was nothing more than a metaphor for society, and his sense of imprisonment in the city.

But today, he decided, standing and stretching, going to the window and throwing back the draperies and gazing out over the misty scene of chimney pots and angled, slate-tiled rooftops, was a new day, and this city his to explore. He did not intend to leave London, though he truly had meant his threat for one brief moment. It had seemed the simplest plan, to take Fanny and Charlotte back to Germany, and then go off on his own with no responsibilities.

He had more fortitude than that, though, and the letter he was writing to Frau Liebner was just to inquire if she had safely arrived at her relatives' in the north of England. He had written a second to his uncle to let him and his wife, Elizabeth, know that everything was satisfactory in their new London home, and a third to the inquiry agent who was searching for Fanny's mother to apprise him of their arrival.

So yes, today was truly a new day. The haze of coal-fire smoke over the city was growing into a soupy miasma, with the humidity in the air the remnant of the rain the previous evening. But the weather, judging from the pearly dawn light creating a roseate glow over the rooftops, was vastly improved. They would not leave, but would stay and see if they could mend the relationship with the Earl of Wesmorlyn, whom Christoph had found a solid and comfortable sort of fellow, ideally suited to take care of his flighty sister. And perhaps marriage and children would calm her down, settling her inappropriate wildness. So, while Fanny and Charlotte went to the dressmaking shop, he would see about box seats to the theater, make an appointment with a renowned music master, and use his family's name hopefully to gain a meeting with a famous violinist and fellow countryman he had heard of as residing in London and taking students. He needed the fellow's help on some violin concertos he had written and wished to perfect.

Siegfried, his valet, entered the room with a terrified look on his young face. One of the sons of Heinrich, his uncle's valet, Siegfried had been trained to follow in his father's footsteps. His uncle Nikolas had thought they might have need of a German servant while in London, and since the boy had expressed an interest in going, he had been added to the party. Rapidly, in German, the young man expressed his fear that the other servants were trying to poison the master.

"No, Siegfried, they are not trying to poison me. What gave you such an idea?"

As the fellow bustled around, preparing his master's toilette with shaving implements placed just so on the nearby table, he spewed a long story about how he had caught the cook sprinkling something in the master's morning coffee, and how he had then tried to stop him, but the ferocious fellow had almost come to blows with him.

Laughing to himself and greatly cheered, Christoph clapped Siegfried on the shoulder. "Calm yourself; I promise you I will get to the bottom of this, but I have a feeling it is a misunderstanding only, and the barrier of language is responsible for the two of you having such a quarrel. I will take care of everything."

That explained why there was no tray by his bedside and no morning coffee, though he had ordered that it be waiting for him at first light.

Siegfried shaved him, then Christoph bathed himself with the hot water provided by a frightened-looking maidservant. As he dressed, he wondered how Charlotte and Fanny were faring. He would have to straighten out the staff situation, and make sure the ladies were comfortable before beginning his day. And he would need to speak with Charlotte. Perhaps he should have the night before, but he had been far too angry at her behavior, and had wanted her to feel his ire. But now he thought he was perhaps too harsh. She was dealing with even more than him, in a way, meeting her fiancé for the first time and finding out he was somewhat of a cold prig. As fine a man as the earl no doubt was, he was also a very cool character, not the kind of romantic fellow young ladies seemed to long for. Perhaps Wesmorlyn needed a little hint to Charlotte's impulsive but generous and loving character.

He gazed at himself in the mirror, putting his cravat to rights. His damp blond hair shone, showing streaks of copper and russet. Yes, he mused, he would straighten it all out this morning, and they could begin anew.

The butler, who had been engaged along with the rest of the staff before they arrived, tapped on the door, entered, and bowed. "Sir, my apologies for my staff and their confusion this morning, but your German valet has thrown them all into

disarray. I will straighten them out. It has come to my attention, though, that something is amiss."

"What is it?" Christoph said, carelessly, turning away from
the mirror toward the portly and dignified fellow. A loud rap-
ping at the front door echoed in the hallway and up the stairs.

The butler held out a folded piece of paper. "This note was
found in Countess Charlotte's bedchamber this morning, on
her pillow."

"On her pillow? Is she not still in bed?" Christoph took the
note, only half attending as he unfolded it, listening to the
commotion downstairs of some guest being admitted. Who
would call this early on the first day after their arrival in London? He glanced at the note; it was in Charlotte's hand, and it
was in German. He caught a phrase that leaped off the page to
him.

"We are gone to find Fanny's mother," Charlotte had written, and he forced his attention on the rest of the note, feeling
as if the breath had been sucked from his body. Fanny and
Charlotte had, it appeared, left London in the night and were
off on an expedition to some unknown place to find Fanny's
mother, Eleanor Dancey!

A footman came upstairs and accosted the butler in the
bedchamber doorway; the fellow listened intently to his un-
derling, and then turned to Christoph. "Sir, I beg your pardon," the butler said, "but it is the Earl of Wesmorlyn. He
sends up his compliments, makes his apologies for the early
hour, but he has something to tell you that cannot wait."

Christoph crumpled the note in his hand, all of his plans
for the day crushed along with the paper. "I cannot go down,
I must . . ." He stopped and thought. *No.* If he wanted to avoid
a scandal of epic proportions, then he had to appear just as if
everything was normal. He would listen to the earl, respond
appropriately, get rid of him, and then he would find Charlotte, pull her all the way back to London by the hair if necessary, and tie her down to one place so she could not embarrass
him ever again. "I will go down and speak with the earl."

Wesmorlyn awaited him in the cold, dreary sitting room
off the equally grim main hall. He turned and bowed at
Christoph's entrance. "I must apologize for the uncivilized
hour of my visit, Count von Wolfram."

"I admit I am surprised, my lord."

"I must trespass further on your good graces by asking to see my fiancée."

"Sir, I do not know about your own sister, but Charlotte, I can assure you, would never arise this early." A neat evasion.

"Ah. Yes, of course. I wished merely to inform her that I had visited the field of honor, and done my duty to her."

"I can give her that message. What was the outcome of the duel? I trust you were not forced to do damage to Mr. Randell? That would be a most shocking outcome."

"No, as a matter of fact," the earl said, with a frown on his handsome face, "Lyulph Randell never showed up at the duel site."

Christoph felt a grave anxiety begin to churn in the pit of his stomach. "Randell never appeared?"

"No. May I see Countess Charlotte a little later? I could come back in two hours. I truly do wish to speak with her, for I feel I have an apology to make to her regarding my behavior last night and some hasty words I said that may have hurt her."

Christoph, with the crumpled note burning in his palm, was rapidly conning over the possibilities. The note had not said so, but was it possible that Charlotte had impetuously eloped with Randell? Or could she have allowed him to accompany her and Fanny on this mad dash to visit Eleanor Dancey? He was no longer certain of anything, and his one instinct was to preserve her good reputation any way he could.

"As a matter of fact, Wesmorlyn, I am told by the maid that Charlotte awoke this morning with a . . . uh, head cold, and I fear she will be in bed for most of the day. Perhaps if we could allow her to rest today, and . . . well, I'm not sure how quickly she will mend." That was terrible; he had stammered through his swiftly concocted excuse with no assurance at all. He took a deep breath and said, "I will not bore you with the details, but the journey was extremely wearing on the ladies, you know."

"She seemed in fine fettle last night," Wesmorlyn said, with a frown pinching his face.

"Just give her time. She'll be well in a couple of days, I warrant. May I see you out?"

Wesmorlyn was soon staring at the knocker on the door of the rented townhome, and feeling the first snarl of what would likely become a festering knot of anger. How dare they ignore him? The count had ushered him out as if he was a tradesman. And to be put off for days, with no idea of when he would next see his fiancée?

Something was wrong. But what?

He returned to his carriage, where Semyaza awaited him. "Something is wrong, Sam, and I want to know what. Watch this house, and if you can, make friends with the staff. They will not have had time to gain any loyalty to their new masters. Something is amiss, and I will know what it is, for I will *not* be played for a fool."

Chapter 5

THROUGH THREE wearying days on the road, staying in inns on both intervening nights, her English money beginning to dwindle, Charlotte worried constantly that they had done the wrong thing. Poor Christoph must be anxious, she thought, over and over until the phrase was like a flail with which she lashed herself. As angry as she had been at his behavior toward her, the hours and days passed, and that feeling mellowed. Everything had been left for him to handle, including making her excuses to the earl. That was wrong, for she should have sent a note to Wesmorlyn herself, ending their engagement. She hadn't thought of it. The only thing that soothed her conscience on that head was the resolution that once they were at Eleanor Dancey's residence she would write a letter. She would simply tell the earl that it was clear they would not suit.

She had certainly had hours to think it over and come to that opinion even if she hadn't already been determined on that course of action, because Fanny was proving to be unexpectedly poor company. She was fussy and particular, not enjoying the food at the inns at which they stayed, and turning up her nose at the linens, saying they smelled musty. It was true, they did, but bad food, poor service, and moldy linens were small inconveniences in exchange for an adventure. With the right companion she would have enjoyed the escapade; she longed to talk to Fanny about it all, but got only sighs in reply to her observations. Their driver was taciturn and unhelpful, beyond making sure they were safely stowed in the inn at night. He apparently spent most of his time drinking, for each morning he looked grubbier and smelled worse, reeking of alcohol.

Their advance into Cornwall had been a revelation. The countryside was barren at times but for "tors," craggy, rocky hills that exhibited a taciturn nature equaling that of Burgess at his worst. And yet it deeply thrilled Charlotte, who found the windswept hillsides and distant views of dark, threatening clouds exciting, almost as much so as her native forests. She longed for the freedom to wander those distant hillsides, unfettered by the bonds of society and its expectation of perfect behavior. Someone with whom to share her thoughts and impressions would have been a boon, but she knew she must be tender of Fanny's feelings, for the girl had other concerns than just the wild beauty of England's most westerly county.

Finally it was evening again, and one more night only would be spent on the road, Charlotte had ascertained, before they would be at their final destination. Mr. Randell, who was supposed to join them at Salisbury to accompany them the rest of the way and introduce them to Miss Eleanor Dancey, had failed them, sending a note by the incredibly speedy English postal service to say that he had been held up in London, but would join them in Cornwall in time to introduce them to Fanny's mother. This had sent Fanny into a gloomy mood of doom that left Charlotte irritated and unable to speak to her civilly, but now, as night fell and they were drawing close to Bodmin, where they were to stay the night before going on the next morning to Moor Cottage, she could no longer maintain silence.

"We're almost there," she remarked, trying to rouse Fanny from her torpor. "Tomorrow you will meet your mother. Aren't you the least bit excited?"

"I suppose," Fanny said, grudgingly, from the gloom.

"If I were you, I would be hopping with anticipation!"

"I've often observed that for sisters we are remarkably un-alike. Night has fallen," she fretted, cupping her hand around her eyes at the glass, trying to see out the side window. "Aren't we going to stop in a village at an inn?"

"Yes. We just haven't arrived in Bodmin yet."

"But isn't it rather late? Shouldn't we have stopped some-where else? Why did we not stop for the night at that place we paused at in Launceston, the Jamaica Inn? That was hours ago! I haven't seen anything outside the carriage for ever so long. Where are we?"

"Good heavens, you are a gloomy puss today," Charlotte said. "Burgess knows what he's doing. Has he steered us wrong so far?"

"Would we know if he had? I don't like him," Fanny said, primly. "He smells of drink, very often."

The carriage halted, and Charlotte sighed in relief. "Thank goodness! We must be at Bodmin."

The door banged opened, and Burgess loomed in the door-way, his surly expression illuminated in a ghostly manner by the interior lanterns.

"Have we arrived, then? Where is the inn?" Charlotte asked, trying to see around the sturdy form of the driver.

"Out," he grunted. "Got a bad wheel, and you'm getting out," he slurred.

"What do you mean?" Charlotte glared at him without moving. "I didn't feel any trouble. If you must get help for the wheel, we shall wait here."

"Out," Burgess said. He reached in and grabbed her by the sleeve, pulling her so hard the material tore.

"What are you doing? Stop it, you drunken fool!"

"Drunken? Ain't drunken, tha gockey mort! Get outta my carriage!" With that he grasped her wrist and wrenched it hard, pulling her forcibly from the vehicle.

She tumbled down to the gritty road surface, crying out at the rough handling. Fanny, giving a wail of fear, needed no such encouragement and jumped out after Charlotte, kneeling at her side and trying to raise her up.

"How could you treat her in this uncouth manner?" she

cried, her voice squeaking in her outrage. "Mr. Randell will hear about this."

"Ar, well, thou hast zealed thy fate, zaucy mort!" Burgess reached into the box in back, pulled out their traveling bags, and tossed them down beside them in the dark. "Thou can fend fer thine oon zelves." He said not another word but jumped up and clicked to his horses, pulling away at a smart pace.

"Burgess!" Charlotte cried, getting to her feet and racing a few paces after the carriage. "Burgess, come back here! You cannot leave us in the dark. What shall we do?"

But he was long gone, just the *clop clop* of hooves on the hard-packed road surface fading in the distance to signal that he had ever been there.

"Oh dear," Fanny said, wringing her hands and sobbing. "Did I say the wrong thing? Why did he leave us here?"

The damp evening air misted on her cheeks, and Charlotte, still stunned, stared down the road into the dark. It made no sense. Burgess had told them something was wrong with a wheel, and that was why they must climb down, but then he had driven down the road smartly enough once they were out. She went back to her sister and put her arm around Fanny's shoulders. "It was nothing you said, Fanny. Either he was drunk, or . . . I don't know. I can think of no other explanation."

"What are we to do?"

Night had closed in around them, the last vestiges of day disappearing in a hint of purple on the western horizon. Fanny shivered, and Charlotte roused herself. "You're cold. At least the villain left us our bags, though my Brunswick is still inside the carriage. Let us get our shawls out of our bags and decide what we should do and where we shall shelter for the night."

"I'm frightened, Charlotte," Fanny sobbed.

Not willing to admit that she, too, was scared, Charlotte, rooting around in her large carpet bag for her warmest shawl, said, "Nonsense. There is nothing of which to be frightened. We are on a main road. Nothing can happen to us."

"But when we were at the inn last night, I heard two maids

speaking of h-highwaymen! What shall we do? Where shall we hide?"

"Aha! Here it is," she exclaimed, pulling out her shawl. "Now, Fanny, you must get something warm for yourself. Here, let me help." Charlotte knelt on the rough shoulder of the road and began searching in Fanny's bag, hampered by the darkness and her sister's lack of attention. "Fanny, calm yourself!" she said, standing and putting her arm around the other girl's shoulders. "It will do no good to snivel now. We must decide what to do, whether to hide by the hedgerow and wait for morning light, or try to make some progress."

"I think we should hide," Fanny said, timidly.

That was Fanny; she would always decide for the safer-seeming of two choices, or the one that required the least decisiveness. "Now, listen to me," Charlotte said. "For all we know we're a mere mile or so from some habitation. I say we walk for a ways down the road and try to find some village, or failing that a farm. Even a barn or shed would be better than the hedgerow, do you not agree?"

"You're right, Charlotte," Fanny said, sounding calmer.

"Of course I am." Charlotte knelt again and pulled out Fanny's warmest shawl. She handed it to her, fastened the bag again, then stood. "We were headed in that direction," she said, pointing down the road, faintly illuminated by the rising moon. "And so I say we continue that way, since we know that we traveled quite far since we last saw civilization behind us. Forward, I say."

They walked, their bags seeming heavier and heavier as they became more weary. The dark was eerie, with sounds in the hedgerow by the road causing Fanny to cry out and dissolve into near hysterics, until Charlotte was close to snapping at her. What good was allowing terror to overtake one, when reason said they were unlikely to be molested by any creatures so small as to hide in a hedgerow?

Exhaustion weighed heavy on Charlotte, doubly so since Fanny insisted on clinging to her, pulling her arm until it felt as if it would come right out of the socket. Fanny started and cried out at every sound, and yanked on Charlotte's arm until it ached. Her bag felt heavier than she would have thought possible, despite its holding only one dress, underclothes, and accoutrements.

Surely even on this lonely moor there must be some sign of habitation soon? She cursed Burgess under her breath, and satisfied herself with everything that she would say to Mr. Randell about his choice of trusted drivers when next they met. Why the fellow had abandoned them, she could not imagine. The puzzle would stay a mystery until they heard from Mr. Randell, but first they must get through this long night and find a village or some place to stay.

Another half hour passed. They had made very little progress, and Charlotte began to feel the first trickle of desperation. Fanny whimpered constantly, and complained that her feet hurt, that she was hungry, and that she was cold and scared. As much as Charlotte loved her sister, adversity did not make her stronger, it only made her complain, and that was becoming worse than annoying.

She let her mind wander instead, trying to defeat the anger she felt toward Fanny for being so fainthearted. Mr. Randell's note at Salisbury had said nothing about his duel with the earl. How had it gone? she wondered. Had the earl been in any way justified in his actions, in challenging his longtime friend and neighbor?

And what was Christoph doing? She felt a pang of bitter remorse. Her brother had been through so much in the last year or so. He had been drugged, abused, and tricked into having a shameful affair with their likewise drug-addled aunt. He had survived losing the woman he had fallen in love with to a rival, and all of the turmoil had culminated in finding out that he was a werewolf, something he told her he had never suspected about himself. At last he was coming to terms with it, finding that it explained much about himself that he had never understood, including why he and his uncle, Count Nikolas von Wolfram, could not live in the same house without constantly arguing and battling over every little detail.

"I don't see any village or town yet, Charlotte," Fanny complained, "and I'm tired and hungry. What shall we do? What if some villain accosts us? Or what if morning comes and we still cannot find any town? What shall we do? I wish we had never made this journey. I wish we had waited for Christoph to—"

"Fanny, do shut up and let me think."

In silent resentment Fanny withdrew her arm from Charlotte's and stopped. She dropped her bag on the road and crossed her arms over her chest.

"I'm sorry, Fanny, but—"

"You needn't snap at me like that," the younger woman said, her voice trembling with weariness and thick with tears.

"I am sorry," Charlotte said, and put her arms around her sister, gazing out over the lonely moor. She hugged Fanny and patted her back in what she hoped was a comforting way. But, what was that flickering light dancing on the moor? She watched the light appear and disappear. Was it some ghost or phantasm come to plague them? Charlotte, weary too and stretched to the limits of her endurance, shivered and watched. But the dancing light, only sometimes visible, did not come any closer. She patted Fanny on the back, then pushed her away and said, "I see something, in the distance. It could be a lantern, or . . ."

Fanny turned and gazed, saying, "I don't see anything at all. Oh wait, yes I do."

"It could be a house."

"Or it could be the campsite of brigands!"

"But it could be a house," Charlotte persisted, straining her eyes to try to see the source of the light.

"I think we ought to continue along the road, or hide in the bushes."

Charlotte thought about it. She gazed down the road into the distance and saw nothing. There was nothing from whence they came. As long as it felt like they had been walking, in her heart she knew that between Fanny's timidity and her own exhaustion, they had actually covered very little distance, perhaps only a few furlongs. "I think we ought to at least creep closer and see. It could be a farmhouse. Think, Fanny, farm-fresh eggs and a rasher of bacon! Bread and butter, perhaps jam! Hot water and a bed to sleep in."

"Or all of our belongings stolen from us and our throats cut or worse!"

"You have the most astonishing bloodthirsty streak," Charlotte commented.

"I read that pirates came from Cornwall and Devon, and that they are all smugglers and wreckers and highwaymen here! And there are ghosts, too. I read about ghosts that will drive you mad."

"Good heavens, you really will have to read some books other than horrid novels, little sister." Charlotte sighed. "Then stay here, if you are afraid, and I will go."

"No!" Fanny said, ending on a shriek. She clung to Charlotte. "Don't leave me on the road alone."

"Then come with me."

"No! Don't go, please Charlotte!"

Taking a deep breath in and letting it out slowly, Charlotte chose her words carefully, gazing into the dimness at the faint paleness that was Fanny's face. "So, your plan is to remain quivering exactly where we are until we are rescued, by some fortuitous circumstance?"

"I . . . I don't know."

"Then you will have to accompany me, because I'm going closer to see if it is a house or farm." She hiked her bag up on her shoulder and left the road, lifting her skirts and scaling down the raised embankment. She approached the hedgerow, looking for a break in it, then took her own bag and shoved it into a thicket, feeling around, finding a thick stick and thrusting it out of the hedgerow at an angle, to mark where she hid her bag. Fanny followed, whimpering. Charlotte took her bag and pushed it in, too. She felt along the hedgerow, found a gap, and pushed through it, dragging a reluctant Fanny behind her. After the bushes, the going was easier, and Charlotte crept forward over the grassy expanse, holding her sister's hand firmly, going carefully to avoid tripping on the rocky outcroppings that dotted the moor.

The light was coming from near a grove of trees. Were the trees hiding a house? It seemed unlikely, but what else could she think?

Moving forward with as much stealth as she could while being cautious of stumbling on rocks, she remembered long-ago hunting expeditions. When she and her brother were young, they would take off for the whole day and hunt, staying out sometimes until long after dark. They had even, on occasion, camped out overnight, making a bed of pine boughs and talking all night while gazing up at the stars and the moon.

It was a rough-and-tumble childhood. As she grew older, her Aunt Adele decided it was not suitable for a young lady to be roaming about the countryside; her adventures were over, even as Christoph was still allowed his freedom. But he didn't go. It would have been dreary, he said, to go without her. She missed Christoph terribly. Tears prickled her eyes, but she squeezed them out and fiercely quelled them. Dropping Fanny's hand, she whispered, "Stay behind if you like. I need to get closer and see what we are dealing with just beyond these trees. I cannot yet tell."

She crept forward, staying in the dark shadows among the brush, her hands out before her to protect her from branches. Voices. Laughter and a musical instrument of some sort; was it a guitar? Someone sang a snatch of song in some language Charlotte did not understand. Who was this? What were they doing on the moor?

The pleasant smell of woodsmoke drifted toward her, and with it the rich scent of food bubbling over a fire. Rabbit stew; the smell of it was familiar from her youth. Her mouth watered. She was so hungry and thirsty! Parting some bushes, she finally saw movement and people. It was an encampment of some sort. There were odd, brightly colored wagons set at angles around an open area where the fire burned brightly. Men sat in groups around the fire, and one did indeed have a guitar, which he played, while laughing and talking with the others.

She felt a tug on her dress, and Fanny whispered, "What do you see? I smell food."

"It's some kind of encampment, but . . ." She didn't want to say that she saw only men. They could not enter an encampment of men, for who knew what would be their fate? But there: bringing a bowl of food to one of the men was a woman, very plump, her hair tied up in a scarf and full skirts flowing around her rotund figure. The man plunged his spoon in and began to eat ravenously. Charlotte's stomach grumbled. The scene was domestic and peaceful. What should they do, approach, or go away?

"Who are you and what do you want?" a voice suddenly cried behind them.

Chapter 6

CHARLOTTE STIFLED a cry as she whirled. Fanny scuttled away into the dark, whimpering at the brambles that tore at her skirts, but Charlotte faced her interrogator, who held up a lantern. It was a young woman, dressed much like the older woman she had already seen, in colorful voluminous skirts and a scarf over her dark hair.

"Who are you?" she said, her melodic voice holding more curiosity than suspicion. "Why are you spying on us?"

"My apologies," Charlotte said, carefully. "I did not mean to spy."

"Then what are you doing creeping up on us like this?" she asked, examining Charlotte's face in the flickering light from her lamp.

"Pardon, but who are *you*? Why are you camped out here?"

"I think you should answer *my* questions first," the young woman demanded, with a proud shake of her head, dark ringlets dancing where they escaped from the scarf. "Why does the other one hide from me?"

"She's frightened. We've had rather a difficult evening," Charlotte answered, keeping her tone even. Fanny had crept back to them, and now was holding onto her hand and squeezing it tightly. "We were on our way to Bodmin to stay the night when our driver abandoned us on the highway. He made us get out of the carriage on the pretext that there was something wrong with the carriage wheel, and then he drove away."

"How odd," the young woman said, with a perplexed frown on her pretty face. "This is a terribly lonely place to be abandoned. The nearest house is some distance away." She examined them for a moment, still holding the lantern high, and then said, "My name is Tamara. You must stay the night with us, for you cannot wander the fields or you will get into trouble."

"We don't wish to impose," Charlotte said, stiffly.

"Oh, you will not impose," the girl said, with a swish of her skirts. "You may pay for your lodging and food. I daresay you have money for that, if you were going to stay in an inn."

Charlotte thought of her bag pushed into the hedgerow. Foolishly, she had left her money in the bag, and it seemed a long way back. She could not tell this stranger her dilemma, though. "We certainly can pay," she said. "But not until tomorrow. Not until we are about to leave."

"Do you think we will keep you hostage?" the young woman said with a harsh tone. "We are gypsies, not brigands."

"Gypsies," Fanny whimpered. She tugged at Charlotte's hand. "We shouldn't stay here. I don't mind sleeping by the hedgerow, really Charlotte, it won't be so bad."

Tamara raised the lantern again. "I promise you," she said, with a gentler tone, one finger raised, "that not a soul will molest or disturb you. You may have my bed in the caravan, and I will sleep by the fire."

Shamed, Charlotte said, "We accept your generous hospitality, Tamara. My name is Charlotte, and this is my sister Fanny." Fanny ducked her head in greeting. "Please, don't mind our ignorance," Charlotte continued. "Where we come from gypsies are . . . um . . ."

"You have *heard* that they are thieves and cutthroats, though you have never met one yourself," Tamara said, with another haughty shake of her head, a few more dark curls escaping the colorful kerchief that held her hair away from her oval face. "How well I know the tales, but that is all they are, tales, told to frighten little children into behaving. Follow me." She whirled, her skirts flying around her.

Charlotte pulled Fanny along behind her and followed Tamara, who led them to the fire, which was mostly deserted now. She approached an older, swarthy man who contentedly smoked a pipe and stared at the flames, and said something to him. He answered, and gestured to the caravan directly behind him. He pointed at Charlotte, said a few words, and Tamara replied in an odd foreign tongue. The man nodded to Charlotte and she returned his polite, wordless greeting.

The younger man with the guitar, the only other left at the fireside, swiftly stood up, set aside his instrument, and approached them, sweeping his cap off his head. "Tamara, who is this?" he asked, speaking softly.

"They are two young ladies who are lost, Romolo. I told them they may stay the night, and I now take them to Mother Sarah, who I think has retired to her caravan for the evening."

The young man bowed. Tamara smiled back at Charlotte and Fanny and said, "This is my brother, Romolo. Romy, this is Miss Charlotte and Miss Fanny."

"Blessings, maidens," he said, with a low bow and a wide, brilliant smile.

"Come along," Tamara said, with a grin. "Do not let my flirtatious brother keep you. Before you have some supper, we must go to Mother Sarah."

"Who is Mother Sarah?" Charlotte glanced back at the young man, but he was watching Fanny with a thoughtful look on his dark, handsome face.

"She is our leader. Come." Tamara led them to one of the caravans, really simply a cart with a tentlike structure erected over it, and circled to the back of it. She pushed aside a brightly colored curtain and gestured for them to climb up.

Charlotte led the way, pulling Fanny behind her, up into the caravan. Ducking her head, for the interior ceiling was not high enough for her to stand, Charlotte crept in.

At the far end of the caravan, which was hung all around with brilliantly shaded and patterned material, sat a woman by a small coal heater. She was swathed in many skirts and shawls, and appeared to be sleeping while sitting. The heat was welcome at first after the misty air outside, Charlotte found, taking a seat along the side of the caravan where a low divan was situated, but soon became unbearable, intensifying the odors of spices and food and sweat. Tamara crept in behind them and shimmied past to approach the old woman. She murmured something and the old woman's eyes flew open.

The first thing Charlotte thought of was Uta, her ancient and venerable aunt who had just passed on in the spring. This old woman had the same small, beady eyes, though the gypsy's were black and set deeply in wrinkled flesh, like currants peeking out of a bun. Also unlike Uta, who was almost blind, she could see, and examined first Charlotte, then Fanny, with piercing interest.

"It is Mother Sarah you may thank for me finding you," Tamara whispered, taking a seat opposite them. "She has the sight, and sent me toward the highway tonight with a lantern. I have been walking for hours trying to find you! She knew someone was coming just after sunset, someone who would be lost and need our help."

"Then why did you question who we were, if you knew you would find us?" Charlotte asked.

"I had doubts," she murmured, shaking her head in dismay. "I had walked all the way to the highway before seeing you both wandering across the field, and I was surprised and uncertain. I should have known; Mother Sarah can see the future!"

Charlotte stared at the old woman in surprise. "She's a fortune-teller?"

"Sometimes. Is there something you would like to know?"

"Yes! Both of us," she said, taking Fanny's hand and squeezing it, "have questions."

"Ask, then. She understands English, though she does not like to speak it often."

"Pardon, but what language were you using? I didn't recognize it."

"It is Romani, the ancient language of my people. That is what we speak among ourselves, for no matter how long we live in this country, still we are Rom. We learn it as children. Now, your questions?"

"I would like to know, for myself," Charlotte said, gazing

down the length of the caravan at the old woman, "should I stay in England or go back home?"

"Where is home?" Tamara asked. "I cannot place your accent."

"We are German, from Hannover. I have thought of leaving England almost immediately." Charlotte bowed her head. "I'm not sure I like this country."

"It is a difficult country to like," Tamara said, gravely. She lowered her head, the lamplight shadowing her long-lashed eyes. "Being island dwellers, these people are narrow-minded, inward-looking. Like a horse that is blinkered, they only see the road ahead of them, and are disturbed by that which does not fit their narrow vision of life. Our people are only tolerated here, and too often not even that."

"It must be a difficult life," Charlotte said, thinking of all the terrible tales she had been told about gypsies, and her family's long enmity with them. What if the old stories weren't true, or were, at the very least, one-sided?

Tamara sighed and smiled. "I should not complain; the English are not alone in abhorring us. Sometimes I wonder if there is a place in the world where we might go and be welcome." She shook her head. "But enough of our woes. How terrible that I am so burdening you! Your questions will be answered." She turned to Mother Sarah and said something in Romani.

The old woman nodded and closed her eyes. When she opened them again, it was to examine Charlotte closely. "You have had a difficult time since landing on these shores," she said, her voice low and her tone ominous. "I see passion, a quarrel, two men fighting. Over you!"

Charlotte gasped and stared.

Fanny squeezed her hand, trembling, and whispered, "How is it possible that she knows this?"

Charlotte cleared her throat. "What else? What am I to do, Mother Sarah?"

"First, you must make an offering," she said, holding out her hand. "Cross my palm with silver."

"I don't have anything right now," Charlotte said. She met Tamara's grave gaze and shrugged. "As I said, I will have money tomorrow, but this moment, nothing."

The young gypsy spoke rapidly to Mother Sarah in Romani, and the woman nodded.

"What did you say to her?" Charlotte asked.

The young woman hesitated, but then said, "I told her to trust you, for I think you are honorable."

"I will tell you more," Mother Sarah said, her voice harsh and grating, "but you must make amends at the first opportunity. I see a quest; you are here for a purpose, but after you fulfill this, it will be death if you stay in this country for any reason but one who loves you more than life itself."

Charlotte gasped; those were almost the exact words in Mr. Randell's letter to her, that he loved her already "more than life itself." Foolishness, but pretty words and flattering.

"Your future," the old gypsy woman said, then fell silent for a long few minutes. Finally, in a sepulchral tone, she said, "You will marry a dark man, black hair I see, and green eyes, or no man at all, unless you wish to die!"

"I do not understand where they can have gone," Wesmorlyn said, as he approached Semyaza, who held their horses in the lamplit inn yard. He looked back at the building, the most prominent inn in Bodmin. "The innkeeper, who seems an honest enough fellow, says he has no such lady in his inn tonight. And yet they left Taunton early this morning headed for Bodmin, and were heard to mention this place. When we stopped at Launceston I was told they had paused to water the horses, but had moved on immediately to Bodmin.

"It is a long stretch, but the innkeeper said given the excellent weather they have had and the moonlit night, they should have been able to make it, certainly by now. But nothing, no sign of them, as if they dropped off the earth. Where have they gone?" The earl took the reins of his mount, leaped up to his saddle, and stared thoughtfully at the inn, bathed in moonlight as it was, a homely scene with golden light in the windows and a crowd of thirsty farmers in the taproom singing a rowdy song in Cornish, the ancient and almost dead language of the area.

"I have no answers, Simeon," Semyaza said, gracefully mounting his gray gelding.

Wesmorlyn nodded. Semyaza had done as much as he could by talking to the servants of the von Wolframs' rented London town house; the staff members, with no loyalty to their new employers, were happy to gossip with the impressive fellow about the strange goings-on, how the two young ladies had gotten into a carriage late at night—the butler was a wakeful and curious sort who seldom slept, and had seen it from his top-floor bedroom window—and how the young German count had ordered a horse saddled directly after the Earl of Wesmorlyn's visit, and had his servant provided with a mount as well.

From there it had been little trouble to follow the progress of the carriage with the two young ladies in it to all of the spots where they had changed horses. Wesmorlyn had just missed them, it seemed, at the two inns where they spent the night on the way to Cornwall, but it still puzzled him that the paths of the two sets of travelers had now diverged.

"We have lost Count von Wolfram, too; I thought he would certainly have headed here, since we have traced the young ladies so far, but he seems to have vanished. I wish he would have confided in me, rather than dashing away from London after his sister while giving me that story of her being ill. It will not wash, Sam," he said, glancing over at his companion. "It will not do to ally myself with a family of such erratic character. I have worked too long at redeeming my family's reputation to have it lost over one young lady with no common sense and little moral fiber."

Semyaza cleared his throat and looked up at the waxing moon.

Wesmorlyn considered what he had just said. "Terribly condemnatory I sounded just now, didn't I?" He sighed. "Still, I wish Christoph had just talked to me."

"He has little reason to trust you, Simeon. He is his sister's guardian and feels a responsibility toward her. It speaks well of his character that he would not expose her to your disapprobation, even when he seems to have good reason to be sorely angry at her himself."

"True. I have done the same, shielding Hannah from the consequences of her own conduct this last little while, haven't I? Well, I don't know what to do." Wesmorlyn flexed his shoulders, feeling the itch between his shoulder blades fiercely. He needed to stretch and relax, take off the constricting jacket and breathe freely for a change. He longed for his estate and the miles and miles of uninterrupted space in which to roam, but he had not planned to return there until late October this year. Normally he would be there for harvest, but Hannah was to stay in London to bespeak her wardrobe for the next spring season, her first officially on the marriage market, and he was supposed to be spending the time getting to know his fiancée.

His fiancée. The vision of her lovely face, with the adorable dimple in the middle of her chin was before him, but he pushed it away. No mere physical attraction would determine his path. The decision to marry was one that would affect not only him, but generations of Wesmorlyn offspring, and he could not afford to make it casually. His agreement to the marriage had been based on careful consideration of the countess's antecedents; her family line was faultless and unblemished from all accounts. Count Nikolas von Wolfram was a steady and sober man, he had learned, and their family connection to the new Princess of Wales was desirable politically, or had been when he made the agreement.

And yet, from what he had seen so far, Countess Charlotte von Wolfram was as unlikely to be a suitable countess to him as the Princess of Wales was a royal helpmeet to her beleaguered husband. He had been misled as to the young lady's character, but as loath as he was to ally himself with folly, Wesmorlyn was committed to the marriage if she wanted it. He supposed in truth that was unlikely, as odd as that seemed to him. How could the girl throw away the most eligible of men with such ease? If he truly wanted out of the marriage, her running away would seem to be the ideal opportunity to disengage himself, but it was not how he chose to end the betrothal. He would face her and hear it from her own lips. If he was completely honest with himself, he was curious. It was a puzzle, a dreadful tangle, and one he must undo, knot by knot.

Semyaza cleared his throat again, and Wesmorlyn was brought back to the present, the dimly lit stable yard. They could not stand their horses so long in this misty night air, but what else was there to do?

A stout fellow, the innkeeper Wesmorlyn had just spoken to, waddled out the door of the inn and bowed low. With great deference and a painfully proper accent, he said, "Honored lord, if you will spend the night here, I would be most grateful. I have a room ready for you, clean and fresh. My good wife has seen to it herself."

Wesmorlyn sighed. "I suppose that is what we will do. Let us find our repose here, Sam, and tomorrow we can try to find out what happened to the countess and her sister."

"SIEGFRIED, I don't know where they can have gone after Taunton," Christoph said, addressing his young valet in German as he paced in the narrow confines of an inn bedchamber in Plymouth. The salty sea air drifted in through the partially open window, and it smelled of freedom and travel and everything the constricting confines of the ballroom and bedchamber stifled. The wildness rose in him, shivering through his body, urging him to run, to succumb to the animal urgency that surged through his body. He took a deep breath, stifling the sensations and choking back every natural part of his mind and heart. "If they did indeed come looking for Eleanor Dancey," he said, carefully, "the last address we had was in Plymouth, at an aunt's home, but the woman appears to have disappeared! Why or where is a mystery, and now my sister . . . *sisters*, are wandering about the countryside in a strange land in who knows what company?"

Young Siegfried, Christoph's only confidant now, had a thoughtful look on his pale face. He sat in a straight-backed chair with his long-fingered hands folded on his lap. "Perhaps, count, we should go back to Taunton, where they were last sighted, and you could pick up their trail, if you understand my meaning." The young man turned a brilliant scarlet, for though he was one of the few serving staff from the castle to know of the family's hereditary ability to transform, he still was not comfortable speaking to his master about it.

Christoph gazed at him steadily, nodding. What a joy a sensible young man was! He clapped him on the shoulder and squeezed. "You are a very good servant, Siegfried, and a good man and perhaps a better tactician than I. You're right of course. We cannot stay in this inn, though I know how tired you are; we must go back to Taunton, and it must be this very night. I will need your aid in my search, and this is how we must work."

He outlined for Siegfried how the search could best be accomplished, given what he knew about himself. He needed to strip down completely and run as a wolf, but for that, he needed a faithful servant to be ready with his clothing at a pre-arranged spot, so he could reassume his manly form and clothe himself. That night would see no rest for them. He needed the nighttime for his unique abilities—though luckily not a full moon, contrary to hoary legend—and he dared not wait another day and night, not with his sisters alone in the English countryside. He would find Charlotte and Fanny if it was the last thing he did, and then he would haul them both back to Germany and deposit them on his uncle's doorstep as too troublesome to manage.

LYULPH Randell staggered up his London terrace home's front step and stumbled through the door. Foster, his butler, waiting up for him as was his custom, caught him and guided him to a bench in the hallway.

"Young Diggory has arrived back, sir," Foster said, "and awaits you in your study."

Lyulph shook his head, then clutched his hand to his forehead as a bolt of pain shot through it. "Damn! Should not have had that last brandy. Bring me some seltzer water," he slurred, "and be quick 'bout it."

In the chilly dimness of the hallway Lyulph waited. Foster brought the drink, and Lyulph downed it and handed the cup back to the butler, then stood again. Good, he was less wobbly this time, and could find his way to the study. He took the steps carefully, though, and headed upstairs, then down the long hallway to his study.

Diggory stood by the fire and looked up as Lyulph entered. He bowed, wordless.

"What news, Diggory? Did you deliver my messages? How were they received?" He cleared his throat and headed to his desk, grateful that he had a good recovery time.

"It will be as you wish it, sir, thems her own words."

"Morwenna's?"

The fellow nodded.

"Did she try to interfere with you in any way? Did she try to get you to take off the charm?" Lyulph watched the younger man's pale face in the flickering light from the fire. Morwenna was a deep planner, and one could not be sure she was going to do what she said she would do.

"No, I don't believe so sir. She were very accommodating. But . . ." He trailed off.

"But what?"

"She offered me her maidservant, sir, for a tumble. Said the girl would do whatever I wanted."

"Hmmm, yes, and then the girl, once she got you into her bed, would ask you to take the charm off, for it would interfere in some way."

"Do you think so?"

"Yes."

"Sir, why do you deal with the witch if you cannot trust her?"

"I find in life, that if you assume you cannot trust anyone, then you do very well." Lyulph sat back in his chair. "And so you delivered both letters?"

"Yes sir. Both messages received and understood."

"Good. Very good. Morwenna is not going to like the change in my plans, perhaps, though her part in my life will remain the same. I haven't dared tell her the whole truth, of course, not with what I have in mind. *If* she will just be content with it, things will go very well, but that is what I'm not so sure of, for she has a tendency to make her own deep plans." Lyulph sighed. *Witches.* As much as a witch was a natural match for a werewolf, they were unreliable and defiant, not heeding their proper place in the scheme of things. If he had not needed her help, he would have discarded her long ago as more trouble than she was worth.

"But now our work in London begins," he went on, to Diggory. "I have a few things to accomplish before I leave. Wesmorlyn has behaved even better than I expected, and has taken off for the country after the countess, though he will not find her easily. At least I hope not, for I need a few days' interval to do what I must. That leaves little Lady Hannah, sweet child, all alone except for her harebrained companion and doddering dowager cousin, the marchioness. My original intention was to use the first opportunity of finding her unguarded by Wes to take her and head to Scotland, but everything has changed." He stared over at the fireplace for a long moment, thinking of golden hair and a dimple in the middle of a sweet, pointed, independent chin. *Countess Charlotte von Wolfram.* "*Everything* has changed."

After a long silence, his faithful servant said, "Sir?"

Lyulph bent over his desk and pulled his writing instruments toward him. "Go get some sleep, Diggory, for you must be weary. But first thing in the morning I will have some errands for you."

"Very good, sir."

WHEN they left Mother Sarah's caravan, Tamara took them back to sit by the fire and gave them tin bowls of fragrant and delicious rabbit stew. Their seat was a thick log that the men had dragged from the grove. At first Charlotte found it odd to be sitting outside by a fire, and yet once her hunger was satiated and she was able to relax, she recalled how on their short hunting trips into the forest around Wolfram Castle, she and Christoph would build a fire in a clearing in the woods and make up adventure stories as they stared into its crackling depths, relishing the darkness and the night sounds around them. They didn't fear wolves or any other animal, both of them at home in the forest. Her younger cousins, Jakob and Eva, had been sent off to school, but neither she nor Christoph had ever left Wolfram Castle. It was all she had ever known, and it had tied her and her brother together in a bond so close it would never be severed.

With the stars sparkling overhead, and the quiet sound of Romolo's guitar, peace stole into her soul. As much as she missed Christoph, and as badly as she felt about deserting him, she knew she had done the right thing. Moor Cottage, where Eleanor Dancey resided, was within quick walking distance, Tamara had told them as they ate, once she became acquainted with their quest, and they could go there first thing in the morning. They were, in fact, on Lyulph Randell's property that very moment; the gypsies were allowed to camp there by his express wish, Tamara said, and they were grateful for his kindness.

"What do you plan to do with your life, Tamara?" Charlotte asked, as Romolo began to sing. Fanny was intently watching and listening to him, and Charlotte was overjoyed that her sister had something to occupy her mind, for she was understandably nervous about what the next day would bring.

"Do?"

"Yes. Do you plan to marry? Or travel?"

The young woman, her olive skin made ruddy by the flickering flames, appeared pensive. "Gypsies do not plan, we live. What God chooses to give us will do for today, and tomorrow? That will take care of itself."

Romolo had moved to sit next to Fanny, who was blushing and giggling at something he was whispering to her. Charlotte watched, smiling. But then she turned back to the other young woman and said, "But don't you have things you would like to do?"

"Do you?"

"So many things!" Charlotte stared into the flames, red, orange, and gold licking at the logs, embers glowing and popping. "*This* is good," she said, "this experience, I mean. I spent so long thinking I never wanted to leave Wolfram Castle, and then I did leave, but only because I wanted Fanny to meet her mother and I knew I was the only one who could help her accomplish it. But now I understand something about myself." She paused and glanced around her. Most of the gypsies had retreated to their caravans and tents, and the sleepy sound of children talking as they were tucked into bed and the soft murmur of the women's voices, the grumble of men's deeper tones, the night sounds of an owl in the grove all satisfied her deeply.

"What do you understand, Charlotte?" Tamara asked.

"I was stifled for so long, and never understood why I was agitated and restless and angry so often. It was a little better as we traveled, but even then, I despised every city, and having to be prim and proper. It was much worse when we got to London, but it evaporated once Fanny and I left that awful city and I found I could love this," she said, waving her hands around. "I don't mind hardship, I can tolerate any amount of dirt and mold and smelly linens. I adore traveling and seeing new places. And meeting new people," she finished, putting one hand on Tamara's smooth-skinned arm.

"I'm so glad you came to us," the gypsy girl replied, deep feeling in her tone, as she put her own hand over Charlotte's. "I've never had a friend my own age before."

Charlotte bit her lip, thinking of Melisande, her friend of two years, now married and living in Russia. She missed Melisande terribly, for no amount of long letters and good wishes from a distance could take the place of talking face-to-face and a warm, companionable hug. "Then consider me your friend, now," she said. She took a deep breath, calming herself. "And Fanny, too. She's a very sweet girl, but shy, and I hope you will come to feel she is your friend as well."

"My brother is certainly taken with her. I have never seen Romolo so intent."

Charlotte watched them, the way he bent his head and spoke to her, the way she blushed and gazed up at him, wide-eyed. "She's very innocent."

"And he is very tender-hearted," Tamara said, softly. "Don't worry about him. He is as much a gentleman in his actions as any lord of this land."

"I meant nothing else," Charlotte reassured the young woman, understanding immediately Tamara's quick defense of her brother, for it is just what she would have said about Christoph.

Finally it was time to retire. Tamara tried to give up her bed, but Charlotte would not hear of it, so all three girls curled up together in a bedroll protected from the elements only by a heavy blanket draped over the side of a cart. Despite deep weariness, they talked long into the night. The differences in their stations in life and in their backgrounds melted away in the face of their youth, good spirits, and willingness from both parties to set aside such vast differences in the interest of friendship. Fanny, though, fell asleep earliest, so the conversation was mostly between Charlotte and Tamara.

"How kind of Mr. Randell to allow you all to stay here," Charlotte whispered as she stared into the velvety darkness and remembered the handsome face and valiant behavior of the man as if he were before her in that moment. It had not escaped her notice that the future husband Mother Sarah had reserved for her exactly fit Mr. Lyulph Randell's description. The universe, it seemed, was conspiring to thrust them together in every way.

"I think there is some ancient tie between our band and his family," Tamara murmured, turning on her side toward Charlotte. "Mother Sarah said it goes back two hundred years, as long as gypsies have lived in England."

"Do you spend a lot of time with Mother Sarah?"

"Yes; she has no children, and my mother is gone, so I think she takes an interest in me. She wishes to teach me the old ways, she says, for the other women are too taken up with caring for the children and cooking."

"The old ways. What are the old ways?" Charlotte could just make out the dull gleam of Tamara's tousled curls in the dark, but couldn't see her eyes.

"Just the old ways, the old language and prayers, that sort of thing."

It was an evasion, but after the young woman's kindness to them, Charlotte did not wish to pry. The day had been long and exhausting, and she felt sleep steal through her. "Thank you, Tamara," she whispered, as she drifted off. "Thank you for everything you have done."

Chapter 7

IN THE morning, after a breakfast of bread and eggs by the fire, Tamara offered to guide them to Moor Cottage. Fanny finally evinced considerable agitation as the three young ladies walked together over the moor, scaling a hill and pausing at the top.

"That is Moor Cottage," Tamara said.

Charlotte stared down the slope at the dwelling and shivered with apprehension. It was not a large building; built entirely of gray, moss-draped stone, it was low with a sloping roof. Separate from it were a couple of small outbuildings, both tumbling down and crumbling in the corners, showing the destructive force of years of moorland storms and wind and rain. The sun had gone behind a cloud, and in the gloomy shadows the cottage squatted in the valley like a toad, malevolent and watchful, waiting for them to approach, daring them to enter.

She shook herself and took a deep breath. *What nonsense!* She had never thought herself imaginative, but supposed the strange events she had experienced in the last months had taken their toll and made her see evil where it did not exist.

"Come, Fanny," she said, taking her sister's arm. "Your mother awaits!"

The girls descended together, but the cottage did not improve on closer inspection. What windows there were overlooking the neglected front gardens were overgrown with thorny bushes that made Charlotte long to take a saw to them. The walkway was mossy and damp, slippery underfoot. Treacherous. They approached carefully.

Fanny was silent, her large blue eyes clouded with trepidation, but whether it was the gloomy aspect of the house that alarmed her, or the idea of meeting her mother for the first time, Charlotte could not tell. "Courage, Fanny," she said, and advanced boldly toward the front door, knocking loudly, a few flakes of peeling paint fluttering down to the stone stoop.

"I have on occasion seen the lady who lives here," Tamara whispered, "though I had not understood her relationship to Mr. Randell to be that of a stranger renting the cottage."

"What did you think their relationship, then?" Charlotte said, glancing sideways.

The young woman blushed, the pink of her cheeks offering a becoming rosiness to her olive-tinted countenance. She merely shook her head, but Charlotte could imagine what she thought and was amused at how wrong things could appear to an outsider who did not know the entire truth.

Fanny twisted her hands together over and over, and Charlotte forgot her amusement at the folly of half-known tales in concern over her sister's agitation. "Fanny, don't make yourself ill," she murmured, taking the girl's hand and squeezing it. "I'll stay with you."

"What if she doesn't want anything to do with me? Maybe I'll be a miserable embarrassment to her. I shall just sink into the ground if she is brisk with me."

"I know it's awkward, but if she is unhappy to see you, then I promise you we will leave immediately, return to London, and leave England." Charlotte swept a few stray curls up under her straw bonnet and said, "At least you will have tried." She patted Fanny's hand, released it, and knocked again.

Tamara stepped back and stared up at the windows of the second floor. "I wonder why there's no answer?"

"Perhaps we ought to go away and come back later," Fanny said, breathlessly.

Just then the door opened and a young girl with vacant eyes and a listless air curtseyed before them.

"Miss Eleanor Dancey, please." Charlotte knew Fanny's voice would be too weak to speak.

The girl curtseyed again and stood back. "Come in to the parlor, if you please," she said, her voice breathy and soft.

The three of them entered the hallway. It was dark and narrow, the paper peeling and blotched with stained patches where dampness crept up the walls and spread like a canker. Charlotte moved blindly into the dank interior but her toe caught on something and she staggered, hitting the wall with her shoulder. Growling and hissing, a smoke gray cat clutched at her leg with all four paws and sank its fangs into her ankle. She cried out and stumbled, righting herself only a second before she would have tumbled to the floor.

Fanny shrieked as Charlotte kicked the animal out of the way, bending down to rub her injured ankle. "Fiend!" she yelped. "It bit me!"

The maid took no notice of the commotion and had gone on ahead into a parlor, where she held the door open and blankly stared at them, waiting for them to pass her. It was exceedingly peculiar, Charlotte reflected, as if the girl was an automaton, like a clockwork figure she had seen once when a traveling circus came to Wolfbeck.

She turned toward her companions, trying to ignore the throbbing pain in her ankle and hoping it wasn't bleeding. "Have you ever been inside this place?" Charlotte whispered to Tamara, as they passed the girl and entered the indicated room.

"No," the gypsy girl murmured, looking around with a wary expression. "Gypsies do not like houses so much, you know. Four walls, floors, ceilings, they confine you so."

"If you had ever seen Wolfram Castle you would not think it confining," Charlotte said, dryly, about their cavernous home.

The parlor was a little better than the hall, with some attempt to ameliorate the gloom of the cottage with brighter paper, but it still was poorly lit, the tiny window overlooking the front of the building overgrown with thorn bushes, as Charlotte had observed from outside, which even crept in through a crack in the glass, the thorny bud stealing along the sill like a malevolent creature intent on invasion.

"I'll get the mistress," the girl said, and drifted away, leaving them to their own devices.

Fanny wrinkled her nose and looked around. "This place smells awfully."

Charlotte opened her mouth to retort that Fanny always said that, and had complained of it all along the way in every inn, but this time she was right. There was a dank odor of decaying greenery that invaded every corner of the place, and overlaying it was a stench of fetid, aging meat. It was almost enough to make her dizzy.

The dark gray tabby slunk in after them and sat in the doorway, glaring at Charlotte. She stuck her tongue out at it but it stared, unmoving, until she looked away uneasily. There was something unnatural in the green eyes of the cat, something knowing and sly.

"Don't mind Hellebore," a woman said, strolling into the room. The cat wound itself around her feet and threw itself on the floor, rolling over on its back and looking once again like any normal cat. "He's really harmless and quite playful."

Charlotte stifled a retort, that if violence was mischief, then the cat was indeed playful. She refrained from mentioning the attack in the hallway at all, but she would certainly avoid the creature.

"Now, what can I do for you? Anne was vague about your purpose in visiting, as she always is. I cannot seem to make her understand that she should ask visitors their reason for coming so I don't have to question them. She's rather doltish, as are all of these West Country dullards."

Charlotte stared at the woman before them. Her skin was pale and waxen, smooth as marble and unnaturally flawless. Hair the color of walnut coiled in perfect curls and gleamed in the dull light from the window. Her eyes were blue, as were Fanny's, but Eleanor Dancey's were the indigo of the storm-tossed sea they had crossed as they sailed from the continental lowlands to England; the color was cold, but had intriguing green flecks in the depths. She was clad simply in a round gown of soft rose-colored material and was very beautiful, blessed with full lips and arched brows that rose at Charlotte's scrutiny. "I beg your pardon, ma'am, but I need to ask a couple of questions of you."

"Certainly," she said, advancing into the room. "Please be seated, though; as humble as this cottage is, I would have you be comfortable."

Tamara and Fanny sat on a settle near the grimy, unused fireplace, but Charlotte took a chair facing the door, trying to ignore Hellebore, the cat, which crouched under a table now, staring at her with chilling intensity.

"Now, then," the woman said, taking a chair opposite Charlotte's, "I suppose I should ask your names, and what it is you wish to know?"

Charlotte was loath to accede to the request; offering the von Wolfram name right away might startle or offend her. So this was Fanny's mother; Charlotte had been a young child when the lady was an inhabitant in the castle. Christoph had a vague remembrance of Eleanor Dancey as a visitor at Wolfram Castle, and of her playing with him and his toy soldiers. But this woman was so youthful. Could she possibly be the *correct* Eleanor Dancey? "Ma'am, if you will be patient for just a moment, there is a reason I am being circumspect. Before I reveal too much of our circumstance, I would like to be sure that you are the Eleanor Dancey for whom we are searching. First, have you traveled outside of this country at any time in your life?"

"What an odd question," the woman said, sitting on the very edge of the straight-backed chair.

Fanny was trembling and would not look up. Charlotte reached over and took her hand, squeezing it. "Please, ma'am, be patient with me. Have you?"

"Well, yes. I did travel on the continent briefly. I was very young." She stared out the obscured window for a long moment, and then returned her gaze to the group opposite her. "It was an unhappy time for me, and when I returned I never left England again." The woman bit her lip, the gesture driving the blood from her rosy mouth. She calmed her expression, cleared her throat, and sighed heavily. "Though I may soon leave forever," she murmured, staring off toward the fluttering curtains.

"Ma'am, excuse me for prying so, but did you stay for a time in Germany before returning to England?"

"Yes, I did," she said, turning her gaze back to the three young ladies. "Who are you? Your accent . . . are you German?"

"My name, ma'am, is Countess Charlotte von Wolfram."

The other woman rose and backed up to the door, her hand over her heart. "You are . . . oh, my, you're little Lotte, as I called you then, a pretty child with blond ringlets."

Charlotte felt a pang in her heart. So, this was the woman for whom her father had forsaken her mother's bed. But Eleanor Dancey had been no more than an impressionable and perhaps lonely girl at the time, younger than Fanny was now. She must not hold against the adult version of Miss Eleanor Dancey the follies of her youth. More important than her own sensitive feelings was that this was Fanny's mother.

"But why are you here?" Eleanor Dancey said, her voice faint. "After all of these years, why come here? Is your father . . . is he . . . ?"

"No. If you're asking if he's still living, ma'am, no, he died long, long ago." Charlotte bowed her head, not willing to relate all of the tragedies her family had endured, beginning with the long-ago terror that took her father and mother within weeks of each other. Fifteen years or more had passed since then, and the reason for being there was Fanny. She stood and pulled Fanny to her feet and over to stand in front of the other woman. "Miss Dancey, this young lady is my half sister, by my father. This is Fanny."

"Fanny? I don't understand."

"Fanny is your daughter."

The woman gasped and fell insensible to the floor in a graceful swoon.

"THERE is some mystery here, Sam," Wesmorlyn said over breakfast in the taproom of the inn at Bodmin. He leaned across the rough board table and spoke quietly, not wanting to share his conversation with the nosy innkeeper, who lingered nearby dallying with a broom while trying to listen in. The rotund fellow had appeared scandalized that the man whom he had evidently pegged as some kind of superior servant was sitting with his lordship, but Wesmorlyn never explained Semyaza to anyone; he wouldn't have dared try, and it was none of anyone's business. Because he was an earl, it was likely written off as an upper-crust quirk, though Wes didn't know and cared even less. "Near dawn I couldn't sleep and came down to ask the landlord what the noise was all about. He was not around, and the taproom was still full of drinkers. I was about to tell them all to quieten down when I heard a couple of fellows laughing together. One of them, a fellow with a very broad Cornish accent, was quite drunk, and he spoke of leaving a couple of young foreign ladies stranded by the side of the road with just their bags and no way to move on. At twilight, he said he did this."

"Do you think it is the young ladies for whom we search?"

"I was doubtful at first; I hesitated, turned away for a minute, and when I looked back, thinking to question him, he was gone. I went outside and looked, but couldn't find the fellow. I don't know whether he saw me staring at him and took fright, or if it was just a coincidence, him leaving when he did. I tried to go back up and get some sleep, but was restless, and the longer I pondered the more certain I became. Surely there cannot be another such party of two young foreign ladies roaming in Cornwall? It is too much to imagine, that there would be another so harum-scarum as Countess Charlotte."

"Do you really think her foolish?"

"I hardly know, Sam. I had so little time with her, and one can make no judgments in a ballroom, you know." He thought about it and drummed his fingers on the tabletop. "I don't believe I made a very good impression on her, as she did not on me. I may think her a flirtatious chit, but she likely thinks me a priggish, crashing bore." He kicked at the table leg.

"Possibly you both deserve another chance to make a better impression?"

"You may be right," Wesmorlyn said, standing and stretching. "Indeed, I think you are, but for that I must find the young ladies and pray nothing has happened to them. I shall never forgive myself if my behavior at the ball drove the countess from London to a bad end."

"The young lady made her own decisions, Simeon. You cannot take credit or blame where it does not belong to you."

"No, perhaps not, but I contributed to the circumstances that may have made her unhappy enough to do such a thing."

Semyaza nodded. "Very well. Then how shall you accomplish this search?"

Wesmorlyn stared at the man. Semyaza knew where the young women were; he knew everything. But his place was not to give Wesmorlyn the easy way out of dilemmas even when there was danger to someone involved, but to observe how he did on his own. The earl's whole life had been spent with the watchful eyes of Semyaza on him. "If this braggart who spoke of dropping the ladies off on the road was indeed their driver, and I strongly feel he must be, then the countess and her sister must, perforce, have found lodging for the night somewhere, and this morning will have found the main road, or an inn. He said he left their bags with them, so at least I can assume they have their money and clothes. In this insular county the wanderings of two well-dressed pretty young foreign ladies will not go unremarked."

"Then we shall wander the countryside after them and search?"

"I have a better idea with which to start, one that will utilize my own particular talents," Wesmorlyn said, feeling the itch between his shoulder blades intensify.

"MISS Dancey," Charlotte said, rushing to the swooning woman, who was crumpled in a heap.

Fanny cried and wrung her hands while observing the scene, but Tamara, resourceful and quick, called out to the maid to bring sal volatile and a glass of water or spirits. Charlotte knelt on the floor and raised the woman's head, and was rewarded by her eyelashes fluttering; finally she regained consciousness.

"What happened?" she said, putting one delicate hand to her forehead.

"T'was my fault. I shocked you to insensibility."

The woman sat up abruptly and stared around her, then rose and fixed her gaze on Fanny, who wept uncontrollably. She crossed the floor even as the maid, Anne, came with the unwanted smelling salts and water. Charlotte stayed the maid with one hand and watched the unfolding drama.

"You are Fanny, my daughter?" Her voice quavered, but the color was still in her cheek and a smile trembled on her lips.

Fanny nodded, and her sobs calmed even as tears still ran down her pale cheeks.

"My dear, I never thought I'd see you! I have suffered these long years, wondering if I did the right thing in leaving you behind. Oh, to see you now, so grown up and a lady!" Miss Eleanor Dancey then took Fanny in her arms and folded her close to her breast. "My own child, my baby. Home at last!"

THE day had turned out to be brilliant after the misty haze burned off. Charlotte strolled back over the moor toward the gypsy encampment with Tamara, leaving Moor Cottage to allow Fanny and her mother to have time together alone. In truth, she was happy to get out of the cottage; it was gloomy and smelled of damp and rot, but Charlotte would not have left her sister if she hadn't felt strongly the two needed time to get to know one another. The woman was clearly still wounded by the events of the past, for she would not speak of her affair with Johannes von Wolfram. Of course, the entire subject must be considered to be very delicate, given the events of that time, the affair's illicit nature, and the unfortunate outcome, so it was hardly odd that Eleanor Dancey was circumspect on the subject, and indeed turned the topic away whenever it reached her time at Wolfram Castle. It was awkward for all of them.

To her credit, she seemed much more interested in Fanny's life and habits. She was somewhat indignant to find her daughter was raised to be a maid to the household, but a little less so when she learned what pains had been taken to give her an education, how light her duties always were, and how much time Fanny was given as an intimate of the family members to whom she was so closely related.

Fanny had been raised thinking her last name was Sanderson, Charlotte told the woman, and that she was the child of the elder Count Jakob von Wolfram's English valet and his wife, a cook's helper in the household, a woman who died the year Fanny was born. It was only in the last few months that Fanny had learned her true paternity, and that she was not Johannes von Wolfram's only illegitimate daughter. If it was a hard fact to learn, it was equally difficult for Charlotte and Christoph to learn they had at least two sisters, Fanny and another girl, Magda, the daughter of a village woman, because of their father's philandering. Magda, at least, was now happily married, but Fanny had no one else but Charlotte and Christoph.

Ameliorating Eleanor Dancey's poor opinion of the von Wolfram family was Charlotte's own stout insistence that Fanny was her and Christoph's sister, would be recognized as such, and would be treated as such for the rest of her life. Charlotte had noted how gratified Eleanor appeared to be to find that it was no difficult feat for her and Christoph to accept Fanny as a sister once the truth was revealed.

Charlotte, as well as wanting to give the mother and daughter time together, was also eager to retrieve their bags so hastily thrust into the hedgerow the night before. She had an awful fear that in the dark she had not been so careful in the concealment, and they might indeed be easily visible from the road by the light of day, and so open to filching by any passerby. She wished to repay the gypsy band for their kindness, too. Without them, she and Fanny would have spent a miserable night shivering, huddled in some woody grove somewhere, alert and frightened of every noise, and finding Moor Cottage would not have been nearly so easy without Tamara's help.

Charlotte breathed in deeply. "This is surely the most beautiful part of England," she said, in an excess of high spirits. She had accomplished what she had come to England for, and was now in charity with the entire nation. As they topped a rise, she paused. Clouds scudded across the broad sky, shadows chasing after them across the scrubby grass of the

moorland plains. In the distance a dark line of spiky hills
loomed, and before them the ground was broken up by outcroppings of jagged rocks. "What wild and lonely country,"
she said, surveying it. There was not a dwelling in sight. "Refreshing after the stifling confines of London. One night in
that city was too long for me." She turned to her companion.
"Were you born here, Tamara?"

"I cannot say where I was born, except not in Cornwall.
My father is vague about such matters, and my mother died
long ago."

She examined the young woman, who returned her gaze
with calm assurance. "Your father was the man by the fire last
night, smoking a pipe. Romolo looks a lot like you, the dark
curls and dark eyes, and he plays the guitar so beautifully; you
must both take after your mother, and she must have been a
very beautiful woman." She paused, thinking of their chance
encounter and good fortune. "Do you know, I have never seen
Fanny so entranced as she was by your brother."

"Nor have I ever seen him so taken with any girl before."

"Do all of you play instruments?" Charlotte asked.

"Most, yes, but Romolo is truly talented. He is brilliant as
a violinist, and equally so on the guitar. My talents are modest, confined more to singing and dancing."

Charlotte smiled and led the way onward. "My brother
also plays the violin, and I sing. Is that how you all make
money?"

Tamara glanced over at her in amusement. "How delicately
you seek an answer to your questions about how we live! I
had not thought Germans so tactful."

"Then we have learned much about each other's culture
this day," Charlotte said, pulling her shawl more closely about
her shoulders as a wind came up and tugged at it. "And perhaps mostly we've learned not to judge. I speak for myself,
for I have been very wrong about many things in my life."

Tamara nodded in silent agreement. "In answer to your
question, music is how we make money on occasion," she
said. "But my father and some of the other men are good at
mending metal, too, being tinsmiths by trade. Also, we sell
things we have bought in other towns, or trade them for food-
stuffs."

"But no steady employment?" Charlotte glanced over at the gypsy girl, wondering at a life that seemed without purpose. "That can't be an easy way to exist. Could you not be a maid? And your brother; he's good with horses I believe you said last night. He could work in a stable and perhaps one day become a coachman."

"Ah yes, your people are very industrious, are they not?" Tamara said, with a fleeting smile that robbed the comment of any sting. "But you were born to wealth and privilege; what do you know of real life?"

Charlotte gazed out over the land and pondered the question without rancor. What *did* she know of life? She had been sheltered within the walls of Wolfram Castle, and though life had never been trouble-free, no struggle for mere existence had troubled her. "But my way of life *is* real life for me. And yet, being here," she said, sweeping her hand around in an arc to indicate the Cornish countryside, "I am feeling that perhaps the essence of myself has been suppressed by my family. Now I begin to understand myself a little better. And as much as I long for the security of my home, I know in my heart I've done the right thing in coming here. Come, let's forget serious topics on such a beautiful day and walk on."

But Tamara said, as they strolled again, "It cannot have been easy, what you've done, breaking away from your family, and even your brother. I can only think that it would be, for me, like being abandoned by my tribe." She shuddered. "That is too awful a fate to contemplate." She frowned and thought for a long minute. "I don't know how to explain my people. Our feeling of safety comes not from having a secure position and a roof over our heads, but from the knowledge that not one of our band would see another suffer. Always, we can depend upon each other. Employment, as you call it, being at others' beck and call, is like death, just like being confined to a house or cottage. We could never live in a city, for we have traditions and beliefs that are different, and would not meld well with *gorgios* ways."

"*Gorgios*? What's that mean?"

"*Gorgios* are all those in this country who are not of the Romani blood."

They climbed to the top of the hill overlooking the grove

beyond which was the gypsy encampment. Charlotte paused to take it all in. "We are still on Mr. Randell's land, true?"

"Yes. He is a vast landowner with an ancient family history, I understand."

"How long have you been camped here?"

"For some time. Mother Sarah has a connection with his family and worked out some sort of exchange with Mr. Randell. We are fortunate to have stayed here this long without being driven away."

The clouds had disappeared and the sun shone brilliant and hot as it rose in the azure sky. Beyond the gentle knolls over which they traversed, on the horizon, was a sharp-edged line of dark, low hills, tors in the Cornish language, Charlotte had learned. It was so different from her home, where the dark forest surrounding the Wolfbeck River gave way to a sharp rise beyond Wolfram Castle, and thence to jagged cliffs and foothills that southward led to the Harz Mountains. It was like living cradled, protected by mountains and dense forest, hemmed in on all sides. Here everything was so exposed and raw, yet she felt a thrill of wayward energy surge through her, an urge to run down the long rocky slope. She suppressed her inappropriate yearning, ruthlessly subjugating it just as she had almost her whole life. "And the Earl of Wesmorlyn's home is near here, I understand."

"So I have heard. Are you acquainted with him?"

"Only briefly." She turned to Tamara, and said, "I need to go up near the highway. Fanny and I, when we were stranded, could not carry our bags all over the place. They're heavy, so I thrust them in the hedgerow, and that is where my money and all of my clothes are."

"I wondered," Tamara said, with an understanding smile. "I misjudged you at first last night, and I'm sorry. I thought you were lying about not having money because you feared being robbed."

Though circumspection was not her natural bent, Charlotte knew enough to keep quiet and not confess the thought did occur to her. The brilliant sun of late summer beat down on them as they slowly made their way toward the highway. When they finally reached the thicket that bounded their side of the road, it took a while for Charlotte to find the spot, since in the dark it had looked so very different. But at long last she found the marker she had left and pulled the bags out. They were intact, and she breathed a deep sigh of relief.

"I'm so weary!" Charlotte said, after their arduous walk. She longed to sit and drink something cool.

"Why don't we go to my camp right now? We can get something to drink and rest before you make your way back to Moor Cottage."

Charlotte gratefully agreed, and Tamara took Fanny's bag. As they began down the slope toward the gypsy encampment, she felt a trickle of perspiration roll down her back. "It's so warm here!" A tiny cloud covered the sun for a moment and offered a very brief relief, but then the heat of the morning sun blazed down on them again.

"I like it," Tamara said, turning her face up to the sun and squinting. "Already the evenings are turning cooler, and soon enough it will be cold. The winter seems so long!"

Charlotte turned her face up toward the sun, too, and squinted. Another cloud passed, and a shadow raced across their faces and over the yellowed grasses. Dazzled by the sun, her vision was blinded momentarily, but when she could see again the cloud had evaporated, as quickly as that. She sighed. "I suppose you're right; we should relish the warmth while it's here."

"I never wish for winter to come."

"It must be difficult," Charlotte said, as they continued on their way toward the camp, "to live in the caravans over winter. I noticed Mother Sarah had a heater last evening."

"She feels the cold and the damp. She is very old, and it bothers her arthritis, she says, and the heater helps."

"Is she truly a seer?"

Tamara nodded. "She is. I don't know how she knows what she does, but she's never wrong about things. As I said last night, it was she who sent me looking for two lost girls. She said I should go toward the highway at dusk; I did, but missed you and had to double back, for you were already on your way to our encampment."

"And we were lucky to see your light. I suppose it must have been your lantern I saw bobbing around in the dark. How remarkable that she should know such specific information!"

Charlotte reflected that it was not unheard of in her own life, though, for her friend, Melisande Davidovich, formerly a guest at Wolfram Castle after escaping the Terror, had developed such talents and had known much for which she could not name a source. She was a healer, too, and a practitioner of magic, though only so much as was beneficial to those for whom she cared. It was heredity, for her grandmother was another such as she. Everyone seemed to have special talents except herself, Charlotte thought.

They circled the grove of trees that the encampment snugged up against. In daylight the little camp looked cheery and quaint, with carts o'erstretched with tents and makeshift shelters. Tamara took Charlotte to see her father, who was a quiet, dark-eyed older man, and while they had a cool drink in the shade, Romolo played the guitar. He really was very good, with a rich voice and sweet tone, and he poured his heart into a melancholy song of love. Then he asked after Fanny, falteringly but with much meaning. Charlotte saw that he was infatuated, though he never said a word to hint at it, even.

She gently replied that Fanny was very well, but would likely not be coming back to the gypsy camp, since she had found her mother at Moor Cottage, and that, after all, was her sole objective in coming to Cornwall. The young man nodded, his expression sad but accepting.

"I must go to Mother Sarah for a few minutes and help her with her morning toilette, and bring her something to eat," Tamara said. "If you will wait, I will help you take Miss Fanny's bag back to Moor Cottage."

Charlotte, happy to linger awhile, agreed. She sat for a few minutes longer watching the bustle of the industrious women as they gathered wood from the grove for the cooking fires, stirred a pot of stew, and peeled vegetables for it. Charlotte swiftly realized she was being watched. Two tiny dark-eyed children with tousled black curls peeped at her from behind a shelter.

She covered her eyes, pretending not to see them, and then uncovered, gasping in surprise that they had crept closer. She repeated the game, and soon there were more than just the two children, there were seven or eight, and all were drawn into the play. The eldest, a beautiful girl with a blue and green kerchief over her dark curls, named them all for Charlotte, and gave her own name, Tully.

"Come, miss, and play with us in the meadow," Tully said, taking Charlotte's hand and pulling her up from her seat.

One of the dark-eyed women nodded and made shooing motions, so Charlotte obeyed, willing to be distracted from her serious and sometimes gloomy thoughts. She danced off, followed by her merry band of children, and they played in the grassy meadow beyond the grove of trees as the sun rose high in the cloudless sky.

STRAIGHTENING his jacket, the Earl of Wesmorlyn approached the gypsy encampment from the direction of the highway, as if he had arrived on horseback. Countess Charlotte von Wolfram, his runaway fiancée, was here somewhere, but where? He heard laughter over a rise beyond the camp, and strode through the long yellowing grass, skirting the grove of trees and so remaining hidden from view. Scaling a low, rocky hill, he saw an extraordinary sight.

Dark-haired, dark-eyed children, seven or eight of them at least, all dressed in the colorful garb of gypsies, danced around; he couldn't keep track of their numbers because they never stayed still. His own land closely neighbored this rocky, hilly estate, that of Lyulph Randell, and he had heard from other landowners that Randell had allowed a group of gypsies to camp on his land. They were unhappy about it; gypsies were unwelcome almost everywhere, tolerated at best, persecuted at worst. Wesmorlyn had wondered if Randell felt an affinity for them, the wildness of their reputations matching the wildness of his heritage, the wolf in him finding an answering untamed spirit.

The children were running in a circle, and at the center of that circle, whirling, skirts flinging out and hair unbound, loosening, and falling in golden waves down her back and over the straw bonnet that hung by ribbons, was Countess Charlotte von Wolfram. Her head was thrown back and her eyes were closed, and she was laughing, the joyous peal like music on the drifting breeze.

Wesmorlyn watched, entranced. Gone was the stiff, un-

happy young lady he last saw, and gone even was the coquet-
tish woman who so infuriated him in the ballroom. Here was
a golden child of God, a happy girl, arms outflung, rippling
hair floating on the wind and tangling with the fringe of her
shawl. One little gypsy girl raced at her and tackled her, and
they fell in a heap on the ground, with the other laughing children piling on, giggles and hilarity ringing out. She wrestled
with them, tickling and laughing, but finally, she cried out that
they were wearing her out.

"Stop! Stop, you little ruffians!" she cried, pulling her bonnet over her head and tossing it aside. "Let me catch my
breath."

"But no, sing us a song, Miss Charlotte!" one little boy
shouted.

"Only if you stop," she groaned, panting.

Wesmorlyn watched. Should he approach? They had not
noticed him yet, for they were turned mostly away from him
now, and he lingered just over a rise, crouching down in the
grass by a boulder, watching. Charlotte caught her flowing
hair and twisted it back into an untidy bun, from which golden
curls escaped and floated down over her shoulders. She put
her bonnet back on, tied the ribbon under her chin and sat in
the grass; the children gathered around her, sitting and lying
in various attitudes of attentiveness.

"I'll teach you a song," she said, and began to sing, in German, a *lied* that Wesmorlyn recognized as being an old folk
song.

Her voice was soft and lovely, tremulous at first, but it
gained strength as she paused and taught the children different parts. They struggled with the unfamiliar language, and
she laughed and started them again, patiently leading them
through the winding story of love and loss, the words to
which they would never know the meaning. It was a maiden's
lament that the man she loved had gone off to war, and would
never come home again, but for the children it was simply a
pretty song in a foreign language.

Through it all Charlotte's lovely voice trembled with feeling and throbbed with sweetness, the honeyed notes calling to
him, twisting and turning through his heart until he could feel
the connection and wondered that she didn't turn from her

students and find him there, watching her, entranced and riveted. He should abhor the raw emotion she betrayed, for it revealed far too much, and he had spent his life ruthlessly quashing even the merest hint of passionate feeling, and yet he was enchanted by her impassioned performance. As she sang on, the children trailing off to listen and watch her, the golden sunshine warmed him and without thought, Wesmorlyn began to sing the lower part, in harmony. One child pointed at him standing upon the rise, and Charlotte staggered to her feet and turned toward him as he started down the hill toward the clustered group.

"Wesmorlyn," she cried. She stiffened, and the children gazed up at her, and then, with resentful expressions, at him, as they rose, too.

All naturalness had fled the moment she looked at him, and his heart throbbed. Was that what he had done? Had he stomped every natural sensation out of her? Well of course, and hadn't that always been his intent with himself and everyone around him? He was speechless, but what he wanted to say was, *Sing . . . sing again, and dance and let your gorgeous hair flow in the breeze and let me watch you, let me feel for one more moment the pure joy of your sweet expressiveness.*

"I was worried for you when you disappeared from London," he said, haltingly, instead.

"Well, as you can see I am just fine."

"Among the gypsies?" It was the wrong thing to say, and he saw it in her eyes. He hadn't meant to sound censorious, but he did. What was wrong with him that he seemed so determined to stamp every sweet and artless expression from her lovely face? "I'm sorry," he said hastily, as she opened her mouth to retort. "I am sorry, Countess, for *everything.*"

"Everything? What do you mean?" She warily watched him, and the gypsy children crowded around her, clinging to her waist and surrounding her. Her arms around the closest and smallest, she held them to her.

"Everything," he said. "I'm sorry for everything I did to upset you. I was wrong, in London, to treat you as I did. You were weary from a long journey, and I was harsh and demanding. I was rude to your sister, Fanny. But I only did not want to dance with Miss Fanny because it was Hannah's first ball, and she couldn't dance with anyone beyond my own party. I so wanted to be her first partner, for she was very nervous of making a misstep." As he talked it all flowed out, his words jumbled in his haste to explain himself. "And I'm sorry I drove you away and was so jealous and hasty and I should never have embarrassed you and hurt you that way. I'm truly sorry." He took in a deep and trembling breath.

When had he ever apologized to anyone? He was accustomed to believing himself right in every action, so this was a new sensation, and he was not so sure he liked it. But then she smiled, and he would have apologized for another thirty minutes to keep her looking so.

"You knew the song I was teaching the children," she said, her head cocked to one side, the sunlight sparkling in her blue eyes under the bonnet brim. "How is that so?"

"My music master was fascinated by folk songs from other countries and so taught me *lieder*, as well as folk songs from Italy and Spain." He smiled self-consciously. "I had a ridiculously thorough education."

"Then help me teach them," she said.

"There is a dance that goes with the song," he said. "Do you know it?"

"Of course."

And so for the next half hour of his life he was a teacher of gypsy children, of all things. The little girls attended well enough, but the boys became distracted and began to roughhouse. One little fellow, racing around in circles, became dizzy and fell down, skinning his knee on one of the rocky outcroppings that dotted the moor. He wailed and wept, and not even Charlotte could convince him that he was unhurt, until Wesmorlyn knelt by him and whispered in his ear, telling him that Miss Charlotte would think him a very brave boy if he would stop crying. The child took a deep, shuddering breath and stopped, and Wesmorlyn then was able to examine his knee—he was wearing short pants, as were all of the little gypsy boys—and pronounce it not too bad, but needing cleaning with a damp cloth.

"Perhaps you could take him back to camp and let his mother look at it?" Wesmorlyn suggested to the eldest girl,

Tully, who nodded wisely. As the leader of the children, she rounded them up and, with one shrewd look at Wesmorlyn, she led them away, through the meadow, around the trees, and over the rise toward the camp.

They were alone, and he gazed at Charlotte. Self-conscious suddenly, she looked down at her dusty dress and hands and patted her skirts down.

"Will you walk with me?" he asked. Everything he had meant to do and say, all of the angry words, the complaints, had flown from him, and for that moment he just wanted to be in her company and to understand who she really was.

Shyly, she said, "All right."

Chapter 8

WESMORLYN TOOK Charlotte's arm, and she felt the connection like a thread pulled tight within her. In their half hour of play with the gypsy children she had seen a side of him that she never would have suspected existed from his stiff demeanor at the ball. His big hand was warm on her skin and a prickle of attraction snaked through her, shocking her with its intensity. Nervous and wary, she looked up at him, wondering what he was thinking, suddenly very aware of her grimy hands, tousled hair, and dusty skirts. She straightened her bonnet on her head and retied the ribbon with a proper bow.

"Do you accept my apology?" he asked, gazing down at her, a grave look in his gold-flecked brown eyes.

Apology; what was he talking about? But yes, he had apologized for his bad behavior, and said it was provoked by jealousy. *Jealousy?* Breathless at his steady stare, she gasped, "Of course." Then, thinking back, she stuttered back into speech. "I didn't realize it was Lady Hannah's first ball. I'm sorry I misjudged you."

"And I'm deeply regretful I was so clumsy as to offend you, but more unhappy if I hurt Miss Fanny's feelings at all."

She felt the tension ease from her at his perspicacious words. It pleased her that he said he would be more sorry if he hurt Fanny, for it meant he truly did understand what angered her most. "I think I was more upset than she," Charlotte admitted, leaning on his arm as they wandered across the sunlit moor. "I'm afraid I don't understand my sister very well."

"Nor do I understand mine, but that may be because I am twelve years her senior and a man."

Charlotte laughed; that was as close as she had ever heard him come to jesting.

"I am very fond of how you laugh," he said, suddenly and fervently, squeezing her arm to him.

She glanced up at him, watching how a random breeze lifted his russet curls off his broad forehead. Most of her anger at him had evaporated with his heartfelt apology, but she was left feeling shy, for he was a stranger to her. "I wish I could say the same, but I'm afraid I have never had the honor of hearing you laugh, sir."

He smiled, and over his solemn face the expression burst like sunshine illuminating shadows. "Do you know, I don't remember the last time I laughed."

"How awful! Life is not so serious that we must spend all of our time frowning over it as though it was a sin to see the humor."

He didn't answer, nor did he respond.

"You think that, don't you?" She observed his face, thinking how different he looked when he smiled and wishing he would smile again. Searching her heart to understand him, she slowly said, still watching his face as they strolled, side by side, "You feel that life is terribly serious, and that it's nothing to joke about."

"I was raised to believe that we are given one opportunity to make a success of life," he said, stiffly. "And that there is so much that needs to be done, so much that needs to be set right, there's no time to make light of it."

She stopped, let go of his arm, and turned to face him. "Life is more than the task at hand, my lord. It is so much more than a race to be run, the goal the only thing worth watching. If you keep your eyes fixed on the horizon, you miss all the beauty and wonder around you. Life is . . ." She trailed off, at a loss for words, then shook her head, gestured around, and swung away from him, twirling in a circle, arms outstretched. "Look at this glorious day!" she cried, closing her eyes and feeling the sunshine on her upturned face and the mossy moor under her feet. She breathed in deeply and opened her eyes, spinning in the sunlight until she was breathless and laughing. "How," she gasped, "can you look at all of this beauty around you and not be moved to laughter or tears. How can you not be joyous?"

He didn't respond, and when she looked over it was to find him staring at her, his eyes wide and an expression of yearning on his face. She stopped, the breath sucked from her lungs. "What is it?" she asked, in a faltering voice.

He shook himself and looked away. "I think we had very different upbringings."

"Perhaps." The dark moments of the past year came back to her, times when she had feared for her life, times when confusion and pain had overwhelmed every other thought and hope was blotted out like sunshine erased by cloud. "That is certainly true, but our experience of life has been different, too. Though you have likely had your share of pain, as have we all, I doubt that you have seen the utter darkness of the soul that I have witnessed."

"What—"

She held up one hand. This was not the time, nor was he someone in whom she could confide. "It is personal, my lord, and painful, but not something of which I wish to speak. Someday, perhaps. But I walked so long in the shadows, my lord, and now, to feel the sunlight and know joy is like heaven on earth."

"Heaven on earth," he echoed, but then shook his head. "Countess, I cannot imagine finding this life to be like heaven on earth."

She searched his eyes. "Then what are you living for, the hereafter?"

"Is that not what we're supposed to do? Our life here on earth is so temporary—"

"And I intend to enjoy it!" she cried. "Every moment of every day. And I will take chances and explore what life has to offer me while I am here."

"Countess, that is not—"

"Please, call me something other than countess," she said, interrupting him again. She watched his face; it reminded her of how the sky, on a cloudy day, would sometimes show glimpses of sunlight peeking through. He was so somber, but was there more beneath that sober demeanor? For the first time she wondered what his life had truly been like. Men were raised differently from women. They were raised to think of duty and honor and responsibility, ideals he evidently valued above all else. Did that have to make one humorless and solemn?

All of the duties and expectations of being a woman seemed like a book she knew by heart, but which she had set aside as irrelevant to her. In her life she was supposed to be silent and submissive and quiet. That was a woman's role, and she understood well the expectations of her and how she failed them, no matter how hard she tried. She was to listen to the men who were to guide her, and accept their decisions about her life without fuss. She should be demure, dainty, docile, and deferential. She'd rather be dead.

Perhaps if her mother and father had lived to raise her she would be just such a young woman: quiet, obedient, and sweet-natured. Much like Fanny, raised in a servant's compliant role. She shuddered at the thought. It was not for her. She did her best to be respectful and considerate, but could not suppress the fire within her forever. Life had been her teacher, and the lesson had been to seize joy with both hands, for one never knew what the next day would bring. Returning to his side and gazing up at him, she said, "If there is no joy in life, then what is there to live for?"

His eyes clouded with doubt. "Why, we live for duty. And to take care of those who mean something to us, and for whom we bear responsibility."

"But none of that means we have to live without joy. Doing our duty doesn't mean we have to do it with a heavy heart and a frown." She gazed up at his face, the sunlight highlighting a faint dusting of freckles over his nobly proportioned nose. His thick chestnut hair was swept back from a broad forehead, but unlike in the ballroom, he was dressed for country pursuits and more handsome for it, in breeches and riding boots.

"But do you understand what it means to do your duty?" he asked, earnestly.

"I understand what it means for a man," she said, "but what does it mean for a woman?"

"Why, that you marry well, and bear children, and raise them to be dutiful to their father."

She felt the constricting panic again, the rising tide of fierce anger and outrage. Boundaries imposed on every side, hemmed in by expectations, it was no wonder she longed for freedom with such passion. She felt a wildness in her heart, an eager need to be free. Turning away from him and stepping up onto a rocky outcropping, she said, "Then I will not do my duty. Or perhaps it is more that I don't even believe that *is* my duty."

"But that is what is accepted! It's in the Bible, and in the homilies handed down through the ages." He shook his head, with a puzzled look. "Why, it's *life*," he continued, frowning up at her on her rocky pedestal. "What is your duty if not those things we have been taught from the cradle?"

He put out his hand to help her down from the rock, but she ignored it and jumped down on her own. "I don't know yet," she said. "All I know is I cannot abdicate the responsibility to understand my life and what it means to me. I can't give over the right to choose what I am to do, to someone else, no matter how much they love me or how well they intend. I just can't!"

Legs spread, feet planted firmly, and arms akimbo, he stood and stared at her. "What else did you come to England for, if not to follow your uncle's dictates and marry me?"

She stared at him in frustration. There they were, back at why they could never suit. She had been right all along; the earl was stuffy and overly correct, and she would die rather than bury herself in the role of countess to such a killjoy.

Wesmorlyn watched her, and it was as if a brilliant light had been covered by a smothering blanket; the joy went out of her expression and her blue eyes dulled. But her joy had a dangerous, intoxicating quality, so perhaps it needed to be tempered and calmed. *She* needed to be calmed, for she exhibited a wildness in her words and thoughts that was alarming. No one could go through life happy all the time. No one could just dance in the sun, laugh and smile and be happy. Could they? Was it possible to do one's duty and yet have joy too? It seemed too much to ask.

"Shall we walk?" he asked, taking her arm.

"I do not need your support, sir," she said, jerking her arm out of his grasp, striding away, and ascending toward the rocky crest of a low hill. "I don't need any man's support." She was vigorous in her climb, as if pursued by the ghosts of future drudgery. When she reached the top, she shaded her eyes and stared out over the other side. Her mercurial mood shifted again, and she smiled. "How *beautiful!*"

He joined her, and gazed out over the rocky slope. Below them wound a sparkling stream and a road followed it, finally crossing the water with the aid of an ancient stone bridge. He glanced at her face and was riveted by her returned expression of joy, her azure eyes alight with a brilliance that rivaled the celestial blue sky overhead. So small a thing as a stone bridge could cause such joy? He couldn't imagine. And yet . . . a memory flooded his mind of Hannah, a child of ten or so, and her joy over finding a tiny gray mouse in the stable. She had cradled it in her hands and exclaimed over it, cooing in a sweet, childish trill of adoration. But he had knocked it out of her hands and stomped it with his boot, and the light had died in her eyes. Even though he explained that it might have bit her, and that they could not allow vermin to flourish in the stables, for they brought disease, he had felt as if he personally stomped the joy out of her expression that day.

Was that his fate, to be the one to kill the joy in feminine eyes? All he wanted was to do his duty, but did that mean being joyless for all the years of his life? He was suddenly afraid of the years ahead, years spent in the calm and plodding pursuit of redemption for the Wesmorlyns, staid, sedate, and devoid of any happiness save the deepest, the kind that came from doing one's duty. What of the other kind, the intoxication she seemed to feel just from nature and beauty? A sudden and blinding need to understand overcame him.

"Teach me," he said, in a desperate panic, his breath coming quick. "Teach me what it is that makes you exclaim over such a poor thing as a dilapidated stone bridge."

She turned to him and stared into his eyes. Her expression

was doubtful; perhaps she thought he was teasing or making fun of her.

"I have never comprehended the picturesque," he said, frowning and squinting into the distance. "Though it has been explained to me many times by despairing art masters, I still don't understand it. Teach me." ·

She shrugged helplessly. "No one can teach you that. It's in here," she said, touching her chest over her heart with the flat of her hand. "Not here," she said, touching her head.

"Then teach me about there," he said, touching her bodice with one finger, staring at her. He felt her heart pounding, and in that moment he longed to flatten his hand, to touch her and feel the vigor of life that she exemplified. Instead he drew his hand away.

She stared into his eyes and bit her lip. "It's like a foreign language to you, isn't it?"

He nodded, numbly.

"I don't know if you can learn it then. I sometimes wonder if some things are innate; we either experience them in our core or they will be lost to us forever."

"Don't say that, please. Try?"

She took in a deep breath. "All right. But you must listen to me and yet endeavor, at the same time, to hear what is in your own heart. Point your body in that direction and close your eyes."

He did as he was told, facing the scene below.

"What do you feel?"

"What? I don't understand. My eyes are closed. How can I feel anything?"

"I said, *feel*, don't look! What do you *feel*? Stop analyzing the words and just listen. Experience the world for one minute without sight."

He stopped trying to think and just let himself be, for a moment. The sun was warm on his face and a breeze chased up the hill and ruffled his hair. It felt good, like tender fingers brushing the hair back from his forehead. Without sight, he experienced the day in a different way, and heard a lark in a distant hedgerow singing, the rustle of the grass bent by the breeze, and then the gurgle of the brook from below came to him, a chuckle of sound more pleasing than the strains of a violin concerto. Had he shut all of that out before? He would have sworn the day was silent, and yet there was a symphony of sound when one stopped to listen.

"Now," she whispered near his ear, "*Now* open your eyes and look."

He did, but if he expected a revelation, it was not to be. He glanced over at her and shrugged.

"Stop *thinking* about it!" she exclaimed, stamping one foot on the ground. "What do you see?"

He stared, and stopped considering the scene from the aspect of a landowner. He tried not to worry about the disrepair of the bridge—the crumbling stone and the anxiety of possible collapse—and just gazed at it, the mossy patterns on the pale gray stone and the sparkling water trickling beneath it, silver and glittering in the brilliant sunlight. The bank rose from it in verdant clumps of tender grass, and a tiny fish leaped to catch an insect hovering too close to the water's surface.

"You're smiling," she said.

"I feel as if I am at the edge of understanding." He glanced over at her, so close to him, and was caught by the loveliness of her pale skin shadowed by the straw bonnet, the rosebud delicacy of her mouth, and the delicious sweetness of the dimple in the middle of her chin. "You're so very pretty," he said, impulsively, "not what I expected at all when I corresponded with your uncle."

She colored, the pink blooming on her cheeks in the same manner that sunset pinkened the sky near twilight. "Do you really think I'm pretty? When you first met me, I sensed you were disappointed."

He *had* been disappointed . . . disappointed that she was so lovely. He couldn't tell her that, for how could he explain it when he didn't even understand himself? "No gentleman could ever look at you and be disappointed, especially after meeting you. I have never seen a lady who so accurately reflects the beauty and freshness of her character in her appearance."

She ducked her head in adorable self-consciousness. Her expression concealed by the brim of her hat, shyly she said, "I have not had very much experience with male attention, sir, and I don't know what I should say in reply."

Her bashful honesty thawed every last bit of his reserve, for at least the moment, and he smiled over at her. "You needn't say a thing." He took her arm. "Will you walk with me down to the stone bridge? I feel oddly like a babe whose eyes are opened to the world around me, and I wish to see things more closely."

They walked and talked for a while, and all of the anxious tension he had felt for many days slipped from him. It was like mist burning off the moor from the heat of the sun; in the sunshine of her presence it just dissipated and finally disappeared. He told her about Cornwall, all the stories his father had told him, about pirates and merchant ships, and the ancient legends of King Arthur, for they were not far from Tintagel. He told her about ancient battles and how his family had come to gain their title, though he didn't delve completely into his family history. There were things in his family's ancient line he spoke of to no one.

Compromises had been made, battles won by foul means and treachery, despicable ancestors for whom to repent. Every moment of his life he had been raised and inculcated to believe that he was the one to set things right, no matter what it took, and no matter if it was the only thing he ever did. If his youth was often grim and cheerless, he had taught himself not to think of it that way, to see in every moment of duty one step up the long ladder to heaven. But now he saw that there was more, and he wondered if he had to miss out on simpler joys after all. With the right companionship it was, perhaps, possible to have everything. She had brought him so far in just an hour; could he trust her with the rest of his life?

Finally he spoke of the physical beauty of Cornwall. "You can see for yourself," he said, with a gesture at the expansive landscape, "though this is Randell's land, and not the best example of Cornwall's best aspects. But it is truly a magical place in every way. Do you know that while the rest of the country suffers through winter, we have an early spring here? Daffodils bloom, and warm breezes awaken the countryside."

She laughed at his unusually enthusiastic speech. "You

sound as though you are trying to sell Cornwall, and I am a prospective buyer!"

He turned and stared steadily into her eyes. "Well, in a way you are, aren't you?"

For the first time she acknowledged how different their expectations were of her arrival in England. It must have been confusing and disappointing to find in her such an awkward, quarrelsome girl when he had expected a gracious, accomplished lady. He had a right to be far more angry at her than he had yet shown himself to be. "You came all this way to find me, didn't you?"

"I was worried when Christoph said you were ill and could not come down to see me, the morning after the ball. I thought something had happened."

"Poor Christoph," Charlotte said, turning and walking again. She strolled along the riverbank, watching the flash and leap of silvery fish and how the sun sparkled on the bubbling surface. "Has he followed me, do you think?"

"He has," he answered, following her, "but for some reason has not come to Cornwall yet, as far as I can determine."

Her cheeks pinkened a deeper shade of rose, and she sighed. "I deliberately did not tell him where we were going, because I didn't know how long I would need for my quest. I knew he might come after us on horseback, and that is so much quicker than traveling by carriage." She paused and gazed back at the earl in consternation. "I feel terrible now! He's probably in Plymouth, knocking on every door looking for us."

"Why Plymouth?"

"That is where he likely thought we were going. I feel dreadful about frightening him, but he would not listen to me." She picked up a stone from the water's edge and tossed it in, watching it sink and a group of tiny, curious fish eagerly dart around the resulting bubbles. "After my appalling behavior at the ball he treated me abominably, and no matter what I have done, I will not stand for that."

Wesmorlyn took her hand. "Please, Countess . . . Charlotte, I'm sorry if my own awful behavior chased you from London."

She met his gaze. "It wasn't you, sir, please believe me. It was a mixture of things, most of which have nothing to do with you."

"But where are you and your sister staying? Why did you come to Cornwall? I have been concerned about your safety, and then last night when we could not find you at the inn in Bodmin, I spent an awful night fearing for you. If I had not overheard your carriage driver laughing about dropping you off in the middle of nowhere, I would never have found you."

"That terrible man!" Charlotte said, a quick flash of anger coursing through her. "I wish I had him here this minute, for I would give him a piece of my mind! It was purest luck, and gypsy sight, that Tamara—she is a girl from the gypsy camp —found us and gave us shelter. But as you can see, sir," she said, dropping his hand and twirling, her dress belling out around her ankles. "I am not worse for the experience."

"You are remarkably resilient," he said, shaking his head. "Most young ladies would have swooned under the experience."

"I have never swooned." She took a deep breath and faced him squarely. "I *am* troubled, sir, about what occurred in London," she said, determined to have it out. "I am concerned mostly about your relationship with Mr. Randell. I dislike being a source of enmity between two old friends. Did you *have* to challenge him? And how did it turn out? I hope neither of you were seriously hurt."

"Friends? We have not really been that for some years, though there is no enmity on my side."

"But . . . your sister named him as a dear family friend," Charlotte said, with a frown.

"She feels more warmly toward him than I. Before the night of the ball I had no real anger toward him."

"But what happened, then, at the duel?"

"Randell did not attend the duel," Wesmorlyn said. "That surprised me. I had not thought him the type to let such a matter of honor slide like that."

"I'm glad he didn't meet you," she said. But if that was the case, she suddenly thought, then what had kept Mr. Randell from meeting them at Salisbury as he had promised? That was a puzzle. "But I must relieve your worry on one account, sir. My leaving London had nothing to do with you. When I came to England, it was partly to find my sister's mother. The woman is still living, and I thought Fanny should have the chance to meet her. And then the very night of the ball I found out from Mr. Randell that not only was Miss Dancey still living, she was a tenant of his! How amazingly fortuitous, is it not?" she said.

His brown eyes were cast down in thought. "You found all this out while you walked in the garden with him?"

"No, it was later, when I was speaking to Fanny on the terrace. Mr. Randell happened to be near—he wished to apologize for kissing me and causing such trouble, which I thought was very gentlemanly—and he overheard the name Eleanor Dancey. He recognized it immediately as belonging to his recent tenant."

"And he understood all just from her name?" Wesmorlyn said, a frown darkening his expression.

"No, of course not," she said tartly. "I explained why we were looking for her, and he kindly offered us the use of his carriage and driver."

He shook his head in grave disapproval. "And so you are going to go meet this woman and see if she is Miss Fanny's mother?"

"We have already done so, sir, and Fanny is now with her. The woman was overcome with joy at finding her daughter, you can imagine, for she was on the point of leaving England forever! Fortune smiles on my endeavor, it seems."

"How do you know for sure this is the correct Eleanor Dancey?"

"Do you not think I asked questions?" Charlotte sighed, exasperated. "You're just as trying as Christoph. You treat me as if I don't have a brain in my head. When we went up to see her, I asked her a few questions, the answers to which proved she was the correct woman. She even remembered calling me Lotte when I was but a child!"

"It all seems so fortuitous," he said, his dark eyes filled with doubt.

"What do you mean?"

He sighed. "You come to England to meet me, and bring Fanny to find her mother. The very first night of your arrival you meet the man, an acquaintance of mine and a close neighbor in Cornwall, who not only knows her, but also has rented her a house recently, and can give you directions."

"And who provided the carriage for us to travel here," she repeated. She explained the original plan, and though it fell apart, and Mr. Randell did not, after all, meet them in Salisbury and the carriage driver abandoned them, it still resulted in success. "He understood completely about how Christoph would behave if I tried to tell him about Eleanor Dancey, and he made available his carriage and driver."

"Who abandoned you by the side of the road," he said, stiffly.

"It is hardly Mr. Randell's fault that his driver is a villain and a drunkard," Charlotte said hotly. How did it happen that she was defending Mr. Randell when she was angry with him herself?

"Nevertheless, it was a rash and risky thing to do!"

Though she understood what he was saying, he was being just as patronizing as Christoph and it sparked her fury. "Perhaps it seems so to you, but I only did it in such a manner because I was pushed by men who will not listen to me! I will *not* be chivvied and patronized as if I have no say in my life." She turned and started back toward the gypsy encampment. "And it all turned out all right in the end, didn't it?" she said, over her shoulder. "Though I am not a believer, perhaps I am wrong; perhaps there is such a thing in life as destiny, my lord, and it was Fanny's destiny to meet her mother. Now, I have been gone too long. I must go back up to the house, for Fanny will worry. She is such a fusser!"

"Wait!"

Charlotte turned back and stared at the earl.

His expression was serious. "Please listen to me; there is much here that I don't understand. I learned before I followed you that Lyulph Randell had not yet left London, and I don't know why that is so, if he was to meet you in Salisbury."

She shook her head. "I will certainly ask him those things when he comes. I understand his home is not too far from Moor Cottage."

"You don't intend to go to his home, do you?"

"What if I do?" she asked, though she had no intention of doing anything of the sort. She was raised properly and did ascribe to some rules of decorum, despite the English population's determined idea that Germans were barbarians. "What if I decided to pay him a visit in his home? Who are you to say anything about it?"

"You are an infuriating girl! I am your betrothed husband," he said, shaking his finger, "and have a right to correct your behavior."

That was it; there was that presumption of privilege. "You have *no* right," she ground out, feeling the iron restraints of male prerogative close around her once again. She stopped herself and looked up to the sky, then back down at him, holding back her temper with an effort. "I know I am not what you thought you were ordering." Her tone mocking, she continued, "Did the catalogue entry state one virginal German bride, dutiful and well-raised, available for delivery?" Her attempt at humor withered and her anger overcame her. "I am *more* than that. I am a grown woman with my own thoughts and opinions, and I will never exchange my feelings for yours. I will *never* use anyone's judgment but my own, flawed and faulty though it may be. Speak to me as if I am a rational being, or do not speak to me at all!"

"I will speak to you as a rational being when you begin to behave as one!" he spluttered, but then calmed, taking a deep breath. He approached her and said, taking one hand, "Charlotte, will you do me one favor?"

She stared down at his bare hand, so broad and long-fingered, encasing hers in his warm grip. "What is it?"

"Will you keep my arrival here a secret for now?"

"Why?" she asked, meeting his gaze.

"Please, I know I have no right to ask such a thing, but just trust me?"

She hesitated, but then nodded, speechless. Arrogant he might be, presumptuous and overbearing, but he was clearly also trustworthy and concerned, and there was every reason to believe that he would have a good reason for any request he made.

"And may I see you again? Here, near the gypsy camp?"

"You shouldn't ask such a thing. A clandestine meeting, a secret between a man and woman: Are not those forbidden?"

She taunted him deliberately, but he would not be drawn this time.

He smiled. "I know. I can't believe I am even asking it of you, for this is completely out of character for me. I have never done such a thing before, but there are things I wish to investigate. Please, do I have your word? I am speaking to you as one rational being to another. I understand if you don't wish to meet me here again, but just keep my secret for a few days?"

"All right," she said, and pulled her hand from his grasp. "But only for a few days." She walked away from him, looking back occasionally to find him staring after her, the expression of intense longing back on his face. What it truly meant, she was afraid she would never know, and she could not explain to herself why it touched her so deeply.

The walk back to the gypsy encampment seemed long; she hadn't realized how far they had wandered nor how long she had been gone. When she approached the camp she heard voices raised in anger.

She rounded the grove of trees and saw the sunlight sparkling off hair very much like her own, but a darker golden in hue. "Christoph," she shouted, overjoyed to see her brother. She broke into a run. "Christoph, you've come!"

Chapter 9

"CHARLOTTE! THANK God!" He caught his sister to him, as she threw herself into his arms, and hugged her, burying his face in her hair under her straw bonnet. His agony of three days was relieved in one sweeping moment. Charlotte, his adored little sister. Through all of the misery and confusion of the last years, even when he could not speak of the terrible things he was going through, she was always there to support him in silence. More than any member of his family she was the one who believed in him implicitly, even when he couldn't believe in himself. She defended him against any slur, and trusted him implicitly, or at least she had until their arrival in England. Their recent rift was more his fault than hers, he realized, and it had torn his heart in two.

He had tracked her as far in the night as the gypsy encampment, but in his werewolf form he could not approach and had been forced to reluctantly return to Siegfried, who followed on horseback with his clothing. And then, such a long night of running and searching, nose to the ground, hour after exhausting hour, had left him drained. Unable to move another inch, he had slept for a few hours before following up on his hunt.

But though he knew she was there at some point, the gypsies had been steadfast in their claims not to have seen two blonde young foreign ladies. What had happened to them? What had the gypsy men done?

His frustration and fury had just been reaching boiling point when Charlotte appeared from out of nowhere to ease his frenzied vexation. "Where have you been?" he asked, holding her away from him. She looked radiant and unharmed, her cheeks faintly sun-kissed as if she had been frolicking in the sunshine without her hat. He was almost angry; she had no right to look so jubilant when he had been suffering agonies of apprehension for the last three days.

"Oh, Christoph, I have so much to tell you! But first . . . you have probably terrified these poor people with your fierce questioning," she said, glancing around at the frightened faces of the children clinging to the women who stood near the shadowy protection of the caravans and the sullen, distrustful faces of the men. She looked toward a caravan at a young woman who was climbing down. "There is Tamara. You must meet her."

She raced over to the young gypsy woman and pulled her by the arm until they were both standing in front of him. Christoph gazed down at her. She was dark-eyed and voluptuous, with tumbled dark curls pulled back by an indigo and emerald scarf; her skin was the rich, warm color of honey.

"Tamara, this is my brother, Christoph; he has followed and found me. Isn't he clever? Christoph, this is Tamara, and she was very kind to Fanny and me last night. She gave us a bed, and made sure we had food. And then she knew where Eleanor Dancey lived and—"

"Wait! What is all of this? What's going on? Why did you leave London and how . . . where . . ." He shook his head, bewildered.

"It's a long story," Charlotte said, touching his arm. "And I promise to tell you all. But first, say hello, for Tamara and I are friends. She is a sweet girl, better than any of those awful English girls I met at the ball the first night we arrived."

Christoph gravely bowed over the gypsy girl's hand. She curtseyed and stared up at him, wide-eyed and wordless, her cherry lips parted. An unwelcome jolt of attraction ripped through his body. She was lovely, doe-eyed and lushly constructed, and he could feel her interest. He smelled it rising from her, a scent of attraction that pulled him, filling him with desire and need. He shut down his body, backing away from the spiraling sensation of arousal. It made him uneasy and uncomfortable, an awful reminder of past confusion and hideous shame.

He swallowed hard and cleared his throat. "Where is Fanny?" he asked, turning to his sister. "We must go back to London. I sent Siegfried ahead to get us a suite of rooms at the inn in Bodmin, but I would rather just hire a carriage and start back to the city today. You left me in a terrible position, Charlotte! I cannot believe how irresponsible you have been, to just run away and leave me to explain your absence to the earl."

"I have been trying to explain to you, Christoph," she said, stiffly, hands balled into fists at her side. "I won't be going back to London. If you would just listen to me you would understand, but you won't. You haven't lately."

He sighed and looked around at the gypsies. Uneasily, he wondered if he would be robbed. The men were glaring at him with distrustful expressions, but they made no move to attack or even to confront him. He took Charlotte's arm and pulled her away. "Take me to Fanny."

She pulled her arm from his grasp. "Stop behaving as if you have some right to tell me what to do. I am weary to the bone of men telling me what to do!"

"Don't be nonsensical! If you will just be more . . . more . . ."

"More what?" she said, her voice rising and her blue eyes glinting dangerously in the brilliant sunlight. "More ladylike? More malleable? More brainless?"

"More *sensible*." He glared at her, and saw the stubborn set of her dimpled chin.

"Listen to me," she said, speaking slowly and clearly making a great effort to be calm. "I'm sorry I frightened you, but you were in no mood in London to listen, and especially after that idiotic scene between Mr. Randell and me. I had to act quickly, or Fanny may not have met her mother. And you were writing that letter, about to take us away when we were on the very brink of accomplishing my goal in coming to this dreadful island. I could not . . ." She paused, putting up one finger. "Wait a moment." Charlotte went and whispered to the gypsy girl, gave her a quick hug, and then turned away, after waving to the other people gathered nearby. Some of the little children waved back. She took Christoph's arm and led him away. "We can walk while we talk. Tamara is going to have one of the men bring my and Fanny's bags to the house later."

"The house? What house?"

"Moor Cottage. I'm trying to tell you if you will just shut up and listen."

So he did, though first he had to surrender to the inevitable and satisfy her curiosity about how he found her in such an obscure place as the gypsy camp. She seemed almost envious at his tale of tracking her movements through the night as a wolf, but he could have told her it had a price in a sweeping weariness deep to the very core of his being. He didn't wish to become distracted, though, and so was terse and to the point, simply explaining that he had then returned to Siegfried, who awaited him near the next village, reassumed his human form, and collapsed in his room at the tiny inn nearby until he awoke later in the morning to finish his search. He didn't go into it, but he had been hideously anxious, fearing she and Fanny were being kept captive, agonizing over the delay in getting back to the gypsy camp, furious over the necessity that had driven him to sleep when he should have been returning directly to retrieve her. Finding her safe and cheerful had been both a relief and maddening, but he knew his sister well enough to know that going into his irritation at that moment would just lead to a long argument. He wanted to know what had taken her from London first.

So at his urging, Charlotte told him a convoluted tale about the night at the ball in London, and how Lyulph Randell, overhearing her and Fanny talking about Eleanor Dancey, volunteered the information that he had rented a cottage to a woman of that name recently, but that the lady had spoken of leaving England for the Canadas.

"What would you have done in that instance?" she asked him, glancing over as they walked. "Be honest, Christoph. If I had told you all of this, with how you were feeling about Mr.

Randell, knowing he is a werewolf, and being angry at me for the scene at the ball, what would you have done?"

He took a deep breath and thought. They had always been honest with each other. "I would have refused to listen," he admitted, scaling a long rise as she easily kept pace with him. "Perhaps only at first, though. You *know* you could have convinced me eventually, Charlotte."

"But I *didn't* know that, and we didn't have time anyway," she said, leading him across the sun-dappled moor, around rocky outcroppings and down the other side of the rise. "I could not trust Fanny's future to my ability to convince you to leave London and head off to Cornwall. Nor would a letter sent by post do in this instance. Really Christoph, how would one frame such a letter? How would one ask the lady by post if she bore an illegitimate child nineteen years before in Germany?"

"And you say you really have found Eleanor Dancey?" he asked, reflecting on her tale. "And she was happy to see Fanny?"

"Ecstatic! Swooning, sighs, tears, just like one would expect." Charlotte gave a little hop of happiness.

He glanced over at his sister. "Is it not all an enormous coincidence, Charlotte?"

"Perhaps not," Charlotte said, pensively. "I have never believed in fate, but could everything that has happened so far be destiny?"

"I don't believe in destiny."

"Yes, well, a few months ago I didn't believe in werewolves nor in witches, either, but there we are," she replied in a dry tone. "Both exist. I am forced to concede that I may be wrong about the existence of destiny at work in our lives."

He experienced a pang at her mention of witches, for his darling Melisande, now blissfully married to a Russian count who also happened to be a werewolf, was just such a one, with breathtaking powers of protection for those in her circle. He had loved but lost her to a man he could not fault, yet the twinge he felt about losing her forever was duller than it had been just a month before. If only he had admitted his feelings sooner, perhaps he could have claimed her as his own, but he couldn't dwell on the past. One day he would think of her without pain, as a friend he cared for deeply.

He turned his mind to his sister's argument. Could Charlotte have something in her determined argument that everything so far, even their trip to England, had been part of some divine scheme to right the past injustices that had separated Fanny from her birth mother? He could hardly discount the possibility that there was some kind of master plan, and they just cogs in the machinery of fate, even though in philosophical discussions about destiny and free will he had always come down on the side of free will. They were creatures of God, perhaps, but free to make mistakes, to forge their own way, he had always thought. What good was the werewolf's eternal struggle, to choose to stay on the path of good and resist the urge to walk on the darker side, if every action was foreordained by some higher power?

But he supposed he must keep his mind and heart open to possibilities. Life had shown him all could change in a heartbeat. "So you think it was no coincidence, but that destiny had some hand in everything that has gone on? If this truly is Eleanor Dancey—"

"It *is* Eleanor Dancey, Christoph, the *right* Eleanor Dancey. Who else could it be? She knew me as a child, and even told me she used to call me Lotte!"

"I don't remember that."

"You were very young; so was I, but she remembered me! And be rational. What motive would some strange woman have, when confronted with two girls at her door, to admit one of them was her illegitimate daughter by a German count? That is surely beyond the bounds of reason. No, she knew his name, Christoph. She knew our father's name, and though she will not speak of him—I fear she was very deeply wounded— she admitted the affair with shame and humility. You'll see." She stopped as they reached the top of the hill they had been scaling and pointed. "There. That is Moor Cottage."

Nestled in the bottom of the valley and with the sunlight beaming softly upon its stone walls and slate roof, it should have been an appealing, idyllic sight, but instead it looked brooding, squat, and gloomy. The gardens, riotous and overrun, gave it the look of a place abandoned and hopeless, devoid of cheer. Two windows faced in their direction, and they looked like heavy-lidded eyes; he felt oddly like the cottage was watching him, waiting for him, anticipating his arrival with sinister satisfaction.

Charlotte was watching him, and he searched for something positive to say, but couldn't. She bit her lip, but finally laughed. "Admit it, Christoph, it looks even gloomier than Wolfram Castle in midwinter!"

He chuckled. "You're right about that. However, onward. Let's go and see this woman."

Charlotte had thought that Fanny and Eleanor would be closeted together catching up on each others' lives in the years since Eleanor had been forced, as a very young girl, to bear her child, leave her behind to be raised in the von Wolfram household, and sent to live in shame in England. But the woman came into the cottage from the kitchen garden beyond the back door, and said that Fanny was upstairs.

Hellebore followed her, as the cat always did, but it took one look at Christoph and hissed, its back arching, spitting with fury. It turned and tore from the house, yowling all the way.

"I apologize most sincerely," Eleanor said, her eyes wide as she stared at Christoph. "I've never seen Hellebore act like that, except when Mr. Randell's game master visited once with his pack of hounds."

Charlotte stifled a laugh. The cat hated her, but was clearly terrified of Christoph. Did it sense that he was a werewolf? "Miss Dancey, this is my brother, Count Christoph von Wolfram," she said, choking back her laughter. "Isn't he clever? He found us, even though he did not know where we were!"

Christoph gave her a warning glance and turned back to the woman. She welcomed him with a shy reserve, but warmly for all that, just as she ought to behave, Charlotte judged. And in fact, Charlotte could see that Christoph was charmed by the retiring, modest woman. Though he offered to go to the inn at Bodmin, she insisted he stay in her humble home, for she would not separate Fanny from the only family she had ever known, she said, her lips trembling with emotion. Charlotte and Fanny would have to share a room, she said, but that being done, he could indeed occupy the third bedroom. She apologized for the modesty of the accommodations, but he thanked her, gravely, and said he would be grateful to stay. First, though, he needed to go to Bodmin and retrieve his manservant, Siegfried, who had gone on ahead of him to bespeak a room while Christoph hunted for his sisters.

Charlotte went in search of Fanny and found her up in the room they were going to share, sitting quietly, reading the Bible. She shared the news that Christoph had found them, and then asked, "So what did you and your mother talk about?" Charlotte plopped down on the high four-poster bed they would have to share.

Fanny looked up from the Bible, frowning into the middle distance, her blue eyes unfocussed. "Well, she did not wish to speak of our father. In fact she didn't wish to speak of Germany at all. She asked how much I knew about her life, and I told her the truth, that I knew very little, except that she was sent to live with a maiden aunt. That is all anyone knew except for Frau Liebner's very brief visit to her quite a few years ago, in her aunt's home in Plymouth. She said that her interest really was in me, and *my* life so far. I could understand her reticence, and did not press her."

Charlotte nodded in understanding. "She likely didn't want to shock you with details of her life best left unmentioned. It must have been so difficult for her when she came back to England, a young girl disgraced and unhappy. I had hoped she would speak of our father, for I remember so little about him, but I can understand her not wanting to remember that painful period in her life."

Fanny was silent, and then continued to read, or at least continued to stare down at the book in her lap. Charlotte watched her for a long few minutes, and noted that she never turned the page, but inevitably her mind turned back to Wesmorlyn, and their walk. He was infuriatingly complicated, offering glimpses of a charming, vulnerable man, easy to talk to, but then he would poker up into that dreadful, stiff caricature of an English nobleman. And the change took place as swiftly as a cloud shrouding the sun.

Why did he not want her to say anything about him being in Cornwall? It made no sense, but she had promised and didn't take that lightly. Perhaps she would see him again at the gypsy camp. She would not soon forget the expression in his fine, dark eyes, the look of yearning as she walked away from him. It had certainly been directed at her, but what did it mean? She sighed, wishing the tangled mystery of the Earl of Wesmorlyn was as easy to unravel as it had been to find Fanny's mother.

Chapter 10

THE MELLOW gold and gray stone walls of Wesmorlyn Abbey glowed in the soft afternoon sun as the earl trudged up the long open hill to his home. He was lost in thought but paused, as he always did, to notice how the stained glass of the Gothic windows glistened, the twin images of Gabriel and Uriel over the door, their hands outstretched in supplication, picked out in brilliant hues of scarlet and azure, emerald and gold. Even without looking he could have said how they looked, though, it was so familiar a sight to him. Every member of his family who had ever entered through the massive doors underneath had looked up, and remembered the old tales of how their eventual redemption rested in the hands of one of them, though *who* had not been foretold. Some, hoping to be the redeemer, had tried to keep to the right path and had failed, while others had not even bothered to try, relishing the power of their position and using it to satisfy their own mortal greed and lust. Centuries had passed in that cycle of sin and suffering and attempts to find salvation.

Semyaza, standing in front, awaited his return. How many generations of his family, upon returning to the Abbey, had looked up to see Semyaza, tall and stern, watching and waiting for them to become worthy? Too far back to ponder, he reflected as he stopped and gazed up at the familiar figure. He slipped his jacket on over his loose shirt and wiped his brow with the back of his hand. The itch in the middle of his back was quiescent, and he was weary, for though his land bordered Randell's, it was still some distance from the gypsy camp to Wesmorlyn Abbey. He had much to ponder and more to discover. Somewhere, at the heart of Countess Charlotte's simple story of finding her sister's mother, lay a mystery.

"Sam," he said, strolling toward the abbey, shrugging his shoulders properly into his jacket and fastening the top button with one hand, "I found them. Both the countess and her sister Fanny are safe. But Countess Charlotte told me a strange tale, one that involves Lyulph Randell. I'm not sure if it is true or part of some scheme."

Semyaza didn't answer, and Wesmorlyn sighed. "I know; these things I need to discover for myself. I'm puzzled. If it *is* true, then it's the most amazing coincidence, or some sort of plan of which I am not a part. But if it is *not* true, then I have to consider that Lyulph Randell has embarked on a scheme that must, through its use of the countess, be aimed at me, and I don't want to think that, not after this many years of mending the enmity between our families. All these years and Lyulph has never once strayed from the right path, not even considering how great the urges are for him." He considered the awful burden under which the man labored, part man and part beast. The earth pulled him, tempted him, and every sense must urge him to become more of what was now only a small part of his makeup. For some reason Wesmorlyn had always been able to vividly imagine it, the excruciating enticement of the physical world, the lure of the seven deadly sins. He had even felt it that very afternoon; the countess's sweet and joyful essence had touched him, and he had experienced the urge to take her in his arms and kiss her until she was breathless.

Battling that impulse, he had begun to question his resolve to stay untainted by earthly lust, but quickly realized that was the danger. He must stay to the path he had determined in the coolness of sober reflection and not be swayed by the heat of human weakness. Better to keep one's eyes firmly pointed upward, Wesmorlyn thought, gazing up at the supplicant angels. Uriel. Gabriel. Better to be working steadily, soberly toward redemption than enticed toward eternal damnation. He met Semyaza's steady gaze again. "I need to find out what Lyulph is up to. I will not have him lead that innocent girl astray."

"The innocent girl he was kissing in the garden?" Semyaza finally said, with a faint smile, moving to allow Wesmorlyn to pass through the wrought iron gates that were pulled aside always to expose the enormous oak Gothic doors.

Wesmorlyn thought about Charlotte's uptilted face in the Cornish sunshine that very day and said, more to himself than to Semyaza, "Temptation comes in many forms, and I must remember that, mustn't I? But also, being led astray can happen in different ways. She is innocent, Sam, in ways other than the corporeal, perhaps. I'll not have that ingenuousness abused by anyone." With that he entered, passing through the gates.

"HAVE some more of the carrots, Count von Wolfram," Eleanor Dancey said, passing the bowl to him with an encouraging smile. "They are from my own garden, and flavored uniquely, I think, with tarragon. It is a hobby of mine, to find unusual pairings of foods and herbs."

"Thank you, ma'am; they're delicious. Very unusual in their flavor."

Charlotte looked askance at the green-flecked carrots and took a bite of the trout instead. The dining room was dark and cramped and smelled, as the whole cottage did, of damp and mold, but the food made up for the inadequate surroundings. The woman was a very good cook, for she insisted on preparing everything, she said, with her own hands. Anne, Eleanor Dancey's maid-of-all-work, was useless for that kind of task. The gypsy men who had brought Fanny and Charlotte's bags had also brought with them fish caught in the stream nearby. They had Lyulph Randell's permission, Eleanor said, to fish and even to snare rabbits and other small animals, and they were kind enough to share them with her, often.

"Mr. Randell must be a very good man," Charlotte said, casting a glance at Christoph as she spoke, "to allow you the rent of this cottage at the nominal rate you said, and to allow the gypsies to not only camp, but also hunt and fish! What other landowner would do such a thing?"

"Without him I would be in a very poor state indeed, for there are those who would drive me to desperation, and all for some imagined slight." This was said with feverish intensity, but Eleanor did not look up from her plate when she said it. "And the gypsies," she added, looking up finally, her eyes moist with emotion, "are so misunderstood! People revile them without reason, even while they make use of their services, enjoy their music, and covet their women. It is shameful the way they are abused for nothing more than their heritage!"

"I feel the same," Charlotte said, eagerly. "No one should be disparaged for the simple accident of where or how they were born. In London, at that dreadful ball, the English girls were so spiteful and horrible, and all because I was German!" She had already spoken of how she had met Mr. Randell at the ball at Lady Harroway's, and his kindness to her.

Christoph sent her a warning look, perhaps because she was being too open, but she didn't care. She was determined to like Eleanor Dancey, despite something odd in the woman's manner. She couldn't put her finger on what it was about Fanny's mother that struck her as peculiar, but thought it was something about her eyes; there appeared to be more beneath their placid surface than she was revealing. But who could fault her for putting on something of a show and for being reticent with her real history? She didn't know them at all, and was feeling the strain of meeting her long-lost daughter for the first time. It was awkward, more so for her, who had so much to regret in her past. Nonetheless, Eleanor Dancey had been kind and welcoming to them, and that was more than Charlotte had felt from anyone in London.

Silence had fallen as everyone ate, so Charlotte continued. "I had never thought of it before, but just so cruelly as we were greeted in London, with sneers and spiteful words, that is how the gypsies must be treated everywhere they go. Reviled for their heritage."

"It is hardly fair to condemn all English girls," Fanny

demurred, "because of the behavior of a couple of representatives."

Eleanor rose and hastily sprinkled some herbs on Christoph's fish. "Please, Count, you do me honor; try this fennel as an enhancer of the mild taste of the fish. I very much fear you will find it bland after such excellent cooking as you must experience in your home."

Charlotte watched in amusement, and noted that Eleanor's concern over the taste of the food only seemed to extend to her brother. He, being a man, likely made her more nervous and she clearly felt the need for his approval. "How do you happen to know Mr. Randell?" she asked of the woman.

"I don't, exactly," Eleanor said, taking her seat again. "My plight was described to him by an acquaintance, and he, always vigilant to do a good deed from what I understand, gave me this cottage very reasonably for however long I needed it, while I decided my destination."

"Are you still determined to leave the country?" Fanny asked, fork poised in midair, a piece of fish on it.

Eleanor reached out and put one hand on Fanny's shoulder. "Your arrival has changed many things, you must know that. For the moment, consider me settled here, in Cornwall."

"And what was your plight? You have never exactly said," Christoph said, taking a bite of the fish and nodding at its improved flavor.

"Christoph!" Charlotte reprimanded. "You must not question our hostess after her kindness to us," she said, giving him a look. Now who was being forward? "It is not our concern."

"No, Countess, please," Eleanor said, color staining her cheeks as she looked down at her hands. She nervously worried the edge of the tablecloth, rubbing it between her fingers. "The count is only worried about my fitness to be a companion to my daughter, and I honor his protectiveness. It is just what I would have wanted for her in a brother." She picked up her knife and fork and continued cutting her food, though she had eaten very little.

Charlotte stared at her, thinking how beautiful she was, and how young she appeared for someone so close to forty. Her skin was smooth and unlined, her figure lithe and youthful, her dark hair glossy. How had a life of care and worry, as she was supposed to have lived, left her so young-looking?

After a pause, the woman laid her fork down beside her plate and said, "The truth is, I made an enemy in a very powerful family."

"How?" Charlotte cried, concerned at the trembling she witnessed in the woman's hands.

"I dared cross a man with great power and many connections," she whispered, fiddling with the tablecloth again, a plain white one with a small embroidered design of green leaves around the edge. "I will not say more. In fact, I cannot say more. I am sworn to silence on another's behalf. It is enough to say that there was a girl," she said, looking up, moisture welling in her eyes. "Perhaps I fancied I saw in her a little of the daughter I had given birth to and had been forced to give up. When she was in trouble, when a man of great power was harassing her, I stepped between them. I gave her sanctuary when she ran away.

"Now I stand accused of aiding this girl—she was the man's ward—to escape his tyranny. It is an offense under law, though I was not aware of that. No matter; it wouldn't have changed what I did. She is back in his care and I can do nothing, but at least I know she is now in London and safe, under the guidance and protection of a woman of excellent reputation and well-known kindness. I feel sure that is my doing, and I can rest satisfied, even though the cost to myself was great. If he knew I was here . . ." She trailed off and sighed.

"Who is the girl?" Fanny said, her blue eyes wide.

Eleanor shook her head. "I promised her never to say her name, and I will not break that promise. My safety rests in obscurity now."

"So that's why you considered emigrating!" Charlotte said. "To escape his influence." Eleanor did not answer.

The group gathered in the sitting room after dinner, but all were weary, for it had been a long day. Charlotte was grateful that night to have a bed, even though she had to share it with Fanny.

The next morning dawned misty again, but the mist burned off quickly, just as it had the day before, and Eleanor suggested they all go down to the gypsy camp for a walk. It was agreed upon, and after a lazy morning spent separately, Christoph writing letters and Charlotte and Fanny walking in the overgrown garden, they had lunch and then set out.

"Did you sleep well, Count von Wolfram?" Eleanor asked, leaning on Christoph's arm as they climbed the hill above Moor Cottage.

"I suppose," he said. "It seems I was restless, for I awoke to find myself by the window."

"You've never sleepwalked before," Charlotte said, glancing over at him in surprise. His pale face did appear haggard, with circles under his eyes. She hoped he was not still suffering the dreams that had plagued him after their awful experience in the spring.

It was one of the reasons she had agreed to come to England, though she would never tell him that; she had hoped the change of locale would rouse him from his looming depression. He needed distance from the setting of so many painful scenes. But right now he looked worried.

"I was just a few feet from my bed. Siegfried came in and found me resting on the window seat."

"Perhaps it is fortunate you have a small room," Eleanor said, gently.

They spent some time with the gypsy children when they arrived at the camp. Eleanor disappeared for a while with a large paper package she carried, saying she always made a habit of visiting the old matriarch of the band out of respect. Mother Sarah was a venerable and wise woman, able to see the future and so protect her people from harm, Eleanor had told them on their way to the encampment. That accorded with what Charlotte had already learned from Tamara. Though Mother Sarah was proud and independent, vegetables and herbs from Moor Cottage garden and eggs from the henhouse were a welcome addition to the tiny tribe's meals; that was what the paper parcel contained. The gypsy men brought Eleanor game and fish to pay her back in some small way. Fanny and Charlotte played with the gypsy children, while Eleanor, having finished her visit with the old gypsy, strolled about with Christoph and showed him the men's handicrafts and the women's intricate and colorful sewing. She explained, too, their cunning travel kits; they were often on the move and so were seasoned and experienced travelers, able to pack up and move in a single hour. Charlotte caught sight of Tamara once, but the young woman stayed in the shadows and did not approach, and then disappeared completely. Charlotte, torn about her role and what she should and shouldn't tell her brother and sister, was somewhat relieved when she saw no sign of Wesmorlyn, and so she did not need to decide if she was going to slip away to find him.

Finally, as the sun began to descend past its zenith, and the shadows of the grove of trees lengthened, they started back toward Moor Cottage. Charlotte had been watching Christoph all afternoon, and knew something was troubling him. It was as if a shadow hung over him, a dark cloud, and it cast her back to the awful old days that were really not so long ago, when he was suffering from the effects of herbal poisons that clouded his judgment, made him hallucinate, and caused him terrible grief.

She had thought it all waning, the awful effects of that time. She had hoped that new surroundings and a fresh start would help him forget. Perhaps it was not to be that simple.

The next day promised to be identical to the one before, and Charlotte was already growing bored and restless. So many things troubled her, and she had not slept well. Christoph was withdrawing again. Though she tried to talk about what was bothering him, he would not speak, merely shaking his head mutely. Eleanor continued to drop hints about the influential family she had offended, going so far as to say they were a Cornish family, very powerful, and holding the title of earl. When Charlotte blurted out the name Wesmorlyn, she had appeared frightened and did not deny it, but would not say anything more. It was irritating to hear only vague insinuations with no confirmation. Fanny, too, was behaving strangely, to Charlotte's mind. Although she professed contentment and gratitude that they had found her mother, she did not go out of her way to spend time with Eleanor, and in fact seemed just as happy to stay in her room and read or sew.

Incomprehensible! Didn't she want to get to know the woman? Why was she not spending every moment of the day with her, drawing her out, getting to know her, and planning for the future?

In a fit of pique, Charlotte donned her straw bonnet and set out after lunch; everyone else had decided to nap or read, but she chose to walk alone down to the gypsy camp, though she didn't tell anyone else that, not even Christoph. *Especially* not Christoph. He was becoming moody and solitary again, but with his protectiveness, he would insist on going with her. She wanted to be alone with her thoughts and free to wander if the occasion demanded it. The cottage, with its damp, dank atmosphere and oppressive darkness, was adding to her fretfulness. Perhaps she could pin Tamara down and find out why she had avoided them the day before.

The walk lifted her sprits and the gypsy camp was picturesque in the midday sunshine. Two women chatted in their incomprehensible language while they washed clothes in a half barrel, their sleeves rolled up past their elbows, and another tended to the fire, stirring a large pot hanging over it. A thin thread of smoke rose from beneath the pot and a tiny child clung to her indigo-dyed skirts. When the woman spotted her, she summoned another child, Tully, the intelligent girl Charlotte had made friends with. Tully listened to the woman, and then raced over to where Charlotte stood, observing the domestic scene.

"Hello, Tully," Charlotte said, feeling more of her edginess ease just from the welcoming smile of the child. "Do you have something to tell me?"

"Yes, miss," the girl said, taking her hand and leading her toward the camp. "Mother Sarah, she wishes to speak to you."

"Ah, I promised to cross her palm, and no doubt she wishes to make sure I follow through with my promise."

"I don't know miss, but we were told to watch for you and bring you to her."

The old woman sat by a small fire in the shadow of her caravan. Tully motioned for Charlotte to sit on an embroidered rug on the grass by her, and she did so.

"My people and yours do not have a happy history," the old woman began, examining Charlotte's face.

"True. But that is history. Between you and I," Charlotte said, steadily gazing into the her beady eyes, "there is no need for enmity."

The gypsy woman nodded. Her hair, still shot with black

among the gray, was confined in a brilliantly dyed scarf; her dark eyes never left their examination of Charlotte. "You are wise beyond your years, child."

Charlotte smiled. "Perhaps, though if my brother heard that he'd say you were being overly kind. Tell me, ma'am, where is Tamara today? I wish to speak with her."

"She has gone to town with Romolo and their father."

"Oh," Charlotte said, disappointed. She stirred restlessly, remembering something from the first night she had come to the camp. "Ma'am, Tamara told me when Fanny and I came that you had known we were coming and had sent her out to find us. Is that true?"

"Yes."

"And that first night you told me I had a quest to fulfill, but that I must not stay in England."

"Unless," she said, waggling her index finger, "you marry a dark man, remember, one with green eyes?"

"But I came to this country already engaged to a man, a man whose hair is not so dark, and whose eyes are brown."

"Ah, but there is another," the old woman said, leaning toward Charlotte. "Another who cares for you, whose lips you have touched, whose heart you have felt touching yours; is this not so?"

Charlotte's heart pounded, remembering the night of the ball and Lyulph Randell kissing her. Was that truly who the gypsy meant? It was just days before, but felt like years, for she couldn't even remember what possessed her to kiss a man she had just met, though in fairness, he had kissed her. She had not offered resistance, but neither had she cooperated with any enthusiasm.

"You do not answer, but it is true, I see it!" The woman closed her eyes and swayed. "I see a moonlit garden, and this handsome man, he kisses you because he feels so much for you, though he has only known you briefly."

"Then where is he? Why did he not follow as he said he would?" Charlotte cried, bewildered.

"He was . . ." The old woman paused, still swaying back and forth in a rhythmic, trancelike state. She hummed while she did so, atonally, but the sound came in waves. Then she stopped abruptly and her eyes flew open. "He was held back from coming by something that happened, something he could not control. Someone is against you. Someone wishes to keep the two of you apart." Mother Sarah leaned toward Charlotte again, and with one long finger laid near her eye, she murmured, "I see someone else, someone who will fill your head with lies, and if you believe him, he will lead you astray. Heed my warning!"

Out of the corner of her eye Charlotte caught some movement from beyond the gypsy camp, just past the grove of trees. A man . . . it was Wesmorlyn! He caught her eye and beckoned to her. This was why she came down to the camp, after all, she thought, acknowledging her own desire to talk to him again, to figure out what it was between them, and if he was the villain she was beginning to fear he was.

"Thank you, Mother Sarah," Charlotte said, rising quickly and getting some silver out of the small coin purse that was tied in to the skirts of her dress.

"Heed me well, girl," the woman said, her tone ominous. She took the silver coins and rattled them together in her bony hand. "Someone wishes to destroy you and your family. Someone tells lies. Be very, very careful who you trust."

Chapter 11

MOTHER SARAH'S words rang in her ears. Eleanor's fearful confidences whispered to her. *Wesmorlyn.* Was young and nervous Lady Hannah the girl that Eleanor had taken in? Was Wesmorlyn the man Eleanor had angered, so much so that she faced prosecution and had run away as a result? Was he the man Mother Sarah warned her against, the one who would tell her lies?

Looking both ways and confident that she was not observed, Charlotte slunk around the elderly gypsy's caravan and ran past the grove of trees to find the earl, who walked, his jacket slung over his shoulder in the midday heat, in the tall grass on the other side of the woods. She stopped and gazed at him.

"Charlotte!" he said, his face lighting up at the sight of her. "I was afraid I wouldn't find you. I came prepared with a note to take to Moor Cottage, to ask you to slip away and meet me."

She stared, silent. His brown hair glinted shiny and clean in the brilliant sunshine and his white shirt was open at the neck, exposing tanned, smooth skin. He must walk his own acres in just that manner, open-shirted and relaxed, for the skin of his throat to be so tanned. And what a tiny, nonsensical observation that was for her to make, she thought. Instead of staring at him, admiring the set of his shoulders and wave of his hair, she should be questioning him. Was he to be trusted? She felt no menace from him, and yet were her own instincts reliable in every case?

"Why the secrecy, sir?" she said, hating how stiff her voice sounded but still disturbed by the gypsy's comments and Eleanor's fear. "It is unconscionable that you would think of meeting me in such a way."

"We're engaged, Charlotte," he said, watching her uncertainly, ducking a little to see her eyes beneath the brim of her bonnet. "It lessens the sin, surely?" And she didn't object to it two days before, his steady gaze seemed to say. "Walk with me?" he asked.

She hesitated, but then nodded; they may as well walk while they talked, and she had many questions for him. First, though, she told him, as they walked away from the gypsy camp, about Christoph's arrival, and his installation at the cottage. She fell silent, as that brought her mind back to Eleanor's dark hints, and her own conclusion that it might be the earl of whom she spoke. But surely, she thought, calming her own fears, he was exactly what he seemed to be, a very moral, upright, and faintly priggish peer of the realm.

He spoke again as he took her arm and left the shadowed protection of the trees to walk in the sunlight up a hill away from the gypsy camp. "I received a disturbing letter from Hannah, my sister, who remains in London."

"Oh?" His nearness was unsettling, she found, his tanned, gloveless hand curled around her arm as he supported her in their walk.

"Yes. She is staying at our cousin's right now, Lady Harroway, with her companion, but through some other girls she knows she has heard disturbing rumors, and they concern you, Charlotte."

"Me?" she said, gazing up at him in surprise.

"I dislike being the bearer of bad tidings, but it is being bandied about town that you ran away from London with a man."

"With a man?" she cried, stopping and staring up at him. "How could such a vicious rumor make its way about?"

The earl shrugged. "I don't know. It was whispered to her that you had eloped with some man, and that I, furious at your deception, had stormed off to find you. She did her best to deny it, but fears that may simply be taken by the ill-natured as confirmation."

"Who would say a thing like that?"

"Can you think of anyone you may have upset or injured in your short stay in London?"

"No. Heavens, I was only there for the one evening, and I certainly hadn't time to make friends or acquaintances. Or enemies." Confusion clouded her mind. How could anyone even know of her departure, much less conjecture she left with a man? What man? In the back of her mind hummed the refrain from the old gypsy woman . . . lies . . . someone would tell her lies and try to cloud her mind. But Wesmorlyn would have no incentive to tell her such a thing if it were untrue. And really, she didn't care about rumors in London. They couldn't hurt her because she had no intention of staying in England, and would never even see that awful city again.

She glanced up at the earl. He saw them as still engaged. She had never broken it off officially, though she had expected that running away from London would end the engagement. Wesmorlyn was not the kind of man to marry a girl who would do such a thing. It was too confusing, for if she was right about that, then he would certainly not be the kind of man to follow her all the way to Cornwall, would he?

For the moment she gave up thinking about it. It was beyond her control anyway. London was long ago and far away, she thought, lulled by the heat of the day and the pleasantness of the moor into a more relaxed state of mind, and no decision about her future had to be made that very second. They strolled together up a long rise punctuated by clusters of gray, mossy stone. She breathed in deeply and could smell the sunshine freshness of Wesmorlyn's shirt, the honest, musky male scent of him filling her nostrils. The muscles of his forearm flexed beneath her fingers where they rested lightly, and a fascination with minutiae filled her: the clear note of a lark that soared above and the grassy smell that rose from under their feet where they trampled the grass as they wove around the rocky outcroppings that dotted the moor. They topped the rise and began down the sloping other side. The tender touch of the gentle wind lifted her curled locks under her bonnet and tickled her neck.

"I hesitate to ask this, Charlotte," he said, finally, as they began to descend the hill. Soon they would be completely concealed from view of the gypsy camp. "But I must. I can't stop thinking about it. Why did you kiss Lyulph Randell in the garden at the ball? I still don't understand."

There was something in his voice, some suffocated anger, still. It was disturbing to her enjoyment of the day. "I'd rather not speak of that," she said, sharply.

"Why not?" His hand gripped her arm. "Tell me honestly; did he force you?"

"No! I would have said so immediately if that was the case."

"But then why? Why did you kiss him? You had just met him, and were at the ball to become acquainted with me. What were you thinking?"

He was walking faster downhill, and she had to trot to keep up. "I don't know! The whole evening was confusing. I was tired, and you upset me. He was kind to me and then he kissed me. I didn't kiss him back, I just let it happen." Finally she pulled her arm away from his grasp, stopping. "I don't wish to walk anymore," she said, out of breath, bracing herself against the steep slope of the hillside. "You're walking too fast. Don't you ever just enjoy the day, instead of making it a footrace?"

He stared at her, the breeze ruffling the tumbled curls over his forehead. He swept back his hair, raking his fingers through it with an impatient gesture. "I'm just trying to understand."

"Don't. Don't try. Just let it be." She gazed at him, exasperated. Now that the peace of their stroll was destroyed, there were many things she wished to ask of him, but would it be betraying the confidence of Eleanor if she did? She had already told Wesmorlyn the woman's name and he had shown no sign of recognition, nor any hint that he was connected to or had any past dealings with her at all. What did that mean?

Should she just ask him? And how would she frame such a question . . . *Did your sister run away, and was she harbored by Eleanor Dancey, and did you threaten the woman with jail or worse?* She couldn't ask that, obviously. Instead, she said, "Your sister seemed so frightened and nervous at the ball. Is she always like that?"

He frowned at the change of subject, but answered, "No. The ball was a new experience for her, and she found it a little overwhelming. She has lived a sheltered life until recently. She didn't go away to school, but instead had a governess at the Abbey."

"Nor did I go away to school. I lived my whole life at Wolfram Castle until we left to come here."

"I didn't know that," he said, staring into her eyes, lost in the blue shadowed into azure flecked with cobalt by the deep brim of her bonnet. "You had never been away from home before. Then you traveled all that way, and only arrived the very day of the ball in London," he murmured. "Do you know, I have always thought myself a considerate fellow, but I had not even given that a moment's consideration until now. You arrived that very afternoon and moved into your new home, and then, out of good manners, you attended the ball, though you must have been bone weary." He shook his head. "I should have sent you a message. I should have told you that if you were exhausted, not to come. I didn't even think of it."

Her expression softened, one corner of her lovely mouth turning up with a trembling smile. "It would not have been so bad if on my way through the crowd I did not hear so many nasty things."

Her eyes clouded even as he looked into them. "Someone dared insult you?"

"I shouldn't be so sensitive!" she said, trying to keep the smile, her lips quivering. "I don't care what those girls think!"

Her valiant attempt to keep the tears at bay touched him, and yet deeply wounded feelings prompted them. "It's natural to feel hurt by an insult, especially," he said, "since you had a right to expect better. What was said to you?"

She pushed her hat off her head and let it drop by its ribbons to hang down her back. Sunlight sparkled on her coiled blond hair, and a few strands escaped her hairpins and danced in wisps around her delicate features. "In the normal course of things I am of a stalwart nature," she said, sighing deeply. "I suppose, as you say, it was just that I was tired. But I was already nervous, and then some girls said spiteful things about my hair, my clothes, and . . ." She stopped and shook her head, looking off into the distance.

"*And?* And what else?"

"About poor Fanny." She met his eyes, and anger sparked deep in the blue of hers. "They said she looked like a maid. Until recently she was, poor girl." She explained, then, about how Fanny was kept in the dark, as were they all, about Johannes von Wolfram being her father. "Since her paternity was discovered I fear it has been a terrible journey for her to make from maidservant to daughter of a count. So when I heard that despicable *voice* saying she looked like a maid, I was overcome with fury on her behalf. I only hope she did not hear them or did not understand."

After that experience and his own haughty behavior, Wesmorlyn reflected, Lyulph Randell's kindness coupled with his natural charm must have seemed a pleasant change. *Then I refused to dance with her.* He glared off into the distance at a bank of clouds gathering on the horizon above the dark line of the tors. Looking back, his lack of sensitivity toward a woman he was supposed to take care of astounded him. He had only been thinking of himself that evening, clearly, worried about appearances, concerned about how things looked to others. "You must have thought me an utter boor, along with the rest of the English." He stepped toward her, and with the tip of one finger he touched her trail of tears. How far she had come, to England from her home, all she had ever known. She was not well-traveled, had never even stepped foot away from Wolfram Castle. If Hannah was sent as bride to some unknown man in a foreign country, how would he want her treated? Surely the very least she could expect would be kindness and understanding, with allowances made for differences in behavior and culture.

"Come," he said, gently, "walk with me, and this time I promise I won't make it a footrace."

They strolled for a time in silence along the slope of the hillside, but he glanced over at her occasionally. Charlotte was not what he would have chosen as a wife; she was far too pretty and vivacious, dangerous qualities in a wife from his own observation of marriages among his circle of friends, for those very traits made her the prey of a certain kind of man who was only interested in young, pretty, bored wives. And yet her appeal lay not just in her loveliness, though that was impossible to ignore. Her heart was tender and open; she was guileless, courageous, energetic, and vivacious.

He stopped and turned toward her. "You know, if those girls at the ball were available in late summer, then it means they did not 'take' in the spring and did not, to be blunt, find a husband." He stared at her; she was watchful, her wide blue eyes alert, searching his, bow lips inviting. "Then you arrived," he whispered, "so lovely, glowing, a golden girl. The remarks you overheard were the screeching of jealous cats." Without thinking he leaned toward her, tipping her head back with his finger under her chin, and kissed her cheek, tasting the salt of her drying tears warm on his lips.

She closed her eyes and sighed; he dropped his jacket on the ground and took her in his arms, lost in a new sensation. Feeling the softness of her lips pouted against his mouth and urged on by his racing pulse, he kissed her chin, the tiny dimple in the center tempting him beyond endurance. She put her arms around his shoulders and kneaded his neck as she leaned into the kiss, and then her hands went down his back and he moved away, panting slightly from the unexpected and unwelcome throb of arousal that pulsed through him, a faint dizziness accompanying it and a pain like a lightning bolt through his backbone.

Her eyes fluttered open and she gazed at him steadily, the dampness of tear trails still evident on her cheeks, and her lips plump from his kissing. Her golden, silky hair was adrift around her face, and she was utterly, adorably unself-conscious. He swallowed, his mouth suddenly dry, the taste of her skin still lingering like brandy on his lips.

"You know," he said, forcing his thoughts away from her lithe body and sweet lips. "I sent a note to my solicitor in London, and he says there are other Danceys . . . one or two even in London."

"I don't suppose it is an extremely unusual name," Charlotte said, watching him, puzzlement clouding her blue eyes.

"And there are some variations in spelling, too. Often it is spelled without the *e*."

"What exactly are you trying to say, my lord? We have already established that this woman is the real Eleanor Dancey. Why would anyone admit to an illegitimate child that was not theirs? What would be the motive for such a ruse?"

He took a deep breath. "I just find it hard to believe in such a coincidence as would bring you to the ball and have you mention the woman's name to Randell, who just happened to rent this same woman his cottage!"

"You begin to sound like Christoph," she said in an exasperated tone. With a swift, agitated movement she put her bonnet back on, her face shadowed by it, the sunlight slanting across and touching only her dimpled chin. She tied the ribbon. "What would be the motive for pretending to be Eleanor Dancey? How would she even know the name? Fanny has no money to tempt tricksters. By German law she has no title, nor is she recognized as a part of our family, the poor girl. My uncle has talked about settling a small competence upon her, but nothing has been finalized and nothing is certain; Miss Dancey is all she has in this world, beyond Christoph and I." Her blue eyes glinted like sapphires as she lifted her chin and the sunlight caught in their expressive depths. "I find it incredible that you spend your time trying to find a way to discredit the woman. What for, sir? What does it gain you?"

He didn't like the note of suspicion in her voice, nor the gleam of distrust in her eyes, and was distracted. "What are you asking?"

"Do you have a personal reason for not liking Eleanor Dancey?"

"What? Whatever do you mean?"

She was silent, simply staring at him.

"I don't know the woman, nor had I ever heard the name before you first said it." He was stunned by the suspicion in her eyes. "I will turn the question, Countess; what reason do you have for doubting me or asking such a question as that?" She was still silent. He examined her shadowed face, trying to read her expression but finding her closed to him. Never in his whole life had his motives been questioned, and he found it unnerving in the extreme.

"I think we both know, my lord, that I am not in any sense what you thought you were affiancing when you agreed by mail to a marriage," she said.

The change of subject threw him off balance. "Don't go on in that thread, Countess, I beg of you." He could see in her eyes a determination to end their engagement, but as unsuitable as she was, as maddening, as independent and forward, and as inappropriately lovely, he was not willing to let her go just yet. The single moment touching her lips with his had left an odd rend in the fabric of his self-assurance. More time with her would either rip the fabric in twain, or mend the tear.

"I think it is simply right to say what must be on your mind," she said, with a haughty tone. "I am not suitable to be your countess. Admit it, at least, Lord Wesmorlyn."

Her manner was coldly formal, at odds with her wind-tossed and adorably sun-kissed appearance. He stood watching her, aware that his hands opened and closed into fists. Why was he so unsure of himself in her presence? He was a leader of men, an employer of hundreds, master of a grand estate, well-known even to the Prince of Wales and his parents, the King and Queen, who approved of him as a confidant, thinking him a steadying influence on their capricious and melodramatic eldest son. And yet this young lady had him unsure of every morally upright, proper, and decorous instinct he had ever had.

He felt as if she had judged him and found him wanting, inadequate to please a lively, intelligent, and vivacious young lady. He was stuffy, her critical gaze seemed to say: stuffy, old before his time, prim, proper, and more priggish than any Mayfair dowager. She could not be sensible and hold such a view—he was the most eligible man in England at that moment, and no one had ever been criticized for being too moral and too upright—and yet he found himself wooed and tempted by hints of her untamed nature to stop fighting the reckless attraction he felt toward her.

"Are you suitable to be my countess?" he asked, sighing and frowning down at his boots. "I just don't know. I begin to think there is much I don't know."

Her stern expression relaxed. "That is the first truly sensible thing I have heard you say, and the most honest."

Relief flooded him. "Then please," he pleaded, "don't break our engagement until you're sure, and I'm sure."

She hesitated, but then nodded. "All right."

He didn't want to say what he had to say next, but he was going to be honest and damn the consequences. "I am still suspicious of this Miss Eleanor Dancey," he said. "No, hear me out!" he swiftly added, seeing the impatient expression of vexation that crossed her pretty, sunlit face. "Hear me out, please, Charlotte. I have asked around, and the villagers of Bodmin say that there was a woman living at Moor Cottage last year, one whose description matches your description of Miss Dancey. But her name was Morwenna Maxwell, and no one was quite sure what relationship she was to Lyulph." He was pleased to see, finally, a look of doubt on her face.

"Is that true? Morwenna Maxwell," she repeated, frowning into the distance. "But a simple description could encompass many ladies."

"True. I'm looking into it. I still cannot imagine why Lyulph would send you down here, say he was going to follow, but then not."

"He may have been detained by circumstances beyond his control."

Wesmorlyn nodded. "True again. I will hope for the best. Lyulph is not a bad sort, though I cannot forgive him for kissing you." He smiled at her. "Though I understand his motivation in doing so; how could he resist?"

She blushed and turned away. "I must get back to the cottage. I've been gone far too long, and I didn't tell anyone where I was going."

He yearned for one kind word, one gentle brush of her lips, but it was unconscionable to think so, nor could he frame such a request in any honorable way. He had already taken advantage of her enough for one afternoon. "Meet me again? Perhaps tomorrow?"

"Maybe," she said. "I'll think about it." And she ran off, looking back just once before disappearing over the hill.

Wesmorlyn watched her, then glumly turned and headed on, away from the gypsy camp. Still too close, he walked on until a couple more hills and valleys were between him and prying eyes. Then he strode out to a big open space where the wind blew briskly, and gazed up at the sun; it was already descending, so it hung about a third of the way down in the western sky toward the horizon. He took off his coat and shirt, rolling them into a bundle that made it easier to carry. It was time to go back to Wesmorlyn Abbey.

He shrugged, and the bony, flexible bundles that nestled between his scapula extended and arched, moving away from his body in a smooth, practiced motion, as the thin gauzy membrane that stretched between the jointed cartilage became taut, as tensely drawn as a drum skin. He folded his bare arms over his broad chest, holding his bundled clothes closely; taking two running steps on tiptoe he soared, magnificent wings beating and thrusting through the air providing unfathomable lift, enough to raise him straight into the heavens.

This was the moment, the infinitesimal instant in time when he understood the thrill of living. Family lore told him that only when they fell to earth did his ancestors understand the euphoria of flight, and the exceptional privilege they had been afforded but come perilously close to surrendering for eternity. Only through a degrading plea for mercy had they won the right to struggle to ascend back into the good graces of the maker. Wesmorlyn was ever watchful and ever vigilant of any taint that would destroy his descendants' chance at redemption.

But in that moment the thrill of flight superseded every other thought and he ascended to the clouds, dipping and swirling, heart pounding. The air was thinner with every furlong he rose, and a familiar, hazy bliss invaded his mind. Finally, though, he arrived at his destination; he approached the bottom of the hill that led up to the Abbey and began his cautious descent, unwitnessed by aught but the beasts in the field. An unwelcome thought occurred to him as his toes touched the earth. Was that heart-pounding euphoria he experienced while flying the same as the bliss that Lyulph and his ancestors felt every time they transformed into wolves and raced through the forests of Cornwall? And if they were akin to each other, how far was he really removed from the bestial Randells?

Chapter 12

SWEET, WARM blood dripped down from his teeth as they tore into flesh, and he savored the rich essence. His fur was bloody and gory, but a good roll in the grass and a long drink from the brook that sparkled in the moonlight nearby would take care of that. Then he would be fit to go home. Home. Where was home? How could he get there? Doubt clouded his mind as he looked down at the creature beneath him, his feast in the moonlight; the skin pale, naked, and furless, gleaming in the silvery light along the ragged edge torn by his teeth.

"Christoph! Christoph!"

Pain hit him in the gut suddenly, and he collapsed and howled, writhing in the agony of involuntary transformation brought about by the repetition of his human name. It shot through his body like a jolt of lightning.

"Christoph!"

Hands on him, shaking him, pulling at his fur; he fought, his paws becoming fists.

"Christoph! It's me, Charlotte; stop hitting out! You're having a nightmare!"

Christoph, panting with fear, awoke to find Charlotte, bonneted and smelling of open fields, staring down at him. The bedclothes were coiled around his limbs and daylight streamed through the window of his tiny bedchamber as a warm breeze fluttered the curtains.

"Christoph, are you all right? I suppose you were just napping and you must have been having a nightmare. Where is Siegfried? I can't believe he didn't hear you." Charlotte looked toward the door in concern as she sat down on the edge of his bed. "Christoph," she repeated urgently, her steady gaze settling back on him, "you were making such a noise! Growling and grunting at first, and then howling."

He rolled up to a sitting position on the edge of the bed next to her and scrubbed his eyes with his fingers, then covered his face. The lurid nightmare lingered as he realized the flesh he had been consuming in his dream was human. He retched and doubled over.

"Tell me what's wrong, Christoph!" Charlotte said, rubbing his back and staring at him as she wrenched her bonnet off with her free hand, letting it trail down her back by its ribbons. "*Tell me.*"

He shook off her hand. "It's all right. *I'm* all right. Forget it." He took a deep breath, stood, and walked to the window, gazing down at the sunny back enclosure, circled completely by a stone wall. Eleanor Dancey was out in her garden picking herbs; it was a tranquil domestic scene. Fanny sat on the stone wall staring off into the distance, swinging her feet. As he watched, Eleanor stopped, turned, and looked up directly into his eyes, as if she was aware that he was watching. Hellebore, her cat, stopped too, sat down on its haunches, and stared up at him. It was unsettling, the intensity of the human and feline stares, so similar. He stepped back from the window into the dimness and scrubbed his eyes with his fingers, feeling the grittiness of sleep still in them. "Siegfried went in to Bodmin to purchase some new neckcloths for me. He is concerned that I am becoming less than perfectly attired, for we left London with a minimal wardrobe."

"Christoph—"

"No, Charlotte, please don't fret about me," he said, gazing over at his sister. Her lovely eyes were clouded with worry. "I'll be all right. Where have you been?" He gazed at her windblown hair and sun-brightened cheeks. "Fanny was asking awhile ago, but I had nothing to tell her."

She blushed and shook her head. "I walked down to the gypsy encampment."

"Alone? Charlotte!" He shook his head and sighed, strolling over to her and taking her hands in his. He squeezed them and released. "Promise me this instant that you will never do that again. It could be dangerous."

She stood and walked toward the door. "I'm not a little doll to be kept on a shelf out of harm's way. Once you shared at least *some* of your worries with me, but you haven't in quite a while. Perhaps it has not yet come to your attention, but I'm a grown woman now, and can take care of myself quite adequately. When you feel like confiding in me once again, I may see fit to share with you, but until then, I will do what I wish." She stalked out of the room and slammed the door behind her.

Confide in her? How could he tell her that he feared very much the encroachment of the dark temptation into his mind and heart? Hunger pulled at him, swayed him, and now entered his dreams. How could he confide how much he dreaded becoming everything that legend said was darkest and most appalling about his kind, about werewolves?

A shivering weakness entered his limbs; he collapsed on his bed and buried his face in his hands. He couldn't even face himself in the mirror anymore without seeing the sharp-fanged monster that was eating his soul alive.

CHARLOTTE stalked away from her brother's room to the bedchamber she shared with Fanny, tossing her bonnet aside on the bed and pacing the small rug in front of the hearth. She had gone to Christoph to tell him about Wesmorlyn's presence in Cornwall, feeling guilty about keeping things from her brother, but he was clearly suffering again, and yet was not willing to talk to her. Couldn't he see that the way to defeat his anxiety was to share it with a sympathetic person, and who was more sympathetic than she? She was not going to add to his burden, as angry as she was that moment, and so she would handle her problems herself.

At dinner she tried to wheedle information out of Eleanor Dancey about her life up until Lyulph Randell had offered her the house to rent, but the woman was reticent, and Charlotte was hampered by her own proper upbringing. One did not force another person to confide their life story; it was rude to push too hard. She did confirm that Eleanor Dancey had never stayed at Moor Cottage before, so that much she could report to Wesmorlyn when she next saw him.

Fanny, too, was frustrating Charlotte; she seemed singularly incurious as to her mother's history and why she did not share her life story with her only child! The questions Charlotte tried to ask would be so much more natural coming from Fanny, but the girl would not cooperate with any normal curiosity.

The evening passed in dull hours of desultory chat, and then an early bed.

Dawn was just graying the eastern horizon when frantic pounding on the front door of the cottage and a high-pitched voice calling out for help roused them. Charlotte, awoken from a restless sleep, was the first downstairs, doing up her robe with one hand as she flew to the door and flung it open.

Tully, the young gypsy girl, was standing on the step, tears streaming down her face and blood on her knuckles from how hard she had pounded on the door.

"Tully! Tully, what is it?" Charlotte said, pulling the girl in from the misty morning air.

Fanny had followed Charlotte down and crouched by the girl, pushing her tousled hair back from her face and trying to soothe her. Anne, the maid, had come from the kitchen where her pallet was; she stared at the scene, wringing her hands together and babbling incoherent questions.

"Go put on the kettle for tea," Charlotte said to the maid to get rid of her. "Now, Tully, what is it?" she asked, turning back to the child. "Calm yourself. Is someone in trouble? Hurt?"

The girl nodded.

"Who?"

"Tamara," she said, her voice reedy with fear. "She's hurt badly, miss, and the men didn't know what to do, so Mother Sarah said to bring her up here, but Tamara refused; she didn't want to be a bother, miss, but finally Mother Sarah got her way, and—"

"What is going on?" Christoph said, bounding down the stairs into the front hall and belting his robe.

Beyond the front door a clattering noise became louder. Charlotte rose and again flung open the door. Romolo, his face red with strain and sweat pouring off his forehead, dark curls clinging damply to his neck, emerged from the mist hauling a handcart down the path toward the cottage door. Tears streamed down his cheeks, and his white shirt was stained with dark streaks. In that handcart was a bundle of clothes or . . . no; Charlotte realized from the whimpering moans that there was a person in the handcart.

"Tamara!" Charlotte cried and raced out the door.

"Her papa collapsed at the camp, miss, and couldn't come," Tully called after her. "He was clutching his chest."

Charlotte barely heard as she reached the side of the cart and looked down at Tamara, who was curled on her side, a blanket around her. She *looked* perfectly fine, though her cheek was paler than usual, and the mist had bedewed it, clinging to the fine downy hairs along her jaw line. "What's wrong?" Charlotte asked, her voice unnaturally loud in the foggy morning quietude. She slipped her arm under Tamara to help the sobbing girl sit up while Romolo, lapsing back into Romani in his agitation, tried to explain with an incomprehensible string of words.

Something warm and sticky coated Charlotte's arm as she helped Tamara sit up, and she examined the other side of the girl's face and neck. Even in the dull light of predawn she could see open wounds, raw flesh and blood that clotted in dark coagulated patches.

"Christoph," Charlotte cried, seeing the blood and feeling it on her arm. "Help me! Carry Tamara into the cottage!" When she got no answer, she looked back. Christoph was standing near the open door, frozen, staring at Tamara with terror on his pale face. He was shaking all over and making unintelligible noises. "Christoph, help me!"

Romolo, finally calming himself, came to her aid and lifted his injured sister, carrying her over the threshold of the cottage just as Eleanor came down the stairs. Charlotte guided him into the parlor and took off her own robe to lay under Tamara on the settee by the hearth.

"What's going on?" Eleanor asked.

"I don't know," Charlotte said. "All I know is Tamara has been hurt."

"Good heavens! Let me look." Eleanor knelt by Tamara and examined the wound, calling out orders; when Anne came back in the room she was told to get clean cloths with warm water and some strips of fabric.

Tamara was being looked after by the surprisingly competent Eleanor, with an anxious Romolo standing over her, so Charlotte pulled Tully aside. "How did this happen?"

"I don't know, miss. It was a while before dawn, and I still slept. All I know is there was some screaming, and then Romolo went out of the camp and found Tamara. She was hurt by someone or something. Perhaps an animal in the woods."

"*Away* from the camp? Why would she be away from the camp at that time in the morning, before dawn? Had she been gone long? Did he find her soon after the accident, or had she been lying out there alone for a while?"

Tully shrugged. "I don't know, miss."

Charlotte watched the scene for a moment. Where was Christoph? She glanced around and saw him by the door to the parlor, watching the scene, a look of horror on his sensitive face. She stood and put one reassuring hand on the child's shoulder. "Tamara is in good hands; you can see that," she said to the child. "Run back to the encampment like a good girl and tell them—especially her father—that she will be staying here at least today, and that she is being well cared for." Charlotte glanced back to the settee. Eleanor had the wounds cleaned, and it appeared that they were not as terrible as they had at first appeared with the blood smeared all around.

"All right, miss."

"Get a cup of tea and something to eat, first, though. You're shivering!" Charlotte pushed Tully toward Fanny, who was already guiding Romolo, in her kindly little housewife manner, to the kitchen. Tamara's brother still had tears running down his olive-complected cheek, but Fanny would no doubt make sure he was fed and had something hot to drink to calm him and steady his nerves. He was certainly doing no good hanging over Eleanor and Tamara. They walked past Christoph, who still lingered in the doorway.

Taking in a deep breath, Charlotte approached her brother. "Christoph, what's wrong?" she said, her voice trembling. "You look awful."

He shook his head and turned away, heading back to the stairs in the hallway and bounding up them two at a time.

"Christoph!"

He didn't respond, nor did he pause.

Charlotte turned back to the parlor and knelt by the settee. "How is she?" she asked of Eleanor.

"She'll be all right, I think," the woman said with a worried frown.

"You *think*?" Charlotte gazed down at Tamara's pale face; the white cloth binding her neck wound contrasted only faintly with her normally olive complexion, paler from shock and loss of blood. "Tamara," she murmured, "Tamara, can you tell us what happened?"

"Mmm," she moaned. "Someone called my name."

"Yes, Tamara, it is me, Charlotte."

"No, someone from the woods called my name. I crept from my bed to see who it was."

"I think she means that is why she was in the woods, where they found her," Eleanor whispered, glancing at Charlotte, and then putting her hand to the gypsy girl's forehead. "She is cool, which is good. No fever has yet resulted."

"Tamara, what happened when you went to the woods?"

"Ahh! No, someone . . . something . . . and I cried out . . . hurt . . . I ran, but it caught me and . . ."

She began to thrash around, and Eleanor said, "No more questions now! She needs rest."

Romolo came in, bowed and said, "Miss, is my sister going to be all right?"

Eleanor looked up at him and said, "Yes, she will recover, but I fear she must stay here, quiet."

"We do not want to bother you, please, lady," he said, wringing his hands.

"Do you know what happened, Romolo?" Charlotte asked.

He crossed the shadowy room and gazed down at his sister, but shook his head. "I do not know. It was dark, still night. I heard screaming and got up from where I lay by the fire. The others awoke, too, and we wondered what to do—we did not know then that it was Tamara, you see—but Mother Sarah said we must go and search, so I did. It was dark, and I found nothing for a while, but then someone brought a torch and we found her. I carried her back to the camp, and we did not know what to do, so Mother Sarah said her wounds needed better care than she could give, and said to bring her here." Tears rolled down his face.

"You did the right thing, young man," Eleanor said.

Fanny entered and crossed the room, putting her slim arm over his shoulders. "Tell them what you told me, Romolo," she said, her voice trembling.

He shrugged. "It is nothing."

"No, it's important. Tell them."

"What is it, Romolo?" Charlotte asked.

When he didn't speak, Fanny gazed down at Charlotte and said, "It was an animal, something big. It ran past him in the woods snapping and snarling, but he could not catch it, nor could the other men. He said"—she stopped, took in a deep breath, and then continued—"he says it looked like a wolf."

Chapter 13

"THERE ARE no wolves in England," Eleanor said, gently. "There have not been for centuries. And Tamara just said that she heard her name being called from the woods. It must have been a man."

Charlotte stayed silent, and would not meet Fanny's steady gaze. She got up and bolted upstairs, going to Christoph's room. If he had not acted so oddly about Tamara . . . she hated herself for doubting him in any way, but she had to know. She pounded on the door. "Christoph!"

"Go away."

Siegfried came to the door and opened it, staring at Charlotte with worry in his blue eyes. In German he said, "The count says he does not wish to see anyone, Countess, not even you. Especially not you."

She pushed past him and stormed over to Christoph, who was sitting in a shabby upholstered chair staring at the empty hearth of the tiny fireplace in his room. "What's going on, Christoph? Why haven't you come down to check on Tamara? Why didn't you stay?"

Siegfried had melted away to the tiny dressing room off

the bedchamber. Christoph didn't answer for a long minute, but then he looked up at Charlotte and held up a scrap of cloth.

Charlotte snatched it out of his hand and looked at it. It was a bloody torn scrap of fabric. She had recently seen a pattern exactly like it, but the brilliant blue and green of it was tainted by dirt and a dark, sticky substance. She held it up to her nose and inhaled, the sharp metallic tang familiar and yet repulsive. Blood, fairly fresh and still damp. "Where have I seen this before?"

He hung his head, silent.

And then Charlotte remembered. She had last seen the pattern on the scarf that held back Tamara's dark hair. "Where did this come from?" she said, dreading the answer.

This time when he looked up at her, there was tragic fear in Christoph's brilliant blue eyes. His voice low and trembling with emotion, he said, "When I awoke to the noise, I was disoriented. I threw on my robe and came downstairs. That was when I realized that the bottom of my robe was damp, as if I had been outside in the dewy grass."

"That doesn't mean anything," Charlotte said, terribly afraid it did, in light of Romolo and Fanny's revelation.

"Yes, it does, don't you see?" he said, bolting from his chair and grabbing back the hank of fabric. "This is from Tamara's kerchief," he said, shaking it in her face. "It was in the pocket of my robe. My robe is wet. I fear if you look out of my window, you'll see them, the footprints." He stared down at the floor. "God help me, there are footprints in the dirt beneath my window at the foot of a trellis. When I awoke, the window was open, but it wasn't when I went to sleep last night."

"That doesn't mean anything," she repeated.

"Yes, it does. Or it might." He passed one hand over his eyes. "I've been having bad dreams, nightmares, and a couple of times when I have awoken, I've been out of my bed near the window. I don't know why." When he met her steady gaze again it was with decision. "Charlotte," he said, reaching out for her hand. "You are the only soul in this world I trust completely. I need you to keep something for me."

"Keep something?"

He strode across the room to his bed and reached under the feather mattress, pulling out a cloth bundle. He unwrapped it and held out to her the contents, a scrap of fur. "Do you know what this is?"

"No."

"It is the wolfskin kirtle of our ancestors. Uncle said eventually I will not need it, but, as far as I know, I still need it to make the transformation from man to beast. If you wish to help me, you will hide it from me and never, *ever* let me have it again."

"You mean until this is over."

"No. *Never*! Please, I cannot bear myself right now."

"Oh, Christoph," Charlotte said, a sob rising within her. "No. I won't believe it, and you mustn't either. You can't truly think that you—"

"No!" he said, putting one finger over her mouth. "Don't say it. I'm afraid for it to be said aloud. I cannot believe I have done anything so heinous as what we fear, but Charlotte, I have had such dreams of late. What if I . . ." He looked around and leaned forward, lowering his voice. "Uta warned me that I would need to beware of the dark pull of evil. But what if it's bewitching me when I don't even know? Help me, I beg of you."

"Of course," she said, taking the scrap of fur. "Did you have this with you in the night?"

"I don't know. It wasn't in my robe, or on my person, but perhaps I hid it in my sleeping state, perhaps . . ." He trailed off on a sob, but regained control of himself. "I just don't know!" he said, grasping his hair and clenching his fists. "If the evil is taking me over, perhaps I'm unaware of what I do. I just don't *know*!"

"On my *life* I will guard this." She scrubbed it between her fingers and a few dark hairs fell loose. Curiosity overwhelmed the horror. "How does it work?"

He took a deep shuddering breath, helped by her calmness, perhaps, to regain his wits. "I don't exactly know. It is a connection to the ancients, to the first von Wolfram who transformed. Aunt Uta told me before she died that the first to use it killed the wolf whose fur it was, and the spirit of the wolf inhabited him."

"No, I mean, how does it work for *you*? What do you do?"

He shook his head and went back to the chair, slumping wearily and kicking at the rag rug by the hearth. "I don't know how to explain it. I hold it and I run. I feel the wildness well up in me, the pain hits, and I collapse, and then become the beast. Now I don't feel the pain so much as I did at first. The transformation is smooth while I run." He put his head in his hands. "And glorious!" he said, choked by a sob. "The wolf in me must be taking over. Listen; take it away, Charlotte, take the kirtle away and destroy it! It is a curse on us all."

She crossed to him and knelt by his side, pulling his hand away from his face and cradling his cheek in her free hand. "No, you listen to *me*, Christoph; you are a good man. I will not believe that what you fear is true. You are a good, kind man, and there is some other explanation for this tragedy. It's something else, I promise you." She stood, not telling him all that she had heard from Fanny and Romolo, for to do so would only make matters worse. She would discover herself what was behind this attack. For too long she had allowed the others in her family to rescue her, but now she was a grown woman and would take care of her brother.

She put one hand on his shoulder. "Why don't you lie down and try to sleep?"

"I'm afraid to sleep!"

"But I have the wolfskin kirtle now, and you can do nothing without it, you said so yourself. I'll tell Siegfried to bring you something to drink, and to stay with you, as you're not feeling well."

He nodded, still staring at the empty hearth.

She did what she said, and saw that Christoph's faithful servant was ensconced in a chair by the empty hearth, then went to her room and changed into a dress. She fastened the hank of wolfskin to her chemise, not feeling comfortable with hiding it in her belongings where it could easily be discovered. Then she descended, to find that with Romolo's help, Tamara had been moved to the tiny room off the parlor that Eleanor used as an office for doing her accounts and writing letters, and laid upon a chaise. She appeared to be sleeping in comfort.

When Charlotte returned to the hallway, Romolo was

preparing to leave, though he was lingering at the door with Fanny. Tumultuous thoughts tumbled through her mind. What was the animal Romolo had seen? What attacked Tamara? Nagging worry pulled at her, but she steadfastly refused to believe that Christoph could ever harm a woman. She had seen him in his wolf form kill another werewolf, but an awesome and dangerous one that had become so by a dark and terrible spell. That attack was to protect the woman he loved and other women for whom he felt responsible, herself among them. How could he even doubt himself?

"Romolo," she said, suddenly, "I'll return with you to the encampment. Fanny, will you go with me?"

She pulled her robe tightly about her. "I'm not properly dressed, Charlotte! And I would rather stay here," Fanny said. She gazed at Charlotte with concern. "But do you think it wise to go? Perhaps I *should* go with you. If you would but give me a few minutes to change."

"No," Charlotte said, making a sudden decision. "I will be perfectly safe; you don't need to go. And perhaps you can help better here with your mother. There's nothing to worry about. I wish to see the scene where this awful attack occurred, but it's daylight now, and everything will be fine."

PACING brought no relief and sleep wouldn't come, so Christoph sent Siegfried away. The fellow's sad expression was too much to bear. Even with the wolfskin out of his possession, Christoph was afraid of sleep now, afraid that the dreams were true and expressed his deepest desires. Was darkness taking him over? He had thought from Uta's description, that evil was in the choices he would be forced to make, and that it would take him over in small increments if it was to happen. But to transform from someone—and something—who was the defender of his family into an attacker of innocent women, and all within a few days . . . how could that happen?

He threw on some clothes and descended, telling Siegfried he was merely going to walk in the garden, though he didn't really know his destination. But in the downstairs hall he paused, caught by a whiff of some sweetness in the air, an intangible and yet alluring scent that drifted to him, pulling him, tangling him in magical relief.

He followed, through the parlor, to a door, and then through the door to a dim, tiny chamber and a dark corner. *Tamara!* He stopped and stared, caught by a desire so swift and intense his knees buckled, and his limbs trembled. Woodenly, he approached the sofa where she lay and sank to his knees beside her.

"I'm sorry," he whispered. "I'm so sorry." He took her small hand in his and caressed the palm, watching her eyes, the lashes fluttering and the orbs under the lids moving. She was dreaming, her lips pursed and relaxed, and she shifted, her lush figure under the light cover unbearably alluring.

She looked fragile and tiny on the sofa, the paleness of the bandages on her slender throat shining white in the dim light from the door into the parlor. Dusky curls, unrestrained by her missing kerchief, spilled in riotous abandon over the pillow. Her fingers flexed and curled around his hand, and tendrils of protectiveness wound through him as he gazed at her. It was a relief to feel that warm connection, and he sat down on the floor by the chaise, a great weariness overtaking him. Resting his head on the edge of the sofa, his eyes became heavy and the dark, blissfully sweet forgetfulness of sleep overtook him.

THE dawn air was thick with foggy dampness, the sun just beginning to rise and burn off the haze. Progress was slow because Romolo was pulling the handcart, but finally they came to the rise overlooking the gypsy encampment. Charlotte gazed down at it, colorful caravans barely visible in the swirling haze that moved like probing fingers through the encampment. She watched for a long minute; figures moved about, but as the mist slowly shifted she could make out the women, going about their chores accompanied by their children, and puffs of smoke from the fire over which a pot hung, stirred by one of the older women. Charlotte looked beyond the camp, to the nearby grove of trees.

"You heard screaming, you say, those of you in the camp?" she asked Romolo, as they descended and approached the fire.

"Yes. Very loud, terrible. My poor sister!"

"Tamara said that she heard her name being called and went to investigate, and then was attacked. It's odd. Almost like it was set up."

Tully ran over to them and grabbed Charlotte's hand. "Will Tamara come back to us?" Some of the other gypsy women clung together and hung back, their dark eyes distrustful, but Romolo and Tamara's father approached, his cap in his hand, his dark eyes filled with worry and his moustache drooping.

"Tamara is in good hands," Charlotte said, loudly, so the words would carry. "She is sleeping peacefully at Moor Cottage. You all know Eleanor Dancey. She is a good woman who knows medicine, and she's taking care of Tamara."

Romolo's father looked doubtful and shook his head. "There is some magic here," he said to Charlotte. "Some *evil* magic. The devils caught my daughter. They lured her into the woods and attacked. Why, I ask? They never did so until you came to us."

Charlotte swallowed hard. "There is no evil and no magic. She was attacked by a wild animal, or perhaps a dog." She turned to Romolo. "Take me into the woods to where you found her."

The happy, sunny atmosphere of the camp had changed. The gypsies watched her with suspicion now, but Romolo guided her past the caravans and tents to a pathway through the grove of trees. "We come this way to gather wood for the fires."

Charlotte pulled her skirts close to her legs and followed him. The sun had not pierced the depths of the woods yet, and fog lingered along the path, clinging to the underbrush. The rustling sound of their progress was the only noise she could hear. No birdsong, no noise of small animals, not even the sound of a leaf turning broke the deadly silence when she paused and listened; no breeze stirred the thick vegetation. It was arduous clambering through the brush and soon Charlotte's heart was pounding and her breath was coming quickly. The woods smelled of damp and rotting vegetation, and a log disintegrated into damp hunks of spongy wood when she put down one hand to climb over it. She dusted her hands together, trying to get rid of the soggy debris, and followed Romolo. Finally he stopped.

"Here," he said in a whisper. "This is the spot where I found my sister."

The brush was flattened, and Charlotte crouched by the spot, tamping down a rush of nausea at the dark blotchy staining that showed where Tamara's blood had flowed freely. "She came all this way because she heard someone call her name? That makes no sense."

Romolo shrugged, his smooth young face twisted in grief. "I don't understand, either."

Charlotte examined the ground around the attack. There had been a struggle; branches were broken and leaves trampled. As the mist began to seep away and the sun to send fingers of light into the gloomy depths, her flawless sight caught dark blotches even on the trunk of nearby trees. How savage had the fight been for that to happen? And what attacked her, man or beast?

Caught on a tangle of underbrush was the scrap of kerchief Tamara had been wearing. Charlotte picked it up and examined it, noting the tear. But if Tamara was awoken from sleep, why was she wearing the kerchief? From Charlotte's experience the night she and Fanny spent in the gypsy camp, she knew that Tamara took it off and braided her hair before sleep. Where the piece was missing, the tear was almost square and looked deliberate. It didn't make sense. She folded the kerchief carefully and thrust it into her tucker.

"Romolo," she said, as she continued to scan the ground. "Have you ever seen dogs roaming near here?" Still crouching, she twisted and gazed up at him. "Dogs from farms, maybe, or from the village or beyond?"

"No, lady. This land belongs to Mr. Randell."

"But that doesn't mean dogs might not get loose and wander. Mr. Randell's game master has hounds, I've been told."

"Yes, miss, but they are kept tied up, and what I saw was larger, much larger than a hunting hound." He shuddered.

"What *did* you see?" she asked, gazing up at him over her shoulder.

He shook his head, his dark eyes wide. "It was still dark, so it was just something large and black; whatever it was, it was big."

"Miss Dancey said there are no wolves in England. Is that true?"

The young man shrugged. "I suppose."

Charlotte's sharp eye caught sight of something snagged by a thorny twig under where Tamara had apparently fallen. She reached out and from the shadowy leaf-strewn forest floor caught between her index finger and thumb a hank of fur. She lifted it to a finger of sunlight; it was dark, almost black, with only some brown near the base of each strand. If this was fur from the creature that attacked Tamara, then it could not be Christoph, for he was silvery when transformed, with darkness only on the outer tips of some of his fur. Who or what, then, did it belong to?

FROM above, the landscape looked serene, dotted with farms and groves of trees, rolling and undulating, green and verdant. No other had ever seen this particular view, Wesmorlyn reflected, and unless he had children, none ever would. There were many others in the world like him, with an ancestry as peculiar and tragic, dating from the fall from grace that had doomed his own family to their odd existence, but they were scattered far and wide over the earth. The intent of the plan set in motion by the ancient anger from the heavens was to keep them apart and make them work toward their reward in solitude and secrecy. They were forbidden contact with each other, condemned to spend forever yearning for the converse of similar spirits.

Doomed to solitude, they worked toward their reuniting with the rapturous glory that would set them free from a long and tedious sojourn on earth. A score of Wesmorlyn generations had not been able to succeed, but he had been determined from a young age that he would, and had bent all his energy, intelligence, and considerable willpower to achieving the reward he knew was only barely possible, held out as a tantalizing hope.

Redemption.

He soared and dipped in the dazzling sunlight of late summer, then came down from the sky near the gypsy encampment but out of sight of it, and with a shrug, folded his gleaming, pearly wings to their resting position, between his shoulder blades. He shook out his bundle and pulled on his shirt, then over it the fawn-colored jacket he wore for walking about the countryside.

Would she be there? Would she come today? News from London had distracted him and held him up, but he had never stopped thinking about Charlotte.

It took a few minutes, for he had landed quite a distance from the gypsy camp, but he finally made it and paused in the shade of the grove of trees to catch his breath. To his surprise he heard a rustling sound from the woods, and voices. He ducked into the shadows and watched, peering into the gloom. Catching a glimpse of golden hair, he knew Charlotte was there, but what was she doing in the woods? Who was she with? He watched and saw her with a young gypsy man, deep in conversation. He followed their progress and crept along the edge, torn as to whether to call out to her, or to wait and try to get her attention. He hated this sneaking around; it went counter to everything he had ever believed in and how he had always conducted himself openly and with nothing to hide but the one central truth of himself.

But he was not done his investigating yet, into the gypsies and Eleanor Dancey. Though other things had pulled his attention away, he did have some information to share with her. His dilemma was resolved when she parted ways with the gypsy fellow and stood deep in thought on the edge of the wooded grove for a long minute, her head down, looking at something in her hand. He approached. "You look so solemn. Is anything wrong?"

"Wesmorlyn!" she said. She sighed and shook her head, balling one hand and thrusting it into her tucker, where it was fastened to her waist. "Yes and no. Something terrible happened last night. Tamara, the gypsy girl who was so kind to Fanny and me, was attacked in the night, we know not by what or whom."

"That's awful!" he said, moving toward her and taking her shoulders in his hands. "Is she all right? Is there anything I can do to help? I understand your concern, but why were you in the woods just now?"

"That is where the attack happened." She glanced toward

the gypsy encampment. They faced the back of the caravans and canvas shelters, but were still within sight of the camp. "Let's walk," she said, dusting off her hands. "I don't wish to go back to Moor Cottage yet."

"It seems that it was an eventful time yesterday and last night."

"Why? What happened?" she asked, looking up at him.

He sighed. Inexplicably, he trusted her. "It's Hannah," he blurted out, thrusting his fingers through his hair and raking it back off his forehead. "She tried to run away. Again."

Chapter 14

"RUN AWAY? Lady Hannah?" Charlotte's mind reeled. He had said Hannah had tried to run away *again*. Did that mean Eleanor's story was true, and that the last time it had happened she was sheltered by the woman?

The earl shook his head. "I didn't really mean to tell you."

"It will stay between us, Wesmorlyn," she said, meeting his gaze. "I hope you know that."

"Somehow, though we have known each other such a short time, I do know that." He took her arm and led her over a nearby hill. "It seems this is all we do, walk and talk."

"That seems a good method of becoming acquainted. Tell me," she said, keeping pace with him, "what's wrong? Why did your sister run away before? And what happened?"

He didn't speak for a long moment, leading her up to the crest of the familiar hill, then down the sloping side. "It has been a tumultuous year, since her mother died. I blame myself, really, for I have not given her the attention she needs, I think. As shy as she is, and as sweet natured, she trusts implicitly and she has been led astray on two occasions, now."

"By whom?"

"I'd rather not say. I fear I'm not being fair. She swears it is all her own idea, and she's honest to a fault, so I must believe her." He kept his eyes forward. "Let us speak of other things."

"No, Wesmorlyn," she said, staying him with one hand on his forearm and making him turn. His brown eyes, sometimes warm, sometimes remote, held worry. She wondered if he really spoke to anyone, or if he always retreated and held his worries close to himself. She had Christoph to speak to, but then they were only two years apart from each other. There were many years between him and Hannah, so he was alone with his troubles. "Please talk to me. This just happened, you said? How did you find out about it if it just happened?"

"That isn't important," he said, hastily. He cleared his throat and took a deep breath, gazing off toward the horizon with squinted eyes. "What *is* important is that she is coming down to stay with me in the country until I can return to London."

"If you need to go back to London, or spend more time on your estate, please don't let me keep you. I have my own needs and my own ideas of what I have to do, but I would not have you change your schedule for me, if that's what you're doing."

He finally gazed at her, his brown eyes thoughtful. "You're very independent."

"For a woman, you mean to say," she said.

"Yes, for a woman. You make it a challenge, the way you add that."

"It *is* a challenge," she said, stepping away from him. A brisk breeze swept up the hill and tugged at the skirts of her gown as clouds began to form and chase each other in a mad dash across the sky. The windswept moor had become her favorite place so far in England, and she didn't think any fine castle or elegant drawing room could ever compete. The open country promised freedom and adventure. "Do you know," she said, gazing up to the top of the long slope they were climbing, "I have spent my life trying to figure out who I am. Perhaps that is not a womanly thing to admit and I know it must make me seem odd in your eyes, but the rules of society make no sense to me." She looked into his eyes; they crinkled slightly at the corners as if he spent a lot of time squinting in the sunlight. "Wesmorlyn, why, because I am a woman, am I to have no sense of myself and who I am?"

"I don't understand," he said, moving toward her. "Who you *are*? You are Countess Charlotte von Wolfram, and my fiancée."

"I don't mean that in a literal sense," she said, impatiently, feeling he was being deliberately obtuse, "I mean who I am underneath. I've made mistakes, and I've witnessed tragedy. One thing I've learned is that my life is too short and far too precious to spend it doing something I will hate."

"And does that mean marriage to me?"

"That's my point, I don't know," she cried, exasperated. She strode away from him to the top of a hill and gazed off toward the far tors, now shaded by charcoal clouds. She would have liked to explore those rocky cliffs, but that was not a womanly ambition either. She should be more concerned with her dress, instead of being happy with wearing the same well-worn gown day in and day out, she thought, gazing down at the dirty hem and torn trim of her green muslin day gown. And she most decidedly should not be trying, on her own, to figure out who or what had attacked Tamara.

But she was just Charlotte, and no amount of fitting herself into a suitable mold would change that, not really. She had tried to be what her family wanted, and it had made her unhappy, so she had vowed to go her own way, finally, for all of their sakes. It seemed simple enough to her, and not too much to ask of life. She turned back and gazed at him, examining his thoughtful eyes and firm lips set in an unhappy scowl. "Don't *you* want to be very sure before taking such an irrevocable step? Marriage is for life, Wesmorlyn. Don't you wish to fall in love with your wife?"

He paused, sober and cautious as always, before he spoke. "It seems wrong, somehow, to be speaking of something so frivolous as love with so much trouble around us. And especially in relation to marriage, which I do take very seriously."

"There," Charlotte said, gazing at him, the lowering sky casting dark shadows across his handsome face. "That is a fundamental difference between us. You think of love as frivolous, and I think of it as something I desperately want, something terribly important to me." She took a deep breath and lifted her chin. "Within marriage or without it."

He stared into her eyes, searching, she almost felt, for her soul. She stepped over to him, reached up, and put one finger to his neck, feeling the heavy thrum of his life's blood through a pulsing vein. A rumble of thunder above them hastened her own pulse, and she cupped the back of his head, drawing his face down close as she watched his eyes. His body was stiff and taut, like a pulled thread that must snap to release the tension.

And then he did snap, pulling her to him hard and claiming her lips, kissing her with suffocating thoroughness. She felt her feet lift from the ground and he bent her back as the rumble of thunder rolled like a kettledrum in the orchestra, echoing against the cloud cover. She surrendered to the floating sensation and grasped him by the shoulders, desperate to maintain her balance, but losing herself in the soft pull of his lips and the delicious sensation of his tongue pushing into her mouth, the shocking intrusion exciting, thrilling her body with tremulous waves of longing.

The skies opened and a curtain of rain descended. He released her, took her arm, and pulled her after him. "Run with me," he said. "We must take shelter under the stone bridge."

He pulled her after him into the shadowy damp dimness under the bridge, but he didn't give her a single moment to think; he pulled her under him and kissed her again, roughly. Too roughly. She got her hand free and slapped his cheek, the sound echoing hollowly against the moss-covered underside of the bridge.

He stopped abruptly and pulled back, his cheek visibly ruddy from her slap even in the gloom. "Isn't that what you're looking for?" he said, gruffly, his expression dark and unlike anything she had ever seen on his face as he stared down at her. "Wasn't that passionate enough for you? Isn't that what I was lacking in your eyes?"

Squirming at his weight half atop her, she replied, breathlessly, "Perhaps that was passion, Wesmorlyn, but passion often exists apart from love; they do not equate to each other. How little you understand women. No wonder your sister ran away!"

"Do not *ever* say anything about Hannah!" he said, grasping a handful of her skirt in his clenched fist.

"I'm sorry! I meant to cast no aspersion on her, you must know. Get off of me!" Stones dug into her back and she shifted herself out from under him, shoving him away as she scrambled to sit up. "Is there no middle ground with you, between coldness and passion?"

"I just don't understand you," he said.

"You would understand better if you would listen to me!"

Resentful, his dark eyes stormier than the rolling waves of thunder around them, he drew his knees up and clasped his arms around them, stopping to wipe the rain from his brow. "I apologize, Countess, for my inexcusable behavior toward you," he said haughtily. "I cannot explain it." He shook his head, and then his voice softened as he said, "I am thoroughly ashamed." He put his forehead on his knees.

"Stop. Just stop!" she exclaimed, and the word echoed back, *stop, stop.* "For once in your life listen to a woman."

Startled, he lifted his head and stared over at her.

"That's better." She scooted around to kneel in front of him. "Look me in the eye when we speak, Wesmorlyn. You would give that courtesy to a man, and I demand it as well. If we are to understand each other *ever*, we must learn to listen. I know I am as guilty as you of wishing to speak more than I listen, but it will not do. Now is your turn to pay attention, though."

She took a deep breath. "I was raised in a home where my uncle and aunt worked together to raise us. He was master of the house, but he listened to my Aunt Adele. Though she is a very hard woman, she's also very intelligent, and neither held anything back from the other. When I was naughty—I blush to say that was quite often—my Aunt Adele told my Uncle Nikolas, and they decided together my punishment. He respected her, you see, and took her advice into consideration. I know that was not a marriage, but I will have the same respect from the man I would marry, or I will never wed. When my uncle *did* marry, just this year, his choice was a woman who would not let him ride roughshod over her; she insisted on sharing every worry he had, and if she was not so, he could not have truly loved her. I don't believe real love can exist within the confines of such an unequal marriage as you would want."

It was a new idea to him, she could see it. "Wesmorlyn," she said, leaning forward, staring into his eyes and making her point directly, "I would not be a comfortable wife, one you could tuck away in the country to bear children and entertain the vicar, as I have heard English lords demand. You would be better to choose someone else for that duty. I cannot be easy to handle, I know that, but I will never be less than I am for any man."

"And I cannot be less of a man just to cater to a wife who will not allow her husband to command her," he said, his expression holding bewilderment. "You would have me behave as a woman."

"Good God, Wesmorlyn!" She rocked back on her heels. "Do you think I would want a man who was less than himself?"

"But the two cannot exist together, can they? An independent woman and a manly man? We would fight all the time! *Someone* must be the master and *someone* must obey."

"*No.* You are describing the relationship of a master and servant, not a husband and wife."

"But the Bible says that a husband must have mastery over his wife."

"It also says to stone a woman who lies with a man before marriage. At least in Germany we don't do that. It seems to me that we *all* pick and choose which biblical verses to obey, and yet all who so choose make specious arguments about why theirs is the only correct interpretation." She hung her head for a moment, deep in thought. How had she come to argue about marriage with him, when she had determined that he was not for her? It seemed ludicrous, and yet she felt something between them. "I don't know what else to say on that account. I will not argue biblical text with you, my lord," she looked up and said, with what dignity she could muster, "but I will not be a subject in my own home. *Ever.*"

"But a boat without a captain will founder and become lost."

"Ah, and a carriage without a horse will go nowhere, and a bucket without a rope will draw no water, and a woman without a keeper will go mad. Don't be ridiculous. I will *not* bow down to analogies or allegories," she said, staring at him. "Marriage is neither a boat, nor a servant/master relationship, nor anything else but a marriage. I know what I want."

"What is it? What do you want?" he said, still exasperated, still puzzled.

What did she want? Perhaps she had been hasty in saying she knew. She thought for a long minute, staring out at the curtain of rain that sheeted off the rocky bridge over their head. A sluice of water flowed down from the side of the bridge, creating a grimy stream that poured down to the creek below, joining it and muddying the water. Rubbing her arms, the dampness beginning to set in as a chill, she finally said, "Perhaps I don't know everything I want, but I do know this; I have seen what marriage *can* be. I want to be respected for my opinion, but not to the exclusion of your own. I want to be heard, but not necessarily heeded. I want you to argue if you don't agree with me, but to yield if I make sense."

"And that is marriage to you?"

"That is a part of it."

"What else? There's more?"

"Of course," she said, meeting his confused gaze. "There is always more, Wesmorlyn. I will grow and change through time, and so will you. If there were ever to be a marriage between us, there must be concessions made for that, negotiations."

"It sounds like a barter."

"Barter is give-and-take so both parties get what they want and need, and so is marriage."

"You make it sound like a business arrangement!"

"Did you not make a business arrangement when you agreed by mail to marry a female you had never met, and ascertained my dowry?" She sighed. "You must recognize that two people, if they are to live in harmony *most* of the time, need to be prepared for disharmony *some* of the time, and they must resolve to love in spite of change and differences of opinion and tragedy and fear and life. I'm not afraid of disharmony and turbulence. Life, Wesmorlyn, if we are going to use analogies, is not a stagnant pond, but a swift-flowing river, ever changing, renewing, moving quickly toward an uncertain future. I will move with it, and so must any man I marry."

"You require so much."

"I know," she said. "Perhaps too much; is that what you think but will not say? I suppose I've spent far more time thinking of what I want than the usual young lady." She gazed out. "The rain's stopping." She made a move to clamber to her feet. "I had better take the opportunity to go back to Moor Cottage."

"Wait!" he said, and grabbed her arm.

His hand was warm through the damp cloth of her dress sleeve. "I have lived my whole life thinking one way," he said, bewilderment in his voice. "You cannot expect me, in the blink of an eye, to change my beliefs."

She gazed down at his hand, the thick, tanned fingers grasping the pale green cloth between them. "I don't."

"But if I don't agree to your ideal of marriage you will break the engagement."

"Wesmorlyn, even if you agree, I cannot say I'll marry you," she said, her voice echoing with a hollow, forlorn sound off the stone bridge overhead. "I'm not sure you even want to marry me, in truth. You're an honorable man and bound to me, you feel, by your word. I release you from that bond here and now."

"What do you want from me, Charlotte? What am I to do?"

She shrugged. "Be yourself." She clambered to her feet, scooted out from under the bridge, and scaled the muddy embankment with some difficulty, casting one long look back at the earl, who had also climbed out from under the bridge. He stared up at her, confusion in his eyes. "Just be yourself, Wesmorlyn, if you even know who your true self is."

She raced back past the gypsy camp and up over the moors to the cottage. Her dress was damp and grimy, and she was going to have to change immediately, or she would come down with some awful fever, no doubt. She thought affectionately back to Melisande Davidovich, her friend, now married to a Russian count and gone to live in Russia. Melisande would always dose her with herbal remedies and somehow it would bring her around. Perhaps Eleanor would do the same, for she spent a lot of time out in her herb garden, cutting and drying and preparing her herbs, though they seemed more designed for culinary uses, from what Charlotte had seen.

The cottage was in view, but the skies again opened and a torrent of rain, carried on a furious wind, battered down on her. She ran the last hundred feet and flew into the front door, gasping for air. The door to her right opened almost immediately and there stood Eleanor Dancey, and beyond she could see, in the parlor, Fanny sitting demurely on a chair, and, rising from the settee by the fire, holding Hellebore in his arms, was Mr. Lyulph Randell.

"Countess!" Eleanor said. "You are soaked to the skin! We have the honor of a visit from Mr. Randell, but you are hardly going to want to come and sit in such a terrible state!"

She was speechless, pushing back her hair from her eyes, and miserably aware of dripping on the rug in the gloomy hall as Mr. Randell stood and approached, smiling. He was much handsomer than she had remembered, his green eyes sparkling with merriment as he approached the doorway.

"Countess," he said, bowing, "even a drenching cannot damage your loveliness!"

"Mr. Randell, you are making fun of me."

Hellebore hissed at her and jumped down from his hold. "No," he said, gently, "I would never dream of doing something so ill-natured, please believe me."

Fanny squeezed past the two into the hall and said, "Oh, Charlotte! I was so worried for you when I saw the rain come down. You're positively soaked to the skin!" She took her older sister's arm. "We must go up and get you something dry to wear!"

"We are about to have luncheon," Eleanor said, "so do not dawdle, girls. Mr. Randell has kindly agreed to stay."

Charlotte, dripping miserably, curtseyed and raced upstairs, trailed by Fanny.

WESMORLYN, battling the winds and rains, donned his soaking shirt and jacket and trudged back up to his home. Entering and glancing around at the stark gray walls and somber décor, unchanged in hundreds of years, he thought how different it could be with Charlotte within it. She was like a twinkling star, brilliant but out of reach. He had kissed her, and yet had no more idea how to attain her than he had before, or even if he should try. Would she make his life heaven or hell? What she wanted from a husband seemed impossible and ludicrous, but he had no doubt she would be steadfast in her determination to either get it or not marry at all.

Semyaza descended the steps.

"Is she here?" Wesmorlyn said.

The sepulchral fellow nodded, but put out a staying hand when Wesmorlyn would have bounded up the steps.

"Hannah doesn't wish to see you yet."

"What? Why not?"

"She is ashamed, I think, and afraid."

"Afraid? Of me?"

"Of your bad opinion. She knows she has done wrong, and I think is afraid to face you."

"She must face me sooner or later. And if she is ashamed that is good; shame has a beneficial purpose in keeping us on the right path."

Semyaza, his thin lips compressed, said nothing.

"Do you not agree?" Wesmorlyn said, stung and agitated. It seemed nothing he thought or said or felt was right to those around him.

The man sighed and looked toward the upper reaches of the vast hall. "Do you truly believe doing right out of the fear of shame and humiliation achieves the higher purpose you seek?"

Wesmorlyn, weary, was about to snap that it was better than nothing, but he paused and thought, hand on the carved finial of the staircase railing. He stared at the wood grain, the perfectly beautiful pattern of nature. If only nature was as reliable a signpost in life as she was a designer of lovely things. But his natural urges were not honorable ones, he feared, not toward Charlotte von Wolfram anyway, judging by the fever that lashed through him in waves of hunger as he held her down and kissed her violently under the bridge. What had possessed him? It was as if the pride and passion that had caused his ancestor's fall had flashed through his blood; the shame of his actions still stung. He looked up and caught Semyaza's eye. "What other guide to what is right do we have, but the knowledge that doing something else will bring us shame?"

"Hannah surely is a good example of how the fear of shame does not always guarantee rectitude," Semyaza said.

"It has always worked for me," Wesmorlyn claimed.

"Have you not had other motives in all you have done?"

"Perhaps." He took in a deep breath. "But I'm no longer so sure."

"And that is your path right now. Examining one's motives on occasion is beneficial." Semyaza looked troubled, an unusual expression for him. "I've had eons to learn that difficult lesson. When I led your ancestor in the fall, I knew I was doing wrong, but I used every reason to justify myself, and failed to examine my motives with the clear eye of awareness. I will pay for my hubris throughout eternity, but you needn't. I think you should perhaps examine, too, whether there is ever an occasion when a person is truly not in control of their own actions, and so not to blame in the slightest."

"What do you mean?"

Semyaza sighed and was silent.

Wesmorlyn thought, hard. *Not in control.* "Do you mean, not in control because of some kind of drug or potion?"

"Or some other force at work. Think of all you know of Hannah, and imagine what, or who, could be behind her misbehavior. But first, give her a half hour to reflect and then go to her—not in anger and wrath, Simeon, but in the tenderness of a brother's love and concern."

He nodded, exhaustion rolling over him in waves. "Send up hot water, please, Sam. I'm filthy and tired."

Some time later he padded down the hallway in the modern section of the Abbey to Hannah's door. He tapped gently, and then entered her pretty, cozy, white-papered room, a reminder of her mother's gentling influence on the stern earl, Wesmorlyn's father, and on the austere household. She was curled up in a chair by the fire, which was lit against the chill dankness of the day. Autumn was on its way, and the rain made everything in the old Abbey feel damp. Hannah's eyes were swollen and red; she had been weeping, judging by the soggy handkerchief in her fist.

The anger he had been trying to defeat evaporated in an

instant and all he remembered was how much he adored his little sister and had from the moment, as a boy of thirteen, she had been placed in his arms hours after her birth, a squirming bundle. He went and knelt by her chair. "Hannah, are you all right?"

"No," she said, her lips trembling. "You must be very, very angry with me, Wes. Are you?"

"I cannot say I have not been very cross with you, but I promise I will not browbeat you, nor will I punish you if you tell me the truth," he said, touching her cheek gently. "Did he do aught to you? Did he tamper with you in any way?"

"No, of course not."

"But he did ask you to run away with him?"

"No. Not even that. It was all my own idea." She hiccupped, and took a drink from the teacup on the elegant little mahogany table next to her. She turned her tragic gaze to Wesmorlyn, and said, "It's over," her bottom lip trembling. "He doesn't care for me. I ran to him, begged him to take me away, but he doesn't love me. He's in love with another woman, he said, and he was leaving London to be with her. That is why I followed him; I couldn't help myself. I went to throw myself on his mercy, so I slipped out. Poor Miss Madison," she said, speaking of her hapless companion, "had no idea of any of it."

"Another woman? He said that?"

She nodded and the tears flowed. "Yes. Lyulph is in love with another woman, and he's going to marry her. What shall I do, Wes? My heart is broken!" She threw herself into her brother's arms and wept.

But as Wesmorlyn patted her back and muttered soothing words, his mind was traveling at lightning speed. All along Hannah had claimed that Lyulph had offered her no encouragement, that it was all her, and he was innocent of any attempt to lure her away from the safety of her family. With that assurance, what could he do in all fairness but tolerate his friend, who had purportedly done nothing wrong? It had been frustrating beyond belief. He had barred her from spending any time with him alone, which was as much as he could do, but even that had not been enough, clearly, to prevent the infatuated girl from making a fool of herself.

Perhaps now she would behave, now that she knew there

was no chance. So Lyulph Randell said he was in love and going to marry. *Who?* Wesmorlyn had never seen any hint that there was a lady in his life, other than catching him kissing Charlotte von Wolfram. His breath caught in his throat; he was stunned by the sudden certainty that Charlotte had to be who Lyulph meant.

Yet that made not a jot of sense. Lyulph Randell was shrewd and business-minded. He was dedicated to his family's legacy as much in his own way as Wesmorlyn was devoted to his more illustrious family heritage. Wesmorlyn had always feared that Lyulph would make a marital alliance with some family of his own ilk from Europe in an attempt to strengthen their dominance in the ways only werewolves knew, but it had never come about. The world of such creatures was mysterious and secret; it was not something Wes had ever delved into, but he had heard that years before, the Randells had gained land using intimidation and a kind of raw forcefulness. Landowners had been known to sell them land and leave, mysteriously, after a visit from the head of the family.

Wesmorlyn had never heard a whisper of Lyulph doing any such thing; he would have strenuously objected to that kind of bullying, if he had seen it. Believing Lyulph Randell was doing the best he could to behave in a civilized manner, Wes had been content with making peace between their two families, erasing the ill feeling their long and tangled history of enmity had engendered. It was an important part of his plan of redemption. Lyulph's apparently rigid determination to stay on the side of the angels was proof, he had thought, that he was doing right.

But all those years of peacemaking had not mattered to him when he had seen Lyulph in the garden kissing Charlotte. He had come as close to rage as he had ever in his life been, though he didn't understand why. How could he feel so possessive of a young lady he had barely met, and whom he didn't feel at all sure would make him a good wife?

There was too much of all of this that involved Lyulph Randell, including the fellow's having the one piece of information guaranteed to take the countess away from London. Wesmorlyn would get to the bottom of the mystery, but first, he had a brokenhearted girl to deal with, and he had no idea how to soothe her hurt pride and wounded emotions. "Tell me, Hannah, how does it hurt, your heartbreak?" he asked, gently ducking his head to see her face. "Is it an actual ache? Help me to understand."

Chapter 15

HER BROTHER'S room was Charlotte's first destination. Finding him groggy but awake, she told him what she had found and pulled the tuft of fur out of her soaked tucker. She was certain it could not be fur from his coat in his transformed state; but it was inconclusive, Christoph replied. He had not seen himself transformed, as Charlotte had, so the evidence bore little weight with him.

Disappointed in his lackluster response, she retired to her room with Fanny, who helped her undress, taking the wet things away as Charlotte tried to clean herself up, brushing her hair and wiping her skin dry.

"What is this?" Fanny asked.

Charlotte turned, and saw her half sister holding up the wolfskin kirtle, damp from being fastened inside her saturated dress. Staring at it, Charlotte was alarmed by a sudden thought; the fur of the kirtle was mottled, with some dark spots, like the tuft she had found in the woods. If Christoph had transformed and gone out that night, could the tuft of fur beneath where Tamara fell be from the kirtle?

"Give it to me," she said, putting out her hand.

Fanny brought it over and handed it to Charlotte. "What is it?" she asked again, wrinkling her nose in distaste.

Charlotte, appalled by her train of thought, turned away from her sister, folded the hank of fur, and tucked it inside her bodice. Instead of answering, she said, "How is Tamara? Is she awake? Is she recovering?"

Fanny said nothing, and so Charlotte turned back to her and looked up, trying to read her expression. "What is it? Tell me."

"It's just odd," she said, coming and sitting on the edge of the bed. "I went to check on her. The room was dark, and so at first I didn't notice, but Christoph was sitting on the floor beside the sofa where she lay, and his head was resting on the pillow beside hers. Both were asleep. I didn't know what to do, but I suppose I made a noise, and Christoph awoke. He stood and almost ran from the room, mumbling something, I didn't hear what."

Charlotte pulled a brush through her blonde hair, untangling it, and thought about her brother. "Has Tamara woken since?"

"Yes. I visited with her for a few minutes."

"Does she remember what happened?"

"She's still very weak. I didn't ask what happened."

Charlotte sighed at such a complete lack of curiosity. But perhaps it was for the best. She wanted to talk to Tamara herself, and in her admittedly slight experience, people's recollections of events became fuzzy and indistinct the more they talked about them with others. They began to embellish upon their first memories with the influence of their own imagination and sometimes with their impression of what others wished to hear. "When did Mr. Randell arrive?"

"Just a half hour or so ago." Fanny helped her with her hair, expertly winding it into a proper style that would not shame her in front of the others. "What took you so long, Charlotte?" she asked, as she tucked in the last stray strand. "You were gone for hours."

"I was waiting until the rain stopped, and then got caught in it anyway." Changed and properly attired once again in the only other dress she had brought with her, an ivory muslin, Charlotte stood. "I have some questions for Mr. Randell. I wish to know, first of all, why he did not directly follow us down to Cornwall as he said he would."

"Oh, but it was not his fault, Charlotte," Fanny said, anxiously, following her sister into the hall and shutting the door. "Truly. He was so very upset about what happened to us on the road. He apologized profusely, and explained immediately that he was unavoidably detained, or he would have met us in Salisbury."

"Immediately?" Charlotte headed down the hall, feeling her way in the darkness and breathing in the suffocating, mold-scented air. "Before he introduced himself to his tenant?"

"What?"

"His tenant, Eleanor." Charlotte looked back at her, making out her features in the dimness. "He had never met her before."

"Oh." Fanny frowned, her expression one of puzzlement.

"You knew that."

"Yes, but they seemed to know each other. Or perhaps that was just my mistake. I was not immediately at the door; Anne answered it and called Mother."

At the head of the stairway, Charlotte turned and stared at Fanny. Something odd was going on. "You didn't like Mr. Randell at first in London. Have you changed your mind?"

"He's very handsome," she said, slowly. "And very kind. He said I was in very good looks, and that I must be happy now that I had met my mother."

"That doesn't answer my question. Have you changed your mind about him? Do you like him now?"

"He's very kind," she said, faintly.

"Countess Charlotte, Fanny, are you coming back down?" Eleanor Dancey's voice floated up into the dim upper reaches of the hall.

At the bottom of the stairs Charlotte, in the dark, didn't see the cat and stepped on Hellebore's tail; the creature yowled and lashed out at her ankle again. She restrained her fury and her earnest desire to kick it as it scuttled away to another dark corner. "Devil beast," she muttered, wincing at the pain. "I swear he lies in wait just to torment me." But she took a deep breath and schooled her expression to a more pleasant one as she crossed the fusty hallway and strolled into the parlor. She moved immediately over to the fire and put her hands out, trying to drive away the persistent damp chill she felt every time she entered Moor Cottage.

"I must see to my patient," Eleanor Dancey said, brightly, glancing from Fanny and Charlotte to Lyulph Randell. "Perhaps you two girls would keep Mr. Randell company?"

"Certainly," Charlotte said. As the woman left the room, Charlotte took a seat on the settee, and the gentleman, who had stood as they entered, sat as well, on a chair by the fireplace. Her mind teemed with questions, none of which she could ask without admitting that the Earl of Wesmorlyn was her source of information.

"You were a long time following, sir, when you said you would be immediately after us on the road to Cornwall."

"As I told your sister, I was delayed by a rather unfortunate business," he said, with a grimace. He shook his head. "It was a sorry thing, I must say, and I would much rather have been free to leave London when I said I would."

Carefully, Charlotte said, "Is this unfortunate business something you can share?"

"I *should* say nothing."

"Ah. Then don't let me tempt you into betraying a confidence, or relaying too much information on a subject best left untouched," she said, watching his face.

"But I feel I can trust you, Countess," he said, with a gentle smile.

"Indeed you can, but you could not know that yet, not upon such a slight acquaintance as may occur in a ballroom."

"I believe one may gauge the trustworthiness of a person by their behavior to those who rely upon them for strength. Your behavior toward your sister certainly shows your sterling character and trustworthiness."

Fanny, bewildered by the rapid pace of the conversation, glanced back and forth.

Charlotte, watching Mr. Randell's green eyes flicker, chose her next words carefully. "Does this unfortunate business have anything to do with another family with which we are both acquainted?"

"How very perspicacious of you, Countess. It does. Unhappily, I was put in a very difficult position by the rather overwrought emotions of a young lady of tender years."

Eleanor came to the door from the hall. "Fanny dear," she said, her eyes bright and her expression tight with a forced smile, "would you come and help me in the kitchen for a moment?"

Fanny half rose from her chair, but then looked at Charlotte and said, "It wouldn't be seemly for me to leave Mr. Randell and Charlotte alone."

"Surely we need not stand on formality here? We'll just leave the door ajar."

"Go, Fanny," Charlotte said. She would have more freedom to get the information to which she was so tantalizingly close without Fanny's dampening presence. "I'll be fine."

Fanny left, but both were silent for another long moment, before Mr. Randell said, "I feel as if I can confide in you, Countess, and ask your advice."

"Oh? Advice? I hardly feel competent to give advice, Mr. Randell."

"But who so competent as a young lady, where another young lady's heart is concerned?"

"Or so incompetent. Careful, Mr. Randell, for one young lady is not interchangeable for another, you know, and to insinuate it is so or that their feelings are easily divined is to invite disdain."

"Nor would I ever think it is so, but you are very special," he claimed, with a warm tone. "I felt from the first moment we met that you have a rare gift for looking into the hearts and minds of many."

She was silent; meeting him again she could see how she had been attracted to him. He was as handsome and persuasive, and there was about him an air of romance, even in the stifling, dismal atmosphere of the cottage. She could not forget that he was a werewolf, one of her own kind, and that with him there would never be a need to explain. Initially that had led her to confide in him, but some of the instant trust she felt had evaporated with her growing assurance on the island nation's soil, and with a broader knowledge of the people. She now wondered if just being a werewolf was enough for her to have confidence in him.

After a pause, he said, "I am in the difficult position of having a young lady infatuated with me, when I have no such feeling for her." He sighed, an expression of worry on his face. "She has been unguarded and imprudent."

"In what way?"

"What am I to do with a girl who will show up at my London residence unescorted and uninvited?" he said, exasperated. He shook his head, and continued, "How am I to respond, especially when she has been a friend and almost like a little sister to me? Perhaps I see now why Wesmorlyn was concerned—" He stopped abruptly and put one hand up to his mouth. "I should not have said that name! I hadn't intended to be so indiscreet. And I spoke so openly of poor Hannah's indiscretion! I should be flayed alive."

There was something false in his movement and protestation, and yet it gibed so well with what Wesmorlyn had said about Hannah's defection, that she had to believe some part of it was true. "Why would Lady Hannah do such a rash and unlikely thing as run to you?"

"She's unhappy at home, I know that. Wesmorlyn, for all of his public face of perfect amiability—and well I know how charming he can be when he chooses to make himself so—is not so amiable in private with those over whom he has power, I fear." He was watching her eyes as he said that.

"Do you mean he puts on a false front with people?"

"He has been known to, to impress them. Why do you ask, Countess? Have you experienced that with him?"

"How would that be possible?" she asked, evasive in the face of such a direct question. "I left London so quickly, when would I have had a chance to see him again and experience aught but the irritating domination he exhibited in the ballroom?"

"True."

"And so you were delayed in London for what reason?"

He sighed. "Wesmorlyn had left Hannah unguarded. Though she was taken to Lady Harroway's to stay, that worthy woman has no notion of how sly a young lady can be when it suits her, and her companion is almost useless. I don't know where Wesmorlyn is, but he is not in London at present." He paused, and his gaze flicked over to meet hers. "I awaited him at the duel site for hours, and I must say I was happy he did not show, as badly as it reflected on him. However, he has disappeared, and Hannah, seeing her chance and knowing me to be in London, slipped away and came to my residence. It was a very sticky situation. I would not be forced to wed the child due to her own frantic attachment to me. Especially not now, when I have another object in mind." He gave her a speaking look of intense yearning.

But Charlotte could not help but compare it to another look of yearning, and it felt practiced and theatrical in comparison. Between the two of them, Randell and Wesmorlyn, she had a definite opinion as to which was the more honest, and it was not Randell. And yet she had not a single fact to back up her impression. All her life she had heard intuition derided as worthless, while reason was put on a pedestal. And yet reasonably, she should not believe in a world where werewolves existed, for it was like believing in alchemy, the transformation of a base metal into gold. But the fact remained: werewolves existed. Perhaps there was a logic to intuition that had as yet to be revealed to the skeptical. "And so what did you do about the poor infatuated young lady?"

"I took her back to Lady Harroway's and bribed a footman to be discreet! But from then on I was quite afraid to leave London, for she swore she would follow me. That would indeed be the ruin of her reputation, if it was known that she had followed me to Cornwall. How could it end? I care for the child as the little sister I never had; if her reputation was in tatters I would . . . nay, I *must* marry her if it would help to mend it, just out of the consideration I bear the family. I am ever careful of any lady's reputation, and where I am a friend, I am a friend for life, no matter what provocation to the contrary."

Fine words indeed, Charlotte thought, *and easy to say.* "So Mr. Randell, was there any gossip about me when I left town so suddenly?" she asked, remembering what Wesmorlyn said.

"No, of course not. Why would there be? It was not known under what circumstances you left, and really, from what I understand your brother left town so quickly after that it must have been considered that you traveled together, if anyone had questioned it at all."

That was not what Wesmorlyn had said; who was telling the truth? "We have had some drama here, you must have heard."

"No, I cannot say that I have. Whatever do you mean?"

"Did Miss Dancey not tell you? How odd. Last night a gypsy girl at the encampment—the one you have sanctioned, you know, and how very kind it is that you allow them to stay on your land—was attacked by some animal or a man, we are not yet sure which."

"Not sure which? How is that possible? Surely the girl knows whether it is a man or a beast that has attacked her."

"In some case the distinction is not so apparent, I'm afraid, as we both know too well."

"You mean . . ." He gasped and looked toward the door. "No, I will not believe it. It is merely a man with a dog or something of the kind, you will find, I'm sure of it."

She watched him for a moment. He had understood her readily, and she took his glance toward the hall door to mean a reference to her own brother, upstairs at the moment, as he must know from the conversation he had with Fanny and Eleanor. "So when did you arrive in Cornwall? Are you staying in your own home?"

"I arrived yesterday afternoon."

"You must have been weary after so long a ride. Did you retire early?" She knew it was impolite to make such an inquiry, but it had struck her in that moment that he, too, was a werewolf. Was he dark furred? Was he vicious?

He gazed at her intently, and said, slowly, "Countess Charlotte, I am a little puzzled as to your sudden interest in my habits, unless you think me responsible in some way for the terrible event you have just told me about. But I cannot believe it would even cross your mind that I would have anything to do with such an awful attack as you say happened on my own property. Just think for a moment what you are suggesting, that I would endanger my life and reputation to attack in such a manner! We have not known each other long, I agree, but I hope you understand me sufficiently to know I am an honorable man, and whatever else you suspect, you will acquit me when I say that though I arrived at my own estate yesterday afternoon, I spent the night at an acquaintance's in

Bodmin, after staying for dinner too late to ride home. The moon is waxing brighter, but clouds obscured it last night."

She sighed. There was no reason in the world to think him involved in the awful attack on Tamara, and every reason to think Christoph guilty; even her brother's own fear spoke to that possibility. But she would never believe that Christoph could do such a thing, and so must consider that Lyulph Randell, a stranger to her, could still be more dangerous than he seemed. She would keep a wary eye on him from now on. Though there seemed no motive for him to attack Tamara, she could not discount the possibility.

Fanny and Eleanor entered then, the older woman carrying the tea tray. "Have you been having a lovely conversation, getting reacquainted?"

Mr. Randell, having stood, bowed, and said, "We have indeed."

"How is Tamara, ma'am?" Charlotte asked. "May I see her?"

"Not at this moment. Please sit and have tea first, Countess." She set the tray down. "Indeed, I have made my special honey cakes with you in mind, for you did say to me that you enjoyed honey above all other sweets."

Had she said that? Not in her memory, but perhaps it was just a polite fiction. "I really would like to speak to her. I'm very anxious for her recovery." Charlotte turned to Mr. Randell. "I don't wish to be rude, but Tamara is truly the reason for Fanny's and my safety the first night, after your carriage driver so rudely dropped us on the side of the road."

A dark shadow crossed the gentleman's face. "I was furious when I heard of Burgess's unforgivable behavior. I had him whipped and sacked on the spot. I cannot apologize enough, Countess, for such a terrible night as you must have suffered."

He appeared sincerely annoyed at his driver. "There was no harm done ultimately," Charlotte replied, "thanks to Tamara and her people."

"Please sit, Countess Charlotte," Eleanor said, with an edge in her tone. "I really have gone to a lot of trouble to make these honey cakes because I thought they might please you, and I shall be wounded if you don't at least try them."

"All right," Charlotte said, with what grace she could muster in the face of such unyielding insistence. She glanced over at Fanny, who was watching her mother with a mystified expression.

Eleanor saw them all provided with cups and tea, and placed a small plate of cakes directly in front of Charlotte. "Please, I really do wish you to try them."

With a sigh, Charlotte did, biting into the moist, dark sweetness. It was delicious. She wolfed it down. She hadn't realized how hungry she was until that moment. She picked up another, pausing only a moment as the others watched her, then giving a little laugh. "You were right, Miss Dancey, this is the best cake I have ever tasted." She ate it, and then the last on her plate, while the others ate their repast more slowly.

"I watched her gather the honey," Fanny said, with her eyes wide and her tone breathless. "It was most amazing. She has a hive down at the end of the garden, you know, and the bees, they swarmed around her but did not sting; she sang a song while she worked."

Eleanor Dancey glanced at Fanny, and then to Mr. Randell. "I've taken the liberty of reviving a hive that stood at the foot of the garden."

Fanny cocked her head to one side and continued, "The song was so pretty, I almost fell asleep listening; it made me so drowsy. She gathered a small bucket of honey, and the bees allowed it! It was truly the most amazing thing I have ever seen."

Eleanor jumped up and said, "Would you like to take a walk in the garden with Mr. Randell, Countess, while Fanny and I clear away the tea tray?"

Charlotte stood. "I suppose," she said, dreamily, not really caring what she did or where she went. She put one hand to her head. "I was going to do something else, but I cannot remember now what it was. What was it Fanny? Do you remember?"

"You wanted to see Tamara," Fanny said, watching her.

"But I'm sure that can wait," Eleanor said, her eyes glowing and bright, a half smile on her lovely lips. "Let the gypsy girl rest for now, and visit her later."

"I suppose." It didn't really matter, after all. She stood

waiting for another suggestion, not quite knowing what to do next.

Mr. Randell rose and put out his hand. "Come, walk in the garden with me," he said, taking her hand and leading her out through the kitchen and the back door to the garden.

The day had become warm and sunny after the misty start, and bees buzzed, visiting flower after flower in the overrun garden. She had once thought the place menacing and tangled, but it appeared lovely and lush in the glorious warm sunshine. Mr. Randell led her to a stone bench near the garden wall, constructed of mellow golden brick and warmly reflecting the sunshine.

"How lovely this place is, is it not?" he said, dusting off the bench for her and urging her to sit with the pressure of his hand on her shoulder.

"It is," she said, looking around. Flowers grew in abundant mounds, a riot of color in great bunches. Butterflies fluttered on the breeze, and a songbird trilled in the plum tree that grew by the far corner of the walled overgrown garden. It was English country perfection, the kind that had convinced Frau Liebner to return with them to England after a few short months in her homeland of Germany. The colors seemed brighter than before, though. *Why is that?* she wondered. And she saw beauty where before she had seen only confusion.

"I have so longed to see you again," Mr. Randell said, sitting down beside her and pulling her attention away from the brilliance of the garden. Hellebore, who had been sunning himself in a corner of the garden, came and wound around his feet, purring loudly. "I have thought of nothing else."

"Oh?"

"Yes, I've thought of nothing but you, and that kiss we shared in the garden at Lady Harroway's ball before Wesmorlyn spoiled it all with his silly challenge."

It seemed an eon ago. She should thank him for all of his trouble in making sure they got to Cornwall safely. But he didn't really ensure that, did he? His carriage driver abandoned them. And he didn't follow when he said he would.

"Have you thought of me?" he asked, turning her face toward his with the firm pressure of his strong fingers.

"I feel a little odd," she said, staring into his eyes.

"I do, too. It is just being together again. I feel so very strongly, Countess, that we were meant by fate to meet and become close . . . so very close." He moved his face toward hers and kissed her.

A weariness overtook her, an inertia. She could not move and slumped against his shoulder as he prolonged the kiss. And yet she felt nothing. Not a thing. She had no will to move away, but the kiss was as dust, uninteresting, unappealing. Not like Wesmorlyn's.

As the kiss ended at long last, she took a deep breath, pulled away, and stood suddenly. "I have to go in and lie down," she said, exerting all of her considerable will to break away from him.

"No! No, you don't wish to do that Countess."

She stopped, confused. Didn't she? Was he right about that? Perhaps she should just stay and let him talk to her some more. He had a lovely voice, and green eyes and dark hair, she thought, staring at him dreamily.

"Sit back down," he said, grabbing her arm and tugging. "You don't want to go back inside yet; it's so lovely out here, and we haven't finished talking yet."

She took another deep breath and shook her head. No, she didn't want to stay! "I *do* wish to go, sir," she said, and pulled her arm from his strong grasp. " Good day, Mr. Randell." She tripped and stumbled away from him and through the kitchen, to the hall, and upstairs. Fanny called after her, but she ignored the summons and headed for her room, where she threw herself down on the bed. After a few minutes of the room spinning, she realized she was feeling a little better. She sat up, took a deep breath, let her head clear, and then went to the window, thinking that she would like some fresh air. She glanced out and there, down in the garden, were Eleanor Dancey and Mr. Randell, and it looked for all the world as if they were having a furious argument, him gesturing and her with her hands up.

Charlotte opened the window, wondering if she could hear them, but at the sound of the sash, both looked up and saw her standing there. He waved and smiled up at her, a tight expression that held no real good humor, and Eleanor waved, then whirled and walked away, out of sight and presumably into the house, trailed by her cat. Randell strode to the garden gate and toward the tiny cottage stable where his horse was, no doubt.

How extraordinary, she thought as she returned to her bed and lay down. She stared up at a damp spot on the ceiling. How utterly extraordinary that two people who supposedly did not know each other should be arguing in such an intimate and passionate manner. Surely an argument like the one she had witnessed could not happen without some degree of familiarity.

There was something quite wrong about this house and these people, but what it was confounded her. One thing was certain, trust was an attribute she was going to abandon for the next while, until she untangled the knotted mystery that was at the heart of everything odd that had happened since they arrived in England.

Chapter 16

"IT WAS the oddest feeling," Charlotte said to her brother, who sat in a chair by his fireplace. Unable to figure out what had just happened, she had joined him in his room and now perched up on his window seat, relating her odd experience with Mr. Randell. "As we sat together, I felt this wave of lethargy; I could not move, and when he kissed me—"

"Kissed you?" Christoph growled, squinting his blue eyes.

"Yes, just listen please; though I didn't like it, I couldn't move away from him. It took every fiber of my being to pull away finally. I went up to my room, for I felt quite dizzy." She leaned forward for emphasis and said, "And listen to this: when I began to feel better I went to my window, and saw Mr. Randell and Eleanor Dancey standing in the garden arguing about something. Why would Fanny's mother, who doesn't know Mr. Randell except as a landlord, be arguing with him?"

"I don't know," Christoph said. "Maybe they were arguing about rent?"

"I suppose, though it seems unlikely." Charlotte thought for a moment about the odd things she had observed while staying in the cottage. "Have you noticed how Anne seems to wander around in a fog much of the time?"

"Yes, but I just thought that was because she was simple-minded."

"Perhaps, but she listens outside of doors. I've caught her a couple of times. And what about Eleanor? Something is just not right about her."

"We ought to leave," he said. "You shouldn't have come here in the first place."

"Don't begin with that again. I did what I thought right for Fanny."

"I know, I know. But there's nothing holding us here now, is there?"

"Christoph, I won't leave until Tamara is well enough, and until we figure out what Fanny's mother is up to."

"All I know is that I have felt peculiar ever since I set foot in this cottage," Christoph said. "And don't you dare make a joke out of that," he said, pointing his finger at her with a flash of his old good humor.

Fanny tapped on the door and came in. "Are you well, Christoph?" she asked. "Mother is asking you both to come down for tea. She seems unhappy about something."

Charlotte took Fanny's arm and pulled her down to sit in the window seat with her, moving a little so both could fit. "What do you think of your mother? How do you feel toward her?"

She shrugged.

Charlotte exchanged a look with Christoph. "Fanny, tell me the truth. You do know that you can tell us anything, don't you?"

"I'm so grateful to you both. You have been through so much trouble for me, and I'm very, very grateful."

"But?" Charlotte stared at her, and saw evasion and unhappiness clouding her clear blue eyes.

"Fanny, is everything all right?" Christoph asked, his forehead pinched in a frown, two vertical lines between his eyebrows. "Would you like to live with your mother from now on?"

"No! Oh, no, please, I wouldn't like that. You won't leave

me here alone, will you?" she cried, grasping at Charlotte's hand.

"Fanny, calm!" Charlotte said, squeezing her hand. She put her arm around her sister's thin shoulders. "We will go nowhere without you, I promise. It's up to you; you have a home with us whenever you need one, you must know that. No one will make you stay here. Do you not like your mother? You've only known her a few days, so it's natural you should feel shy with her. Has she been unkind to you?"

"No," Fanny said, slowly. Tears welled in her eyes and she sighed deeply. "I just don't feel comfortable. She doesn't feel like a mother; I can't explain it. She's always kind to me, though she is often short and cruel to poor Anne when she doesn't know I am watching. That's why Anne is so nervous, I think."

"We were just speaking of her, actually. Why doesn't the girl leave for another position?" Christoph asked.

"I asked her that, but she mumbled that she can't, that she is bound to the lady."

"To Miss Dancey."

"She never says her name. She only ever says 'the lady'."

Charlotte, still feeling the lingering effects of the strange bout of lethargy she had suffered, sat back in the window seat, thinking. She had tried time and again for the few days they had been there to speak with Anne about her mistress, but the girl was frightened and often blank, just staring as if she didn't understand. Was the girl an imbecile, as Christoph had suggested? At times it seemed so, but at other times the girl had quite a sharp, intelligent look in her eyes, like when she was listening at doors.

"So will you come down?" Fanny said to them both.

Christoph stood and stretched. "I suppose we should. You know," he said, addressing Charlotte, "I think it quite rude that Wesmorlyn has not answered the letter I wrote to tell him where we are. Since we are in his part of the country, I thought he might come down and we would see him. I think it imperative, Charlotte, that you apologize to him for your behavior, but we could ask him some questions about Lyulph Randell, too. Who knows the man better than the earl?"

Charlotte shifted guiltily. To tell or not to tell?

Eleanor Dancey tapped and entered the room; looking around brightly, she said, "Why are you not outside on such a beautiful afternoon?"

"Christoph has not been feeling well, ma'am," Charlotte said, watching her. She rose from her seat and continued. "I wish to see Tamara. May I speak with her?"

"Certainly," she said, her gaze flitting from Fanny, to Christoph, and then to Charlotte. "Yes, I do think my patient is up to some company now."

As she turned and exited, Charlotte followed, thinking of what Fanny had said about her unkindness to her maid, but that girl's insistence that she was "bound" to the lady. *Bound.* Was she indentured? Perhaps when Eleanor Dancey intended to go to the colonies Anne offered herself as an indentured servant to earn her way. But with the woman's humble life after her fall from grace surely she would not be able to afford another's passage? Charlotte descended behind her, wondering what mystery lay behind her reticence.

"Miss Dancey," she said, carefully. "I am so interested in your time in Germany. If you feel up to speaking of it, I would like to hear your impressions of Wolfram Castle and of my father and mother, if you please. I don't wish to be indelicate, but you must understand my interest, given how young I was when they died. The impression of an outsider would be valuable to me, as I only have my uncle and aunts' recollections to go on."

They reached the hallway, and Miss Dancey turned, her face shadowed by the fading light from the open door into the drawing room. Hellebore padded over to them and wound around Eleanor's legs, purring loudly. "Of course, Countess," she said, in her gentle, noncommittal tone. "We'll speak about that. It was a painful time for me, but if you insist, I'll tell you what I remember. But not right now."

Evasion again. Charlotte pressed on, determined to learn more. "What were you and Mr. Randell arguing about in the garden, ma'am? When I looked down from my window you were having a heated discussion."

"Really?" Eleanor said, with a puzzled expression. "How odd that it should appear so; we had no argument, I assure you." The big tabby cat leaped up into her arms and growled at Charlotte. "Hellebore, behave," the woman said, and then, with a placid look on her lovely, perfectly smooth face, continued. "It must be a mere mistaken impression from your viewpoint. I have nothing but good things to say about the gentleman, for after all, he saved me from a very difficult situation."

"Yes, a difficult situation. So you have said over and over."

Christoph had pulled Fanny aside and was speaking to her. Charlotte moved closer to Eleanor Dancey, and in a low tone, watching the woman's face, said, "Very handsome, too, isn't he? He truly seems to be enamored of me, for he's *so* persistent! He's hinted at marriage, but I'm undecided. I very much feel the lack of a mother right now. Perhaps as an *older* lady you can help me make up my mind." She watched the woman's eyes, how they squinted in the dimness.

"I can feel how very much he cares for me," Charlotte continued, pushing it a little farther. "From one lady to another, it took all of my willpower to break away from his kiss." Was it her imagination, or did the woman's jaw clench? She certainly tightened her grip on Hellebore, for the creature squawked indignantly and leapt from her hold, slinking off down the dim hallway into the darkest shadows. "But how much do I know of him?" Charlotte said, keeping her tone low and confidential. "It's a big decision; should I allow his advances? And what about when he declares himself and offers me his hand? What should I do?"

"I have no advice to give you, Countess. Tamara will no doubt be happy to see you," she said, her tone abrupt. "I spoke to Mr. Randell about the attack at the gypsy camp and he is concerned, of course, since it occurred on his property. He's going to look into it. Perhaps *that* was the discussion you saw and misinterpreted." She turned to Christoph and Fanny. "Will you come to the dining room? Tea is almost ready, Count. I've made more honey cakes just for you, since you didn't join us earlier." She motioned them ahead of her, and then went down the hall past them toward the kitchen.

Tamara was sitting in the parlor by the front window overlooking the rose garden when Charlotte entered. Her hands were folded in her lap, and she gazed longingly out the window.

"How are you, dear girl?" Charlotte said, swooping over to

her and embracing her in a strong hug. She stood and gazed down at her new friend, taking in the paleness of her cheek and the bandage that covered the wounds on her neck. They were stained pink, her wounds still seeping.

"I'll be all right, Charlotte, though I still feel tired and so weak. I don't know why. I've slept for hours. Though I couldn't bear to stay in that poky, dark room another minute, it took every ounce of my energy to move from my bed to this chair. I don't think I could make it back again on my own," she admitted, a catch in her voice.

That reminded Charlotte of what Fanny had said about finding Christoph by Tamara's side, sleeping. She had meant to ask him about that, but became distracted by other things. "You've gone through an awful experience." She examined her carefully. Tamara's dark lustrous hair was brushed and tidy, confined at the nape of her neck with a blue ribbon. Of course: her head scarf was torn to shreds. Charlotte swallowed and refused to think of the scrap of fabric in Christoph's dressing gown pocket, and the remnant she had found in the forest. She took a seat and asked, "Can you speak of it now? What happened? We only got bits of it from Romolo and Tully."

Tamara gasped. "Romolo! Is my poor brother all right?"

"Yes, yes," Charlotte said, putting one hand on her arm. "Hush, Tamara, he's just fine. I accompanied him back to the encampment and told them you would recover after some rest. I'll get word to them that you're doing well."

"Can't I just go home? This cottage"—she shook her head and glanced around—"it doesn't feel right. I'm not used to walls on all sides, and a ceiling instead of the sky. I can't breathe here."

"It's not just you, trust me. This cottage is no place I want to stay for long. But you must recover first before you go back. We won't leave until you're well enough to go, too."

"But I'm well enough, really, and I could . . ." She stood, but wavered and then collapsed into the chair again, her coloring a little more sallow.

"You're *not* well enough. Just stay the night, at least, and then we'll see tomorrow if we can get your brother's handcart and take you back to your family that way."

Tamara leaned toward her friend and murmured, "But this cottage doesn't *feel* right."

Charlotte, curious to hear Tamara's impressions, asked, "What do you mean?"

Eleanor Dancey's voice berating Anne floated to them. Tamara just shook her head. "I don't know," she whispered. "It's all confusing. I'm just not accustomed to staying in a house, enclosed, fettered; that's likely why I feel so uneasy here. That *must* be all it is."

Charlotte examined her; the golden light of late afternoon filtered through the grimy window and touched the girl's eyes, making their warm brown almost an amber color. Tamara met her gaze and offered a weak smile, through tears that clung to her dark lashes. Charlotte would never believe that Christoph had attacked the girl, no matter what he himself feared. "Please, tell me what you remember, Tamara," she said, reaching out and taking her hand, trying to infuse some of her own strength into the gypsy.

She stared out the window, a frown wrinkling her brow. "I awoke in the night, I don't know why."

"A noise, perhaps?"

She shook her head. "I think I heard my name. I'm almost certain of that. I arose and—" She stopped, her lips parted as if to continue, but she stayed silent.

"What is it? Tamara?"

"I just can't understand it," she said, her gaze focused in the middle distance, her brow still furrowed in thought. "I *did* hear my name, and I got up and went out of the camp and toward the woods. But that seems ridiculous. Why would I do such a thing?"

"Just tell me what happened in your remembrance," Charlotte said. "Don't try to figure out *why* yet."

Tamara took a deep breath and nodded. "All right. I entered the woods; I could see somehow, though it was very dark. I don't remember what I was thinking." She blushed and turned her face away into the shadows.

"What is it? Tamara, you *do* remember what you were thinking," Charlotte said, squeezing her hand. "What is it?"

But she shook her head. "I walked," she whispered. "Then I stopped. I don't think I remember what happened next."

Charlotte, her heart pounding, remembered how Tamara had stared at Christoph when he came to the camp. She had seemed entranced by him, fascinated and attracted. If she saw him in the woods, would she admit it? Taking a deep breath and letting it out slowly, Charlotte decided she wanted to know the truth no matter what, and she would deal with the consequences later. Even if Christoph was there, it didn't necessarily mean he was the one who hurt her. "You must remember something. Did you see anyone you recognized? Or hear a voice you had heard before?"

"No," the gypsy said, and then she met Charlotte's gaze. "No, I didn't see or hear anyone I recognized. I swear it. I *was* thinking of someone, I admit, wondering if I would ever see him again, and then . . ." She paused and put her free hand to her forehead. "It all happened so quickly. I was thrown down, and I think I heard growling and felt an awful pain, and then I suppose I screamed and fainted. That's all I remember."

"You didn't see a face, didn't feel human hands?"

Tamara shook her head helplessly. "I just don't know."

"But you must know if whatever attacked you was an animal or a person?"

"No! I tell you, I just don't know." She pulled her hand out of Charlotte's grasp and broke down, weeping.

Aghast at how pushing for answers had weakened the poor girl, Charlotte said, "All right, all right." She touched Tamara's bare arm and felt her shaking. "We'll figure this all out, don't worry. You're getting better, and I hope by tomorrow you'll be well enough to leave here."

CHARLOTTE, Christoph, and Fanny made a pact not to eat or drink anything that had not been prepared before their eyes, and so refused anything but the tea Fanny made that afternoon. Then the young ladies became extremely eager to help in the kitchen, Charlotte going so far as to say she had always been fascinated by cookery, a colossal lie. They remained in the kitchen for the rest of the afternoon, observing, helping when they could, watching when they couldn't. Eleanor Dancey was becoming more and more irritated as the day wore on, and even more so at dinner when she wanted to add some herbs to Christoph's meal, as she had gotten into the habit of doing, but he put his hand over his food, preferring to taste the "natural" flavor, as he said, of the trout that would be the main course.

What exactly they suspected was not clear even to Charlotte, at whose instigation the changes took place, but to her there was some connection between the odd feelings both she and Christoph had been experiencing and Eleanor Dancey. The woman constantly tampered with Christoph's food, sprinkling dried or fresh herbs over his plate, even insisting on serving him personally. And yet Charlotte's own bad spell had not been preceded by anything of that kind, though she *had* eaten the honey cakes Eleanor prepared. Nothing made sense yet; it was like a human figure seen through a mist, the whole was amorphous and shrouded in mystery, unrecognizable without some key element that they did not yet possess or know. It was unthinkable to accuse the woman when they had not a clue of what to accuse her, and so they must leave it be.

The next day dawned and promised to be lovely, with golden sunlight burning off every vestige of dampness early. Charlotte impatiently waited through the morning. Christoph reported with a relieved smile that he had had no recurrence of the awful dreams, but he still did not feel confident that he was not the one to attack Tamara. When Charlotte offered to return the wolfskin kirtle, he asked her to keep it.

After lunch Charlotte made an open statement that she and Fanny were going to go down to the gypsy encampment, though Fanny was in truth going to stay in the cottage and try to go through Eleanor's things while Christoph and Tamara kept her occupied downstairs. Fanny was not the one Charlotte would have chosen for that task, but Christoph was out of the question—if he was found in her room it would have caused a terrible commotion whereas Fanny could have a plausible explanation if pressed—and Charlotte had her own reasons for going to the gypsy camp.

She left the house with Fanny, and then, when Eleanor had been called on some pretext to the small office where Tamara was sleeping, they snuck Fanny back in and up to Eleanor's bedroom. Charlotte crept back out of the cottage and bounded away, over the hills and toward the gypsy camp. She was taking back news of Tamara's recovery to Romolo and their father, but also, unbeknownst to anyone else, she was keeping her eye out for Wesmorlyn.

She delivered her message that they hoped Tamara would be well enough to come home later that day, or the next morning. Romolo was grateful but not inclined to keep her there without Fanny to stare at longingly. He was content to receive the news, relay it to his father, and then go back to his task of fashioning a new halter for one of the horses.

The day was gorgeous, warm and inviting in the way only late summer could be, with sunlight dappling the grassy hillocks beyond the gypsy encampment. She walked and walked, with no real destination, but very much hoping Wesmorlyn would meet her, for she had questions for him. Lyulph Randell's admission that Lady Hannah was infatuated with him, and that she was chasing after him in a most unladylike manner, was disturbing. Having met her at the ball, Charlotte had formed an image in her mind of the girl that did not accord well with the kind of young lady who would follow or try to entrap a gentleman into marriage, as he implied she was doing.

Perhaps Wesmorlyn would have found something out to help the puzzle pieces fall into place. At this moment it was all mysteries and no clues.

And yet as much as she needed to speak with the earl, she was troubled by her tenuous friendship with him. Perhaps it would be easier if he would just use empty flattery and obviously worship her as Mr. Randell did. Instead he kept trying to understand her, and how was that possible when she didn't understand herself? She clearly was not ready for marriage, which was no surprise, since she had formed the resolution not to marry, or at least not to marry the earl. And yet his kisses had left her trembling. Why? What was different about him from his stiff demeanor in the ballroom? Why did the handsome and flattering Mr. Randell not affect her in the same way?

All she knew was that she thought of Wesmorlyn constantly, drawn by something strong and comforting in his demeanor, and yet repelled by the other side of that, an inflexibility that irritated her free-spirited self. When he did let loose his natural self he was overwhelmingly enticing, exciting, attractive, but that happened so seldom. He would briefly reveal how wonderful he could be, then he seemed to box up that uninhibited side of himself and return to being the stuffy, judgmental prig of the ballroom.

The sun warmed her, and she untied her bonnet and pulled it off, letting her hair come loose from its pins and tumble down her back as she strolled. She had walked a long ways from the gypsy camp, strolling in the direction Wesmorlyn always came from. As she topped a hill, she saw a figure walking alone. It was the earl, and he had just crested a far hill with his shirt and jacket undone. He was thinking deeply as he strode, a frown on his regular features, his hair wildly tousled and his shirttails fluttering in the breeze, revealing the smooth golden skin of his chest and abdomen. He was powerfully built, with sharply defined bones and sculpted muscles.

She stopped, riveted by the sight. He was always so tightly buttoned and done up. She had thought him a prig, with not a natural bone in his body. This picture of him, distracted, loosely striding with an open gait, his clothes rumpled, completely overturned any lingering impression she might have had of him as controlled and self-conscious.

He looked up, and their eyes met across the distance.

Chapter 17

HIS MIND clouded by worry, Wesmorlyn strode to the crest of a hill and looked up, finally, to see where he was. That was when he first saw Charlotte. She stood on a hill a ways away, staring at him. The wind lifted her golden curls into a tangle, and her lithe body swayed in the breeze as if she was a beautiful flower in a meadow; she was more lovely than the most exquisite and sought-after London diamond, and with a heart and mind that he found endlessly fascinating, bewildering, infuriating, and utterly captivating. Both of them stood for a long minute staring. Then, as if they were magnets irresistibly drawn by the force of nature, they quickly went toward each other and met in the waist-high grass of the lonely meadow at the bottom of the hill. Compelled by a greedy yearning that had not left him since their last kiss, Wesmorlyn took Charlotte in his arms and kissed her, feeling the softly pouted lips against his and the seductive litheness of her form against his body.

Her hands sought his chest and touched his naked skin, sending radiating shivers through him. A wave of dizziness drove him to his knees before her and he took her down, enfolding her body in his arms, every sensible urge of his brain, every nagging little voice that tugged at his conscience dispelled with the rush of connecting emotion and bodily sensation. It was overwhelming to feel his heart and mind come together, and her acceptance, the readiness she displayed to kiss him and hold him and touch him, heightened the new sensations he was experiencing.

Her bonnet was crushed and she laughed and tossed it to the wind as he pushed her wild blonde curls away from her face and stared into her sky blue eyes.

She stilled beneath him and her laughter died. "Wes, what is it?" she asked, one hand to his cheek. "You look so fierce, so—"

But he smothered her words with another kiss and she wrapped her arms around him, kneading his shoulders and arms. Her heartbeat was strong. The scent of her hair and the tender skin beneath his tongue and lips made his body thrum with desire. Dizzy with hunger, he lost himself to every sensible thought and for once in his life just felt his body and a strange, intoxicating joy that had nothing to do with the future, nothing to do with his hopes and plans, but just emanated from that very moment and the sun on his back and the woman beneath him. She touched his soul, challenging every firm belief, every thought, giving him a sense that life was just beginning and stretched before them, instead of the doomed sense he had always had of trudging inevitably toward the grave and the reward beyond.

Charlotte, caught off balance by his wordless physical greeting, was swept along on the tide and soon could think of nothing but this man expressing the yearning she had seen over and over in his eyes. This moment might never come again. With every tender kiss and every caress, he was asking something, and she answered by releasing her tightly controlled craving for physical contact.

Pushing his shirt and jacket down off his shoulders, she marveled at the enticing sinew and hewn muscle. His upper body was chiseled like a sculpture, hard and sleek and warm beneath her hands. As he shivered with excitement, he pushed eagerly at her clothing, tugging at the unfamiliar feminine garments, so she helped him, shedding her outer pieces of clothing in a shameless and abandoned freedom that was exhilarating.

The sun beat down on them and the breeze that tousled the deep grasses within which they were sheltered swept over their heated skin; whatever happened, this sweet moment was for the two of them an exploration, a chance to see what it was that drew them together repeatedly. Her garters had come undone and she kicked off her stockings, slid off her petticoat, and began to unbutton the fall of his breeches as he pulled off his boots and tossed them aside.

His breathing was raspy and harsh, and his heart pounded as, propped on one elbow, he watched her fingers undo his buttons. He met her eyes, a question deep within the brown depths of his. In answer, she kept undoing, and as he rose slightly, pushed his breeches down over his slim hips, gazing steadily and with quickening breath as his penis sprang out, just as hard and sleek as his muscles, rising triumphant and lusty from a mass of brown curls. He awkwardly shed the breeches, kicking them away into the grass to rest in a tumbled heap over his boots, and knelt before her.

She had no fear. With trembling fingers she touched the fascinating length, remembering her affair with Dieter, her dancing master. He was only twenty, and she just fifteen when she lost her virginity. He was shy and gentle and she had seduced him shamelessly; she remembered the hurried meetings, the attic room she had taken him to, the secrets she had hugged to herself as a charm against the all-pervasive power of her uncle and her rebellion against it. Their lovemaking had been fumbled hurried affairs, enjoyed more as a strike against her Aunt Adele and Uncle Nikolas's dour rule and the tensions that seethed in the house than for any physical pleasure she may have wrung from each event.

But this—being with Wesmorlyn in the brilliant English sun, studying his body, wondering what it would feel like to make love with him—this was completely different. She was not a child any more, though even at fifteen she had been headstrong and had known exactly what she was doing.

She stared up at him, examining his flushed face; his whole body quivered with restrained passion as he wordlessly watched her fingers stroke him, stirring him to thicken and lengthen. Then she rose and knelt in front of him, clad only in her chemise, and put her arms around his neck, gazing steadily into his eyes as she kissed his lips.

"Charlotte," he moaned, "We must not—"

"Shhh," she murmured and pulled him down beside her, her dress beneath them as protection from the prickly yellowing grass. "Don't say a word."

"But what shall I do?"

"You should follow your deepest desires."

He kissed her then, and ran his hand up under the short skirt of her chemise, feeling the tender skin of her thighs and bottom, cupping and fondling, exploring as if he had never touched a woman before. And in turn she touched him, running her hand along the hard edge of his hip, feeling the jutting hipbone, trailing her fingers down to the dark hair at his groin and tickling it with her fingers, feeling his stomach muscles spasm and flex.

But she felt a growing impatience as his fingers delayed, moving so very slowly to the juncture of her thighs that she thought she would go mad from the suspense. Then, slowly, his fingers eager and fumbling, he touched her, and she spread her legs, inviting his intimate touch. She kissed him deeply, suckling his tongue, laving his lips.

When he finally slipped one finger into her, her whole body rocked at the sensation and he withdrew immediately, murmuring an apology, but she took his hand and guided it back, whispering that she liked it very much, and that he shouldn't stop. Her movements meant she liked it, she explained, feeling faintly foolish that she had to tell him that, but not ashamed or apologetic.

She softly closed her hand around his penis and felt how much it had thickened. Her breath coming faster, she whispered, "Let me feel it."

"Feel it?"

Impatient, she pushed him off her and rolled him onto his back, then moved to straddle him. This was where she preferred to be anyway, she thought, looking down at him as she slowly, teasingly, lowered herself over him and rubbed softly against the thick knob, relishing the gush of warmth from the tip and shifting her hips to rub, wetting his length with their mingled juices and quivering through her whole body with desire.

Perspiration had beaded on his forehead and his upper lip, and he closed his eyes, spanning her hips with his broad hands and digging his fingers into her waist. A shudder of lust ripped through his body and he pulled her down onto his shaft, and in one swift movement had thrown her on her back and begun to stroke eagerly, suddenly demanding.

Astonished but not unwilling to be taken so enthusiastically, she gasped and spread wider, receiving his length with some pain but more pleasure. His powerful thrusting took her close to some quavering aching fulfillment, but with a roar of carnal pleasure he released and his body jolted with orgasmic fury as he deepened his movements, burying himself inside of her and holding her tight as he collapsed on top of her, kissing her neck as he stilled.

All very well, but she was left with no such satisfaction.

"Ah, but we are not done, not nearly," she whispered in his ear, shifting to feel him better. His size had diminished some as had his stiffness, and yet that actually aided the pleasure she was seeking. She urged him with soft movements and kisses to help her, and without seeming to understand, he was willing enough; he kissed her deeply and began to move, thrusting with renewing eagerness, swelling and thickening with astonishing speed.

She stretched and wrapped her legs around him, taking him deeply into her until she could feel the pressure begin to build toward some distant and yet attainable goal. With trembling hands he stripped her of her chemise and she lay naked under him, his male heat competing with the brilliant sunshine for dominance. She cried out as he took her close, and he paused, but she dug her heels into his buttocks and pulled him closer, begging wordlessly for more of him. He responded with fervor until she felt it rise, the tension, so close, and then it burst over her in a shower of sensation, flooding her being with fiery delight.

For one long moment time stopped, and she felt deep within herself an innate knowledge that she could, if she so chose, in her moment of elation, give over to him all of her werewolf capacity, but she swiftly turned away from that choice, shifting slightly, concentrating instead on her own needs and wants. The moment passed, and she knew then that she would never give away a part of herself that existed deep within her soul, the latent werewolfism that only lay dormant in a woman's body, ready to be given to her sons.

He didn't stop, and the tension quickly built up again; a second crashing wave of ecstasy rolled over her, rocking her body to the small of her back. He thrust deeper and finally released with a guttural cry of fulfillment.

She felt like laughing and crying, knowing that never in all her years, first with her brief experience of having a lover and then on her own, exploring the female heart of her sexuality, had she experienced such a deep sense of release and glorious bliss. As it dwindled, it left her feeling peaceful, drained, and yet oddly energized.

He had rolled off of her and lay at her side, sated and deeply breathing, almost asleep. But he opened his eyes and gazed at her, then reached out and cupped her chin, trailing a thumb over her lips. "I'm so happy, Charlotte. And deeply grateful."

She smiled over at him and curled provocatively close to his body. "You can thank me best by doing that again, only this time—"

"Have a little mercy! I don't think I can do that again for a while," he said, with a weak smile.

"No, I suppose not," she said with a delirious giggle.

"I'm so glad our first time was together. We'll always have this memory."

She almost stopped breathing and propped herself up on her elbow, looking into his dark eyes. The long grass around them fluttered and bent in the breeze, the sound like waves washing on the shore. "Do you mean that was your very first time making love?"

He kissed her chin, touching her dimple with his tongue. "Of course," he said. "When I was a student, there were girls in town who were ready and willing to make themselves available. Other fellows took advantage, but I always knew I would wait to do that with the woman I was going to marry."

Marry. The word resounded in her brain, chasing down the notion that it was his first time, while it was not hers. *First things first.* "Wes," she said, then took a deep breath and continued, "that was not my first time."

It was a terrible blow to him, she could tell, but he said not a word. His expression was solemn, but not stiff.

As she curled close to his naked body she told him about her youthful rebellion against her uncle's strictness, and poor Dieter, sent away for his dalliance with her, but even more for how he had mindlessly acquiesced to her plan to run away together.

"I understand," he said, carefully, stroking her hair back from her face. He gazed into her eyes and trailed one finger down her neck to her collarbone. "I promise I'll never hold against you your youthful indiscretion."

She examined his expression carefully; there was no sign of reproach, though his words had made her pause for a moment. She had had to quell the first tart retort that came to her tongue, which was that she did not regret it even now, and did not feel it to be an indiscretion, but rather the natural rebellion of a high-spirited girl kept too confined. And yet she knew that many men of his status and makeup would have reviled her for her offense against morality. She put her arms around him and touched his back, running her hands up until . . . she felt between his scapula where there ought to have been a tracery of his spine. She gasped and felt, touching some kind of bone and tissue. "What is that, Wes?"

He smiled and said, "My little secret. It seems we both have secrets."

"And yours is . . . ?"

He stood, blotting out the sun, and shrugged; slowly, with startling grace, wings unfolded from his back and spread. Great, gauzy wings, the sun beaming through the pearly silken structure that was supported by thin bony extensions.

Wordless and gasping for breath, she stared. He was beautiful, his naked body a golden, muscular contrast to the ethereal splendor of his astounding wings. "You're an angel!"

"Well, not exactly," he said, his expression growing serious.

"Can you fly?"

He nodded.

She leaped to her feet and jumped up and down, clapping. "Let me see you!"

His heart pounded as he watched her small breasts bob enticingly, her slim figure perfectly pale in the glorious sunshine but for one small mole near her sharp collarbone. Sinuous curves, marble-pale skin, rosy, peaked nipples jutting upward, the soft, downy hollow at the juncture of her thighs: if he thought too much about what had just happened, he would become aroused all over again. He may never have experienced sexual fulfillment with a woman, but his own body was familiar to him, arousal an old challenge, a demon to be wrestled and defeated. This time instead of defeating it he had allowed his desire to have fulfillment, and now they were wed, in his own heart; she was his wife, and he was overwhelmed with joy. He could even forgive her sexual experience with another man. His wings beat slowly and the lift, when it came, was controlled. He took two giant steps on tiptoe and soared straight up, swooped down over her head, and then landed behind her.

She whirled and bounced up and down, her blue eyes round with amazement. She clasped her hands together under her chin. "How I wish I could fly! It must be thrilling!"

"I never realized how much I glory in it until these last few days. I think I was ashamed to love it so, but I do."

"How could you not love it? It is glorious. *You're* glorious." She smiled at him and held out her hands. "I too have a secret, though, other than my past experience with Dieter."

"Oh?" he said, coming to her and wrapping her in his arms, folding his great wings around her too. It created a sheltered world with just the two of them encased in the pearly, luminous cocoon, the sun glimmering through with hazy warmth. He kissed her then, reveling in the sweet urgency of her ardent response.

If it could only stay like this, if he could shelter her from the world, he thought, feeling the building passion, he wouldn't care another moment about anything in her past. Outside of this meadow the world awaited, though, and her unconventionality went bone deep. And yet he was committed now, forever. He had sworn an oath that his first sexual experience would be with his wife, and so she would be. But how would they go on? Could he teach her to restrain her inappropriate wildness? She must learn to subjugate her will to his or there would be no peace in their home.

He set all that aside and concentrated on Charlotte, and her radiant face uplifted to his. "What is your other secret?" he murmured.

Shyly, she said, the pearly glow of sunshine making her blue eyes shimmer with opalescent light, "My family has long been . . . well, I know you know about Lyulph Randell and accept him as a friend. Our family has the same curious history."

"What?" he cried, not understanding at first. But then, as he saw her expression turn serious, the shock hit him in his gut and he released her, staggering back, his wings folding swiftly to protect themselves between his scapula in reflexive action. And yet she couldn't mean what it sounded like, she couldn't possibly . . . they couldn't be . . . his mind reeled.

"We are werewolves," she said, frowning and covering her nakedness. "Or at least the von Wolfram men are all werewolves, and the women, well, we . . . we pass that on to our sons." She watched him, puzzlement in her blue eyes. "What's wrong?"

He shook his head and stared at her, her nakedness a reminder of his own lack of control and sexual gluttony in her arms. He had been seduced utterly by her animalistic abandon to discard all of the prudent planning and self-restraint of his entire adulthood. He had known her barely two weeks and every carefully laid plan and closely held tenet of his life lay in ruins around him.

Werewolves! Horror filled him, crowding out every other thought and feeling. She was of a werewolf family, and he had done the unthinkable. Their tainted blood made them walk the fine line just above the abyss of eternal damnation, and he had fornicated with her, joining their bodies in lusty abandon, dangling his family's only hope of redemption above that deadly abyss with no regard.

He was devastated. He collapsed on the ground and drew his knees up to his forehead. What would become of him now? In four hundred years of living on neighboring estates, no Wesmorlyn had ever married nor had children with a Randell, and yet, with all his good intentions he had broken the most sacred of vows every Wesmorlyn son made his father, never to contaminate himself. He had been less reserved than his own little sister and had allowed this wolf-woman to devour his good sense with her fevered attraction.

He looked up at her; her expression betrayed shock and anguish, but he had no reassuring words to offer. What would become of them? They could never make love again, for he had sworn not to mingle his bloodline with that of a werewolf. He struggled to his feet, weariness overwhelming him.

"I never guessed, though I should have," he said, feeling bile rise in his throat at the thought of the danger he had been toying with. Revulsion twisted through him. "Your tainted blood makes you attractive," he whispered, still aching for her, still wanting her with a treacherous yearning. "Like flames, you and your people are hypnotically beautiful, and wickedly perilous. I never guessed, not once. And Christoph?"

She watched him, all of the joy gone from her lovely face. "Of course. He's my brother; Christoph is a werewolf."

"And responsible for the attack on the gypsy girl?"

Her expression darkened, the blue of her eyes becoming smoky and her chin rising. "No! *Never!*"

"Do you know for certain? Can you vouch for him?"

"I don't need to. You do not understand my brother one bit," she said, her accent coarsening in her anger. "Though he has suffered heartbreak in his life and has faced terrible things no man should have to face, he is still the finest, most principled man in existence. And I am including you among those over which he is superior, sir!" She shivered and began methodically to dress, frowning at grass stains on her dress and bundling her unused stays and stockings into a tight ball. "I thought I could trust you," she said, her words ground out between clenched teeth. She would not meet his eyes. "I thought you would understand, being different. I thought finally I had found someone with whom I could just be myself."

He didn't believe that for one second. She had never trusted him, never fully relied on his judgment and constancy. "If that was true why did you not tell me before we made love? Charlotte—"

"Don't speak to me. I was right all along. You are a coldhearted prig, with no more human emotion than . . ." She paused and finally looked at him. "Human emotion. Why should I expect that, since you're not even human, are you?"

A deep freeze had taken hold of him and was stiffening his limbs, making even his face expressionless, he feared. "Yes, I am human," he said carefully.

"How can that be? Half angel, half man?"

"It is a long and complicated story," he said, on a sigh. He swiped his hand over his face, weariness shuddering through him.

"Then it is best not told, is that true? For then you would have to linger in my tainted presence and suffer my perilous attraction," she said, resentment in every line of her body and every word that dropped from her lips like shards of ice.

Patiently, he said, "You don't understand, Charlotte, how long I have labored to raise my family up to be worthy, and how in one afternoon . . ." He couldn't go on. He didn't want to hurt her, but the truth was that she would be the death of his ambitions for redemption for his family in their generation. The damage may have been done already, and he could not even right the immorality in which he had indulged by marrying her. Though he had felt them to be wed, joining with her in that intimate union was unthinkable now.

His heart throbbed with a swift ache of fear. Had they already made a child? Had he been tricked into creating that unknown and unknowable creature, a half-breed of the wolf blood and the humanus angelus? While he had thought her his future bride, it hadn't mattered if she became pregnant. But now, knowing what she was, seeing clearly for the first time how he had been drawn in and used, he was furious.

And yet she was staring at him with heartbreak in her lovely eyes and he realized in that instant that there had been no intent to soil him. She hadn't known, of course, what he was, just as he had not known what she was.

"I never want to see you again," she whispered, her words carried up on a breeze.

He held out one hand to her in a gesture of peace. "Come, Charlotte, don't be so melodramatic."

She laughed, a sharp bark of sound in the quiet day. "Melodramatic?" She clutched at her gown, struggling to keep it on since it was still undone. But she retained every scrap of her dignity as she drew herself up and said, "You are an angel and despise the fact that I am of the werewolf blood. I think we have the very definition of melodrama here, the recipe perfect, the circumstance enviable." Her tone rose, and hysteria seeped into the laughter. "We have made love, or what I thought was making love but was clearly, to you, just an insufferable allurement, a trap set to drag you down into the filth and muck within which my family roils endlessly."

"I didn't mean that."

"Yes, you did," she said, calming. A light breeze drifted down the hillside and teased her curls into movement. She stood, proud and perfectly still, staring at him. "Yes, you meant that. And that is the tragedy of it. To be so unfeeling and yet imagine yourself compassionate, to be so judgmental and yet think yourself honorable. You are unspeakably revolting. I meant what I said. I never want to see you again." She turned to walk away, but then turned back, slowly, not meeting his eyes, but just staring down at the grassy patch where they had lain in their loving embrace. "I may never know what has been behind this odd episode of Eleanor Dancey and Lyulph Randell, but I deeply feel that Eleanor is not good for Fanny. My poor sister feels no connection and thinks herself at fault. My shame is that it was my choice to bring her here; my decision has led to all of this unhappiness. But at least I have learned a lesson and been humbled. England is poisonous to us all, I think, and so we'll take our filthy selves away, back to Germany, back home, where we are valued and loved."

With that she whirled and ran, her golden hair fluttering in the breeze and her abandoned, broken straw hat tumbling after, chasing her. He had no heart to stop her and nothing to say. He picked up the hat. She topped the distant hill and looked back, once, before disappearing down the other side.

Wesmorlyn looked down at the trodden grass where they had lain and made love. It was over.

Chapter 18

LYULPH RANDELL, as he strode over the moor, growled in fury under his breath, feeling the wolf rise in him, restrained only by the sunlight that kept him human. He needed to either vent his ire, or contain it. Mother Sarah had been right about where Wesmorlyn and Charlotte were, and Lyulph had found them with little trouble, even though they were some distance from the gypsy encampment. The sight would haunt him forever, perhaps. The moment he had crested the hill and seen Wesmorlyn and Charlotte together, in the meadow—she naked, gorgeous and gloriously alive and he not deserving of such passionate bounty—he knew she belonged to him body and soul.

He had been unsure of his path, wondering if he had made a terrible mistake in deserting his original plans, but now the fierce bite of jealousy had sunk its teeth into him like a parasite and would not abate. Charlotte von Wolfram was his mate. He must separate her from Wesmorlyn and convince her of her destiny, which was to unite with him and bond to the depth that only another of the wolf blood was capable.

And she must *never* be with Wesmorlyn again. He kicked

at a rock with his booted foot, wanting to howl with rage, but he strode on, topping another rough tor. He should never have let it go so far, nor listened to anything but his own instinct. Charlotte's most fertile time was fast approaching. He had been able to tell the moment he had seen her again at Morwenna's cottage; any sexual contact she had in that period of days would absolutely end in bearing a child.

A child. It must be *his* child. He stopped, took in a deep breath and let it out slowly, calming his heart rate and tamping down his fury, containing it with ruthless will. Long ago he had learned the bitter lesson that allowing his most dramatic emotions free expression would only garner contempt and disappointment among his peers. As unwolflike as it was, restraining his natural impulses was necessary.

He must think rationally. If he was the one to impregnate Charlotte, then he would be the one to whom she would be bound for life. That had been the way of their people since time immemorial. Even if she was unsure, bearing their child would give him a say in what she did and where she went; by law the child would be his, and a woman like her would never stray from her baby.

He sniffed the air, discerning myriad scents; the gypsy encampment was east of him, downwind, and yet he could still smell their fire and the stewpot. Horse dung, laundry drying in the sun, fecund women: all were other smells from the gypsies. But the stream that divided his property was nearby, and with the freshwater scent that teased his nostrils was something else, the smell of sex and sweat. *Wesmorlyn.* Why the earl did not flutter home on his pretty wings was not a mystery to Lyulph.

Charlotte. Drawn by the sight of them together in the lonely meadow, Lyulph had crept close and had seen her lithe, pale, perfect body intermittently through the tall grasses, urging the stuffy earl on to sexual feats that would certainly be beyond most males. It had made him hungry just to watch— her slender back arched, her inviting bottom rhythmically moving—and with a throbbing erection filling his breeches it had taken every fiber of his being to restrain natural urges that would require her body devoted to his needs to sate. That time would come. Soon. Self-control would be rewarded.

Lyulph had to hand it to the earl, he had kept up with her, almost. Now all of his energy would be required just to walk out of there. He would need to recover before flitting off to Wesmorlyn Abbey.

And there he was; Lyulph spotted the earl sitting on the crumbling stone bridge that crossed the stream. Now he would find out if Mother Sarah, his faithful servant, had been right after all; had the earl and Charlotte's enormous dissimilarity in personality taken its toll and made the rift he had witnessed in London even wider, into a vast, unfathomable chasm? From the scene of sexual excess he had witnessed it did not appear so. He had desperately wanted to challenge Wesmorlyn, but that was a fight that he might win, or might not.

And regardless of the outcome of the battle, an open challenge would be the end of any hope he might have of taking Charlotte not only bodily, but her mind and heart, too, for though some women liked men fighting over their favors, she didn't appear to be one of them. He believed he still had a chance to attract her, despite her unexpected resistance to even the bewitchment Morwenna had been inflicting upon her group.

Mother Sarah had been firm in her belief that it would end badly between Wesmorlyn and Charlotte. But if the gypsy was wrong, and the prophesied rift had not occurred, then he would need to solve the problem himself. He would tell Wes her family secret and see if that would make her abhorrent to him, for he was getting desperate and must separate them somehow.

He sauntered toward the earl. The hairs at the base of his skull stood on end, and it was an ordeal not to bare his teeth in aggression, but he forced the snarl into a smile. "Well, well, well," he said. "What are you doing so casually on my property, Wes? Out strolling, so far from the Abbey?"

Wesmorlyn scrambled to his feet. "Randell! I will be on my way."

"For heaven's sake, calm yourself."

"No, I'll go."

Lyulph stopped and examined Wesmorlyn's face and attitude. It was not that of one glorying in the sexual conquest of a fulfilling lover. His shoulders were slumped and he was slovenly, not the prim and perfect earl he always was. His shirt and jacket were undone, his boots scuffed, and his chestnut hair tumbled over his forehead and lifted in the breeze. "She told you, didn't she?" he said without thinking, sure of his conclusion.

"What?"

"I saw the countess just a while ago storming across the moor," he fabricated. "The two of you were just together and she told you."

A wary expression clouded Wesmorlyn's eyes. "What are you talking about?"

Impulse had led Lyulph so far, and now it must be his plan for the moment. "I know about you and Charlotte. Mother Sarah, the gypsy queen, has told me that you and she have been meeting on the moor. I didn't see it as my business to interfere, but I was frankly surprised. I thought you better than that, better than skulking around in shadows spying and taking advantage of a sweet girl like the countess."

"You don't know anything about it!"

"Oh, yes I do," Lyulph said, gaining more assuredness as he watched the earl's eyes. Something had happened after Lyulph retreated, and the countess had told the earl her family secret, which he had not known before. There was just something in Wesmorlyn's slumped shoulders and wary gaze that told him it was true. "Countess Charlotte told you. Don't deny it; I can see it on your face. She told you her family secret."

"You know about them?"

"Of course I do," Lyulph replied, carefully watching his nemesis's expression. "I knew the moment they entered the ballroom at Lady Harroway's. One of the wolf blood always recognizes another immediately. My hackles rose at Count Christoph's entrance."

"So you knew all along that she was of that same kind."

"Well of course, *she* is of the same blood as her brother. And she told you that today, didn't she?"

"Yes," he said, hanging his head.

It was unbearably funny to watch Wesmorlyn, the self-righteous prig, now faced with his worst nightmare, union with a werewolf family. He had thought that if the earl found out about the von Wolfram legacy he would see the opportunity that existed, of joining his unique heritage with that of a werewolf female. It was enthralling, the idea of such a union . . . at least to Lyulph. Lady Hannah, the insipid little angel girl, had little attraction to him but as a tool toward revenge on her family and mother to a new breed of human. What would their children be? It had given him chills of anticipation just wondering. And yet he had given up that plan for a chance at the enticing Charlotte. If he could just win her, the trade would be worth it.

"Why didn't you tell me, Randell?" Wesmorlyn said, his voice thick with misery.

"It wasn't my secret to tell, Wes, old man. But it must have been a blow to you, given how you have always thought of werewolves as lower than the serpent that slithers across the rocks."

"I've never treated you badly," the earl said, sharply.

"Not openly, but it was in your eyes. You hold us in disgust."

"It's not disgust I feel," Wesmorlyn said. He opened his mouth to speak, paused, but then said, "But my family, we're . . . we have other desires and aims than the earthy and corporal. You indulge yourself, with no restraint." His chin went up, and his expression became disdainful. "How can we help but conclude that our family line must not be corrupted by yours? Don't forget, Lyulph, I knew you as a youth," he said pointing one finger. "You may have learned discretion as you have matured, but I saw you in all of your excess."

Lyulph nodded. "I knew it. You never said a word, but my women, the drinking, the fun I had . . . it was all a sign of how soiled I was by my so-called animal impulses."

"The whores and the alcohol," Wesmorlyn said as he shuddered and shook his head. "I'm sorry, Randell, but that is how I feel. You were beneath me, if I am to be honest. I never wanted to say that, and never, by any word, wished you to feel it."

Lyulph restrained himself with great difficulty from launching himself headlong at the imperious earl. "But now you have descended . . . is that it? Is that what is rankling?" He watched Wes's face, and then said, with spiteful sarcasm,

"But I suppose she seduced you, teased you. Was that it? Our kind is corrupt, but attractive, and she seduced you away from your pious perfection with her animal attraction."

"Careful, Randell," the earl said, his voice throaty and harsh.

The truth came to him then in a blinding insight. All their confrontations at school and later, among mutual friends, came back to him in a rush, but with a new explanation. "All that time, at school and after, you and your clique of pure, high-minded friends . . . you *envied* me!" he crowed, and laughed out loud, the harsh sound drifting away on the quickening breeze. "You were jealous of my freedom, and the merriment, all while you toiled away at your books being the perfect student, the perfect little gentleman."

"Never! I would *never* have lowered myself to frolic in the filth with your kind!" Wesmorlyn said, his face suffused with a dull brick color.

Lyulph pushed his face into the other man's. "But now you have! Ah, poor fellow," he mocked, "did she draw you in and subjugate you? She is very beautiful, and very alluring, a tempting little morsel. That is what happened to me in the garden, at the ball, I'm sure you understand now. I was drawn in by her wanton ways; the little trollop enticed me into losing my diffidence."

Wesmorlyn balled his fists, trying to keep down a wave of fury that ripped into him at Lyulph's taunting words. "I would stop talking about her that way now, before I am forced to hurt you."

"Ah, I see. She has dug in more than just her sexual claws. She has burrowed directly to your heart. She's not good enough for you, old man. She's just a little whore. Give her to me," he said with a knowing leer. "I know what to do with her. I'll keep her busy in my bed."

Wesmorlyn's fury boiled and he launched himself off the edge of the bridge at the other man, tackling him to the ground and rolling with him down the embankment into the stream. His hands closed around Lyulph's throat and he throttled him, his vision blurred, everything covered in a haze of red. Even the cold water flowing around him could not cool his rage.

"Stop it you fool," Randell said, struggling to talk. He

flailed out at Wesmorlyn, catching him on the chin and sending him flying back. "Just stop it!" he said, staggering to his
feet and retreating a few yards, dripping wet and disheveled.
"Don't be an idiot."

Wesmorlyn, soaking wet, heaving, and feeling the exhaustion beat him down so much he could not stand, was sick to
his core at this ridiculous compulsion he had to fight Lyulph
whenever they met now. What was wrong with him? He had
never in his life allowed emotion to make his decisions, but
now he was no better than an animal, the way he let anger rule
his actions. He covered his face and let the cold water on his
hands run down and cool his heated cheeks and neck.

"You *know* I'm right," Randell said, clutching at his throat
and coughing. "She's not good enough for you. You can't
marry her, not now, knowing the truth. That's it, isn't it?
That's why you're so upset." He paused and cleared his throat,
taking a deep breath. "What shall you do now about your engagement?" he said, pushing and prodding his rival. "You feel
honor-bound, but you cannot marry her and bring forth the
next generation of Wesmorlyn heirs. A she-wolf countess?
Wolf-angel babies? The thought sickens you, doesn't it?"
Lyulph recovered quickly with another deep shuddering
breath, and straightened. "Tell you what," he said, straightening and watching the earl's red face, "I'll take her off your
hands." He shook off another shower of water and passed his
hand over his hair.

"You say it as if she is a mare you would consider purchasing," Wesmorlyn said, resentfully.

Lyulph shrugged. His dark hair glistened in the brilliant
sunshine and he swiftly restored order to his impeccable
clothes, damp but hardly damaged at all by their scrap. With
a slight smile, he said, "Despite our differences, Wes, I have
always considered you a worthy fellow. Any enmity has never
been on my side. I may have envied you at times, but beyond
that I consider you a valuable neighbor and an ally." With
studied grace, he leaned one hip against the stone bridge abutment and gazed at Wesmorlyn as he struggled to his feet. "I
like Charlotte. She is, perhaps, a little wild and uncouth, and
you can see that she is too willing to succumb to the lusts of
the flesh, but for me that is not such a problem as it is for you.

You are an earl; your countess will be expected to dine with dukes and princes, hostess elegant parties, perhaps even sponsor Lady Hannah's first season. She must meet the Queen. Can you see her doing any of that?"

"No," Wesmorlyn agreed. She was impetuous and headstrong, and yet every fault in her character he would have overlooked, if only she did not possess the fatal flaw; her blood betrayed them both. He couldn't abandon the principles of a lifetime for Charlotte; what would that say about his character? He had sworn to uphold the tradition of his ancestors. No Wesmorlyn could ally him or herself to one of the wolf blood.

And yet, she was not an animal to be traded between them. He met Lyulph's steady gaze, searching his eyes, as he left the stream and waded up the embankment. Did he genuinely care for Charlotte, or was this some kind of charade? Could he bear thinking of them together, seeing them, as he inevitably would if Lyulph and Charlotte wed? Wesmorlyn touched the bruising at the corner of his mouth and winced. "You have a rather good left, there, Lyulph. Better than in our school days."

"I was untrained and undisciplined then. Wild. Unmanageable. I have seen the benefit of harnessing my energy toward a goal."

Chilled, Wesmorlyn watched Randell's green, changeable eyes. There was something behind them, an implacable will that had never been there in his youth when he had been unruly but good-hearted and warm. "It is not my place to discuss the countess's future," he said, stiffly. "Her last words to me after we argued were that she and her brother and sister are going back to Germany, and that is for the best, I believe."

"Really." The other man backed away and bowed, saying, "Take your time recovering, Wesmorlyn. If you need help getting back to the Abbey, the gypsies will loan you a horse . . . for a price. I hope I didn't hurt you too badly."

"No more than I hurt you," he replied.

As Randell walked away, disappearing over the far tor, Wesmorlyn contemplated all that had just occurred. His whole body still registered the shock of Randell's accusation that he was jealous of his freedom and always had been. It couldn't be true, could it? Perhaps it was; seeing Lyulph transform for the first time had been appalling and exhilarating at the same time, and after that his own uniqueness, his wings, had seemed tame and drab by comparison. And Randell's friends had always seemed more exciting and dashing than his own. But now was not the time for morose reflection; something was not quite right and he needed to figure out what it was. He should have asked about Eleanor Dancey while he had the chance, but it was too late now. He supposed he could run after the man and ask, but perhaps there were other ways of getting the information. He didn't think he could bear another moment of Randell's mocking company just then.

With energy renewed by necessity, Wesmorlyn stood and took off his jacket, squeezing the excess water out of it and folding it carefully, then removing his shirt and doing the same, his actions methodical and practiced. Then he shrugged his shoulders and tested his wings. Home was not an impossible distance and the need was great. He would take the chance. His great wings slowly beating, he lifted from the ground and ascended to the blue and golden heavens, becoming, for those on the ground, just another bird soaring overhead.

THE dinner hour had arrived and the homely dining room of the Whip and Wheel coaching inn was full of solitary men eating pasties, pies, and homemade sausages. The taproom across the dreary, narrow hallway was low-ceilinged and dark, and was equally as busy. This was the place where Burgess, the coach driver in Randell's employ, was said to spend his evenings, Wesmorlyn had heard. Smoke from a dozen pipes drifted like fog and men bent their heads together in earnest conversation, much of it in Cornish, the blurred and thick accent buzzing through the hazy pall kept down at head height by the low-beamed ceiling. Bare wood tables lined the walls; seating was confined to benches polished by decades of broadcloth-clad bottoms. Wesmorlyn strolled along, peering through the dimness. Some conversations stopped as he passed, but he did his best to ignore them and slouch convincingly through the room.

Dressed in old clothes discarded by his coachman, he was hoping to be taken as a carter or driver passing through, but clothes alone would not do it. His attitude and speech must convey the correct status. He shoved his hands in his jacket pockets and plastered his unshaven face with what he hoped was a dour expression. It was not as difficult as it would normally have been, because he felt a deep shaft of hopelessness piercing his heart, so he let his emotions show on his face instead of schooling his expression to a bland mildness. The bruise by his mouth helped; he looked like a ruffian who fought regularly.

Though deeply disturbed, he felt truly alive, and could feel the blood pulse through his veins. Even as he tried to defeat it, desire and passion for Charlotte still overwhelmed him, and he didn't know how to eradicate those earthy sensations, or even if he wanted to. Making love with her had taught him lessons that had eluded him in life. His human side was stronger than he had ever been willing to acknowledge. And loving a woman was more than a physical act; it took every bit of him, human and angelic. Corners of his soul that had never been explored were now illuminated with the bright light of self-examination, and he wasn't sure he was proud of what he saw. It was unnerving and enthralling, all at the same time.

But self-knowledge would have to wait. There was a more important task at hand. He must get to the bottom of the mystery of why Randell had lured Charlotte to Cornwall. A lifetime of living in Cornwall must aid him in reproducing the distinct West Country accent, for he would need to be authentically Cornish. He ambled through the barroom.

There, by the standing bar, was the fellow described by Charlotte, his unusual broadness of shoulders, swarthy features, and one drooping eyelid marking him as Burgess, the carriage driver who dropped them in the middle of nowhere. He was alone; he flirted with a comely barmaid and flipped her a coin, which she caught in midair with practiced ease.

"Thou bist handy at that, lass," Wesmorlyn remarked as he approached, broadening his accent, and adopting the mannerisms he knew from a youth spent in the stable, grooming his own horse and listening to the men tell tall tales of their conquests among the local lasses.

"'Ow thee do prate," the young woman said with a saucy wink, eying him favorably in comparison to the swarthy Burgess, and then asking his preference in beverage. He ordered stout, and one for Burgess, too, which won from the man a nod of thanks. But the gratitude was scant and overlaid by a wariness Wesmorlyn knew would be hard to overcome in a West Country fellow.

So he didn't say a thing for a while, just kept refilling their tankards with stout. The noise increased as the dinner hour passed and men began to drink in earnest, and Wesmorlyn felt he must say something or go mad from the smoke and hum of conversation, like a swarm of bees in his ears. The other men in the room avoided Burgess, casting him surly glances or ignoring him, as was their inclination. Wesmorlyn had heard the fellow was not liked by anyone because of his willingness to take offence and beat others up when he was in his cups.

Wesmorlyn's eyes teared from the pipe smoke and his stomach began to rebel against the liberal downing of dark beer. He felt it coming before he knew it, and a mighty belch erupted, relieving the gas building in his stomach. He would have been horrified, except the barmaid just glanced over from her conversation and giggled, and Burgess clinked his tankard against Wesmorlyn's.

Finally, his mood mellowed by gallons of good beer, the coach driver began a guarded conversation with Wesmorlyn, which the earl gradually guided to a conversation about a humorous story he had heard doing the rounds of a couple of young foreign lasses being dropped off in the middle of nowhere as a good lark. He laughed drunkenly, and then hiccupped; the brew had gone to his head, and he would need to keep his wits about him.

"Ar, forrin' lasses they were," Burgess said, with a slow wink.

"Don't tell me tha knowst the tale?"

"Summat," the man said, with a mysterious nod and another wink.

"What zay thee then? Who be th'lasses, and who the

driver?" Wesmorlyn said, employing his thickest accent.
Would Burgess admit his part?

"Hush, naw," Burgess said, but then leaned forward and
continued: "Harkee here, zur and I be trauthful, dedent oy
juzt be the one? T'were twa forrin lasses, and long side
th'road didst dump them, loike to be trash." He chuckled.

Wesmorlyn burned inside at Burgess's gay recitation of
dumping the two girls along the side of the road as if they
were garbage, but he held back his fury, for the driver had not
done it on his own. Why would he have? There must be some
reason behind it, and Lyulph Randell must have had a hand.

So he led the conversation along, letting it weave tipsily,
knowing that too direct a questioning would sober even the
inebriated Burgess. The driver admitted dropping the girls at
a preplanned spot on the way to Bodmin. He didn't know
why, but his master was a deep thinker, and had ordered it so.

And then, Burgess said, glowering, "Bloody minded
bastard."

"Bloody minded? 'Ow zo?"

Burgess, with many pauses to down more beer, drunkenly
related to his captive audience how his employer had a hatred
for one enemy in particular so deep his whole life was bent
to destroying the man, no matter what it took. Wesmorlyn
was puzzled; was he this enemy? And what did any of it have
to do with Charlotte and Fanny?

He cautiously probed for more information. It seemed that
Lyulph Randell was consumed by this hatred, and had hoped
to take away not only the man's sister, but his home and even
his life. Not, the fellow added hastily, that it would be murder. Oh no, his master was a deep thinker, and would certainly not kill the man outright. There were other ways of
destroying a man until he withered away and died or took his
own life. Wesmorlyn, sobered by the awful implications of
what he was hearing, shakily asked who the object of his employer's hatred was, but Burgess, even staggering drunk,
would not give a name. Not that it needed to be spoken.

"Ar naw, whut dost thou care?" the man asked, suspicion
thick in his tone.

Wesmorlyn called for more beer, and the man took a long
drink from the tankard, his whole face disappearing before he

came up for air, foamy ale dripping off his chin. He forgot his suspicion enough to speak on, wending through a long tale of the Witch of Bodmin Moor, who had confused and bewitched many a fair lad into doing her dirty work. Fair of face she was, Burgess confided, but foul of deed. She stole souls, draining the weak and unwary until there was nothing left but a husk, like chaff from wheat.

"Tha'st met her?" Wesmorlyn asked, wondering how to get back to the man's employer and his enemy.

"Ay, harkee, bra aand saucy I be," he said, claiming bravery and impertinence, as he leaned close and exclaimed, his malt-soured breath puffing out the words, "but naw would'st I go to herr, nay matter th'lure, fur she be m'maister's doxy."

Wesmorlyn frowned into the smoky gloom; Burgess claimed he would not respond to her allurements no matter what, for this supposed Witch of Bodmin Moor was Randell's mistress. As well as he knew Lyulph Randell and as much as he had been in his company this last spring and summer, he had heard no word of any mistress in his keeping. Unless a woman who had once resided at Moor Cottage, he thought, with a sick feeling in his stomach, a woman he had heard tell of as Morwenna Maxwell, was she. But then was this the same woman as the one now claiming to be Fanny's mother?

It was confusing and inconclusive. But a few things were certain. Randell had ordered Burgess to dump Fanny and Charlotte by the roadside and had some ulterior motive for doing so. Far from firing the man for the deed, he had rewarded the driver. And if the woman at Moor Cottage was known to him intimately and he had lied about it, then she was certainly not Eleanor Dancey. But why? How did luring Fanny and Charlotte away from London with a false story benefit Randell? Unless, as he now suspected, the entire plot was aimed at Wesmorlyn all along. But still, the plan was hazy and uncertain.

Burgess stood, woozily, wavering on his feet. "Got ta go naw. Big doin's, aand me wid no wits." He put his hand to his head and took a deep breath, trying to sober up.

"Big doings?"

He shuddered drunkenly. "M'maister did zay, I mait be

one whut did that deed, nor mait be Diggory, dedn't I chuse
zo. Pure Diggory . . . haw ist bewitched, und effen he doan
do whut maister zay, he smart's turrible fur it."

Burgess was in no shape to do anything that night, so the
hapless Diggory, that Burgess spoke of as bewitched and
obliged to obey Lyulph Randell, would be forced to do whatever was to be done.

Wesmorlyn watched him leave. Why, he wondered, thunderstruck by the information he had just received, did Lyulph
Randell want him destroyed? He was forced now to believe
that everything, all the plotting and everything that had so far
happened to Hannah, Charlotte, Christoph, Fanny, and even,
likely, the gypsy girl, could be laid at Lyulph Randell's door.
But why? And how?

Questions teemed in Wesmorlyn's logical mind, adding
up to sums he could not calculate. How long had Lyulph Randell been concocting plans to destroy him? For years? Since
they were in school? And was poor Hannah's devastating attraction to him, resulting in her self-destructive and unfathomable behavior, part of the plan?

One thing was clear: the Eleanor Dancey residing at Moor
Cottage was not the real lady, not Fanny's mother. Despite
the terrible terms on which he and Charlotte had parted, he
could not let the von Wolframs suffer, not when he had
knowledge that they needed, and especially since it all
seemed ultimately to be a scheme to destroy *him*; they had
been caught up in it only because of their ill-timed appearance in London. Something was coming to a head. Tonight
was perhaps the night, or tomorrow, but he had to get word to
Charlotte immediately.

"IT is all falling apart around me, I tell you!" Lyulph said,
pacing in the kitchen garden immediately by the back door of
Moor Cottage. Twilight was falling, and the light from the
kitchen window cast a faint buttery glow over the green, lush
herbs that grew in riotous overabundance. "Your witchcraft
isn't working. Charlotte doesn't trust me now; how can I
achieve my goals without her trusting me?"

"And just what are your goals, Lyulph?"

Lyulph stopped pacing abruptly and stared at his mistress, signaled to be watchful by something in her voice, a tone, a hint of asperity or something else. She was not one to toy with, nor to betray, at least not openly. His change in plans had not been communicated to her, for he was sure she would not be sanguine about the adjustment. His deepest fear was that she had her own plans, and had not shared them with him. "What is it, Morwenna? Are you troubled about something?"

"Troubled? No, Lyulph, I am not *troubled*," she said, her voice silky and seductive. "But I wonder if you have been completely frank with me about your plans."

"I've told you everything," he said, carefully, his nostrils flaring. He scented danger. "I cannot have another werewolf family in England; it just will not do. My plan is to drive the von Wolframs from England by disgracing them all."

She simply stared at him, her hypnotic eyes holding his gaze.

"To do that," he went on, compelled by her stare, "I need complete mastery over them. It is imperative that they trust me if I am to thoroughly destroy them. That's why you've been feeding them your potions; I need them wholly in my power."

She just stared at him.

"I've told you over and over; I will not allow another werewolf to settle in England and begin to breed. My family worked for centuries to establish dominance and drive the last of our kind away, fending off every challenge. I am on the very brink of eliminating any threat from Wesmorlyn and forcing Lady Hannah into marriage."

"Then why do you dally with Countess Charlotte?"

Ah, so she had sensed his confusion and ambivalence of the last few days; he must be careful that she not discern his growing need for the countess. There was something about Charlotte von Wolfram that attracted him as no other woman had ever done. Of course the werewolf blood that flowed through both of their hearts was a connection deeper than he had ever thought possible. He hadn't foreseen his feelings, but then he had never met another of his own kind. Charlotte was wild at heart, and he had not been able to get her out of his head since their kiss in the garden in London. That interest had grown into his current obsession. Perhaps Morwenna already felt it, for her senses about such things were heightened during the time of her menses and she had often come close to invading his mind at such a time. Always powerful—to his detriment he had angered her more than once and felt the sting of her abilities—during that time of her cycle she was formidable, her connection to the rhythm of nature intensifying her energy tenfold.

He had to keep her content, and in such a way that she detected no deceit. He took her in his arms, blanking his mind of every thought about Charlotte. Instead he let himself feel Morwenna, and their powerful physical attraction for each other reasserted dominance in the human and sensible part of him. He became fully aware of her lush curves pressed to his body, and experienced a surge of arousal as he bent to kiss her in the shadows of the door overhang. She was his kind of woman, full-bodied, curvaceous, and wide-hipped, bound to the earth through something more than animal instinct. Her dark eyes were clouded with desire as he released her. She sighed and licked her lips.

"Does that convince you, my own bewitching Morwenna?" he said, huskily, his hands sliding down to her waist and around, locking them behind her back and holding her firmly to him. "What I do, I do for us, for our future," he murmured. "I have promised you offspring, children that unite our unique abilities and who will continue our heritage, but first, to protect my legacy, to ensure the fruit of my loins becomes as powerful as I plan, I must use my own abilities to disgrace forever and thus drive the von Wolfram siblings from our shores. *Trust* me!"

She stared up at him. "I do trust you," she said, softly, cupping his cheek with her warm palm. "I trust that you know where your best interest lies. I trust you will be intelligent and not anger me. If you betray me, you must know you will feel my wrath. I will never leave you in peace, and though I am forbidden to kill, I can make you wish for death!" She tightened her grip and pulled his face down to hers. She whispered in his ear, "You have made promises to me, Lyulph Randell, vows to which I will hold you, and I have made my bond with you. Our offspring will be more powerful than either of us could dream. You will marry that little wench, Lady Hannah, and break Wesmorlyn under your heel, and then it will all be ours."

She kissed his ear and nibbled his earlobe. Too late Lyulph felt her slip her tongue into his ear, the poison of her innate cruelty deeply implanted. He pulled back and clapped one hand to his ear, feeling the seething coil of treachery wind into him. "What have you done?" he said on a groan.

She smiled, her eyes darkening to coal. "I have ensured that you will be faithful and do what you have vowed to do, and come back to me," she whispered, her voice a soft and sibilant hiss. "If you betray me, you will feel the sting and be driven mad by it. Unless you remain devoted to me your very soul will drain from you like lifeblood."

He saw, then, the danger in which he had placed himself, but it was too late. Morwenna, cunning, beautiful, and ruthless, was using him as much as he had ever thought he was using her. It was a disaster. "What have I done to deserve such malice?" he moaned.

She ran her fingers down his arm and squeezed his hand. "I feel the change in you, my love. You have become enamored of that despicable little wolfling girl. But I will not have you deny me your seed."

"I never for one moment planned to deny you your wishes," he whined, cringing as her fingernails dug into his palm.

"It was not your plan, but that is how it would have ended. The bowl has told me. Now, I will send that simpering little miss out to you, and you will do what you must. You can depend upon my help only so far. Destroy the family and send them scampering back to Germany before I go mad from having to share a roof and floor with them."

He stood still, trying to think what to do. He could feel the inexorable progress of her poisonous maggot burrowing into him. Morwenna's magic would eventually make him her slave, if he let her, and yet what could he now to defeat her plan? It was already too late, and he must do exactly what she wished or die. Or *was* it too late? The deep pairbond he would create with Charlotte could help him fight the poison, and Mother Sarah could help him the rest of the way. It might be his only opportunity now to keep from being enslaved by the treacherous power of Morwenna, the Witch of Bodmin Moor.

Chapter 19

CHARLOTTE SIDLED out the door, but kept her distance from him.

"Will you walk in the garden with me?" he asked, his tone gentle. Lyulph's mind raced as he tried to imagine how best to escape this new and alarming dilemma.

She looked back into the kitchen, and then met his gaze with her clear, focused, bright eyes. "You and she are in league together, don't even try to deny it," she said, sharply.

"Why would you think that?" he said, putting his hand over his heart. He swallowed, struggling with the confusion that overwhelmed him. Morwenna had him in thrall, the maggot inflicting him with the dreadful curse of mindless obedience, but his heart and body were working to overcome the spell. Her orders were to humiliate the von Wolframs and send them racing back to Germany, but he had other plans. Charlotte von Wolfram, lovely, intelligent, and with the blood of the wolf in her veins, called to him in ways Morwenna, with all her beauty and treachery, could never match.

And now he *needed* Charlotte if he was to escape the curse set within him. Morwenna's poison was already infecting him, and soon he would be nothing but an automaton carrying out her commands. He had one chance, and he must act quickly; he had to convince Charlotte von Wolfram to believe him and rescue him from his fate. He could not submit to being ruled by Morwenna. Death by her horrible spell would be preferable, for he was beginning to understand how dark her arts were and how ambitious she was.

"All right," he said, looking over his shoulder. He could see movement in the kitchen, shadows that altered the faint light from the oil lantern. Hellebore slunk out of the door, throwing himself down in the gloom under a shrub and licking one paw, pretending to be an ordinary house cat. "Her name is Morwenna Maxwell, and it's true," he murmured. "She and I were in league together to try to send you and your brother and sister away, because I had plans to marry Lady Hannah."

"You *did* lure that poor girl away!" Charlotte hissed, her face getting pink with agitation.

"It was a mistake, and I knew it. I changed my mind and sent her back! I swear to you," he whispered, the words tumbling over each other like polished stones in a stream, "that I did not know the extent of Morwenna's treachery." He reached for her hands but she snatched them away and put them behind her back.

"Morwenna Maxwell. So she is not Eleanor Dancey, but a witch?"

How she had guessed that Morwenna was a witch, he couldn't imagine. Perhaps that explained why she was not befuddled by the herbal potions his mistress had been feeding them all. Charlotte was supposed to be mindlessly obedient and malleable by then, but her clear, skeptical gaze told him she had eluded enchantment. "Yes," he admitted, forced to tell some of the truth, "a very dangerous one. But when I told you she was Fanny's mother and sent you down here it was not to put you in her clutches, it was simply to get you safely out of London. I had no idea she had her own plans."

"I wish I could believe that."

"It's true! But I was wrong to go along with her plans. I didn't understand how dangerous she would become." He glanced up, watching through the window for her shadow. Could she see him? Could she hear him, even? He didn't think so. Not yet, anyway, but soon unless he got away and sealed his bond with Charlotte. He clasped his hands together before her in a gesture of supplication. "Please believe me; I only wish to help you now."

"Are you telling me the truth?"

"Yes. *Yes*!" he cried, softly.

"Why should I believe you?"

He gazed at her lovely face, the tender lips drawn down in distrust. "I don't know," he admitted. "All I can tell you is the truth." He stared at her. "I love you, and I want to protect you."

Hellebore got up and darted into the cottage through the open kitchen door.

She took a deep breath and shook her head. "Even if I believed you, that wouldn't change how *I* feel, though. I don't love you. Your witch mistress thinks my senses are dulled with her herbal poison," she murmured, "but they aren't. She tried to bewitch *all* of us, but we've dealt with such things before. Her potions are as nothing to us. Tonight Christoph, Fanny, and I will be taking Tamara out of here. Then you and Wesmorlyn can continue whatever contemptible battle you have going. However this struggle for power ends between you, I don't care, just leave us alone."

So she had figured out that she was merely a pawn in a scheme that went deeper than her family's involvement. But everything had changed for him, and now it was a blow to hear her say she was leaving England. His situation had become desperate now that he had lost Morwenna's trust. If Charlotte would not bond with him and strengthen him, he would have to leave England or submit to becoming a mindless slave.

"You're not going to marry Wesmorlyn then?" he asked, remembering the flashes of her naked body in the meadow, the jealousy and anger he had struggled with, and the glory of knowing Wesmorlyn was such an ass as to toss away this breathtaking girl. Now he had the confirmation that she had broken irrevocably with the earl. One night with her and he would be whole again. His future would open before him like a glorious vista of power and strength and supremacy. Desperation lanced through him, sharp and fierce. "Are you?" he urged, when she hesitated.

"No. He's made his choices, and his precious sense of his 'duty' to his family's destiny comes before anything else. I told him the truth about the von Wolframs, and he seems to think that I'm soiled with the tainted blood of my forefathers." She tipped her chin up. "I will not apologize for being what I am."

Impressed by her fortitude, he saw finally the difference between a woman of strength and a woman of menace. Charlotte and Morwenna. His breath caught in his chest; he deeply admired her, and his path, newly minted, seemed even more right than he had thought. She would be his. She might not see his reason yet, and she may be too distracted to give herself over to him completely, but she *would* be his.

But his time was dwindling. "Listen to me," he said, leaning toward her and speaking hurriedly. Hellebore was yowling inside, and Lyulph had never figured out how much the cat understood, and how much he could relate to his mistress. "Instead of leaving England, marry *me*! Come away with me tonight and we'll be bound, in old handfast tradition, and then by the church as soon as I can get a license."

She reared back in surprise. "What are you saying?"

"Shh!" he said, putting one finger up to his mouth. "Be quiet! Come with me," he said, grasping her hand. "We'll defeat them all by combining our blood, tonight! I, too, have been made to feel like dirt by Wesmorlyn, and together we could raise a generation of werewolves that would defeat the 'humanus angelus,' as his kind have styled their precious selves." Now he had risked everything. She had fire in her veins, just like he did, and together they would overcome magic and angels.

"You must be joking," she said, jerking her hand away with an incredulous expression on her face.

It was as if she had poured a bucket of cold water over his head, to see the distaste on her face. "No, of course I'm not joking."

"You would marry me to make me into a vessel for your own despicable plans for domination? You've taken leave of your senses. Good luck to you, Lyulph Randell," she said, turning away, "but as for myself, I'm going home to Wolfram Castle."

"Wait," he said, grabbing her arm and pulling her back.

"Let go of me!" she said, wrenching her arm out of his grasp.

He had no choice; if Morwenna heard and came, he would be dead for this desperate act of mutiny. He grabbed Charlotte and yanked her hard. She lost her balance, tumbling into his grasp, and he pulled her to him, putting his hand over her mouth. She struggled, trying to bite his fingers, but he was done being gentle. She was going to see sense or he would make her do so. He pulled and tugged her down the garden path toward the gate, even as she thrashed about. Her squirming only fired his determination; he dragged her away from the cottage.

Once through the gate, out of earshot of Morwenna and almost to his mount, tied up to a tree on the other side of the stable, he threw her over his shoulder and carried her. She beat on his back with her fists and howled, screaming at him to let her go, and though he knew he would have bruises from it, he relished her fury, determined to tame her and turn that fire into passion before long. He had seen how she could be, free and wild, and now he would experience it for himself, claiming any bit of her that still yearned for Wesmorlyn. He would make her over into his mate.

"TAMARA," Christoph whispered, coming to the door of her tiny chamber. "Are you feeling any better?"

No answer.

He daren't go any closer. "Tamara?"

Still no answer, and yet he could make out her form on the couch. It was imperative that he talk to her though, because neither he nor Charlotte were willing to leave Moor Cottage without her, and they were determined to leave that very night.

He felt the pull of her as he heard her soft, even breathing; she slumbered deeply. Heat roiled through his body, and he rolled up his shirtsleeves as a trickle of sweat rolled down his back. Hunger burned him like an ember in the pit of his stomach every time he was in her presence, and the sensation left him filled him with guilt. Would he never feel whole again?

The anger turned inward, a fury that such natural feelings suffocated him with self-loathing.

He feared the attraction he felt for her whenever they were alone, and yet *had* to speak with her. "Tamara," he said, approaching the sofa. She was awakening, and her movement, as she rolled over onto her back, displayed her lush bosom and the womanly swell of her hip.

"Christoph?" she said, reaching out her hand.

Just the touch of her fingers brushing against his naked forearm sent shivers over him, and he drew his arm out of reach. He knelt on the floor near the sofa and stared through the dark, grateful in one sense for the heightened abilities his wolf side left him with: excellent night vision, superior sense of smell, and an acute awareness of every tiny sound. He could tell exactly where she was and each movement of her body and hands, and so avoid that provocative nearness. And yet those same things drove him to the brink of madness when associated with the seductive innocence of Tamara's voice and feminine scent. It was like waves of physical sensation. He opened his mouth and let it drift over his tongue, to the back of his nose. Arousal swiftly followed, even as he tried to close himself off from those physical feelings.

"What is it, Christoph? You are upset, fearful. What is it?"

"How can you tell that?" he asked.

She shrugged and rolled to sit up, sweeping her tumbled locks away from her face. "I don't know. I've always been able to tell things about people. My father says my mother was like that. I can hear it in your voice, and can feel it. It rolls off of you like waves crashing on the shore."

"I have grave concerns for the safety of all of you ladies in this cottage. This is not a good place to be. Charlotte told me you feel the same way."

"There is evil here," she whispered. "I feel it."

So she also had a sense of the menace the cottage held for them. "I sent Siegfried, my valet, back to London to find out what he could about Eleanor Dancey, but that was before we figured out that this woman is not who she says she is. We must get out of here; are you well enough to leave tonight? With what we suspect of this woman, it is wisest if we go. Charlotte and I both feel this way."

"I can make it."

"I don't wish to frighten you, but we feel sure she is some kind of witch, and so shall do this in secrecy, the better to escape her undetected." He stood.

"Christoph," she said, softly.

He felt a shiver down his spine. "Yes?"

"Have I done anything to upset you?"

"Why do you ask?"

"You avoid me."

He took in a deep and shaky breath. She must never know how he felt, for she would turn away from him in disgust; any decent woman would, given his past. "You've done nothing. Please don't concern yourself. My sisters and I have nothing to do with this country, and soon we'll be gone, leaving you in peace."

She was silent for a long moment, then said, "I will be ready to leave whenever you say. Do you think my people are safe from whatever may occur?"

"I think so. They're not involved in any way, and should completely escape the witch's wrath."

She stood and moved close to him, so close he could almost taste her scent. Without another thought he put his arms around her and held onto her tightly. In the dimness, he saw her upturned face and his will crumbled. He dipped his head and hungrily he kissed her, his grip tightening convulsively as the sweet intoxication of lust overtook him.

She responded, pressing her body to his, full breasts squashed to his chest, surrendering to his passionate embrace. Lost in the feelings, he felt the pulse of arousal, and his hold on her tightened even as he felt her squirm and gasp. "Tamara," he murmured against her lips, pushing her down to the sofa, "Tamara, let me—"

"No, Count, please, you're hurting me!" she cried out, her words smothered by his insistent kiss.

He released her instantly and staggered away, shame filling him. How could he have abused her trust that way? "I'm sorry," he groaned. "Please forgive me!"

"I didn't mean for you to stop kissing me," she said, breathless. "It's just that your grip was so tight, it hurt. Come back to me!"

But he shook his head and stumbled back to the doorway. Shame and anger overwhelmed him, and all of the terrible associations of sexual hunger flooded back, filling him with self-loathing. "Be ready when I come back for you," he said, from the doorway. "I'll make sure you get back safely to your father and brother, and I swear on my life and honor I'll not molest you again." He turned and fled back upstairs.

CHARLOTTE had been taken against her will before by someone she had thought she could trust. That time, the man had ended up dead, through no action of her own. This time Lyulph Randell had made good his escape, though, and she was being transported through the twilight, across fields and over streams and hills, slung over a horse's back like a sack of goods. Her ribs ached and she was nauseous, the motion and flickering light of the moon when she could see it leaving her feeling faint and sick. Finally, after straining to get away and twisting and turning trying to figure out where she was, she resolved to save her strength for when she best had a chance to use it.

Lyulph slowed the horse, pulling back on the reins.

"Where are we? Why are you doing this?" she said, fighting back a wave of fear as she saw a dark house looming nearby. It was black and lifeless, isolated by its situation on the edge of a dark forest that stretched off into the distance.

To her surprise his voice, when he spoke, was mild in tone. "I just need somewhere to keep you for a while. I promise you on my life no harm will come to you." He threw his leg over the horse and slid to the ground, then helped her down. Her legs were wobbly, and she staggered against him. He righted her with gentle hands. "There you go," he said.

She tensed her muscles and was about to run when he grabbed her hard and pulled her back against his chest, binding her close to him with strong arms.

"Don't trespass on my kindness by thinking you can run. Where would you go? You don't know the way back to Moor Cottage, nor to the village. The moors, my fierce one," he said into her ear, "are wild and lonely, and the tors full of crags and rocky cliffs. Four hundred years ago Wesmorlyn's ancestor fought mine to a standstill; he was awarded the plum, the land that was farmable and gentle. We got the rocky, wild, craggy tors, the land Wesmorlyn's kin disdained." He awkwardly hauled her with him as he moved toward a small stable. "But it's mine, and I know every inch of it; even the people who live on it are faithful to me. If you run you will have nowhere to go. This is my land, and *you* are mine, now, too."

"I am *not* yours!" she said, twisting and turning. His brutal grasp was bruising her, but she would rather be black-and-blue than stay his captive.

"You will be, and you'll be happy about it, if you just settle down and give me the chance. If you ran," he still growled into her ear, holding her tightly against his chest in a strong embrace, "I would run after you as a wolf, and I am very fast indeed. You would not like how I would be forced to hold you in that form. By my teeth, my dearest Charlotte, by my big, white teeth."

"It was you who attacked Tamara!" she cried, her voice trembling with a mixture of anger and fear.

"I'm not proud of that, but I didn't hurt her badly. I could easily have killed her, but I had no wish to; all I wanted was for you to think your brother had done it."

"Why?"

He sighed. "Forget it!"

"How can I? I never for a moment believed it was him, but you made him so unhappy, you and your trollop!"

"You're testing my patience, Charlotte. We were trying to sow the seeds of discord in your tight little group. It was a wicked thing to do, and I apologize."

He said it so casually, as if such a heinous offense could be swept away by a few careless words of apology. Her voice low and trembling, she said, "Did you taste human blood when you terrorized poor Tamara?"

He shuddered, his body jolting. "Yes. But it was unavoidable."

That was not the answer she had hoped for. She swallowed hard against the terror that welled up within her, the taste bitter in her mouth. She wanted to scream, to fight, to make him suffer, but for the moment, with her arms pinned at her sides as she staggered forward, it seemed useless. She kept talking, trying to work her arms free. "My great aunt said that the way of a werewolf is hard. If he once begins to walk toward the dark side, he is pulled relentlessly until it is all he can be, all he can do. Have you done that? Have you given yourself over to evil?"

"I didn't know the German people had such a flair for drama." He pushed her knee with his, urging her forward.

"It has nothing to do with drama. You tasted human blood. Listen to me, Lyulph Randell," she said, twisting to look up at him in the gloom, as he forced her to walk beside the agitated, restless horse. "You *must* stop now and fight what is happening to you, or you'll be drawn into the abyss. I'm speaking to you as one of the wolf blood; stop, or you're in danger of losing your soul."

With one arm he held her still, and with the other he led his horse into the pitch blackness of the stable, leaving it there and shutting the door as he tugged Charlotte back out. "Come," he said, one hand still clutching her arm, the other tangled in a mass of her clothing. "Resistance will do neither of us any good. I have no desire to hurt you, but I'll use whatever force is necessary to make you behave yourself as a young lady ought."

She was exhausted from struggling. He was too far into his plan to listen now, she feared. He had abandoned his witch mistress and now ran in fear of her wrath, that much she understood. But surely reason would still have some sway. "You said you loved me," she said, twisting and tugging, trying to get free. "What has become of the chivalrous gentleman I thought you were?"

"Chivalry is just a thin veneer with which men coat their baser instincts, my dearest Charlotte. It is a ruse to gain the trust of the ladies. After marriage men show their true colors. Be grateful you'll know the worst about your husband before we're wed."

Wed? He was deluded. "I don't believe any of that." Even as they spoke, she was trying to figure a way out of her dilemma, for she didn't want to go into the house he was hauling her toward. But he was stronger than she had expected. When she dug her feet into the earth, he simply picked her up, with little enough effort, and half carried her, both arms around her again, binding her arms to her sides. Never had she resented male strength more than that moment. "You only think that because that is what you are, base and despicable." She tried to jam her elbow into his gut, but could not move it. She lifted her foot to bring it down on his, but he shifted her and threw her off balance. She was ready to scream with frustration, but who would hear her? The blackness of the night was unrelieved by any illumination save the moon, which was just beginning to rise.

"Believe what you will," he said, as he guided her toward the door of the dark, timbered dwelling, opening it and pushing her through. "I do love you, my sweet little wolfling, but if you will not succumb to my charming self, then you must be made to see reason. I have no time for dawdling."

It was dark in the house, and he shoved her hard; she stumbled in the inky interior, feeling around to figure out where she was. It was a hallway, she supposed, and there was a staircase nearby. She stood and clung to a newel post, attempting to orient herself, trying to think of a way out of her predicament. He seemed to be able to see quite well, for he shot a bolt across and she could hear a lock snick into place. Of course, he was a wolf, and Christoph had said once that all of his senses were heightened from the first time he had transformed, and that those powers became stronger with usage.

"No one knows where you are," he said, his voice deceptively gentle. He pulled her against him. "And this house is fast, prepared as a snug retreat. It would be best for you if you accept the truth, that I truly do care for you. If you will just submit and bind with me, it will go better. I wish you no harm. I do love you Charlotte, and I promise, do as I ask—marry me—and I will allow your brother to leave England, and to take your half sister with him."

"He is a werewolf, too, as you well know, and—" She stopped abruptly, stricken by the knowledge that fastened to her underskirts was Christoph's only way of transforming.

He turned her around and sought her lips, but she twisted away. He jammed his fingers into her hair, turning her face toward his, and said, "Charlotte, I don't know what you're thinking, but if you're contemplating running, forget it. Even if you could get out, you have no idea where we are, and I could hunt you down in a trice. I know what you did with Wesmorlyn, rutting with him in the open field, and I know you were no simpering virgin even before that. I don't mind. I'm not a judgmental sort, nor am I jealous as a rule."

He pulled her head back and kissed her throat, touching the pulse at the base of it with his lips and breathing deeply, inhaling her scent. "But you will be mine," he said, twisting her head and whispering into her ear. "There is room for only one werewolf family in England, and it will be ours, a dynasty of such power as the world has not seen. Let Wesmorlyn try to regain heaven for himself and his offspring. I am content with earth for mine." He bit her earlobe and drew blood.

Chapter 20

"WELL WHERE is she then, if she's not here with you?" Christoph asked Fanny, who stood, bewildered, in the middle of the room she shared with her sister.

"I don't know. She went down to the kitchen to get a cup of milk, but has not yet returned. I thought perhaps you and she went to speak to Tamara together."

"No. Where is she, I wonder?" Christoph thought for a moment, not willing to jump to conclusions, especially where his sister was concerned. Charlotte was more than capable of taking off in her own direction, with her own ideas.

"Christoph," Fanny said, agitated, "we must go down to make sure she is still here."

"You stay here," he said, putting out one hand. "I'll find her. I don't want to alert that witch woman to our plans." He descended, quietly; the house was eerily still. Tamara was still in the room where her narrow sofa was, he could tell just by feeling her in his mind. Every pore of his body was alive to Tamara's rich female scent and the delicious perfume of her fecundity, and now that he had tasted her lips he would never forget the sensation, the sweet heady rush of desire. He shut down such forbidden thoughts. That part of life was dead to him forever, for he was unworthy of such purity and innocence as sweet Tamara possessed.

But where was Charlotte? He stopped in the hallway and stilled himself. He didn't know if he could feel Charlotte. She was his sister, and they were close, but it was not at all the same as with Tamara. He blanked his mind and closed his eyes, standing still and hearing the night noises around him. Mice in the walls, a branch rubbing against the roof of the cottage, a breeze rustling through the herb garden outside. Tamara paced restlessly, waiting for him to return. Fanny, too; he didn't need his excellent senses to hear the floorboards creaking above him.

The kitchen. Who was there? He paced quietly through the hall toward the back of the house, and pushed open the door. Anne stood to one side, her shoulders slumped, the flickering light of the hearth fire dimly lighting up her blank eyes and lackluster expression. The worktable in the middle of the small room had a large copper pot on it, and the woman he knew only as Eleanor stood, peering down into it, her normally neatly restrained hair a wild tumble of chestnut locks. Hellebore, her cat, had his paws up on the edge of the bowl and he was staring to its depths, too, in a weirdly human attitude. At some movement or sound he made she looked up and her eyes were wide, her irises and pupils a glowing silvery shade.

"Where is Charlotte?" When she didn't answer, he strode into the room and said, "Where is my sister? What have you done to her?"

Hellebore crouched and growled, spitting and screeching at him.

"I have done nothing. But here, look to the water and you will see what is happening to your littermate." She smiled a wide, weird smile and backed away from the pot, motioning toward it as the cat leaped down and scuttled away.

He crossed the room in two steps and gazed down into the depths of the large copper vessel. It was filled with silvery water, and images flickered across the surface. At first he couldn't make them out, but then he saw, as the surface settled, Charlotte. She was clinging to a wooden bedpost, and a man dressed in black with his back turned knelt by her, doing something. When the man stood up, Christoph could see Charlotte was chained to the bed. The man turned. It was Lyulph Randell.

HANNAH was feverish; she tossed and turned and her ancient nanny, Mrs. Howe, a devout woman who had been her nursemaid all her life, sat by her and patted her forehead with a damp cloth.

"What's wrong with her?" Wesmorlyn cried, pacing. "I don't understand."

Semyaza, standing quietly by the door, said, "There is magic at work here."

"Magic?"

"She is suffering the end of a spell. When one is under magic, the diminishing of it leaves a void in the soul; something must fill the void."

The nanny wept and prayed, holding the girl's slim hand. Wesmorlyn stopped and stared at Hannah, and then turned to Semyaza. "What are you talking about? She was fine when she arrived from London."

"But still under a spell. At first I thought it was just glamour; Lyulph Randell's kind have a sort of magic of their own. Sometimes they are not even aware they're using it, though Randell knows. But this seems like more to me, perhaps a potion or a spell. Someone has been luring her with magic."

Fear clutched at Wesmorlyn, fear for his precious little sister, and for the others, for Charlotte and Christoph and Fanny. "Randell sees me as his enemy, I'm still not sure why. Could he have done this magic?"

"No. He is not a magician and this is beyond his reach. His lure dies with distance from him, whereas this had dug deep into her like a burrowing slug, consuming a part of her."

Burgess's words came back to haunt him. The man had said the woman at Moor Cottage was capable of weaving a spell that would consume a soul. "The woman who calls herself Eleanor Dancey; she's the one they call the Witch of Bodmin Moor!" he exclaimed.

Semyaza nodded, encouragingly. "Bound in some way to Randell, through love or perhaps just ambition."

"And that means the others are in danger from her. I had intended to warn Charlotte of Lyulph Randell's part in her abandonment by his coachman, but now I must warn them against that woman, too. But how can I leave right now, when Hannah needs me?" Wesmorlyn went to his sister's bedside and gazed down at her, then turned to Semyaza. He had returned to check on her before going on to Moor Cottage, but had found Hannah in anguished torment. "Sam," he said, his voice breaking, "will she be all right?"

He nodded, a ghost of a smile on his thin lips. "Now she will. The magic is dwindling. Nanny Howe, with love and prayer, is filling the empty part of her soul with all that is good and wise and healthful. She will be weak after this, but I think will recover fully."

Wesmorlyn crossed back to the door. "Semyaza, my old friend, I must go, but will you stay with her through this terrible night?" he asked, putting one hand on his guide's lean arm. Semyaza nodded, and Wesmorlyn looked back at his little sister, her sweet face finally calm in the candlelight as Mrs. Howe prayed and held her thin hand cupped in her own blue-veined ones; he regretted every harsh word he had said to her about her flight to Lyulph Randell's residence and his disbelief of her protestations that she didn't know why she did it. He had believed Randell over his own sister, and he ought to be horsewhipped through the village for his brotherly failings.

With a whispered prayer he left, racing through the Abbey, and to the stables. A hair shirt would not fix the current dangerous situation. He must act rather than contemplate, as soothing and refreshing as a trip to the Wesmorlyn chapel would be at that moment. In the past, he would have turned to prayer and contemplation, but now saw that in some instances, no amount of prayer would substitute for action. As late as it was, he must go to Moor Cottage and alert the von Wolframs that they were staying in the viper's den and would be poisoned by her venom if they did not leave that moment. He'd drag them away if he must, especially Charlotte, who was in the most danger. He certainly couldn't scoop her up and fly away with her in front of the others, so he must ride;

if both Fanny and Charlotte needed to escape, he would let them share his horse. His groom already had his horse saddled, and he rode out into the gathering gloom of twilight, as the moon began to rise.

He still could not stomach the thought of what Charlotte had told him about her family, and yet the hours preceding her revelation had been a wild tumult of new feelings and sensations, and the burgeoning sense of what love could be between a man and a woman content to be merely human. Could something that was so wonderful and sweet and full of joy be wrong? And the natural, earthy act of lovemaking . . . now he understood why men sought it so vigorously. That precious hour in the meadow with her, allowing nature to command him, had taught him that he was not beyond physical passion.

He couldn't say now with any certainty whether he had made a mull of his future or not; was a union with a woman of werewolf blood really so out of the question? He had to ponder that. For the first time his heart was speaking to him, and it was beguiling him with tender thoughts and hope. All that mattered this moment, though, was that Charlotte was in danger and he must help her.

The steady beat of his mount's hooves thudded his urgency. He hoped to heaven he was not too late. He prayed that the von Wolframs did not suffer for what he suspected was a legacy of Randell anger directed at the Wesmorlyn's.

THE room was small and dark, the light of one candle the only illumination. The only furnishing was a broken settle in the corner and a four-poster bed with just a ticking-covered feather mattress on it.

"Don't you see," Lyulph said for perhaps the tenth time, "that together, you and I could produce the most powerful breed of werewolf the world has ever seen? My family has had centuries to become as we are, dark and formidable. Your legacy is fresh and vibrant."

"Ours goes back centuries as well, to the dark times, I've been told." Charlotte, chained to a bedpost and battling fear, kept her tone even, despite the lunacy with which she was faced. He had been talking at her for a half hour, but she remained steadfast in her determination to keep him at bay.

"But somehow your family line has remained untainted by time." He gazed at her steadily. "Mine is powerful, but diluted by hundreds of years of living among ordinary humans. Perhaps it's the secrecy your family has maintained, and your isolation, but I felt it from your brother. He has the potential to be a giant among our kind, pure in his spirit."

Charlotte watched his eyes when he said that; the green of the irises disappeared as his pupils, large and dark, dominated, making his gaze menacing. His words sounded mild enough, but there was a threat there. He would not suffer Christoph to remain in England unchallenged. He intended, she realized, to marry her and then drive Christoph away somehow. But she didn't think that had been his original plan. "That purity, or whatever it is, is because Christoph has never given himself over to the darkness. Don't you sense the danger?" She didn't know what she was talking about, but would say anything to keep him distracted.

"No, no danger. Power, Charlotte . . . unlimited power. The strength of two werewolf family lines joined. Our children," Lyulph Randell went on, his tone sly and insinuating, "would be vigorous and tough, uniting the best of what we are, severally and together. We could perhaps take by might what I had planned to obtain by marriage. It's a chance. It might not even succeed. But for *you* I would be willing to upset the plans of a lifetime and boldly venture."

"You've crossed the line from sanity to lunacy, can't you see that?" Charlotte said, staring at him and shivering in the chilly, damp night air.

"I'm not mad," he said, his tone indignant.

She was wise enough not to pursue that line of reasoning; madmen never admitted it, she had experience enough to know. "This was not your plan initially."

"No. Meeting you changed everything."

"How?"

"I didn't know that Wesmorlyn's intended would be from a family such as yours. How could I? Even those families acknowledged among our kind exist in secrecy, or we would be hunted down and murdered! We *must* take whatever we can from the others, for nothing will ever be given to us! They fear us, don't you see that?" he said, urgently, leaning toward her. "It's us against them!"

"No!" She sneezed once and rubbed her nose. The house was ancient and had clearly not been inhabited for some time, for the musty smell, much the same as at Moor Cottage, was driving her almost as mad as Lyulph Randell's wicked, crazy schemes. He had been warped, it seemed to her, by a lifetime of persuasion, to think that plotting and planning was the only way to live. Perhaps reason would work. "Do you truly think that any nation in our day could be overruled by force? Or that a sane, sober government would stand idly by while you rob another man of his birthright?" she said, referring to some part of his plan that she surmised involved seizing Wesmorlyn's land. "We live in more civilized times, sir, and though your ancestors may have been robbed of land and power by force, the same will not gain you those back."

"I'm not an idiot! I know how to get what I want." He knelt by her. "I had little simpering Lady Hannah in the palm of my hand," he said through bared teeth, his expression twisted by frustrated ambition as he held his hand out, palm up. "I could have married her and blended her family's legacy with my own. I would have suppressed Wesmorlyn then, brought him to his knees somehow."

"You mean by Morwenna's spells and potions!" she gasped, astonished at the depth of his deviltry. Would he have poisoned Wesmorlyn, murdering him even? Seducing her in the garden on the night of the ball was just one more battle in a war of his own making.

"The world has never seen the offspring of such a union as werewolf and angel," he said, regret in his tone. He stood and paced, frustrated ambition in every movement. "I could have taken over not only Wesmorlyn's land, joining it with my own—his is one of the rare earldoms that will pass to a female member of the family should he die without issue—but I could have used Hannah and my offspring to gain more. And what we could not gain by marriage, we would take by force. I had it all planned." He stopped, and stared into the distance. "What have I done? I gave it up, and for what?" He swung his gaze back to her in the flickering candlelight. "For the hope of you. For the *chance* of you!"

"Then you gave it up for nothing," she said, watching him. He didn't seem truly mad, just furious that she would not go along with his plans. She was trying, as they spoke, to figure a way out of her predicament, but the chains at her wrist were indestructible. "You aren't doing any of this for me, but for yourself."

He collapsed in front of her, then reached out and touched her hair, the tumbled golden locks shining in the dim moonlight from the window. "But I *love* you, Charlotte."

He stared into her eyes and she felt the lure, the ache of passion that rose within her, and yet it was false. She knew that now. Every tender moment with Wesmorlyn had been real: every trembling longing and even every angry moment, every feeling of affection mingled with pain, all had been honest emotions with truth behind them. Nothing with Lyulph was real, not his friendship, nor his passion, nor his spurious claims of love. Wesmorlyn, for all his faults, was just trying to puzzle life out as she was. Lyulph was the most dangerous of creatures, in her estimation; he was one of those who thought he had it all figured out. He manipulated through the use of some kind of power he wielded over women. And as she thought that, the fascination abated and she was left in peace. She met his gaze and cared nothing for it.

He saw it and growled in fury. "You will do what I want, or . . ."

"Or what?" she said, triumphant. "Your power is nothing over me now. You can hold me here as long as you want, but you cannot make me marry you." She watched his eyes, holding back her own fear that he would force her to give in to his physical demands. But she saw in his eyes that for some reason he couldn't, or mustn't. There was so much her family did not know about their own powers, she thought, wishing she knew more, wishing she could say with confidence that he could never force her into lying with him.

"I *will* have you," he growled. He stood and paced to the door. "Think about this while I'm gone; I am offering you the chance at a life with me, and the power that will come of uniting our destinies. What could you ever have with Wesmorlyn but his shame and penance and that endless, whining, *cringing* wish to get back into heaven? It is nauseating, and I have had to listen to it my whole life. I don't need heaven, not while I have earth. You and I together could defeat him and gain mastery, dooming his legacy to die with him and his puerile sister."

"I don't want power," she said, "and I don't want a husband. Choose between the two of you? I choose neither. I don't want you and I don't want him. I'll *never* acquiesce!"

"We'll see," he muttered.

She could hear his voice floating out behind him as he clattered down the stairs to the main floor.

"We'll see!" he shouted.

She kicked at the bedpost in impotent fury. How was she going to get out of this quandary? She would have to think of a way.

Chapter 21

WOULD ELEANOR know they were leaving, Christoph wondered? Would she care? He had no idea; he only knew that Fanny and Tamara were his responsibility, and he must get them out before finding Charlotte.

Christoph crept down the stairs with Fanny, and paused in the hallway, holding one finger to his lips. Though he felt a powerful connection with Tamara, would she experience it too and feel him calling her? He put all his energy into it, reaching out, trying to touch her mind, and he was rewarded when he heard the faint creak of the door to her sleeping chamber. A shadowy figure crept through the parlor door and he knew without a doubt that it was her.

"We must leave this very minute," he whispered. "I will explain all when we get outside."

"What about Charlotte?" Tamara murmured, her dark eyes mere blots even to his sensitive eyesight in the windowless, dank hallway.

He took her arm, led her to the front door, and opened it, trying to be silent. Fanny to one side and Tamara to the other, he led them out and left it open, not willing to risk the sound of it closing. He hastened his steps, leading them to the gate that opened on to the moor, but something made him glance back; Eleanor stood motionless in the doorway. And yet she did nothing, just stood and watched.

He feared that he was doing exactly what she expected and wanted but he could think of no other way out, so he led his sister and Tamara through the gate and to the open moor. "Charlotte has been taken by Lyulph Randell. I'll handle him, but first we need to get you both to safety. Do you know your way by heart back to the gypsy encampment?" he murmured to Tamara.

"Yes. I know it well, even in the dark."

"Then take us there. It's too dark to take my horse; I'll come back and get it after you, Fanny, and Charlotte are safe. The gypsy camp is our only hope as we need somewhere to stop until I can figure out where Randell is keeping Charlotte. I don't even know if I can trust what I saw in that woman's damnable witch's bowl," he said, and explained the vision he had seen in the kitchen. "If I can, then I don't think we have long to rescue her."

Fanny began to weep silently, her body shuddering with every stifled sob, and Christoph cursed his thoughtlessness. It was an arduous journey over the hills in the dark, and Fanny stumbled often. He almost regretted not bringing his horse for her sake, but it would likely have taken just as long or longer, given the number of rock outcroppings across the moor.

"I don't understand why Mr. Randell would steal Charlotte away like that," Tamara said, as they walked. She had tugged Fanny to walk between them so they could both help her when she stumbled, which in her emotional state was often.

Christoph couldn't tell her what he suspected. Randell, knowing the von Wolfram family secret, was either using Charlotte to lure him out to destroy him as a rival, or he had decided—and given his behavior of late it seemed the most likely explanation—to make Charlotte his mate, hoping the werewolf in her would strengthen his own family line. But a werewolf could not take a mate by force. That was the one thing his Uncle Nikolas had been adamant about, not that Christoph ever would, but his uncle had told him as a piece of necessary information to pass down in the family. Charlotte wouldn't know that, though, he realized, and would be suffering terror because of it.

But a werewolf in human form was just a man, a very strong, vigorous, and dangerous man. And as a man, if she refused to bond with him as his mate, Randell could still intend to use her as no woman should ever be used; Christoph would fight to the death before he would allow his sister to be so violated. He hastened his pace, dragging the two young women after him.

WESMORLYN, guided by the glittering moon that ascended the sky in its nightly journey, rode swiftly along the highway. When he had to leave the road to approach lonely Moor Cottage, it was painfully slow, picking through the hummocky grass and rocky outcroppings. He didn't wish to forewarn the witch woman of his presence, and knew he would need to be quiet in his approach; how then would he manage to alert Charlotte and Christoph to the danger they faced?

His mount's hooves swished through the grass and the wind whispered around him. From a distance he saw that the front door to the cottage was open, and could make out the form of a girl staggering down the path toward the gate. He rode faster, risking a stumble, and dismounted quickly, fearing he was too late. But as he pelted forward, through the gate and to the front garden, he could see that the young woman was a stranger to him. Wesmorlyn had no time to ascertain more before another woman, long dark hair streaming behind her, came racing out the door after her, laughing.

"Go then," she cried. "Go! You're no more use to me anyway."

"What's going on?" Wesmorlyn shouted, striding toward the cottage.

"She's a witch," the younger woman cried, stumbling to him. "She has cursed me, and now I'll die!"

He caught her in his arms as she fell weeping to her knees. Gently he helped her back to her feet, pushed her behind him, and shielded her from the other woman. She was treacherously beautiful, her skin waxen and white, her hair dark and long, coiled in curls. "You're Morwenna Maxwell," he said, certain that he was right. "You are a witch, and Lyulph Randell's leman."

She stopped, her dark, flat eyes wide open but strangely reflecting the rising moon off their glassy surface. "Who are you, to know my name? No, wait, don't tell me. I know." She paced down the sidewalk as the girl cowered behind him. "You are he, Lyulph's mortal foe," she whispered, staring up at him. "But more, you are one of the fallen. He never told me that. Why did he never tell me that?"

"Where are Countess Charlotte and her sister and brother?" Wesmorlyn asked, turning to the girl, whose white face shone with desperate fear.

"They have gone," the girl said, haltingly, "Gone. Gone." Her repetition was a hollow echo, forlorn and empty of meaning.

He took her shoulders in his hands and shook her. "Gone where?"

The woman laughed, a low seductive chuckle. "She is almost completely drained of sense, poor little dear. I have used her up. Why don't you ask *me*, angelic one?"

When he turned to face her, she strolled the rest of the way down the walk to him and stared up into his eyes. "Where are they, then?" he asked. Black anger filled him; this was the demon who had used her dark arts on Hannah. Her witchery on her maidservant had the same foul stamp, the draining of intelligence leaving behind a feverish, mournful vacuity.

"How beautiful you are," she said, reaching up to push his chestnut curls off his forehead.

He swatted her hand away. "Where are they?"

"Countess Charlotte was taken away by the man, her lover!" the girl cried, pointing at her mistress. She wailed after speaking and fell to her knees again, as if the effort gave her great pain.

"Anne, shut up!" the woman shouted, pointing at the girl. "I forbid you to speak again."

"Lyulph took her? Where? Where did they go?" Wesmorlyn said, fury and fear ripping into him. But he knew he would receive no answer, so he turned and was about to return to his horse when the girl cried out. He whirled and saw that the witch had Anne by the hair. "Let her go!" he shouted.

The witch released her and the girl fell to the ground. Morwenna walked down the path, swaying, her hips twitching; she whispered something in another tongue as she walked, but he hardened his heart against any spell she might try to weave.

The moon's reflection glittered in her opaque eyes. Stopping before him she put out one hand and touched his face, her fingers trailing over his lips. She left a path of sparking heat where she touched. Her expression full of delight, her smile wide and weird, vacant of true joy, she said, "You are one of the fallen—or rather, one of the descendents of the fallen. Am I right?"

"You're right." He watched her, filled with dread, faced with a creature he had never in his life expected to meet. She was a witch, one of the oldest forms of half-mortals. Her eyes were empty, or no, not empty, he realized, staring into them, lost in the shifting silvery shadows that chased through their fathomless depths; they were full of cruelty and a horrible, aching hunger that would never be satisfied. Perhaps that insatiability was the terrible price she paid for her power. Thunder rumbled in the sky above and the moon flickered between swiftly coursing clouds, reflecting in their silvery void. Mindless ambition and pitiless determination had drained them of any humanity she might have possessed. He was seared by a dreadful knowledge; he was in danger of becoming as she was. If he abandoned the human side of him in his striving for redemption, he would become vacant of humanity, lacking any warmth. She had made the choice to abandon her half-mortal heart in favor of darkness; he had been on the verge of abandoning *his* humanity in walking toward the light. The decision was one that faced all who were other than merely mortal.

Would he choose the angelic side of him or the human? This was not the time to make that decision, but he hoped he was wise enough to decide correctly, and not out of fear or pain. Or perhaps he could learn to walk the fine line between them.

Her eyes glowed brighter with the silver light of the moon. "This explains so very much that I did not understand, for I have felt in all of our planning a resistance in the ether. Lyulph never told me we were plotting against an angel!"

"I'm not an angel."

"No, perhaps not, fully, but you do have the pretty, pretty wings, don't you?" she said, smacking his cheek with each word.

He was tempted to strike out at her, but it wasn't worth the time or effort. He had other priorities, so he just pushed her away and focused his attention on the girl, who had collapsed on the walkway. Human compassion filled his heart as he saw the silent tears rolling down her pale cheeks. "I must go and find Charlotte and the others. Come with me," he said, gently, holding out one hand. "Come." Trembling, she clambered to her feet and started toward him.

"Stop!" the witch commanded.

Anne stopped and stared at Wesmorlyn, yearning in her eyes, her gaze going beyond him and beyond the gate to the open moors and freedom. He couldn't leave without her, though his heart raged at the delay. Fanny and Christoph had clearly already left, possibly to the gypsy camp with Tamara, or perhaps to help Charlotte. He couldn't afford another second, and yet couldn't just abandon the girl to the witch's cruelty.

"Anne, come with me."

"Why don't you leave her alone, pretty angel," the woman said, strolling toward him yet again, her expression one of excitement mingled with fascination. "She is of no use to you."

"I won't leave her with you," he said. He held out his hand. "Anne, come, now!"

The girl tried, but, weeping hysterically, stopped when the witch laid one hand on her shoulder.

"Why don't you let her go?" Wesmorlyn said. "She's of no use to you now, you said so yourself."

"One more moment and I will release her." She stopped and stared at Wesmorlyn. "You interest me. Your kind was barred from redemption by your ancestor's action."

He was silent.

"Those ancestors . . . their greatest sin was breeding with human women, creating the anakim, the giants that once roamed the earth," she said, cocking her head to one side. "Do I have the ancient story correct?"

"Yes, yes, of course," he said, impatiently. He didn't need a lesson in his family's history from her.

"And now you are merely shrunken butterflies. Why don't you leave it behind, this desperate attempt to reclaim heaven? It is a fool's ambition," she chided. "Come to me, and we can become something more beautiful, darkness and light, heaven and hell, eternal balance." She added some words in another tongue.

But nothing she could say nor any magic spell could stay him in his path. "I think I'll stay with my fool's ambition to regain the hope of redemption for my children."

"There is no true ambition but personal ambition," she said, with disdain. "All the rest is shadows and dreams."

"So you say." *Enough talk.* He must ask once more. "Where has Lyulph Randell taken Charlotte?"

"Why would I tell you that?"

He watched her for a moment and had a flicker of the truth occur to him. "Do you not care that Charlotte has supplanted you in Lyulph's affections?" he said, watching the light in her silvery eyes. "Doesn't it infuriate you that he has plotted to win her? I saw them kissing; I know what passion he feels for her. Has she taken your place?"

Her expression darkened to anger, but she defeated it easily. "I have him in my power; Lyulph Randell will not dare go against me."

"But you'll always know he chose Charlotte over you."

"That doesn't matter. My own plan will win out anyway; all others will be destroyed and he'll remain faithful to me, or die." She reached out one hand and held it close to Wesmorlyn's head, searching his eyes. "One of the fallen," she whispered. "I had heard that you were beautiful, and that is true. Tell me, what was the name of your first ancestor?"

"I may not say that on pain of death."

"Pain of death." A dark expression crossed her beautiful face and shone in her eyes. "I have been betrayed and deceived before this night, but no more. Do you wish to know your fate? I can show you, in my bowl." She stepped back toward the house, crooking her finger in a beckoning gesture. "Come with me, beautiful angel, and I'll show you your fate."

He wasn't tempted. "Come Anne," he said, putting out his hand and staring at the girl, willing her to trust him and defeat the residual power of the witch. "She has not taken your soul, and her power is not limitless. The magic has drained much of your vital being, but I promise, you can regain yourself."

"I can't," the girl wailed, her arms over her stomach.

"You can!" he said, urgently, his hand still stretched out to her. Time was wasting away, and he must find the others. "Come with me and I'll make sure you are safe and secure in my house. You'll be replenished with good things, love and prayer and hope. You can regain your soul with the courage you've already displayed."

The witch haughtily said, with a flicking motion of her hands, "I am becoming bored. Be gone. Go to your fate."

Anne finally broke free and grasped his hand, a tranquil expression on her face. As she joined him in walking to his horse, Wesmorlyn uttered a silent thanks to Semyaza for the information that might save the girl from being lost forever. Though the witch might be angry at his intervention, she seemed disinclined to interfere. He knew her unwillingness to take any action, though, was because she had a much larger plot brewing, the end of which was now in sight. He feared that he had unwittingly furthered those plans with his own resistance to the truth he felt in his bones; he loved Charlotte von Wolfram with a frighteningly human intensity that he still did not know how to acknowledge or handle.

But they had already been there too long. He *had* to find the others, and quickly, for they might know where Randell had taken Charlotte. Wesmorlyn turned to Anne. "Sit up on my horse and we'll follow the others. Do you know where Christoph, Fanny, and Tamara went?"

"The count took the ladies to the gypsies."

It was far too dark to risk riding over the moors; Wesmorlyn helped Anne up onto the horse and they walked away, the earl leading his mount. The walk was not long, but for the entire length of it Wesmorlyn tried to plan. He was not so naïve as to think that the witch's decision not to interfere in their leaving meant she had no further intentions. Him following the others to the gypsy camp might even be a part of some elaborate plot, or she might think him inconsequential and powerless. But there was nothing else to do; he had to find Charlotte and rescue her from Randell's clutches. Christoph might know where she was.

"DRINK. Drink more of the wine. Are you not increasingly thirsty?" Lyulph said, holding a stemmed silver goblet out to Charlotte.

"I've had enough, I tell you!" Charlotte, free of her chains, knocked it from his hands, and the wine spilled over the floor, a dark trail of liquid seeping into the floorboards.

"Damn you!" he exclaimed and wiped his hand on his jacket. "Why won't you drink more? Aren't you thirsty?"

She watched him in the dim light from the one candle in the dark room. He had left, but had not been gone long, and when he came back it was with food and wine for her. She didn't answer his query.

He knelt beside her and touched her hair, fury darkening his face when she shrank away from his touch and made an exclamation of disgust. "Come, you must care for me a little. Remember how you kissed me in the garden at the ball within minutes of meeting me; don't you feel the same this minute?" He pushed his face close to hers and tried to kiss her cheek, but she swatted him away like a pesky insect. He grabbed her shoulders and shook her but then stopped abruptly, putting his hands up and saying, "I'm sorry! I just wish you wouldn't treat me so coldly. Don't push me away, Charlotte, please."

"You've taken me against my will and hold me prisoner. What do you expect from me?"

He leaped to his feet, pacing. Then he stopped and crouched before her again. "I expect you to recognize your mate for life! We're the same, you and I," he said, thumping his chest for emphasis. "I *like* your challenging nature. I *appreciate* your spirit. Can you say the same for precious Wesmorlyn? Does he value your wildness, your independence?"

Charlotte blinked back tears. "No. He hates our kind."

"He despises us as animals, no better than his hounds. I've always known that beneath his feigned kindness to me was that arrogance, that presumption that because he is from a race that once ruled the heavens, he's better than those of us who are bound to the earth and happy for it."

She bowed her head. "Your truth does not mean I'll turn to you as I turn away from Wesmorlyn."

He poured another glass of wine with shaking hands. "Drink," he said, pushing it at her. "Drink more, please!"

"No, I told you, I've had enough!" she said, batting it away again. She stared at him; there was an expression of thwarted determination in his green eyes. "What's in the wine?" she asked. "Poison?"

He was aghast. "Why would I try to hurt you? I only want you to care for me, Charlotte."

"Is it some kind of love potion?" She saw the truth in the shame in his eyes.

Lyulph, frustrated by her recalcitrance and even more so because he could not force her into anything or it would work against his plans, began to realize one very important thing. Every step of the way, as he thought Morwenna was aiding him, she was really furthering her own plot. She had sensed the change in his plans, and perhaps she feared his desire for Charlotte. The love philter she had provided him with was likely nothing more than colored water. This avenue was futile.

Why did everyone oppose him? He didn't ask much, just that she go along with his plan. It would benefit them both, after all! He had promised Morwenna offspring, a blend of the witch and werewolf. All she had to do was help him achieve his goal, though that had changed from his original plan to marry Lady Hannah and subvert her family's supposed destiny, altering it to suit his own needs. Meeting Charlotte had changed everything, he thought, looking down at her.

Everything. If she would just see that together they would be magnificent, siring a generation of leaders and conquerors. He felt the power within her, and perhaps a call to her inner determination would work.

"Charlotte," he said, sitting down on the floor in front of her. He examined her pale face, her hair a tangled rats' nest of blonde curls and dirt smudged on the tip of her nose. She was never more desirable. "Listen to me. I'm being candid, more

so than I have ever in my life been. I care for you." She turned
her face away. "No, don't shut yourself off from me," he said,
turning her face gently back to him. "I care for you in a quite
unexpected way. I offer myself to you wholly, without reser-
vation, and will give you whatever you want."

She stared at him in the gloom, her brilliant blue eyes full
of questions. "Do you really care for me?"

"Yes! Yes, I do."

"Then let me go."

"No!"

"Then you don't care for me. You keep spouting nonsense
about destiny and sharing everything, and yet you keep me
prisoner!"

He grasped his hair in his hands. Taking a deep breath, he
pushed back his frustration. "If I let you go, will you marry
me?"

"You would let me go if I promised to marry you?"

It was a trap, and he saw that before he stepped in. "I
would need more than a promise. My vicar could marry us in
the old tradition, a handfast marriage."

"Handfast," Charlotte repeated.

"Yes; that means—"

"I know what handfasting is," Charlotte grimly stated.
"And I know what follows. Do you think me uneducated? Or
my people? If you have your way, you and I would handfast,
or betroth, and then we would consummate the marriage
through sexual intercourse, which would solemnize the ceremony and make it binding."

A greedy light entered his eyes. "How bright you are. I had
thought I preferred the dim and dull for marriage, but I find
your quick mind enticing. It offers so many opportunities for
educating you in the ways you could please me. Consumma-
tion. Yes, we'll have that, but I would make it quite pleasant,
sweetness," he said, taking up one of her matted blonde curls.

"I am not sweet, so do not choose some idiotic pet name
for me like I was a puppy," she said, swatting his hand away.
"And don't touch me. There will be no handfast, and no con-
summation. And the last wish I have is to please you."

The spirit he so loved in her had an unfortunate side. She
was indomitable. He stood and looked down at her. This was

going nowhere, and he had one other unexplored option. There was one whose loyalty was beyond question, one whose bond to him went back generations. Mother Sarah, while not a witch, was a creator of potions and philters. It was she who had told him not to interfere in Charlotte and Wesmorlyn's secret meetings, because she said she could see the disharmony between them, and how it would end in anger and disenchantment on both sides, and she had been right. Perhaps he should have gone to her from the beginning rather than relying on Morwenna, who Mother Sarah warned had her own plans.

"I'll leave you to think over my deal." He took up the chains again, but she shrank back.

"Please," she said, her whole heart in that one word. "I *hate* the chains. I feel like I can't breathe!"

"That is the wolf in you," he said, fingering the metal links. "No wolf can tolerate the chains and bonds that dogs willingly bear to be near humans." He thought about it, and said, "I won't chain you if you promise me that you won't try to get out."

She stared at him for a long minute and then bowed her head. "I can't promise," she mumbled.

It moved him that she was honest. Any other woman would have easily lied. "As a sign of my good faith, and in the hope that you will not try to get out—the attempt would be useless, my dear, anyway, for I shall lock the door behind me—I'll leave you unchained only to prove that, unlike Wesmorlyn, I don't wish to break your spirit or change you in any way. I treasure the wolf in you, that unfettered wildness, and together we could find such bliss as I have only heard about in old stories," he said, gently. "Think about that."

He left the room, locking it after him with a padlock. What she could not know is what he had sensed the moment he had entered; Morwenna had at least done as he asked and put a protection spell on the house. No point of egress or ingress was available to anyone but him. He could well afford to make this touching display of trust, because she could not get out no matter what she did.

And now, to the gypsy camp to get from Mother Sarah what Morwenna had failed to give him. A love philter or charm of some kind. One way or another Charlotte would be his. Even if she would not submit to a handfast ceremony, all he needed was for her to say "yes" and allow him to create within her his child. Then nothing could touch them, for the wolf in her was so powerful, nothing else would matter but the baby she carried and her bond to him, as the father.

Chapter 22

"WHAT HAVE you done to him? What have you done?"

As Wesmorlyn arrived, that was the anguished lament he heard from a young woman he assumed was Tamara, the gypsy girl who had befriended Charlotte; she knelt by a prone Christoph von Wolfram. The young German count rolled on the ground in agony, doubled over.

"What has happened?" Wesmorlyn asked, speeding his pace as he arrived at the gypsy encampment leading Anne, who listlessly and awkwardly rode his horse over the rocky and treacherous moor.

"My lord," cried Fanny, running to him as he approached. "It's my brother! That awful old gypsy woman has given him some potion that has made him ill!"

An ancient woman sat a little distance away, with a secretive smile on her face, the flickering flames of the nearby fire giving her a demonic appearance. But as Wesmorlyn came closer her expression sobered and she stared at him with dread in her dark eyes. He felt her trepidation; it emanated from her in waves, and he knew that somehow she could sense his secret. Why would she fear him, though? He had no special ability other than flight, and he was duty-bound to eschew violence, though he had kept to his vows poorly in the last weeks.

Was there something about him intrinsically that she feared? "What's wrong with him?" he said, striding over and staring down at Count Christoph. The sounds the fellow was making were awful. He was retching and moaning. "Has he been poisoned?"

Trembling, the beautiful gypsy girl, holding a damp cloth to his forehead and trying to calm his agony, looked up at him, tears in her eyes. "I didn't know. I swear I didn't know!"

"Didn't know what?" he asked, bewildered.

"Some of our elders are bound to Lyulph Randell," she said, sobbing. "They are promised to him as to a liege lord, and do his bidding whenever necessary. I never would have thought such a promise possible. Our people promise allegiance to *no one*! And yet they have done this thing. In return we have been promised protection from the English. I did not know this until a short while ago; Mr. Randell was here and consulted with Mother Sarah, who gave him a corked earthen bottle, and then he left again."

"Randell was just here?" Wesmorlyn said, anger and urgency rising up in him like a tidal wave. He grabbed her shoulders and stared into her dark eyes. "Where is he? What was he doing?"

She said, "He *was* here, but just for a few minutes, and then he left again."

"Where has he gone? And where is Countess Charlotte?" he asked, crouching down by her. Christoph still moaned, and the girl's attention was divided as she mopped the count's forehead, sobs catching in her throat while Fanny, behind them, wrung her hands and wept. One of the young gypsy men was trying to calm her to no avail.

"I don't know where she is!" Tamara's eyes narrowed, and she continued, "Lyulph Randell must have her close by, though, or he could not so easily have come here on foot."

And if he was dressed, Wesmorlyn reflected, then he must have come as a human, and not as a wolf. "I must find her," he said, feeling his stomach clench into a knot. "But what does any of this have to do with Christoph? What has happened to him?" he asked, kneeling by her side and putting two hands on the younger man's shoulders; he had finally stopped groaning and rolling around. The count opened his eyes, as startling blue as his sister's, and gazed up at Wesmorlyn, but his expression was blank and he appeared not to know the earl. "Are you sure this is not some residual effect of the witch's sorcery?" Wesmorlyn asked the gypsy girl, thinking of Hannah's belated agony.

"I don't think so," she answered. "This terrible torture began the moment he drank ale given him by Mother Sarah." She pointed at the old woman huddled by the fire. "He dropped to the ground in agony and became as you see him."

Fanny still wept and wailed in the background; the young gypsy man patted her shoulder, trying in vain to offer comfort.

"You know all this and assume the old woman is responsible," Wesmorlyn said, "and yet you claim you knew nothing of your band's reliance on Lyulph Randell?"

"Do not blame my sister! Tamara didn't know, nor did I," the young gypsy man said, stepping forward, "because the old ones kept it a secret from all of us younger, and yet this night, in her glee at the count's agony, Mother Sarah revealed the truth. She said they did not tell us young ones because they knew we had different ways, that we felt differently about the people of this land."

"Romolo, don't try to excuse our ignorance," Tamara said, sitting back on her heels, calmer as Christoph appeared to fall asleep.

Christoph von Wolfram's pale face was now composed, and his breathing was deep and even. Fanny, though, was still sobbing that Christoph was going to die, as Tamara patted his forehead with a damp cloth and tenderly brushed his golden hair off his forehead. Romolo watched Fanny, hopeless yearning and pain in his dark eyes, helpless to ease her misery. Wesmorlyn felt like his eyes had been opened as he watched, alive to the powerful human passions of all who gathered, where in the normal course of events he took great pains to shut himself off from those terrible, painful, and sometimes touching emotions. A few of the young women, children clinging to their skirts, looked confused and frightened, while their men seemed suspicious of him. Though they appeared to wish

Christoph no ill, neither would they help him if the elders did not allow it.

It was almost overwhelming, the sudden onslaught of knowledge that came to him now. He felt like he had knowledge thrust into his brain, a profound awareness of human passion opened to him since his intimacy with Charlotte von Wolfram. Now he saw the many faces of love: Fanny's sweet devotion to her brother; the powerful passion Tamara carried in her heart for Christoph, over whom she crooned in desolate sorrow; and the young gypsy fellow's hopeless adoration of Fanny. It was beautiful and terrible, both at the same time, overwhelming him with conflicting sensations of hope and agony. Everything that it was, was irrevocably a part of him now. Once acknowledged, it could not be turned away from, and he felt a humbling desire to help if he could.

"Your brother is right, Tamara," Wesmorlyn said. He took a deep breath and let it out. "You cannot be held responsible for what you did not know."

Then one old man stood. Romolo watched him, and from the resemblance between them it was evident to Wesmorlyn that they were father and son.

"We have too long listened to this woman," he said, his voice quavering as he pointed to Mother Sarah. "She has preached hatred and fear of the English. What has this brought us but trouble?" He looked at Fanny and then to Wesmorlyn, resolution in his dark eyes. "I vow the young German will be safe here while these women look after him," he said, indicating the younger women of his tribe.

"And this English girl," Wesmorlyn said, indicating Anne, who listlessly slid from the saddle and stood, quiescent and mindless.

"And the English girl," the man agreed, gesturing to one of the men to help her. A young mother with kind dark eyes held a lantern for them as the gypsy fellow helped Anne over to sit by the fire.

The old gypsy matriarch had been watching and listening, but now grunted in disgust. "Pah! Idiocy. You do not know what you are saying," she said, pointing to Romolo and his father. "You overstep your boundaries! These are *gorgios*, not

Rom!" Mother Sarah rose, her ponderous girth swathed in flowing robes of many colors.

"But they are *gorgios* who have done us no harm," Tamara said, taking in some of the other gypsies in her encompassing glance. "Lyulph Randell is *gorgios*, too; why should we cause pain on his command? Why should we pledge ourselves to him?"

"My only concern is for Countess Charlotte," Wesmorlyn said, putting up one hand in a gesture of peace. He had to find her, desperation seizing him at this delay. "Among you she stayed in peace, but your liege lord, he to whom you have mistakenly given allegiance, has taken her. That is where he has likely gone now, back to where he has hidden her! I fear for her life. This is her brother," he said, one hand on Christoph's shoulder, "and he has done no one harm. His only wish is to save his sister and leave England. Do *any* of you know where Lyulph Randell would keep her?" The gypsies shook their heads.

But Tamara met his gaze across the prone form of Christoph. Trembling, she said, "My lord, I *may* know how to find her."

"Where is she?" he asked. "Just tell me where she is and I'll go this instant."

But she shook her head. "I do not know to *tell* you where she is, I know in other ways. I can find my way to her, for she is here," she said, hand over her heart. "She's my friend, and I know I can find her."

Wesmorlyn must have displayed his skepticism, because the young man, her brother Romolo, stepped forward. "Please, my lord, don't doubt my sister. She has the sight. It is why Mother Sarah kept her close, I think; she feared her powers."

"She has no power," the old woman scoffed, but was ignored. She slumped back down on her seat, the fire gone from her eyes as her people paid no attention to her outburst.

"Will you lead me?" he asked of the young woman, and she nodded. "Can you do so in this darkness?" She nodded again. "Then let's go." It seemed a faint hope, but it was all he had to cling to.

Tamara gazed down at Christoph, swept his blond hair off

his forehead, and kissed it. She murmured some words in his
ear, and then looked up at Fanny. "My brother will protect you
both from harm, and so will my papa. Trust Romolo."

"I do," Fanny said, her voice quavering, but calmer, responding to Tamara's composed strength.

Once more Tamara bent over Christoph, her hair shielding
her from view; she was motionless for a long moment, then
rose. "I'm ready now. I can find Charlotte." She turned and
started toward the woods beyond the gypsy encampment.

EXHAUSTED, Charlotte sat on the floor, her knees up and
her arms wrapped around them, dust and dirt clinging to her
and her hair a ratted mess. She was cold and weary and miserable. She had been trying to find a way out of the room ever
since Lyulph left. The window would have seemed a logical
choice, but it resisted every effort of her hands to open, and
when she tried to break the glass it was as if she was hitting
water, for though she could put her wrapped fist through it, it
closed up again when she withdrew her hand. Witchcraft at
work.

The awful dilemma she was in finally hit her, and the tears
ran down her grimy face, though she would not give in to the
weakness of weeping outright. The candle guttered and died,
and she was plunged into utter darkness. A sob welled up
from her gut and burst out, against her fiercest attempt to quell
it. But she was not one to concede; after a few fainthearted
minutes, Charlotte took a deep, gulping breath and fought
back the tears, anger building in her heart. She would not be
defeated, not until her last breath was taken and her last heartbeat stilled. She couldn't change the past, but she could determine her future.

So she began to methodically search the room in the dark
for any weapon she could use on Lyulph Randell when he
came back. In the darkness, as she searched slowly, blindly
reaching out and feeling around her, she looked back over
every step she had taken that had brought her to this moment
in time.

She had left Germany intent on finding Fanny's mother,
though she had led her uncle and brother to believe she was

seriously considering the Earl of Wesmorlyn as a husband. There was no need for regret there. How else did men expect women to behave if they would not listen to them and treat them as rational beings? Subterfuge was the resource of the powerless.

That feeling of powerlessness over her own destiny was what had led her to *all* the mistakes of her youth, even her misguided affair with poor Dieter, her young lover, though she could hardly blame her uncle for concluding from it that she was a danger to herself. She was a wild young girl, unhappy, turbulent, difficult, and at fifteen, to throw herself at her dancing master as she did, betrayed an unsteadiness of character that would have led to even worse disaster in the broad world. Though she shuddered to think of the risk she had taken of becoming pregnant, she still couldn't regret her behavior even now. Some would say that indicated how low her character was, but she didn't care. Her fault had not been in seeking love and affection, but in trying to inflict upon the mild-mannered young man a plan to take her away from Wolfram Castle. Her Uncle Nikolas had learned of the plan, and thus began a distrust of her that had never waned. Through it, she had learned to fear her own feelings and doubt her instincts.

She grabbed the iron leg of the bed in the dark and felt for a way to disassemble it; would it come apart? Could it be used as a weapon against Randell?

Wryly, she thought that if her Uncle Nikolas could see her now he would be shaking his finger and saying that he knew it would come to a bad end. But once she was in England, with the best of intentions to help Fanny find her mother, she didn't see how she could have known to behave any differently, given the string of events beginning at the ball her first night in London.

Damn the iron bed! Frustrated, she gave up trying to get the leg off. It was firmly welded on and she was just straining herself to no purpose. She tried instead to figure out if there was any other piece of the bed that would come apart. It was evident to her now, she thought as she worked, that Lyulph Randell, who had appeared to be such a fast friend to Wesmorlyn and Lady Hannah, was really plotting their downfall.

But how could she possibly have known that then? Even Wesmorlyn had been in the dark about Lyulph Randell's plan to marry Hannah and thus take over the earl's estate. If anyone had a reason to be chagrined at not knowing the truth, it was Wesmorlyn. She had trusted Lyulph Randell because he appeared to be a solid member of their society, and an intimate even of her approved fiancé.

She supposed if she had stayed in London and gone along with the plan to wed Wesmorlyn, Randell would have just come up with some other plan to thwart his enemy, as he had repeatedly called the earl. He saw her and her brother and sister as an impediment, first, and then a tool. Now he seemed to have some wild plan to make her his wife and create a generation of powerful offspring to fight his battle. It was absurd, but he would not listen to reason.

There was no escaping her own responsibility, ultimately, though, no matter how she tried to justify her behavior. She should never have trusted someone she didn't know. Blinded by her instant dislike of the earl, flattered and taken in by Randell's persuasive charm, and pushed relentlessly by her brother's insistence that they were going back to Wolfram Castle immediately, she had taken matters into her own hands, with these disastrous results. It didn't matter one bit that it may all have turned out the same if she had not interfered, for she *had* interfered, and this was on her head.

She gave up on the bed, for it was indestructible, and put her forehead on her knees. Then there was Wesmorlyn, the center of her misery. How had it happened that a man she had despised from the moment they met had become so important to her, then tenderly valued, and then a betrayer? For she could think of it as nothing less than utter betrayal, that he should take their most tender, intimate moment, and what she shared with him in that time, and turn it against her. He had twisted it into something terrible, despising her for her honesty, failing her test of trust. If they had only worked together, and if he had not been the kind to despise her for what she was, then perhaps it would have all turned out differently.

His own revelation of his unique heritage had, after all, been a complete shock to her. But she had taken it in stride and honored him for his uniqueness, feeling perhaps they were drawn together to balance each other out—the earth and the sky, wild and disciplined. It had led her to believe that as unusual as he was, he would understand and appreciate her own distinction. So the disgust evident in his expression when she told him her family secret had been doubly a betrayal, and she had not foreseen it. Perhaps that was why it still stung so badly.

A noise made her look up; Lyulph unlocked the door and strode into the room, lantern in hand. He thrust forth a bottle and said, "Drink this!"

"No!" she cried, blinking at the light and covering her eyes.

"Please," he said, falling to his knees and pushing the bottle toward her. "Charlotte, if you do, I will do anything, I promise. Anything you ask of me."

"Liar."

"You're impossible," he hollered, fury in his expression, frustration in the tense line of his body. "Drink!" He shoved it at her.

"No!" she cried again, hitting his hand away from her face.

They quarreled for a time, but Charlotte no longer felt his lure. He was just a scheming, jealous, pitiful wretch pushed and prodded by his envy of Wesmorlyn's family holdings and unblemished history to try to steal it all away. He could pretend it was some grand, diabolical scheme, but in the end it came down to petty jealousy. As her resistance remained intact, he became more frustrated and louder in his demands. But she would not be bullied.

"Give up, Randell," she finally said, "for I will never willingly go along with your scheme, and I suspect you cannot take me unwillingly, or—"

"But I *can* take you unwillingly," he said, his voice hoarse with anger. He set the lantern aside, stood, and pulled off his jacket, tossing it across the filthy floor, out of his way. "Our bond will not be the same. You won't be my wife and lifelong partner, but since you refuse me anyway, then I will *take* what I want and follow through with the rest of my plan." His eyes had darkened with fury and anguish, but he paused and stared at her, his expression softening, the grim set of his mouth slackening. "Charlotte, please," he said, pacing toward her with measured steps, his boots striking the wood floor with a thudding beat, " I give you one more chance. I have restrained myself until now out of respect for you, but if you will be so foolishly stubborn, then you leave me no other choice but to—"

"There is *always* another choice," she cried, fighting back her fear, skittering back against the wall. "You can stop now, and let me go!"

"No! You don't understand."

"I don't, and I never will!"

His eyes widened, and there was terror in the green depths, fear of some unknowable horror, it seemed to Charlotte. "I have no choice!" he said, crouching by her and holding out one hand. She batted it away. He sighed, scrubbed his face with both hands, and then stared at her. "Charlotte, this is the only way for me now, the only way I can break away from Morwenna. She has planted a terrible magic within me, and to fight it I need to bond with you, or leave forever." He leaped back up to his feet. "If you persist in this stubbornness," he said, pacing in agitation, "then I must make you with child. You will bear my son and then I will take him away from you, raising him to—"

"Shut your mouth," she said, fear and fury mingling in her tone. She slid along the wall to the bed, some of her courage fleeing at his growled threat.

He stopped pacing and stared at her as he unbuttoned his shirt and pulled the bottom out of his trousers. He unbuttoned the fall of his breeches and pulled his shirt off. His pale skin, sleek musculature, and the wiry dark hair over his chest and forearms riveted Charlotte's gaze. Grabbing her by the arm he threw her down on the mattress, but she kicked out at him, catching him on the shin. He yelped in pain, but didn't let go of her until she summoned every bit of her strength and kicked him in the groin. Staggering, he knocked over the lantern and it went out; the smell of lantern oil filled the air and a tiny flame trailed across the wooden floorboards as the fire ate the fuel and licked up to the bed mattress.

At that very moment, a noise outside drew their attention. The glass in the windows rattled as something or someone pounded on the outside door. Lyulph stumbled to the window and threw it open, gazing down below. "Damn!" he shouted. "Damn him, *damn* him! How did he find us, and so quickly? Why did Morwenna not delay him as she said she would?"

Charlotte leaped to her feet and raced to the window; she pushed Lyulph aside, looking down. "Wesmorlyn," she hollered, as she saw his chestnut hair gleaming dark gold and copper in the pale platinum light of the moon. Flames began to light up the room, as they caught on the bare mattress.

"Charlotte!" he cried, as he looked up. He took off his jacket and shirt and threw them aside, and in front of Tamara, who gaped at him in awe from a few yards away, he unfolded his mighty wings, the twelve-foot span arcing away from his body and the tips unfurling. "I can come to you. If you will cast yourself out of the window, I'll carry you away from this madman!"

"I can't," Charlotte said, as she tried, but was pushed back by a force that was like hands on her chest, keeping her inside. She beat at the wooden window frame, trying to find a weak spot, but it was useless. "Some magic is at work, and the house is locked to me; I can't get out! And the room is on fire!"

"It is time this was over," Lyulph, behind her, growled.

She turned in time to see that he had stripped off his last articles of clothing, tossing them to the flames, and she staggered back in horror as before her eyes, he sprouted dark fur, as dark as that found after the attack on Tamara, and his body convulsed in change, his snout forming, big white teeth bared. A howl of pain and glory erupted from his throat. And then, as she backed away, he leaped at the window, breaking the wooden frame to splinters. He landed on the ground and faced the earl.

Charlotte turned back to the room and saw that the rush of air had fueled the flames, which licked up the papered wall and raced across the wood-paneled ceiling.

SOMEONE groaned. Who was that, Christoph wondered, blinking and rolling over.

"Christoph, are you all right?" Fanny asked, crouching by him in the dark.

He realized it was he who was groaning and stopped. "Yes," he said, his voice strangely hoarse. "I'm all right." Confusing memories bubbled to the surface of his consciousness, but overlying it all was a sense of urgency. He bolted upright. "Charlotte!" His vision went black for a moment, and he put one hand to his head and moaned again.

Fanny cried out, "Christoph, Christoph!"

But it was another's voice he remembered. Tamara had spoken to him as he drifted in a condition of stasis, conscious but unable to move or indicate that he heard her. She had leaned over him, kissed his lips with sweet fervor, and whispered, *"Come to me; you will always be able to find me now, from this moment forward."*

And he did know where she was; she was near Charlotte, who was in danger. He couldn't explain to anyone how he knew this, but he did. He must go to them, and he must go as a wolf. But he was without the wolfskin kirtle; could he make the transformation without it? He staggered to his feet and shook himself. He had to try. Fanny stood nearby wringing her hands and weeping.

"Fanny, stop crying," he whispered, taking her shoulders in his hands and moving her away from the firelight, into the gloomy shadows of one of the caravans. "Do you wish to help me save Charlotte?"

"Yes, oh yes," she said, gulping back tears. She took a deep breath and straightened. "How?"

He glanced around at the gypsy camp. The old woman who gave him the ale when he arrived at the gypsy camp—Mother Sarah, she had been called—was embroiled in a bitter argument with some others, but the discussion was carried on in their own unintelligible language. Children wept and clung to their frightened mothers, their soft sobs carried on the breeze to his sensitive ears. Others of the group lingered in the shadows, including Tamara's brother, who administered to a young girl he recognized as Anne, the witch's befuddled maidservant from Moor Cottage.

"I need to get away," he murmured, turning back to Fanny, "and I need you to be very brave." He stared into her eyes and felt the force of his own personality emanate, transferring courage to his nervous half sister. "I know how frightened you are of werewolves, but can you be brave, Fanny? Can you gather your courage and help me, for Charlotte's sake?"

She took a deep shuddering breath and stared into his eyes, the blue of hers almost disappearing around her dilated pupils. "For Charlotte," she said, faintly. "For her I will do anything."

CHARLOTTE looked down from the window and saw Lyulph the black wolf dart at Wesmorlyn, leaping and tearing at his beautiful but fragile wings. Tamara screamed, and Lyulph turned toward her, snarling.

"No!" Charlotte screamed. "Tamara, run away! Run! Protect yourself!"

"I will not leave you!" she cried. "I see fire. Can you climb out yet? Is the magic still working?"

It was; she tried again to climb out the window, but it still barred her. She could feel the heat from the fire on her back, and knew she would die if she stayed in that room for much longer. The ceiling was engulfed. Flames rushed toward her, eating everything in their path like some ravenous insatiable monster.

Fury ripped through Charlotte, and then an odd, preternatural calm. She was *not* going to die, not now, and not this way. Lyulph had turned back to Wesmorlyn; with his mighty wings the earl soared and beat at the wolf, which leaped and snapped, its great jaws closing occasionally on the wings. Charlotte heard a sickening crunch, and the bony tip of one wing hung limp, shattered by the powerful teeth of Lyulph, but Wesmorlyn did not stop. He soared straight up, and then came down, striking at Lyulph with his heel, but it was a glancing blow off the wolf's broad head, and only stopped him for a moment.

A confidence entered Charlotte, down to her soul. She was a von Wolfram through and through; she now knew something she had never known before, and was willing to take the chance no other woman had ever taken. She rapidly stripped her clothing off, feeling the heat from the flames lick at her feet and blister her naked back. Then she climbed up to the windowsill, holding aloft the wolfskin kirtle as she fought back her fear and settled deep into her mind, finding the darkest recesses, the most secret knowledge of her core. The answer to the enigma of her life resided deep within her; she had the power. She always had.

It trembled through her and she felt the transformation, the gut-wrenching evolution of her body into its elemental form. The wolf within her had always longed to get out to express the wildness of her soul, and now it shivered to life. Slim but strong, silver and golden all at once in the pale moonlight and glittering firelight, wrapped in the warmth of thick wolf fur and agile in ways no human ever could be, she leapt from the third floor, no longer bound by the spell on the cottage, just as the first flames danced and flashed out the window.

She landed on all fours. The world was different; vision shifted and she could see only in shades of light and dark, but for every loss of color and depth of perception she could feel a ferociously powerful sense; Tamara whimpered, so softly no one but a wolf could hear it, and Wesmorlyn was beginning to wheeze, his breath coming quickly. The fresh scent of the grass upon which she had landed was overlaid by the acrid stench of the crackling fire that was now consuming the entire third floor of the building. Lyulph had not tired a bit, but when he whirled and saw her, he yelped in utter astonishment, and she felt his mind, the roar of anger in his soul. For him, she was his mate, even more so now that he saw her as a wolf, but to her, he was nothing but a danger that must be destroyed.

She raced at him, leaping at his neck and sinking her teeth in, glorying in the sensation of breaking skin and the flood of warm blood. But he was stronger than she and bigger, as well as far more experienced in wolfish behavior. So as he shook her off and scrambled to try to recover from the shock, she knew that she had but a few precious seconds left to hurt him before he would regain his equilibrium and she could be killed.

But Wesmorlyn, horror on his beautiful face, gazed at her. "You're an animal," he cried, and heaved, retching as he staggered back, his wings beating to try to maintain his balance. "A beast, just like him!" He shook his head, the horror twisting his mouth, but then, as Lyulph growled and leaped at Charlotte, he rejoined her in her battle against the giant wolf. He soared and stomped again, and the wolf yelped in pain, rolling, stunned on the ground.

His expression a grimace of fury, Wesmorlyn kicked Lyulph again and again, as Charlotte, determined to keep Lyulph down, leaped on him, going for the jugular. It was not a conscious decision she was making, but the rapid response of instinct over thought. She must stop him before he hurt someone, and so she held him by the throat. Wesmorlyn ran to her side and reached out, but in that second Lyulph leaped to his feet, shook off Charlotte and pounced on Wesmorlyn, pinning him to the ground and ripping into his left wing, clamping down on it and pulling with all his might. A sickening snap of bone and the pop of a joint being pulled, and Wesmorlyn cried out in agony, the wail of pain echoing in the night as he writhed.

But he would not be defeated so easily; even as Charlotte, the fierce animal part of her mind failing her and the woman watching in horror, leaped forward to tackle Lyulph, Wesmorlyn rose, his golden skin emitting a blinding light that rivaled the consuming fire for brilliance, his fury translating into superior strength. Lyulph twisted to meet Charlotte's attack and the earl yelled, "No!" He lunged at the animal, his one injured wing dragging on the ground, and gripped the huge dark wolf in both hands, digging his fingers into the fur. As it yelped in shock, he picked up the robust beast and heaved it against the stone wall of the house. It lay in a heap by the bushes at the foundation, howling in pain as embers and ash from the fire above rained down on its head. The bitter scent of burning fur wafted on the damp night air, the stench filling Charlotte's nostrils.

At that second, across the moor, came another silver wolf, slim, and slightly larger than Charlotte. She howled in joy; it was Christoph! He skidded to a halt at the sight before him, and his mind reached out, touching hers. *Charlotte?*

It is me, she said to him with an excited yip. He raced to her, they rubbed muzzles, brother-wolf and sister-wolf. Lyulph had risen and was trying to limp off into the night, blood gleaming on his dark fur and dripping off his snout. Charlotte, overjoyed by their collective victory, wanted to race after the badly injured werewolf, but a howl from Christoph stopped her in her tracks.

There on the ground lay Wesmorlyn, pale and unconscious, his beautiful wings stretched out and torn, ripped to shreds and battered. One hung loosely from its joint between his scapula. His head was bleeding from the fall he had taken when Lyulph had pulled him down by the wing. But his fists were still closed around the hanks of fur he had pulled from Lyulph's hide in his stalwart attack, the one that had finally defeated Lyulph Randell and forced him to retreat.

Tamara knelt by him and looked up at the two wolves. "He does not breathe!"

Chapter 23

CHRISTOPH RACED off after Lyulph, no doubt concerned that their formidable foe would come back. Charlotte rushed to Wesmorlyn; only when she saw Tamara pull back did she realize that as a wolf, she would never be able to take him in her arms or touch his face. She leaped away and willed herself to come back to her human form. The transformation hit and she rolled on the ground in agony, howling in pain and hugging the wolfskin kirtle to her breast. As her body returned to human form, quivering and naked in the damp night air, she understood at last the danger inherent in werewolfism. As jealous as she had been of Christoph's magical ability, it was a burden to be assumed not lightly, but with great trepidation. Panting and shivering, still feeling the awful torment of the change, she accepted it willingly, stronger now and sure of herself and her place in the world. She was a wolf-woman, perhaps the first, perhaps the only.

Tamara, stalwart even in her shock at the von Wolfram family secret, ran to her and put her own cloak around Charlotte's shoulders, covering her nakedness. "We have to get away from this building before it comes down," she cried, looking up in fear at the burning house.

"Wesmorlyn," Charlotte cried, staggering to her feet and stumbling to him, collapsing at his side. She threw herself over him, and then felt, as she wept with relief, the faint sound of breathing in his chest, and a tiny puff of air from his mouth. "He's breathing! He's alive!"

Fanny, holding a bundle of clothes, raced out of the nearby copse and joined them, her pale face betraying her fear and horror at the events of the night. She cried out at the sight of the fire. Charlotte leaped to her feet, hugged the poor girl, and hurriedly explained all that had happened. "We have to get Wesmorlyn away from this place before it comes down," she commanded, as a cracking sound overhead announced the splitting of a support beam. A heavy charred piece of wood landed near them.

Fanny shrieked and danced away, but then stared at the earl again. His broken wing was stretched out at an odd angle. "But what is he?" Fanny cried, staring at Wesmorlyn. "I don't understand!"

"Never mind that now, just help me, *both* of you!" Charlotte shouted, over the increasingly savage roar of the inferno. Together, the three girls pulled Wesmorlyn far enough away, to safety.

Fanny, panting, told Charlotte that she had Christoph's clothes, and asked where he was.

"He has followed Lyulph Randell," Charlotte said.

She eyed the earl. "I still don't know what he is. I don't understand any of this."

"He's a kind of angel, Fanny; hush." Looking around, fearful and uncertain, Charlotte tried to think, but her gaze returned to Wesmorlyn, motionless and bruised, the gorgeous golden aura he had emanated as he vented his wrath on Lyulph now extinguished. "We need to decide what to do now. How are we to get him back to his home?"

"Romolo has the earl's horse safely tied up at our encampment; he can help get the gentleman back to Wesmorlyn Abbey," Tamara said, her olive complexion made golden by the flames that now had consumed the uppermost floor of

Charlotte's former prison. "It's not far from here, and my brother knows the way."

A floor inside gave way and crashed, the sound echoing in the night, the smoke spilling out of windows and billowing upward, blotting out the moon as sparks flew up in clouds. Fanny cried out and clung to Charlotte, who said, "But what about Christoph? How will he find us?"

"I'll stay behind and help him follow," Tamara replied, calm in the face of everything that had happened.

"Are you sure?" Charlotte asked, kneeling by Wesmorlyn and cradling his head on her cloaked lap. It would be a relief to have help with Wesmorlyn and Fanny, and Romolo had impressed her as calm and courageous as his sister. "But after all you've seen . . . don't you even want an explanation?"

Tamara shook her head. "No. You're my friend; we don't need words. Wait here. I'll go get Romolo, as well as some clothes for you; you must leave here as soon as possible." She gazing up at the blazing building. "I'm afraid this fire may spread. I'll send Romolo to you with the horse and clothing; you three take the earl, and I'll wait for Christoph and guide him to Wesmorlyn Abbey."

"But how will you know where to go?" Charlotte asked, exhaustion beginning to wear her down.

"I led Wesmorlyn to you tonight. I'll know the way, for I will always find you, my friend."

Charlotte stared at Tamara and then went to her; they clung to each other, and she felt it. It was true; there was no need for words. They were bonded friends, down to the soul, and Charlotte was grateful for the young woman's steady good sense in this hour of terror.

She supposed it took a half hour, and in that long interval, Charlotte stared up at the rapid progress of the fire consuming her prison. But finally Romolo, leading the earl's horse, found them and handed Charlotte a bundle, sent along by Tamara. She dashed to the copse of trees, dressed as well as she could and put her friend's cloak back on over it all. Then Charlotte accompanied Romolo, Fanny, and Wesmorlyn, who slumped on his horse, cloak over his battered and torn wings. As they walked away from the disastrous scene, a horrible rumbling noise shook the ground and Charlotte looked back; the roof had finally collapsed and the walls were now just jagged fingers pointing skyward, outlined in orange and crimson by the shooting flames. If she had not transformed, she might have been a burned skeleton lying in the ruin.

They walked for hours, until Charlotte thought she would go mad from fatigue. Light glimmered in the eastern sky as they finally wended their way up a long, crushed-stone lane toward a sprawling golden stone castle.

A tall sepulchral man stood before the great open gates in front of Gothic arched oak double doors. His expression was impassive as he strode forward and pulled back the drab, filthy cloak that covered Wesmorlyn. As pale as he had appeared, Charlotte saw his gaunt face bleach to the color of finest white linen, a whiter pallor than humanly possible, as if he had no blood in his body. "This I feared from the beginning."

He pulled the earl off the patient horse, gently folded his broken wings, and easily bore him through the gates and the enormous oaken doors that swung open as he approached. Romolo led the horse away, around to the back.

"Who are you?" Charlotte cried, gathering up her gypsy skirts and following into the Abbey. "Don't you wish me to explain? Don't you want to hear—"

"I need no explanation. Rather I will tell you. You are the Countess Charlotte von Wolfram, affianced to this man, the Earl of Wesmorlyn. Having made hasty and unwise choices, you found yourself in terrible trouble, and the earl went to your succor. He persevered and defeated Lyulph Randell, suffered greatly in the event, and now is damaged, and perhaps has given up his lifelong goal of justifying his family's return to the fold."

"Who are you?" she whispered, her voice echoing like the hushed sound of leaves falling in autumn.

He still walked across the flagstone floor of the vast great hall, bigger even than that of Wolfram Castle, the earl limp in his outstretched arms. Charlotte followed, trembling with exhaustion, weary and sick at heart, but Fanny sank down into a chair, murmuring that she was exhausted, without even the energy to climb the stairs. The man did not answer Charlotte, and what did it matter? Her curiosity died with the acknowledgment that there was nothing for her here. The man's disapproving speech proved that the vast chasm between her and Wesmorlyn was wider than she had even imagined. What did an angel and a wolf have in common that could possibly make any link between them viable?

As they reached the third floor, Charlotte mindlessly following, not knowing what else to do and hoping to see the earl stir, at least, before leaving the castle forever, a door down the hall opened and Lady Hannah bolted out.

"Semyaza!" she cried. "What has happened to Wes?"

Charlotte stared at the girl, remembering what the earl had said about her running away, and her obsession with Lyulph Randell. Randell must have been using his odd power on her; his scheme had been to marry this girl and destroy Wesmorlyn. All of his plans had been upset the moment Charlotte and Christoph entered the ballroom and he realized that his nemesis's proposed wife was of a family of werewolves.

And yet his interest may have been served better if he had not lured Charlotte away with the false promise of Fanny's mother. If she had stayed in London, if she had not allowed Randell to influence her and lead her astray, her initial dislike of the earl may have hardened into something worse. London, to her, after her brief acquaintance with it, did not seem fashioned to bring about any better end, for the falseness of its society, the dreariness of its atmosphere, and the stultified company they would have been to each other in the brief drawing room visits allowed a young man and his fiancée could never have explained them to each other as time alone on the moors had.

So her engagement with Wesmorlyn was doomed from the beginning either way, she supposed, ultimately. The dull ache in her heart as she remembered their fleeting fervent encounter on the moor pained her still, but she would have to forget it and carry on as best she could.

Hannah followed them, and both young women entered a bedchamber after Semyaza, who strode across the huge room in a couple of long steps and laid the earl gently on a velvet-draped bed. "What happened?" Lady Hannah cried, sobbing and folding her hands as if in prayer. "What is that awful smell? Why is he hurt? His wings—his beautiful, *beautiful* wings—are shattered and singed!"

"He saved my life," Charlotte said, her tone hollow and vacant. "Lyulph Randell attacked me and Wesmorlyn intervened," she continued, remembering his awesome strength as he picked Randell up and threw him against the stone building. "He risked his life to save mine, even though he saw me in a form that revolted him. Still, he saved me."

Semyaza turned, and gazed at her, the diffused light from the curtained window shadowing his hollow eyes. "What did you just say?"

Charlotte rubbed her arms, swallowed hard, and repeated her words, then said, "And now he's dying, perhaps, and it's all my fault!" She coughed, feeling the effects of the smoke in her throat.

Semyaza nodded in acknowledgment, but then said, "Yes, perhaps, but don't blame yourself for what happened, Countess. It was one more necessary step in this young man's progress," he said, touching the broken wing with gentle fingers. "The earl was doing the right thing, and learning a most important lesson. You have helped him by demonstrating your own passion for life and family. He needed to know this, for he has never understood that the human part of him is equally as important as his angelic heritage."

Charlotte shrugged, not caring about lessons in life at that moment. She glanced over at Hannah, who crouched and wept at her brother's bedside; her heart ached, for she knew what it was to despair for a brother so deeply and yet be powerless to help him. "Shouldn't we be doing something for him?" she asked, her voice thick and strange to her own ears. "Shouldn't you get him a physician, or . . ." She trailed off.

"You should be helping him."

"Me?" she asked, horrified, meeting the tall man's penetrating gaze.

"Yes, you."

She shook her head and backed away, but Semyaza took Lady Hannah's arm and hauled her out to the hall and then closed the door behind them, leaving Charlotte inside. "But sir!" Charlotte cried as she heard Hannah wail mournfully. She raced to the door and pulled at it, but it was locked from the outside. "I can't help him!" she cried, pounding on the door. "He needs a doctor!"

"No doctor can mend his wounds." The man's hollow voice was muffled by the thick wood of the door.

"But what can I do? I almost got him killed!"

"Think but a moment and you will understand. Go to him!" the man said, his voice commanding.

Hannah's sobs echoed down the hall, diminishing as the man led her away. Pounding on the door and wailing would not move him; Charlotte knew it somehow, and stopped. She put her forehead to the wood door, weary in body and spirit. But finally, there was nothing to do but obey. She returned to the earl's bedside and stared down at him. He was utterly beautiful in his stillness, his skin golden, though smudged with ashes, his brown hair dirty and tightly curled, sweat on his brow. She sat on the edge of the bed. How could she help him? She was no healer. It didn't come naturally to her as it did to some women of her acquaintance. His wings were broken and burned, and she was no angel's surgeon, nor was she anything but a wolf-woman, wild and untamed. She wouldn't take back her transformation even if she could, for with it had come a knowledge that a part of her she had always suppressed as evil and unwomanly had been released. Strength was not unwomanly, nor was vigor. Protecting those she cared for was not unwomanly, nor was sexual need and the satisfying of it, no matter what those at home would say. She was more a woman now, where she was a girl before.

And yet still, she felt deep within her the pain of becoming repellent in Wesmorlyn's eyes, when once, before her metamorphosis, those eyes had looked upon her with desire and affection. She was about to stand and leave the bedside, but he stirred, and she paused. He had risked his life to save her, even after she had told him the truth about their family, and even seeing her in her animal form. What was that if not the ultimate test of fidelity and courage? She couldn't abandon him now. She knelt by his bedside, and rusty as her prayers were, she began to speak to whatever power governed the universe, for she was not sure if she believed in the god of her childhood, the unyielding, wise, and stern master of all. Did she even believe in the god of these fallen angels, an angry, all-knowing, all-seeing god?

"Please," she whispered, "take this man-angel and return

him to health, for he is good and kind and wise, and his sister needs him, as do those in his care and employ. Even abhorring my family legacy as he does, even seeing me as a wild wolf, still he came to my aid and saved me from Lyulph Randell, whom he knew to be full of anger and ambition." Tears welled in her eyes.

He moved, and his broken wings stretched out. She gazed through a veil of tears, and reached out to touch them, feeling the torn, gauzy material, like fragile silk stretched between brittle ivory bone, shredded by the sharp fractures of the bone shards. The edges were singed and crisped by the fire, and they were blackened at the tips. Tears dropped and stained, spreading on the gossamer fabric like water on blotting paper.

"Heal him," she whispered, smoothing the diaphanous web between her hands as she closed her eyes, tears raining down to her fingers. She laid her cheek against his chest, feeling the smooth warmth of his skin and hearing the steady *thump-thump* of his heart. Pressing her lips to his skin, she murmured, "Come back, Wes, and know that though we'll be apart, I will always understand how much you risked for me and be grateful to you. Your life is here with those who need you. Come back for Hannah's sake."

She wept softly, knowing that a fractured part of her heart would always be devoted to him, and as much as he was revolted by her wolf essence, he must care for her, too, or he wouldn't have made such an incredible sacrifice. But their differences were too great and the pain of knowing she would always repulse him, no matter how he tried to get over it, made it an impossible bond to maintain except apart. When she was back home she would remember his lovemaking, his kindness, and his courage, and would do her best to forget the moment of horrified revulsion when he saw her for the first time as a werewolf. And in turn she hoped he remembered their golden afternoon together and would forget everything else.

Hours passed. She talked and prayed and found some solace, knowing that as much as she had done wrong, she had learned and would be better and stronger in the future. Being a wolf might seem an ugly thing to some, but for the first time in her life she felt whole and at peace in her heart. She rubbed her cheek against his lovely wings and then slept, eventually.

They had arrived at Wesmorlyn Abbey just after dawn; when she awoke, day had dwindled into early evening. Twilight made a golden glow in the room as the sun set. She was sitting on the floor against the bed, stiff and aching all over. Not a soul had come to the room all day, and she wondered what had happened, realizing with a start that she had not even thought about Fanny, Christoph, or Tamara all day. When she finally stood and gazed down at Wesmorlyn, it was to see that he slept peacefully now. His outstretched wings were mended, the filmy gauze beautiful, translucent, and repaired. The broken wing tip, which had been singed and hanging limply, was healed and strong again. He was still dirty and smudged with ashes, but he was whole.

She sighed, relieved at his miraculous recovery. His breathing was even, and he slumbered deeply, his expression peaceful at last. How had it happened? She couldn't believe she had any part in it, though she had prayed for his recovery. Another time her curiosity would have plagued her, but this was one of the things she would likely never know, and she would have to live with that. It was enough that he was recuperating; how it happened was not important.

Tapping at the door lifted her from her reverie. "Yes?"

Her brother entered. "Charlotte?"

"Christoph!" she cried and ran to him, hugging him hard. "You returned! Did you find Lyulph Randell? Where did he go? What did you do?"

"He escaped," Christoph said, frustration in his voice. "He left a trail of blood, for Wesmorlyn's mighty throw and your attack left him badly hurt. I tracked him as far as I could, but lost him eventually. I can't tell whether I'm grateful or angry about that."

"Where did he go?"

"I think he may have returned to Morwenna. When I got to the cottage, the door was wide open and the place was abandoned, and his blood was on the doorstep."

"Oh." A sense of dread swept over her as she thought about Lyulph and Morwenna together, their anger building. But she was safe now. Lyulph Randell couldn't hurt her. "What about . . . about . . ." She put a hand to her forehead and wavered. "Oooh," she groaned. "I feel so weak."

"When did you last eat?" he asked.

"I don't remember," she admitted. "Yesterday? What time is it?"

"It's about half eight in the evening. Fanny, poor girl, was exhausted after the ordeal. Hannah was very kind to her, she told me when I arrived, and even though she was worried frantically about the earl, nursed our little sister very kindly. Fanny slept most of the day. I'm not sure I understand this household; Lady Hannah seems to rely utterly on that fellow, Semyaza, who I thought was a servant, at first."

"I don't think he's a servant, Christoph. I'm not sure what he is, but he is very grand and solemn, and yet kind enough, I suppose, though he locked me in with the earl." She put one hand on Wesmorlyn's bare arm, feeling the steady pulse of his blood through his veins.

"What?" Christoph appeared horrified that she had been locked in, but Charlotte, after one lingering look at the earl, explained it all to him as he helped her up and out of the room, guiding her to the stairs and down.

"What about Tamara?" Charlotte asked.

When he didn't answer, she glanced sideways at him. If there was one thing she knew, it was that Tamara had fallen in love with him almost the moment she saw him. He, though, to the best of her knowledge, was still aching over his lost love, Melisande Davidovich. His pain was raw, like a burn, and Charlotte could not bear to hurt him by probing the wound, so she didn't pursue the matter.

"Tamara and her brother have gone back to their tribe," he said, finally, leading her along a modern hallway to a lovely dining room.

"Oh," she replied, experiencing a sharp ache of sorrow. She would never see them again, because they would no doubt go back to London immediately, and from thence would return to Germany. "I hope you said good-bye for me," she said, her voice thick with unshed tears.

"I did. Tamara didn't speak much, but Romolo told me he and his sister were going to make sure that their tribe does not suffer any retribution from Lyulph Randell. They are going to leave Cornwall now, forever."

Semyaza, Christoph went on to say, had ordered all who

came from their party to be made comfortable and given rooms to sleep in, food to eat, and fresh clothes to wear. Fanny, who was waiting in the dining room, rushed at her and hugged her. Charlotte rocked back on her heels.

"Fanny, Charlotte needs some food," Christoph said. "Release her."

"Of course, Christoph." Fanny guided her to a chair and piled a plate high with food, serving her as she had always done.

Charlotte put out one staying hand, grabbing her arm. "Fanny, stop! You are *not* our servant."

"I know that," Fanny said, putting her free hand over Charlotte's, "but it's natural to me to help wherever I can. I'm not strong, nor am I intelligent, but I can make people comfortable." She shrugged. "That's what I can do."

"Fanny, you're so much more than that, and I hope you learn that someday," Charlotte said, affectionately, hugging the girl.

They ate, and no one from the castle staff interfered, except to bring fresh dishes and hot water when necessary. A maid came in and closed the curtains against the purple twilight outside, then lit the candles as the three talked. The old gypsy woman had used wolfsbane on Christoph, he told them; that was what was in the ale she gave him. But he had been exposed to it before, in Germany, and so recovered swiftly. Fanny, Christoph said with pride, had gathered all of her courage to assist him in his transformation into a wolf. Their younger sister colored, and ducked her head shyly at the praise.

"What about poor Anne?" Charlotte asked, beginning, as she ate and drank some wine, to at least feel alive again, after the traumatic events of the past while.

"Anne was beginning to recover when last I saw her," Fanny said. "She was afraid of the gypsies at first, but I think she will be grateful to them and may stay there, with Tamara. I don't think they'll allow Mother Sarah to deceive them again, now that they see how she will lead them into trouble and danger."

"Poor Romolo," Charlotte said, watching her sister's face. "He cares for you a great deal."

"I said good-bye to him before he left," she said, calmly, "and thanked him for all of his help." Taking a deep breath she sat up straighter. "Where shall we go now? What shall we do?"

Her desire to change the subject was evident, and Charlotte and Christoph exchanged glances.

"I thought we should return to London and continue the search for your mother, your *real* mother," Christoph said. "If it is truly what you want, Fanny."

"But what about the earl?" Fanny said, looking at Charlotte.

Feeling the pain deep within her, Charlotte looked down at her hands and said, "He's well cared for here, and will get better in time, I have no doubt. He made it quite clear that my being who I am revolts him, and no matter how I feel, I could never love someone who didn't care for me exactly as I am."

"You don't need him," Christoph said, his tone dark with anger. "You don't need any of these English. We'll return to Germany where you are valued and loved."

Charlotte nodded, afraid to talk for the tears in her voice. She conquered her emotion and finally said, "But first, Fanny, you didn't answer. Do you wish to find your mother? I was wrong before to push you. I didn't really take your feelings into consideration. What do you *truly* want?"

"I would like to find my mother," Fanny said, hesitantly. "I may never live with her, and she may not want to see me, but I would just like to know that she is all right, and didn't suffer for bearing me."

"All right then, that is what we'll do," Christoph said. "We can leave for London in the morning at first light."

"I'll tell Semyaza," Charlotte said.

She didn't need to search for him. The moment Fanny and Christoph left the room, Semyaza materialized as if out of nowhere.

"You have made a decision," he said to her, his gaunt face sallow in the golden candlelight.

"Yes," she said, folding her hands together on the mahogany dining table to keep from twisting them in her anxiety. "First, will the earl recover now?" she asked, breathless. This man would know.

"Yes, he will recover in time, thanks to you. Do you know what you did?"

She shook her head.

"You may not understand," he said, gently, kindness in his pale gray eyes, "but you gave him a part of yourself, a part that he needed to heal. He has learned a valuable lesson from you, and will be a better man for it."

Her breath caught in her throat and she held back a sob. "Then I repaid him for his valiant effort to rescue me, and no debt exists. Good. We're leaving in the morning."

He nodded.

She cleared her throat, still raw from the smoke she had inhaled. "May we use one of the earl's carriages? It would facilitate our move."

"Of course."

"Thank you. Will you make our farewells to Lady Hannah? It's late, and I don't wish to disturb her, especially as she has not been well lately, nor will she be up when we are ready to leave in the morning."

"I'm sure she would wish to see you before you leave."

"No. No, I just want to go. I'll write her a note of farewell. It will be easier that way."

"Then it shall be as you wish," Semyaza said. "Everything will be prepared for your journey."

Chapter 24

BRIGHT MORNING sunlight slanted through the window and directly into Wesmorlyn's eyes. He was dazzled as he awoke, stretching and yawning, wondering at the wild dreams he had had, of werewolves and fire, a ferocious battle, and Charlotte weeping over him, her tears dripping down on his wings. He flexed his shoulders and sat up in bed.

"Wes, finally, you're awake!" Hannah cried, leaping up from her chair, which for some strange reason was by his bedside.

"What are you doing in here, Hannah?" he said, holding the sheets up over his naked chest. His little sister had never invaded his sanctum before.

"Waiting for you to awaken. You must get up," she said, taking his wrist and tugging him in an unusual display of vigor. "She's gone and I didn't know what to do. You've been asleep for days and days, but Semyaza said it was all right, just to let you sleep. But Charlotte saved your life, but she left and she didn't even say good-bye, though she left me a sweet note. But she's gone! What shall we do?"

He threw his legs over the edge of the bed and touched his

head, which ached fiercely. There was a bandage at his throat. He pulled it away, touching almost healed wounds. Memories flooded back to him, of the battle and his fury at Lyulph, and then the one moment when time stood still, and he saw, up in the window, flames leaping behind her, his beautiful, naked Charlotte. And she changed into a wolf. The intense attraction he had felt toward her had not disappeared, not even knowing what she was, and that was a revelation to him. But he had experienced an intense moment of revulsion, and knew that must have showed in his expression. Putting his head in his hands, he closed his eyes; how could he have let that show? His reaction must have hurt her. Perhaps that was why she had left before he regained consciousness.

The hazy memory of joy and contentment in her company came back to him, and with it the intriguingly erotic sensation of joining with her body and soul. What would have happened between them if her revelation of werewolf blood had not followed his so swiftly? Would he have asked her to marry him?

Would she have said yes?

He looked up and met Hannah's worried gaze. He had thought himself a considerate and exemplary brother, but had failed in some elemental way. If he had really listened to Hannah and given her credit for her excellent moral fiber, if he had just dug deeper, he would have discovered why she couldn't help her behavior around Lyulph; Randell had been trying to destroy his family by luring Hannah into either disgrace or marriage.

In the golden light of truth, he saw that he had become proud and cold and inhuman. He had felt his family to be above others, most especially the Randells, and not solely because of their secret life. Though Lyulph Randell's behavior couldn't be excused, he didn't think the fellow was always so angry. Many years before he had been just a carefree, cheerful youth, with none of the brooding anger of the last while. Wesmorlyn's haughty disdain for the fellow was the root of much of his need for vengeance. He had sowed the seeds of this discord with his own behavior, and that stung deeply. Had he done the same to Charlotte?

And in his attempt to rescue his family from eternal damnation, had he condemned them all to hell on earth? It was humbling to find that in trying to do the right thing, he had so completely missed the mark in every respect.

But for a few hours, at least, he had forgotten his distrust and distaste for all things passionate and human. In Charlotte's arms he had been whole for just a while, and simply a man, giving and taking in equal measure, feeling bonded with another human in a way he had never been before and likely never would again, now that he had driven her away so brutally.

Semyaza entered and gazed steadily at him.

"I've made a complete ass of myself and ruined everything, haven't I?" he said to his watcher. "I put myself and my family up on a pedestal, and forgot that most of our composition is human and fallible, and that our connection with humans, though it initially was our downfall will also be our—" He stopped, mouth open, and stared out the window, awareness seeping into his soul, understanding that was prompted by Charlotte's beautiful spirit and radiantly human soul. "Of course, that's it. Our salvation lies in our humanity!" he whispered.

He took Hannah's hand in his and watched the silent tears roll down her soft cheeks. "We'll *never* be perfect," he said, thinking out loud. "To gain redemption we have to keep trying and failing, over and over, working at it day by day, just like all humans do. There is no end, just the continual struggle, and as hard as that is, there's also great joy. And love." He squeezed his sister's hand. "We must take chances and opportunities, love and be loved. Connect to other imperfect spirits." He looked up at his guide. "I was so afraid of failing that I wouldn't give of myself, no emotion, no love, no true compassion. I tried to hold us apart, doing nothing, giving nothing."

Semyaza deeply sighed. "Imperfect you began, and imperfect you shall always be."

"Isn't there a ring of hell dedicated to those who do nothing, neither evil nor good? I believe I was headed there. Hannah," he said, putting one arm around her slim shoulders, "I never was the loving brother I should have been."

"But you were. I felt the love in everything you did."

He was humbled and grateful, and knew there was some truth to it. There must be an innate side of him that was loving, and Hannah had always had that deep brotherly devotion, from the very first moment of her birth. "I held you as a little baby, and now look how lovely you are." He turned and stared at Semyaza's gaunt face and ghostly eyes. "Sam, I've driven Charlotte away, idiot that I am. She was the one sent to teach me the truth, to show me how human I truly am, and I've driven her away. I have to go find her!"

"Then you must go to London," he said, with a faint smile on his thin lips.

A letter awaited Charlotte, Christoph, and Fanny in London. Their old friend, Frau Liebner, now on her way back to London to join them, had found out the fate of the real Miss Eleanor Dancey. The reason the woman had left Plymouth was a happy one; she was married and settled in a comfortable home in Chelsea with three stepchildren, and would be happy to see her long-lost daughter.

"So we need not even have left London to find your mother," Charlotte said, staring at the letter. They sat together at a table near the window overlooking the street in the dreary sitting room of their rented London townhome. "And I put you all through so much because of my impatience. Taking us off to Cornwall like that! Perhaps Uncle Nikolas is right after all. I'm imprudent and hasty, unfit to make my own decisions."

"That's your weariness talking, Charlotte," Christoph said, putting one hand over hers and meeting her gaze.

"No, Christoph, you're very kind, but I was foolish and hasty, and I must apologize," she said, humbly. "I put you all through so much, and I'm very sorry."

"I've been thinking of this," he said, releasing her hand and sitting back in the dusty, ornately carved side chair. "And you were right the night of the ball when you accused me of behaving badly because of my confusion over how to handle meeting another werewolf. Perhaps now that you have transformed you'll understand what it's like. I knew it wouldn't end well. I must challenge him or he must challenge me; one or the other of us must submit or leave."

Fanny, wide-eyed, said, "What would you have done?"

A hard gleam entered Christoph's blue eyes. "I would not have submitted, I can tell you that much." His expression softened. "I suppose I sensed some threat from him, but I'm still inexperienced and I wasn't sure of my conclusions. But my point is, by my recalcitrance and bad temper that evening, I drove you to your actions, Charlotte."

"No, it's kind of you to try to ameliorate my own opinion of myself, but it will not do." Self-knowledge came with a price, Charlotte found, and the price was conceding one's faults. Though she would never again allow anyone to make her decisions for her, neither would she be hasty in making them herself. "Deep inside I knew you would not, nor could you, make me leave if I wasn't ready. I wanted an adventure, and I got it. I was wrong to haul you all into it with me."

"But Charlotte," Fanny said, timidly. Her brow wrinkled and she took a deep breath. "If I had been stronger, I could have said immediately that I didn't like that awful witch-woman, and we could have left Cornwall before things went as far as they did."

Warm tears begin to slip down Charlotte's cheeks and she put out both her arms and pulled her siblings to her. "I am grateful, my loves, for your kindness." She released them, laughing at Christoph's discomfited expression, and took in a deep breath. "But this is not a night for tears, this is a night for celebration," she said, picking up the letter and waving it. "Fanny, tomorrow you will truly meet your mother. I'm so happy for you!"

Christoph retrieved his violin and played a merry tune, then laid it aside. "Tomorrow." He took Fanny's hand and squeezed it. "We'll be at your side, my dear, don't worry."

The next day Fanny was unnerved and pacing, alternating between tears and laughter. Morning was too early for the visit, and so she tried to occupy her time, but failed miserably, ending up simply staring out the front window at the gloomy little park opposite their rented townhouse. Charlotte left it to her to choose how the day was to proceed, and she decided she would like her brother and sister with her. If things went well, then she would let them know she was comfortable enough for a private visit with the woman.

A maid answered the door of the snug Chelsea house, just

a street back from the embankment, and guided them up the stairs to a first-floor parlor. Flanking Fanny, Charlotte and Christoph entered the room just slightly behind her, both with a hand at her elbow in case she should feel faint or need an encouraging squeeze.

A woman, sitting by an unnecessary fire, stood, nervously twining her hands around each other. She stared, her blue eyes big and round, but her belly even bigger and rounder. She was heavily pregnant, and seemed to tremble on the verge of tears, ready to drop back down into her seat. "My daughter," the woman said, her voice breathy and quavering.

Fanny broke free from her siblings and dashed across the room, taking the woman by the arm, guiding her to sit back down. "Some water for Mrs. Prudholme," Fanny said to a lingering maid, looking down at the woman, who had her eyes closed and had leaned her head against the chair back.

Any tension there might have been was diminished by this domestic scene, and after a short interlude for the woman to regain her breath, the four sat together, the tea tray in front of them, though no one could think of eating or drinking at the moment. Mrs. Eleanor Prudholme had taken hold of Fanny's hand and had not yet let go.

"I've never stopped thinking of my little girl all these years," she said, gazing at Fanny with tears in her eyes and voice. "You were such a beautiful baby, so perfect and sweet and well-behaved. How I longed to take you away with me! But I was young and frightened, and for a long time, even during my trip back to England and after, I was ill. The von Wolframs were kind—especially Countess Adele—but pointed out that they had already secured a wet nurse, while I . . . I didn't have the first idea how to care for you. My aunt, with whom I lived until she passed from this life a few years ago, advised me just to forget it all, but I never could."

"We love Fanny very much," Charlotte said, catching her sister's eye, "and you can be proud of the young woman she has become." Her voice broke on the last word, but she took a deep breath and stiffened her spine.

They spoke for a while about Eleanor's time in Germany, and she talked about Charlotte and Christoph's mother and father, confessing her own shame over events, but soon the conversation turned from painful subjects to happier things, and then as the daylight hours dwindled, it was time to go.

Charlotte drew Fanny aside and asked her what she wished to do; she had an invitation to stay in the house. They had briefly met Eleanor's husband, and he was a kindly, studious gentleman, absentminded but tenderhearted and doting on his heavily gravid wife. He was many years older than her, and a little nervous, he said, about having a baby in the house.

"I think I'd like to stay for a couple of days to become acquainted with her," Fanny said, looking back to the scene by the fire. Her mother had three stepchildren, and the youngest child, a girl of about seven years, sat at Eleanor's feet, one hand on her stepmother's enormous belly, while the two elder children were at a table in the corner playing a game.

"I think that would be good," Charlotte said. "But if you need me, or wish to come back, please just come. We're at your command."

"I wish matters between you and the earl had ended on a better note," Fanny said. "I feel terribly guilty having so much happiness when you—"

"Stop, Fanny!" Charlotte said, putting her forehead to her sister's and petting her hair. "Stop fussing. You are *such* a fusser. Take your happiness; you deserve it, and have paid amply in your life for what contentment you now can enjoy."

They left Fanny in Chelsea surrounded by her new family. Returning to their dreary rented house—the moldering rooms, the surly servants—was all the worse for her absence and the contrast between what they endured and the chaotic warmth and shabby charm of the Prudholme abode. Charlotte had not realized how, in such a short time, she had become so attached and dependent upon Fanny's presence. For all her fussing and occasional depression, she had become precious to both von Wolfram siblings.

And so, at dinner in the dark dining room, Charlotte and Christoph stared at each other across the scratched oak dining table. They had talked at length about Fanny's new family and had exhausted the topic. There were other things of which neither of them wished to speak, and so Charlotte's amazing transformation was all that was left.

"You are a werewolf, too," Christoph said, gazing at her

with an odd mixture of puzzlement and pride. "No woman has ever become one of us, one of the transformed. Not even every man born to our race can do what you've done. It is oft times only one man in each family or generation, but you did it, and so easily."

"Not easily," she said, with a deep sigh, pushing a dry piece of fish around on her chipped plate. "My fear of the fire and the anxiety of the moment facilitated the change, along with having the kirtle in my grasp. It was the only way I could escape the enchantment on the house, too, for that spell contained only the human me. I would have died in that fire if I hadn't transformed. I understand now, Christoph, what you and Uncle Nikolas have said about the sacrifice and the temptation and the burden of responsibility. I was jealous, but I know now it's not a gift, but an encumbrance."

"You can't go back now, though," he said, "or you would become . . ."

He didn't need to go on. The fate of the *unveraendert*, or untransformed, was familiar to them, the awful weakening and fading of the ones who refused to transform, refused to accept the burden and temptations and rewards of their unique heritage. Eventually the untransformed faded from life, but not into death, just into a kind of gray existence, where they walked among men unseen and unnoticed, banished forever from the joys of the flesh, and yet forbidden the relief of death. They had seen a man well on his way to such a death-in-life, and neither would consider it. It was a selfish and weak path, they both agreed.

"How did you know you could do it?" Christoph continued, determinedly cheerful, taking a fork full of the tasteless fish.

"I think I always felt it, the wolf within me, but I never knew what to do with it. No one ever told me it was possible; it was something I had to figure out on my own."

"I wonder if any woman has ever done what you have done?"

"I don't know."

Silence for a long few minutes.

"There's a lot, I think, that I don't know about what went

on between you and Wesmorlyn," Christoph said, still toying with his fish fork. He watched her intently.

"Trust me, Christoph, there is much more that I don't understand myself." She shook her head and pushed her plate away. "But all that really matters is that we shall not suit, as they say, and the engagement is broken irrevocably."

"You're sure of that?" Christoph said, gently.

"I'm quite sure."

FOR the first time in his life, Wesmorlyn acted purely on instinct. Semyaza assured him that Charlotte would be in London, and so he headed there, flying on the wings she had mended with tears of sorrow and humility and human forgiveness. But once there, he was unsure of himself, doubting everything but that he didn't deserve her forgiveness. What would he say? How should he approach her?

Not willing to face Christoph, he watched the house until she exited alone the morning after his arrival; she headed across the street to the small garden opposite and walked in the shade of the golden trees. Trembling with excitement to see her again, to say all he had to say, he followed her.

"Charlotte," he whispered.

Charlotte turned, and there was Wesmorlyn, impeccably clad in city clothing, his brown eyes full of yearning, the same melting look she had seen on the moor, the same look that had driven her into his arms. But this time she didn't believe it. It was a lie, a sham intended to make her feel that he cared when she knew that he didn't. Not really. Not for her. And she would never settle for less than bone-deep love. "I am happy to see you returned to health."

"Not so cold, Charlotte, please; don't be so chilly toward me." He took a step toward her.

"You say that as if you merit otherwise, when you scorn all that I am, all that my family is," she said, taking a step back, trembling as anger surged up within her heart. "You treat us like beasts; you behave as though because your ancestors did something dreadful and were cast out of paradise you are somehow better than we are. You're intolerably smug, judgmental, cold!" A chill wind blew through the park, and the leaves overhead trembled, some pulling free and fluttering down to rest at her feet.

"No, Charlotte," he said, putting out one hand. "That is how I *was*, not how I *am*."

"Can you truly say from your heart that you think differently now? Can you truly say that there remains within you no hint of censure, nor even a scrap of disgust?"

He blinked at her vituperation. "Charlotte, you must understand, the Randells have been my family's only experience of . . . of your kind. At times in their family history they have been brutal and cruel."

"And have your ancestors always been saints?"

He ignored that question, saying, "Please understand; I was raised to think of one objective only, and that was to regain what was lost, to better my family until we became worthy of deliverance."

"And you thought the way to do that was to become cold and emotionless?"

He approached, both hands outstretched. "That's how I *was*, Charlotte, but I've learned from you how far from worthy I was, how much I had yet to learn, how far I had to go. How far I *still* have to go."

"So you've learned a valuable lesson, and I'm sure that will be a comfort to me as I make my way back to Wolfram Castle." Another leaf fell from the tree above, fluttering down to her, and she caught it in one bare hand, savoring the leathery texture of the golden surface before letting it go to drift down to the ground.

"You're leaving?"

"Why would I stay in England?" she said, watching his eyes. The breeze lifted his russet curls off his nobly proportioned forehead. He was perfectly dressed and styled, and yet she thought he had been far handsomer in Cornwall, with careless attention to his attire and hair. In the dark night her heart still pounded with passion when she thought of him, his shirt and jacket undone, striding toward her over the moors with ardor lighting up his brown eyes.

"Give me another chance," he said, still slowly pacing toward her. "I know that somewhere in your heart you've forgiven me for treating you so badly. Now give me the opportunity to prove I can be what you want me to be."

"I think our time has passed."

"Please, Charlotte, don't say that."

His beautiful brown eyes held that expression of yearning again, and she couldn't bear it. Choking back tears, she turned away, and said, "I will never forget the look of revulsion on your face when I became what is, for me, the essence of my being. I'm a wolf-woman, and will always be, now, for once one of us has taken the step, we can never go back." She turned to see his expression, and caught the look; the faint shadow of distaste was still there.

"Surely you can go back," he said, stopping a ways away from her on the walk. "Can you not suppress it?"

She shook her head. Sighing, she said, "There, you see? You haven't changed."

"Yes, yes I have! I didn't mean that you *should* suppress it, just if you wanted to—"

"All right," she interrupted, "I'll say it differently, though what I just said is still true. I have taken the step and I would no more wish to go back than I would wish . . ." She paused, gazing at him through a haze of unshed tears. "I would no more take back my transformation than I would wish we had never made love. Would you take *that* back if you could?"

"No."

But she could see in his eyes that a part of him would take it back. "You're lying," she said, her tone harsh, her tears drying.

"No, I'm not." He had stopped and his head was bowed. "I would never take that back; it's my most precious memory. But I was raised to believe one way, and I cannot in one leap undo the teaching of a lifetime. I just wish we had waited until our marriage vows were said."

"That should be my speech," she said, dryly. "It makes me realize how unsuited for each other we are. We would be a constant reproach to each other. We would always want something from the other that was never going to be fulfilled, and the frustration would drive us apart no matter how much I I—" She stopped abruptly midword and turned away from him.

"What were you going to say?"

"I'll never deny that I care for you, Wes, but I will not be reproached for who I am every day of my life. I need to be myself. I need to transform and run as a wolf." She met his gaze, needing to make him understand what separated them. "How could I do that with the revulsion on your face, and knowing to you it is a dirty secret?"

"But we can work that out!" he declared. "You once told me marriage would be compromise and working things out as we went along."

"No. Some things, yes; but this, no."

"Please, Charlotte."

She turned away and headed out of the park, her shoes crunching on the falling leaves. "Let me go, Wes," she said, over her shoulder. "It will benefit neither of us to prolong this."

"No!" he roared. He bounded after her in a few quick steps, caught her, turned her swiftly, and jerked her into his arms. "I love you," he said, then pressed his lips to hers, binding her tightly in his arms.

She pushed him away and wiped her mouth, her hand trembling. "Perhaps love isn't enough," she said, and walked away.

"One more chance, Charlotte."

"Leave me alone, Wesmorlyn," she said, pausing at the edge of the park, and looking back at him. The overhanging trees, beginning to lose their summer leaves, shadowed his face. "Let me think. I need some quiet in my mind." She ran back across the street as a carriage passed, and then up the steps and into the gloomy townhouse as a light rain began to patter down on the pavement.

Chapter 25

THE MOON, waning to a half disc, was silvery, but with a yellowish haze surrounding it. Charlotte lay in bed and stared at the window, thinking of home. She really wasn't sure she belonged there anymore, but where else was there to go? With all the changes she had undergone, her uncle was going to have a difficult time dealing with her. No other woman in their family had ever gone through the transformation, and he might be appalled, though he would try to hide it if he was, no doubt. It wasn't that he would ever be unkind, it was just that his idea of what a young lady ought to be and her true self were at distinct odds. It occurred to her that she would excuse her uncle's behavior, and yet she was holding Wesmorlyn to a far higher ideal.

Ah, but if she couldn't *blame* Wesmorlyn, then she would have to admit that she loved him and wished, despite their vast differences, they could marry. *Marry.* The word had an oddly appealing ring. *He is the man I would like to marry*, she thought. Having a home away from her family, staying in Cornwall, having an exciting new life with Wesmorlyn, loving him every day and night: it was an enchanting idea, and she could too easily imagine herself happy at Wesmorlyn Abbey. She sighed and turned over, restless, but then she flipped back again to stare out her window, from which she had drawn back the curtains.

It just wouldn't do to envision some ideal life with Wesmorlyn. Living with a man who found such a vital part of her as her wolfdom revolting would be soul crushing. Being angry at the earl was self-preservation. It was simple fact that he couldn't help but be disgusted by that part of her.

That part of her. Looking back, she knew that the wolf side of her was always trying to surface, and the wildness she felt, the appalling need to be free, was what had led to her horrible indiscretion with her hapless dancing master. It would not have happened if she had known what to do with those feelings. The werewolf side of her released all of that pent-up energy, as she had learned from running with her brother through the midnight streets of London the previous night. It was exhilarating and freeing and she felt, after, refreshed and relieved of tension.

Ultimately it was a part of her, and she knew that her sexual desires were a part of her too. The relief and deep sense of freedom after making love with Wesmorlyn had been similar, though the connection lovemaking had forged between them had been soul-shattering and unexpected. They would always be a part of each other now, she supposed, even if they lived forever apart. And what was she to do with those emotions if they were not to be together?

She turned over and beat her pillow. The expression on his face as she left him in the park that afternoon haunted her, the look of painful hunger on his face, the haughtiness he had always displayed beaten down and hammered into humility. She remembered again their glorious afternoon in the Cornish sunshine, and the blissful moment of transport, the golden instant when, his body connected to hers, she had wholly entered a state of euphoria she was unlikely ever to experience again. Closing her eyes she drifted, half asleep. Dreams might be her only refuge now.

A noise startled her, the sound of something or someone tapping at her window—her *third-floor* window. She threw the covers back, slipped from bed, and ran to it, lifting the sash; there, in the glimmering, hazy moonlight, was her lover and former fiancé perched on the railing of her narrow balcony, glorious wings outspread, aiding his balance.

"What are you doing here?" she asked, breathless, staring up at him. Her gaze traveled from his broad chest up to his intense eyes, golden brown and gleaming in the moonlight.

"I can't stand it, Charlotte," he cried, his voice crackling with emotion. "I won't let you turn me away. Please, can we talk about this? I won't leave you alone, I swear it, not until you hear me out. I'll follow you wherever you go, even to Germany."

"But you must leave me alone," she said, hammering her fist on the windowsill. "Just go!"

"No," he said, his tone hard and his expression determined. "If I leave you alone you'll leave England."

It was what she intended, though she hadn't had the courage to tell him so outright. "How do you know that?"

"Because it's the easier choice. The *safe* choice."

"When have I ever made the safe choice?" she exclaimed. She glanced back into her room, afraid her voice would carry. "When have I *ever*?" she said, in a softer tone. "I'm no coward."

"You will this time, I just know it." He balanced precariously on the railing, one foot slipping and his gleaming wings beating to keep him balanced. It was a breathtaking sight, gloriously unearthly. "Come with me for an hour!" he said. "I want to show you something."

"No!"

"Please," he said, his pearly wings drooping. "I'm *begging*."

She couldn't stand to see him so humbled. That was not what she wanted for him, she realized, to be abject and humbled by her. She sighed and said, "How? How can I go with you anywhere?"

"Step out of the window and come to me," he said. He stretched out one hand to her, his magnificent wings outspread.

She looked down three floors to the paving below. "I will crack my head open if I fall."

"I won't let you fall," he said, his tone gentle and brimming with meaning. "Come, trust me. Dare to have this adventure."

Taking a deep breath, she lifted her nightgown and clambered up to the railing until she was toe to toe with him. She felt herself slipping and waved her arms to keep her balance; it was a precarious position, but he folded his arms around her, holding her close to his chest.

"I won't ever let you fall or abandon you, Charlotte," he whispered in her ear.

His warm breath tickled her ear and left her feeling oddly breathless. She was enfolded in a world of his warm, golden skin, as the sound of his wings, and the heady sensation of being lifted up and rising above the city made her giddy. He shifted her slightly so she could see, and she clung to him, curled in his protective embrace, their legs entangled as her nightgown skirt drifted in the breeze, and yet she was free to see below her the city and the river sparkling dark and sinuous, rolling its way through London.

No one else had ever seen the city this way; the Thames curled in and around it like a twisting snake, a pall of smoke clung to the buildings, and spires soared, pointing heavenward, giving hope of redemption and a blameless afterlife to all who aspired. They left the city proper, and, following the river, came to a great walled garden in Chelsea. Wesmorlyn gently descended and set Charlotte down on her bare feet on a walkway.

"Where are we?" she whispered, feeling a shiver run down her spine at the breeze rustling through a hundred trees and bringing the luscious scent of greenery wafting to her with the hushed murmur of the leaves.

He shrugged, folding his glorious wings back, between his scapula, and took her arm, guiding her down a walk. "This is the Physic Garden."

They walked and talked for a while, and he told her the history of the garden, how it was created by the society of apothecaries to identify and keep valuable medicinal plants, but soon they fell silent. The peace of the place filled her, and Charlotte wondered if that was Wesmorlyn's plan in bringing her there, that in such a green and gracious spot she would more readily listen. If so, it was working, for she wanted to hear him again.

"You said, when we last spoke, that you would wish that we had waited for our marriage vows before we committed to each other bodily." She looked up at him as they strolled.

With a faint smile on his face he said, "And you said, that should be *your* speech."

"It should if I was a proper young lady. But I must tell you why I would not have waited." She didn't speak, though, for a few minutes, ordering her thoughts. Her whole life long she had been imprudent and hasty. What good was all that had befallen her, if she learned nothing about being more circumspect and discreet? It did not elude her notice that she only came to that conclusion when all of her wildness and vigor had a natural channel in her being a wolf sometimes.

But he didn't rush her, nor did he demand. His company, arm through hers, pace suited to her shorter steps, was calm and sweet, warm and gentle. He was different, more accepting and open, and she could feel it in the lack of tension in his powerful body next to hers. She glanced up at him again. His chestnut hair was tumbled by the wind, and his naked skin glowed golden in the yellowish light of the moon. He carried a golden aura with him, gleaming light emanating faintly from his skin. He had changed, too, and that thought gave her comfort.

"Have you always known how strong you are?" she asked, remembering his mighty heave as he tossed Lyulph the wolf at the burning building. It was certainly strength beyond what other men possessed.

"No," he said. "I'm learning much about myself that I never knew, nor even suspected." He closed his eyes for a moment, and the golden aura deepened. "This is all new, this glorying in my powers. I suppose I've always just accepted my heritage, using flight only when necessary, but now . . ." He trailed off and shook his head. "I can't explain the change. But I think making love with you had something to do with it, for I felt a shift within me then, one I've been trying to comprehend ever since. I have a lot more to learn about what it all means."

She nodded. "I understand." She decided not to share, at

that moment, the feminine ability of her kind to give the gift—or curse—of werewolfism, and how she had decided never to give it away. It wasn't important to tell him, and there were other things she wanted to say. "I discovered, while we made love, what it was to feel intimately joined to a man; I felt your body's pulse within me. It was unlike anything I've ever experienced." Or ever would again she supposed.

He closed his eyes and sighed. "I think about it all the time," he said. He glanced down at her and squeezed her arm. "But what was that beautiful act for, if not to confirm that we were meant to be together?"

She was silent for a long moment. She was tied to him, it was true, but that didn't mean she could be what he needed and wanted in a wife and lover. "I don't know if I believe in destiny anymore, or that two people are meant by some higher power to be together. I believe in choices." She stared down at the pathway beneath her bare feet.

"You don't think destiny took you away from London, and gave us our time in the sun?"

"No," she said, regretful but suddenly sure. Belief in destiny was attractive because it took away the necessity of making difficult choices and standing by them no matter the consequences. And if you could *blame* destiny for disastrous choices, you never took responsibility. "The choice I made to go to Cornwall was the result of things beyond your knowledge at the time, and even beyond my own. Lyulph Randell skillfully manipulated me. You following was your own choice. And our coming together, that was a choice, too, made by both of us. We would not have made love if something about the two of us was not matched."

"I think I prefer to believe it was destiny."

"No," she whispered, "no, I don't, because that makes it an accident of fate that we came together, when it was so much more."

"Or it's the plan of the supreme power. Do you believe in that?"

She stopped and looked up at him, meeting his warm brown gaze. She evaded the question of her belief or lack thereof in an all-powerful being. "You don't understand. I would rather have you *choose* to be with me, than to be compelled by some supernatural force."

A wave of emotion shuddered through him. "Charlotte," he said, clutching her shoulders in his big hands. "I *choose* to be with you! And I don't regret what we did. How can I, when what we did and who you are all adds up to one sum? I *love* you. The attraction I felt immediately, and the tenderness I came to feel for you, has melded into more, much more, and now, wanting you, thinking of you, seeing your honor and strength and beauty and—"

"Stop," she laughed, holding up one hand. "I'll get a big head if you go on."

"No, you deserve it all. I don't think you understand how truly fine you are, how intelligent, how compassionate. You were right about so many things. You accepted my secret life immediately, and I, to my shame, did not accept yours."

"To be fair," she said, on a deep, trembling sigh, "my secret life is a little more difficult to accept."

"No, that's not true, and if I made you feel it was so, I was wrong." He pulled her close and held her for a long, silent few minutes. Then he gazed down into her eyes. "I've thought a lot about this, even since this afternoon. My whole life I've considered . . ." He trailed off and stopped.

"Don't stop," she said. She looked up into his eyes and saw them clouded with doubt. "If you're worried about hurting me by being honest, don't. I'm stronger than I ever knew I was."

He nodded. "I *am* afraid of hurting you, but you must understand, what I'm about to say is what I used to feel, not how I feel now." When she nodded, he continued. "I used to think that Randell's werewolfism, if we can call it that, meant that he was somehow inferior. But I've thought about this long and hard. You and I are much more alike than we are different. Those things—my angelic heritage and your werewolf legacy—are two sides of the same coin. I won't call it destiny, since you don't like that concept, but we are the perfect balance for each other, earth and sky, both beautifully simple and exquisitely complex."

Wesmorlyn stared at her, the delicate loveliness of her face, the piquant dimple in the middle of her chin, the spark of fierceness in her blue eyes, and continued, "Seeing you as a wolf-woman frightened me. But it was not for who or what you are, but for the fear of such an intense, powerful, earthly bond it implied. I didn't know how to handle that. My whole life I've avoided such a tie, and then to have it presented to me as part of the woman with whom I want to spend eternity, I was afraid of all it implied."

"What did it imply to you?"

This was the crux of the problem, and what he had just come to understand after watching her walk away that afternoon and feeling a part of him go with her. It had terrified him that he now felt that they were part of a whole, and what would happen if she kept to her decision to leave England forever. He would follow her if she went, that he now knew. "I feared that I would never understand that part of you because I was too far removed from the natural human part of me, and yet I was more afraid of accepting that half of me was so human and needed your love. I had deliberately separated myself from that part of my being, but it's still there; it was all along. I understand now that what revolted me was not you, but myself, and the powerful need in me for you, and all that you represent."

She shook her head and frowned.

He took her shoulders and pulled her down to earth. Kneeling before her, he stroked her golden hair off her face. How could he ever explain? "When I contracted our marriage, I pictured a relationship where I would be your lord, and you my subject. There would be obligation, duty, maybe even friendship between us, but nothing more. But I *love* you." Words failed him. How could he express how he felt? He cupped her cheek and rubbed with his thumb. "What I feared was what you called up in me, my connection to the roots, to the earth, to this place," he said, waving a hand around at the trees overhead and the greenery surrounding them. "My whole life has been spent looking up, but in doing so I forgot to make roots, forgot that I'm more human than anything, and should honor that part of me."

She opened her mouth, but didn't speak for a long moment. "Oh," she finally said. Her brow furrowed. "You were afraid I would drag you down?"

"No! Oh, no, it was how I feel about you that frightened

me." He kissed her brow, and then moved to her pink cheeks, to her nose, then sought her lips, bending to her and warming her with his body.

"How you feel about me?" she murmured against his kiss.

Peace overwhelmed him. "I love you with all my heart." He gave himself over to it, sinking into the kiss and letting the love swell within him just as his body changed with the desire he experienced.

She gave in to his ardor and their tongues met and tasted each other, their mouths melding sweetly. After a long few minutes, she broke away, breathless, and stuttered, staring up at him, "B-but what about redemption, your family, your ancestors?"

"Redemption," he said, looking into her heaven-blue eyes as they shone with hope, "if my family ever achieves it, will come from being a part of this world, not from separating ourselves from it."

"But what of children?" she murmured. She cradled his cheek in her palm and rubbed her thumb over his lips, searching his eyes. "If we come together, what will happen to our children?"

He had thought of this long and hard. Semyaza had once told him that he needed to learn to trust himself, and not be so rigid in thinking he had to meet some impossible standard of perfect behavior. It had taken him a long time, but perhaps he was beginning to trust himself. If it was truly wrong for them to marry and create new life, he would know somewhere in his heart. He held her close and whispered, "Perhaps they'll be wolf, like you, or have wings, like me, but either way, they will have someone who can explain life to them, and make a better world for them than either of us has experienced."

"Wes, I believe you. And I love you."

His heart soared with joy at her trembling words.

The soft warm scent of the garden, green and fresh, enticed her, and she leaned into his kiss and then pulled him down to the soft bed of greenery beneath them. She rubbed his naked shoulders, feeling his chest pressed against the filmy fabric of her nightrail and the growing evidence of his feelings for her. His broad hand ran up her leg and pushed the fabric further, as he stroked her thigh and pulled her to him, cupping her bottom with his hand and pressing himself to her ardently, whispering against her lips words she could not understand, but the meaning of which became clearer as his breathing quickened.

"You're not afraid of me any longer?" she teased, closing her eyes and feeling the passion well up, coiling tightly like a spring within her.

"Yes, I'm terrified," he whispered, covering her with his body. "I'm drowning in love, and have completely lost balance, but you are far wiser than I in the balance between human and other, for you seem to effortlessly move through it."

"But I've only just begun to understand that about myself," she said, opening her eyes and gazing up at him in the moonlight. She pushed his dark curls off his broad forehead. "How can you trust me so readily?"

"That was the hardest thing for me, but I do trust you," he said, staring into her eyes. "Perhaps you've only just discovered that you can transform, but the wolf-woman was in you all along, bursting to get out. You had the balance ready long before the need for it arose."

"I'm the first of my kind in my family; no other woman has ever transformed. I don't know what to make of it, and I don't know what it means for children I may have."

"I think that was what Lyulph feared all along," Wesmorlyn said, the golden light of his skin glowing around them. "He was intent on making you his because he feared the unique power of offspring of a union such as ours. He was afraid that what he intended to create with Hannah would be ours."

"He's gone from England with or without Morwenna, Christoph thinks, perhaps forever."

"I don't care. I will handle him if need be, but he'll never touch you again. *Ever!*" Wesmorlyn said, his tone feverish as he pushed against her, ardent and yearning, hungry with love and desire.

Eagerly she sought the fall of his trousers as his lips met hers and his tongue dove into her mouth; he sucked on her lip, nipping wildly. His sturdy and willful member sprang from its prison into her hand and she touched him, stroking with unnecessary movements.

"Stop," he cried, his stomach muscles tightening as he

spasmed in need. Gently he spread her legs with his hand and touched her, groaning at the wetness he found and diving his finger in, readying her with quick, fumbling strokes and then parting her legs further with his knee as he mounted her.

The first touch of him as he pushed gently to begin entry made her cry out in delight at the sensation rippling through her body. He was bigger than before, more needy, harder, longer, much more urgent. His first stroke was vigorous and pushed her bodily, driving her into the earth, almost, with reckless abandon.

"Gently," she whispered into his ear, biting the lobe and feeling the rumbling moan in his chest as he slowed.

"I'll learn, my love, I will learn."

A ready student, he listened as she whispered hints, eagerly begging her to tell him what she needed, and she felt a veil of madness begin to descend as his quickening strokes and eager hands, tickling and kneading her until she was delirious, took her to the very brink of sweet release. "Yes, yes," she cried out, her voice echoing back to her strangely as a bird, disturbed in its slumber, took wing and fluttered away. She locked her heels behind his back to accept him deeper.

His great wings unfolded, then, and he beat them slowly, lifting her into the air until all she could feel was the sensation of him inside of her; every stroke, each teasing touch, raised the tension until the wildness erupted. She was transported, hovering above the earth, and while the ecstasy exploded within her, Wesmorlyn, driven to rapture, deepened his thrust and the juices flowed, filling her with his profound adoration with every thrust and every whispered "I love you." They tumbled over and over in air, buried in passion, transformed by love.

Then gently, he brought her back to earth, cradling her in his arms while, trembling, she felt tears pour down her face as she understood, finally, that his love was forever.

"I must take you home while my strength allows it," he whispered. He gathered her up in his arms and soared high, carrying her back over the city.

They entered her room, and he carried her to her bed, laying her gently down. Not willing to have him leave, as he clearly intended, she grabbed his arm and with a tug, pulled him into her bed. She climbed atop him and said, "You aren't going. Not yet. Maybe not ever."

"Tell me first," he said, pushing up against her, the proof of his eagerness again evident, "that you'll marry me, or I'll *make* you say it."

"How?" she asked, breathless, the sweet darkness enfolding them, and her single word coming as a sigh. His golden glow had faded with weariness, and she could no longer see his face; his disembodied voice echoed in the dark room.

With quick movements he yanked her nightrail up over her head. He pulled her roughly toward him and began raining kisses over her breasts as he undid his own trousers this time. Straddling him as she was, she could feel him lengthen and harden as he began to slow his movements, swirling his tongue over her nipple, drawing it in, suckling and making her moan with the sweet madness that began once again to envelope her.

"Where did you learn that?" she gasped, throwing her head back. "Not from me."

"Instinct."

"Don't stop," she cried, and then moaned at the sweetness of the sensations trilling through her body.

"Marry me or I'll stop this instant," he murmured against her breast, then rubbed his lips against her wet, peaked nipple.

She giggled. "You cannot extort a promise like that from me now!" she said. "It's not fair!"

"Oh yes I can, and I don't wish to be fair." He drew her breast into his mouth and nipped the tightly budded rosette, then positioned himself to enter her again, tickling her above their juncture with his free hand. "Marry me," he said, pausing in his enticement.

"What a time to ask! I can't think," she moaned, her body feverishly hot.

"Good. I don't want to think either. We both think too much."

"But this isn't the time to make an important decision."

"Mine is already made. Isn't yours?"

"Yes," she sighed, pushing down on him. "Yes. I love you. I have since making love on the moor!"

"Then say it," he said, drawing out, pushing her up with his other hand. He grasped her bottom and squeezed. "Say you'll marry me, and quickly."

"Yes, yes, I'll marry you, and quickly," she gasped. "Now stop teasing!"

"Never," he grunted, pulling her down onto him and taking her other nipple into his mouth, his nipping teeth almost painful in their attentions, but not quite.

"You've become quite masterful," she said, with a chuckle, looking down at him. A faint hint of light, now that her eyes were adjusted to the darkness of the room, illuminated his forehead, where beads of perspiration trickled, making his hair damp with sweat. She moved on him and was rewarded by the sight of his eyes rolling back and his body arching under her. "But now it's my turn to master you, my angel."

After, they lay in a tangle of blankets and talked long into the night. He confessed his fears, and she hers.

Could he make her happy, truly happy, that she had left her homeland? Would she miss her family too much? Those were his fears.

Would she fit in London society? What kind of a countess would she make? And what kind of mother? Her fears were more far-reaching and unanswerable, perhaps, except by time and trust.

But even as they fell asleep in each other's arms, they both knew the answers to all those questions lay in the future, and that together they would find the solutions to every problem.

MORNING came and light leaked into her room around the edges of the drapes. Charlotte stretched and yawned, but was not prepared for the sight of the door opening; a young maid bearing a tray stood in the open doorway.

Christoph following, saying, "Charlotte, I need to speak to you. Something dreadful has happened and—"

He stopped, and he and the young girl both stared at the sight that greeted them. Wesmorlyn, naked and just now awakening, was tangled in the blankets, his muscular bare leg thrust out over the covers. Charlotte held the sheets up to cover herself. "Go! Go away, Christoph," she cried, laughing and blushing.

Christoph shoved the gaping servant out the door, but stormed back in and over to the bed, grabbing Wesmorlyn by the hair. "You! You miserable sneak, what are you doing here? How did you get in? What are you doing in my sister's bed?"

"No! Christoph, no! It's all right," she cried, holding up one hand. "Let him go, for heaven's sake! We're to be married. Soon."

Christoph fell back in amazement and stared at them both. "I don't understand."

"It's true, I love him," she said, looking over at Wesmorlyn, his sheepish expression and sleepy eyes adorable to her. "We're going to be married right away."

Christoph's expression was grim. "All right. Get dressed. You, Wesmorlyn, have a lot of explaining to do. She is in my care while we are here, and—"

"Christoph!" Charlotte interrupted. "I am in no man's *care*. I'm my own woman, and I have decided to marry him."

Wesmorlyn, his face red, said, "I'll be your brother, Christoph. I've never had a brother and will be honored to call you mine."

Christoph looked from one to the other of their faces, and said, "This is what you both want?"

"Yes," Charlotte and Wesmorlyn both said, so eagerly that they ended on a laugh.

"Well Uncle Nikolas will be happy."

"And so will we," Charlotte said, winding her arms around Wesmorlyn, who was turning a brilliant scarlet, but looking very pleased with himself. "So will we. But what were you going to say, Christoph, when you came in?"

He paused for a moment, but then said, hoarsely, "Romolo is downstairs. Lyulph Randell has taken Tamara and says he will kill her unless we do exactly what he says."

"No!" Charlotte bolted upright. "What are we to do?"

"You two need do nothing. This is a challenge to me directly, for he says I must leave England, taking you with me, if she is to live. But I will allow no man to tell me what to do. No man, nor any wolf. I should have killed him when I had the chance."

Charlotte stared at her brother. She had never heard him

say anything like that before, and a glimpse at his harsh, dark expression made her shiver.

"You'll have my help whether you wish it or not," Wesmorlyn said, sitting up and throwing his legs over the side.

"And mine," Charlotte said. "We're in this together, or not at all."

"I'll see you downstairs, then." Christoph left the room.

Trembling, Charlotte asked, "What does it mean, Wes? Why has Lyulph done this?"

"I should have taken care of him years ago instead of trusting him." Wesmorlyn leaped from bed and pulled on his breeches. "This is, in truth, my responsibility, not your brother's."

"I've never seen him so angry," Charlotte said.

"I have got to take care of this. I won't have your brother harmed for my weakness."

She slipped out from under the covers and wound her bare arms around him. "I think, my love, that you must accept that we are all in this equally, for we have all had a hand in creating this particular problem."

Wesmorlyn gazed down into her blue eyes as the morning sun flooded the room with light. It was true; she was his partner now, and he would never underestimate her again. "I love you," he whispered, lowering his face to hers and kissing her deeply, sweetly.

She felt it, then, felt the bond strengthening with every moment together. He trusted her now, wholly, and she had learned to trust him. He would never let her go or abandon her. "I love you," she returned against his mouth. "And I always will. Whatever happens next, we'll handle it together."

THE BUTTERFLY BOX

'Thoroughly readable . . . old-fashioned romance.'

Evening Standard

'Absorbing.'

Vogue

'Refreshing . . . imagination, charm and delicacy. Santa is the new Rosamunde Pilcher. Delightfully written.'

Daily Mail

'[An] escapist, passionate romance.'

Dorset Evening Echo

'This is a good, old-fashioned saga with all the classic ingredients. Federica has genuine pathos and charm, and those qualities permeate the whole book . . . both engaging and charming.'

Penny Vincenzi, *Mail on Sunday*

By the same author

Meet Me Under the Ombu Tree

About the author

Santa Montefiore was born in England to an Anglo-Argentine mother, and read Spanish and Italian at Exeter University. After a year teaching English on an Argentine estancia, she spent much of the nineties in Buenos Aires. She lives in London with her husband, journalist and author Simon Sebag-Montefiore and their daughter, Lily.

THE
BUTTERFLY
BOX

Santa Montefiore

CORONET BOOKS
Hodder & Stoughton

First published in Great Britain in 2002 by Hodder & Stoughton
A division of Hodder Headline
First published in paperback in 2002 by Hodder & Stoughton
A Coronet paperback

6 8 10 9 7 5

A CIP catalogue record for this book
is available from the British Library.

ISBN 0 340 76953 X

Typeset in Bembo by Hewer Text Ltd, Edinburgh
Printed and bound in Great Britain by
Mackays of Chatham plc, Chatham, Kent

Hodder & Stoughton
A division of Hodder Headline
338 Euston Road
London NW1 3BH

To my parents

I would like to thank Gibran National Committee for granting me permission to quote from Kahlil Gibran's *The Prophet*.

Gibran National Committee
PO Box 116–5487
Beirut
Lebanon
Fax (961–1)396916
Email:k.gibran@cyberia.net.lb

I would like to extend my deepest gratitude to my cousin, Anderly Hardy, for her guidance on all Chilean matters and to Susan Fletcher, my editor and Jo Frank, my agent for their advice, wisdom and support.

Love gives naught but itself and takes naught but from itself.
Love possesses not nor would it be possessed;
For love is sufficient unto love.

Kahlil Gibran, *The Prophet*

PART I

Chapter One

Viña del Mar, Chile, Summer 1982

Federica opened her eyes onto a different world. It was hot, but not humid for the sea breeze carried with it a cool undercurrent from where it had dallied among the waves of the cold Pacific Ocean. Her room was slowly coming to life in the pale morning light that spilled in through the gap in the curtains, casting mellow shafts onto the floor and walls, swallowing up the remains of the night, exposing the regimental line of sleeping dolls. The constant barking of Señora Baraca's dog at the end of the street had left the animal with little more than a raw husk, but he still continued to bark as he always did. Some day he'd lose his voice altogether, she thought, which wouldn't be a bad thing; at least he wouldn't keep the neighbours awake. She had once tried to feed him a biscuit on her way to school but her mother had said he was probably riddled with all sorts of diseases. 'Best not to touch him, you don't know where he's been,' she had advised, pulling her six-year-old daughter away by the hand. But that was the problem; he had never been anywhere. Federica breathed in the sweet scent of the orange trees that floated up on the air and she could almost taste the fruit that hung heavily like lustrous packages on a Christmas tree. She kicked off the sheet that covered her and knelt on the end of her bed, leaning out through the curtains onto a world that wasn't the same as the one the sun had set on the day before. With the rising of the new sun a quiver ran through her skinny body, causing a broad smile to spread across her pale face. Today her father was coming home after many months travelling.

Ramon Campione was a giant of a man. Not only in stature – at well over six feet he was tall for a Chilean and tall for an Italian, which was where his family originated from – but in his gigantic imagination, which, like the galaxy itself, seemed never-ending and full of surprises. His adventures took him to the far corners of the earth where he was inspired by everything different and everything beautiful. He travelled, wrote and travelled some more. His family barely knew him. He was never around long enough for them to find the person behind the writing and the magical photographs he took. In the mind of his daughter he was more powerful than God. She had once told Padre Amadeo that Jesus was nothing compared to her father who could do so much more than turn water into wine. 'My papa can fly,' she had said proudly. Her mother had smiled apologetically to the priest and rolled her eyes, explaining to him quietly that Ramon had tried out a new contraption in Switzer-land for flying off the mountain on skis. Padre Amadeo had nodded in understanding but later shook his head and worried that the child would only get hurt when her father toppled, as he surely would some day, off the tall pedestal she had so blindly placed him upon. She should focus such devotion on God not man, he thought piously.

Federica longed for it to be time to get up, but it was still early. The sky was as pale and still as a large, luminous lagoon and only the barking dog and the clamour of birds resounded against the quiet stirring of dawn. From her bedroom she could see the ocean disappearing into the grey mists on the horizon as if the heavens were drinking it up. Her mother often took them to Caleta Abarca beach, as they didn't have a swimming pool to cool off in, although the sea was almost too cold for bathing. Sometimes they would drive to the small seaside village of Cachagua, about an hour up the coast, to stay with her grand-parents who owned a pretty thatched summerhouse there surrounded by tall palms and acacia trees. Federica loved the sea. Her father had once said that she loved the sea because she was born under the sign of Cancer whose symbol was a crab. She didn't much like crabs though.

After a long while she heard footsteps on the stairs then the high-pitched voice of her younger brother Enrique, nicknamed Hal after Shakespeare's 'Prince Henry'. That had been Ramon's idea – although his wife was English she had no interest in literature or history unless it was about her.

'Darling, you're dressed already!' Helena gasped in surprise as Federica jumped across the landing and into Hal's bedroom where she was dressing him.

'Papa's coming home today!' she sang, unable to remain still even for a moment.

'Yes, he is,' replied Helena, taking a deep breath to restrain the resentment she felt towards her absent husband. 'Keep your feet still, Hal darling, I can't put your shoes on if you keep moving.'

'Will he be here before lunch?' asked Federica, automatically helping her mother by opening the curtains, allowing the warm sunshine to flood into the dim room with the enthusiasm that belongs only to the morning.

'He'll be here sometime before noon, his flight gets in at ten,' she replied patiently. 'There, sweetie, you look very handsome,' she added, smoothing back Hal's black hair with a soft brush. He shook his head in protest and squealed before wriggling off the bed and running out onto the landing.

'I put on my best dress for him,' said Federica, following her mother down the stairs with buoyant footsteps.

'So I see,' she replied.

'I'm going to help Lidia cook lunch today. We're making Papa's favourite dish.'

'What's that then?'

'*Pastel de choclo* and we're making him *merengon de lúcuma* as a welcome home cake,' said Federica, flicking her straight blonde hair off her shoulders so that it fell thickly down her back. She had pushed it off her forehead with a hair-band, which along with her small stature made her appear younger than her six years.

'Papa's coming home today,' said Federica to Hal as she helped her mother lay the table.

'Will he bring me a present?' asked Hal, who at four years of age remembered his father only for the presents he gave.

'Of course he will, sweetie. He always brings you presents,' said Helena, placing a cup of cold milk in front of him. 'Anyway, it's Christmas so you'll be getting loads of presents.' Federica supervised Hal while he dipped his spoon into the tin of powdered chocolate and dropped it into his milk. She then grabbed the cloth from the sink to mop up the chocolate that hadn't quite made it to the cup.

'Fede, the croissants are ready, I can smell them beginning to burn,' said Helena, lighting a cigarette. She looked anxiously at the clock on the wall and bit her lower lip. She knew she should take the children to the airport to pick him up as other mothers would. But she couldn't face it. The awkward drive from Santiago airport to the coast, all the while making conversation as if everything was positively rosy. No, it would be much better to see him at home, the house was big, more space for them to lose each other in. How silly, she thought bitterly, they had lost each other a long time ago somewhere in the vast distances they had placed between themselves. Somewhere in the faraway lands and imaginary characters that seemed so much more important to Ramon than the people in his life who were real and who needed him. She had tried. She had really tried. But now she was empty inside and tired of being neglected.

Federica buttered a croissant and sipped her iced chocolate, chattering away to her brother with an excitement that made her voice rise in tone, irritating the raw nerves of her mother who stood by the window blowing smoke against the glass. Once they had been in love, but even hate was an expression of love, just a different face. Now Helena no longer hated him, that alone would have been a good enough reason to stay. But she felt indifference and it frightened her. Nothing could grow out of that. It was a barren emotion, as barren as the face of the moon.

Helena had made a life for herself in Chile because she had believed, as did her daughter later, that Ramon was God. He was

6

certainly the most glamorous, handsome man Polperro had ever seen. Then his article had appeared in *National Geographic* with photographs of all the old smugglers' caves and crumbling castles Helena had shown him, and yet somehow the photographs were suffused with a light that didn't belong to Nature. There was something mystical about them that she couldn't put her finger on. Every word he wrote sung out to her and stayed with her long after she had turned the last page. Now she recognised the magic as love, for it had followed them for the first six years, converting even the most mundane things, like filling the car up with petrol, into a magical experience. Their lovemaking had pertained to another plain far above the physical and she had believed that the power was within him and in him alone. Only after it had gone did she realise that the connection had been cut – like electricity, their 'magic' had been caused by the two of them and ceased the minute one of them felt disenchanted by it. Once it had gone it was gone for ever. That kind of sorcery is of high energy but low life span. At first they had travelled together, to the far corners of China, to the arid deserts of Egypt and the wet lakes of Sweden. When she became pregnant with Federica they returned to settle in Chile. Their 'magic' had followed them there too where the white powder coast and pastoral simplicity had enchanted her. But now it echoed with the emptiness she felt within her own being because the love that had filled it had drained away. There was no reason to stay. She was tired of pretending. She was tired of pretending to herself. She longed for the drizzly, verdant hills of her youth and her longing made her hand shake. She lit another cigarette and once more eyed the clock.

Federica cleared away her breakfast, humming to herself and skipping around the kitchen as she did so. Hal played with his train in the nursery. Helena remained by the window.

'Mama!' shouted Hal. 'My train is broken, it's not working.' Helena picked up her packet of cigarettes and strode out of the

7

kitchen, leaving Federica to finish clearing up. Once the table was wiped and the crockery washed up she put on her cooking apron and waited for Lidia to arrive.

When Lidia bustled through the gate she saw Federica's small eager face pressed up against the glass, smiling broadly at her.

'*Hola*, Señorita,' she said breathlessly as she entered the hall. 'You're ready early.'

'I've even cleared away the breakfast,' replied Federica in Spanish. Although her mother spoke excellent Spanish they had always spoken English as a family, even when her father was home.

'Well, you *are* a good girl,' Lidia wheezed, following the child into the kitchen. 'Ah, you angel. You've done all the work,' she said, casting her dark eyes over the mixing bowls and spoons already laid out on the table.

'I want it all to be perfect for Papa,' she said, her cheeks aflame. She could barely contain her impatience and suppressed her desire to run by skipping instead of walking. That way the nervous feeling in her stomach was indulged a little but not too much. Lidia struggled into her pink overalls then washed her swollen brown hands. She suggested Federica do the same.

'You must always wash your hands before cooking, you don't know where they've been,' she said.

'Like Señora Baraca's dog,' giggled Federica.

'*Pobrecito*,' Lidia sighed, tilting her round head to one side and pulling a thin, sympathetic smile. 'He's tied up all day in that small garden, it's no wonder he barks from dawn till dusk.'

'Doesn't she take him out at all?' Federica asked, running her hands under the tap.

'Oh yes, she takes him out occasionally, but she's old,' Lidia replied, 'and we old people don't have as much energy for things like that.'

'You're not old, Lidia,' said Federica kindly.

'Not old, just fat,' said Helena in English, walking into the

8

kitchen with Hal's toy engine. 'She'd have much more energy if she didn't eat so much. Imagine carrying that bulk around all day, no wonder she wheezes all the time.'

'*Buenos días,* Señora,' said Lidia, who didn't understand English.

'Good morning, Lidia. I need a knife to mend this blasted train,' said Helena in Spanish, not even bothering to force a smile, however small. She was too anxious and impatient to think of anyone else but herself.

'I wouldn't worry about that, Don Ramon will be home soon and he can fix it. That's men's work,' said Lidia cheerfully.

'Thank you, Lidia, that's very helpful. Fede, pass me a knife,' she said edgily. Federica handed her the knife and watched her walk out again.

'Oh, it's so exciting that your Papa is coming home,' enthused Lidia, embracing Federica fondly. 'I'll bet you didn't sleep a wink.'

'Not a wink,' she replied, looking up at the clock. 'He'll be here soon,' she said and Lidia noticed that her small hands trembled when she began to cut the butter up into pieces.

'Careful you don't cut yourself,' she said gently. 'You don't want your Papa to come back to a daughter with only seven fingers.' She laughed, then wheezed and coughed.

Helena, who was usually very deft at mending things, broke the engine. Hal started to cry. Helena pulled him into her arms and managed to cheer him up by promising him another engine, a bigger, better one. 'Anyway, this engine was old and tatty. What use is an engine like that? The train looks much better without his engine,' she said and thought how much she'd like to be a carriage on her own without an engine. She lit another cigarette. The doors to the garden were open, inviting in the gentle sea breeze that smelt of oranges and ozone. It was too hot to be sitting in suburbia, they should be down on the beach, she thought in frustration. She wiped her sweating brow with her

9

hand then looked at her watch. Her throat constricted. His plane would have landed.

Federica and Lidia buzzed about the kitchen like a couple of bees in a flowerbed. Federica loved to be included and followed Lidia's instructions with great enthusiasm. She felt like a grown-up and Lidia treated her as one. They chatted about Lidia's back pain and her stomach cramps and her husband's verruca, which was giving him a lot of trouble. 'I'm afraid of putting my feet where he's put his,' she explained, 'so I wear a pair of socks even in the shower.'

'I would too,' Federica agreed, not sure what a verruca was.

'You're sensible like me,' Lidia replied, smiling down at the skinny child who had a manner well beyond her years. Lidia thought she was far too grown up for a child of almost seven but one only had to look at her mother to understand why. Helena gave her so much responsibility, too much probably, that the child would be quite capable of running the entire household without her.

When Helena entered the kitchen the smell of *pastel de choclo* swelled her senses and her stomach churned with hunger and tension combined. Federica was drying up while Lidia washed the utensils and mixing bowls. Helena managed to grab the remains of the cream before Lidia's podgy hands pulled it into the soapy water. She scraped her finger around the bottom of the bowl and brought it up to her pale lips. 'Well done you, sweetie,' she said, impressed. She smiled at her daughter and stroked her hand down her shiny blonde hair. 'You're a very good cook.' Federica smiled, accustomed to her mother's changeable nature. One minute she was irritable, the next minute she was agreeable, not like her father who was always cheerful and carefree. Helena's praise delighted Federica as it always did and her spirits soared until she seemed to grow an inch taller.

'She's not only a good cook, Señora, but she's a good housekeeper, too,' said Lidia fondly, the large black mole on her chin quivering as her face creased into a wide smile. 'She cleaned up all the breakfast by herself,' she added in a mildly accusing tone, for Señora Helena always left everything to her daughter.

'I know,' Helena replied. 'What I would do without her, I can't imagine,' she said nonchalantly, flicking her cigarette ash into the bin and leaving the room. She walked upstairs. She was weary. Her heart weighed her down so that even the stairs were an effort to climb. She walked along the cool white corridor, her bare feet padding over the wooden floorboards, her hand too disenchanted even to deadhead the pots of pale orchids as she passed. In her bedroom the white linen curtains played about with the silk breeze as if they were trying to open all by themselves. Irritably she pulled them apart and looked out across the sea. It lay tremulous and iridescent, beckoning her to sail away with it to another place. The horizon promised her freedom and a new life.

'Mama, shall I help you tidy your room?' Federica asked quietly. Helena turned around and looked at the small, earnest face of her daughter.

'I suppose you want to tidy it up for Papa?' she replied, grabbing an ashtray and stubbing her cigarette into it.

'Well, I've picked some flowers . . .' she said sheepishly.

Helena's heart lurched. She pitied her daughter for the love she felt for her father in spite of the long absences that should have made her hate him. But no, she loved him unconditionally and the more he went away the happier she was to see him when he returned, running into his arms like a grateful lover. She longed to tell her the truth and shatter her illusions, out of spite because she wished she still shared those illusions. She found the world of children so blissfully simplistic and she envied her.

'All right, Fede. You tidy it up for Papa, he'll love the flowers, I'm sure,' she said tightly. 'Just ignore me,' she added, wandering into the bathroom and closing the door behind her. Federica heard her switch on the shower and the water pound against the enamel bath. She then made the bed, scenting the sheets with fresh lavender like her grandmother had shown her and placed a small blue vase of honeysuckle on her father's bedside table. She folded her mother's clothes and placed them in the old oak cupboard, rearranging the mess that she found there until all the shelves resembled a well-organised shop. She opened the windows as wide as they could go so that the scents of the garden and the sea would spirit away the dirty smell of her mother's smoke. Then she sat at her dressing table and picked up an old photograph of her father that grinned out at her from behind the glass of an ornate silver frame. He was very good looking with glossy black hair, swarthy skin, shiny brown eyes that were honest and intelligent and a large mouth that smiled the crooked smile of a man with an irreverent sense of humour and easy charm. She ran her thumb across the glass and caught her pensive expression in the mirror. In her reflection she saw only her mother. The pale blonde hair, the pale blue eyes, the pale pink lips, the pale skin — she wished she had inherited her father's dark Italian looks. He was so handsome and no doubt Hal would be handsome just like him. But Federica was used to getting a lot of attention because of her flowing white hair. All the other girls in her class were dark like Hal. People stared at her when she went into Valparaíso with her mother and Señora Escobar, who ran the sandwich shop on the square, called her 'La Angelita' (the little angel) because she couldn't believe that a human being could have such pale hair. Helena's best friend, Lola Miguens, had tried to copy her by dying her black hair blonde with peroxide, but had lost her nerve half way through so now she walked around with hair the colour of their terracotta roof, which Federica thought looked very ugly. Her mother didn't bother to look after herself like Chilean women who always had long manicured nails, perfect lipstick and immaculate clothes. Helena bustled about with her hair scrunched carelessly up onto the top of her head and she usually had a cigarette hanging out of her mouth. Federica thought she was beautiful when she made an effort and judging by old photographs she was once very beautiful indeed. But recently she had let herself go. Federica hoped she would make an effort for her father.

Helena stepped out of the bathroom followed by a puff of steam. Her face was pink and her eyes sparkled from the moisture. Federica lay on the white damask bedspread and watched her mother dress and prepare herself for her husband's return. Helena could smell the lavender and the ripe scent of oranges and refrained from lighting another cigarette. She felt guilty. Federica was so excited she quivered like a horse in the starting gate while *she* awaited Ramon's return with trepidation and the secret knowledge that any moment now she'd gather together her courage and leave him for good. As she painted her face she watched her daughter in the mirror while she didn't know that she was being watched. She stared out of the window across the sea as if her father was arriving by boat and not by car. Her profile was childish and yet her expression was that of a grown woman. The anxious expectation in her frown and on her trembling lips betrayed too much awareness for a child her age. She worshipped her father with the devotion of a dog, whereas Hal worshipped his mother whom, Helena felt, was more deserving of his love.

When Helena was ready, in a pair of tight white trousers and T-shirt, her hair scrunched up on her head, still damp and knotted, she sat on the bed beside her daughter and ran a damp hand down her face.

'You look lovely, sweetie. You really do,' she said and kissed her innocent brow affectionately.

'He'll be here soon, won't he?' said Federica softly.

'Any minute,' Helena replied, masking the tremor in her voice with a deftness that came from years of practice. She got up abruptly and hurried down the stairs. She couldn't smoke in the bedroom, not after Federica had prepared it so lovingly, but she was in desperate need of a cigarette. Just as she reached the bottom, her espadrilles landing on the cold stone tiles of the hallway, the front door swung open and Ramon filled the entrance like a large black wolf. Helena gasped and felt her stomach lurch. They stared at each other, wordlessly assessing the frigid estrangement that still grew up between them whenever they found themselves together in the same room.

'Fede, Papa's here!' Helena shouted, but as impassive as her features were her voice croaked with repressed emotion. Ramon's dark brown eyes pulled away from the stony countenance of his wife in search of his daughter whom he heard squeal with delight from the landing before the soft patter of her small feet scurried across the floorboards and skipped down the stairs two at a time. She jumped past her mother and into her father's sturdy embrace. She wrapped her thin arms around his bristly neck, nuzzling her face into his throat and inhaling the heavy, spicy scent that made him different from everyone else in the world. He kissed her warm cheek, lifting her off the ground and laughing so loudly she felt the vibration shake against her body like an earthquake.

'So you missed me!' he said, swinging her around until she had to wrap her legs about his waist to stop herself from falling.

'Yes, Papa!' she laughed, clinging on as her happiness almost choked her.

At that moment Hal ran into the hall, took one look at his father and burst into tears. Helena, grateful for the distraction, ran to him and picked him up in her arms, kissing his wet cheek. 'It's Papa, Hal darling, he's come home,' she said, trying to boost her voice with a bit of enthusiasm but her tone was dead and Hal sensed it and cried again. Ramon put his daughter down and walked over to where his son was weeping in his mother's arms.

'Halcito, it's Papa,' he said, smiling into the child's frightened face with his large, generous mouth. Hal buried his head in Helena's neck and wriggled closer against her.

'I'm sorry, Ramon,' she said flatly, sensing his disappointment but secretly taking pleasure from the child's rejection. She wanted to tell him that he couldn't expect his children to love him when he took no part in their lives, but she saw Federica's love set her cheeks aflame and the admiration shine in her pale, trusting eyes and knew that it wasn't entirely true. Nevertheless, he didn't deserve his daughter's love.

'I've got a present for you, Hal,' he said, walking back to his bag and unzipping it. 'And I've got one for you too, Fede,' he added as his daughter placed an affectionate hand on his back as he rummaged around for his gifts. 'Ah, this is for you, Hal,' he said, walking over to the little boy whose eyes opened wide at the brightly painted wooden train that his father waved in front of him. He forgot his fear and held his hands out. 'There, I thought you'd like that.'

'I broke his engine today,' said Helena, making an effort for the sake of the children. 'That couldn't have come at a better time, could it, Hal?'

'Good,' Ramon replied, retreating to his case.

'Now, where's yours, Fede? I've got you a very special present,' he said, looking up at her expectant face. He felt her hand on his back again. It was so typical of Federica who always had to have some sort of physical contact to feel close. His hands burrowed deep into the bag that was filled not with clothes but with notepads, camera equipment and souvenirs from faraway countries. Finally his fingers felt the rough surface of tissue paper. He pulled it out, taking care not to knock it against the hard metal of his equipment. 'Here,' he said, pressing it into her trembling hands.

'Thank you, Papa,' she breathed, unwrapping it carefully. Hal had run off into the nursery to play with his new train. Helena lit a cigarette and smoked it nervously, leaning back against the banisters.

'So how are you?' he asked without approaching her.

'Fine, you know, nothing's changed,' she replied coldly.

'Good,' he said.

Helena sighed wearily. 'We have to talk, Ramon.'

'Not now.'

'Of course.'

'Later.'

★　　★　　★

15

Federica unwrapped the paper to discover a roughly carved wooden box. It wasn't pretty. It wasn't even charming. She felt the tears prick the backs of her eyes and her throat constrict with disappointment. Not because she wanted a nicer present, she wasn't materialistic or spoilt, but because Hal's present had been so much more beautiful than hers. She understood his presents as a reflection of his love. He couldn't love her very much if he hadn't even bothered to find her a pretty gift.

'Thank you, Papa,' she choked, swallowing back her tears in shame. 'It's very nice.' But she didn't have the strength to rebel against her emotions. The excitement had been too much, now the disappointment threw her into a sudden low and the tears welled and spilled out over her hot cheeks.

'Fede, *mi amor*,' he said, pulling her into his arms and kissing her wet face.

'It's nice,' she said, trying to sound grateful and not wishing to offend him.

'Open it,' he whispered into her ear. She hesitated. 'Go on, *amorcita*, open it.' She opened it with a shaking hand. The little box might have been plain on the outside, ugly even, but inside it was the most beautiful thing she had ever seen, and what's more it played the strangest, most alluring tune she had ever heard.

Chapter Two

Federica stared into the box in awe. The entire interior was covered with neatly cut stones of every colour that shimmered as if each little gem contained a small heart of light all its very own. There was not one patch of wood, not even a minute piece, that lay exposed between the mesmerising crystals. From within, the box appeared to be made solely out of jewels and not out of wood at all, like the core of a crystallised piece of rock. On the floor of the box trembled the delicate wings of a butterfly that varied in colour from a dark ink blue against her body to the palest of aquamarines and finally amber. So delicate were they that Federica placed a finger onto the surface in order to convince herself that they were really stones and not drops of glittering water from some enchanted pool. A strange, iridescent light caused the butterfly to shudder as if about to extend her wings and fly away. Federica moved the box about slowly to see where the light was coming from and at once she was taken by the magical movement of the butterfly who, as she tilted the box, seemed to change from blues to pinks, reds and oranges. She caught her breath and put the box straight again. The butterfly returned to her cool sea tones before changing once more into fire as Federica tilted the box again.

'It's beautiful,' she sniffed without taking her eyes off the sparkling treasure chest.

'Beauty isn't always on the outside, Fede,' he said softly, hugging her. He looked up at his wife who still stood stiffly against the banisters, blowing smoke into the air like a dragon. She sighed impatiently and shook her head before walking out of the hall into the corridor, the smoke floating eerily behind her like a phantom. She wanted to tell him that he couldn't buy his daughter's love with presents all the time.

But regretfully she knew he didn't have to buy it at all; he already had it for free.

Ramon stood up and tore his eyes away from the trail of smoke, which, along with the ill feeling, was all that remained of his wife. He looked down at the radiant face of his daughter, oblivious to the tension that caused the atmosphere to quiver with the invisible force of disappointment. He ran a hand over his unshaven face and down his dirty black hair that was long and reached his shoulders. It was hot. He needed air and he needed a swim. He had looked forward to returning home, built it up in his mind, romanticised it. But now he was home he wanted to leave again. Home was always a rosier place in the mirages of his mind. It was better to leave it there.

'Come, Fede,' he said. 'Let's go down to the beach, just you and me. Bring the box with you.' Federica jumped to her feet, clasped her treasure against her thin chest and, taking his hand, she followed him out through the front door.

'What about Mama and Hal?' she said, delirious with happiness that she had been chosen to go with him and she alone.

'Hal's happy with his train and Mama's with him. Besides, I want to tell you how I found your box. There's a very sad legend attached to it and I know how you like stories.'

'I love your stories,' she replied, skipping along to keep up with his lengthy strides.

Helena watched helplessly as her husband left the house, taking with him the overbearing weight of his presence and suddenly she felt cheated, as if the pressure that had built up inside her chest had been for nothing. The house felt still and somehow bigger than when his powerful body had dwarfed it and she bit her lip in frustration. 'How dare he leave us,' she thought bitterly, 'why can't he just stick around for once?'

* * *

The midday sun was scorching in spite of the sea breeze that cooled it off around the edges. They walked down the street, passing Señora Baraca's dog who pulled on his leash and let out a frenzied round of barks when he saw them. Federica told her father how the dog barked all the time because he wanted to run about and wasn't able to in his small garden.

'Well, let's take him out then,' said Ramon.

'Really? Can we?' she replied in excitement. She watched with pride as her father rang the bell. They waited in the shade of an almond tree. The sound of children playing in the street resounded through the air, their laughter like the song of sea birds on the beaches. Federica didn't wish to be with them. She wished only that her father would stay this time and never go away again.

'*Sí?*' came a voice from behind the door. It was deep and guttural, muffled by the phlegm that caught in her throat.

'Señora Baraca. It's Ramon Campione,' he said with the assertiveness that pertained to everything he did. Federica pulled herself up, copying her father who always walked tall.

'Ramon Campione, indeed,' she replied, venturing out of the house like a timid crow. She was old and bent and wore a black dress of mourning even though her husband had died more than ten years before. 'I thought you were the other side of the world,' she croaked.

'I'm home now,' he replied, softening his voice a little so as not to frighten her. Federica held tightly on to his hand. 'My daughter would very much like to take your dog for a walk on the beach. Perhaps we could do you the favour of exercising him.'

The old woman chewed on her gums for a moment. 'Well, I know you, so you won't be stealing him,' she replied. 'Perhaps you could shut him up for me. If I don't go insane with grief, I'll go insane with the barking.'

'We'll do our best for you,' he said and smiled courteously. 'Won't we, Fede?' Federica cowered behind him and lowered her eyes shyly. Señora Baraca's knotted fingers fumbled clumsily with the lead, the hairs on her chin illuminated like cobwebs by the sun. Finally she opened the gate and handed the dog to Ramon. The dog stopped barking and began to jump about, puffing and snorting with the enthusiasm of a freed prisoner.

'His name is Rasta,' she said, hands on hips. 'My son gave him to me before he disappeared for good. That's all I have left. I'd rather have my son, he made much less noise.'

'We'll bring Rasta back before lunchtime,' Ramon assured her.

'As you wish, Don Ramon,' she replied, blinking into the sunlight with the discomfort of a creature grown accustomed to the darkness of her melancholy.

Ramon and Federica strode down the hill towards the sea, half running to keep up with Rasta who jumped and skipped in front of them, straining at his leash, thirsting to sniff every gateway and post, every patch of grass or tree, cocking his leg indiscriminately everywhere the scent of another animal lingered. He was pathetically happy. Federica's heart floated with joy as she watched the skinny black mongrel experience freedom for the first time in perhaps many months. She looked up at her father and her cheeks burned with admiration. There was nothing he couldn't do.

They crossed the road that ran alongside the coast, then made their way down the paved steps to Caleta Abarca beach. One or two people walked up and down, a child played with a small dog, throwing a ball into the sea for it to chase. Federica took off her sandals and felt the soft sand, like Lidia's flour, between her pink toes. Ramon changed into his bathing shorts, leaving his clothes and leather moccasins in a heap for Federica to look after while he went and washed himself off in the cold waters of the Pacific. She watched him jog towards the sea, followed eagerly by Rasta. He was strong and hairy, with the powerful physique of a man capable of climbing mountains, yet he walked and moved with surprising grace. Ramon Campione's imagination was as deep and mysterious as the sea, full of shipwrecks and sunken continents. Federica had grown up on his stories and somehow those stories had made his absences less acute. When she looked back on her short life she saw only the long rides through her father's fertile mind. Those were the adventures she remembered, not the many months of drought. She watched him splash about with Rasta in the glittering water. The light caught the tips of the waves and the silk of his hair and if she hadn't known better she would have thought he were a playful seal. She placed the box on her lap and ran her hand over the rough wooden surface. She wondered to whom it had once belonged. A shudder of anticipation careered up her spine at the thought of another magical story. She opened the box to the ringing of little bells and marvelled once again at the glittering gems that caused the butterfly's wings to quiver.

Finally, Ramon's wet body sat down next to her on the hot sand to dry off in the sun. Rasta, unwilling to stop enjoying his liberty even for a moment, galloped up and down the beach, playing tag with the sea. Ramon was pleased his daughter liked the box. She deserved it. After all, Helena was right, he wasn't a good father. Good fathers gave their children their time. He couldn't be that sort of father. It wasn't in his nature. He was a wanderer, a nomad. His mother used to tell him that children give according to what parents put in. Well, he must have done something right, for Federica loved him and her love showed all over her face. He cast his eyes out over the blue horizon and wondered how long he'd last on this shore before the itchiness in his feet got the better of him and the winds of new adventures blew outside his window to lure him away.

'Tell me the legend, Papa,' said Federica. Ramon lifted his daughter between his legs so that he sat behind her with his arms around her body and his rough cheek against hers. They both looked into the mosaic of crystals and listened to the light clatter of tiny bells.

'This box once belonged to a beautiful Inca princess,' he began. Federica gasped in delight. She loved his stories and nestled in closer, for she knew this one would be special. She kept the box open on the folds of her yellow dress, running her hands over the stones and turning it from side to side to watch the colours mysteriously change as if by magic. 'The Inca princess was called Topahuay and lived in a palace on the hillside village of Pisac in Peru. The Incas were an ancient Indian civilisation who worshipped the sun, Inti, and paid homage to their Emperor, the ruling Inca. Beneath the Emperor were the nobility, the "Capac Incas", the true descendants of the founding Inca, Manco Capac. Topahuay was a member of one of these ruling houses called *panacas*. She had smooth brown skin, a round open face, sharp green eyes and long black hair that she tied into a plait that fell down her back, almost to the ground. She was admired by everyone and all the young men of the nobility longed to marry her. But Topahuay was secretly in love with a man of lowly birth, a member of the *yanakuna*, a domestic class who served the *panacas*. A marriage between these two such distinct classes was unthinkable. But Topahuay and Wanchuko, which was his name, loved each other so fiercely that they defied the laws of their land and saw each other in secret. Sometimes Topahuay would disguise herself as a woman from the *yanakuna* and they would walk the streets unnoticed, hold hands away from the suspicious eyes of her relatives and even kiss when no one was looking. Now, Topahuay was only thirteen years old. You may think that is very young for a girl to be thinking of marriage, but in those days thirteen was the beginning of womanhood and her parents were scouring their society for a worthy husband for her. Topahuay felt trapped in a world of strict social codes with no escape. She knew in her heart that she would have to marry a nobleman and relinquish Wanchuko for ever. So Wanchuko decided to make her a box that was so unremarkable she would be able to take it with her wherever she went without attracting suspicion, but which contained a secret message within that only she would ever see, to remind her of his love. So he set about making a plain wooden box. He made it so plain that it was almost ugly.

'Once the box was made he searched the hills and caves for the most beautiful stones he could find. Some were precious, some were simply crystals, others were rare gems he found at the bottom of the lake of such exquisite blues and greens that he believed them to have been made out of the water itself. Once he had gathered all his stones together he locked himself in his small room from dawn to dusk where he chiselled and carved, setting each stone carefully into the wood. Then he fashioned a much smaller box, which contained a special mechanism he invented so that when the larger box was opened a strange music, like the tinkling of tiny bells, resounded within. Legend has it that the box was a magical box, made with the very force of his love that was not of this world. It was due to that higher vibration that the stones were set in place, as if by enchantment. You see, he didn't use a type of glue, as others would have, instead the stones are held together by each other, like a magnificent mosaic. If you were to take one stone out they would all fall away and the picture would be lost for ever. So you see, it must have been made with magic. There is no other explanation. On the bottom of the box he designed a butterfly to symbolise Topahuay's entrapment and her beauty. When he gave it to her she cried large silver tears and said that she wished she had wings like a butterfly so that she could fly away with him. What Wanchuko didn't know was that the symbolism of the butterfly would go beyond entrapment and beauty. Butterflies only live for a day. Topahuay's life would be cut short, just like the butterfly's, at the height of her magnificence.

'The Inca Empire was also at the height of its powers. It was the largest and most potent empire that South America had ever known. But it was all to go drastically wrong.

★   ★   ★

23

'The Spanish arrived to conquer Peru in one of the bloodiest episodes in the history of the empire. It was then, when all hope had drained away and the blood of thousands of Incas ran in rivers down the hills into the valleys that they sacrificed their most beautiful and cherished Topahuay to their god of war, in the desperate hope that he would save them. Clasping the box to her breast she was dressed in exquisitely woven wools, her hair plaited and beaded with one hundred shining crystals. Upon her head was placed a large fan of white feathers to carry her into the next world and frighten the demons along the way. Wanchuko was unable to save her. He could only watch, helpless and heartbroken, as she was led up the small mountain path together with an entourage of high priests and dignitaries. As she passed him her large green eyes gazed upon him with such intense love that a light ignited about her head, a light not of this world. His lips trembled and his outstretched hand grabbed her woollen cloak in an effort to save her. But it was no good, the entourage passed him and continued up into the mists of the mountain. Up to the bridge that joined this world to the next, a bridge that Topahuay would have to cross alone. He was too angry to cry, too afraid to run after her. He stood petrified, waiting, wanting it to be over. When he unclenched his hand he saw a brightly woven piece of wool sitting in his shaking palm. A moment later he heard a short, piercing scream. He turned his eyes to the mountain where the scream echoed momentarily off the jagged peaks before disappearing into the wind. When he looked down at his hand the piece of wool had transformed itself into a resplendent butterfly. He watched, aghast, as she stood quivering in his palm for a brief second as if stunned by her own metamorphosis. Then she lifted her fragile wings and flew away. Topahuay had become a butterfly after all and her spirit was free.'

Federica was so moved a tear trailed slowly down her shining cheek, dropping off her lip onto her chin and finally into the box where it seeped into the crystals. 'How did you get the box,

Papa?' she whispered, as if the sound of her voice would shatter the tenderness of the moment.

'I found it in a village called Puca Pucara. Topahuay's family had managed to salvage it before she was buried on the mountainside. They brought it down to their village where they kept it for a while until the Spanish came with their weapons and their slaughter. It was then that Topahuay's mother gave it to Wanchuko, for she had always known what her daughter's secret heart contained, and told him to leave Peru until it was safe to return. So Wanchuko left as he had been told only to return many decades later as an old man. He had never married for he had vowed in his heart to love only Topahuay. He had wandered the world alone, thinking only of her. In dreams, when he was awake as much as when he was asleep, her open face and smiling eyes would come to him and comfort him through his lonely life. When he returned to Pisac he recognised no one. His family had been slaughtered along with Topahuay's; in death there were no social divides. They had all died together, emperors and servants alike. On the brink of despair he climbed up the same path that Topahuay had walked that fateful day, all those years ago. At the top, to his surprise, he saw a little old woman sitting on the grass, looking out across the kingdom of mountain peaks. She was quite alone. When he approached her he recognised her as Topahuay's sister, Topaquin. Time had warped her skin and shrunk her bones, just like his. But he knew her and when he came closer, she too recognised him and invited him to join her. There they talked about Topahuay, her short, tragic life and the Spanish armies of destruction who had stamped out their culture and way of life for ever. Wanchuko gave Topaquin the box, telling her that the spirit of Topahuay danced in the light of the crystals and sang with the music of the tiny bells. Then he lay back on the spot where Topahuay's life had been so cruelly taken from her and died. He, too, crossed the bridge that joins this life to the next. But, he wasn't alone, for Topahuay was with him and her love was there to guide him so no evil could touch him.

'The box was taken to Puca Pucara and remained there for all

25

that time, handed down from one generation to another. The strange thing is that an old woman gave it to me. She said that it has special powers. She said that I needed it more than she did. So, she wrapped it up and handed it to me. It must be priceless, Fede, like you. So you treasure it, for it was made with love and must be cherished with love.'

'I'll cherish it for ever, Papa. Thank you,' she replied, overwhelmed with gratitude and so moved by the story that her lips seemed to lose their colour and turn pale.

Ramon glanced at his watch while his daughter sat transfixed, stroking the butterfly with an unsteady hand. 'We should go home for lunch,' he whispered into her ear, stroking the soft skin of her white neck with tender fingers. 'Where's Rasta?' he chuckled, casting his eyes up and down the beach. He stood up and stretched before putting his clothes back on again. Federica followed his lead reluctantly. She closed the box and got to her feet. She straightened out the creases in her pretty yellow dress and called for Rasta. Still full of energy he appeared wet and sandy with a ball in his mouth.

'Here, Rasta,' she said, patting her thighs. He trotted up to her and dropped the ball on the ground. She shook her head. Some poor person would probably want that ball back, she thought, picking it up with a finger and thumb so as not to dirty her hands. She looked around but saw no one. 'What shall I do with this ball, Papa?' she asked.

'Oh, I think he can keep it. Poor old Rasta. He doesn't have anything else to play with and I can't see anyone looking for it,' he replied, slipping his feet into his moccasins. Federica threw the ball up the beach. Rasta scurried after it. 'Come on, let's go,' he said, taking her hand and leading her back up the steps.

'That was such a beautiful story, Papa.'

'I knew you'd like it.'

'I love it. I love the box. I'll treasure it for ever. It will be my

26

most treasured possession,' she said, clutching it against her chest again.

Ramon was pensive as they walked up the hill towards home. He had a dark premonition that Helena had given up. There was a distant look in her eyes that hadn't been there before. A resignation of sorts. The feisty expression was no longer set into her features, as if she'd grown tired of battle and wanted out. He sighed deeply. Federica was still far away in Pisac with Topahuay and Wanchuko and walked up the hill beside him in silence.

They returned Rasta to Señora Baraca who was grateful that he no longer barked, but panted heavily and wagged his thin tail with pleasure. She said that Federica could take him out whenever she wanted. 'As he hasn't bitten you, he must like you,' she said without smiling, chewing on her gums.

Federica followed her father up the street. 'Mama says I shouldn't touch him. She says we don't know where he's been,' she said to her father.

'We do now,' he replied, smiling down at her. 'Still, I'd do as she says and wash your hands before lunch.'

'I cooked your favourite lunch with Lidia,' she said proudly.

He grinned, his gleaming teeth whiter against his dark skin. 'Pastel de choclo,' he said and she nodded. 'I don't deserve you.'

'Oh yes you do. You're the best father in the whole world,' she replied happily, hugging her magical box and gripping his hand so tightly that he knew she meant it.

Chapter Three

Federica followed her father across the midday shadows of the leafy acacia trees, through their front gate and up the path towards the front door. Just before they reached it Lidia appeared, scarlet-faced and anxious.

'Don Ramon! Señora Helena is waiting to have lunch. She told me to go and find you,' she puffed, her heavy bosom heaving with exertion.

Ramon strode up to her, disarming her with his wide smile. 'Well, Lidia, you won't have to now as we're back. I hear there's *pastel de choclo* for lunch,' he said, walking on past her into the hall.

'*Sí*, Don Ramon. Federica cooked it all by herself,' she said, closing the door behind her and following them into the kitchen.

'Smells delicious,' he said, inhaling the warm aroma of onions. 'Don't forget to wash your hands, Fede,' he added, running his under the tap. Federica's eyes sparkled with happiness and she smiled without restraint. After washing her hands she rushed into the sitting room to tell her mother about the legend of the box.

'Mama!' she cried, skipping up the corridor. 'Mama.'

Helena emerged cross-faced and weary, carrying Hal in her arms.

'Where have you been, Fede?' she asked, running her hand down the child's windswept hair. 'Hal's dying of hunger.'

'We went to the beach. We took Señora Baraca's dog, Rasta. You know he doesn't bark any more, he just wanted to be let out to run around. Poor thing. Then Papa swam and I looked after his clothes. Rasta swam, too. Then Papa told me the legend.'

'What legend?' Helena asked, humouring her daughter as she ushered her into the dining room.

'About Topahuay and Wachuko. The Inca princess. This box was made for her.'

'Really. How lovely,' said Helena, patiently. She looked up at her husband as he walked into the room, filling it with his presence and the tense atmosphere that had once more returned to the house. They locked eyes for a moment like two strangers curiously looking each other over for the first time. Helena averted her eyes first.

'I want to sit next to Papa,' Federica announced happily, pulling out a chair and patting the placemat possessively.

'You can sit wherever you like, sweetie,' said Helena, dropping Hal gently into his chair. 'I hope you washed your hands,' she added, remembering the dog.

'Oh yes. Señora Baraca looks like a witch,' Federica laughed.

'She does, actually,' Ramon agreed, chuckling, attempting to lighten the atmosphere.

'Well, I hope she didn't cast a spell on you,' said Helena, making an effort for the sake of the children. Her throat was tight and her chest constricted under the pressure of having to perform. She longed to talk to Ramon on his own. She needed to release the burden of her thoughts. She needed to resolve the situation. They couldn't go on like this. It wasn't fair on either of them.

'Oh no. She was very grateful we had walked her dog for her,' said Federica.

'I want to see the dog,' Hal whined, wriggling in his chair with impatience. Lidia entered with the steaming *pastel de choclo*.

'Fede made this for you this morning,' said Helena, sitting down at the other end of the table from her husband.

'So I'm told. You're very good to me, Fede,' he said truthfully.

'She certainly is,' said Helena dryly. She would like to have added that he was wholly undeserving of her affection, but she restrained the impulse with a gulp of water from her glass. 'She worked all morning, didn't you, Fede?'

'Papa hasn't seen his room yet,' she added and a bashful smile tickled her face.

'What have you done to my room, you naughty monkey?'

'You'll have to see for yourself,' she said.

'Fede picked flowers this morning,' said Hal disloyally. 'Didn't you, Fede?'

'Mama!' protested Federica in frustration.

'Have you enjoyed your train, Hal?' Ramon asked in an effort to distract the child from giving anything else away.

'It's brightly coloured and goes very fast,' he said, making 'chuga chuga chuga chuga' train noises. Lidia placed a hot plate of food in front of him. 'I don't like sweet corn,' he grumbled, sitting back in his chair and folding his arms in front of him.

'Yes, he does,' said Federica. 'He's just pretending because I made it.'

'No, I'm not.'

'You are.'

'Not.'

'Are.'

'All right you two. Enough of this,' said Ramon firmly. 'Hal, eat your corn or you go to your room without lunch or your train.' Hal scowled at his sister, his brown eyes darkening with resentment.

Ramon and Helena's conversation revolved around the children. If the children went silent, which they often did after an argument, they would be forced to talk to each other, which neither wanted to do, not with that false politeness, like a couple of actors in a badly written play. Ramon let Federica tell her mother the story of the Inca princess, only interrupting her when she turned to him for help over some detail that she had forgotten. Ramon was surprised at how much she had managed to remember. Helena listened, turning to answer her son once or twice when he whined 'Mama' just to get attention. Federica was used to being interrupted by her brother, she was also used to her mother indulging him by saying 'What is it, my love?' in a slow, patient voice. She didn't mind. One often tolerates things purely out of habit.

'Darling, what a delightful story. And the box is now yours.

You are a very lucky little girl,' said Helena. She didn't add 'and I hope you'll look after it', as other mothers would, because she knew Federica was more responsible about things like that than she was herself.

'I thought we could drive up to Cachagua for a couple of weeks,' Ramon suggested casually as if everything were normal, as if he hadn't noticed the change in Helena's countenance. 'Spend Christmas with my parents. They'd love to see you and the children.'

'Oh, yes please, Mama!' squealed Federica in delight. She loved staying with her grandparents. They had a cosy, thatched house overlooking the sea. Helena wished he hadn't brought it up in front of the children. They needed to talk first. He hadn't consulted her. Now if she said they couldn't go, she'd disappoint them. She couldn't bear to disappoint them. Hal gazed up at her with hopeful brown eyes.

'Yes! Yes!' he cried, knocking his fork on the table. He also loved staying with his grandparents. They bought him ice creams and took him for pony rides up the beach. His grandfather read him stories and carried him about on his shoulders.

'Okay, we'll go to Cachagua,' she conceded weakly. 'Ramon, I need to talk to you after lunch. Please don't disappear off with Fede again.' She tried to sound casual so as not to alarm the children. She knew in her mind what she wanted to say to him and feared that her thoughts might seep through her words and betray her.

'I won't,' he replied, frowning at her. There was something final in the tone of her voice and he didn't like it. Women always had to tie everything up with bows. Everything had to be worked out. Helena was like that. She was incapable of just going along with things and seeing how they turned out. She had to make decisions and formalise them.

After the first course, for which Ramon thanked his daughter by kissing her pale forehead fondly, she skipped out with Lidia to put the final touches on the welcome home *merengon de lúcuma*. While she was out Helena and Ramon talked to Hal, anything rather than talk to each other. Hal began to show off with all the attention and started singing a song he'd learnt at school about a donkey. Both parents watched him, anything rather than watch each other. Finally, the door opened and in walked Federica holding a white meringue cake with a single candle flickering on top. Hal sang Happy Birthday. Ramon and Helena both laughed and for a moment the strain in Helena's neck and chest lifted and she was able to breathe properly.

Federica placed the cake in front of her father and watched as he blew out the candle. Hal clapped together his small hands and giggled as the candle caught alight again as if by magic. Ramon pretended to be surprised and blew at it again. Both children laughed at the joke, certain that their father was truly baffled by the inextinguishable flame. Finally, he dipped his fingers in his water glass and pinched the wick. The flame was smothered and smoked away in protest. 'Welcome home!' he read out loud Federica's curly girlish handwriting, written with brown icing sugar onto the white frothy cream that resembled a choppy sea. 'Thank you, Fede,' he said, pulling her into his arms and kissing her cheek. Federica stayed on his lap while he cut it. Hal waved his teaspoon at the cake, catching a bit of meringue on the end, which he then hastily put into his mouth before anyone could tell him not to. Helena pretended she hadn't noticed. She was too tired to use the little energy she had left for her talk with Ramon on her mischievous child.

After lunch Federica reluctantly joined Hal in the garden while her parents went upstairs to talk. She wondered what they needed to talk about and resented her mother for dragging her father away. She carried the box into the garden and, sitting under the shade of the orange trees, she opened it and reflected on the story her father had told her.

'Can I see your box?' Hal asked, sitting down beside her.

'Yes, if you're careful.'

'I'll be careful,' he said, taking it from her. 'Wow!' he enthused. 'It's very pretty.'

'Yes, it is. It used to belong to an Inca princess.'

'What's an Inca?' he asked.

'The Inca were a race of people who lived in Peru,' she replied.

'What happened to the princess?' he asked.

'Didn't you listen to my story at the table?' she said, smiling down at him indulgently.

'I want to hear it again,' he said. 'Please.'

'Okay. I'll tell you again,' she agreed. 'But you must listen and be quiet or I won't tell you.'

'I'll be quiet,' he said and yawned sleepily. It was very hot, even in the shade. The low hum of bees in the flowerbeds and the distant roar of the sea were a soothing backdrop to the languid hours of siesta time. Federica placed her arm around Hal's body and let him rest his head against her.

'Once upon a time in deepest Peru,' she began and Hal closed his eyes and looked into a strange new world.

Ramon followed his wife upstairs. Neither spoke. He watched her walk down the corridor with her shoulders stooped and her head hung. As he approached his room the scent of lavender reached his nostrils and reminded him of his mother's house in Cachagua. As if sensing his thoughts Helena told him that Federica had prepared his sheets with fresh lavender from the garden.

The room was breezy and clean and smelt also of oranges and roses. He cast his eye around the place they had shared for the best part of seven years of their twelve-year marriage, but he didn't feel he belonged there. In spite of Federica's flowers and loving preparation it was his wife's room and the coldness of her demeanour told him that he was no longer welcome.

He placed his suitcase on the floor and sat on the edge of the bed. Helena walked over to the window and looked out across the sea.

'So, what do you want to talk about?' he asked, but he knew the answer.

'Us,' she replied flatly.

'What about us?'

'Well, it's just not the same, is it?'

'No.'

'I'm tired of pretending to the children that everything's fine. It's not fine. I'm not happy. It's all very well for you, travelling the world like a gypsy, writing your books of stories. But I'm the one trapped here in this house without you. Without any support. I've brought these two children up almost single-handedly,' she said and felt the strain in her neck rise to clamp her head in its vice.

'But you always knew that was my life. You didn't have any expectations. You said so yourself. You gave me freedom because you understood that I couldn't survive without it,' he said, shaking his head and frowning.

'I know. But I didn't know how it was really going to be. In the beginning we travelled together. It was a dream. I loved it and I loved you. But now . . .' Her voice trailed off.

'Now?' he ventured sadly.

'Now I don't love you any more.' She turned to face him. Noticing the hurt cloud his face she added quickly, 'Love has to be nurtured, not left to rot with neglect, Ramon. I loved you once, but now I don't know you any more. I wouldn't recognise love if it slapped me in the face. All I know is that I'm tired of being alone and you always leave me alone, for months on end. You always will,' she said and the tears cascaded down her cheeks, one after the other, until they formed two thin streams of misery.

'So what do you want to do?' he asked.

She walked timidly over to him and perched next to him on the bed. 'If you were afraid of losing me, Ramon, you'd stay and write here. You'd change for me. But you won't, will you?' He

34

thought about it for a moment, but his silence answered her question. 'Do you love me, Ramon?' she ventured.

His shiny conker eyes looked at her forlornly. 'Yes, I do, in my own way, Helena. I still love you. But I don't love you enough to change for you. If I stayed here with you and the children I'd shrivel. I'd dry out like a plant in the desert. Don't you see that? I don't want to lose you, or the children, but I can't change,' he said, shaking his head. 'I arrive home and the first thing I think about is when I can get going again. I'm sorry.'

They both sat in silence. Helena cried with the relief of having given vent to her feelings. She felt the heaviness lift and the tension ease on her temples. Ramon sat wondering what she was going to do. He didn't want to lose her. She was his safety net. He liked to have a home to come back to. Even if he rarely used it, he still liked it to be there. He loved his children. But he wasn't used to the day-to-day routine of children. He wasn't a family man.

'So what happens now?' he said after a while.

'I want to go home,' she replied, standing up again and walking over to the window.

'You mean to England?'

'Yes.'

'But that's the other side of the world,' he protested.

'Why should you care? You're always the other side of the world and you always will be. What difference does it make where we are? You'll always be on another continent.'

'But the children?'

'They'll go to school in England. We'll go and live in Cornwall with my parents.' Then she rushed to his side and knelt on the floor at his feet. 'Please, Ramon. Please let me take them home. I can't bear it here any more. Not the way it is now. Without you there's no point, don't you see? I don't belong here like you do. I would have belonged, I had planned to, but now I want to go home.'

'What will you tell them?'

'I'll tell them that we're going home. That you'll come and see

35

us, the same as you always have. We'll just live in a different country. They're young, they'll accept it,' she said firmly. She looked at him imploringly. 'Please, Ramon.'

'Do you want a divorce?' he asked impassively.

'No,' she replied quickly. 'No, not divorce.'

'Just a separation then?'

'Yes.'

'Then what?'

'Then nothing. I just want out,' she said and hung her head.

His premonition had been right. She was leaving him. She needed his permission to take the children out of the country and he would give it to her. How could he deny her that? Their children were more hers than his if one judged it by the amount of time they both spent with them. She was right, what did it matter where they were, he was always thousands of miles away.

'All right, you can take the children back to England,' he conceded sorrowfully. 'But first I want to take them to see my parents in Cachagua. I want to give them a family Christmas, so they'll always remember me like that.'

'Ramon,' she whispered, for her voice had gone hoarse with emotion, 'you will come and see us, won't you?' She searched his eyes, afraid that by cutting herself off from him he would no longer make the effort to be a part of their children's lives.

'Of course,' he replied, shaking his shaggy head.

'The children will miss you terribly. You can't desert them, Ramon. They need you.'

'I know.'

'Don't punish them for my actions. This is between us as adults, not them.'

'I know.'

'Fede loves you, so does Hal. I couldn't live with myself if you deserted them because of me.' She sat up abruptly. 'I won't go if leaving you means depriving my children of their father. I will sacrifice my own happiness for theirs,' she said and began to sob.

Ramon was confused. He ran his hand down her blonde hair. 'I won't desert them, Helena,' he said.

She looked up at him with glassy eyes. 'Thank you.'

Suddenly his mouth was on hers. Without understanding their actions their bodies rebelled against the cold detachment of their minds. They clawed off their clothes like thirsty animals scraping at the ground for water. Helena felt the sharp bristle of his chin against hers and the soft wetness of his lips and gums. For the months he had been away she had only dreamed of making love to other men. She had had opportunities but she had rejected every one for the simple reason that she was the wife of someone else, if only in name. Now she abandoned herself to the touch of a man, even though she felt nothing for him now but gratitude. In these intense moments of intimacy they could have been mistaken for believing their love to have been re-ignited. But Helena knew that sexual pleasure alone was a false love, as illusory as a mirage. She closed her eyes, blocking out the sad reality of her situation and allowed herself to take pleasure as his hands stroked the curves of her body as if exploring them for the first time.

It had been many months since they had last united in this way. They had both forgotten what the other's body was like. As if she had no control over her impulses, her fingers followed the ridge of his spine and caressed the hair on his shoulders like they used to do when they had been driven by love. She ran her tongue over his skin and it tasted of the sea mingled with the scent of man. When he kissed her, his mouth on her mouth, his face only inches away from hers, she opened her eyes to find his were closed. She wondered whom he was dreaming of and whether he too had had opportunities on his travels. She didn't want to know. Then he was inside her, awakening her dormant desire that had endured many months of hibernation and she thought no more about the other women he might have had. They both forgot the other as they moved like one writhing beast, oblivious to the low groans that escaped from their throats and the delirious sighs that vibrated deep within their bellies.

When they lay sweaty and exhausted, the heady scent of their skin mingling with the sweet fragrance of lavender and rose, they both stared up at the ceiling and wondered why they had allowed themselves to get carried away.

Helena was too embarrassed to look at him and covered her steaming body with the bedspread in shame. A ridiculous action after he had tasted it so intimately. She fumbled in the bedside table drawer for a cigarette. Finding one she lit it with a trembling hand and inhaled impatiently. How strange it is, she thought, that we can be as close as two people possibly can be then suddenly, in the space of a second, lie here side by side but thousands of miles apart. She looked over at him and he turned to face her.

'That was nice,' he said.

'Yes, it was,' she replied tightly.

'Don't regret it, Helena. It's okay to indulge in the pleasures of the flesh, even if you feel nothing but physical desire.'

She inhaled again. 'I don't regret it,' she said. She didn't know whether she did or didn't. Had she really made love without love? She waved the thought away with the smoke. It no longer mattered. She was going home.

Chapter Four

Ramon watched his wife dress in the dim light of the bedroom. Neither spoke. The smell of cigarettes masked the lavender Federica had pressed into the linen and the garden flowers she had so lovingly picked and placed on his bedside table in the shiny blue vase. The messy bed was all that was left of their passion. He wondered if there was anything left of their love. Then he heard Federica's soft voice singing in the garden and he realised that his children were the physical expressions of a love they had once happily given to each other, and he shuddered at the thought of being without them.

Helena's body was still firm and slim with that translucent pallor that had first attracted him to her twelve years before. She was now thirty years old, too young to be on her own without the attentions of a loving man to nurture her. When he had found her on those cold Cornish beaches she had been young and ready to sacrifice everything just so that she could be near him. They had travelled the world together, united by his thirst for adventure and her desire to be loved. It had worked until domesticity drove them apart. He watched her brush her long blonde hair and pin it onto the top of her head. He preferred it when she wore it down her back. Once it had reached her waist. Once he had threaded it with jasmine. She had been beautiful then. Now she looked tired and her disenchantment drained her face of colour so that her pallor, once so alluring, no longer glowed but lay stagnant like a diminishing waterhole in the dry season. If he didn't let her go there'd be nothing of her left.

She caught him watching her in the mirror but she didn't smile like she once would have done.

'When do you want to go to Cachagua?' she asked.

'Tomorrow. I'll call my parents, tell them we're coming.'

'What will you tell them?'

'About us?'

'Yes.'

He sighed and sat up. 'I don't know yet.'

'They'll think I'm heartless. They'll blame me,' she said and her voice quivered.

'No they won't. They know me better than you think.'

'I feel guilty,' she said and stared at her reflection.

'You've made your decision,' he said impassively and got to his feet.

Helena wanted him to beg her to stay. She had hoped he would fall to his knees and promise to change like other men would. But Ramon wasn't like other men. He was unique. It had been his uniqueness that she had fallen in love with. He was so self-sufficient he didn't need anyone. He just needed the air to breathe, his sight to take in all the wondrous places he travelled to and a pen to write it all down. He hadn't needed her love but she had given it to him, desiring nothing in return except his acceptance. But it is human nature to always want more than one has. Once she had won his love she wanted his freedom too. But he had been unwilling to relinquish it. He still was. He had been as difficult as a cloud to pin down, she should have known he would never change, that there would come a time when she would be alone, for the world possessed his soul and she hadn't the strength to fight for it any more. But she still wanted him to fight for her. How could he still love her but refuse to fight for her? He made her feel worthless.

Helena stepped out into the garden, squinting in the white glare of the sunshine, to find Hal asleep in the shade of an orange tree while Federica sang to herself on the swing. She knew Federica would be broken-hearted leaving Viña, but her parents' separation would hurt her so much more. Helena watched her swinging in the sun, ignorant of the dark undercurrent that swelled beneath her perfect day. When she saw her mother standing in the doorway she leapt off the swing, picked up her magic box from the grass and ran towards her.

'Have you finished talking to Papa now?' she asked.

'Yes, I have, sweetie. We're going to Cachagua tomorrow,' she replied, knowing how happy that would make her.

Federica grinned. 'I told Hal the story of the Inca princess. He's asleep now.' She laughed. Hal lay on his back, his arms and legs spread in blissful abandon, his chest gently rising and falling in the afternoon heat.

'Well, let's not wake him,' Helena said, watching her child with tenderness. Hal was so like his father. He had Ramon's dark hair and conker eyes without that maddening glint of self-sufficiency. Federica was happier on her own but Hal needed constant attention. He was the part of Ramon she had loved and been allowed to hold on to. Hal needed her and loved her unconditionally.

Federica skipped into the house to find her father in the sitting room, talking on the telephone in Spanish. She walked up to him with her box and perched on the armrest, waiting for him to finish so that she could talk to him. She listened to the conversation and realised he was talking to her grandmother. 'Tell Abuelita about my box,' she said excitedly.

'No, you tell her,' he said, handing her the receiver.

'Abuelita, Papa's bought me a box that once belonged to an Inca princess . . . yes, a real princess . . . I will, I'll tell you tomorrow . . . so am I . . . a big kiss to you, *yo también te quiero,*' she said and blew a kiss down the telephone, which made her father chuckle as he took back the receiver.

'We'll see you in time for lunch, then,' he said, before hanging up. 'Right, Fede, what shall we do now?'

'I don't know,' she replied and grinned, for she knew her father always had something planned.

'Let's go into town and buy your grandmother a present, shall we?'

'And buy a juice,' she added.

'A juice and a *palta* sandwich,' he said, getting up. 'Go and tell your mother we'll be back in time for tea.'

★   ★   ★

Mariana Campione put down the receiver and shouted to her husband Ignacio who was lying in the hammock on the terrace reading, round glasses perched on the bridge of his aquiline nose and his panama hat pulled down over his bushy eyebrows – an indication that he did not wish to be disturbed.

'Nacho, Ramon's back and he's coming to visit with the family tomorrow,' she said in delight. Ignacio did not move, except to turn the page. Mariana, a full-bodied, large-boned woman with silver-grey hair and a kind open face, walked out through the French doors to where her husband was lying in the shade of an acacia tree. '*Mi amor*, did you hear me? Ramon's home. They're coming to visit tomorrow,' she repeated, her cheeks stung with joy.

'I heard you, woman,' he said without looking up from his book.

'Nacho, you don't deserve to have grandchildren,' she said, but she smiled and shook her head.

'He disappears for months without so much as a letter, what sort of a man does that to his family? I've told you before, Helena will lose patience with him eventually. I lost my patience with him years ago and I'm not married to him,' he said firmly, then glanced at his wife over his book to see her reaction.

'Don't be silly,' she chided gently, 'Helena is a good wife and mother. She's loyal to Ramon. I'm not saying he's right to desert her like that all the time, but she's an old-fashioned woman. She understands him. I'm thrilled they're coming to stay.' Her large face creased into a tender smile.

'How long are they staying for?' he asked, still looking at her.

'I don't know. He didn't say.'

'Still, I suppose we should be grateful,' he said sarcastically. 'Out of our eight children Ramon's the one we see the least so when he shows up it's more of an event.'

'Now you're being petulant.'

'For the love of God, Mariana, he's a forty-year-old man, or thereabouts, it's high time he grew up and took some responsibility before he loses everything. If that long-suffering wife of his leaves him he'll only have himself to blame, and I'll be on her side one hundred per cent.'

Mariana laughed and retreated into the cool interior of the house. She had listened to his argument enough times to know it by heart. Ramon was just a free spirit, she understood him like Helena did, she thought, wandering into the kitchen to inform their young maid, Estella, about the change in numbers. He was so talented it would be very wrong to tie him down and stifle such precious creativity. She read and re-read all his books and articles and felt immense pride when people told her how much they too enjoyed his writing. He was celebrated in Chile and he had earned every bit of the respect he was given. 'I know I'm his mother,' she said to her husband, 'but he really does write most beautifully.'

Estella had awoken from her siesta and was already chopping the vegetables for dinner when Mariana entered the kitchen. As in most Chilean households of the well-to-do, the kitchen was part of the maid's quarters, along with her bedroom and bathroom, which were situated at the back of the house, hidden behind thick perennial bushes and bougainvillea trees. Estella was new. After Consuelo, their maid for twenty years, had died the previous summer they had been very fortunate to have found Estella, through friends who had a summer house in Zapallar, the neighbouring village. Mariana had liked her immediately. Whereas Consuelo had become too old to clean properly and too sour to cook with any enthusiasm, Estella had set to work immediately, polishing, sweeping, scrubbing and airing with an energy bestowed on her by her youth and with a smile that bubbled up from her sweet nature and desire to please. She was courteous, discreet and a quick learner, which was vital, for Ignacio was impatient and pedantic.

'Estella, my son Ramon is arriving tomorrow at lunchtime with his wife and two small children, please make sure that the blue spare room is made up for them and the room next door, I know how my son likes his space. The children can share, it's more fun that way.'

'*Sí*, Señora Mariana,' she replied obediently, trying to conceal her excitement. She had heard an enormous amount about Ramon Campione, seen his picture in the papers many times and even read a few of his articles. The poetry of his descriptions had stirred her heart and she had longed to meet him from the moment she had realised who her new employers were. She enjoyed wandering about the house, gazing at the photographs scattered over tables and mantelpieces. He was so handsome and romantic-looking, with his long black hair, acute brown eyes and generous mouth that seemed too large for his face but at the same time utterly captivating. She had spent long moments polishing the glass that protected his face from the dust. Now she was going to meet him, she could barely contain herself.

'Scent the linen with lavender and I want fresh flowers in all three bedrooms. Don't forget the flowers. Federica appreciates nature. She's a sweet girl. Clean towels, fresh drinking water and fruit,' said Mariana, not forgetting a single detail.

'How long will they be staying, Señora Mariana?' Estella asked, trying to control the tremor in her voice lest it betray her.

Mariana shrugged. 'I don't know, Estella. Ten days, maybe more. I'm going to try to persuade them to stay for New Year, although it'll be hard pinning my son down. Ramon takes every day as it comes, he never makes plans,' she said proudly. 'One minute he's here and you think he's here to stay then suddenly he'll get up and leave, just like that. Then we don't see or hear from him for months. That's the way God made him so I don't complain.'

'*Sí*, Señora Mariana,' said Estella.

'My grandchildren love *manjar blanco*, please make sure there is enough in the house, I'd hate to disappoint them,' she added before leaving the room.

Estella sighed with pleasure. She set about preparing the rooms at once. She swept through the children's room like a tornado, making up the beds with real Irish linen sheets, sweeping the wooden floorboards and dusting the surfaces. The marital room she arranged with more care, scenting the linen with lavender

44

and opening the shutters to the fresh sea air and sound of chattering birds hopping about in the eucalyptus trees. When she opened the door to Ramon's room she breathed in deeply before making the bed slowly and tenderly, smoothing her elegant brown fingers over the pillow to flatten any wrinkles. She imagined him lying there, gazing up at her, beckoning her to join him. Then she lay on the bed and closed her eyes, breathing in the heady scent of tuberose she had set in a vase on the dresser. She smiled as she thought that perhaps tomorrow his head would lie where hers was lying now and he would never know how close they'd been.

She hoped he'd stay for a long time.

Ignacio put down his book and rolled out of the hammock. He felt sleepy and lethargic. The evening was cool, the shadows lengthening, the tide edging its way up the shore like a nightly predator. He stood on the terrace, leaning against the railings, looking out over the smooth surface of the sea that sighed hypnotically. He felt uneasy. His weathered face crinkled anxiously as he tried to discover the root of his ill-ease. The light had ripened to a warm orange as the sun hovered behind the horizon about to dawn on another shore. Perhaps it was the natural melancholia of sunset that had brought on this feeling, he thought hopefully. But he knew it had more to do with his son than with nature. He sensed things weren't as they should be.

Mariana wandered out to join him with his nightly glass of whisky and water. 'Here,' she said, handing it to him. 'You're very quiet this evening,' she added, smiling at him.

'I'm sleepy,' he replied, sipping from the glass.

'You've been reading too much.'

'Yes.'

'It can make one subdued, all that reading,' she said kindly, patting him on his weather-beaten brown arm.

'Yes,' he repeated.

'Still, you'll have Ramon and Helena to entertain you to-morrow, and those adorable children.'

'I know,' he agreed, nodding solemnly.

'He's given Fede a box that once belonged to an Inca princess, or so she tells me,' she said, watching the sun flood the sea with liquid gold.

'That sounds like one of Ramon's stories.'

'Yes, it does, doesn't it?' she chuckled. 'Typical Ramon, his imagination never ceases to amaze me.'

'An Inca princess, indeed.'

'Fede believes it.'

'Of course she does, Mariana, she worships her father,' he said, shaking his head. 'She worships him and he just abandons her. It's too bad.'

'Oh, Nacho, really. Is this what your silence is about? Ramon's lifestyle? It's really none of our business. If it works for them it shouldn't concern you or me.'

'But *does* it work for them?' he said, looking at her steadily. 'I don't know that it does. I feel something in my bones.'

'They're old bones, Nacho, I'm surprised they still feel anything at all.' She smiled.

'They're old bones, woman, but they're as sensitive as they always have been. Will you walk with me up the beach?' he asked suddenly, draining his glass.

Mariana looked surprised. 'Now?'

'Of course. We old people have to strike while we're still able to. Tomorrow may be our last.'

'What nonsense, *mi amor*, you really are very miserable to be with sometimes. But, yes, I'll walk with you up the beach. We can take our shoes off and get our feet wet, hold hands like we used to.'

'I'd like that very much,' he said, removing his panama hat and kissing her soft cheek.

'You old romantic,' she said and laughed at their foolishness. They were too old to play these games.

★   ★   ★

Ramon tucked Federica into bed. He noticed the box was on the table beside her.

'I'm frightened the box might not be here when I wake up,' she said suddenly, her smooth face creasing with anxiety.

'Don't worry, Fede, it will be here when you wake up. No one's going to take it while you're asleep, I promise.'

'It's the most beautiful thing I've ever had, I don't want to be without it, ever.'

'You won't be,' he reassured her, kissing her forehead. 'Have you noticed Señora Baraca's dog isn't barking tonight?'

'He's happy and tired, like me,' she said, smiling up at her father.

'He's exhausted.'

'What about tomorrow, can we take him out before we go to Cachagua?'

'Of course we can,' he said, touching her cheek with the tips of his fingers. 'We can take him up the beach again.'

'I feel sorry for Señora Baraca,' she said.

'Why?'

'Because she's so sad.'

'She chooses to be sad, Fede.'

'Does she?'

'Yes. Everyone has a choice, they can either be happy or sad.'

'But Mama told me her husband died,' she protested.

'Mama's right. But her husband died over ten years ago, before you were born. Now that's a long time ago.'

'But Wachuko was sad for his whole life.'

'Yes he was. But he didn't have to be. Sometimes it's better to move on rather than dwell on the past,' he said. 'One should learn things from the past and then let them go.'

'What should Señora Baraca have learnt from her past?' Federica asked, yawning.

'That she should spend more time looking after her dog than mourning her dead husband, don't you think?' he laughed.

47

'Yes,' she said and closed her eyes. Ramon watched her as she drifted off into the world of princesses and magic butterflies. Her long lashes caught the light that entered from the corridor, giving her a celestial beauty. Her face was long and noble, generous and honest. He felt his throat tighten with emotion at the thought of leaving her and while it didn't weaken his resolve it just made it a little harder to accept. He bent down and kissed her forehead again, feeling her velvet skin against his dry lips. He smelt the fragrance of her soap and the clean scent of her hair. He wanted to wrap her up in his arms and protect her from the harsh reality of a world that would only disappoint her.

Before he went to bed he crept into Hal's room to watch him as he slept. He didn't feel so close to his son. The child was only four and barely knew him. He was more attached to his mother and gave his father little attention. Hal didn't need him like Federica did. He watched the little boy suck on his thumb and cuddle his toy rabbit as he slept. Hal looked as if he embodied the qualities of an angel, as though he had been dropped into bed by God himself. His skin was flawless, his expression serene and contented. Ramon ran his rough hand over the boy's hair. Hal stirred and changed position but he didn't wake up. Ramon left as quietly as he had come.

The bed was cold in spite of the warm night. Helena slept curled up at one side, almost falling off the edge in her effort to avoid him. Ramon lay on his back staring up at the icy moonlight that crept across the ceiling. Neither recalled the fevered interlude of the afternoon. They didn't want to. Helena wished it hadn't happened and flushed with shame when she thought of it. So she pretended it simply hadn't happened. She felt him next to her, not because he moved, he didn't, but because the atmosphere was so heavy it was as if a third person occupied the space between them. She felt afraid to move or make a sound so she breathed shallow breaths and lay as rigid as a corpse. When sleep finally overcame them it

48

was tortured and fragile. Helena dreamed of arriving in Cornwall but not being able to find Polperro. Ramon dreamed of standing on the beach while Federica drowned out to sea. He did nothing to save her.

Chapter Five

When Federica awoke she was disappointed to see the sea mist swirling dense and grey outside her window, obscuring the morning sunshine and silencing the birds. It was chilly and damp. Her mother always told her that the sea mist was sucked into the coast by the heat in Santiago. If it was really hot in the capital Viña was misty. Federica hated the mist. It was depressing. Then she forgot all about the dreary skies and pulled her butterfly box onto her lap. She opened it, moved it about, ran her fingers over the stones, pleased that the light was still there causing the iridescent wings to shudder and tremble. That was how her mother found her, absorbed in Ramon's magic world of make-believe, somewhere amongst the mountains of Peru.

Helena had barely slept at all. Or at least she felt she hadn't slept. Her head was heavy and pressured. She had taken pain-killers and hoped they'd be quick to take effect. She padded into Federica's room in her dressing gown, followed by Hal who was already dressed and playing with his new train. When Federica saw her, pale faced and grey around the eyes, she noticed immediately and asked if she was all right.

'I'm fine, thank you, sweetie,' Helena replied, forcing a thin smile. But her eyes didn't smile. They remained dull and expressionless. Federica frowned and closed the lid of the box.

'You don't look very well, Mama. Shall I make you breakfast? Where's Papa?' she asked, jumping off the bed.

'Papa's still asleep, so best not to wake him. Why don't you put on your dressing gown and we can make breakfast together?' she suggested, patting Hal on his shiny head as he passed her making train noises. Federica scrambled into her dressing gown and wondered whether her father would remember his promise to take her to the beach with Rasta. She hoped he'd wake up and not spend all morning in bed, as he was apt to do. She skipped lightly down the stairs, through the hall and into the kitchen. Hal sat on the floor running his engine over the terracotta tiles, under the table and chairs, talking to himself and still making the noises of a train.

Federica helped her mother lay up for breakfast in the dining room. When her father was at home they stopped eating in the kitchen, which was an English habit of Helena's that she had never dropped, and ate like Chileans in the dining room. Lidia would arrive at ten to clean the house and cook the lunch. Ramon rarely went into the kitchen. He had grown up with staff, unlike Helena, whose family kitchen had been the very heart of her home.

Ramon awoke to find himself alone in the strange bed. It took a moment for him to remember where he was and for the heavy feeling of his wife's unhappiness to find him again. He cast his eyes to the window where the curtains danced with the cold breeze that came in off the Pacific bringing with it the damp sea mist. He didn't want to get up. The atmosphere in the room was stiflingly oppressive. He wanted to cover his head with the sheets and imagine he was far away on the clouds, above the mist and the misery that hung dense upon the walls of the house like slime. He lay there with a sinking feeling in his chest, suppressing the impulse to get up, pack his bag and leave.

Then he heard the gentle footsteps of his daughter. The sinking feeling turned to one of guilt and he peeped out over the sheets.

'Are you awake, Papa?' she asked. He saw her expectant face advance, her large blue eyes blinking at him hopefully. She treaded softly so as not to wake him if he was still sleeping. She moved slowly like a shy deer uncertain whether the animal in the bed was friend or foe. Ramon pulled the sheet down so that she could see he wasn't sleeping. Her face lit up and she smiled broadly. 'I've made you breakfast, Papa,' she said and her cheeks shone proudly. 'Can we go down to the beach, even though it's misty?'

'We can go to the beach right now,' he said, brightening up at the idea of getting out of the house. 'We'll take Rasta with us. You'd like that, wouldn't you? Then we'll head off to Cachagua.'

'Mama says it'll be sunny by the time we get to Cachagua,' she said, jumping from one foot to the other impatiently.

While Ramon was in the bathroom Federica skipped around the room, opening the curtains and making the bed. She was used to looking after her mother, but looking after her father gave her more pleasure. It was a novelty. Ramon ate his breakfast for Federica's sake. Hal had finished his and was playing quietly by himself in the nursery. His interest in his train far exceeded his interest in his father, whom he looked upon with suspicion because he sensed the strained atmosphere as all small children do. Helena sat at the table sipping a cup of black coffee. Ramon noticed her eyes were red and her face sapped of colour. He smiled at her politely, but she didn't smile back until Federica bounced in with hot croissants. Only then did she sit up and make an effort to act as if everything were normal.

After breakfast Ramon once again took Federica by the hand and led her down the road to the beach, the other hand holding onto Rasta's leash. Federica no longer cared whether it was sunny or misty. She was with her father, just the two of them. She felt special and cherished and she hugged the butterfly box tightly against her chest. They took off their shoes, Ramon's large brown explorer's feet made Federica's small pink ones look even smaller and more vulnerable. Together they walked up the beach, letting the sea catch their toes and cover them with foam. Ramon told her stories of the places he'd visited and the people he'd met and Federica listened transfixed, begging for another one until they were on the road to Cachagua, driving through the mist up the coast.

As they left the town behind them the road ascended into the pastoral charm of the countryside. They passed small villages of brightly painted houses with crude corrugated tin roofs and glassless windows into dark interiors. Open fruit stalls spilled out into the road and mangy horses and carts ambled up the sandy tracks driven by weathered Chileans in ponchos. Skinny dogs sniffed the dry ground for something to eat and grubby-faced children played with sticks and faded cans of Coca Cola, their large black eyes staring at the car with curiosity as it sped by. The road was dusty, with the odd precarious hole here and there. They stopped after a while for a break and a drink. The mist was beginning to lift and the sun push through. The shade of the slender acacia trees darkened as the light intensified behind them, fighting its way through the fog. Federica sat drinking a large glass of lemon soda while Ramon chewed on an *empanada*. The dark Chilean children sat in a huddle against the bleached wall of the shack, watching Federica and Helena with wide eyes, whispering behind their hands, longing to creep up and touch their white angel hair to see what it was made of.

Helena and Ramon each felt much better being out of the house, away from the place that represented nothing but un-happiness for Helena and disappointment for Ramon. With the emergence of the sun they began to smile at each other and abandon themselves to the cheerful chatter of their children. The strain in Helena's eyes lifted and the colour returned to her cheeks. Ramon hoped that perhaps she might change her mind. A couple of weeks away would do her good.

Mariana and Ignacio took breakfast in the dining room as the sea mist made it too unpleasant to eat outside on the terrace. When Estella entered with the coffee and toast, in her clean blue uniform with her raven hair shining and loose down her back like a glossy pony, Mariana noticed there was something dif-ferent about her and mentioned it to her husband.

'Looks the same to me,' he said, raising his eyes above his glasses to see her better. 'The same to me,' he repeated, returning to the large puzzle he was busy putting together.

Mariana watched her pour the coffee. She definitely looked different. It wasn't the hair, because she often let it down. It was something about her face. She was wearing more make-up. Her cheeks were pink and her eyes shone like wet pebbles. She smelt of soap and roses and her skin glowed due to the oil she had rubbed into it. Mariana smiled and wondered why she had made such an effort.

'I think she's got a "friend" in Cachagua,' she said to Ignacio, who wasn't remotely interested in the private life of his maid. 'Yes, she must have a suitor, Nacho. Now I wonder who that could be?' she said thoughtfully and rubbed her chin with her sensible brown fingers. Estella noticed Mariana watching her with a knowing look on her face and blushed. She smiled back nervously and turned away, fearful that Señora Mariana might guess the reason behind her blushes.

By midday the sky was a majestic blue, the last of the mist burnt off by the fierce heat of the December sun. Mariana sat in the shade on the terrace, listening for the sound of the car, quietly doing her embroidery while Ignacio wrote letters inside. She had been to check the bedrooms and bathrooms and came away very pleased with their new maid who had carried out her every command, forgetting nothing. She liked the fact that the girl had initiative. She went that little bit further without being asked. Mariana swept her soft grey eyes over the dark wooden terrace, at the pots of plants and tall palm trees that gave it respite from the sun and noticed they had all been watered. Now she hadn't asked Estella to do that, she had taken it upon herself without waiting to be asked. That was initiative, she thought to herself contentedly.

As the car descended the sandy road into Cachagua, Federica rolled down the window and poked her head out. Cachagua was the most charming of seaside villages. A low wooden fence, partly obscured by rich green ferns and palms, surrounded each thatched house. Sometimes the only visible proof that a house lay concealed behind such an abundance of nature was the tall water tower that rose up to catch the rain. It was an oasis of trees – palms, acacias and eucalyptus. Their sweet scents mingled with the salt of the ocean and the bushes of jasmine buzzed with the contentment of bees. The sandy track weaved its way through the *pueblo* down to the long golden beach and navy sea. Ignacio and Mariana's house was the nicest house in the village. Obscured behind frothy trees it resembled a log cabin on stilts with a large terrace overhanging rocks at the water's edge. Inside it was sparsely decorated with brightly woven rugs and deep crimson sofas. Mariana had always had beautiful taste and Ignacio hated clutter. He had been known to throw his hands impatiently across surfaces that he felt were too busy, knocking everything onto the floor. He had a violent temper, which only Mariana could assuage with her calm, soothing voice and gentle manner, always detecting it early by the sudden swelling of his ears.

As the car drove through the gates into the sandy driveway, Ramon beeped the horn. Mariana's heart jumped in her chest, more out of surprise than delight, for she had drifted off and forgotten to listen out for their arrival. She called to her husband and, getting up slowly – age didn't allow her to leap to her feet as she used to do as a young woman – she made her way through the house to greet them.

Estella's hands were clammy with nerves. She leant back against the kitchen sink and smoothed down her pale blue uniform. She heard the excited voices of the children, the bubbling laughter of Señora Mariana as she hugged and kissed their eager faces, then the deep, gravelly voice of Don Ignacio. She strained her ears to find the voice of Ramon Campione but the low chatter of adult voices made his unrecognisable. She didn't even know what he sounded like.

Federica skipped onto the terrace holding her box out for her grandmother to admire. Helena gently told her to be patient, Abuelita would have all the time in the world to look at it later, once she had had a chance to talk to Papa. Federica retreated obediently to the hammock, where she curled up like a dog and watched as her grandparents chatted to her parents. Hal sat on Helena's knee with his train, which he rolled up and down the table. After a while Federica grew tired of waiting and opened the box to gaze into her secret world of make-believe.

'How long will you be staying?' Ignacio asked bluntly, noticing the impatience in his son's eyes. Ramon shrugged and glanced warily over at the hammock. Federica was no longer listening.

'I don't know,' he replied.

'You will stay for Christmas, won't you?' Mariana said. 'Surely you weren't going to leave again before Christmas?' she added, appalled at the thought.

'Of course not,' Helena said and smiled tightly.

'Then why don't you stay here until New Year? I don't know who's coming yet, probably Felipe and Maria Lucia and Ricardo and Antonella. No one tells me anything, you just all turn up when you feel like it,' she said, pretending to complain but smiling happily. Ramon looked at Helena, but their art of silent communication had been lost long ago with their intimacy.

'We'd love to,' Helena replied, thinking of the children and the extra week they would have with their father. They could return to England after New Year. A new year and a new start, she thought and sighed heavily. Mariana noticed the strain between them and her buoyancy subsided a little. She glanced at her husband who could feel her thoughts even without looking at her.

'Good,' he said and nodded gravely.

At that moment, just when an uncomfortable silence was about to slip into their conversation, Estella appeared on the terrace with a tray of *pisco sour*. She kept her eyes focused on where she was walking for fear of stumbling and making a fool of herself. Ramon leapt to his feet to relieve her of it.

'Careful, it's heavy,' he said, taking the tray.

She looked up at him from beneath her thick dark lashes and replied in a soft chocolate voice, 'Thank you, Don Ramon.'

He smiled down at her and she felt her stomach lurch and her cheeks burn. She lowered her eyes again. Her face was so smooth, so innocent and generous that Ramon's immediate impulse was to study it some more, but he could feel his parents and wife watching them. Regretfully he tore his eyes away, turned and placed the tray on the table. When he glanced behind him the maid had disappeared into the house leaving only a faint smell of roses.

Ramon poured the traditional Chilean drink of lemons and *pisco* and handed them around. Once he had sat back down he noticed the maid appear once again with two cups of orange juice for the children.

'Estella's new,' said Mariana quietly. 'She's wonderful. Do you remember Consuelo?' she asked. Ramon nodded absentmindedly, with half an eye on the ripe young woman who padded tidily across the terrace. 'Well, dear old Consuelo died last summer. I was at my wits' end, wasn't I, Nacho? I didn't know where to look.'

'So how did you find her?' Helena asked, glad the conversation had begun to flow again.

'Well, the Mendozas, who have a summer house in Zapallar, found her for us. She's the niece of their maid Esperanza. The one with the bad squint,' she said, then added as an afterthought, 'poor old Esperanza.'

'So you're happy with Estella?' Helena asked, wiping the hair off her son's forehead and kissing his soft skin tenderly.

'Very. She's efficient and hard working and gives us no trouble at all.'

'Not like Lidia then,' Helena laughed. 'She's always got something wrong with her. If it isn't her back it's her front, her foot or her ankles that swell in the heat. She can barely walk around the house, let alone tidy it up. Dear old Federica does everything.'

'Surely not!' Ignacio exclaimed, appalled.

'Well, she likes it,' said Helena quickly.

'She seems to,' Ramon added in her defence. 'Helena's a good mother, Papa,' he added, glancing at his wife in the hope of winning a smile. She remained tight-lipped as if she hadn't heard him.

'Of course she is,' said Mariana. 'Fede, come here and show me your lovely box,' she called to her granddaughter, who rolled out of the hammock and walked hastily over to her.

'I want to see it too,' said Ignacio, pulling the child onto his lap.

Federica placed the box on the table. 'This once belonged to an Inca princess,' she said gravely. She then paused for effect before slowly lifting the lid. To her delight her grandfather caught his breath and dragged the box closer to get a better look. He pushed his glasses up his nose and peered inside.

'*Por Dios*, Ramon, where did you find this treasure? It must be worth a fortune?'

'I was given it in Peru,' he replied. Federica shivered with pride.

'In Peru, eh?' he mused. Then he ran his fingers over the stones.

'It's a magic box, Abuelito,' said Federica.

'I can see that,' said Ignacio. 'Here, woman, have a look at this. It's extraordinary.' He pushed it across the table to Mariana. Helena felt guilty that she hadn't paid it more attention.

'My dear, it's beautiful,' she said admiringly.

'If you move the box about the wings move. Look!' said Federica, pulling the box back and holding it up, tilting it from side to side. They all stared into it in amazement.

'My dear, you are absolutely right,' said Mariana, shaking her head in disbelief. 'I've never seen anything like it.'

'Papa, can I tell them the story?' Ramon nodded and Federica, her large blue eyes shining excitedly, began to tell them the legend of the butterfly box. They all listened quietly as Federica recounted what her father had told her.

Without being seen Estella stood behind the French doors

watching Ramon's raffish face smiling at his daughter with great tenderness. He was more handsome than he was in photographs and had a charisma that filled the house and overwhelmed her. She stood in the shadows, as still as a marble statue, and left her eyes to gaze upon him while her mind drifted into the realm of fantasy.

After dinner, when the children had gone to bed, Ignacio and Ramon took their drinks onto the beach and walked in the foam of the surf as Ignacio had done the night before with his wife. The sky was bright and tremulous, the sea lit up by the phosphorescent moon that hung weightless above them. At first they talked about trivialities, about Ramon's latest book and his latest adventures. Finally his father drained his glass and stood in front of Ramon.

'What's going on, son?' he asked bluntly.

Ramon fell silent for a moment. He didn't really know. 'She's leaving me, Papa,' he said.

Ignacio stopped walking. 'She's leaving you?' he repeated incredulously.

'Yes.'

'Why?'

'She doesn't love me any more.'

'What a load of rubbish!' he growled. 'She's crying out for attention, any fool can see that. What else?' he demanded.

Ramon shuffled in the sand, making piles with his toes. 'I'm not there for her.'

'I see.'

'She wants me to change.'

'Why can't you?'

'I can't.'

'You're too selfish,' said his father grimly.

'Yes. I'm too selfish.'

'What about the children?' Ramon shrugged his shoulders. 'You love them, don't you?'

'Yes, I do, but—'

'But! There are no "buts" when it comes to children, son. They need you.'

'I know. But I can't be what they want.'

'Why not?'

'Because I just can't be a family man, Papa. I'm not cut out for it. The minute I come home I want to leave again. I get this claustrophobic feeling in the pit of my stomach. I need to be on the move. I need to be free. I can't be tied down.' He choked.

'Grow up, Ramon, for God's sake,' he said impatiently. Ramon stiffened. He felt like a little boy again being chastised by his father. They stood in silence, staring at each other through the twilight. Finally, they began to walk back up the beach towards the house, each alone with his thoughts. There was nothing more to say. Ramon couldn't begin to explain the claustrophobia he felt and Ignacio knew his advice was unwelcome.

Helena was relieved when Ramon suggested he sleep in the next-door room. She smiled at him gratefully. He didn't tell her about the conversation he had had with his father. She wasn't his ally any more. They were strangers. Polite, distant, mistrustful.

Ramon slipped into bed. He could smell lavender and tuberose and thought of Estella. He thought of her hands making the bed and placing the flowers in the vase. There was no point suppressing his desires as he would have done in the old days, before adultery had become a way of life. In those early days he had desired no one but his wife. She had loved him like he believed no one else could love him. He'd close his eyes and still be with her; later he'd close his eyes to be with someone else, anyone else. Now he closed his eyes and thought of Estella. Her timid expression, fearful yet brazen somehow. Her trembling lips that begged to be kissed and her glowing skin that failed to cover the longing that lit her up inside like a fire. He wondered where her bedroom was and whether she'd be surprised to find him standing in her doorway. He almost climbed out of bed to find her, but he cautioned himself against such recklessness. It was all very well when he was on his travels, alone with his secrets. But here in his parents' house was incorrect. He sighed and rolled over onto his back. The breeze was cool, slipping in through the gaps in the shutters, but he still felt hot and restless, his loins wracked with desire.

Then he did something completely crazy. He got up and walked down to the beach. In the silvery light he slipped out of his towel and walked naked into the sea. The cold water stunned his senses and he gasped for breath. He swam out until his feet no longer felt the bottom and his body was so cold it no longer felt desire. There he lay on his back, steadying himself with his outstretched arms, paddling gently with his hands. He gazed up into the inky sky and wondered what lay beyond the stars. He drifted on the current until he felt the humiliation of his father's unkind words no more. In the silence of his watery bed he no longer cared about anything. His mind was numb and his heart cold and unfeeling. When he finally pulled himself up he saw that he had drifted much further out than he had meant to. Frantically he swam back to shore, his mind clattering with the many stories he had heard as a child of men being swept out to sea and drowned. When he was able to stand his heart quietened and he waded back towards the beach, grateful to be alive.

Estella stood on the terrace anxiously watching the beach for Don Ramon who had disappeared into the sea. She had been unable to sleep knowing that he was sleeping under the same roof. Her body trembled with a yearning she could scarcely control. So she had walked out onto the terrace to breathe the air and clear her head. It was then that she had seen him wander up the sand, drop his towel and wade naked into the sea. She had had to hold onto the balcony to stop herself from following and declaring her feelings to him. But then minutes had passed and he hadn't returned. She knew of people who had drowned in these cold waters and her stomach had churned with the thought that he might join them.

To her intense relief she spotted his dark figure wading out of the water. He was alive. He was safe. She could breathe again. Hidden by the darkness she watched him pick up his towel and roughly dry himself. Then he began to make his way back towards the house with the towel casually draped around his neck. She stepped back against the wall as he neared her. She couldn't help but watch as he strode towards her, ignorant of her curious eyes that feverishly consumed his naked body. Once he had disappeared she collapsed onto the wooden floor and put her head in her hands. She was going mad. What would he think?

When Ramon once more slipped between the sheets he felt cool and less disturbed. He closed his eyes and listened as his heartbeat slowed down and his breathing became heavy with sleep.

Estella retreated to her room as agitated as before, where she lay on her bed, tormented with frenzied thoughts of him.

Chapter Six

The following morning Ramon awoke to the sounds of the children playing outside. He lay staring at the shutters, at the lucid shafts of light that streamed in through the gaps in the wood, searching him out. He thought of Estella and the thought of her made him climb out of bed with enthusiasm. He opened the shutters. He could hear Federica's excited voice on the terrace and the calm, indulgent tones of his mother. He pulled on a pair of shorts and a shirt and walked barefooted into the sunny corridor. Noticing that the rest of the family were outside he stole into the kitchen hoping to find Estella. He was disappointed. The kitchen was still and gloomy. She had been there for the bread was out on the table and the vegetables in neat piles on the sideboard. He could smell the fragrance of roses mixed with something that belonged only to her. Like an animal he sniffed the air. He waited but she did not appear. Frustrated, he walked into the sitting room, following her scent that got increasingly stronger until he knew she was somewhere close. His heartbeat quickened with the excitement of the chase.

'*Buenos días*, Don Ramon,' came a voice from behind him. He turned to find her crouched down changing the record. He noticed her exposed thigh and the neat curve of her ankle. He wanted to reach out and touch her.

'*Buenos días*, Estella,' he replied and he saw that her cheeks stung crimson at the mention of her name. He smiled down at her until the pressure of his gaze caused her to turn away. With a shaking hand she placed the needle on the rotating disc of the gramophone. Cat Stevens resounded through the room. 'Do you dance, Estella?' he asked. She stood up and looked embarrassed.

'No, Señor,' she replied, blinking at him nervously from under her long lashes.

'I love to dance,' he said, swaying to the music and the lightness in his heart that compelled him to move. Estella smiled. When she smiled her whole face came alive, he thought. Her teeth were gleaming and white against the milk chocolate colour of her skin. Her silky black hair was pulled off her face into a thick plait that fell down her back. With an unsteady hand she curled a piece that had come astray behind her small ear. He watched her every move and she felt his eyes upon her and blushed. 'Do you like it here?' he asked, attempting to engage her in conversation.

'*Sí*, Don Ramon.'

'My mother tells me you do a very good job.'

'Thank you,' she said and smiled again.

He was suddenly disarmed by the charm of her radiant face. 'You look beautiful when you smile,' he said impulsively. She recognised the longing in his voice and shuddered because she knew she was unable to hide the longing in hers.

'*Gracias*, Don Ramon,' she said hoarsely, lowering her fevered eyes that burnt when she blinked.

'Did you put the lavender in my room, and the flowers?'

'*Sí*, Señor,' she replied breathlessly, suffocated by his proximity. He was so close she could smell him.

'They're lovely. Thank you.' He watched her hover, not knowing whether to leave or stay, knowing she should scuttle back to the kitchen but unable to tear herself away. She licked her dry lips with her tongue. He stepped closer. She caught her breath and with startled eyes watched him watching her.

'You find me attractive, don't you?' he said softly, smelling the sweat that seeped through the pale cotton of her uniform.

'I do find you attractive, Don Ramon,' she whispered and swallowed hard.

'I want to kiss you, Estella. I want to kiss you very much,' he said, inching closer towards her. The chatter from the terrace faded with the roar of the sea. It was only him and Estella and the doleful melody of Cat Stevens that sang out 'Oh baby baby it's a wild world' on the gravelly record behind them.

'Papa, shall we go down to the beach soon?' said Federica, skipping into the sitting room, pleased to find her father up and dressed. Ramon stiffened. Estella's shoulders tensed and she turned with the grace of a panther and slipped back to the cool sanctuary of the kitchen where she leant against the table and fanned herself with her cookbook. Her heart jumped about like a frightened bird and her legs shook as if she were walking on them for the first time. She felt the sweat trickle down her back and between her breasts. She was excited that he desired her too, yet afraid because she knew she shouldn't sleep with a married man whose wife and children were in the same house. She knew she could lose her job. She also knew that he just lusted after her, wanted nothing more than to make love to her then cast her aside and return to his marital bed. But she didn't care. One night, she prayed, God give me one night and I'll never misbehave again. She couldn't help herself. She was powerless to resist. She bent over the table and began to chop up the vegetables to calm her agitated nerves.

Ramon followed his daughter reluctantly out onto the terrace and sat down at the table, glad to be able to hide the excitement that strained against his shorts. He poured himself some coffee and buttered a piece of toast. Helena was sitting at the other end of the terrace with his mother and Hal. She looked happier and more relaxed but Ramon didn't notice, all he saw was Estella and all he could think about was how he was going to engineer it so that he could make love to her.

Federica sat on the chair next to his with her legs swinging in the air impatiently. She placed the box on the table in front of her and opened and closed it, turned it around and tilted it but Ramon was too distracted to give her the attention she wanted.

'Good morning, son,' said Ignacio, emerging with his panama hat placed firmly on his head, in a pair of loose ivory trousers and a short-sleeved, sky-blue shirt. 'I thought we could go and have lunch in Zapallar today then drive on to Papudo. I know someone around here who wants to ride on the ponies,' he said and chuckled as Federica leapt down from her chair and ran up to him.

'Yes please!' she cried, throwing her arms around his waist. Ignacio patted her white hair and took off his hat to fan himself. It was hot and the air was sticky with the scent of the eucalyptus trees.

'That's a lovely idea, Nacho,' said Mariana. 'The children would love that. You'd like an ice cream, wouldn't you, Hal?' she said to Hal who was playing with the box of toys Mariana always kept in the house for her grandchildren. Hal nodded before once again busying himself with his game.

'I'm going to take Fede down to the beach,' said Ramon, who had no intention of going to Zapallar for lunch. He was going to spend the afternoon making love to Estella.

'I'll come with you, Ramon,' said Mariana. 'I could do with a walk. Will you be all right here, Helena?' she asked.

Helena smiled and nodded. 'I'll be fine with Hal, thank you,' she replied. She hoped Ramon would tell his parents of their plans, because she didn't think she had the courage to tell them herself. She watched them disappear back into the house. She had slept well and woken in a good humour. Mariana and Ignacio's house was serene and cool, away from the tension that seemed to cling to the walls back in Viña. Here she felt liberated. They had separate rooms and she had her own space. Ramon was diluted with his parents. He didn't seem so big and oppressive with them as he did when he was alone with her. She lay back in her chair and thought of Polperro.

Ramon and Mariana wandered down the beach while Federica skipped and jumped, playing tag with the waves that rushed up onto the beach. It was too early for people to start filling up the sand with their towels and their oiled bodies, so they had the beach to themselves.

'I'm so pleased you've come back, Ramon,' said Mariana

happily. She had taken off her sandals to reveal her painted red toenails that ate into the sand as she walked. 'We do miss you when you're away. I know you and understand you,' she said sadly, 'so I'm not complaining. You do give us such pleasure.'

'Mama,' he said, taking her hand. 'You give me pleasure too. I don't know why I can't stick around for long, something inside me just tells me to keep moving.'

'I know. It's your creativity, *mi amor*,' she said as if that excused everything.

'I wish I were married to someone like you,' he sighed.

'Helena understands you more than you think. It's good for you both to get away together. She looked very strained yesterday, but the colour has come back to her cheeks today. She seems much happier.'

'Does she?' he asked. He had barely noticed her.

'Yes, she does. You know she needs a bit of time to get to know you again each time you come back. You have to be patient and not expect too much.'

'Yes,' he said. He was glad his father hadn't shared their conversation with her. He knew he should tell her the truth himself. That Helena was leaving him, leaving Chile, leaving to start again on a distant shore. But he knew it would break his mother's heart to tell her that she wouldn't watch her grandchildren grow up and he couldn't bear to upset her. She was so happy to see them, now wasn't the moment. So he just smiled down at her.

'Mama, do you mind if I don't come to Zapallar with you all. I'm weary. I'd really appreciate some time alone. I know you understand me better than anyone. I want some quiet time without the children,' he said carefully, knowing how to get around his mother from years of practice.

Mariana concealed her disappointment. 'Well, seeing as you're spending so much time with us I'll let you off,' she said and chuckled.

'Four weeks,' he said.

'Is it really that long until New Year?' she asked in amazement. 'No, it must be less, *mi amor*, we're already in December.'

'Well, just under.'

'What have you got the children for Christmas?'

'I don't know,' he replied truthfully. He and Helena had been so preoccupied with their own troubles they had completely forgotten about Christmas.

'You gave Fede that stunning box. I think she's so happy with that she won't expect anything else,' said Mariana, remembering the staggering beauty of that strange object.

'Oh, Helena has bought them trunkloads of gifts. In that department they are certainly not lacking,' he chuckled.

'How lucky they are. We'll have a lovely Christmas, you'll see,' she said, squeezing his hand.

Federica was disappointed her father wasn't joining them for lunch in Zapallar and swallowed back her tears. Helena suffered a confusing mixture of emotions. On one hand she was relieved and looked forward to some time without the unsettling weight of his presence, but on the other hand she was drawn to him like a reckless fly about the head of a bull. She felt compelled to be near him if only to provoke a reaction. Ignacio commented dryly that he had already had three months on his own, but after their conversation the night before he understood that his son wanted time, not on his own, but away from his wife and that saddened him. He hoped they would wake up and realise their marriage was worth saving.

Ramon watched the car disappear up the sandy track and waved at Federica who waved forlornly back with her small, pale hand.

It was very hot. The midday sun pounded against the earth with its full force. He wiped his sweaty brow with his sleeve then headed back into the house. He went straight into the kitchen in search of Estella, but she wasn't there. So he walked hastily onto the terrace, his heart pounding against his chest in anticipation, but she wasn't there either. His eyes scanned the sitting room with impatience. He didn't want to lose a moment. Finally he strode down the corridor towards his room. He heard the rustle of linen and the low hum of her voice as she sang happily to herself.

When he appeared at the door of his room Estella sprung around in fright. No one had told her that Don Ramon wasn't going to Zapallar with the rest of the family. She remained startled, blinking at him with uncertainty. 'Don Ramon, you scared me,' she said and her voice was breathless. She placed her hand about her neck as if attempting to loosen the clamp that had taken hold of it.

'I'm sorry, I didn't mean to sneak up on you. I didn't know you were here,' he lied.

'I can do your room later,' she said, dropping the sheet and walking around the bed towards him with the intention of leaving.

'Yes, you can do it later,' he replied, stopping her from going by grabbing her upper arm. She gasped. He then placed both hands on her arms and pushed her up against the wall. Her breasts heaved expectantly. He noticed a bead of sweat cling to the soft skin that formed the valley between them. He placed his finger there and lifted it off her body.

'Are you nervous?' he said, his dark eyes studying her anxious face.

'You're married,' she replied foolishly.

'Only in name, Estella. Only in name,' he said regretfully. Then he lowered his lips and brushed them softly across hers. She swallowed to release the tension that made her throat ache and closed her eyes. He kissed the moist skin of her neck, running his tongue up towards her ear. It tasted salty and smelt of roses. His hands found the bottom of her uniform and crept up inside it, his fingers tracing the soft curve of her thighs and hips. She caught her breath. Overwhelmed by the force of his charisma she felt her body go limp and surrender to a will far greater than hers. Moments such as these were the stuff of dreams and she was determined to steal her pleasure because tomorrow it might be gone. The bristle of his chin on her neck distracted her momentarily so that when his mouth fell on hers she realised his fingers were playing with the edge of her panties and caressing the damp skin of her upper thighs. When his tongue began to explore the smooth interior of her mouth she lost herself completely. His fingers pulled her panties aside and found the core of her longing where she ached to be touched. They remained pressed against the wall, their breathing heavy and in unison, their hot bodies bathed in each other's sweat. His fingers felt the velvet of her most tender places and he enjoyed watching her eyelids flutter like butterflies as she abandoned herself to his caresses.

He laid her on the bed and lifted her dress over her head to reveal even brown skin and generous breasts. He had seen her body in his fevered dreams; it didn't disappoint him in reality. He gently slipped off her underwear and gazed upon her bare sensuality with appreciation. She opened her eyes and looked up at him dazed with pleasure, her eyelids heavy and half closed. She was no longer shy or ashamed. She lay wantonly, waiting for him to do with her whatever he wished. He scrambled out of his shirt and shorts and stood before her, showing her the full glory of his naked body. She allowed her eyes to linger on it admiringly. Her face was aflame and her lips stung crimson from his kisses. She was beautiful and her beauty lifted him out of the misery of his marriage and he bathed in it and forgot himself.

When they lay entwined on the half-made bed, illuminated by the shimmering sunlight that crept in through the shutters Estella had closed to keep the room cool, Ramon felt the satisfied aching of his loins and the slowing thud of his heartbeat. He looked down at her burning face and long ebony hair that spread out across his chest in a glossy fan. She noticed him looking at her and smiled contentedly. He ran his hand up and down her naked back, his fingers playing with the bumps on her spine absentmindedly. Most women he wanted to get rid of the minute he was finished with them, but there was something warm about Estella. He wanted her to stay.

'You're very nice to lie on,' he said at last.

Estella felt drunk with love. 'Thank you, Don Ramon,' she replied, wanting the afternoon to last for ever. She could hear his heartbeat in his large chest and feel his hair against her face. He was soft and warm to lie on too. She wanted to tell him but in spite of their physical closeness she knew they were oceans apart by the very nature of their places in the world and cautioned herself against speaking out of turn.

Federica rode the little pony up and down the beach. Helena even let her trot by herself while she led Hal's pony by the reins. Papudo was a pretty fishing village overlooking the sea, nestled at the foot of hazy blue mountains. Mariana bought them ice creams while Ignacio sat in the shade of the eucalyptus trees drinking coffee and guarding Federica's precious butterfly box while he played Solitaire. Helena had enjoyed lunch in Zapallar, the children had enchanted them all with their innocent conversation and laughter and she had barely thought about Ramon.

Federica hadn't stopped thinking about Ramon. She missed him. She had wanted him to watch her riding and remembered how he had once built her the prettiest castle in the sand decorated with white petals and shells. When they piled back into the car to drive home for tea she felt her spirits rise with the thought of seeing him again.

Ramon made love to Estella for the second time. She was a delicious feast and there were parts of her he hadn't yet tasted. Once he had satisfied his lust and his curiosity he pulled her laughing and protesting into the shower where they reluctantly allowed the water to wash away all traces of their adultery. It was only when he towelled himself dry that he looked at his watch. It was late afternoon. They would be back any minute. He told Estella to go and change her uniform that was creased and stained with sweat. She panicked when she saw the state of the room and thought of all the chores left undone that might expose her. But Ramon wandered out onto the terrace where he sat in the sunshine, picked up his father's book and began to read with a contented expression softening his rugged face.

Estella ran into her room where she hastily tied her hair in a plait, changed her uniform and patted her skin with cologne. She then set about making up the rooms without further delay. She hadn't time to dwell on the sweetness of the afternoon, the languor of their lovemaking or the passion that had made everything else seem unimportant and dispensable. When she heard the voices of the children as the door in the hallway was thrown open she gasped because they would be expecting tea and she hadn't even begun to make it.

'Papa, I rode a pony all by myself!' Federica cried, rushing to her father's side. He was in a good humour and pulled her onto his knee.

'All by yourself, you clever monkey,' he exclaimed and chuckled, kissing her hot cheek.

'Hal rode too, but Mama had to lead him, he's still too small to ride by himself. Abuelito looked after my box. He guarded it all afternoon,' she said proudly, placing it on the table.

'I hope you don't forget it one of these days,' he said.

'Papa! I will *never* lose this box,' she replied, astounded that he would even, for one minute, think she could mislay her most important possession.

'Fede rode all by herself,' said Mariana, fanning herself as she wandered slowly onto the terrace.

'You look exhausted, Mama.' He smiled fondly at her.

'I am, Ramon. It's been hot and tiring. But it was lovely. We missed you, *mi amor*.' She sank into an easy chair.

'Well, it's been very quiet here,' he said, yawning. 'I've done nothing all afternoon but read Papa's book. It's rather good.'

'*Me alegro*.' She sighed. 'I'm glad you had a nice time.'

'How about you and me go for a swim this evening before

bedtime?' suggested Ramon to Federica, suddenly wanting to make up for not having joined her for lunch.

'Yes please, Papa,' she enthused. 'Abuelito can look after my box again,' she said and watched him come out into the sunshine in his crooked panama hat. 'Can't you, Abuelito?'

'What's that, Fede?' he replied, opening his eyes wide, pretending to look startled. Federica giggled; she loved it when her grandfather pulled faces.

'You can look after my box while I'm swimming with Papa in the sea,' she said.

'Careful the crocodiles don't eat you,' he said humorously.

'There are no crocodiles in the sea, silly!' she laughed.

Estella emerged with a heavy tray of tea, cake and biscuits. Ramon helped her unload it onto the table. Their eyes met and there passed between them the silent bond of complicity. She looked the same as she had that morning except the corners of her mouth curled up with satisfaction in spite of her efforts to dissemble.

'I think Estella has a lover in the village,' Mariana commented once the maid had retreated back into the house.

'*Dios*, Mariana, what does it matter?' said Ignacio, slicing the cake.

'Oh, it doesn't matter, Nacho, I'm just rather curious as to who it is,' she replied, taking a cup and saucer and handing it to Helena who emerged with Hal from the dark sitting room.

'What makes you think she's got a lover, Mama?' Ramon asked, amused.

'Because she glows. It's a woman thing. I can sense it in her step and in her eyes.'

'You perceptive old devil,' he laughed. Helena sat down next to Federica and lit a cigarette. The sight of her husband made her feel uneasy.

'I might be old, *mi amor*, but I'm not a devil,' Mariana replied, her pale grey eyes smiling at her son affectionately.

'So what if she has a lover,' said Ignacio, shrugging his shoulders.

'Who's got a lover?' Helena asked, handing Hal a piece of cake.

'Estella.'

'I agree,' she replied. 'It's a woman thing, as Mariana says. It's in her eyes.'

Ramon laughed heartily. 'Good girl. No wonder she looks well. She looks satisfied,' he said with pride.

'Well, if he's compromised her I hope he marries her. Some men aren't as honourable as they should be,' said Mariana sternly. 'Poor girl, I hope she knows what she's doing.'

Ramon chewed on the cake. 'Good, isn't it, Fede?' he said, smiling down at her. She grinned up at him and nodded. Mariana watched her granddaughter and noticed that she never took her eyes off her father. She loved her mother too. Helena was a good mother. But there was a very special bond between Ramon and his daughter. She was saddened that he had to rush off and leave her all the time. She watched the child's adoring face and felt pity for her.

Chapter Seven

The next few weeks were hot and languorous. Mariana took time to enjoy her small grandchildren and give Helena a break from domesticity. She noticed that her daughter-in-law was often tense and unhappy, usually when she was with her husband, for then she smoked twice as many cigarettes as usual. She also noticed, however, that she was constantly watching him. When she spoke it was for his benefit and when he didn't react she would go silent as if intent on forcing a reaction. At times Ramon barely acknowledged her presence. But Mariana refused to believe that their marriage was disintegrating and put it down to the natural estrangement bred during their long months apart.

Federica and Hal played on the beach, dipped in the cold sea and entertained themselves drawing pictures and showing them to their proud grandparents and parents who applauded them and loved them, making them feel cherished and secure.

Ignacio watched his son with increasing gloom. He disguised his pessimism behind the face of a clown that he put on for his grandchildren to play the fool. But inside he knew that unless his son settled down and looked after his family properly, Helena really would leave him. He wondered whether that would mean she would leave Chile altogether. It would break their hearts if she took her precious children to England. They would grow up on another shore, with other grandparents and forget their Chilean family. It would be all Ramon's fault. He was selfish and irresponsible. That marriage had been doomed right from the start.

Ramon's liaisons with Estella were snatched whenever they were able to steal some time alone together. She would creep into his room in the middle of the night when moonlight bathed the bed in silver and the scents of jasmine and eucalyptus rose up on the heat to wrap them in their heady perfume. They would make love in the secrecy of the small hours when the rest of the house were far away in their private worlds of dreams. At first Estella had captured Ramon's curiosity and desire; she never even hoped to capture his heart. But little by little, in those magic moments when they lay together separated only by their skin, Ramon felt a strange power within her that ensnared him and refused to let him go. He missed her when he played the husband and father during the day and longed for the languid nights when she would appear to love him again. He saw her face whenever he closed his eyes and felt her presence long before she entered the room. Her unique scent of roses clung to his nostrils and reminded him of their passion and their tenderness and he longed to carry her away with him.

Christmas came and went. His two brothers, Felipe and Ricardo, joined them with their wives and children, so that Federica and Hal had their small cousins to play with and the house disintegrated into a large playroom with toys scattered over the floors and laughter echoing through the rooms. It was only after they had left that Ramon and Helena sat down with Mariana and Ignacio to inform them of their plans.

'We're separating,' Ramon announced flatly, staring at the floor so that he didn't have to suffer his mother's disappointment. There followed a heavy pause during which Mariana's eyes welled with tears and Ignacio rubbed his chin trying to think of something to say. Helena had lit a cigarette and smoked it nervously, hoping that they wouldn't see her as the villain of the plot.

Finally, Ignacio spoke. 'When are you going to tell the children?' he asked.

'Do you have to tell the children?' Mariana choked, wiping her eyes. 'They'll be so hurt, especially Federica. Can't you just go on the way you are? You barely see each other as it is.'

'Helena wants to take them back to England,' said Ramon accusingly. Helena stiffened.

'To England?' Mariana gasped. She felt winded, as if someone had punched her in the stomach. She tried to breathe regularly but her breaths were short and shallow.

'I feared the worst,' said Ignacio.

'All the way to England?' Mariana repeated sadly, dropping her shoulders in defeat. 'We won't see them grow up,' she whispered.

'I can't go on like this,' Helena stammered, apologetically. 'I want to start again.'

'But why England, it's so far away?' said Mariana helplessly.

'Only to you. To me it's home. To me Chile is the other side of the world. We'll come and visit and you can come and see us. Ramon will, won't you, Ramon? You said you would,' she replied quickly.

'Yes, I will.'

'You can't desert your children, son. You spend half your life in faraway places, England won't be much out of your way,' said Ignacio gruffly.

'I don't want to hurt the children. But I'm unhappy and they feel it,' Helena explained weakly. 'Ramon isn't at home to be a proper husband and help me raise them, I can't do it on my own. I've had enough of this kind of life.'

'But doesn't it worry you how the children are going to take it? Especially Fede, she's so sensitive. She'll be devastated. I just have to watch her gazing up at her father with that adoring face to know that this will break her little heart,' Mariana sobbed, taking Ignacio's hand for support.

Helena felt wounded; Federica loved her mother too. 'I know. I've thought about that. But they're young. I can't live my life for my children. I have to think about me too,' said Helena, taking a long drag with a shaking hand. She wanted to add 'because no one else is going to'.

'Ramon, can't you try? Can't you stick around at least for a few months and give it another try?' Ignacio suggested. But he knew his powers of persuasion weren't as strong as they once might have been.

'No,' Ramon replied emphatically, shaking his head. 'It won't work. Helena and I no longer love each other. If we stay together we'll end up hating each other.'

Helena swallowed hard and blinked back her emotion. He had said earlier that he loved her.

'So this is it, then?' said Mariana sadly, lowering her head.

'This is it,' Helena replied, sighing heavily.

'So when will you go?' Ignacio asked bleakly.

Ramon looked at Helena. Helena shrugged and shook her head. 'I don't know yet. I suppose it will take a while to pack up our things. I'll have to tell my parents. We'll have to tell the children. I suppose we'll leave as soon as we're able to,' she replied, then began to bite her nails with impatience. She wanted to leave right away.

'Divorce will not be easy,' said Mariana, thinking of the Catholic Church that prohibited it.

'I know,' Ramon replied. 'We don't want a divorce. We don't want to marry anyone else. We just want to be free of each other.'

'And I want to go home,' said Helena, surprised that she and Ramon were at last agreeing on something.

Ramon thought of Estella and wished he could take her away with him. Helena thought of the shores of Polperro and felt herself getting nearer.

'When are you going to break it to those dear little children?' Mariana asked coldly. She thought their actions wholly selfish. 'Think very carefully before you do it,' she warned. 'You'll hurt them beyond repair. I hope you know what you're doing.'

'We'll tell them tomorrow, before we go back to Viña,' said Helena resolutely, watching her husband warily. How far did she have to push him? she thought, his heart must be made of stone. Mariana pulled herself up from her chair and retreated sadly into the house. She suddenly looked old.

'At least they'll have their grandparents around to comfort them,' Ramon said with bitterness, looking at his wife accusingly.

'This isn't my fault, Ramon,' she said in exasperation. 'You're the one who is refusing the change.'

'It's no one person's fault, Helena,' Ignacio interrupted. 'It's the fault of the both of you. But if that is what you want it's the way it has to be. It's life and life isn't always a bed of roses.' Ramon wished it were a bed of Estella's roses. 'Tell them tomorrow and be kind,' he added, but he knew there was no gentle way to tell children that their parents no longer loved each other.

Helena was too emotional to sleep. She sat outside beneath the stars, devouring one cigarette after another, watching the smoke waft into the air on the breeze before being swallowed up by the night. She was deeply saddened and anxious about telling her beloved children, but she knew it couldn't be avoided. It would have been crueller to pretend nothing was wrong. They'd suspect something in the end, or at least Federica would. She imagined her daughter's innocent face and felt a stab of guilt penetrate her heart. She dropped her head into her hands and wept. She tried to convince herself that it would all be okay once they were settled in Polperro. They would be gathered up by her parents, whom Federica had met a few times and Hal only once. They would love England and make new friends. She thanked God she had always spoken English to them, at least that was one obstacle they wouldn't have to overcome.

It must have been about one in the morning when she trod softly down the corridor towards the room where her children were quietly sleeping. She crept in and watched their still bodies in the dim moonlight. They slept unaware of the earthquake that was going to shatter their lives on the morrow. She ran her white hand down Hal's brown face and kissed him on his cheek. He stirred and smiled but didn't wake up. Then she tiptoed over to where Federica slept, her magical butterfly box on her bedside table where she could guard it, even in her sleep. She picked up the box and studied it without opening it for she didn't want to wake them with the music. Her heart lurched when she recalled Federica's happy face gazing up at her father in gratitude, holding his gift against her chest, treasuring it as much because it was from him as for the box itself. Suddenly she was overcome with remorse. She couldn't do it to them. She couldn't tell them. She couldn't deprive them of their father. As much as she needed to leave for herself she suddenly felt unable to use her children as innocent pawns in her battle with Ramon. She would have to think of another strategy, another plan.

Weeping she ran down the corridor to Ramon's room. She wanted to tell him she had thought again. That she had realised she wasn't able to tear their children away from everything that was familiar to them. Gasping for breath, the tears blurring her vision, she stood trembling outside his bedroom door, afraid to go in. She placed her hand on the doorknob, about to turn it, when she heard voices. Surprised, she held her breath and listened. Appalled, she recoiled. He was making love to someone. She recognised his sighs immediately and the slow rustle of sheets. When the low, contented laughter of a woman resounded off the walls she felt her stomach churn with fury. She wanted to storm in and expose them. But she was afraid of Ramon, she always had been. Pressing her ear to the door she strained to recognise the voice of the woman. She heard whispering and more laughter. It revolted her that he could be making love to another woman under the same roof as his children. Then it all fell into place. The woman could only be Estella. She then remembered their conversation about Estella and her lover and recalled the look of pride that had inexplicably swept across his conceited face. No wonder he had been so pleased with himself. She could scarcely restrain her anger and her disappointment. She had been ready to sacrifice her happiness. It was plain that he wasn't ready to sacrifice his – not even for his own children. She stepped back and, blinking away tears of pain and self-pity, she walked defeated up the corridor to her room.

The following morning Helena awoke early. It wasn't surprising she had slept badly, a shallow sleep tormented by disturbing dreams brought on by anxiety. She had tossed in her sheets, struggling with the implications of her husband's infidelity. She had been so close to changing her mind, but now nothing could alter it. Not even repentance. The carefree chatter of birds and the timid dawn light nudged her back to consciousness and she was relieved the night was over. She showered and dressed before lighting a cigarette to give her courage. She was going to talk to Ramon.

She opened the shutters and blew the smoke out into the fresh morning air. The sea was pale and smooth, gently caressing the shore with the rhythmic motion of the tide. It reminded her of Polperro although the sea was very different in Cornwall. There the waves came crashing into the land. They used to throw themselves against it as children and surf onto the beach, which was dense like clay and good for building castles. The smells were different too. The salty ozone, the damp and the coarse sand full of crabs and rock pools lined with prickly urchins. Her heart lurched for her home and hardened her resolve. She stubbed her half-smoked cigarette into the ashtray and taking a deep breath walked purposefully towards the door.

She hesitated outside his room. The voices were now silent and she could feel the contented sleep of satisfied lovers seeping through the gap below the door. Recalling the horror of her discovery she turned the doorknob and marched in. Ramon was lying on his back. Estella was curled up against him with her head on his chest. His hand was flopped over her long black hair that lay loose and wanton down her back. They were naked except for the sheet, which did little to cover them. Helena stood with her arms folded in front of her, her mouth little more than a thin line of bitterness. Ramon felt her presence in his dreams and opened his eyes. He didn't move, but stared at her as if trying to focus, not sure whether he was still in the realm of fantasy. He blinked. Helena stood staring back at him in disgust. He then realised that blinking wasn't going to send her away or wake him up because he was already awake. He nudged Estella who writhed in that pleasurable state of half-sleep. He nudged her again, this time more urgently. She opened her eyes in alarm to find Helena smouldering at the end of the bed. She gasped in horror, leapt off the mattress with a cry and hastily gathering her clothes, ran from the room, sobbing in shame. Ramon put his hands behind his head and glared at her.

'What do you think you're doing, Helena?' he said, as if she were guilty of intruding.

She shook her head in disbelief. 'What do you mean, what am I doing?' she snapped in fury. 'You're fornicating with the maid under the same roof as your wife and children. Don't you have any respect?'

'Calm down, Helena,' he said in a patronising tone. 'We both know our marriage is little more than a shoddy bit of paper. You're the one who wants to end it. I don't. I don't want to tear our family apart, you do. What does it matter to you whether I sleep with the maid or anyone else?' He sat up.

'It doesn't matter to me whom you choose to fornicate with, Ramon. But I would have thought you'd have some human decency left. Your children are in the room down the corridor. What if Fede had had a nightmare and come looking for you?' she reasoned, her eyes livid with exasperation.

'She didn't,' he said flatly.

'Thank God.'

'Look, it's your decision to leave me and take them to England,' he said, raising his voice.

'Only because you don't want us any more,' she replied, almost shouting at him in frustration. 'You said so yourself, the minute you arrive home you long to leave again. How do you think that makes us feel? We're not a family any more and you know it.' She wanted him to protest that they could be, that he wanted to try to make it work, but he just narrowed his empty black eyes and stared back at her.

'Okay. We've already discussed this,' he said and yawned. 'We'll tell the children today as planned and you can leave as soon as you're ready. I won't stop you.'

'No, you won't, because it doesn't suit you to stop me. I'm giving you your freedom. All of it,' she said. 'Now you won't have to come home ever again.'

In the brief pause that followed, while they both simmered at each other with loathing, the deep, heartbroken sobs of Federica trickled under the door. Helena gasped. Ramon went pale. 'Oh my God,' he murmured, standing up and scrambling into his trousers as he rushed towards the door. They both opened it at the same time to find their daughter in a crumpled, shivering heap on the floor. She had heard everything. Estella had run past her bedroom sobbing, waking her up and sending her to her mother's room in a panic, only to find her mother wasn't there. She reached her father's room in time to hear them shatter everything she had grown up to believe in.

'Fede, sweetie,' said Helena, crouching down and gathering her into her arms. 'It's all right. Papa and I were just having a silly argument.'

'We didn't mean everything we said,' Ramon added, trying to take her from her mother's embrace.

'Leave us alone, please, Ramon,' said Helena in a voice of raw steel. Ramon pulled away, surprised by the force of her tone. He watched helplessly as his wife lifted Federica into her arms and carried her down the corridor to her room. Once inside she closed the door, shutting him out. He suddenly felt a tremendous wave of loneliness. He walked back into his room and sat down on the bed. He didn't know what to do with himself. His chest burned with guilt and remorse. He hung his head in his hands and wept.

Helena sat on the bed with her sobbing daughter clinging to her in despair. She wrapped her arms around her and gently rocked her, kissing her fevered brow and running her hands down her long hair in an effort to soothe her. It broke her heart to see her suffer so and she felt the resentment towards her husband rise in her stomach like bile.

'It's all right, Fede. Papa loves you very very much,' she said. 'We both love you very much.'

'Papa doesn't want us any more.' The child sobbed. 'If he wanted us he wouldn't go away all the time.' Helena wanted to shoot her husband for the pain he caused his children. They were innocent victims of an adult world which they were too young to understand.

'Papa does want us. At least he wants you and Hal. He loves the two of you so much. That's why we're both so unhappy. Because we want you and Hal, but we don't want each other.'

'Don't you love Papa any more?'

'It's not that simple, sweetie,' she said, trying to lessen the blow. 'Papa travels so much, it's his work and he has to do it. It's not because he doesn't want to be with us. You know all those wonderful stories he tells you?' Federica nodded. 'Well, he wouldn't have those colourful tales to tell you if he didn't go to wonderful places around the world. He comes back full of fantastic adventures to tell you, and of course the magic box he found you. If he didn't love you he wouldn't have given you that box. He wouldn't spend so much time with you. So don't doubt his love, sweetie. Mama and Papa just don't want to be together any more. But that's nothing to do with you and Hal. This is to do with us, and only us. Do you understand?' Federica nodded. 'Now we're going on an adventure. You, me and Hal,' she said, trying to make it sound exciting.

'To England,' said Federica gloomily.

Helena winced at the proof that she had heard their entire conversation. 'Yes, to England,' she said. 'Now you'll love England. We're going to a beautiful town by the sea. There are lovely big seagulls that fly over the beaches. The rocks are full of crabs and shrimps. You can go fishing with Grandpa and Granny will take you to the fair. There are ruined castles to explore and new friends waiting to know you.'

'But will I ever see Abuelito and Abuelita again?' she asked forlornly.

'Of course you will. And Papa will come and see us just like he always has done. Except we'll have a different house and no one will speak Spanish. We'll live with Grandpa and Granny, so you'll see them all the time.'

'Can I take the butterfly box with me?'

'Of course you can, sweetie. You can take anything you like.'

'I won't see Rasta any more,' she said in panic. 'Who will walk him?'

'Someone will walk him. Don't you worry.'

'He'll start barking again.'

'Maybe we can buy you your own dog. Would you like that?' Helena suggested, desperate to make it up to her child.

Federica sat up and wiped her nose with her hand. Her eyes opened very wide with a tremor of excitement. 'Can I have a dog of my very own?' she asked. Suddenly England didn't sound so bad.

'Yes. You can have a dog all of your very own,' Helena said, relieved that Federica was smiling again.

'When are we going to England?' she asked.

'As soon as we have packed everything up at home.'

'Can I go and tell Abuelita that I'm going to have my own dog?' she said, slipping off her mother's knee.

'I'll come with you. Let's get you dressed first and wake up Hal.'

When Ramon walked out onto the terrace, Helena was at the breakfast table with Federica, Hal and his parents. His eyes darted from one to the other anticipating his wife to have told them everything. Federica watched him warily over her cup of chocolate milk. Hal chattered away as if nothing had happened. Ramon sat down next to his mother and waited for someone to speak.

'Fede tells me she's going to get a dog of her very own when she gets to England,' said Mariana and although she smiled her eyes showed their strain. She only had to imagine them leaving for her vision to cloud with misery.

'Really, Fede? That's wonderful,' he said sheepishly. 'What are you going to call it?'

'Rasta,' she said but she didn't smile. Ramon felt his heart ache.

'Why can't I have a dog?' Hal whined, looking up at his mother.

'You can enjoy Rasta too,' she said wearily, trying to sound happy when all she wanted to do was hide away and cry.

'I want a rabbit,' he said. 'Are there rabbits in England?'

'If you get a rabbit, Rasta might eat him, Hal,' Federica said not unkindly.

'Lidia doesn't like dogs, so Fede will have to leave Rasta in England when we come back,' he said, taking his mug in both hands and gulping down his iced chocolate.

Ramon and Helena caught eyes where they both remained for a long moment, staring at each other helplessly. Helena hadn't had the courage to tell Hal that they wouldn't ever be coming back.

When Estella appeared on the terrace, pale and ashamed, Ramon realised that Helena hadn't told anyone about his adultery, for Mariana commented on her appearance with the same curiosity she had shown earlier.

'Oh dear. I think Estella's had a fight with her lover. She doesn't look very happy,' she said, sipping her coffee.

'She'll get over it,' said Ignacio with indifference.

'Yes, she will,' Helena agreed without looking at her husband. 'Some men are not worth the tears,' she added caustically.

Estella returned to the kitchen and once more burst into tears of shame and self-pity. She recalled Señora Helena's face, twisted with fury, as she stood as still as an icon of the Virgin Mary at the end of the bed. Don Ramon would never speak to her again. It had been heavenly but now God would surely punish her. She had only asked for a night and she had been given so much more. But it wasn't enough. She loved him. She knew she shouldn't. He wasn't from her world and the class divides were as wide as they were severe. But her heart was ignorant of the boundaries and yearned for him still.

After breakfast Helena tried to encourage Federica to play with Hal, but all she wanted to do was curl up on her mother's lap and suck her thumb, which she had stopped doing a long time ago. Helena wanted to talk to Mariana. She had only managed to tell her that Federica had been told as gently as possible that she was going to live in England. Federica had then rushed in and told her grandparents that she was going to be given a dog.

Ramon offered to take Federica down to the beach for a swim, but she held her magic box to her chest and curled up closer against her mother. Ramon felt crestfallen. Ignacio went with him instead and they talked man to man. As Helena had only informed them that Federica had been told, Ramon didn't enlighten his father on any further details. He didn't want to be cast in a bad light. His parents didn't need to know any more. He thought of Estella, pictured her bowed head and the hurt in her eyes and longed to go to her.

Federica helped her mother pack their clothes while Hal made a nuisance of himself unpacking everything they put into the cases. Federica chose to carry her box herself, she didn't want to lose it among all their clothes and Christmas presents. Ramon hurriedly searched the kitchen for Estella. He knew he didn't have much time before they had to leave and he didn't want to be caught again. He wandered around the house pretending to search for his camera. He found her finally in her room, weeping on her bed into the cotton and lace *pañuelo* her grandmother had made her. When he stood in the doorway she sniffed and told him to leave. But Ramon knew better than to believe that was what she wanted. He sat down next to her and cupped her tear-stained face in his rough hands.

'I'm not leaving you,' he said. 'I'll come back for you, I promise.'

She looked at him, startled. Her trusting brown eyes gazed up at him in bewilderment. 'But I will have to leave,' she stammered.

'Why? Helena didn't tell my parents. They think you've had a fight with your lover,' he said. 'Helena is going to England with the children. I'll come back for you.' It seemed so simple, so easy.

She threw her arms around him in gratitude. 'Thank you, Don Ramon,' she said and sobbed into his neck.

'For God's sake, call me Ramon.' He laughed. 'I think we're intimate enough now to be rid of those silly formalities.'

'Ramon,' she breathed. She liked the sound of that and said it again. 'Ramon.'

He touched her feverish face with the palm of his hand and pressed his lips to hers, breathing in her scent and tasting the salt of her tears.

'Wait for me, Estella. I will come back. I promise.' He stood up and left her crying once more into her *pañuelo*.

But her tears were no longer of grief but of hope.

Mariana and Ignacio hugged the children with sadness, unsure of whether they'd ever see them again. They embraced their daughter-in-law, repressing the resentment they both felt, wishing her a safe journey to England. Mariana secretly blamed her for the breakdown of the marriage in spite of her reasoning that told her Ramon was more to blame. It felt unnatural to begrudge her son and she had to begrudge someone. She kissed Ramon with a love that was unconditional and wilfully blind. Ignacio wasn't so blinkered. He had predicted this would happen for some time. Now it had he was deeply saddened but realistic. He hugged Ramon and wished them both well. 'Don't let them drift away, Ramon. They need you,' was all he said before his son climbed into the car and the subdued family disappeared up the track. With sad old eyes Ignacio and Mariana watched until all that was left was the dust the tyres had kicked up and the sorrow that weighed heavily in their hearts.

Estella moved away from the window, afraid of being seen, and retreated into the kitchen. She sat down to chop the vegetables and wait, as he had instructed.

Federica sat in the back of the car in silence. She wanted to cry but she knew she had to be strong for her mother. Crying would only make both her parents sad. So she swallowed hard and strained her neck to prevent the tears. She looked across at her brother who was oblivious to the sudden change that was about to rock their lives. She remembered every word of her parents' fight and wondered whether it was true that her father didn't want her any more. In spite of her brave efforts a fat tear trickled down her cheek. Hastily she wiped it away before anyone spotted it. She opened her box and tried desperately to find in its magic her father's love.

Chapter Eight

The next few days were suspended in a surreal limbo. While Helena packed up the things that were precious to her and her children, Ramon took Hal and Federica for long walks up the beach with Rasta and into Calle Valparaíso for *palta* sandwiches and juice. Everything seemed normal. Beneath the surface, however, things were far from normal.

The night they returned Federica awoke crying. When her mother rushed to her she discovered that her daughter had wet her bed. She pulled her child into her arms, kissing her damp cheeks, reassuring her that it was okay; even grown-ups wet their beds occasionally. Federica didn't understand what had happened and buried her face in her mother's bosom in shame. But Helena understood only too well and longed for life to settle down in Polperro. She would have taken Federica to her bed had Hal not already occupied the space between Ramon and herself, the space usually left for indifference and self-pity. He had shuffled into his parents' room crying, having had a nightmare. But Helena knew that his nightmare was nothing more than a symptom, like Federica's incontinence, of the stress their marriage breakdown was causing them. They only had themselves to blame.

When Ramon slept he dreamed of Estella. When he was awake he fantasised about her. It was only because of Estella that he was able to get through the traumatic few days that ensued. Long days of packing up the house, organising estate agents to put it up for sale, travel agents to arrange Helena and the children's trip to England. He longed to be on the road again, free from the turbulence Helena had invited into their lives. He'd buy an apartment in Santiago, somewhere to have as a base. Somewhere for him alone, without the constraints of domesticity, where he could come and go without explanation. He arranged to wire money to England, enough for them all to live well. Helena should have been grateful, his offer was generous, more than generous, but she only felt bitterness. Like his gifts, Ramon found it easy to buy people's affection, as long as he didn't have to invest his time, or himself. She accepted because she had to, for the sake of the children, but she would have preferred to have thrown it back in his face.

Federica curled into a ball. The light from the street lamp scattered her room with an orange glow. The light used to be reassuring. It used to make her feel secure. But not any more. She pulled her knees up to her chest and sucked her thumb. She had gone to the bathroom at last twice in ten minutes. Not that she needed to go, but because she was afraid of wetting her bed again. Her father had kissed her goodnight. He had even told her a story. One of his adventures. She had listened, seated on his knee as usual. But when he had kissed her goodnight she had found herself wanting more. A longer kiss, a longer hug. When he had left the room she felt deprived, as if he hadn't loved her enough. She no longer felt secure and cherished. She felt needy. She longed for her mother to embrace her and hold her against her body. She lay awake in bed devising plans to justify going into their room in the middle of the night. A nightmare was Hal's excuse, she had to think of something different. So she pretended to be ill. Her mother had been sympathetic and allowed her to sleep in their bed on the second night, but on the third Hal had had another nightmare so she was swiftly taken back to her room where she cried herself to sleep. She was frightened about going to England. She didn't want to leave Viña del Mar, or Chile or Abuelito and Abuelita. She didn't want things to change. Most of all she wanted Mama and Papa to be friends again. But as much as they put on a show, she knew they no longer liked one another. She had heard everything.

Finally the day of their departure arrived. With solemn faces they watched as Ramon loaded up the car with their cases. Federica couldn't stop herself crying. She didn't want to leave her father. She didn't know when she would see him again. In Viña she had been happy to wait, after all it was his home, he was bound to come back at some stage. He always had. But now her new home wouldn't be his home.

He picked her up in his strong arms and held her tightly, kissing her face. 'Papa loves you, Fede. Papa loves you so much. Just remember that, *mi amor*. Papa will always love you, even if he's not with you. When the sun shines and you feel that heat on your body, that's Papa's love. You understand?' Federica nodded, too distressed to speak. She didn't want him to let her go. But he had to. They had a flight to catch and the taxi was waiting to take them to Santiago. Helena had thought it less traumatic for the children if Ramon said good-bye to them at the house and didn't accompany them to the airport. He picked up his son, who didn't really understand what was going on, and kissed his plump face. 'Papa loves you too, Hal. Be good for Mama, won't you,' he choked, closing his eyes, burying his face in the child's glossy black hair.

Federica clutched the box against her and waved at her father who stood forlornly in the road, waving back with an unsteady smile, like a clumsy giant. She turned to look out of the back of the car and waved until they had turned the corner and he had gone. Then she sat slouched against the window, watching the houses pass by, numb with sadness. She felt as if her insides had been scooped out, leaving a gaping hole that only her father could fill. She worried all the way to the airport about Rasta. She worried that no one would walk him and that he'd start to bark again out of sheer boredom and misery. It was only when they were on the plane that she stopped crying. She had never been in a plane before and it fascinated and excited her. She took her mother's hand as they careered up the runway. Helena smiled down at her lovingly and squeezed her hand.

When the lights were turned out and Hal and Federica lay sleeping in their seats, Helena reflected on the past few days, relieved that they were over. She would put Chile behind her, Ramon too. She'd start a new life in England. She felt drained of energy, depleted of emotion. She replayed the telephone conversation she had had with her mother and found the tears welling in her somnolent eyes. She had been so busy playing the glad game for the children she hadn't allowed herself the luxury of crying. Now they were asleep she wept silently, relieving the strain in her neck and jaw. The thought of her mother's voice made her stomach flutter with longing. She had heard her father in the background and suddenly she had wanted more than anything in the world to run to them, as she had done as a child, and let them soothe her with their gentle words and reassuring presence. They had been saddened to hear that Helena had decided to leave her husband, but glad that they were coming home.

Jake and Polly Trebeka had watched helplessly as their daughter had married and gone to live on the other side of the world. They had both liked Ramon in spite of the vast difference in culture that had prevented them from understanding him. They were never given the time to get to know him properly. Both would have preferred a gentle Cornishman for their daughter. But Helena had been consumed by him almost from the minute she met him. The first indication of his feelings for her and off she had gone to follow him wherever he chose to go, like an adoring shadow. Of course, Polly knew all about their troubles and blamed Ramon entirely for the disintegration of their marriage. She had had her reservations right from the start. He was from a different world, a wanderer and it was all very well while they floated about just the two of them, but there would come a point when Helena would want a family. Ramon had always been selfish. The world revolved for him alone and she doubted he'd ever change his ways for anyone. Well, now it had imploded. Jake and Polly were distraught but realistic. Helena was still young, only thirty years old. There was plenty of time to find a nice, kind Cornishman to look after her as she deserved to be looked after. Ramon was an unfortunate error; but he was now in the past.

Polly immediately set about preparing for their arrival. She spent hours deliberating whether Hal and Federica would like to share or whether they'd prefer to have their own rooms. The house was large. There was space enough for everyone. Finally, after having discussed it with her husband she decided to give them their own, each with twin beds, so that if they felt lonely they could share. She aired Helena's old bedroom, still with the clothes and trinkets she had left behind packed neatly in the cupboards. She had never cleared them out. She hadn't had to. As far as she was concerned that room had always belonged to Helena.

Chapter Nine

Ramon walked up the beach and experienced for the first time in his life the hollow pangs of bereavement. It was evening and he was alone. He hadn't even been able to take Rasta for a walk, for without Federica there didn't seem much point. So he had walked past the dog's small prison looking the other way and ignoring the animal's excited breath and husky barking. His heart ached with remorse and self-loathing and yet he didn't consider changing his ways as Helena had asked him to. He hadn't even offered to try. He wallowed in his misery, enhanced by the natural melancholy of the dying day. He turned his weary eyes to the sea and tried to imagine their new home in England. He remembered Polperro and the first time he had seen Helena. He imagined it the way it was then.

He sat on the sand and rested his elbows on his knees looking out over the choppy Pacific Ocean that stretched out before him, untamed and free. He had been like the sea then, going wherever the tide of his imagination took him. Those were the days when he was young and adventurous and blessed with immortality. Or so he had thought. He could do anything he wanted. So he had travelled, sometimes sleeping under the stars, other times boarding with strangers generous enough to take him in. He had been born into a world of privilege and yet money had never meant a great deal to him. As long as he was on the move he was happy. At first he had written poems, which a friend of his father's, who owned a small publishing firm in Santiago, had published for him. It had been immensely exciting seeing his work in print for the first time, with his name in big letters, positioned in the bookshop window for all to see. But he didn't care too much for fame either, he was happier wandering the world unnoticed. Then he had written a collection of short stories, inspired by his adventures and embroidered with his fantasies. After that he was no longer an unknown in Chile; he began to be recognised. His book sold in bookshops all over the country. His picture appeared in *El Mercurio* and *La Estrella* and alongside the articles he wrote for various magazines such as *Geo Chile*. His desire to be creative was insatiable, nothing could pin him down. He'd stay in Chile long enough to see his family and then he'd be gone again, as if he were afraid his own shadow might catch up with him.

When he first met Helena he was writing a piece for *National Geographic* about the historic sights of Cornwall. He had been inspired to write the story having met a weathered old seaman who had grown up in St Ives before joining the Navy and finally ending up in Valparaíso. He had woven a compelling tale of the land of King Arthur and Ramon had been struck with the urge to go to see it for himself. He hadn't been disappointed. The villages and towns were stuck in the past as if the modern world had not yet discovered them. The houses were whitewashed and built into the rich green hills that fell sharply into the sea. The bays were solitary coves haunted by the ghosts of smugglers and shipwrecks. The roads were little more than narrow, winding lanes lined with tall hedgerows scattered with cow-parsley and long grasses. He had been enchanted. But if it hadn't been for Helena he would only have scratched at the surface.

Helena Trebeka had been sitting on the quayside in Polperro when Ramon had first seen her. She was slim, carefree, with long wavy hair of such a pale blonde that he was immediately struck by it. He sat down to watch her, making mental notes in order to put her into one of his stories. He imagined she was the granddaughter of a smuggler. A girl with a wild nature and rebellious inclination to do exactly as she pleased; he wasn't far wrong. She caught him staring at her and stared back in defiance. Not wanting to offend her he walked over and placed himself next to her so that their legs dangled over the edge together.

'You're very beautiful, like a mermaid,' he mused, smiling at her. She was caught off guard. Englishmen were never that poetic or daring and most of the men she knew were afraid of her.

'Well, I'm sorry to disappoint you, I have legs not fins,' she said and smiled back vivaciously.

'So I see. Much more practical, I should imagine.'

'Where are you from?' she asked. He spoke with a heavy accent and his black hair and brown skin were new to her, as were the leather moccasins he wore on his feet.

'I'm from Chile,' he replied.

'Where's that?' she asked, unimpressed.

'In South America.'

'Oh.'

'There is a world outside Polperro, you know,' he teased.

'I know,' she said tartly, not wanting him to think her provincial. 'So what are you doing here in my little town?' she asked, unable to curtail her curiosity.

'I'm writing an article about Cornwall for a magazine,' he said.

'Do you like it?'

'What, Cornwall?'

'Yes.'

'So far, I like it very much.'

'Where have you been?' she asked, smiling, for she knew he wouldn't have been to the secret places that weren't to be found in guidebooks. So he listed the towns he'd visited and some of the history he'd picked up.

'You know, my grandfather was a smuggler,' she said proudly.

'A smuggler.' He laughed, congratulating himself on his acute powers of perception.

'A smuggler,' she repeated.

'What did he smuggle?'

'Brandy and tobacco, that sort of thing. They used to cart it by the wagon-load to Bodmin Moor where they would hide it. They'd sell it for a fortune in London.'

'Really?'

'Yes. Now that's the sort of thing you should be writing in your article. Everyone's bored of King Arthur. Why not write something original?'

'Well, I—'

'I could show you all the secret coves and bays and Dad could fill you in on the details,' she said impulsively. Ramon thought that sounded like a good idea. At least if the smuggling story didn't work he'd have some time to get to know this intriguing character who was presenting him with a tempting challenge. She wasn't like other girls he'd met. She was outspoken and confident.

'Okay. I'd like that,' he replied, surprised at her forwardness that contradicted sharply her almost angelic looks.

Jake and Polly Trebeka were appalled when Helena skipped in for lunch to tell them that she had made a new friend, a writer from somewhere in South America, whom she was going to show around all the old smuggling sights.

'You can't go picking up strangers, Helena. You don't know anything about him,' said Jake sternly, carefully hinging the miniature wooden door on the model boat he was making.

'He could be a murderer,' Polly added wryly, as if murderers were commonplace. She took a steaming vegetable lasagne out of the Aga and placed it on the table. 'Where the devil is that brother of yours? Toby!' she shouted. 'Toby!'

'Mum, he's not a murderer,' Helena protested.

'Well, you'll only find out when it's too late.' She chuckled heartily, wiping her hands on her woollen skirt. Polly was a large woman, not fat, but big-boned and strong. She thought diets were frivolous and spending time in front of the mirror a wasteful indulgence of the very vain. Like a magnificent galleon she dwarfed her husband who trailed behind her like a crude sailing boat. Not that Jake was slight; he might have been small in stature but he could knock the breath out of any man who caused him offence. They looked an odd couple but they were immensely fond of each other and agreed on everything as much out of habit as out of a united opinion. Jake owned a thriving joinery business and Polly ran the house, raised the children and the beds of flowers that blossomed every spring. They were comfortable but not rich. 'What do I need a lot of money for?' Jake would say. 'I can't take it with me when I die, can I?'

Toby descended the stairs, the loud thumping noise of his feet on the wood shaking the entire building. 'What's for lunch, Mum?' he asked, smelling the heavy aroma of his mother's celebrated cooking.

'Vegetable lasagne,' she said briskly, placing a water jug on the table.

'My favourite,' he enthused. Jake had always said that Toby must have holes in the soles of his feet because he had an amazing capacity for food but never gained weight. He was slim and lithe like a rubber plant, with the gypsy black hair of his father and the good humour of his mother. When it came to food he had an appetite that far exceeded both theirs combined.

'Jake, can't you finish that after lunch?' said Polly impatiently. 'Why we need another model boat is beyond me.' She sighed, casting her eyes over the rows of models that cluttered up her surfaces like the shelves of a toyshop.

'What if I bring him here to meet you, then you can judge for yourselves?' Helena persisted.

'Bring who here?' Toby asked, dishing himself a large portion of lasagne.

'Helena's met a man in Polperro who wants her to show him all the old smuggling sights for an article he's writing,' said Jake.

'Oh yes?' Toby exclaimed. 'That's a good one.'

'No, he really is writing an article,' Helena insisted.

'Why, did you see it?' said Toby.

She pulled a face at him. 'Of course not, stupid. He hasn't written it yet.'

'All right, all right. Enough you two,' said Polly as if she were talking to a couple of rowdy dogs. 'Tell him to come here for tea, then we can meet him for ourselves.' Helena smiled triumphantly.

'How old is he, Helena?' Jake asked seriously, pulling out a chair and joining them at the table. He dug his fork into the lasagne.

'Mid to late twenties,' she replied and shrugged because she didn't really know. He was bristly and hairy, well built and confident. He could have been anything between twenty-five and forty.

'And he's travelling alone?' he said, chewing on his food. 'Polly, this lasagne is really very good,' he added as his wife sat down and helped herself to what was left.

'Looks like it,' said Helena.

'At eighteen you might think you're a woman, but when I was your age I had to have a chaperone,' said Polly.

'As if you needed a chaperone, Mum, you could flatten the strongest of men with one wave of your big hand,' Toby chuckled irreverently.

Ramon met Helena as planned on the harbour wall. She was embarrassed to tell him that she had to introduce him to her parents before they'd allow her to go anywhere with him.

'My mother thinks you're a murderer,' she said and sighed.

'Well, you can never be too sure.'

'You come from a strange country, how are we to know, you might be a cannibal.' She laughed.

'Well, if I were I think you'd be pretty tasty.'

She smiled coyly but didn't lower her eyes or blush. She looked at him with her steady blue eyes, assessing him. 'You think so,' she replied loftily. He nodded and grinned at her. Her arrogance amused him although he was sure it wasn't meant to. 'Well then, I think you'd better come and meet my parents. We live just outside Polperro so you can either travel as I do by bike or walk.'

'I'll find a bike,' he said. 'We can go together.'

They cycled up the hill out of Polperro, leaving the sleepy harbour and whitewashed houses that were stacked up the banks of the hill like dolls' houses. It was a clear summer day, the seagulls floating on the salty breeze and the bees humming in the cow-parsley. As they cycled together Ramon told her about

Chile and his book of tales. When he told her he was a well-known writer, she didn't believe him, retorting that she had never heard of him. 'Well, if you come to Chile you'll hear about me,' he said.

'Now, why would I want to go to Chile?' she replied.

'Because it's beautiful and a girl like you should see the world,' he said truthfully.

'I'll see the world one day. I'm only eighteen, you know.'

'You have plenty of time.'

'And lots of more important places to see first,' she said. Ramon laughed and shook his head. He was suddenly overcome with the urge to kiss her, but he bicycled on. There would be time enough for that later.

Helena's house was a pretty white building crawling with an abundance of clematis that climbed up the walls and onto the grey tiled roof above like the tentacles of a floral octopus. Ramon noticed a family of pigeons hopping about by the chimney, watching him from their lofty height with shiny black eyes. 'Well, it ain't much but it's home,' she said, dismounting and throwing her bike against the wall. 'Let's get this over with,' she added, winking at him mischievously.

Polly Trebeka was not as Ramon had expected. She had pale hair like her daughter which was streaked with a silver grey and tied into a rough bun which left curly wisps floating about her neck. Her face was completely free of make-up. She seemed the sort of woman who never bothered with creams yet her skin was soft and youthful and her smile that of a young girl. When he was introduced to Jake Trebeka he saw where Helena's pale blue eyes came from. They were almost the colour of aquamarines. In Jake they were more evident due to his swarthy skin and jet-black hair. He looked like a strange gypsy with the eyes of a hawk. Helena had inherited their best features and was more refined than both of them.

Toby had taken special care to be present for this meeting. He had noticed the excitement burn in his sister's cheeks when she spoke about this man and was curious to see what it was about him that made him different from all the other young men in Polperro who fell in love with her.

'Please sit down, Mr . . .' said Jake politely, looking to his daughter to introduce them. Helena, of course, didn't know his name. Toby caught her eye and grinned. She shot him a look to tell him to behave himself before turning back to her parents.

'Campione, Ramon Campione,' said Ramon and sat down on the sofa. His presence was somehow too big for the small sitting room. Helena was undeterred by the amount of sofa he took up with his long arms and legs and sat down next to him.

'I'm Jake Trebeka and this is my wife Polly and Toby, our son. It's a pleasure to meet you. My daughter tells me you're a writer,' he said.

Ramon nodded. 'Yes, I've written a couple of books of poetry and some short stories,' he said and his heavy Spanish accent sounded out of place in such an English home.

'But you're not here for a book,' said Polly, putting down the tray of tea. She noticed Ramon's long glossy hair which she thought could have done with a good cut and the mahogany colour of his intelligent eyes. He was so totally foreign. She had never spoken to a foreigner before.

'No, Señora, I'm writing an article for *National Geographic*,' he said.

Polly's eyes widened and she looked at her daughter in exasperation. 'Why didn't you tell us he was writing for *National Geographic*, Helena?' she said, placing her large hands on her round hips. 'I love that magazine, so does Toby, don't you dear?' she enthused, feeling more comfortable now she was able to place him in a familiar box.

'We love it,' Jake agreed, impressed. 'What's the article on besides smuggling?'

'Well, it's meant to be on the land of King Arthur,' Ramon explained. 'But Helena suggested the smuggling idea. I haven't passed it by the editor, though.'

'Oh, the land of King Arthur. What a magical idea,' enthused Polly.

'No it's not, Mum, it's unoriginal,' said Helena bluntly.

'Helena's right, it's very unoriginal,' Toby agreed, grinning at his sister.

'That all depends on how it's written,' said Ramon, his shiny brown eyes smiling at Helena playfully.

'Well, I said I'd show him the haunts and you, Dad, could fill him in on the history,' said Helena breezily, smiling back at Ramon.

'I'd be happy to help,' said Jake. 'The *National Geographic*, eh. Now that's a prestigious magazine. Do you take the photographs as well?'

'Everything,' said Ramon. Polly nodded in admiration.

'So you see, he's not a murderer, is he?' said Helena. Polly glared at her. Jake laughed. Toby nearly choked on his tea.

'I hope not,' he chuckled. 'Be sure to show him Crag Creek,' he added.

Helena beamed triumphantly. 'I'll show him everything,' she said.

Helena and Ramon spent the following ten days cycling around the coast. She showed him places he would never have found without her help. She'd prepare picnics for them, which they'd eat on the beaches, chatting with the familiarity of two people who have known each other for a good many years. They talked to people in pubs and fishing boats, explored caves and creeks and swam in the sea. Ramon had wanted to kiss her from the first moment he had endured the arrogance of her conversation. His chance came after a couple of days when they were picnicking quietly on a remote beach. Helena had only packed one piece of her mother's chocolate cake. Ramon suggested she halve it. Helena refused and placed the whole piece into her mouth at once, giggling triumphantly.

'Well I'll just have to go and get it then,' he said. Helena tried to stand up, silently protesting with her hands for her mouth was too full to speak. But Ramon was too quick for her. He lay on top of her and pinned her onto the sand with his hands. She glared at him with ice-cold eyes that a moment before had been warm and inviting. But to his amusement she couldn't refuse him verbally, so he placed his mouth onto hers with his Latin ardour and kissed her chocolate lips. Then he devoured the curve in her neck and the rise of her collarbone. Finally she swallowed hard and was able to speak.

'Ramon! What are you doing?' she protested.

'Shut up, I've heard all I want to hear from you for the moment. Now, relax and let me kiss you, I've been longing to from the first moment I saw you in Polperro,' he said and placed his lips on hers again to silence her. She relaxed as he had instructed and closed her eyes, aware only of his warm mouth and the light feeling in her stomach.

Ramon left Polperro after two weeks. He kissed Helena good-bye on the quay where they had first met. She was too proud to show her sorrow so she smiled at him as if she didn't care. Only afterwards did she cry into the spongy bosom of her mother. 'I think I love him, Mum,' she sobbed. Polly wrapped her arms around her and told her that if he loved her he'd come back for her. If he didn't then she wasn't to waste any more of her time on him. 'Summer romances are lovely things in themselves, dear, sometimes they're best left as they are.'

But Ramon hadn't forgotten about Helena. He had tried to. He had written up his article and sent it off to his editor. Then he had gone to his parents' house in Cachagua where he had moped around like a lovesick schoolboy, sat on the beach watching the sea with a heavy heart, thinking of Polperro and the mermaid he had left there. He tried everything to forget her. He slept with a few girls he picked up, but that only made his ardour stronger. He wrote poems about her and a short story about the daughter of a Cornish smuggler. His parents were delighted. He had never been in love before and they had almost despaired of his cold heart and lonely wanderings. So Mariana had talked to him, told him to follow his feelings instead of fighting them. 'They're not going to go away, Ramon,' she had said. 'Enjoy them and indulge them. That's what love is for. You're lucky to feel like that, some people go through life and never experience it.' So Ramon had called his editor and asked to add one small paragraph.

'What's that then?' his editor asked curiously. He liked the article very much, but they wanted to run it immediately. 'I hope it's not long, I won't have space,' he said.

'No, it's not long. I'll dictate it to you.'

'All right. Go ahead.'

'The most beautiful and magical place of all is Helena Beach in Polperro, a small cove of silver white sand with a pale blue sea of such translucence that she lures you into the depths of her mysteries until your heart is captured and your soul enslaved. I left knowing that I would never be the same again and that I would be hers for ever. It is only a question of time before I go back to give myself to her, body and soul.'

'Quite a beach, Ramon,' said the editor dryly. 'I shouldn't allow it to go in, but as it's you.' Then he added with a smile, 'I just hope none of our readers try to find it, they might be disappointed!'

When Helena received the copy of *National Geographic* she knew it was from Ramon, although there was no note attached. She tore open the paper and leafed through the pages with a trembling hand. Then she sat at the kitchen table and read his article. She wept at the photographs, taken together, and the way he wrote which was uniquely poetical and touched her heart. When her eyes found the paragraph about 'Helena Beach' they were so misted she could barely read it. Blinking away her tears she had to read it again in case she had read too much into it. Then she smiled because she knew that he loved her and that he'd come back for her. He had been worth waiting for after all.

*   ★   ★   ★

Ramon sat on the beach, thinking of Polperro, thinking of his wife and children sitting on the quay in the harbour and his heart lurched for them. He thought of the way he first felt about Helena and the way he now felt about Estella. Love, he sniffed, what's the use? It always goes sour in the end, he thought bleakly. How could he love Estella when he hadn't even been capable of loving his wife properly? It was better not to love at all.

Later when he returned to the house he had made up his mind. He would leave immediately and forget about Estella. He should have forgotten about Helena all those years ago, at least he wasn't about to make the same mistake twice.

Opening his maps he cast his eye to India and nodded. India, that's as good a place as any.

Chapter Ten

England

Toby Trebeka had stayed the night in London in order to be close to Heathrow airport for his sister's arrival the following morning. He had volunteered to go. He didn't like to think of her having to take a train or a bus down to Cornwall, especially not in her fragile state of mind. His parents had told her she had decided to leave Ramon. He was saddened. She had been so happy at the beginning. Wasn't everyone? He felt sorry for the children, torn between two people like that, feeling themselves to blame for their parents' failure to love one another. It always affected children more than people realised. Still, he thought, one can't live one's life entirely for one's children. Not that he'd ever have that problem.

Toby had always been different from the other boys growing up in Polperro. In spite of being of an athletic build he hadn't enjoyed sport, except for fishing, which the other boys thought incredibly dull and antisocial, especially because he always threw back the fish he had caught. He refused to eat meat – 'anything with a mother or a face' he explained. But Toby had sailed off in his father's small boat to look at the fish in spite of their mockery. He used to sit out there in the rough sea for hours on end with only the seagulls for company and the sound of his own voice humming the bad love songs he listened to on the wireless. He was handsome with pale luminous skin and sensitive eyes that cried easily, usually at things other people wouldn't have even flinched at, like the sight of a shimmering shoal of fish beneath the surface of the sea or a lone crab running for cover beneath a rock. It was only his cheery nature and sharp wit that prevented him from being bullied at school and because he was so much brighter than the other boys. He earned their respect by humour and by his readiness to laugh at himself. He collected insects, which he kept in large glass containers with all the luxuries they could possibly need from foliage to food, and spent hours nurturing and studying them. He read books on trees and animals and subscribed to the *National Geographic*. He knew he was different. His mother had told him to 'make a feature' of his differences. So he hadn't tried to like football or rugby, he hadn't tried to like smoking and sitting in pubs discussing girls. For that matter he hadn't tried to like girls either – well, not in the way the other boys expected him to 'like' them.

When he was about fifteen and the only boy in the class never to have kissed a girl he forced little Joanna Black up against the wall and kissed her in front of everyone just to prove that he could. He had hated himself for it. Not only because he had hurt Joanna Black and sent her running into the classroom sobbing with the force of a woman robbed of her virginity, but because he hadn't liked it. It hadn't felt right. The boys patted him on his back with admiration. Joanna Black was one of the prettiest girls in the school. But the hot rush of pride to his head had been quickly replaced by a burning shame that tugged at his conscience. Joanna Black never spoke to him again. Even when he saw her in the grocery shop years later, she still stuck her nose up and stalked out without so much as a glance. He had tried to apologise, but it felt silly apologising for something that had happened so long ago.

In the sixties, when Toby was a teenager, he had more 'girlfriends' than any other boy in Polperro. Girls adored him. He was funny, enjoyed gossip and intrigue, treated them with respect and was never nervous with them or too shy to say what he thought. He was attractive in an endearing way with those lucid eyes that assured them he understood them better than other boys. His large smile was honest and his kind face approachable. They all loved him and yet he never loved them in the way they longed for him to love them.

The sea was an escape for Toby when he wanted to avoid the

boys in the pub discussing girls and how far they'd got. He would sail out into the salty mists where he could be himself, where he didn't have to conform to anything. He remembered his mother's advice, but he couldn't make a feature out of homosexuality without offending the entire town. He had known he was gay from a very early age, but homosexuality was vehemently outlawed by their sheltered society and Polperro was too small to hide in. So, in 1967, at the age of eighteen, he chose to leave Polperro and look for work in London. His parents hadn't understood why he needed to go off and work in London, there was plenty of work locally for an intelligent young man like Toby. His father wanted him to work with him making windows and doorframes but Toby couldn't explain that he winced at the very idea of cutting magnificent trees into little pieces. He couldn't explain so he didn't. He just packed his bags and left. His mother was devastated, his father angry. 'You sweat blood to bring them up and then the ungrateful sods leave without so much as a thank you,' he growled. By that time Helena was travelling the world with Ramon. Jake and Polly found themselves more alone than when they had first married, because they knew what it was like to have the house filled with the laughter of their children. Now all they had left were echoes, which were louder than the silence had been in those pre-children days.

It had taken years for Toby to find a job. Not because he wasn't employable – he had left school at eighteen with good grades – but because he couldn't find something that he enjoyed doing. As he explained to his parents, 'If I'm going to be working for the rest of my life it had better be something I love or it's not worth living.' They couldn't help but agree with him, which is why they were confused by his decision to leave Polperro. There were no fishing boats in London, no wide-open sea for him to lose himself in. Toby had tried working in the City but only lasted three weeks. He brushed off his hasty departure with a cheery smile stating simply that he wasn't cut out for the City. He tried his hand at everything from selling to marketing to designing kitchens. But he soon grew disheartened and behind the smile he presented to his friends as each new failure defeated him lay the frightened soul of a man confused and alienated. He didn't belong in London, or the City, or the offices of Mayfair. He didn't belong in the world of married couples and children either. He knew where his world lay, but it might as well have been at the foot of the rainbow for he was too afraid to find it. He longed for his home, for the sea and for the security of that fishing boat hidden in the impenetrable ocean mists. Then one night in a bar he met a flaxen young man called Julian Fable who changed his life for ever. They both had too much to drink, Toby to drown his misery, Julian to give him courage. When they left the bar Julian turned to Toby and, taking his forlorn face in his hands, he kissed him. Suddenly Toby felt an enormous release, as if the shadow he had been was at last covered with a skin that felt comfortable to live in. Finally in 1973, at the age of twenty-four, he returned to Polperro with Julian, complete and contented. They bought a cottage outside Polperro where Julian built a dark room for his photography and Toby bought a boat, which he christened 'The Helena' and started up his own business taking tourists for rides around the coast, and at last he settled down. He had found himself.

For the first few years no one thought it was in the least bit strange that Toby Trebeka was living with another man. But when people began to notice that they never dated nor chased girls, gossip and rumour started to rise like the sea mists until it became overwhelming and impossible to ignore. Toby had been happily going about his own business, never interfering with anyone else's. It deeply saddened him that he should have to explain himself to anyone. But he was left no choice. He arrived one evening at his parents' house for dinner. They were curious as to why he should invite himself for dinner in the middle of the week and an uneasy feeling invaded their home. Jake and Polly had both suspected he might be gay, but as long as it wasn't discussed or flaunted in front of them they ignored it. Pretended it wasn't there. Like hiding a stain in the carpet with a potted plant, they were happy to leave it unattended in spite of the friends and neighbours who talked about it behind their backs.

'How is everything?' Jake asked warily while Polly stirred the vegetable soup with a firm hand.

'Fine, thanks, Dad,' said Toby, swallowing down a gulp of wine to give him courage.

'So all's well then,' said Polly from beside the Aga, her tight smile betraying her anxiety.

'Look, Mum, Dad. I'm gay,' Toby said bluntly. He had the same direct approach as his sister yet it still managed to take both parents by surprise. He sighed heavily and let the wine feel for him. Jake knocked back his brandy. Polly stirred the soup with vigour. For a while no one spoke. Left alone with their thoughts the silence isolated them from each other. Only Toby's heart soared weightless in his chest, more buoyant than ever.

'So Julian's your . . .'

'Lover, Dad. Julian's my lover, my friend. I don't expect you to understand, just to accept that this is the way I choose to live. I don't want people gossiping about me behind your backs. You have a right to know,' he replied, looking at his father steadily.

'I've always taught you to be independent,' Polly began, approaching the table.

'To make a feature of our differences,' said Toby wryly.

'To make a feature of your differences,' she said and chuckled. 'Well, I'm proud of you. It takes a lot of courage to go against the tide.'

'I think I've been swimming against the tide all my life,' Toby mused, smiling sadly.

'Well, I'll swim with you, Toby dear,' said Polly, bending down to kiss him.

He put his arms around her thick waist. 'This means a lot to me, Mum,' he choked.

'I know,' she replied, patting him on the back. 'I know.'

Jake accepted it as his son had asked him to, but he never spoke about Julian or wished to see him or entertain him in his house again. Toby was mortified that suddenly a wall had been erected between them. His father had liked Julian before, but now, out of sheer prejudice, he saw him as a threat and decided to go against his initial judgement and turn against him. However, Polperro was a small village and they simply couldn't avoid each other. When they did eventually meet one hazy Saturday morning on the quay, while Julian moored Toby's boat, *The Helena*, and Jake walked past on his way to his own boat, they nodded politely, but that was as far as it went. Jake had acknowledged him without venturing further than his good manners pushed him. Toby was pragmatic. At least he had told them, there were no secrets to pull him down. The only road ahead was up.

Federica and Hal arrived at Heathrow airport dazed and exhausted. The flight had been long, stopping in Buenos Aires, Rio, Dakar, and finally Heathrow. Their world had been reduced to the small interior of the aeroplane for what had felt like an eternity. They had played games with the pencils and paper the air hostesses had given them and slept as much as they were able to, using their mother as a cushion and comforter combined. But they were restless hours punctuated by frustrating stops and once the novelty of flying had worn off they had both wept weary tears. Helena had tried to keep them distracted and she had even asked Federica to tell her the story of her box again just to use up a few more empty minutes with something.

Finally Toby's long, smiling face loomed into focus, as he waved at them madly when they walked slowly out through customs. Neither Hal nor Federica recognised him. But Helena ran into his arms, the sobs spilling out of her lungs as the pressure of having to be strong for her children burst with relief. She rejoiced at the familiar feel of his body and the familiar scent of his skin. She was home. The nightmare was over.

'I'm your Uncle Toby,' said Toby, bending down and shaking

Hal's hand, which was immediately swallowed up by his long fingers. Hal clung onto his mother's legs and looked at the strange man with suspicious eyes. Federica extended her hand and said 'hello' politely but without smiling. 'You are even prettier than your mother described you,' he said, taking Federica's hand and shaking it gently. Then noticing her box he added, 'What's that you're carrying?'

Federica clutched it in her hand possessively. 'Papa gave it to me. It's a magic box,' she replied quietly.

'I bet it is. You'll need a magic box in Polperro.' He chuckled.

'Why?'

'Because there are magic caves and mysterious creeks and haunted beaches,' he said and watched her tired eyes flicker momentarily with interest.

'Really?' she exclaimed and her mouth lengthened into a thin smile.

'Really. I'm very pleased you've brought your box,' he said, then stood up. 'You must be exhausted, Helena. Let's get you to the car immediately, the children can sleep on the back seat.'

Toby pushed the trolley laden with their cases, while Helena walked holding her two children by the hand. When they got to the car, Toby loaded the luggage into the back and then settled the children on the rear seat, which he had prepared with pillows and rugs. It was a long seven-hour drive to Polperro. 'I can't believe you've put all this together for the children,' said Helena gratefully. 'They'll sleep like kings in there.'

'It's an arduous drive. Poor lambs, they look shattered and bewildered,' said Toby, shutting the door. Federica closed her eyes and leant her aching head against the pillow. She had no time to reflect on her situation for sleep overcame her, numbing her senses like a drug.

'Oh Toby. I can't tell you what I've been through. I've left Ramon and broken my children's hearts all because I couldn't cope any more,' said Helena, the tears glistening in her bloodshot eyes.

'Don't blame yourself, Helena, it's life. They'll cope. Don't worry. It's happened to tons of children before them and they've survived,' he said, patting her on her arm. 'Now do get in or you'll catch a cold. I don't imagine you thought of bringing coats,' he said, looking at her shivering in her sweater and slacks.

She shook her head bleakly. 'Of course not, it's midsummer in Chile,' she said, thinking suddenly of Ramon and wondering what he was doing.

'When the children are asleep you can tell me all about it,' he said, climbing into the car.

Helena watched the grey cloud hang low in the sky like a shroud and yet it didn't make her feel depressed as bad weather often did, but gave her a contented feeling of reassurance. It was all so familiar and so comfortable. As they drove towards the motorway she cast her eyes about her at the naked trees with their branches stiff from the cold and the sleek black rooks that pecked at the winter fields. She remembered England like this and smiled inside.

'It's good to have you back, Helena,' Toby said, glancing in the mirror to check the children were asleep. 'Poor darlings, they're shattered. Look.' Helena turned her head around wearily. Hal and Federica were asleep curled up against each other like a couple of puppies. She thought of Ramon and wondered whether he was missing them or whether he had simply deleted their memories and moved on. More countries, more books, no commitments.

She sighed. 'It's been a while since I last talked to you. How's Julian?' she asked, staring at the moving ground in front of them, blinking away her fatigue.

'Julian's doing well. He spends a lot of time in London on assignments. He's getting lots of work and becoming rather successful. He'll be keeping me in my old age,' he chuckled.

'Lucky old you!'

'Not really. Dad's the same.'

'That doesn't surprise me. He's a man's man. Proud with it. He probably blames himself,' she said.

'It undermines his own masculinity.'

'He'll come round one day, don't expect miracles. There are far more important things to get upset about. You haven't killed anyone.'

'No, not yet.' He smiled. 'But it's been two years since I told him and he still hasn't spoken to Julian. When Julian first arrived in Polperro he was only too happy to embrace him into the family as my friend. He was charmed by him. How narrow-minded can a person be to ostracise someone because of their sexuality, which is a private matter anyway? Especially as he liked Julian very much as a person.'

'That hurts, doesn't it?' said Helena, noticing his white knuckles grip the steering wheel in frustration.

'Yes, only because we've always been so close. It's not the same now. You'll see.'

'He just pretends Julian doesn't exist?'

'Yes.'

'How does Julian feel?' she asked, trying to take an interest but all she could think about was her own pain.

'He's so laid back, he doesn't care. He's far too interested in his photography to worry about whether Dad likes him or not. Anyhow, he's thirty-nine years old, he's seen it all before and it doesn't faze him. I mind for me, that's all.'

'Dad probably feels you've been led astray by an old pervert.' She watched Toby's mouth twist into a reluctant smile.

'Hardly old, Helena.'

'Seven years older than you. To Dad you're still a baby.'

'Well, this baby knows what he wants.'

'Then that's fine. To hell with Dad. Who cares! As long as you're happy. You have to think of yourself, you know, and not live your life for other people,' she said, considering her own situation and the two heartbroken children who slept innocently on the back seat.

'We both have to think of ourselves, Helena. No one else is going to,' he replied gravely then fell silent and watched the grey road stretch bleakly out in front of them.

★   ★   ★

Helena and Toby had always shared all their secrets. Even though he was younger than his sister by two years he had always been more mature than other boys his age. That's what comes of keeping secrets, it wears one out and makes one furtive, Helena reflected. She had known Toby was gay long before he had decided to tell his parents. She had always known he wasn't interested in girls, that he was happier with his books on worms and beetles than going to nightclubs. It wasn't that he was frightened of women, he wasn't. He adored his sister, admired his mother and had lots of good girl friends. Toby just wanted their friendship; the idea of physical contact was as alien to him as football. When Helena's friend Annabel Hazel fell in love with him, crying hopeless tears of unrequited love onto her shoulder, Helena began to wonder whether Toby might be gay. He never dated anyone. He could hardly marry one of his unfortunate beetles. Helena was usually too distracted by her own desires to have the time to notice anyone else's, but Toby's sexuality intrigued her and wrenched her out of herself. She watched him closely. It was in the Chilean summer of 1972, that Toby had flown out to spend a few weeks with his sister who had settled happily into married life with Ramon.

Helena was distressed to see that Toby had grown fat with misery and taut with anxiety. He was suppressing his feelings and choking on his efforts. He was unemployed and unhappy and his usually buoyant smile could barely manage to float. They walked up and down the beach and talked as they had never talked before. Toby spoke of his difficulty in finding a job in London, how the fumes of the cars made him sick and the noise made him nervous. 'I just don't feel me any more,' he explained hoarsely.

'Well, you're not going to get a boyfriend by being miserable,' Helena said nonchalantly. Toby stared at her, his face at once pink and white and his eyes full of terror. 'It's okay to be gay, you know,' she continued and smiled at him in understanding.

'You're still my darling Toby.' Toby sat down on the sand and put his head into his fumbling hands and sobbed as he hadn't done since his dog, Jessie, had been run over that hideous winter morning fifteen years before. Helena sat next to him and placed her arms around him. 'You're fat because you're not happy, you're not happy because you're confused. You always have been. That's why you went to London because you couldn't cope with your secret in Polperro. I don't blame you.' She laughed. 'That town is way too small for you. But you know, it's where you belong and it's where you'll be happy.'

'I know.' He sniffed. 'I want to go home. I hate London. But,' he sighed heavily as if the weight of his secret was being released through his breath. 'I want to be loved like everyone else.'

'And you will be. There are lots of gay people all over London, all over the world. You only have to have the courage to find them.' Toby turned and looked at his sister with shiny blue eyes that resembled a clear sky after a heavy rainfall.

'How come you knew?' he asked.

'Because I know you. Because I care,' she said. 'I've known for a long time. Ever since you rebuffed Annabel Hazel. I began to think about it then. You never dated anyone, you were more interested in those wretched insects of yours. I thought there was something strange about that. No one else did, mind you, because you had always been eccentric. But no one was as close to you as I was.'

'Still are,' he said and smiled with a gratitude that made her eyes water with emotion.

'So,' she said, blinking happily, 'if we're going to get you a boyfriend we've got to get you looking good. You're far too fat!' Toby laughed bashfully. 'The diet starts today, and you're staying more than a month. Ramon and I aren't travelling again until March and I'm not sending you back to London until you're ready, understand?' He nodded. 'Love is the best thing in the world. I want you to have the sort of love I have,' she added.

'For the first time ever I feel it's possible,' Toby replied, taking her hand and squeezing it. Suddenly he felt lighter and more positive. As they walked back up the road to Cerro Castillo where Ramon and Helena had a beautiful house overlooking the sea, Toby felt as if he was seeing the world for the first time in many years. He wanted to take a boat out and lie under the sun, rocking gently on the waves, gazing out onto the horizon that suddenly held so many promises he wanted to run to it and embrace it.

Toby looked across at Helena who now lay sleeping against the seat belt, her troubled eyes shut to the turmoil of the last month, dreaming of better times no doubt. Her breathing was slow and deep as if even in sleep she recognised the familiar air of her home country. How life has its ups and downs, he thought, at least after a down one can only go up. He glanced at the children in the mirror and noticed the gentle stirring of their bodies as they left the comfort of their secret worlds to open their eyes onto unfamiliar countryside. He wished it were spring, then England wouldn't look so bleak.

Federica sat up and blinked out of the window at the passing fields, scattered white with a thin covering of frost.

'Are we nearly there?' she asked.

'Not quite, Fede,' he replied jovially. 'Tell me about your magic box?' he asked, watching her open and close it absent-mindedly.

She sighed and her face lengthened sadly. 'All right,' she said, recalling her father's secure embrace and inwardly wincing because with that memory invaded the less pleasant one of the conversation she had overheard in Cachagua. But as she began to tell him the story of the Inca princess the colour returned to her cheeks and her spirits lifted. By the time they stopped for lunch in a quaint village pub she no longer felt sad but intrigued. Intrigued by all that was new about her.

Chapter Eleven

When they turned the corner into the narrow lane that wound its way down to the house where Toby and Helena had grown up, Helena felt her heart turn over. She rolled down the window to smell the familiar scents of her childhood. But it was January and the air was frosted so she smelt nothing. This did not dampen her enthusiasm. As they drove through the gates and onto the gravel the white house rose into view like a steady old friend, exactly as it always had been, pretty in spite of the winter that left its walls naked and exposed.

On hearing the car, Jake and Polly, who had spent the previous hour pacing the rooms in agitation, hurried out of the front door to welcome the weary travellers home. Polly noticed immediately that her daughter was thin and gaunt but she was surprised at how well the children looked. Federica ran into her arms and embraced her in excitement.

'You have your own room, Fede, and I've even made you chocolate crispies for tea because I remember how much you liked them when I made them for you in Chile,' said Polly, hugging the skinny child who held on to her waist like an orphaned monkey. Hal clung to his mother's legs and begged to be picked up.

'Hal, sweetie, you're too big to be carried. You're four and not a small four either,' Helena laughed, kissing her father with emotion. 'God, it's good to be home. I feel better already.'

'Do come in out of the cold. It's warm in the kitchen, let's all go and talk in there,' Polly suggested, ushering Federica in with her capable big hands.

'Well driven, Toby,' said Jake, patting his son stiffly on his back. 'It was very good of you to pick them up.'

'No trouble at all, Dad,' he replied, grateful for his father's praise. He didn't get much of it these days.

Polly laid the table with a chipped teapot that Toby had once dropped and an odd collection of mugs she had acquired over the years. She then loaded up a tray with chocolate crispies, biscuits, cake and Marmite sandwiches. Unlike other Chilean children Hal and Federica had grown up on Marmite which Polly had sent out regularly to Viña along with the Mary Quant make-up Helena couldn't do without. Polly looked at her daughter with worry. She was still good looking but her radiance had faded like a dried flower. Neglect had sucked the juice out of her and left her dehydrated. Polly wanted to wring Ramon's neck, but she was careful to wait until she was alone with Helena before she talked about her errant husband. The children warmed up in front of the Aga, eating their way through the tea like hungry locusts. They settled in quickly and Hal overcame his shyness when he saw the chocolate cake.

'It's so wonderful to be home again. It's just like the old days. Nothing's changed,' said Helena, surveying the room in one swift glance while she lit a cigarette and inhaled slowly, savouring the first rush of nicotine. Her mother had barely aged in the last few years. She was an agile sixty-year-old with plump honey skin that seemed too smooth to dry into lines and the shining eyes of someone blessed with a strong constitution and good health. If it hadn't been for her greying hair that she twisted into an untidy bun and the matronly clothes she wore, she wouldn't have looked a day older than fifty. Her father's hair was now a dignified silver which softened his craggy features and made him look less like the swarthy smuggler he had resembled when it had been black. He still said little but observed everything. When he did speak everyone listened.

'It's lovely to have you back,' Polly enthused, her ruddy cheeks hot from the excitement of seeing her child and grand-children again. 'I've got the perfect friends for Federica and Hal,' she added happily. 'Do you remember the Applebys?'

Helena looked at Toby. 'What, that mad family who live at Pickthistle Manor?' she replied, smiling at her brother because as children they had always tried to engage old Nuno Trevelyan in conversation whenever they saw him because he was Polperro's most entertaining eccentric. He had been in his early sixties then, walking on the balls of his feet with a very straight back, nodding his tortoise-shaped head at people as he passed them as if he were mayor. He had been born in Cornwall and yet, because he had spent much of his youth in Italy studying art, he spoke with a pseudo-Italian accent and had changed his name from Nigel to Nuno. He lived in Pickthistle Manor with his daughter Ingrid, an avid bird watcher, and her writer husband Inigo and their five wild children.

'Well, they're not mad, dear, original perhaps, but not mad,' Polly replied.

'Original!' Jake chuckled, grinning a lopsided smile that revealed one crooked wolf's tooth. 'And I usually count on Polly to say it like it is.' He laughed.

'Ingrid and Inigo have five children,' said Polly, ignoring her husband. 'Let me see, there must be one or two compatible with Fede and Hal.' She squinted her pale blue eyes as she tried to remember them.

'Well,' interrupted Toby, 'Sam must be about fifteen, so he's no good.' He recalled the rather arrogant boy who rarely spoke to anyone and always had his nose buried in a biographical dictionary.

'Goodness no, I'm talking about Molly and Hester,' said Polly.

'Ah yes. Molly must be about nine and Hester seven,' said Toby. 'Perfect playmates. They both go to the local school so it could work very well.'

'That would be nice for Fede,' said Helena, watching her children who now laughed happily, playing with the presents Ramon had given them.

'Lucien and Joey are little, Hal's age more or less,' Polly added. 'I think we should invite them over for tea sometime soon.'

'I remember Ingrid,' Helena laughed, 'just as crazy about animals as you, Toby. If there was a wounded creature within five miles she'd find it, box it and nurture it back to health in her airing cupboard.'

'Well, if they weren't wounded they pretended to be, that airing cupboard was like the Ritz,' Toby chuckled. 'Do you remember those flea-ridden hedgehogs she kept in the scullery?'

'And the goose who was so vicious they couldn't use their kitchen for a week until its leg had recovered. *You* can hardly talk with all your insects installed in five-star incubators,' Helena added, grinning at her brother.

'She still spends most of the day on the cliff painting seagulls,' said Polly. 'She paints beautifully.' She sighed in admiration. 'Mind you it's all at the expense of those dear children who live like gypsies.'

'Rather grand gypsies, Polly,' Jake interjected wryly.

'Yes, grand gypsies, but they run wild. Ingrid's so vague and Inigo spends all day locked in his study writing or tearing through the house grumbling about everything. Best to stay out of his way I always think. Still, they are charming children even though there's not an ounce of discipline to share between them.'

'Do you think they're the right sort of children for mine?' Helena asked anxiously, flicking her ash into the bin.

'Of course they are. Federica could do with a little freedom,' said Polly, remembering how Federica wasn't allowed out of her front garden without the supervision of a maid or her mother. Police patrolled the streets and the military enforced the curfew. Viña del Mar was carefree enough but a suburb was no place to bring up children. 'The countryside will do them the world of good,' she added, taking joy from the idea of them playing on the beaches and running through the fields with their new friends. Federica was still a child although she seemed like a young woman in a child's body. Polly thought it was high time she was allowed to enjoy her childhood, or at least the few years she had left.

When Federica was tucked up in her new bed she lay on her side and stared at the butterfly box that sat on her bedside table. It was so dark that she had asked her mother to keep the door open onto the landing so that the light could flood in and dilute the night that seemed all-consuming in this unfamiliar country. She looked at her box and took courage from it, a little piece of home in a strange land, a little bit of her father to cling onto until he arrived to love her properly.

Helena had allowed Hal to share her bed for the first night. She didn't realise at the time but she needed him as much as he needed her and he would consequently share her bed for the next six months, until Polly finally intervened and tactfully suggested that perhaps it wasn't healthy for a young boy to be so dependent on his mother. But that first night had been important for both of them. Helena clung to his warm body hoping to reassure him and assuage her guilt at having torn him away from his father and home. She knew her children were young enough to cope with the trauma of uprooting, she knew they'd make friends and one day almost forget they had ever lived in Chile. Certainly for Hal, Chile would pale into a murky memory whereas for Federica it would be harder. She thought of Molly and Hester Appleby and her hope rested with them. She resolved to introduce them as soon as possible. Federica hadn't had many friends in Chile, she was by nature more of a loner, probably due to having had three years as an only child. She closed her heavy eyes and let sleep wash over her, drowning all the unpleasantness of the past and leaving her to dream about the wonderful new life that was opening up to them. But every now and then Ramon's imposing will would invade her thoughts and claim her once again while she was powerless to fight him.

'Poor Helena,' Polly sighed, pulling the covers above her matronly breasts. 'She's done the right thing though. I hated thinking of her out there in Chile without anyone to watch out for her. Now she has us, we'll take care of her.'

'Don't let her get you running around for her, Polly. You know what she's like,' said Jake, climbing into bed.

'Helena needs us.'

'Yes she does. But go easy or you'll end up her slave just like the old days,' he said, rolling over and turning off the light.

'She's different now. She's been through a hard time and she needs our support,' she insisted.

'Don't say I didn't warn you,' he mumbled before sighing heavily, indicating that he was too tired to talk any more.

Molly and Hester Appleby were intrigued by the thin, trembling girl who stood shyly before them. Their mother had invited her mother to tea telling them that Fede, pronounced Fayday, had just arrived in England and had no friends. They were to make her feel welcome. In typical Ingrid style she threw the children together and told them to run off and play while she caught up with the girl's mother.

'Fede's a funny name,' said Molly, narrowing her green eyes suspiciously.

'It's short for Federica,' Federica replied hoarsely.

'That's funny too,' said Molly.

'My father's from Chile,' she said, then noticed the two girls' faces staring blankly back at her. 'That's in South America,' she explained. They both understood South America from the map which their nanny had painted on the nursery wall and nodded.

'Is your Daddy black?' Hester asked.

'No,' Federica replied, shocked. 'He's got black hair though,' she added and smiled as she thought of him.

'Our Daddy has black moods,' said Molly and laughed. 'We'll show you around if you like.'

Federica nodded.

Federica borrowed a pair of Wellington boots and a coat that was much too big for her and followed them out into the winter garden. Their house was a large white manor with tall sash windows and a wide terrace, descending onto the lawn by way of an imperial set of large stone steps. The ground was hard and glittered with crisp white frost that Federica had never seen before. She had seen snow, because her father had taken them skiing a few times in the Andes resort of La Parva, but she had never seen frost. They wandered down the lawn towards the lake that lay flat and icy at the bottom of the garden. 'Let's ice skate,' Molly suggested, padding carefully onto the lake. Federica followed her, wincing as she took her first faltering steps over the slippery surface.

'Careful you don't fall,' said Molly.

Federica didn't want to go on the ice. She was frightened it might break. But she watched miserably as the two unfriendly girls skated their way into the middle of the lake and knew that if she wanted them to be her friends she would have to follow. Reluctantly she stood unsteadily on the shiny surface. Relieved that it felt sturdy and secure she skated stiffly after them. 'Come on, Fede!' Molly shouted, smiling at her. 'Well done!'

'Bet you never did this in Chile,' said Hester. She was right. Federica nodded.

'Isn't this fun? I'd like to skate properly with proper skates,' said Molly. 'I wish Daddy would buy me a pair, then I could twirl around.' She demonstrated a shaky twirl. Hester tried to copy her but fell on her bottom. They laughed and Federica laughed too, feeling the first thrill of camaraderie. She practised a few turns which resulted in her falling onto the ice as well.

'Like this,' Molly instructed, taking large steps and lifting one leg into the air. Hester and Federica copied her, giggling at their hopeless efforts.

'Look, there's Sam!' Hester shouted, waving to her brother who descended the lawn towards them.

'Get off the ice!' he shouted. 'It isn't safe.'

'Spoilsport,' said Molly under her breath. 'Come on,' she sighed, skating off towards him.

Suddenly there came a deep cracking noise, like the awakening groan of a monster from the deep. Molly roared with laughter, Hester screamed in alarm and Federica, some way behind them, began to run in her effort to get off the ice. She didn't realise that one shouldn't run on ice. The groan got louder and more threatening. She ran faster but her feet started to falter. Suddenly they slipped up from under her and she landed on her chest winding herself, knocking her chin against the surface with a terrifying crunch. When she tried to get up she saw blood on the ice and cried out in terror. As she raised herself onto her knees, barely able to breathe because of her fall, it gave way and she slid into the freezing water of the lake. Panic seized her around her throat so that her cry was nothing more than a pathetic whisper. She tried to grab onto the ice that surrounded her but it crumbled in her hands like icing on a cake. Her coat was too big and restricted her movements. She tried to kick with her legs but she felt nothing but the cold. She began to sink and squealed in fright as the water reached up to her neck.

'You're all right,' came a calm voice. She raised her bloodshot eyes to see the pale face of Sam Appleby looking down at her from where he was lying above her on the ice. He grabbed her arms. 'It's all right, I've got you,' he said, locking his eyes into hers to reassure her. 'Now, I'm going to pull you up so when I say "go", start kicking with your feet,' he instructed.

'I can't feel them,' she sobbed.

'Yes you can. Now GO!' Federica began to kick furiously as Sam slowly pulled her out of her black hole. The ice creaked ominously again, but Sam continued to pull and Federica continued to kick as her very life depended on it. 'Good girl,' he kept saying to encourage her. Finally she lay on the ice like a heavy wet seal, panting and whimpering with shock. 'Now we're going to slide along, okay? We're not going to walk, you understand?' She nodded, her teeth chattering as much out of fear as out of cold. Sam put his arm around her and together they wriggled their way towards the grass. Her body was so numb she could barely move it. It seemed an age before they touched the solid ground. Once on the land Sam wasted no time in lifting Federica into his arms, striding urgently up the garden to the house with Molly and Hester following behind like a couple of breathless geese.

The girls rushed into the sitting room to tell their mother and Helena while Sam stalked up the stairs shouting for Bea, the children's nanny, who was in the nursery supervising Lucien, Joey and Hal. When she saw the sobbing child in Sam's arms she gasped in horror and led them into Molly's bedroom. 'What happened?' she cried as Sam put the child down.

'Molly again. Stupid girl!' he exclaimed hotly. 'That child could have died. Get her out of those clothes at once before she catches pneumonia,' he instructed before leaving the room. Helena and Ingrid rushed up the stairs and into the bedroom where Federica, naked and shivering, fell into her mother's arms and sobbed all over again.

'Did you think you were going to die?' said Molly later, when Federica was warming up in front of the sitting room fire, dressed in Hester's clothes, roasting marshmallows in the hot flames for tea.

'Yes, I really did.'

'You were so brave, crawling over the ice like that,' said Hester in admiration. 'Was that the first time you had been ice skating?'

'Yes. I don't think I'll be going again for some time,' she replied and laughed.

Molly handed her another marshmallow. 'These are good, aren't they? You really deserve them. I'm so sorry,' she said and smiled sheepishly, curling her auburn hair behind her ear.

'That's okay. You couldn't have known that the ice would break,' said Federica kindly.

'So lucky that Sam was there,' said Hester.

'Big brothers have some uses,' Molly laughed. 'He is a bit of a hero though,' she conceded.

'He was very brave. He saved my life,' said Federica, chewing on her sticky marshmallow and feeling light in the head with the thought of Sam carrying her into the house. 'How old is he?'

'Fifteen,' said Molly. 'I'm nine and Hester's seven like you. Mummy had two miscarriages in between Sam and me otherwise we'd be seven.'

'I'd like to be seven,' said Hester.

'Well, we're six now,' said Molly, grinning at Federica.

'Oh, yes, so we are,' Hester agreed happily. 'Better show you around the house then,' she added, looking at her sister for approval.

Molly nodded. 'Grab a piece of cake and I'll introduce you to Marmaduke,' she said.

'Who's Marmaduke?'

'The skunk Mummy rescued last week, he lives in the cupboard in the attic because sometimes he makes such a smell he has to have the whole floor to himself.'

Helena watched the girls disappear through the sitting room door and felt a tremendous wave of gratitude, not only towards Sam who had saved Federica's life, but to the girls for liking her and embracing her so readily. 'Your girls are very kind,' she said to Ingrid who sat smoking out of an elegant lilac cigarette holder and wearing the most extraordinary patchwork coat that looked like a quilt. Her hair cascaded over her shoulders in wild, auburn curls and around her neck hung a large gold monocle that she put to her eye every now and then to see better. Helena had never noticed before but one eye was blue and the other green.

'Molly's rather like Sam, they both think they're better than everyone else, because they're clever,' said Ingrid. 'Hester's sweet and not very bright. She's a good painter like me.'

'I owe Sam a huge debt of gratitude. If he hadn't been there I dread to think what might have happened.'

'Oh, she would have died, for sure,' said Ingrid, flicking the lighter to light Helena's cigarette. 'Molly always has to go one step too far.' She sighed. 'I'm sorry about Ramon.'

'So am I,' said Helena, inhaling the nicotine with an unsteady hand.

'It'll take a while, but you will recover,' said Ingrid, noticing the cigarette shaking in Helena's hand. 'You know, I remember when you ran off with Ramon. You were so young. I must be a good ten years older than you. I remember thinking how incredibly romantic it was. He was dark and foreign and you were pale and English. There was something wonderfully exotic about it. Mind you, I did worry for you, out there the other side of the world. It's not like going to live in Leicester, is it?' She laughed, revealing crooked white teeth. When Inigo had courted her all those years ago he had told her she resembled a beautiful portrait hung crooked on the wall. She liked things to be imperfect, there was nothing duller than perfection.

'Well, it was exotic and wonderful at the time. It just went sour. Sad for the children, but I have to admit I feel different already,' said Helena.

'Children need stability – one parent can give them that. Really, two is an extravagance,' Ingrid replied, playing with one of the fat curls that bounced around her neck. 'I've brought the children up single handed, almost. Inigo's children are his books. I only wish people would buy them. They're frightfully dull though. I can't get beyond the first page. Philosophy has never been an interest of mine. I prefer things one can touch.'

'Like animals?' Helena suggested.

'Quite.'

At that moment old Nuno shuffled in on the balls of his feet.

'Ah, two delightful virgins to greet,' he said in a heavy Italian accent and bowed theatrically.

'Pa, you remember Helena Trebeka, don't you?' said Ingrid.

'Why, of course, Helen of Troy was not more fair. "Sweet Helen, make me immortal with a kiss!" It is a pleasure to see you,' he said, bowing again. Ingrid frowned. 'Marlowe,' he added, raising his feathery eyebrow at her in disapproval. 'Young Samuel would know that one.'

'Helena's left Chile to live here again,' said Ingrid, ignoring him.

'Far too chilly in Chile I should imagine.'

'Where the heart is concerned, at least,' Ingrid laughed. 'Would you like some tea, Pa?'

'I'd like something much stronger than tea, *cara*. Ignore me, I'm not really here,' he said, shuffling behind the sofa towards the drinks cabinet.

'You're not easy to ignore, Pa.'

'I hear young Samuel is to be knighted for bravery. He is now Sir Samuel Appleby and I shall bestow on him the Order of the Skate to remind us all of his *coraggio*.'

'I'm so grateful to him,' said Helena, wishing Toby were there to laugh with her at the Polperro eccentric.

'I think he has won the fair maiden's heart, like in tales of yore,' said Nuno, raising his bushy eyebrows suggestively.

'Well, that wouldn't surprise me,' said Helena. 'I'm in love with him too.'

'Hearts have been won by lesser feats that that,' he said, picking up his glass and wandering out of the room.

'He came, he drank, he commented, he left,' Ingrid sighed, flicking her ash into a Herend dish.

'And he's married off my daughter, I'd say that's a good day's work done, wouldn't you?' They both laughed and poured more tea.

When the time came for Federica to leave with her mother and Hal, she wished she could stay for ever. Molly and Hester had introduced her to Marmaduke who gave off such a vicious smell it sent the three of them running down the corridor holding their noses, giggling profusely. She had met the fox cub who lived in the airing cupboard and the jackdaw who perched on Ingrid's kitchen chair and drank tea like the rest of the family. A strange pig, which Federica thought looked more like a miniature brown cow, snuffled about the house as if he were the family dog and answered to the name of Pebbles. He even ate from a dog bowl in the scullery along with Pushkin, the Bernese mountain dog, who managed to clear a whole tabletop with one swish of his white-tipped tail. Federica was enchanted.

But at six years of age Federica was now in love with the gallant hero who had saved her from an icy grave at the bottom of the lake. When he appeared in the hallway to find out whether she was okay she was suddenly overcome with shyness and her words came out as mere husks with no substance. 'You look better,' he smirked, running his eyes over the awkward child who blushed up at him gratefully. 'Your lips were blue. Mine go blue sometimes because I put the wrong end of my fountain pen in my mouth.' He laughed.

'I cannot thank you enough, Sam,' said Helena. Sam was tall, almost six feet, and looked down his nose at her loftily.

'My pleasure, I would say any time, but to be honest it was a bit cold, so I'd rather not plunge in again, at least not for a while,' he replied and laughed again.

Helena ushered Federica and Hal to the car. Federica climbed into the back seat and watched as Sam waved good-bye on the steps with his sisters who broke into a run and chased the car down the drive.

'Charming people, aren't they?' said Helena.

'I really like them,' Federica agreed. 'Can we come back soon?'

'You'll be going to school with the girls, Fede, so you'll see them all the time.'

'Good,' she replied and gazed dreamily out of the window.

Chapter Twelve

Cachagua

It had been four months, four days and four hours since Estella had last kissed Ramon Campione in her small, breezy room in Cachagua. She had waited for him to return as he had promised, but she hadn't heard anything, she hadn't even received a letter. Yet she waited as he had asked her to, as she had reassured him she would. She now sat on the beach, the soft autumn light receding into evening, flooding the horizon with an amber luminosity that poured melancholy into her heart. She placed her hand on her belly and felt the growing child within; Ramon's child. She smiled sadly to herself as she remembered those tender moments when they had been one, free from the social distinctions that separated them. Love has no boundaries, she thought optimistically, then wondered whether he had changed his mind. Whether he had realised their affair had been nothing more than a summer romance by the sea, as unreal as the fantasies he wrote about. She had found his books in his parents' bookshelves and taken them to her room where she had read every one. They were magical, surreal and compelling. Poetic stories of love, friendship and adventure set against the exotic landscapes of countries she had never even heard of. She had recognised his voice in each word as if he were some place near, whispering to her, loving her. She longed for him to come back. She longed to tell him about the life they had created together. God had given them a child and God didn't make mistakes.

Estella's future was uncertain. For the last few months she had been able to hide her secret. She had even managed to hide the sickness that had awoken her every morning and sent her running to the bathroom with the bile rising in her throat. Yet she hadn't minded, she had taken pleasure from it because everything from Ramon was a gift, so she cherished it. However, now her belly was beginning to swell and she found she tired easily which made her slow to complete her tasks. Señora Mariana watched her with narrowed eyes, in fact, Estella suspected she probably already knew. Señora Mariana had a sharp intuition about such things. If she could just get through the next few weeks, then Don Ignacio and Señora Mariana would return to their home in Santiago until the following summer. At least the next six months would be secure. If they discovered her condition before they left she feared she would have to leave her job and return in disgrace to her parents in Zapallar. They would be mortified because no man would want to marry her in that condition. What man could want another man's child? Her mother had always told her that any man worth his salt would want to marry a virgin. She was lost for sure. But as bleak as her future appeared she still believed that Ramon would return. He had not only promised, he had fervently promised as if he couldn't live without her, and she had agreed to wait because she loved him and believed he loved and needed her too. Yes, she thought, I know he'll come to find me.

She wandered back up the beach towards the house and remembered that time she had watched him from the shadows as he walked naked towards her. She had desired him then and she desired him now. Yet she didn't dream about making love to him but about lying next to him with his protective arms around her, his proud hand on her belly. She dreamed about him as the father of her child. When she entered the house Señora Mariana was waiting for her in the hallway.

'We need to have a talk, Estella,' she said, leading her into the sitting room. Estella knew she had been discovered and the beads of sweat collected on her brow. It was all over, for sure, she thought, and her chest constricted with panic.

'I have taken the opportunity to talk to you tonight as my husband is not here. Woman to woman,' said Mariana, smiling kindly at the trembling girl who perched on the edge of the sofa in discomfort.

'Sí, Señora Mariana,' she replied obediently.

'You are pregnant, are you not?' she asked, her grey eyes resting on Estella's swollen stomach. She noticed the girl lower her eyes in shame and a large tear roll down her beautiful face. 'I'm not angry with you, Estella.' Estella shook her head in despair. 'Surely this young man you've been seeing will marry you?'

'I don't know, Señora Mariana, he has gone,' she stammered.

'Wherever has he gone to?'

'I don't know, Señora Mariana. He's just gone.'

'Might he come back?' she asked gently, observing the girl's obvious distress and feeling her heart sag with pity.

'He promised he would. I believe him.'

'Well, that's all we can do, can't we? If you believe him then so do I,' she said and smiled sympathetically. 'We must find someone to replace you while you have your baby. Don Ignacio and I will be leaving for Santiago in a few days and won't be returning until October. That will be near the time when you have your child, I imagine. Please don't cry, dear, we'll muddle through. If he promised to come back I'm sure he will. You're too beautiful to leave in this condition,' she said, patting Estella's shaking hand.

'You were right, Nacho, she's pregnant,' said Mariana later when her husband returned for dinner.

Ignacio rolled his eyes and nodded. 'So I was right,' he said.

'Sadly, yes,' she replied and sighed heavily. 'What should we do?'

'Who's the father?'

'She didn't say.'

'Did you ask?'

'Well,' she shrugged, 'I tried to.'

'The point is will he marry her?'

'Of course not, he's scarpered, hasn't he?' she said crossly, folding her arms in front of her. 'It's really not fair.'

'It's the way it works in their world,' he said, dismissing her class as a group of uncultivated savages.

'It shouldn't be. She's so beautiful and charming, what sort of a man would do that to her then run off?'

'It happens all the time in their world. There's no honour among thieves.'

'Really, Nacho, they're not all like that.'

'No?' he challenged. 'I'll bet you they are. In their world women are victims. That's the way it is. She's no different. She'll have her baby, go back to her family in Zapallar and eke out a living somehow.'

'Nacho!' Mariana exclaimed in horror. 'You're not going to fire her?'

'What do you want me to do?' He shrugged.

'She can work for us *and* look after her baby,' she suggested calmly.

'We're not running a charitable organisation here,' he retorted firmly. Mariana noticed his ears go red, usually a sign that he was on the verge of losing his temper.

'I can't bear her to lose her livelihood as well as her fiancé. We can't be so heartless, Nacho. *Mi amor*, let's not talk about it any more, we have five or six months to think about it.'

He nodded gruffly and watched her walk out onto the terrace. The problem with people, he thought to himself, is that they take no responsibility for their actions. Ramon is just as bad as Estella's lover, he concluded, he brings shame on his own class.

Ramon had slept with several women since he had left Chile and yet he still couldn't erase the sweet memory of Estella that dogged his mind and refused to give him any peace. On top of that he felt guilty. He had told her to wait for him. He knew she would. The right thing would be to write and put her out of her misery and yet he couldn't. He didn't want to lose her. He wanted to keep the door open in case he woke up one of these mornings with the urge to go back to her. Sometimes he woke with a gnawing longing that racked his loins as well as his conscience and yet he managed, every time, to persuade himself that he couldn't love her the way she wanted to be loved, the way all women wanted to be loved. Just like Helena. He couldn't be there for her. He couldn't be there for anyone.

Ramon sat on the old rickety train that cut through the arid western Indian desert on its way to Bikaner. The sun blazed down upon the roof of the train, cooking up a sweltering heat inside that smelt of sweat and the intoxicating aroma of spices that clung to his nostrils and made his throat dry. The compartment was crowded with the dusky brown faces of men in turbans of saffron and fuchsia, their dark-eyed children watching him with innocent curiosity and giggling behind grubby hands. They knew he was a foreigner in spite of his homespun kurta pyjamas and chappals. When he had entered at Jodhpur he noticed the women arrange their veils in front of their aquiline faces with an almost ethereal movement of their long bejewelled fingers to ensure their modesty. Their timid eyes were at once lowered behind their veils like exotic birds in mist. After a while they forgot he was there, watching them with the scrupulous gaze of a voracious storyteller and they chattered away among themselves in a language he didn't understand. He loved Indian women. He was enchanted by their delicate femininity and their virtue, the graceful way they moved behind their glittering saris, bright flowers against so dry a desert. He didn't prey on these women, they were paragons of virtue, but he found the mysterious theatre of their world too compelling a spectacle to tear his eyes away from them. He felt that if he made too abrupt a movement they would fly off to settle in the green leaves of one of those banyan trees that miraculously survived in such barren terrain.

The dust entered through the windows like thin smoke and settled wherever it could. A bony old Indian sat cross-legged in the corner under a scarlet turban and unloaded his tiffin box, arranging the aromatic food and utensils around him with the ritual of a priest. He had taken up two seats in spite of the weary passengers who crowded the corridors for lack of places. A small child watched the man arrange his food, dribbling with hunger and hopeful that if he stared hard enough the man might offer him a bite.

Suddenly the train screeched to a frantic halt. Ramon looked out of the window through the horizontal bars. The compartment erupted out of its somnolent state into confused chatter as the passengers left the train to see why it had stopped. Ramon watched them all spill out onto the desert like ants. Soon the heat grew too intense for him to stay inside without being fried alive and he too joined them to choke in the dust under the sun. As he descended he noticed a beautiful European woman move through the crowd with the gracelessness of a mule walking through a herd of elegant sambar. Just like Helena, he thought to himself and guessed she must be British. She was striding impatiently towards the throng that had gathered around the railway track. Her face was pinched with irritation and yet she still managed to look down her nose with a haughtiness more at home in the days of the Raj. She wore a pair of white trousers and knee-high riding boots, revealing long legs and a shapely bottom.

He grinned to himself and strode up to her. 'Do you want some water?' he asked in English. She blinked at him from under her hat that resembled a pith helmet.

'Thank you,' she sighed, taking the bottle from him. After gulping down a large swig she exploded into complaints. 'What the bloody hell has happened? The train was late leaving and now we'll be late arriving. Nothing goes when it says it will in this country.'

Ramon laughed. 'This is India,' he said, looking her up and down.

She narrowed her pale blue eyes and scrutinised him back. He could have been Indian but his accent gave it away.

'Angela Tomlinson,' she said, extending her hand and looking at him steadily.

'Ramon Campione,' he replied, taking it.

'Spanish?'

'Chilean.'

'More exotic. I'm afraid I'm from England,' she said, smiling at him. 'That's not very exotic.'

'Only to the British,' he said. She laughed and wiped her freckled face with a firm hand. 'I think England's very exotic.'

'Well, you must be the only one. Aren't I lucky to have found you!' she chuckled.

'I imagine it's an animal on the line, or a person,' he said, squinting into the sun but he couldn't see past the multitude of Indians clamouring to see for themselves what had fallen onto the track.

'How horrid. Will it take long?' she asked, screwing up her nose in distaste.

'Why are you in so much of a hurry?'

'I'm meant to be in Bikaner already. Meetings, you know. I'm boringly punctual, I'm afraid. Hate to keep people waiting.'

'What's your business?'

'Hotels. I'm a consultant. We're constructing a new hotel, the one I'm to stay in will be much less glamorous I should imagine.'

'But infinitely more charming,' he said, imagining the kind of monstrosity her company was constructing.

She smirked flirtatiously. 'What takes you to Bikaner?'

'The tides,' he replied. She looked at him, impressed.

'That's all?'

'That's all.'

They stood chatting for a while, during which time a dead cow was dragged off the track and laid out on the sand for the flies and birds to peck at. Slowly the weary passengers wandered back to the train and into the throbbing heat of the carriages. Ramon followed Angela into her first-class carriage and the train lurched back into motion once again. First class wasn't all that different from the crowded carriage he had been travelling in before, the aroma of spices and wafts of dust invaded the compartment, which was also overcrowded with chattering Indians and desperately hot. Angela sat beside the window allowing the wind to cool her down. She closed her eyes and let it wash over her. She reminded Ramon in a strange way of Helena and he found himself wondering about her and his children. He was so far away it was difficult to imagine them in England, settling into Polperro, forgetting that he ever existed. But Angela possessed the same gracelessness as Helena, that very same directness that belonged only to the British and he found himself, in spite of his efforts, missing her.

Angela had arrived too late for her meeting. 'God, I'll be hung, drawn and quartered,' she complained, fiddling with her watch in agitation.

'You're not going to change the time by playing with it,' said Ramon, ushering her past the throbbing crowd of people and into a taxi, where a wizened old man sat at the wheel of a dusty car embellished with tinsel, carrying on his shoulder a small grey monkey who played with the swinging pack of plastic gods that hung from the mirror.

'I know. It's just so unlike me,' she whined.

'Look, this is India. They'll know the train was late – nothing runs on time. You can have your meeting tomorrow. One of the many reasons I could never work for anyone else is because I couldn't hack someone controlling the way I spend my time,' he said.

'Lucky old you,' she exclaimed.

'Why don't you branch off on your own?' he suggested.

'I'd be far too lazy and irresponsible.'

'Sometimes it's fun to be irresponsible.'

'Yes.' She sighed and caught him looking at her intensely. 'I suppose you're going to invite me out for a drink now?'

'If you like.'

'I think I need one.'

'Good.'

'Let's go to my "infinitely more charming" hotel,' she said and laughed.

'Good idea. I hadn't thought about accommodation.'

'Just going with the tides.'

'Exactly.'

'Well, darling, you've been washed up on my shore,' she said and placed her hand on his. 'Lucky me.'

Making love to Angela only reminded Ramon of his wife and of Estella. Her English accent made his stomach lurch with the memories of his last few days with Helena and consequently turned his thoughts to his children, yet the scent of her body and the taste of her skin only encouraged him to miss Estella by virtue of the fact that Estella tasted infinitely sweeter. It was a disappointment. He may as well have been a horse for she rode him furiously with the stamina of a professional jockey. When she was satisfied she had flopped onto the bed and fallen asleep like a man. He looked across at her pale blotchy skin and knotted hair and knew that he couldn't spend another minute in her bed. He got up, dressed and left without so much as a good-bye note.

He walked out into the sultry night air. The dawn was already seeping gold into the cracks in the sky and the monkeys were skipping on the rooftops, chasing one other across the shadows. He felt melancholy. Bad love always made him morose and he craved the poetic love of Estella. Sitting under the vast desert sky he pulled out of his rucksack the pen and paper he had stolen from Angela's hotel room and began to write to Federica. He wrote with the intention of it being read by Helena. He missed her, which was strange, as that feeling had been covered in dust for many years due to lack of use. He had never missed her before. But he missed the idea of her. She was no longer there for him. He felt he couldn't just 'rock up' like he used to. He missed Federica's adoring face. He even missed Hal whom he had never really bonded with. His base camp had gone. Now he had nowhere to go home to. Not even in his dreams.

He wrote a story for Federica about a mysterious girl who followed him about on his travels. 'She must be an angel,' he explained, 'for her hair is long and flowing and the colour of clouds at sunrise. She's beautiful, not only on the outside but on the inside, which is the most important and the most rare. I first saw her in a dream. My longing for her was so great that when I awoke she was sitting on the end of my bed, watching me with pale, luminous eyes filled with affection. And so she has accompanied me everywhere. Up the Himalayan mountains where yaks roam the snowy peaks down to the huge lakes of Kashmir where large exotic birds feast on flying fish, catching them in the air and carrying them off into the sky. She enjoys all the wonders of the world just like me. She makes me very happy. Now I realise, of course, after many days and nights travelling in her company, that she isn't real at all, but imaginary. I realised only after I had tried to touch her and my arms went right through her, rather like a ghost. But she isn't a ghost because I know she really lives in Polperro with her mother and brother Hal. So I don't try to touch her any more, I just watch her and smile. She smiles back and that to me is the most miraculous part of all.'

Chapter Thirteen

Polperro

'How's Federica getting on at school these days? Better?' asked Ingrid who was bent over her easel painting a portrait of Sam reading on the lawn. 'Blast!' she exclaimed hotly. 'I'm so much better at painting birds.'

'Fine,' Molly replied absentmindedly, concentrating on the daisy chain she was making.

'Oh, I am pleased. It can't be easy moving to a new country and having to make friends all over again.'

'She was very quiet at first, but Hester says she's happier now. She's more Hester's friend,' said Molly, who was a couple of years older and bored by their childish games.

'The summer term is always much more fun anyway,' said Ingrid, sitting back on her stool and exchanging her paintbrush for her cigarette that smoked in its elegant lilac holder on the table beside her. 'Sam darling, don't move a muscle,' she instructed, putting the monocle to her eye and studying her painting in detail.

'Mum, I haven't moved for the last hour, why would I want to move now?' said Sam, who was lying on his front reading Maupassant's *Bel Ami*, unamused at being disturbed. Ingrid grinned at him from under the wide brim of her sunhat.

'It's a precaution, darling. I don't want you to ruin my picture.'

'Is it any good?'

'Quite. But it would be better if you were a seagull or a hawk.'

'Sorry,' he replied and the beginning of a smile tickled the corners of his petulant mouth.

'Federica fancies Sam,' said Molly, putting down her daisy chain and patting Pushkin who lay panting beside her in the heat.

'She's got very good taste,' said Ingrid, lifting her eyes over the easel and smiling at her son with pride.

'What do you think, Sam?'

'I simply don't think, Molly,' said Sam, irritated.

'You seem to think about everything else,' she said.

'Perhaps, but I don't think about Federica Campione.'

'Darling, she's a very sweet girl,' Ingrid interrupted.

'Exactly. A girl,' said Sam. 'If I fancied anyone she would be a woman, not a girl.'

At that moment Hester skipped out onto the lawn followed by Pebbles, the Vietnamese pig, and cradling a snuffling hedgehog in her arms. 'I think Prickles is better now,' she announced. 'He can walk again.'

'Thank Heaven for that. Have you fed him?' Ingrid asked, momentarily looking up from her work.

'Yes. He drank all his milk. He's still covered in fleas, though. Nuno says you shouldn't have brought him into the house, he says he's been scratching ever since.'

'Your grandfather's very impressionable. If you hadn't told him about the fleas he wouldn't be scratching.'

'Fede's coming for tea,' said Hester.

'Good.'

'Her mother lets her bicycle now.'

'About time too. She's somewhat overprotective. Mind you,' said Ingrid thoughtfully, her paintbrush poised, 'after what that poor child has been through it's hardly surprising.'

'What has she been through?' Hester asked innocently.

'Well, she's had to leave her home and start again in a new place,' said Ingrid.

'She hasn't seen her father since she left Chile,' said Molly, plucking another daisy from the overgrown lawn. 'I don't believe she's even received a letter from him. I bet he's really horrid.'

'You can't call someone horrid when you don't know them, Molly. Anyway, I don't think he's intentionally horrid, just selfish and irresponsible.'

'Poor Fede,' Hester sighed. 'She talks about her father all the time.'

'I bet he doesn't think about her ever, or her mother. Have they divorced?' Molly asked dispassionately.

'Goodness no!' replied her mother, licking the end of her paintbrush. 'They've just separated. I'm sure they'll get back together in the end. I imagine it was hard for Helena living out there. It's not England you know.'

'Helena will probably fall in love with someone else,' said Molly, relishing the idea of a scandal.

'You've been reading too many romantic novels, darling,' Ingrid laughed, shaking her head at her daughter with the same indulgence that had allowed all her children to behave exactly as they pleased all their lives.

'Hester,' said Molly. 'Is or isn't it true that Fede fancies Sam?'

'Leave it, Molly,' said Sam, without looking up from his book. 'Mum, if they don't shut up I'm going to read in the orchard.'

Ingrid sighed. 'Girls.'

'Yes, it's true. Ever since he rescued her from the ice,' Hester replied, unable to resist her elder sister.

'Girls, Sam is trying to read. I'm sure he's very flattered that Federica has taken a shine to him, but really, he's fifteen years old and has much more important things to think about than the infatuations of a six-year-old child.'

'He should be grateful anyone fancies him at all,' added Molly, who always liked to have the last word. Sam ignored her and turned the page.

'What glorious sunshine!' exclaimed Nuno trotting out onto the lawn. ' "As night is withdrawn from these sweet-springing meads and bursting boughs of May," ' he said, surveying the tranquil scene before him.

'Robert Bridges, *Nightingales*,' said Sam casually, turning another page of his book.

'Quite right, dear boy,' said Nuno, nodding his approval with the slow inclination of his head as if he were on the stage.

'You must be thinking of Italy, Nuno, weather in this country is usually foul whatever the month,' said Molly sulkily.

'Oh dear! Moody Molly is like a *grande nuvola* obscuring the sun. I simply cannot tolerate the whining of a capricious child.' He sniffed. Molly rolled her eyes and smirked at Hester. 'Don't think I don't see the silent communication between you and your accomplice,' he added, glaring at them in mock anger. 'You'll both be shot at dawn. Now, Ingrid, let's see your *opera d'arte*.' He leant over his daughter's shoulder and peered at the canvas with great self-importance. 'Not bad, our Italian masters might not celebrate your achievements with a glass of Chateau Lafitte in Heaven but neither would they recoil in horror,' he said slowly in the clipped Italian accent that he had cultivated over so many years he was now unable to speak without it. 'There is no mistaking that it is Sam, my dear, only which end is his head and which end are his feet?'

'Oh for goodness' sake, Pa, go and scratch somewhere else,' Ingrid sighed, inhaling her cigarette once again in a gesture of dismissal.

'On that not so pretty subject I might add that animals with fleas are not hygienic to have in the house. I am being driven mad by scratching and no amount of bathing will relieve me. The hedge pig has to go.'

'Hester, you'll have to let Prickles go,' she sighed.

'What an unimaginative name for a pet,' said Nuno disapprovingly, straightening himself up. 'With a name like that he's not worthy of being invited into the house in any case.'

Federica was fast becoming a regular visitor to the Applebys' rambling manor. At least her name was Italian so she was immediately embraced by Nuno who remarked that with a name like that she was not only ensured great beauty and charm but also a touch of mischief which, he added imperiously, was as vital as a dash of Tabasco to the most enticing spaghetti napoli.

Hester was thrilled to have found a new friend. She had always trailed behind her elder sister, Molly, who bossed her around because she was older and cleverer then dismissed her when she found better company at school. Federica made Hester feel important. She cycled eagerly up the lane to see her almost every day and gratefully allowed her to take the lead. They indulged in childish games without the inhibitions that crept in when Molly was around. They clambered down the cliffs to the hidden bays and coves where they would find caves to hide in and share secrets. The sea was different in England, dark and murky, filled with seaweed and smelling strongly of salt and ozone. But Hester showed Federica how to love it, how to build castles in the thick sand and how to find shrimps and crabs in the many rock pools that collected during the high tides. They built a raft for the lake, fashioned fishing rods out of sticks and roasted marshmallows on the fires they were only allowed to build if supervised by an adult. As winter thawed into spring and the days lengthened and warmed, their friendship blossomed with the apple trees.

Sam had O levels to take at school. He didn't do much work. He didn't need to. He was by far the cleverest boy in the school and looked on most of the other children as either slow or just plain stupid. He rarely read the books he was supposed to, preferring to read nineteenth-century French authors such as Zola, Dumas and Balzac that his grandfather Nuno gave him. He still managed, somehow, to come top of every class, even maths, which he didn't consider himself very good at. With sandy blond hair, large intelligent grey eyes and a smile that curled up at the corners, he was charismatic and arrogant. He knew he was different from everyone else.

So Federica fancied him. He had smiled to himself in amusement and then forgotten all about it. Most girls fancied him. What other boys failed to realise was that girls liked boys who excelled. Whether they excelled on the games field or in the classroom, it didn't matter. Girls wanted boys who were commanding and confident. Boys who shone.

Sam shone. He didn't enjoy football or rugby – he hated group activities. He was good at tennis but only played singles. Doubles bored him. He liked to run around and get as exhausted as possible. He bored easily of girls, too. He wasn't unkind. In fact, when he liked a girl he was romantic, phoning them and writing to them. His intentions were always good. But rather like a new book, once he had read it he moved on to the next.

His mother told him that his behaviour was only natural in a young man of his age. 'Sow your wild oats, darling,' she said, 'one day when they're tamed oats you'll be glad that you did.' Nuno said that women weren't worth wasting his time on and gave him more books to read. ' "Alas! The love of women! It is known to be a lovely and a fearful thing," ' he said, to which Sam dutifully replied, 'Byron, *Don Juan*.' His father, on the odd occasion that he emerged out of his philosophy books, advised him to go for the more mature woman, as there was nothing more unattractive than a man who didn't understand the complexities of the female body; an older woman would teach him the art of good love.

So Sam was determined to find an older woman. The girls he knew were far too young to hope for anything more than a kiss. A kiss was fine, up to a point. He had now reached that point. The point where his loins ached with a longing that was beginning to distract him from his schoolwork and drag his mind off his much-beloved nineteenth-century French literature. He found himself thinking about sex at the most inopportune moments, like in a car or on a train, usually when he wasn't alone to indulge in his private fantasies. If he didn't find a woman soon he'd go out of his mind with frustration.

Federica had spent the morning with her Uncle Toby and his friend Julian in his boat, *The Helena*. The sea was as calm as a lake allowing them to sail for miles with the help of a firm but warm southerly wind that sent the boat slicing through the surface like the fin of a shark. Federica liked her uncle very much. He had taken her to his cottage and shown her his collection of insects. He had explained to her how ants built their hills and how hard they worked, like a little army of very disciplined soldiers, carrying pieces of food, sometimes twice their size, back to their nest. They had hidden in bushes at night to watch the foxes and badgers and he had built her a tree house in his parents' garden so that she could wait for the rabbits to steal into the kitchen garden and nibble on Polly's cabbages. In April when they had found an abandoned baby blackbird who had most probably fallen out of its nest they had immediately driven up to the Applebys' manor to give it to Ingrid to nurse back to health. Toby and Federica had visited every day to check on its progress. Federica had been too shy to visit on her own, especially as she was afraid she might find herself alone with Sam and not know what to say. He wasn't in the least bit interested in her. Why would he be? She was a child. But she couldn't stop thinking of him. The bird had been promptly christened Blackie, another unoriginal name for Nuno to complain about, and no amount of coaxing would encourage it to fly away. 'Life's much too good!' said Nuno as little Blackie perched on a coffee cup in the sitting room and ate breadcrumbs out of an adoring Hester's hand. After that Hester had insisted Federica visit every day. She had been reluctant at first, but soon her desire to belong far exceeded her awkwardness and she found herself cycling up the lane daily for afternoon tea.

Hester had supported Federica during her first term at school like an overprotective nanny. Having been a shy child herself the teachers were surprised at how much she had grown in confidence in one term. Thanks to Hester, who included her in everything, Federica had made friends for the first time in her life. In Chile she had always preferred to be on her own. She had been happy that way. Now things were different. She needed

Hester and to her delight Hester needed her too. But nothing could replace her father, not even Uncle Toby.

When Federica returned home from sailing she found her mother crying on the sofa in the sitting room. 'Mama, what's happened?' she asked, her heart at once filling with dread that something might have happened to Hal or her grandparents.

'It's a letter from your father,' Helena sniffed, handing her daughter the tear-stained piece of paper. 'Sorry I opened it, sweetie, I thought it was addressed to me.'

She lied. She had been unable to resist. She hadn't heard from Ramon since they had left in January. When she recognised his handwriting she hadn't wasted a moment, but tore it open in a sudden fit of rage and longing. It was written from India on hotel writing paper and had taken a month to reach them. He had written such an enchanting story for Federica that the tears had welled in her eyes until they had spilled over, running down her face in a stream of jealousy and resentment.

'I hate Ramon for what he has made me become,' she explained to her mother later that evening when Federica had gone to bed. 'I'm jealous of my daughter because he wrote to her and not to me. He loves her. In his hopeless way he loves her. Then I resent him for maltreating her. For writing this letter which will only bring her hope. He's not coming back. It's over, for all of us. For Federica too. But this letter will only make it worse. He raises her hopes only to dash them later. He's always been like that, impulsive. Suddenly gripped by remorse or homesickness or God knows what, he writes this epistle of love, but he'll have forgotten all about it by now. That's what sickens me. He's so damned irresponsible. If only he'd come clean and tell her to forget him then she wouldn't be constantly on the brink of having her heart broken. I can't bear it for her. He doesn't even write a message to me, not even a few words at the bottom. Or Hal, it's as if we don't exist. He's Hal's father too.'

★   ★   ★

Federica read the letter while her heart inflated like a happy balloon, filling her chest with excitement. Surely this must mean that he will be coming to visit soon, she thought, biting her lip to contain the impulse to scream with joy. Then she ran into her grandfather's study to find where India was on the map. It wasn't too far from England. Not that far at all, she deduced, turning the globe around to find Chile. Chile was the other side of the world. But India was close. Close enough for him to stop and visit on his way back to Santiago. She read the letter several times before placing it in the butterfly box that sat on her bedside table. As she listened to the light clatter of tiny bells she was comforted by the certainty that he loved her and was thinking about her. That letter made up for the four months of silence during which she had almost given up hope that he remembered her at all.

'I received a letter from Papa today,' Federica told Hester as they sat on the raft in the middle of the lake. 'He'll be visiting us soon.'

'That's nice, what did he say?'

'He wrote me a story. He writes wonderful stories,' she said, her cheeks burning with pleasure.

'Is that his job?'

'Yes. He writes books. He once wrote about Polperro for the *National Geographic*. That's how he met Mama.'

'Really, how romantic.'

'It was. He wrote a secret message in the article that only she would understand. She realised then that he loved her.'

'Molly says your parents are divorced,' said Hester suddenly before she had time to stop herself. Federica gasped in horror and her face stung crimson.

'Divorced? No, that's not true. Who told her that?' she asked tearfully.

'I imagine she made it up,' said Hester quickly.

'Well, it's not true. They aren't divorced. Papa's coming to visit soon. Tell her that. If they were divorced he wouldn't write me such a nice letter, would he?'

'Of course not. Molly makes up loads of things,' Hester said, wishing she hadn't mentioned it for Federica's face was now grey and agonised. They sat in silence while Hester was tortured with regret and Federica with uncertainty.

'If I tell you a secret, will you promise to keep it for ever?' said Federica quietly, blinking sadly across at her friend.

'For ever. You can trust me. You know you can,' said Hester, wishing to make it up to her.

'Don't tell anyone about this. Anyone at all.'

'I won't, I promise.'

'Not Molly.'

'Especially not Molly,' said Hester firmly.

'Well, we were in Cachagua, staying with my grandparents. I overheard my parents arguing,' she began hesitantly.

'What about?'

'Mama was accusing Papa of not caring about us, that's why he spent so much time in other countries. I didn't tell you before, but Papa always travelled a lot. We hardly saw him. He'd suddenly turn up out of the blue after a few months. Sometimes one month, sometimes more. He'd never say when he was coming home, he'd just arrive. She said that their marriage was only a bit of paper and that she was giving him his freedom. She said he'd never have to come home again.' Federica's chin wobbled with despair.

'But he's written you this letter,' said Hester, shuffling up to her friend and placing a comforting arm around her shoulders.

'I know. He wouldn't have written it if he wasn't coming back, would he?'

'Of course not. If he didn't want to see you again he wouldn't have written at all, would he?'

Federica shook her head. 'No, he wouldn't have written,' she agreed.

'So there's nothing to be sad about. In fact there's everything to be happy about. He'll be coming to visit soon. Maybe very soon.'

'If they were divorced, I'd know about it, wouldn't I?'

'Yes. They would have told you.'

'Mama said that we'd live in England and Papa would come and see us just like he always has done.'

'Well then, that's the truth,' Hester conceded. Federica wiped her tears with a hanky that she pulled out of her pocket. The only person Hester knew who carried a hanky in their pocket was Nuno. 'You know, my mother says that people often say things they don't mean when they fight.' She added, 'My father says terrible things, but we don't really worry about them because when he's angry he's a different person. I think your parents were different people when they fought. I doubt they meant it.'

'Me too,' Federica agreed, feeling a lot better.

'Why don't we ask Sam to light a fire for us, then we can roast some marshmallows?' Hester suggested happily.

Federica blinked across at her friend with gratitude then focused her thoughts on Sam. At once she forgot about her father and the conversation she had overheard in Cachagua. Paddling furiously, they made their way across the glassy lake to the long reeds and bulrushes.

Sam was not happy to be distracted from his book. They found him lying on the sofa in the sitting room, eating a packet of salt and vinegar crisps and listening to David Bowie. He told them to go and find someone else.

'But there is no one else, Sam,' Hester said.

'What about Bea?'

'It's Saturday, silly,' she replied.

'Well, she's here because I heard her,' said Sam, taking another handful of crisps.

'Well, if she won't do it, then will you?'

'I'll jump that when I get to it. Just go and call her,' he instructed. Hester walked out into the hall and shouted for Bea. Federica followed sheepishly behind her not wanting to be left in the room with Sam. While Hester called for Bea, Federica watched Sam through the crack in the door. He was so handsome she wished she were fifteen too, then he would notice her.

When Bea trotted down the stairs she looked completely different to the scruffy nanny who had helped Federica out of her clothes that winter day when she had fallen through the ice. She was dressed to go out in a very tight black dress with high stiletto shoes and a froth of wild blonde curls that bounced as she walked. Her face was painted like a doll with thick black eyelashes and shiny red lipstick. 'What do you want, Hester?' she asked, leaning over the banisters. 'I'm about to go out.'

'We wanted you to light a fire for us,' said Hester.

'Well, I can hardly do it dressed like this, can I?' she replied and smiled sympathetically.

'Sam won't do it.'

'Why not?'

'Because he's reading.'

'For goodness' sake, he's been reading all day. Where is he?'

'In the sitting room,' said Hester, watching as Bea tottered passed them to confront Sam.

Sam sighed and raised his eyes above his book with impatience. When he saw Bea towering over him with her long naked legs strapped into shiny black stilettos he put the book down and sat up in amazement. 'Sam, can't you tear yourself away from your book for five minutes and light the girls a fire?' she said, but Sam wasn't listening. He was watching her scarlet lips and imagining what they could do for him.

'Sorry?' he stammered, shaking his head in order to shatter the image he had conjured up.

'I said, please can you light the girls a fire?' Bea repeated impatiently.

'Yes, of course,' he replied beneficently.

Bea straightened up. That was easy, she thought to herself in surprise. Usually it was impossible to get Sam to do anything he didn't want to do. 'Thank you, Sam,' she said, self-consciously pulling her skirt down her thighs as Sam's eyes crept up it.

'My pleasure, Bea,' he replied, regaining his composure. 'You look very nice tonight, where are you going?'

'To the pub with friends,' she replied unsteadily.

'Well, you'll outshine them all,' he mused appreciatively.

'Thank you.'

'Make sure you're escorted, I wouldn't trust any man to keep his hands to himself with a dress like that,' he said and smirked at her. Her face flushed.

'Really, Sam,' she muttered, pulling it down again. 'Is it too short?'

'Not too short, Bea. In fact, it's too long,' he replied, imagining what she would look like without a dress on at all.

'You're too young to make comments like that.' She laughed and walked out of the room with faltering steps. 'There you go, girls, Sam will light your fire,' she said.

Sam overheard and chuckled to himself. Given half the chance he'd light *her* fire.

Chapter Fourteen

It was late when Bea crept across the shadows and into her bedroom. She didn't want to wake the children by turning on the light on the landing so she let the moonlight guide her. She had drunk too much wine and flirted too much with the strange men in the pub. It didn't matter, weekends were for having fun. After all, the rest of the week she was tied to the nursery and all girls needed to let their hair down every now and then. She closed the door quietly and slipped out of her heels, kicking them across the room.

'Ouch!' came a voice in the corner as one of the flying shoes met with flesh. Bea caught her breath and stood as rigid as a dog that has just smelt danger. With a trembling hand she felt across the wall for the light switch. 'Don't turn on the light,' continued the voice, now so close she could feel his breath on her neck.

'Sam!' she gasped in relief. 'What are you doing in here?'

'I had a nightmare,' he said and she could detect a grin sweep across his face.

'Go back to bed,' she stammered, trying to blink herself back to sobriety. Sam ran a finger up her neck. She shrugged him off. 'For God's sake, Sam. What are you doing?'

'Don't pretend you don't know,' he whispered.

'You're a child,' she protested.

'Well, teach me then.'

'I can't,' she said and giggled at the absurdity of their conversation.

'Why not?'

'Because I'll get the sack.'

'No you won't.'

'I will.'

'Who'll tell?'

'I don't know that you can be trusted,' she replied coyly.

'So it's not that you don't want to then?' he said and placed his lips on the soft flesh where her neck met her shoulders. She shivered with a pleasure she wished she had more strength to resist.

'You're a boy,' she repeated weakly.

He took her hand and placed it on his trousers. 'Is this the behaviour of a boy?' he asked.

She felt the solid evidence of his desire and giggled again, more out of nervousness than merriment. 'I suppose not.' She chuckled.

'I'm ready for you,' he breathed into her ear.

Bea couldn't help but find the situation amusing. She suppressed her laughter. 'I'll bet you don't know what to do with it,' she said, gently squeezing it with her hand.

'I'd like you to show me,' he said. Suddenly Bea felt like a temptress and she liked the sense of power it gave her. The wine had made her reckless, dulled her reasoning so that tomorrow seemed another lifetime and tonight a magical limbo in which anything was possible. She turned and allowed him to kiss her. As his wet mouth descended onto hers she forgot that he was a fifteen-year-old boy, the son of her employers. He kissed like a man. It was only when they fell onto her bed that she was jolted back to reality. He was hard and energetic and yet he was ignorant of the complex labyrinth of the female body. After the initial kiss she lifted his fumbling hand off her breast and resolved to teach him how to make love like a man.

The following morning Bea was thankful it was Sunday so that she could spend the entire morning in bed. Before Sam had returned to his room in the early hours he had boasted that he could have gone on all night and probably all weekend. She had believed him. He was a quick learner and like any child with a new toy had been reluctant to put it away and go to bed. She smiled to herself in that pleasant heavy-eyed limbo between consciousness and unconsciousness and recalled with pride her eager student who by five o'clock in the morning had mastered the art of a soft touch, a slow kiss but not quite managed the patient restraint. That would come, she thought to herself, with maturity. Then she panicked as she remembered he was only fifteen years old and she sunk deeper beneath the blankets.

She was awoken a short time later by a sensual licking of the spaces between her toes. She writhed in her sleep as a warm sensation crept up her legs and into her belly. When the feeling of a wet mouth on her thigh became too intense to be imaginary she managed to open her eyes and peer down her body. 'Sam. Not now,' she protested and rolled over.

But he persisted. 'You can't send me away, I know how you like it. You can't resist me,' he said, running his hand over her naked leg.

'Just watch me,' she replied, pulling the pillow over her head. But Sam was right. She was defenceless. He knew her vulnerable places and how to stimulate them. She was powerless against the responses of her body in spite of her mind that cried out for more sleep. She allowed him to coax her onto her back where she feigned reluctance as he practised the lessons of the night before.

Sam could think of nothing but sex. Seducing Bea had had the opposite effect to the one he had hoped for. Instead of toning down his lust it had only intensified it. He was now less able to concentrate on his studies than before and spent most of the day gazing out of the classroom window imagining what he was going to do to Bea when he next saw her. The fact that it was illicit made the whole affair irresistible. He enjoyed sitting across the breakfast table having sneaked out of her bed only a few minutes before, talking to her with his usual indifference, relishing the fact that no one knew of their nocturnal adventures.

He took her wherever possible whenever they found them-selves alone. Behind the pool house, in the barn, beneath the apple trees in the orchard, down on the beach or in the hidden caves that still echoed with the urgent whispers of long-dead smugglers. Bea worked hard in the day looking after Lucien and Joey, who needed constant supervision and entertainment, then serviced their elder brother through the night. She was exhausted but she couldn't refuse him. He gave her too much pleasure.

Sam didn't boast about it at school. He didn't need to. He had changed and the other boys sensed it and admired him for it. Ingrid was too vague to notice her weary nanny or the self-satisfied expression on the face of her eldest son. Inigo rarely left his study and the girls were too preoccupied with their childish games to pay attention to their little brothers' nanny. They considered themselves too grown up for a nanny.

'Come down to the orchard with me,' Sam suggested, running a finger up the inside of Bea's forearm.

'I can't. I should listen out for the boys in case they need me,' she replied, withdrawing her arm.

'They've never needed you before. They're asleep,' he retorted, smelling the sweat on her body and feeling once again the ache in his groin.

'It's not safe. Anyone could discover us.'

'Don't be silly. Mum's on the cliff painting, Dad's in his study where he always is, the girls are at Federica's house and Nuno, well, who cares about Nuno.' He chuckled.

'I don't want this to get out of hand,' she said, trying to sound sensible. 'You're just a boy.'

'You've made me into a man,' he teased.

'I shouldn't have done.'

'Well, nothing can stop me now. I desire you.'

'You desire anything in a skirt and I'm the closest thing available,' she replied.

'That's not true, Bea. I like you. I really do,' he said, trying to sweet talk her into the orchard.

'Sure.'

'I do. Look,' he said, taking her hand and putting it on his trousers.

Bea sighed and smiled at him fondly. 'There's more to

relationships than him,' she said, shaking her head and retracting her hand.

'Don't pretend you don't want him. You taught him how to satisfy you. Now he can't get enough of you. Doesn't that make you feel desired?'

'Yes,' she conceded. 'But I have to keep reminding myself that you're only fifteen.'

'Almost sixteen, actually.'

'It doesn't matter. Sometimes you're so adult you could be any one of my friends. But you're not.'

'Does it matter?' he asked. Bea wanted to tell him that she was falling in love with him, that she lay awake at night pondering on the ten-year age difference and trying to figure out how a real relationship might work. But she knew in her heart that he wanted her only for sex and that he didn't love her. He wasn't even in love with her. He'd grow up and be off, breaking hearts all over the country, she thought wistfully. She gazed into his shallow grey eyes that had yet to deepen with the experiences of life and onto his mop of sandy hair that fell over his trouble-free forehead. His grin was mischievous with the charm of a monkey and yet his gaze was lofty, as if he knew he was cleverer and more beautiful than everyone else.

She sighed and ran a hand down his cheek. 'I may as well enjoy you while I can,' she conceded, smiling at him thought-fully. He returned her smile with a twinkle in his eye as he followed her down the stairs and out into the garden.

It was evening. The scent of hay lingered in the cool air as the dew stitched her diamonds into the freshly mown lawn and surrounding flowerbeds. The sky was pale and receding as the sun was chased away by an impatient moon. The distant roar of the ocean and the sad cry of seagulls faded into the background as Sam opened the gate into the walled orchard and pulled Bea into his arms to kiss her. She had no time to savour the melancholy of the twilight or taste the scent of ripe apples, for at once Sam was pressed up against her, his mouth on her neck and her shoulders and then on her breasts that he released from her brassiere with one swift movement of his fingers.

He liked her breasts. They were large and soft like the marshmallows Molly and Hester were always roasting over fires. Pale, pink and pert, they were always enthusiastic, always responsive. He knew how to run his tongue around them. She liked it gentle. She barely liked to feel anything at all except a rapid teasing sensation that she had told him sent the blood rushing straight to her belly. She was large and curvaceous, all woman, every bit of her, and he enjoyed exploring again and again those female places that never ceased to fascinate him. She released him from his trousers to find he was as alert and impatient as ever. Falling to her knees she took him in her mouth with the enthusiasm of a woman desperate to do anything to keep her man. It was at that moment that Nuno trotted up from the other end of the orchard on the balls of his feet. Neither Sam nor Bea noticed him for his footsteps were light and his amusement such that he didn't want to disturb the sensual scene being played out before him.

Sam stood with his eyelids fluttering with pleasure, his mouth open, his jaw loose. Nuno thought he looked quite beautiful, like a golden youth from mythical times, a young Adonis or Hercules. He turned discreetly to face the rose bed while his grandson reached the *moment critique*, he didn't want to ruin the boy's pleasure. He felt immensely proud that his grandson had discovered the joys of the flesh. About time too, he thought, it must have been the influence of Zola's *Nana* that stirred his budding sensuality.

Sam gave a moan and then a long, satisfied sigh. Bea giggled and got to her feet. Then Nuno turned around and coughed, loudly. ' "The only way to get rid of a temptation is to yield to it," ' he said, then raised his thick grey eyebrows at Sam.

'Oscar Wilde,' said Sam dutifully.

'*Molto bene, caro.* Now you have yielded perhaps Miss Osborne had better return to the nursery.'

Bea nodded numbly and ran through the gate without so much as a parting glance. Her face burned so red it throbbed. She was mortified. She wanted to die of embarrassment. But Nuno was greatly amused.

'Come with me, young Samuel. I think I have to adapt your reading list,' he said, wandering out of the gate that Bea had left swinging on its hinges.

Once in his library Nuno stood before the dusty bookshelves, running his hand over the spines of his beloved books. 'These give me much pleasure, Samuel. My admiration for women was shattered when I discovered they were not as perfect as the ancient Greek sculptures I studied as a boy.'

'How come?' Sam asked, throwing himself into his grandfather's leather sofa.

'I only made love to your grandmother once.'

'Really? You must have been fertile, Nuno.' He chuckled.

'Indeed I was, as luck, or the Gods, would have it. No, my dear boy, when I discovered women had pubic hair they toppled for ever from the heavenly pedestal I had so innocently placed them upon.'

Sam laughed. 'All because of pubic hair? You can't have believed women to be literally like those sculptures?' he said in amazement.

His grandfather pulled out a couple of books and lovingly stroked their covers. 'Indeed I did, Samuel. They were never quite the same after that.'

'Poor Grandma.'

'She was devoted to me. Devoted. You'll learn that the pleasures of the flesh, the entwining of loins, the stimulation of the genitalia,' he said, clipping his words for emphasis, 'are nothing more than illusions, dear boy. False love. You lose yourself in them momentarily, then they are gone and you are left lusting after the next fleeting pleasure. You can chase it all your life, but you can never hold onto it. No, dear boy, love is something more profound. That is how your grandmother loved me. Not like an animal but like a divine being. Yes, a divine being. *Ecco,*' he said, handing Sam the books.

Sam took them and eyed them suspiciously. 'Casanova's *Memoirs* and Oscar Wilde's *The Picture of Dorian Gray,*' he read.

'The first will teach you about the joys of the flesh, the second will teach you not to abuse them,' said Nuno wisely.

'Thank you,' said Sam, getting up.

'Sexual pleasure can be a weapon as well as a wand, young Samuel. Use it well.'

'You won't tell Mum, will you?' Sam said, hovering by the door, shuffling his feet.

'It's your business, dear boy, but might I suggest you keep your loving to the dark hours when there is no chance of someone walking in on you.' He turned back to his books.

'"Love ceases to be a pleasure when it ceases to be a secret,"' replied Sam, grinning smugly.

'Aphra Behn, *The Lover's Watch*,' said Nuno pompously, without turning around. 'It is still a secret from the rest of the household, dear boy. Enjoy it,' he added, and smiled proudly because he had taught his grandson to appreciate literature.

Helena stood at her bedroom window and watched Federica playing in the garden with Hester and Molly. She was glad that Federica had settled into their new home. Her first term at school had been a great success. Hester had taken Federica under her wing and made her feel part of their family, which was what Federica needed, a large, loud family to take her mind off her absent father. When the term had finished they had spent many long afternoons on the beach, building sandcastles, picnicking on the cliff, exploring caves and listening to Jake's old smuggling stories. Uncle Toby had taken her out in his boat with Julian and taught her how to fish, except that Toby always threw them back into the water again. He hated to hurt any living creature. Federica had developed a crush on Sam Appleby, which didn't surprise Helena at all, Sam was a very beautiful young man. At least that took her mind off her father. All to the good, she thought. But what of her?

Helena was tied to the house, looking after Hal. She had been mortified to read the letter Ramon had sent to Federica. She found she missed him in spite of her efforts and caught herself more than once recalling that strange moment in Viña when their impulses had overcome their reasoning and they had made love. She had then remembered discovering him in bed with Estella and felt that nauseating anger all over again, as if it had been yesterday. She had hoped that she would have left all her memories of Ramon in Chile, along with the sentimental nonsense collected during their first happy years together. But it was harder to let him go than she had predicted. He clung to her thoughts in order to torment her. As much as she tried to shake him off she was plagued by images of him. She wondered where he was, whether he ever thought about her, whether he would turn up one of these days and tell her that he had made a mistake, that he would fight for her after all, that he would make an effort to change. How could he love her and not fight for her? She couldn't understand him.

Then there were the children. She couldn't comprehend that someone could love their children and yet care so little for them. He had written once but he hadn't visited. It was now August. She often heard Federica listening to her butterfly box, miles away, riding on the mesmerising waves of her father's stories as if that would bring her closer to him. Suddenly she was overcome with the possibility that something ill might have happened to him. She hadn't considered that as a reason for his silence, she had been too busy blaming him for neglecting them. Defeated by guilt and remorse she pulled herself away from the window, lit a cigarette and dialled his parents' number in Santiago.

'*Hola*,' responded the maid in a distant voice. Helena tried to ignore the lengthy delay and asked to speak to Mariana. She waited with a constricted heart as Mariana came to the telephone.

'It's me, Helena,' she said, trying to sound buoyant.

'Helena. How nice to hear from you,' Mariana replied, her tone at once betraying her resentment. She had thought so often of her grandchildren, wondering how they were and whether they were happy in their new home. She had minded very much that they hadn't written. She had waited for their letters with growing impatience and disappointment. But she didn't want to reveal her feelings to Helena in case she put the telephone down and shut them out for ever.

'I haven't heard from Ramon since I left. Is he all right?' Helena asked quickly, but she could tell from her mother-in-law's voice that nothing dramatic had happened.

'Hasn't he called you?' said Mariana in surprise.

'No. He wrote to Fede,' she said weakly, trying not to get emotional. She wasn't meant to care any more.

'Is that all?'

'Yes.'

'Well, he's now back in Chile. He's bought an apartment here in Santiago. He's got a new book coming out next March, it's getting quite a lot of attention.'

'I see.'

'How are the children?'

'They're happy here. Of course they miss you both. They're enormously fond of you and Nacho. So am I,' she said, inhaling the cigarette held with a trembling hand. Suddenly she felt a stomach-wrenching homesickness that took her by surprise.

'Are you happy?' Mariana asked, sensing her daughter-in-law's distress across the wire.

Helena paused. She wanted to say that she was happy, but she didn't know whether she was or not. She only knew that for some strange reason she missed Ramon and needed to hear from him. 'Yes,' she replied impassively.

'I am pleased,' said Mariana, not convinced.

'It's just taking a while to get used to living here again,' she said. 'I'm lonely,' she added to her amazement, then wondered where the devil that had come from.

'You'll settle in. It's a big thing starting all over again in a new country. Sometimes the grass is greener on the other side until you discover that your problems follow you wherever you go.'

'Yes,' Helena replied automatically. Suddenly she realised that Mariana was right. Her problems had followed her to Polperro.

She was still lonely. Still dissatisfied. She had believed that coming home would change everything, that she would be able to return to her childhood, to that idyllic state before responsibility and domesticity had changed her.

'You don't often know what you have until you have lost it,' Mariana added gravely. 'What shall I tell Ramon?' She still hoped they might see sense and realise that what they had was worth holding on to.

'Tell him that his children miss him. Tell him to call or write or, better still, to come and visit,' she said, unable to prevent the bitterness from seeping into her words. 'Tell him not to desert them because they need him.'

'And what about you, *mi amor*?'

'Nothing. I'm calling for the sake of the children,' she retorted flatly.

'*Bueno*. I'll tell him,' she replied. 'Please send the children all our love, we miss them terribly. Perhaps they could write, we would love to hear from them.'

'Of course. I'm so sorry. My mind has been elsewhere,' said Helena guiltily and made a mental note to get the children to paint pictures of their new home for them.

When Helena put the telephone down she sank into an armchair and watched the shadows edge their way into the room and into her head, where they grew, casting doubt into her mind. Had she perhaps been too hasty? She tormented herself with memories of Chile. Having despised it she now longed for it. She thought of her friends, the sunshine, the beach, the smell of the orange trees in the garden, the sound of children playing in the street, the barking of Señora Baraca's dog. She remembered the days when Ramon would return home to her outstretched arms, carrying her straight up to their bedroom where they would lie for hours discovering each other again after long weeks of separation. Those had been happy times. He had even managed to satisfy her when she had hated him. Such was the power of his nature. She had been eaten up with bitterness because she had been unable to possess it, to tame it. Here she was now, the other side of the world, still longing to possess him. She didn't dare ask herself whether she might have brought her children to England in order to get him to react, because he hadn't reacted in the way that she had hoped he would. He had let her go. So now what?

When she turned out Federica's light she told her that she had spoken to Abuelita, that she had sent her love and that she wanted her to paint her a picture of her new home. At first Federica had been pleased. She closed her eyes and imagined the picture she would draw and the letter she would write. But then she felt her heart lurch with longing. She remembered her grandmother's gentle face, the summer house in Cachagua that she loved so much, the navy sea and the soft sand so unlike the sand in England. She remembered her grandfather in his panama hat, the horse ride on Papudo beach and Rasta. Then she recalled her mother's promise of a puppy and she began to cry. Not because she hadn't been given a puppy but because the promise had been made to distract her from the argument she had overheard. 'Now you won't have to come home ever again.' Her mother's words echoed about her head until it throbbed with pain. Finally, when she could no longer bear her desolation she opened the butterfly box on her bedside table and allowed her mind to drift into the secret world of her father's stories. The pain began to subside as she floated across the Andes mountains, chased lions in Africa and sailed high above the plains of Argentina in a hot air balloon. As she drifted off to sleep she felt the sun on her face and the heat on her body and basked in her father's love.

Chapter Fifteen

Santiago, Chile

When Mariana told Ramon that she had spoken to Helena, he felt his stomach churn with guilt. He had only written once and he hadn't telephoned, even though he could well afford the expense of the call. He knew he should have. The only explanation he could give was that he had been busy travelling. Too busy finishing his book. In reality he had deliberately lost himself in India. He had rented a shack on the beach and written his novel. He had tried to forget Helena and the children. He had tried to forget Estella. He had succeeded in the former because things didn't feel very different. He was used to being alone on his travels so as far as that was concerned nothing much had changed. But Estella was a different matter altogether. He missed her all the time.

In spite of his apparent neglect his conscience was alerted to the misery he might be causing her. He had told her to wait and he had no doubt that she *was* waiting for him, dutifully, in the kitchen, chopping vegetables, floating through the house leaving the warm scent of roses as she went about her chores. He didn't want to telephone her or write to her, he didn't know what to say. He couldn't say what she wanted to hear, because he knew he could never commit to anyone ever again. He had hurt Helena and the children and he didn't want to do the same to Estella. Perhaps he would return in the summer and make love to her again.

When he considered the possibility of Estella falling in love with someone else the jealousy rose in his stomach like an uncontrollable demon to take possession of his mind and torment him to the point where he nearly packed his few belongings and returned to Cachagua to claim her. But then his reasoning had assuaged him. She loved him and a woman in love was as faithful as a dog. So he spent unsatisfactory nights loving strangers, imagining they were Estella, no longer possessed by the demon but looking forward to returning in the summer to find her again.

When he returned to Chile at the end of August he went directly to Santiago where he moved into his new apartment in the barrio of Las Condes. But it didn't feel like home. In fact, he longed for Viña and he longed for his family. He was bereft without them. Suddenly, after having spent months on his own in India, he was no longer comfortable with himself. He wasn't used to a solitary existence in Chile and it just didn't feel right. So he partially moved into his parents' colonial house in Avenida el Bosque. His mother was delighted to see more of him and took over the domestic side of his life like an adoring wife. His father was less enthusiastic.

'He's got a wife, woman. He's too old to need his mother,' he growled one evening when he came home to find the sitting room carelessly cluttered with Ramon's camera equipment, piles of prints and other belongings.

'Nacho, *mi amor*, he's going through a painful time. He's lonely on his own,' she protested, following him into his study.

'Well, why doesn't he ask Helena to come back? It's very simple. But if you're always there for him he won't make the effort.'

'He doesn't know what he wants,' she said, her voice dripping with pity.

'He wants the bread and the cake, Mariana. I don't know where we went wrong, but for some reason he is unable to commit to anything.' He shook his head dismissively. 'He didn't want Helena to leave him, but he wasn't prepared to change his ways for her or ask her to stay. He would have liked everything to tick on as always like a familiar although somewhat tiresome clock. I don't blame her for leaving him, though I suspect she had hoped she might force his hand.'

'What do you mean?' Mariana asked slowly, sitting down on the worn armchair that Ignacio used for reading in the evenings after dinner.

'I think she hoped that by leaving him he might be forced to change in order to keep her. I hoped he might make the effort. But he's an avoider. He let it happen and then disappeared for months to pretend it hadn't. That's why he's come home to live with us, because he misses them now he's back in Chile.'

'I wouldn't have believed you had I not had that strange call. I think Helena misses him too.' She recalled Helena's strained tone of voice and now recognised it as an unspoken cry for help.

'I bet she does.'

'Do you think she regrets leaving?'

'The grass is always greener.'

'Perhaps not as green as she had hoped.'

'Perhaps not.'

'We have to force him to question what he has done. Something's got to jolt sense into him. He hasn't quite grasped the seriousness of it all. He just can't treat people in this way. Someone's got to teach him the value of life.'

'You're right,' she said, lowering her eyes. 'What do you want me to do, Nacho? Turn him away?'

'That would be the best thing. He's not going to miss his wife if you're buzzing around him looking after him.' He noticed the dejected expression in his wife's grey eyes. He sighed and shook his head again. 'I'm not going to insist that you do it. How can I? You're his mother.'

'I want what's best for him,' she said and pulled a thin smile.

'Then tell him he can't move back in with us.'

Mariana laughed bitterly. 'Oh no, Nacho, I'm not going to tell him. It's your idea so you tell him.' She left the room.

*   *   *

Ramon arrived on time for dinner. Ignacio rolled his eyes at his wife as if silently to indicate his exasperation at his son's ever-increasing presence in their house. Mariana pretended she hadn't noticed and poured Ramon a glass of whisky on the rocks. 'There you are, Ramon, have you had a busy day?' she asked kindly. But Ignacio spoke before Ramon had time to.

'Have you decided what you're going to do about Helena, son?' Ignacio sank into an easy chair opposite Ramon who managed to take up most of the sofa with his long legs and arms. Ramon sipped at his whisky as if playing for time. Ever since childhood he had been unable to avoid his father's questions and he still felt pathetically weak every time he answered them, like an obedient schoolboy.

'I think my next trip will be to England, Papa,' he said, trying not to give too much away.

'When will you go?' he persisted.

'Oh I don't know, perhaps in a couple of months,' he replied vaguely.

'A couple of months? Why can't you go sooner?'

'Ramon is very busy with his work,' Mariana interrupted in her son's defence.

'I'm not asking you, woman,' said Ignacio firmly. 'Ramon is old enough to answer his own questions. For God's sake, you're forty years old.'

'Forty-one,' said Ramon and grinned at his mother.

'Exactly. You're a man. You should have settled down by now, not be wandering the globe like a gypsy.'

Ramon wanted to tell his father to mind his own business, but then he remembered that he was virtually living in their house so he had a right to know his plans. 'I'd like to spend some time in Cachagua, start a few projects. The weather's getting nicer now . . .'

'You can take the house,' Ignacio said breezily. 'It's yours when you want it,' he added, avoiding the confused expression that had alighted across Mariana's face.

'But there's no one to look after him,' Mariana protested, still frowning.

'What about Estella?' Ramon asked quickly. He then checked himself to avoid showing too much. He knew his father well enough to know that the slightest change in the tone of his voice would be noticed and analysed.

'Oh poor, dear Estella,' Mariana sighed, dropping her shoulders. 'That dear child, she was such a sweet girl. No one looked after the house like she did. I don't know what we'll do without her.' She looked at Ignacio accusingly. Ramon's eyes darted from his mother to his father, aware that his heart had plummeted to his stomach, leaving only a throbbing anxiety in its place.

'It had to be done, woman. She can't look after us and a baby at the same time,' he replied, shrugging off her accusations. 'Ramon, she's pregnant.'

'Pregnant?' Ramon repeated slowly.

'Pregnant,' said Mariana. 'Poor child. You know that young man she was seeing last summer in Cachagua?' Ramon nodded gravely. 'Well, the fool got her pregnant then ran off.'

'It happens all the time, Mariana,' Ignacio argued wearily.

'But I liked her. She didn't deserve to be treated like that. She was a good girl, not one of those women of easy virtue that hang about the port in Valparaíso. She was too trusting. I'd wring that boy's neck if I ever got the chance.'

'So where is she now?' Ramon asked, feeling sick in the stomach and dizzy in the head. He drained his glass and swallowed uncomfortably.

'Ignacio sent her back to Zapallar,' said Mariana in a clipped voice.

'I said she could come back when she's had the baby. Perhaps her mother can look after it during the day when she works,' Ignacio said with forced patience.

'I know, but she was so upset. You know, Ramon, she believed he'd come back. He told her he would and she believed him. I didn't want to shatter her hopes so I just agreed with her. But as far as I know there's no sign of him. *Dios mio*, the indignity of it all.' She sighed again.

'Did she tell you the man's name?' Ramon asked carefully.

'No, she wouldn't say. She was too ashamed, no doubt.'

'Enough, woman, my head is spinning,' Ignacio said with irritation. 'Ramon can have the house. If he wants a maid he can look for one.'

'Temporary, of course. Estella may come back and I'd like to leave the job open for her,' Mariana repeated anxiously.

'That's fine by me,' said Ignacio. 'When do you want to go?'

'Tomorrow morning,' Ramon replied automatically. His mind was whirring like the internal machinations of a clock. 'I'll just go and wash my hands before dinner.' When he looked at himself in the mirror he noticed his features had completely drained of colour leaving his complexion grey and sallow. He rubbed his cheeks with his fingers in order to encourage the blood to return, but it was useless, his shock showed all over his face.

'Why are you giving him the house?' Mariana asked her husband while Ramon was out of the room. 'I thought you were going to tell him not to live with us any more.'

'Because time alone at the summer house might just remind him of his wife and children. He may find his senses out there on the coast. I don't know. I'm clutching at straws, woman, but maybe the sea and the sunshine will remind him of the good times he shared with Helena, before it all went wrong.'

Mariana placed an affectionate hand on her husband's arm and smiled at him reassuringly. 'We suffer almost more than he does,' she said, remembering Federica and Hal with sadness.

'For sure we suffer more than him. That's the trouble, he doesn't suffer at all,' said Ignacio. 'Quiet now, I can hear him coming.'

When Ramon returned to the sitting room his parents were already standing up and moving slowly into the dining room. Mariana looked at him and smiled sympathetically. Ignacio was less tactful. 'Are you all right, son, you look pale?'

'No, I'm fine,' Ramon replied flatly.

'Look, I understand this has not been an easy time for you. I just think you've been avoiding the issue.'

'I haven't, Papa, I think about Helena and the children all the time,' he lied.

'Then why don't you go and see them? What are you afraid of?'

'I'm not afraid. Helena needs time on her own,' he began.

'For God's sake, son, that's the problem, she's been on her own far too long,' Ignacio interrupted edgily.

'She needs time to settle into Polperro. The last thing she needs is me whipping her up again.'

'Then write to the children, call them from time to time, be a father, Ramon. Don't avoid your responsibility.'

'I think of that dear little Federica and how much she loves you, *mi amor*. Your father is right. You mustn't neglect them,' Mariana said, touching her son's forearm and patting it fondly.

When Ramon set off the next morning for Cachagua, Helena, Federica and Hal could not have been further from his mind. All he could think about was Estella. He had spent a tormented night fighting off the demons of guilt and remorse that had flown about his bed, pinching him and pulling him, making sleep an impossibility. He had fought them off by trying to focus on the new book he was going to write, but Estella had kept surfacing to the top of his mind like a rosebud in a pond that refused to sink.

At first he had tried to convince himself that the child wasn't his, but that was useless wishful thinking. There was no mistaking that the child was his, it couldn't have been anyone else's, not only because of the timing which confirmed the summer conception, but because he knew Estella. She wasn't the type to sleep around. That in itself made him wince. He had seduced her and then abandoned her. That would have been bad enough, but he had abandoned her with child. Even he was repulsed by his own conduct. He had longed for morning, but every time he had looked at his clock it was always only a few minutes on from the previous time. He would have gone there and then had it not been for the curfew that prohibited anyone from leaving their houses between two and six a.m. Finally, when dawn had torn apart the night's sky and the light had poured in, he had grabbed his bag, clambered into the car and set off. It was six in the morning.

It was only when he caught sight of himself in the rear mirror that he realised he hadn't shaved or washed his face. He looked like a tramp with long knotted black hair, a dark shadow across his face and weary, bloodshot eyes. He would normally have stopped along the way, had a cup of coffee or a lemon soda, then he could have splashed his face with water and wet his hair, but he didn't have time. He didn't want to leave Estella alone for another minute. He pressed his foot on the accelerator pushing the limit as far as he could go without risking being caught by the police for speeding. When he arrived finally at Zapallar he hurriedly parked the car and strode out into the bright morning sunshine.

He didn't know where to look. He didn't even know Estella's last name to ask, and anyhow he didn't want the entire village to know about it. He would surely be recognised by someone. He wandered up the beach hoping that perhaps she might be there, that perhaps he might pass her on her way to buy the bread or simply taking a stroll. But there was no sign of anyone. An early spring was beginning to inject the surrounding trees and bushes with a new vitality and the air was distinctly warmer. He half expected to smell her scent of roses and follow it until he found her. But that was the kind of romantic notion he might have written into one of his novels, it wasn't real life. After walking up and down the beach for a while he realised that he would simply have to ask someone. He'd have to describe her and risk the whole village knowing about it. There was no other way. He was desperate.

When he saw an old man sitting on a bench gazing out to sea he suppressed his embarrassment and approached him. 'Good morning, Señor. I'm looking for a young woman called Estella. She's heavily pregnant, long black hair, down to her waist, about so high,' he said, indicating her height with his hand. The man eyed him bleakly through tiny black eyes that watered and blinked at him dispassionately. He leant with brown leathery hands on a knobbly wooden stick and chewed on his gums for he had no teeth to grind. 'She lives with her parents, must be about twenty or so. She used to work in Cachagua. She's very beautiful,' he continued, then sighed in disappointment. 'You'd recognise this description if you knew her,' he added, turning away. The man continued to chew without muttering a word. Then something prompted Ramon to add that she smelt of roses and suddenly life returned to the old man and he began to mumble something about her scent reminding him of his mother's funeral.

'They buried her in a grave full of rose petals,' he said wistfully. 'They said it would soothe her in the event of her waking up and not knowing where she was.' He turned and cast his eyes over to where Ramon was standing hopefully in the shade of a eucalyptus tree. 'Your Estella lives up the road, about half a kilometre, on the hill overlooking the sea. You'll recognise the house because it's yellow,' he said, nodding to himself. 'Whenever I go to the cemetery I can still smell them. One day I'll go there and never come back.'

'One day we'll all go there and never come back,' Ramon said to the old man's astonishment. He didn't think the young man was still there. He waited for Ramon to go before he continued his solitary conversation about the dead.

Ramon walked up the hill with hasty strides. It was still early. A light mist smudged the edges where the sea joined the sky so that they merged into one shimmering blue horizon. As he looked about him for the yellow house he remembered those lazy days the summer before when he had loved Estella without distraction, without guilt, without remorse and without this terrible fear of entrapment.

When he saw the house he stood on the dusty track and watched. It was still and shaded beneath the budding trees that were beginning to reveal the almost phosphorescent green of their new leaves. The house was a small bungalow with about two or three rooms. It was neatly kept with a little garden that looked well tended and cared for. He could hear a dog barking in the distance and the staccato voice of a mother berating her child that sent a ripple of commotion through the sleepy village. He continued to watch but still nothing moved. Finally impatience led him to her door where he stood anxiously and knocked. He heard a light rustle of movement come from within. For a moment he panicked that he might have got the wrong house, but then he smelt the heavy scent of roses waft through the open window and he knew she was there and his heart inflated in his chest.

When Estella opened the door and saw Ramon towering over her like a wolf, blocking out the light, her face went white before the blood was pumped urgently around her arteries in an effort to revive her. She would have cried out but she had no voice, it was lost along with her reasoning. She blinked and then blinked again. When she was sure that it was indeed Ramon who stood in front of her and not some apparition inspired by the herbs her mother gave her for her pregnancy, she threw her arms about his neck and allowed him to sweep her off her feet and carry her into the cool interior of the house.

He laid her gently on her small bed and gazed down at her adoring face that glowed with happiness. 'I knew you'd come back,' she sighed, running a soft hand over the rough bristle on his face. Falling into her beautiful features he was suddenly filled with confusion and wondered what had possessed him to leave her. What had possessed him to fear her? As he kissed her grateful lips he believed he would never leave her again. He breathed in her unique smell and tasted the salt on her skin. Then he placed a hand under her white cotton nightdress and over the swell of her naked belly.

'This is my child,' he said and was certain he felt a life stir within. Estella smiled the smile unique to expectant mothers, tender yet proud and fiercely protective.

'If he is a boy we shall call him Ramon,' she said.

'And if it's a girl, Estellita,' he replied and buried his face in her neck.

'So you are not angry?' she asked, looking up at him timidly.

'No, I'm very happy,' he said truthfully, surprised by his own reaction. 'I'm sorry I—'

'Don't be sorry, my love,' she said, placing her finger across his lips to silence him. 'You've returned as I knew you would and I'm contented.'

He kissed her finger and then the palm of her hand, up her arm and finally on her heavy swollen breasts. 'I want to see you naked,' he said suddenly, overwhelmed by the sensuality of her fulsome body. He unbuttoned her nightdress with trembling hands and pulled it over her head, then he sat back to admire her.

Estella lay proudly before him watching his eyes as they traced the voluptuous curves of her new body. She was like a shiny, plump seal. Her skin was glossy and smooth and glowed with an internal ripeness that lit her up from within. He wanted to lose himself in her and yet didn't dare for fear of hurting her or his child. So he kissed her shoulders and her breasts, her belly down to her feet. 'I want to take you away from here, Estella,' he said, kissing her lips again.

'I don't want to leave Zapallar, Ramon. Not until after the baby is born.'

'Then at least come and live with me in Cachagua, then we can think about what to do.'

'What about your parents?' she asked with a shudder.

'They won't be coming up until October. It'll be just you and me.'

Estella didn't need to be persuaded, she had already envisaged every possibility over the last six months. It was what she wanted. 'Just you and me,' she said, smiling with pleasure.

Chapter Sixteen

Estella had grown strong over the last six months, ever since she had been fired by Don Ignacio. She had returned to her parents in Zapallar and told them about the dark bear of a man who had stolen her heart and left a part of him growing inside her womb. Her mother had wept copious tears. Her father had thumped his fist against the wall leaving a large hole in the plaster that still remained months later as they didn't have the time or money for repairs. He had vowed that if he ever laid eyes on the scoundrel he would personally cut off his penis with a carving knife. 'If he can't trust himself to use it properly, he shouldn't have it at all,' he bellowed, nursing his swollen hand. Estella had tried to convince them that he would come back to her. She told them he had promised and she believed him. But they gazed at her with wise eyes that had seen almost everything during the rough course of their long lives and shook their heads in despair.

Pablo and Maria Rega were almost too old to have a daughter of twenty-two. They had married young and tried for many years to have a child. But after her fragile womb rejected seven babies they had given up hope of ever having a family. More tears, more fist-bashing until finally they had resigned themselves, too weary to fight any more. Pablo had thrown himself into his work caring for the cemetery that overlooked the sea, talking to the unknown unfortunates who lay in the earth beneath his feet about his longing and his regret. 'They can't help me,' he told his wife, 'but they're good listeners.' Maria continued to work in the grand house of Don Carlos Olivos and his wife Señora Pilar, cleaning and cooking from dawn till dusk. She had always helped herself to food from his fridge, but when she had finally resigned herself to the fact that she simply wasn't made for producing children she had eaten to dull the pain and to fill the hours she would have spent thinking about her brood. When she was young they had called her 'Spaghetti' because she had been as thin and as fragile as a strand of pasta. But when she started eating she couldn't stop. Her misery clung to her body in the form of thick rolls of fat until she was so large she could barely climb the big staircase in Don Carlos's house without wheezing and holding onto the banisters for support. Pablo liked her better that way. He would mount her and lose himself in the rolling plains of her body. There was more of her to love.

Then one morning Maria had just managed to reach the top of the staircase after a long climb, during which she had had to pause on every other step in order to catch her breath, when she had fainted onto the floor, only to be discovered by Don Carlos's mistress, Serenidad, furtively leaving his bedroom on tiptoe. Serenidad would have liked to ignore the woman who lay on the wooden floorboards like a heaving ox, but her conscience overcame her revulsion and she called for her lover, fanning Maria with the wad of notes Don Carlos had given her to pay off her debts. So embarrassed was Don Carlos at having been discovered with his mistress that he sent Maria immediately to the private hospital in Valparaíso where she was informed by a kindly doctor that she was in labour. Don Carlos's chauffeur drove Pablo into Valparaíso to join his wife. They held hands as Maria pushed, but she didn't feel any pain or any discomfort. Their baby slid out of her body like a newborn seal, with silky brown skin, shiny black hair and the correct number of little fingers and little toes. Maria and Pablo were too in awe of the miracle to cry. They watched their child as if she were the first child ever to have been born into the world. 'She shall be called Estella,' said Maria with reverence, 'because she is a star loaned to us from the heavens.'

Maria lost weight. It didn't happen gradually, but within the short space of a month. She was never again the 'Spaghetti' of her youth, but Pablo liked her that way. Now he had two people to love.

★   ★   ★

Pablo had always found it difficult to communicate, even to his wife. So he talked to his subterranean dead – an ever-increasing audience – with a fluency that evaded him when he spoke to the living. He patted his favourite tombstone that marked the grave of Osvaldo Garcia Segundo who died in 1896 from a single shot in the head delivered by the man whose wife had meant to run away with him. The wife had killed herself afterwards, with the same gun. But her husband had refused to have her buried anywhere near her lover and threw her body into the sea. Pablo wondered whether Osvaldo Garcia Segundo could see her from where he was, high up there on the cliff. He hoped so. That story had always touched him. He now unburdened his worries about his daughter and the man who had not only stolen her heart but her future in one short, useless affair, because he felt that Osvaldo would understand.

'She'll never marry now, you know,' he said, tapping his fingers on the gravestone. 'Not now. Who'll have her? She's pretty enough, but her belly will put them all off. Who'd want another man's child? She believes this young man will come back, but you know that's not the way life is. I don't know who's been feeding her these romantic ideas but they'll come to no good. Mark my words. No good at all. I don't know what to do. Maria has flooded the house with her tears and I put my fist through the wall. What's going to become of us?' he sighed, remembering his little girl as a child and the pleasure she gave them. 'You give them everything you have, your possessions, you earnings, your love, your dreams and what do you get in return? Nothing but ingratitude,' he continued, staring out across the sea. 'Ingratitude.'

Estella had grown strong. She had temporarily sunk into despair after being dismissed from her job. But then she had pulled herself up by focusing on the two important things in her life – Ramon and her child. While she still believed he would come back for her she had the will-power to put her job behind her and think only of the future. She hadn't listened to the ranting of her parents. She had waited as Don Ramon had asked her to and all the while she waited she had considered her dreams, like a pharmacist weighing out medicine. Don Ramon would return, of that she had no doubt, but what would become of her? He was still married. She wouldn't want to go and live in the city; she had no desire for a glamorous life. She had no desire to see the world, either. She didn't want to tie him to a life that wouldn't suit him. She simply wanted to breathe the same air as him, make love to the distant roar of the ocean and bring up their child with love. She had longed for him to come back so that she could tell him she didn't want any more of him than that.

She had worked out his reservations from the conversations she had overheard between Don Ignacio and Señora Mariana as they discussed their 'irresponsible' son. Señora Mariana had been forgiving, explaining to her husband that Ramon was a free spirit, a being blessed with an unquenchable creativity. That explained why he couldn't stay in one place for very long, why he was incapable of being a proper husband and father to his wife and children. Don Ignacio's ears had throbbed with blood and he had sent his fist crashing onto the table, stating cuttingly that it was about time Ramon grew up and stopped behaving like a spoilt, petulant and selfish child. 'The world will continue to revolve without him setting it in motion with the burning soles of his feet, woman,' he had growled, 'but Helena and those children will be much the worse off without him.' Estella had vowed not to be like Helena. She would give him his freedom in return for his love.

Estella left Zapallar with Ramon, leaving a note for her parents telling them that her lover had returned as she always knew he would. Ramon had had no desire to meet them and Estella hadn't insisted; she worried that her father might carry out his threat. So they had returned to the summer house in Cachagua where the memories of their affair echoed off the walls to remind them of the way it was then, when they had made love in the dark hours, claiming the night for themselves, enjoying each other without a thought for the future. Now they had a future they had to wrench themselves out of the present and decide what they were going to do with it.

They walked up the beach. The sun had set leaving the coast cold and blustery. They held hands and reminisced about the summer before.

'I watched you swim that night you couldn't sleep,' said Estella, smiling. 'I couldn't sleep either, so I watched you from the shadows.'

'You did?'

'Yes, I watched you walk naked up the beach. I wanted you so much, I didn't know what to do with myself,' she said huskily.

'What are we going to do with you now?' he asked and his voice betrayed his uncertainty.

Estella sighed. 'I've spent the last six months preparing speeches for you. I planned what I would say when you came back, but I haven't told you any of it yet,' she said, looking down at her bare feet as they sank into the fine sand.

'I think I know what you want to say,' Ramon said, squeezing her hand.

'I don't think you do.'

'All women want the same things,' he said, as if it were an accusation.

'So what do all women want?'

'They want security. They want marriage, children and security,' he replied bleakly.

'You're not wrong. That's what I always wanted for myself. But then I met you and you're not like other men. So that's not what I want.'

'What do you want?' he asked in surprise.

Estella stopped walking and stood opposite him, looking at him steadily through the dusk. She put her hands in the pockets of her wool cardigan and shuffled her feet in preparation of giving the speech she had practised. 'I want your love and your protection,' she began. 'I want it for myself and for our child. I want him to know his father and to grow up with his love and guidance. But I don't want to chain you to a home. Travel the world and write your stories, but promise to come home to us every now and then. I will store up your kisses in my heart but once they run low you must come back to fill it up again. I don't want to find it empty.' She smiled at him as if she understood him better than he understood himself.

Ramon didn't know what to say. He had expected her to beg him to stay with her and not go away, as Helena had when Federica was born. But Estella blinked at him with confidence. He knew she meant it.

Pulling her into his arms, he kissed her temples and her cheekbone, breathing in her rose scent and feeling closer to her than ever before. He searched about the pit of his stomach for that familiar feeling of claustrophobia yet it was nowhere to be found. Estella was prepared to love him enough to give him his freedom. But neither had prepared themselves for the wrath of Pablo Rega.

Pablo and Maria had returned home at dusk to discover Estella's neatly written note.

He's come back for me like I promised you he would. Please don't be angry. I'll come back soon.

Pablo would have thumped his fist carelessly against the wall had it not been for his wife who threw herself between him and the hole he had left the previous time, begging him to calm himself and think rationally.

'It's a blessing he came for her,' she insisted, rubbing her hands together in anguish. 'No one else would have her.'

'How respectable can he be?' he argued furiously. 'He didn't even bother to ask for her hand in marriage.'

'Marriage?' stammered Maria.

'Of course. He can't plant his seed in her womb and not marry her.'

'Perhaps that's why he didn't want to meet us. Maybe he has no intention of marrying her.'

'He'll marry her. By God he'll marry her or I'll damn him to Hell!'

'Where are you going?' Maria cried, watching helplessly as her husband stalked out of the house.

'To find them,' he replied, climbing into his rusty truck and disappearing down the hill, leaving a thin cloud of dust behind him.

Pablo Rega didn't know where to start searching, he knew he just had to look or he'd go out of his mind with madness. He drove down the coast towards Cachagua. The sun hung low in the sky like a glowing peach, causing the ripples on the sea to glimmer with a warm pink light. He thought of his daughter and the miracle of her birth. He wasn't going to let some irresponsible ruffian ruin it all now. Not after they had sweated blood to raise her. As he neared the village of Cachagua he decided to ask at the house of her former employers, Don Ignacio and Señora Campione. He had no idea where to find her and their house was as good a place as any to start.

He drove down the sandy track into the village that sat in the quiet evening light, apparently deserted except for a three-legged mongrel that sniffed the ground hungrily. When he saw a car parked in the driveway of Don Ignacio's house his heart leapt in his chest – at least someone was home. If Estella needed help of any kind he was certain she would run to Señora Mariana whom she liked very much. He looked at his reflection in the mirror, licked his hand and smoothed it over his thin hair in an effort to make himself look respectable. Then he jumped out of the truck and dusted down his shirt and trousers. He did up the buttons as far as his chest, leaving the remaining few loose to expose the silver medallion of the Virgin Mary that he always hung about his neck for luck, and to protect him against the odd evil soul who cursed him in the cemetery. Then he inhaled deeply, remembering afterwards to hold his stomach in and his shoulders up, and made his way towards the front door.

He hesitated a moment before ringing the bell. The tall acacia trees towered over him like sentinels. The house was as big as a fortress. Suddenly he felt humbled and embarrassed that he had come at all. Besides, he wouldn't know what to say. The living muted him. He was about to turn and leave when he heard voices coming from the other side of the house. He stood and listened. There was no mistaking that the laughter was Estella's. She had a very distinctive laugh, like the bubbling of a merry river. Pablo loved that laugh more than any other sound on earth and he felt a suffocating fury grip his throat again. He clenched his fists and ground his teeth like a bull about to be taken on by the bullfighter. He rang the bell.

The laughter ceased immediately, dissolving into urgent whispers and the light patter of feet. Pablo rang the bell again. Then he waited completely still as if conserving all his energy for his fight. The door opened after a long pause and Don Ramon Campione stood in the doorway.

'Can I help you?' he asked politely. Pablo searched for the right words but he had never been very good at expressing himself in syllables to living people so he simply pulled his arm back and sent his fist crashing into the proud jaw of his adversary, sending the larger man reeling back into the house where he fell to the floor and glared up at Pablo Rega in astonishment.

'*Hijo de puta!*' he exclaimed, taking his hand away from his wound and examining the blood. 'What the hell was that for?' But he knew.

'Papa!' Estella cried. 'What have you done?' she gasped in horror when she saw Ramon stagger to his feet, his face dripping with blood.

'How dare you steal my little girl?' Pablo stammered angrily, his fist poised to hit him again.

'He didn't steal me, Papa, I came willingly. Didn't you get my note?' she interrupted in exasperation, bravely placing herself between her father and her lover. 'Enough, Papa,' she ordered. 'You've done enough!'

'Marry her, Señor!' Pablo pointed a threatening finger at Ramon, who looked down at the squat little man with impatience.

'There's the slight problem of me being married already,' said Ramon flippantly.

Pablo's face swelled crimson and his lips began to tremble. 'So what are you going to do?' he asked hoarsely, shaking his head incredulously.

'Papa, please come in and we can discuss this calmly,' said Estella, taking her father by the arm and leading him into the house. Ramon watched them walk through the hall and sitting room and out onto the terrace. He noticed how her confidence had grown with the baby and he admired her for it. He remembered the shy little girl he had seduced and smiled in spite of his throbbing jaw.

Pablo slumped into a chair and looked up at his daughter with weary resignation. Estella sat opposite him, placing her hands on her large belly. Ramon stood by the door with his arms folded in front of him. He let Estella do all the talking; he had no desire to sweet talk the old man. As far as Ramon was concerned, his affair with Estella had nothing to do with anyone else but them.

'Papa, I love Ramon. He is the father of my baby and I want to be with him. I don't care about marriage. Ramon will buy us a house in Cachagua and make sure we are looked after. This is what I want,' she said calmly.

'Your grandmother would turn in her grave,' he muttered, gazing at his daughter with watering eyes.

'Then she'll have to turn, Papa,' Estella replied resolutely.

'You're committing adultery. God will punish you,' he said, instinctively touching his silver medallion of the Virgin Mary. 'He'll punish you both.'

'God will understand,' said Ramon, who hated the way the church kept everyone in line by filling their hearts with fear.

'You are a godless man, Don Ramon.'

'Far from it, Señor, I am a believer. I just don't blindly believe the garbage I'm told by weak mortals who call themselves priests and claim to be in constant dialogue with God. They are no more holy than I.'

'Papa, Ramon is a good man.'

'He's lucky he's not a dead man,' Pablo replied, getting up. 'Go on then, live in sin. I don't know you any more.'

'Papa, please!' Estella begged tearfully, throwing her arms about him. 'Please don't turn your back on me.'

'As long as you're with this selfish, godless man, I don't want to see you,' he said sadly. Estella followed him out to his truck. She tried to persuade him to give Ramon a chance, but Pablo refused to listen. 'After all we've done for you,' he said, turning the key in the ignition.

'Papa, please don't leave like this,' she sobbed.

But he drove up the road without so much as a glance in his rear mirror.

Estella gave birth to a baby boy in the same hospital in Valparaíso that she had been born in twenty-two years before. Ramon was as proud as any new father and held the tiny creature in his big hands, declaring that he be named Ramon. He placed his lips on his mottled forehead and kissed his son. 'Ramon Campione,' he said and smiled at Estella. 'We don't need marriage when we have Ramoncito to bind us together.'

Estella missed her mother dreadfully. The birth had been painful without her herbs and soothing words. She longed to contact her but she was afraid of their rejection. Her father's harsh words had inflicted a deep wound that had left her feeling isolated and more dependent on Ramon than ever. A month after the birth they had moved into a pretty beach house that Ramon had bought just outside Zapallar so that she could be near her parents and the friends she had grown up with. He reassured her that her father would forgive her in time.

'Time heals everything,' he said knowingly. 'Even my father might forgive me one day for letting Helena go.'

At the end of October Ignacio and Mariana had moved to their house in Cachagua for the duration of the summer. Mariana had hired a new maid called Gertrude, a sour old woman who had nothing pleasant to say about anyone and complained constantly about the state of her health. Ignacio liked her because she was so disagreeable he didn't have to make the effort to be nice to her. In fact, she responded better to his cantankerous nature than she did to Mariana who tried to mollify her with kind words and smiles. Gertrude never smiled. When Mariana had foolishly mentioned Estella, Gertrude took it upon herself to inform her that there was a rumour that Estella had given birth to a monkey as a direct result of her getting pregnant outside wedlock. 'That's what happens to those who disobey God's commandments,' she crowed gleefully.

It never occurred to Ignacio and Mariana that their son might be the father.

'I miss Estella,' Mariana said to her husband.

'Yes,' he replied, laying out the pieces of a monumental puzzle on top of the card table in the sitting room.

'How could Gertrude be so unkind? A monkey indeed.' She sighed despairingly. 'Where do these people hear such rubbish?'

'It's folklore, woman,' Ignacio replied, adjusting his glasses.

'Well, any intelligent human being must know it's untrue.'

'You believe in God, don't you?'

'Yes.'

'But you have no proof.'

'Nacho!'

'It's just an example, woman.'

'On a completely different level.'

'As you wish,' he replied, hoping she'd leave him alone to concentrate on his puzzle.

'You know, I might find out where Estella lives and go and visit her. You know, just to make sure she's all right.'

'*Como quieras, mujer*,' he said impatiently. Mariana shook her head and left him to his puzzle. 'The minutiae of my wife's world never cease to amaze me,' he sighed once she had gone, and sat down to commence his task.

Ramon watched his son sleeping in his cradle. The baby didn't move, didn't even twitch. Once again he panicked that his son might be dead. He bent into the cot to listen for his breathing. When he heard nothing he put his face to the baby's in order to feel his breath on his cheek.

'*Mi amor*, you're not worrying again? Ramoncito is alive and well,' Estella whispered, placing the clean washing on the chest of drawers.

'I just had to be sure.' He grinned at her bashfully.

'You've forgotten what it was like,' she chuckled, planting a tender kiss on his cheek.

'Yes, I have.'

'Go and see them,' she said suddenly.

'What?'

'Go and visit your children, Ramon,' she said.

'Why?'

'Because they need you.'

'I can't.'

'Yes you can. If you left me and started a family with another woman I would like to think that you would still be a good father to Ramoncito.'

'I'm not going to leave you, Estella,' he said firmly.

'That's not what I mean. Those children need you to be a father. Whatever went wrong between you and Helena has nothing to do with them. If you don't go, they'll blame themselves. They must miss you. I look at Ramoncito, he's so vulnerable and so innocent. He needs us both.'

'I'll go sometime,' he said casually.

★   ★   ★

Estella was the first woman he had ever been with who didn't beg him to stay. He was surprised that she had suggested he go. Suddenly he worried that she was growing tired of him. She was twenty years younger than he. Perhaps she longed for a man of her own age. Then he reassured himself that she couldn't possibly want anyone else. He was the father of her child. She had also promised him that she would never complain if he left as long as he came back from time to time. The irony was that now he didn't want to go anywhere. He could write at their beach house, take long walks in the sunshine, swim in the sea, make love in the afternoon and enjoy watching his baby grow each day. He found that his poems came easily. He didn't have to find the words in faraway places, they were right there in their beach house. Estella read them and when she understood them she wept. She never asked when he was leaving and she never again suggested he go. But her words had settled into his conscience and grown. He knew she was right. He knew he should go and see his children. But he always put it off until tomorrow. Tomorrow was a long way away.

Chapter Seventeen

Polperro

Federica bicycled down to the post office with Hester to post the picture she had painted for her grandmother. It was of her new house and her new friends Molly and Hester. She had included Sam, painting him in bigger than everyone else, even bigger than her mother and grandparents. Hester had admired it. 'You should be a painter like Mummy,' she had said. 'But Mummy can't draw people, they all end up looking like birds.'

'Oh, I think she's rather good.'

'Well, when you know Mummy better you won't be too shy to say what you really think.' She had laughed. Federica also had a letter to post to her father. She hadn't told her mother and as she didn't know her father's new address she had popped the letter into the envelope addressed to her grandmother. She knew Abuelita would pass it on. She had told him that she missed him and that she thought of him every day when she woke up and every night before she went to bed, because those were the times she reserved for her butterfly box. She told him that he was right, the box was magical, because when she opened it her mind automatically drifted off to faraway places where she rode on clouds, fished pink fish out of silver rivers and ate delicious fruit unlike any fruit she had ever seen before. Then she asked him to come and see them because she was growing up fast and if he didn't come soon he wouldn't recognise her. Satisfied that he would surely come, she had sealed the envelope with a wish.

Federica had spent almost the entire summer with the Applebys, leaving her mother to concentrate her attention on Hal. Polly cooked, cleaned and cared for Helena as if she were a child again. Nothing was too much for her to ask. Jake just rolled his eyes as he watched his wife run around after their daughter as if the last ten years had been but a blink. Polly insisted that she was only doing what any other mother would do for her child. Jake couldn't disagree; he didn't know what other mothers would do but he only had to look at Helena running around after Hal to know that there was at least a certain amount of truth in his wife's excuses.

Hal could do no wrong, if only in the eyes of his mother. He had his father's glossy black hair and dark, heavy eyes into which Helena would fall and disappear for hours. During those periods there was very little anyone could do to get her attention. She would laugh at all the quaint things he said, play whatever games he suggested and praise him even when he hadn't done anything worth praising. At four years of age Helena felt he was the brightest, most charming child she had ever seen. Well beyond his years. She refused, however, to acknowledge his moods that swung from absolute affection to blind fury and loathing, for no apparent reason. When Hal swelled with rage not even Helena could reach him. Somehow she found excuses for these tantrums and if anyone mentioned them she turned on them with all her defences. Federica knew instinctively when to leave her mother and Hal alone together and play on her own. Her mother didn't love her less, she understood that, Hal just needed her more than she did. After all Hal didn't have any friends like Molly and Hester. Lucien and Joey included him at their tea parties, but Hal wasn't an honorary member of the Appleby family like she was. He was too little.

Federica wanted to join Hester for Christmas, but Helena insisted she stay at home with her own family. 'You're not an Appleby, you're a Campione,' she said, much to Federica's disappointment because she was beginning to feel more like an Appleby every day. Ingrid began to decorate the manor in October. Instead of tinsel she made garlands of flowers made out of crêpe paper, which she hung up the banisters and around the cornices in the hall and sitting room. The tree was hung with large goose eggs that she painted in festive colours and lit with a conventional string of Christmas tree lights. On the top she made a nest for Blackie to sit in. To Federica's surprise Blackie was delighted with her new bed. None of the Applebys were in the least bit surprised, for when it came to animals Ingrid had the touch of Saint Francis. But the most surprising of all was Nuno. Apparently every Christmas Nuno made the pudding. It was a ceremonial affair, which was taken very seriously indeed. The entire kitchen had to be cleared for a day. No one except Sam was allowed in so the rest of the family had to have lunch at the pub while Nuno floated about the kitchen in a state of rapture. Even Inigo was dragged out of his philosophy books and his black mood and forced to join in the fun at The Bear and Ball. Nuno believed himself to be a phenomenal cook.

'It's not so much about the right quantity of ingredients, dear boy, but the way the pot is stirred,' he told Sam.

'I don't see the point in cooking,' Sam replied. 'It takes much too long to prepare and is much too brief to eat.'

' "Kissing don't last. Cookery do!" ' said Nuno in his clipped Italian accent.

'That one's lost on me,' Sam admitted in irritation, after having thought about it for a while.

Nuno widened his glittering eyes and tapped his wooden spoon on the butcher's table. 'Come come, dear boy, think.'

'Sorry, Nuno. I can't,' he replied, defeated.

'Meredith Middleton.'

'Of course. "Speech is the small change of silence," ' Sam sighed, shaking his head. 'That was an easy one.'

'It's always the easy ones that get us, Samuel. And we're always got in the end.'

For Federica Christmas with her grandparents was going to be very dull in comparison to the Applebys'. Polly and Helena decorated the house with conventional streamers and the tree with tinsel and shiny baubles. Federica would have joined in had she not preferred to help Hester make presents for all the animals. Jake thought Christmas highly overrated and began to build a new model ship, leaving glue and pieces of wood all over the house, much to Polly's chagrin. Helena found her daughter's daily jaunts up the lane excessive and decided that Hal and Federica were going to paint pictures for their grandparents' presents and set them to work at the kitchen table. 'I want the most beautiful paintings you can do, and if it doesn't take at least a week you're obviously not doing it properly,' she said, directing her comments at Federica. Federica's heart sank. She set about her task with little enthusiasm, wondering at every moment what Hester was doing up at Pickthistle Manor.

Toby had told his parents that he was going to spend Christmas with Julian's family in Shropshire. They were hurt. No less hurt than they had been the Christmas before or the Christmas before that. But Toby wanted them to be sorry. As long as his father refused to have Julian in the house he would make him suffer by staying away too.

Helena was furious and confronted her father about it. 'He's my brother and I won't stand by and watch you treat him in this way. He's not a leper, you know, he just happens to be in love with a boy. What's the big deal?' she said angrily. But Jake didn't want to discuss it with his daughter. He wasn't able to speak about his son's homosexuality to anyone, not even to his wife. He was too ashamed. Helena didn't give up. She spoke about Julian at every opportunity. 'I went up to Toby's today with Hal. Really, Julian is so sweet with him. I left them together while Toby and I went for a walk. He couldn't have been in safer hands. I'd trust him with my life,' she would say, but Jake would ignore her and either leave the room or bury his nose further into the bowels of his model ships. But Helena was determined their family shouldn't be wrenched apart because of some old-fashioned, irrational, misguided prejudice. She didn't know how she'd do it but she was confident she could rectify the situation given time. In the meantime she was saddened. Christmas would be deeply lacking without Toby.

By the time Christmas arrived a thick covering of snow had transformed Polperro into an ice kingdom. The sky was pale and timid, the sun no more than a resplendent haze that hung low in the eastern sky. The trees had retreated into themselves, leaving only their frozen shells to fend off the bitter wind and in spite of their naked branches a few rooks and the odd robin braved the cold and sought shelter there. Federica and Hal were enchanted by the snow. They awoke early and pressed their noses against the frosted windows to marvel at the white garden that lay silently in the emerging dawn light. They had been so excited by the snow that neither had noticed the fat stockings which lay full of presents at the end of their beds.

Scrambling into Helena's bed Hal and Federica excitedly tore open the tissue paper on each carefully wrapped present. 'How come Father Christmas found us in England?' Federica asked her mother, squealing in delight as she pulled out a brand new paint box.

'He's very clever,' she replied, watching as Federica folded each bit of wrapping paper neatly in a pile while Hal threw his on the floor for someone else to pick up later.

'I hope he found Papa in Santiago,' said Federica, remembering how both parents used to get stockings too. 'I wish he were here,' she said wistfully, turning one of her gifts over in her hand thoughtfully. She wanted him to see her opening her presents although she knew no present would ever beat the butterfly box he had given her. 'Where's yours, Mama?' she asked, noticing that Helena didn't have anything to open.

'Father Christmas left it outside your bedroom by mistake,' said Polly, entering in her dressing gown and slippers with her greying hair long and wild about her shoulders. She handed her daughter the stocking.

'Thank you, Mum.' She smiled at her mother, making space for her on the edge of the bed.

Polly sat down and touched her daughter's cheek with her large hand. 'Don't thank me, thank Father Christmas,' she said and winked.

Federica ate her breakfast in silence. She had loved her presents, especially the Snoopy dog that came with lots of different outfits so that she could change him for each new occasion. Her grandmother had put little gifts on their places at breakfast and her grandfather had turned the Christmas tree lights on making the house look festive. She loved the snow and longed to run outside and play in it. But nothing could make up for the absence of her father. She tried not to think about him, she wasn't meant to be sad on Christmas Day and she didn't want to spoil it for her mother by sulking, but in spite of her smiles she missed him so much she wanted to cry.

Helena noticed her shiny eyes and knew immediately what was wrong. 'Why don't you and Hal finish breakfast now and go and play outside. You can build a snowman if you like,' she suggested kindly, hoping that the snow might distract her. But nothing could.

Federica didn't want to go to church even though she knew the Applebys would be there. She didn't feel like it. She didn't feel like watching all the other children with their fathers, looking at her and wondering why she didn't have one too. She wanted to hide. But her mother wouldn't let her and told her that she had to go to church to thank God for all the wonderful things He had given her during the year and to thank Him for giving the world baby Jesus. On the way to church she thought about what her mother had said. God had given her lots of wonderful things, Hester, for example, and she liked Polperro. But she couldn't help but feel deeply let down. If God could give her Hester why couldn't He give her back her father? She resolved to ask Him in her prayers.

The church was said to be so old that it was listed in the Doomsday book. Toby had taken Federica there when she had first arrived in Polperro to show her the grave of Old Hatty Browne, the witch burnt by the villagers for sorcery in 1508. Toby added darkly that on very clear nights she was often spotted in the yard picking herbs for her potions, with which she would minister to the dead. Federica had been enchanted and wanted to know more, so they had sat among the daffodils and talked until sundown.

The church itself was small and quaint with a sloping roof and rickety porch, surrounded by snow-capped graves and a low brick wall to keep the dogs out. For some inexplicable reason there was nothing they liked better than to cock their legs on the gravestones. Nuno said it was due to the pungent scent of the deceased that rendered the earth irresistible to them but Inigo lamented their lack of respect and said that they enjoyed 'pissing on the deceased because they couldn't piss on the living'. The nave and balcony only managed to seat about fifty people but due to the unlikely charisma of the Reverend Boyble there was rarely a spare seat in the place. Helena had brought her children up in the Catholic faith, because Ramon was Catholic. But now she was back in England and on her own she had reverted to the Protestant faith with which she had been raised. It gave her a sense of belonging.

Everyone was dressed in their best coats and hats. Federica had squeezed into an old tweed coat of her mother's that Polly had kept sealed in a large white box with tissue paper. She didn't like it because it was scratchy and a little too small, but Helena thought she looked very smart and refused to let her take it off. Consequently she tugged at the collar throughout the service. The church smelt of pine tree and perfume, mingled with the waxy scent of the candles. Old Mrs Hammond played the organ with faltering precision, her shrivelled face pressed up against the hymn book because she was too proud to admit she needed glasses. A murmur passed through the congregation when the Appleby family entered and took their places at the front of the church. Nuno trotted in first on the balls of his feet with his tortoise nose in the air and a devout expression frozen onto his face. 'Girls, you're not a pair of pious penguins. Hold your hands together in front of you like vestal virgins,' he hissed to Molly and Hester whose shoulders hunched up and shuddered as they tried their best to suppress their giggles. Hester caught Federica's eye as she passed and winked at her. Federica forced a thin smile in return but she didn't feel like smiling. Ingrid swept by dressed in a velvet turban and long green velvet coat that reached to the ground and trailed along behind her as if she were an ageing bride. She greeted everyone with a gracious nod of her noble head but she didn't see any of their faces because her eyes had misted over with the beauty of the music. Inigo shuffled down in a mangy brown duffel coat and felt hat pulled low over his ill-tempered face followed by Sam, who was already bored, Bea in a short skirt, Lucien and Joey.

Once the Applebys had settled into their seats the Reverend Boyble sprang into the centre of the nave like a jolly frog. His bulbous brown eyes swept cheerfully over the attentive faces of his congregation and he smiled a very wide, charming smile. 'Welcome,' he enthused in a surprisingly high, thin voice. 'Welcome everyone. Today is a very special day because it is Jesus' birthday.'

Sam yawned, opening his mouth wide like a hippo. The Reverend Boyble noticed his yawn and chuckled. 'I see some of you would prefer to be in bed on this glorious morning, or perhaps you're tired of opening all those presents. I thank you for making the effort to come.' Sam sat up stiffly and tried to prevent his face from flushing by focusing on the crucifix that hung above the altar.

'Effort, hmmm . . .' murmured Reverend Boyble thoughtfully, rubbing his thumbs over the surface of his prayer book. 'Effort is a virtuous thing. It's all too easy to allow laziness to lead us down the path of evil. I wonder whether you all know the story of the two frogs in the milk bowl.' He cast his eyes about the faces that stared back at him expectantly. 'They were stuck and couldn't get out. It would have been quite easy for the stronger frog to have stepped on the weaker frog, thereby ensuring him a swift leg-up to safety. But the stronger frog didn't go for the easy option. Instead he continued to kick and kick together with the weaker frog in an enormous effort to throw himself up the side of the bowl. Well, his efforts were rewarded. They kicked so hard and for so long that the milk turned to butter, thereby allowing them to simply hop out with no trouble at all. That is effort, my good people. It brings its own rewards.' A murmur of admiration rippled through the congregation. 'Today is Jesus' birthday, so let us celebrate with the first carol on your service sheet, "Away in a Manger".'

Federica knew some carols because they had sung them at school in Chile, although the words had been in Spanish. It had been an age since she had last spoken Spanish, she thought unhappily, and she attempted to sing along quietly the way she had been taught in Viña. Suddenly all the homesickness and longing she had suffered silently for so long rebelled against her failing will and clawed their way into her throat, causing her eyes to water in discomfort and her chin to tremble. In her mind's eye she saw scenes of her past opening up to her like a vision of a lost world. Her heart stalled when she saw the dark face of her father emerge in all its magnificence and as much as she tried to hold back the tears they cascaded down her cheeks because she searched his eyes for love but found only indifference. At once she felt desperately empty and sad. All those wasted hours believing he'd come and visit. How naïve she had been. He had obviously forgotten about them because it was Christmas and he had never missed a Christmas, ever. She knew now that he would never come and her spirits sank lower than they had ever sunk. Helena placed a hand on her shoulder, sensing her daughter's distress. She too missed Chile and in a strange way, Ramon. But she was more practised at hiding her melancholy and sang more heartily than ever.

During the sermon Reverend Boyble spoke about the meaning of Christmas with great enthusiasm. 'Christmas is a time for love and forgiveness,' he preached. Federica listened to him but she felt no love or forgiveness, just an aching wound that refused to heal. As the full enormity of her father's rejection reached her understanding, her vision misted until the candles glowed like small suns and Reverend Boyble was reduced to a black blur, his voice no more than a low hum in the distance. She felt the heat prickle on her skin as she made one last effort to suppress a sob, but her chest was too small to withstand such a violent tirade. Abruptly she stood up and shuffled blindly past her grandparents who looked at each other in bewilderment. She then ran up the aisle, pushed open the heavy oak door and burst out into the snow where she was finally able to let herself go and howl into the icy air.

Holding her stomach she bent over and cried at the injustice of the world. She loathed Christmas and she loathed England. Suddenly she felt a heavy hand on her back. She stopped crying and straightened up. Wiping her face with her glove she lifted her eyes to find the dark eyes of her father staring into hers with love and remorse. She swallowed hard and blinked.

'Papa?' she croaked, catching her breath in her throat with surprise.

'Fede. I'm sorry.' He drew her kicking and screaming into his arms.

'I hate you, I hate you!' she sobbed, as he held her in a firm bear hug, burying his face into her hot neck, whispering words of tenderness and encouragement. As she felt herself enveloped in the familiar smell of his body she closed her eyes and stopped fighting, giving in to the security of his embrace, conquered by her love for him. Finally he crouched down and held her by her narrow shoulders.

'I missed you,' he said emphatically, searching her expression for submission. He wished he had missed her much sooner. 'I got your letter,' he added, grinning at her sheepishly.

'Is that why you came?'

'No. I was always going to come and see you. I've just been

Chapter Eighteen

the service was over the church turned into a parochial
ail party as the village wished each other a very happy
tmas. Ramon shook hands with Jake and kissed Polly on
ff cheek as if he had seen them the week before. He lifted a
ant, wriggling Hal into his arms and kissed his face before
ng him back to Helena.

es it surprise you that he doesn't recognise you?' she hissed.
mon lowered his eyes and shook his head. 'I'm sorry. I
mean to leave it this long,' he replied, ashamed.
u never do,' she retorted bitterly.

erica took him by the hand and led him through the
g of strange people to meet the Applebys.
is is my father,' she said proudly to Ingrid who extended
nd graciously.
a great pleasure to meet you. Fede has told us so much
you,' she said and smiled broadly.
u must be Hester's mother,' he said.
rid's face expressed her surprise. 'Why, yes I am,' she
l, wondering how he had worked that one out.
le's lucky to have a best friend in Hester,' he said. Federica
ed his hand because he knew nothing about Hester except
he had told him outside.

rid placed her monocle in her eye to study him in more
He was devastatingly handsome with the remote, mys-
eyes of a wolf. She also found his accent most charming;
genuine, Nuno's was not.
me with me, I'd like to introduce you to the rest of my
' she said, gesticulating to her father and husband who
alking to each other because they found the after-church
t with the village superficial and tiresome. Both longed to

very busy. But your letter made me realise that I couldn't leave it
any longer.'

'I'm glad you're here,' she said and smiled timidly.

'There, that's better.' He wiped her face with his thumbs.
'You have so much to tell me. You've been living an adventure.
I want to hear everything. Do you like England?'

'Sort of. I have a best friend called Hester.' She sniffed,
cheering up.

'What about that dog Mama was going to buy you?' he asked.

'She hasn't yet.'

Ramon rolled his eyes. 'Oh dear. Do you want one, as a
Christmas present?'

'No thank you. You're my Christmas present and I couldn't
ask for anything else.'

Ramon had forgotten how much he loved his daughter. It had
been too easy to forget. But now, as he held her against him
again, his heart reeled with tenderness.

Suddenly the door opened with a low groan and out walked
Helena. When she saw Federica in the embrace of a strange man
she was about to object. But then she recognised the wide
shoulders and the strong back and felt her head swim with
uncertainty. When he turned around to face her she stood
blinking at him with her jaw open, not knowing what to say
and fighting the impulse to slap him around the face and slate him
for not having come months ago.

'Helena,' he said and smiled at her.

Helena stared back at him, her face pale in the blue winter
light, her lips quivering, anxiously trying to find the words.
'Ramon,' she replied in confusion. Then added clumsily, 'What
are you doing here?'

'As there was no one at the house I presumed you'd be at
church,' he replied casually, as if he dropped in all the time.

'Yes, we are at church,' she retorted stiffly, finding her wits
again. 'We're at church. Now if you'd kindly let Fede go we'd
like to finish the service,' she said tightly, taking Federica by the
arm.

'I'm not leaving him,' Federica hissed, grabbing onto his hand.

'Fede, he'll be here when we come out.'

'I'm not leaving him,' Federica repeated before dissolving into tears again.

'It looks like I'm going to have to join you,' said Ramon with a smirk, squeezing his daughter's hand.

Helena pursed her lips together and let out a long-suffering sigh. 'There's very little room,' she argued, not wanting to incite the curiosity of the congregation by walking back up the aisle with Ramon.

'I'll find somewhere,' he said, shrugging his big shoulders.

'As you wish,' Helena conceded, reluctantly opening the door.

Ramon followed her into the church, which he dwarfed with the sheer scale of his charisma. As they walked down the aisle Helena felt innumerable pairs of inquisitive eyes settle on her husband, eager to know who the strange, dark foreigner was. But Federica placed a proprietorial hand in his so that no one would be in any doubt that he was her father.

Jake's and Polly's eyes widened with surprise when Helena asked them to move up to make space for Ramon. They sat staring at him with their mouths agape like floundering fish. Fortunately Reverend Boyble was still merrily giving his sermon about the meaning of Christmas so they didn't have the opportunity to ask questions or voice their shock. Federica grinned up at her father and held his warm hand in both of hers to prevent him from getting away. Hal squeezed closer to his mother, sensing her uneasiness and feeling fear but not understanding why. Helena wished she hadn't been so un-friendly, but she was in shock, what did he expect? He could have let her know. A letter or a telephone call would have been nice. She sat scowling into her prayer book trying to draw some peace from the words written on its pages, anything rather than look at him. She struggled with her pride, which longed for him to see her happy and settled and regret letting her go, and her heart, which suffered the weight of her memories and yearned

for him still. Ramon sat back and glanced around him. Then he settled his gaze on tear-stained face glowed with love and pri had come.

be back at the manor with their books. 'Pa, Inigo, it gives me great pleasure to introduce Ramon Campione,' she said and smiled broadly. 'Isn't he quite the most handsome thing Polperro has ever seen?'

Ramon chuckled to hide his discomfort but Federica's grin increased until it was in danger of swallowing up her entire face.

'Really, darling, you shouldn't judge people by their appearance. I apologise for my wife,' said Inigo, shaking Ramon firmly by the hand.

'"It is only shallow people who do not judge by appearances,"' said Nuno, bowing to Ramon.

'Ah, you're an admirer of Oscar Wilde,' he replied, bowing back.

Nuno's eyes flickered their approval. 'So are you. Now I hold you in great esteem. When can you come to lunch? I would like to show you my library,' said Nuno, turning to his daughter and raising an eyebrow. 'I could tell young Federica comes from a learned family.'

'Ramon is a famous writer,' said Ingrid, who knew all about him from Helena. 'He's highly regarded in Chile.'

'I understand you have taken my daughter under your wing,' said Ramon. 'I'm very grateful to you.'

Ingrid patted Federica on her head as though she were a rather well behaved dog. 'It's a pleasure. My daughters adore her. My father is right, Ramon, you must come for lunch. How long are you staying?' she asked, hoping he was going to stay for a long time. She liked nothing more than colourful people.

'I don't know yet.'

'Divine! I love a man who takes every day as it comes. Much the best way to go through life. It lasts longer that way,' she said and laughed. Then she leaned in closer to him and whispered, 'We have invited the vicar to lunch today, so I think we had best be heading back to Pickthistle Manor. You will come to lunch, won't you?' she added. 'Tomorrow?'

'Of course. It would be a pleasure,' he replied with a courteous inclination of his head.

'Good. Tomorrow it is then. Bring Helena and the children. It's always a delight to see your wife.'

Helena was furious. 'You want to go around presenting as a family?' she raged. 'How dare you show up here and take everything over.'

'I'm not taking anything over. I came to see my children. Isn't that what you wanted?'

'You sweep in without a single apology for not writing, not calling, not being there when your children need you.'

'I'm here now,' he replied.

'You're here now, but gone tomorrow. I had given up on you. It was easier to give up. Now you're back I don't know where I am any more.' She folded her arms in front of her obstinately.

Ramon shrugged his shoulders and sighed. There was simply no point in arguing with her. He watched her rigid features; the bitter line of her mouth, the pinched skin and frozen eyes and remembered why he had let her go. 'What more can I say? I'm sorry,' he ventured in an attempt to alter her expression.

Her lips twitched as she pondered her next move. 'I don't want Fede to hear us arguing again,' she said. 'Let's go for a walk and discuss this calmly.'

They walked up the lane, through a mossy wooden gate and into the field and woods beyond. Helena lit a cigarette and blew the smoke into the icy air where it floated on the cold like fog. Ramon was dismayed to find that Helena hadn't changed at all in the months that they had been apart. She was just as unhappy as ever. She hadn't even bothered to wash her hair for church. He was disappointed. He sensed a strange feeling of *déjà vu* along with those familiar contractions in his gut, that summoned him away.

'So how long will you be staying?' she asked as they walked up the field, their boots scrunching into the melting snow.

'I don't know yet,' Ramon replied, struggling against the

impulse to return as quickly as possible to the serene and untroubled home Estella had forged for him.

'Nothing's changed, has it?' she sighed. 'Well, I'll tell you how long you'll stay, a week, perhaps ten days, then we'll begin to bore you and you'll be off again.'

'You and the children never bored me,' said Ramon seriously.

'No?' she retorted grimly. 'Well, that's what it felt like.'

'Look, Helena. I'm sorry I didn't call. I wanted to surprise you,' he said, placing his large hand on her shoulder. She shrugged it off. 'Fede was pleased to see me,' he added and smiled a small, pensive smile.

'Of course she was. But you haven't been around for the past eleven months wiping her tears. Not a day has gone by when she hasn't thought that perhaps, just maybe, today will be the day Papa turns up. What sort of a childhood is that, Ramon? If you just wrote regularly, kept in touch, let her know your plans then she wouldn't live in such an uncertain world. It makes her very insecure, you know, and I suffer with her.' Her voice dripped with bitterness.

'I'll try,' he conceded.

'And what about Hal?' she continued. 'It's as if he doesn't exist. You write to Fede but not to him. He's your son and he needs you just as much as Fede does. More so, because he's never experienced your affection like she has.'

'You're right,' he said simply. 'You're right about everything. I haven't come here to fight with you.'

Helena blinked in surprise and kept her eyes fixed on the snow-laden trees in front of them. She hadn't expected him to be so compliant.

They walked up the path until they came to the high cliffs which cut straight down to the sea. Helena led him to a small iron bench where she often came to sit alone and gaze out over the waters. There, the view that stretched out before her into the mists of infinity would take her soul back to the sweet days of her past before acrimony had seeped in to sour it. Now she sat down and surveyed the frosty sky and icy clouds with the man whose love had once been as intense as the sun. Once more the horizon dragged her spirits out of the shadows of her unhappiness and she remembered how it had been then. She felt her heart thaw in the midst of such splendour, in the midst of such vivid memories. She burrowed in her coat pocket for her cigarettes and lighter. With a shaking hand she lit one. She felt Ramon's overbearing presence and the desire to cry. How did it all go so dreadfully wrong?

'So, how are your parents?' she asked after a while, placing a hand on her aching temple.

'Well. They're in Cachagua.'

'I miss Cachagua,' she said quietly, almost as if she were talking to herself. She didn't look at him but continued to stare out over her memories. 'I miss the heat, the sea, the smells. I never thought I would miss it, but I do.'

'That's the trouble with loving two countries, you always want to be in the one you're not in. It gives one too much choice,' he said. 'Sometimes it's better not to have the choice.'

'Your life must be very hard indeed, you have the whole world to choose from,' she said and chuckled resentfully.

'You have two, sometimes that's harder.'

'Oh, I'm very happy here. Very, very happy,' she said, but Ramon was not convinced and neither was she.

'Have you got one of your headaches?' he asked, noticing her massaging her temple with her hand.

'Yes, but I'm fine, they come and go,' she replied dismissively.

'Come here,' he said, moving her so that her back was facing him. She tried to object but he silenced her with his assertiveness and placed his hands on her head and started massaging her.

'Really, Ramon. I'm fine,' she argued weakly as the sensation of his touch caused her skin to prickle with nostalgia.

'You're not fine. But I'm going to make you fine,' he said and laughed.

She resented his cheerfulness and wondered why everything was always so straightforward for him.

Ramon's fingers working into her skull were too pleasurable to resist so she ceased to fight and leant back against them, taking in a long, deep breath. As she relaxed her head his hands moved down to her shoulders, moving beneath her coat and sweater to her skin.

'Tell me how the children have been?' he asked and she told him about Federica's infatuation with the Applebys, her crush on Sam and her progress at school.

'She adores the Applebys,' she said. 'She never had many friends at school in Viña, but they've become like a second family to her. It's done wonders for her confidence.'

'That's good.'

'Oh, it's wonderful. At first England frightened her. It was so cold and grey, not like the blue skies of Chile. It's good we moved to the sea though, at least that's familiar.'

Then she told him about Hal and her shoulders eased up and her throat loosened until she began to laugh without bitterness or resentment.

'At least they are happy here,' he said.

'They seem to be.' She closed her eyes to the luxurious feeling of his fingers sending the blood back into her dried-out muscles.

'But what about you?' he asked.

'Oh, Ramon. I'm fine.'

'I'm asking you as a friend, not as your husband.'

'You're still my husband,' she said throatily and smiled, recalling a lost age when their shared happiness had eclipsed the impending unhappiness that would overwhelm them.

'Okay, so I'm asking you as your husband.'

'I don't know,' she replied, shaking her head.

'What do you do all day?'

'I look after Hal.'

'What do you do for you?'

'For me?'

'For you,' he repeated.

She thought about it for a while. She didn't know what she did for her. She sometimes accompanied Federica up to the

Applebys for tea, or took Hal to the beach. She visited Toby and Julian, chatted to her mother. But she couldn't think of anything she did purely for her own pleasure.

'I don't know, Ramon. I can't think of anything,' she said bleakly and felt her throat constrict again with emotion. 'The children give me enormous pleasure.'

'Of course they do. But that's domesticity. I mean an indulgence. A selfish pleasure which you don't share with anyone.'

Helena considered his question – Ramon was a master of self-indulgence and she of sacrifice, that's why it had all gone so wrong.

'Everyone needs time to themselves,' he continued. 'A long bubble bath, a trip to the hairdresser, I don't know what makes you happy.'

'Well, I've lost touch with myself,' she sighed, 'because I don't know either.'

'Perhaps you should start thinking about you. I give you enough money?' he asked.

'You give me more than enough money.'

'Well, go and spend it, for God's sake. I don't know what you girls do, but buy a new dress, go to a beautician, enjoy yourself. Don't chain yourself to the nursery; you're not a domestic. If you need a domestic, hire one. If you need a house of your own, buy one. I don't care but you have misery written all over your face and it's not very attractive.'

Helena was stunned. She couldn't remember the last time they had talked so frankly. She couldn't remember the last time he had thought about her and her happiness. She felt her stomach stagger with the recollection of what it had been like when they had been friends. They had talked without pause, about everything and anything, laughed at the smallest things and communicated without words across the lines of love. She wondered when their conversation had dried up and why. She dared not turn around because she knew if she looked into his eyes she would close up again with uncertainty, so she kept her eyes shut in an effort to extend the moment.

'I moved the children to England for me, but ironically they are the ones who enjoy it. Not me. I wonder, I don't know, I wonder . . .' She hesitated.

'What?' he asked quietly.

'I wonder, oh God, Ramon, I can hardly say it.'

'Say it. You'll feel a hell of a lot better if you do.'

'Have I made a huge mistake?'

Ramon stopped massaging her shoulders. She sat up and turned to face him. He looked at her with dark, impenetrable eyes and she felt herself slowly closing up again with inhibition and shame.

'Have you made a mistake?' he asked seriously, thinking of Estella and hoping she wasn't suddenly going to change her mind.

'I don't know whether I've made a mistake leaving Chile. I miss it. Perhaps it's nothing more than nostalgia,' she added dismissively.

'Perhaps,' he agreed thoughtfully.

'I don't know.'

'I think you need to give it a chance here,' he said. 'You need to throw yourself into it like Fede has.'

'It's much easier for children. They just get on with things and don't brood.'

'Look,' he said. 'It was your choice, Helena. I never asked you to leave. I didn't want you to. But I understood why you did and I support your choice. I think you are encountering the same problems here as the ones you faced in Chile. You're a mother on her own who's dedicated her life to her children. I think you'll find if you dedicate some of that time to you your feelings might change. You're young, you're good-looking.' She blushed and turned her face away. 'You need to find a hobby, something that takes you out of yourself and out of the home.'

'Perhaps you're right,' she said, feeling happier. 'You know, we haven't talked like this for years.'

'I know. We were too busy resenting each other, we now know where we both stand.'

She looked at his diffident profile as he stared out across the sea. Then lowered her eyes. 'Yes,' she said sadly. 'We do.'

Federica was so happy to have her father back that she was unable to sleep. Her parents slept in different bedrooms, but she didn't mind. She was grateful that he was there at all. Jake and Polly accepted his sudden arrival once they saw how he and Helena got on much better than they had predicted. There were no fights, no tantrums, no bitter comments, no tears. Helena washed her hair, applied make-up and even bought herself some new outfits in town. They disappeared every day as a family. They went for walks along the beach with the children, explored ruined castles and hidden caves. In fact, they did all the things that they had done when they had first met. The only difference was that they didn't kiss and they didn't laugh quite as much. But Helena was less resentful and Ramon more attentive to her needs. She no longer felt numb inside but regained her awareness. Her indifference had, after all, been nothing more than a rebellion of the senses, a stagnation of the heart. As her anger dissolved she discovered she cared. While they retraced the paths of their courtship she began to find the man she had fallen in love with behind those dense eyes and her spirit stirred for him again.

Ingrid was enchanted by the swarthy foreigner who had suddenly appeared in their midst. He had come for lunch on Boxing Day with Helena and the children and entertained her with stories which he recounted in his thick accent and foreign intonation. She wished she spoke Spanish because she would have bought every book he'd ever written. But he charmed her none the less with stories he invented off the top of his head and tales of his adventures that he embellished with his rich imagination until he had captivated the attention of the whole table, even the lofty Sam who was usually bored by the men his mother suddenly 'took shines to'.

The weeks that ensued were punctuated with invitations to Pickthistle Manor. Helena felt herself swelling with pride as Ramon dazzled everyone with his presence and his uniqueness. The atmosphere was charged with a rare energy when he was present and no one felt it more than his wife.

'Why you're the other side of the world from this delightful young man is beyond me,' Nuno said to Helena one day over lunch.

'Oh, Nuno, it's not that simple. You don't have to live with him,' she laughed.

'No one else will have me besides Ingrid so it's not an option,' he replied, looking down at her loftily with intelligent blue eyes. 'Sometimes one realises what one has lost when it is too late. I hope, my dear, that you won't suffer the same fate.'

'He's here for the children, not for me,' she said coolly. But she looked across the table at Ramon's animated face and wished he had come for her. She wished he could just bury his pride and beg her to come back to him. She wished he could change for her. But her heart sank because she knew the true nature of the man. He was like the wind and he always would be – he'd never know where he was going to blow next.

'Ramon's the same as ever, Nuno, when he's with you, you feel there's no one in the world more special to him than you. Take Federica, for example.' They both looked over at the small child who clung onto every word her father said. Everything she did was for his benefit; her laughter, her jokes, her stories, her comments, her smiles. She worshipped him. 'Federica believes he loves her more than anyone else in the whole world. Right now he does. I really believe that. He's full of remorse that he didn't come earlier, that he never wrote or called. He's mortified. Wracked with guilt. But then he'll be off soon and we won't hear from him for months, perhaps years. Because with Ramon, out of sight is out of mind, I'm afraid.'

'Love is understanding someone's faults and loving them in spite of them,' said Nuno philosophically.

'Is that a quote?' she chuckled.

'No. It's mine, but unfortunately not terribly original. None the less, it's true.'

'Ramon and I spent years trying to understand each other until we gave up trying.'

'It's never too late to try again.'

'I don't know. I think we've always misunderstood one another.'

' "To be great is to be misunderstood," ' Nuno quoted. 'Ralph Waldo Emerson. A very perceptive man.'

'So I see.'

'He also said another very acute thing, my dear.'

'What is that?'

Nuno leant over to her and whispered in her ear. ' "We are always getting ready to live, but never living." '

Helena thought about that all through lunch and throughout the afternoon. Indeed, for some reason she was unable to think of anything else.

'Fede?' said Hal, brushing his teeth over the basin.

'Yes?'

'Do you think Papa is going to stay?'

Federica hung his wet towel over the radiator. 'I don't know,' she replied, not wishing to voice her hope in case she raise her brother's unnecessarily.

'Maybe he'll take us back to Viña,' he added, spitting into the running water.

'I don't think he'll take us back to Viña, Hal,' she replied carefully.

'Why not?'

'Because we live here now.'

'I would rather live in Viña,' he said decisively.

'But you love it here with Granny and Grandpa,' she insisted.

'I miss Abuelito.' He pulled a sad face.

'So do I, Hal.'

'Grandpa doesn't carry me on his shoulders or swing me around by the arms,' he complained.

'I know.'

'Or take me riding.'

'He's very busy.'

'I want to go back to Viña. I think Abuelito misses me.'

'I'm sure he does. I'm sure they both do,' she said wistfully. 'It's bedtime now, Hal. Shall I read you a story?'

'Where's Mama?' he asked, padding out of the bathroom in his bare feet.

'At Joey and Lucien's house.'

'She's always up there.'

'I know. She likes the Applebys.'

'I don't.'

'Yes, you do.'

'No, I don't.'

'You always play with Joey.'

'I don't like Joey.'

Federica sighed in anticipation of a row. 'Come on. I'll read you a story,' she cajoled brightly.

'I want Mama to read me a story,' he insisted. 'I won't go to bed until she does.'

'What about Granny then?'

'I want Mama,' he whined and folded his arms in front of him stubbornly.

'All right,' she sighed. 'Get into bed and wait until Mama comes back, she shouldn't be long.' But Federica knew that by the time she returned they'd both be asleep.

It was late when Federica heard the wheels of the car scrunch on the gravel in the driveway outside her window. The light penetrated her bedroom for a moment before she was once more plunged into darkness as the engine was switched off. She listened for their voices as her parents hurried in out of the cold. They were laughing, but she couldn't make out what they were saying. She hadn't heard her mother sound so happy in a long time. She sat up in bed and strained her ears for some indication that her father might stay, but she only heard muffled voices that revealed nothing except a growing friendliness between them.

'I really enjoyed tonight,' said Helena, climbing the stairs. Federica cowered in the darkness, watching as her mother came into view through the crack in the door.

'Me too,' Ramon agreed, following closely behind her.

Helena hesitated outside Federica's room. 'I'm glad you like the Applebys,' she said softly so as not to waken her children.

'Nuno's an original,' he chuckled. 'As for Inigo.'

'You're the only one I know who gets Inigo's point. He barely talks to anyone, shuts himself up in his study all the time. It must be exasperating for Ingrid.'

'I have to admit I find him fascinating.'

'I can't imagine what you talk about.'

'Everything.'

'Really?'

'He's learned and wise. You just have to penetrate his disappointment.'

'Disappointment?' She frowned.

'He doesn't have Nuno's ability to rise above the world.'

'Like Ingrid.'

'Exactly. He spends his days pondering life and dwelling only on the negative. If we look hard enough we can find ugliness in anything. The trick is not to look for it.'

'I don't know what you're talking about,' she said lamely and chuckled to hide her ignorance. 'Thank you for making such an effort with Hal these last few days.'

'He's a sweet boy,' Ramon replied.

'He is, but you never knew him. It's important for him to feel your affection. I know Federica's more interesting to you. She's older and more outwardly loving. But Hal loves you too, he just doesn't understand it.'

'It's been good for me to see them.' He nodded then yawned.

'It's been good for us, too,' she said and looked at him steadily.

He caught her eyes and smiled ruefully. 'It has,' he agreed in such a low voice, that Federica hardly heard him.

'I'm glad you came.'

'Me too.'

They both hovered awkwardly before Ramon walked on up the corridor. 'Goodnight, Helena.'

'Sleep well, Ramon.' She watched him go with tenderness. Then she too disappeared out of sight.

Federica felt a shudder of anticipation cause her skin to shiver as if it were cold. But she felt very hot and very excited. She squeezed her eyes closed and hoped that what she had just witnessed was the beginning of a new love affair between her parents. She was sure then that her father would stay.

Helena lay in bed and thought of Ramon. She then thought about what Nuno had said. 'We are always getting ready to live, but never living.' She repeated it again and again in her head, pondering on the meaning and how it applied to her. Nuno was so right. Ramon was living. He didn't bother about preparation; he just rushed off to live as much as he could, whereas she was always preparing to live. Ramon was like a large bird. For him there were no frontiers, he just flew where he wanted, when he wanted. She envied his spontaneity yet resented his lack of responsibility. He didn't answer to anyone, not even the pleas of his children. Much less the entreaties of his wife. But, he was certainly living. Ralph Waldo Emerson would have approved of Ramon.

She lay in solitude and yet, tonight, her solitude felt heavier and more uncomfortable than ever before. She stared up into the blackness and remembered those early days with Ramon when she had curled up in the warm reassurance of his embrace and slept without doubts. She felt his presence in the house because it was as dense as smoke and hot like fire. She was powerless to ignore it and unwilling to fight it any longer. She remembered Ralph Waldo Emerson and climbed out of bed.

She slipped into her dressing gown, opened her bedroom door and crept down the corridor towards Ramon's room. She didn't hesitate outside his door as she had done that terrible night the previous January, but opened it quietly and walked into the darkness. 'Ramon,' she whispered. He stirred beneath his bed-clothes. 'Ramon,' she repeated. He stirred again. She felt her way to the bed and prodded him. 'Ramon.'

He woke up. 'Helena?' he mumbled. 'Are you all right?'

'I'm cold,' she said, because she couldn't think of anything better to say. Her body was trembling all over, surprised by the impetuosity that had suddenly overcome it. 'Can I get in?'

Ramon shuffled to make room for her. She climbed in beside him and pulled the covers about her. 'What do you want, Helena?' he asked. But she ignored the impatient tone of his voice and persisted.

'I want you to stay,' she said.

He sighed and pulled her against his warm body, wrapping his arms around her and breathing into her hair. 'I can't.'

'Why can't you?'

'Because my home is Chile.'

'Can't you just stay for longer? You can write here. You don't have to be in Chile. The joy about your work is that you can take it anywhere.'

He sighed again. 'I can't change,' he said flatly.

'Why can't you, Ramon? Because you don't want to?'

'Because I can't.'

'But we've become friends again. We haven't enjoyed each other like this for years. We're getting to know each other again. No, let me finish,' she said when he tried to interrupt her. 'I thought I didn't care about you any more, let alone love you. I felt this dead indifference and it scared me. I thought there was nothing left of our relationship. So I came home. I thought it was the only option. But I was wrong. I see that now and I pray that it isn't too late. We can make it work, I really believe we can.'

'But we'll face the same problems we have always faced. It doesn't matter where we are, our problems will follow us.'

'I need you,' she said, then swallowed because she heard the desperation in her voice and it frightened her.

'You don't need me, Helena. You need a life.'

'But you didn't want me to go, are you saying now you don't want me back?'

'I'm not saying anything at all. I'm just saying that we both need this time apart.'

'Then you don't want me at all,' she said with resignation, ashamed that she had declared herself so carelessly.

'I want you, Helena,' he said and kissed her forehead. 'I would make love to you now, happily. I have always enjoyed you.'

'Then why don't you?'

'Because I'm not going to stay.'

'Because you don't desire me any more?' she said, defeated.

'Because the holes in our marriage are still there, Helena.'

'The holes were made by me. I was confused. I was hurt. I felt dejected.'

'You were right. You were dejected. Nothing's changed. Nothing's changed at all.'

'You said you loved me then,' she choked.

'And I do, but not in the way that you want to be loved. You want a man who can love you every day. I'll be gone soon and then you'll be left alone to feel dejected. I can't help that.'

'Then there really is no chance?'

'Of what?'

'Of trying again?' she said, and her voice trailed off in humiliation.

Ramon stroked her hair and lay staring up into the darkness. He thought of Estella and the confident way that she loved him. There was something very needy about Helena and he felt that old, familiar sense of claustrophobia suffocate him once again. He still loved her. But he couldn't change her and as long as she enveloped him with her needy love he couldn't love her in the way that she longed to be loved. He felt the wind of change blow outside his window and knew that it was time to leave.

The following morning Ramon came down to breakfast with his bags packed.

'You're leaving?' said Helena tightly. Her headache had returned and she was filled with shame. She wished she could rewind the tape and erase the previous night. She could barely look into his eyes. When she did they were once more dark and impenetrable. She had gone too far and ruined everything.

'I'm leaving,' he replied, then sat down next to Federica.

'You're leaving?' she stammered. 'Now?' She watched her father's grim face nod at her sadly. Had she dreamed the night before when they had talked on the landing with such affection? She was certain they were falling in love again. How could it all have gone so wrong in one night? She didn't understand.

'Don't be sad, *mi amor*.' He touched her forlorn face. 'I want you to write to me and tell me how you're getting on and what you're doing. Don't miss out a single detail.' He wiped a tear off her cheek with his thumb. 'You be good and don't cry, because I'll be back very soon to see you.'

But Federica's face crumpled into misery and she threw her arms around his neck and sobbed. 'I don't want you to go,' she choked. 'Please don't go.'

'I can't stay for ever, *mi amor*. I'll be back, I promise,' he reassured her. 'Remember to write to me,' he added and kissed her wet face.

When he gathered Hal into his arms the child squirmed and cried out for his mother. Helena soothed him with gentle words and gathered him up, where he clung to her like a frightened monkey. Ramon didn't pursue it. There was nothing more to say. He kissed Helena's stony face, then he was gone leaving a feeling of emptiness in their hearts and a terrible sense of loss.

Helena wondered when he'd come back. She had a premonition that it wouldn't be for many years.

Federica ran upstairs and slammed her bedroom door behind her. She threw herself onto her Snoopy duvet and cried. How could he rush off like that with no warning? She had invested all her hopes in him. She was sure he was going to stay. Besides, he had enjoyed it in Polperro. They had had fun. He liked the Applebys but most of all he had appeared to like her mother again. They had become friends. What went wrong? When she had tired of crying she pulled the butterfly box onto her knee and opened the lid. She stared down into the glimmering crystals and watched the butterfly extend her wings, changing from reds to blues as if in sympathy. In the mesmerising shades of the ancient stones she hid from her unhappiness and the sudden sense of rejection that gripped her heart with cold claws. Slowly she lost herself in her memories that seemed to resonate in each tiny gem. She saw her grandparents on their balcony in Cachagua and Rasta running up Caleta Abarca beach. She saw the house where she used to live and then the wide open sea, she smelt the lavender and felt the sun on her face. Dizzy with the invasion of so many recollections she closed her eyes and drifted on her father's love.

Chapter Nineteen

Cachagua

It was just before Christmas that Mariana finally made the effort to visit Estella. A Christmas visit of goodwill. She would take her a silver necklace that she had bought in Santiago as a present. After all, it hadn't been her idea to sack her. In fact, Mariana had done everything in her power to persuade Ignacio to keep her on. She had liked her and she was the first maid she had ever had who did the jobs without being asked and used her initiative without being prompted. Estella had been far too intelligent to reduce her talents to cooking and cleaning but she seemed to enjoy it.

Mariana had been forced to ask the ill-tempered Gertrude to find out where Estella was now living. She was unable to discover her whereabouts on her own, especially now that rumour had it that Estella was no longer living with her parents. Gertrude had been quick to point that out. She had added with glee that according to her cousin who lived in the same village as Pablo and Maria Rega, not even they knew where their daughter's house was.

So Mariana had driven herself to Estella's beach house, following the directions that Gertrude had given her. The old woman had offered to accompany her but Mariana had graciously declined her offer with a shudder. She could barely spend more than five minutes in the maid's company in her own home, let alone in the claustrophobic interior of a car. The thought of it made Mariana's mouth curl downwards with distaste. Not only was Gertrude insolent but she also had a strange tendency to smell strongly of aniseed. Mariana was old fashioned and liked the parameters between employer and employee to be clearly defined. Gertrude hurled herself against those parameters without thinking and always caused offence. Ignacio dealt with her firmly by shouting at her to 'know her place', to which Gertrude responded with a scowl but also a reconfirmed sense of duty and commitment to her job.

When Mariana first saw Estella's beach house she was immediately impressed by the size and quality and curious to how a woman in her position could afford such luxury. It was built into the bank overlooking the sea and had the good fortune of being the only house for some distance. It was painted white with an American-style veranda and large green shutters to keep the interior cool in the summertime. The roof was thatched and the walls supported an abundance of sky-blue plumbago which had managed to weave its way over the veranda where it hung down and fluttered in the wind like butterflies. Mariana had never suspected Estella's errant lover to be rich. She had assumed he came from the same world as she did. She had been wrong.

The door was open and she could hear Estella singing inside and the cheerful gurgles of a baby. Mariana recalled Gertrude's vicious comment about the monkey and smiled with satisfaction. That was most certainly not the noise of a monkey. She hesitated a moment before calling for Estella because she noticed evidence of the presence of a man. A man's shirt hung on the back of the chair on the veranda and a pair of moccasins were placed by the door. Well, she thought, if he's here I may as well meet him too. So she called out 'Estella' and waited.

Estella recognised the voice immediately and she stood rooted to the ground, stunned with panic. Ramon was in England yet all his belongings were scattered over the house. In the brief moment between Mariana's call and Estella's thin reply she tried to remember what items of Ramon's were where and which would give him away. Finally she laid Ramoncito in his cradle and walked up the corridor to the door where Mariana was inching her way in, curious to cast her eyes about the house.

'Señora Mariana, what a surprise,' said Estella firmly, attempting to hide the tremor in her voice. 'Let's talk outside, it's very hot in here,' she said, ushering her former employer out onto the veranda. Mariana was disappointed. She had wanted to see the house. But her good manners prevented her from requesting a tour.

'I'm sorry I came unannounced. Are you alone?' she asked.

Estella noticed her eyes rest on the pair of shoes by the door. 'Yes, I'm alone,' she replied casually. 'Please, sit down and make yourself comfortable.' She gesticulated to the chair with the shirt hanging off it. Estella removed the incriminating item and placed it inside the front door along with the shoes. Mariana noticed everything and wondered why she was so embarrassed. Then it suddenly occurred to her that perhaps the man sharing her house was not the father of her child.

'I see you are quite happy,' said Mariana tactfully. 'You have a beautiful house.'

'Thank you, Señora Mariana.'

Mariana noticed how nervous the girl was and concluded that it was only natural after Ignacio had so brutally asked her to leave his employment. 'I'm so sorry about your job,' said Mariana, desperately trying to put the girl at her ease. 'Ignacio can be very insensitive. He doesn't mean to. It's his way. But not everyone understands him like I do. Are you being taken care of?' It was a clumsy question but Mariana couldn't resist. Estella stiffened and her eyes lowered as if she were ashamed to look at Mariana directly.

'I am very content,' she replied simply.

'You have a little baby now. A boy?' Estella nodded and she smiled without restraint. 'He's obviously giving you a lot of pleasure. I adored every one of my eight children and grand-children,' she sighed. 'Grandchildren give me the same pleasure all over again.' Then she thought momentarily of Federica and Hal and her eyes misted. 'What is he called?' she asked, deliberately forgetting her own melancholy.

Estella's cheeks burnt with guilt. She could tell the truth and risk suspicion or she could lie. She raised her eyes to Mariana's and decided that lying was without doubt the only option.

'I have not decided yet,' she said, looking steadily at the other woman in an effort not to appear shifty.

Mariana was surprised. 'You haven't decided yet?'

'No.'

'Well, you must call him something!'

'I call him Angelito. My little angel,' she said quickly.

Mariana smiled. 'Angel. That's a nice name,' she said, but her intuition told her that something wasn't quite right.

'I'm glad things turned out well for you. Last summer I was very worried.'

'Me too.'

'But you have a lovely house, a little boy and' – she hesitated but then threw aside her reservations and continued without inhibition – 'you have a man to take care of you.' She watched as Estella's face burned again and her eyes shone awkwardly. 'Don't worry, my dear, I'm not prying,' she reassured her quickly, thinking of Gertrude and wishing that she hadn't gone so far. 'I don't need to know who he is, it just makes me happy that you're happy. I am very fond of you, Estella, and it gave me much grief to see you suffering. You're a good girl and you didn't deserve to be treated with such callousness. There are plenty of girls who deserve that sort of treatment, but not you, you're a cut above them. I wanted to tell you that if you ever need anything to come and see me. I'll always try to help you in any way that I can. A reference perhaps or advice. I'm here to talk to if ever you need someone who's detached from your family. An outsider. I would only be too happy.'

She watched Estella's face relax and the colour drain away again as her embarrassment was replaced with gratitude. 'You're very kind, Señora Mariana. A girl like me is very lucky to have a protector like yourself. I'm very privileged and I thank you,' she said, wondering how Mariana would feel if she knew they were Ramon's shoes in the doorway and Ramon's shirt that had hung over the back of the chair. Estella doubted she would offer her protection if she knew her son was committing adultery with a lowly maid.

Mariana rose to leave. She swallowed her curiosity and restrained herself from asking to see inside the house. But before she left she felt it wasn't unreasonable to ask for one thing. 'Estella, I would dearly love to see Angelito,' she said.

Estella went pale. 'Angelito,' she repeated.

'Yes. If it's not too much bother. He's obviously a good baby as he hasn't made a squeak.'

'He is a good baby. But he might be asleep,' said Estella, trying to make excuses.

'Then I can come and take a peek. I won't wake him,' she insisted.

Estella had no choice. If Mariana came into the house she would no doubt recognise her son's belongings. 'No, I'll go and get him and bring him out here,' she replied quickly, retreating into the house. Mariana thought her behaviour most strange. If her child had really been a monkey she would have reacted in the same way. For a brief moment Mariana wondered whether there was perhaps something wrong with the child. If the child was in some way deformed it was quite wrong of her to insist on seeing it. But before she had time to tell Estella not to worry, the young woman appeared out of the shadows carrying a small bundle in her arms. Mariana felt an itchy heat crawl about the skin on her neck and prepared herself for the worst.

Estella hoped that Mariana wouldn't recognise her son in Ramoncito's conker eyes and languid smile. But when she saw the baby blinking up at her sweetly Mariana's face opened like a flower and a wide, genuine smile swept across it expressing her delight.

'He is quite the most beautiful baby, Estella. Can I hold him?' she enthused, pressing her hands against her cheeks in wonder. 'Adorable, completely adorable,' she sighed, taking the child from his mother and pressing him against her bosom. Estella smiled too, relieved that grandmother hadn't recognised grandson and she was able to breathe again.

Mariana sat back down in her chair while the baby smiled happily up at his grandmother. Estella brought out a tray of iced lemon and the two women sat under the plumbago and talked about the baby. 'He is so like you, Estella. Such a pretty baby. Look at his long eyelashes and dark eyes. He'll be breaking hearts all over Chile. Won't you, Angelito?' she clucked, gently rocking him.

'He's a good baby. He rarely cries,' said Estella proudly.

'I bet he eats well, too.'

'He does. He's growing so quickly.'

'I can see.'

'I love being a mother. I have a purpose in my life now. I feel needed,' said Estella thoughtfully.

'Motherhood is a wonderful thing. It changes your life for ever. Suddenly there's this little person who needs you more than anyone else in the world. He's from your own body. Imagine that bond, how strong it is. He's a part of you and even when he's grown up and gone he's still connected to you, because you made him, gave birth to him and suckled him.'

'You're so right,' agreed Estella and she told Mariana about how she felt when he was growing inside her.

The two women began to talk as equals about the duties of a mother, the joys and the sorrows that were the two sides of the privilege of motherhood.

'We feel their pain and their pleasure. We can't help it. It's our lot,' said Mariana, remembering Ramon and the break-up of his marriage. 'But they are individuals and have to make their own choices. We can only advise and be there when things go wrong. But I would never change any of it for a second. Motherhood is the most wonderful gift of life, and I'm very fortunate to be a woman,' she said and smiled at Estella.

'Me too,' Estella replied, smiling back.

When Mariana finally got up to leave the midday sun was high in the sky. She looked at her watch and realised that she had been there for well over an hour and a half. 'Goodness me, look at the time!' she exclaimed, handing the child back to his mother. 'Angelito must be hungry.'

'He's always hungry. I think he's going to be a big boy,' she said, kissing his forehead tenderly.

'Thank you for letting me see him,' said Mariana gratefully. 'He really is very dear.'

'It was a pleasure,' Estella replied. 'Thank you for coming.'

Mariana was no more than ten steps from the house, reflecting on the delightful baby Angel, when she put her hand in her pocket and felt the silver necklace she had bought for Estella. She sighed in frustration at her own forgetfulness and turned back. Estella had disappeared inside, leaving only the wings of the plumbago flowers to flutter about the walls of the beach house in the cool sea breeze. Mariana stood once again in the frame of the door, uncertain whether to knock or walk straight in. She smiled with tenderness as she heard the excited tones of Estella playing with her child.

'Ramoncito, my little angel. Ramoncito,' she laughed as the baby squeaked and gurgled back.

Mariana's smile slowly slipped off her face. She held her breath as the blood drained from her head to her feet, fixing her to the ground when all she wanted to do was run away as fast as her old legs could carry her. When Estella repeated his name Mariana was left in no doubt that she had heard correctly and arrived at the right conclusion. With great effort she turned as quickly and as quietly as she could and hastily made her way back to the car, her temples throbbing with the sudden sporadic appearance of thousands of unpleasant images.

Once inside she sat behind the wheel with her heart thumping like a maddened bat inside her breathless chest, as if she had just witnessed a murder. With a trembling hand she turned the key in the ignition. It was only when she was on the open road that she began to breathe again. The father of Estella's child was none other than her own son, Ramon. There was no doubt about it. It all made complete sense. The camera in her mind had at once been turned into focus and she could see clearly the events of the summer before. Estella's lover had been Ramon. He had seduced her, impregnated her then left her. That sort of callous, irresponsible behaviour was not limited to the lower classes, as Ignacio had maintained, but to their own flesh and blood.

Mariana was repelled by the thought of adultery. They were clearly living together; Estella couldn't afford a house like that. Now she understood the girl's reluctance to show her the baby and her unease. Ramon's possessions littered the house. Mariana thought of Helena and her children and suddenly felt consumed with resentment and regret. When her old eyes welled with unhappiness she was forced to pull the car up on the side of the road and give way to her tears. She couldn't understand Ramon. But she loved him and tried desperately to justify his actions. She blamed Helena for driving him into Estella's arms and Estella for being too beautiful for him to resist. But her arguments paled in the light of her reasoning, which told her Ramon was guilty. He was a victim of his own selfishness. He wilfully sacrificed everything he loved for a vacuous freedom, which would inevitably leave him lonely and full of regret. He would leave Estella too.

By the time Mariana returned home she had decided not to tell Ignacio. She had also decided to look out for Estella. The girl didn't know it yet, but she would need support.

Mariana knew her son better than anyone.

PART II

Chapter Twenty

Polperro, Spring 1989

Federica bicycled up the hill, her breaths staggered and short as she sobbed and pedalled, barely able to see the road for the tears in her eyes. The warm May sunshine had tempted the trees and bushes into blossom and bud, the unlikely snowfalls in April were now over for good. But Federica didn't care for the beauty of nature. She didn't even notice the armies of bluebells in the woods or the sweet smell of fertility as the ground woke up from her winter sleep. Her heart felt as if someone had wrenched it from her chest, beaten it about, then carelessly put it back again.

The ride up the lane to Pickthistle Manor seemed much longer than normal. Her face was red and sweaty from exertion and her eyes swollen like two baked apples. When she cycled into the driveway she was greeted by Trotsky, the rather arrogant Great Dane that Inigo had given Ingrid to console her after the death of her favourite dog, Pushkin. Trotsky was honey-brown with skin like velvet and the intelligent face of a Cambridge scholar, his eyes surrounded by dark circles which gave the impression that he was wearing little round glasses, much to everyone's amusement. Hence the name Trotsky, which he lived up to with great pride and dignity. Federica patted him absent-mindedly as she passed. He sensed her distress and bounded after her with long, leisurely strides.

She threw down her bicycle on the gravel then rushed inside shouting for Hester. She held her breath and listened for a reply, but none came. Only the sound of Inigo's classical music escaped under his study door and floated through the house. She didn't want to disturb Inigo who was obviously working so she wandered through the rooms hoping to find one of the girls. She was mortified to discover that the house was completely empty except for Sam who sat at the kitchen table eating a large peanut-butter sandwich, reading the Saturday papers. When he saw her standing awkwardly in the doorway he put down his paper and asked her what was wrong.

'I'm looking for Hester,' she said quietly, wiping her face with her hands and hoping he wouldn't notice she was crying. She took a deep breath and forced a smile.

But Sam wasn't fooled. 'The girls have gone shopping with Mum and the boys are having a picnic tea on the beach,' he said, then smiled sympathetically.

'Oh,' said Federica, not knowing what else to say. She had always felt suffocated when alone with Sam. He was too handsome to look at, too clever to talk to and much too grown up to be interested in her. So she began to back away through the door, mumbling that she'd find Hester later.

'Why don't you have a peanut-butter sandwich?' he asked, holding up the jar. 'They're extremely good. Mum calls this type of food "comfort food" and you look as though you need some of that.'

'No, really, I'm not hungry,' she stammered, embarrassed by her own incompetence.

'I know. But you're unhappy,' he said and smiled again. 'At least have some to make you feel better.' He pulled out a couple of slices of bread and began to prepare a sandwich for her. She had no choice. She walked up to the table and sat down on the chair that he had pulled out for her. 'I'm afraid I can't resist a weeping woman,' he said. Federica laughed as the tears blurred her vision again. A month off thirteen she could hardly be considered a woman, not even by a long stretch of the imagination. She lowered her eyes and took a timid bite of her sandwich. 'You know,' Sam continued, 'women's tears are their secret weapon. I know I'm not alone. Most men go weak at the sight of them, or they don't know how to handle them so they leave themselves vulnerable to every sort of manipulation. They'll do anything to bring a smile to the lady's face. What can I do to bring a smile to your face?'

'There's nothing you can do. I'll be fine,' she replied, staring down at her sandwich, anything rather than look at him.

'Well, there's nothing worse than sitting about inside on a sunny day like this feeling miserable. Why don't you join me for a walk? The bluebells will cheer you up and by the time we get back the girls will probably have returned. How does that sound?'

'You must have better things to do,' she said, not wanting to be a bore.

'Now you're sounding like Eeyore. Try and be more like Pooh, or Tigger. Actually,' he said, grinning at her, 'you're more like Piglet.'

'Is that meant to be a compliment?'

'Definitely. Piglet is a fine fellow. So how about a stroll in the hundred-acre wood?'

Federica rarely saw Sam. He had left school and travelled for a year before taking up his scholarship at Cambridge. The long holidays were usually spent travelling, weekends up in London at parties. When he came home he'd only stay for a couple of days, locked in Nuno's library or in heavy discussion with his father. Federica would bicycle up the drive, her heart in a state of quivering expectation, hoping that his green and white Deux Chevaux would be parked outside the house indicating that he was at home. When the space on the gravel was empty she'd still keep her ears open and hope that perhaps during the course of her visit he might very well turn up and surprise them all. But he rarely did.

During the previous seven years Federica's crush on Sam had neither waned nor tempered. If anything it had grown more intense, teased by the fact that she so rarely saw him. She knew he was too old, she knew he would never look at her as anything other than his little sister's friend, but still she fantasised about him. Molly and Hester knew of her crush. The whole family did and they all found it charming, even Sam, whose ego wasn't immune to the blushes of a twelve-year-old child. But no one ever spoke of it in front of Federica. She was shy and ill-equipped for their type of humour.

It was warm. The bluebells flooded the ground like a violet river, drowning the disintegrating winter foliage beneath them, shimmering in the breeze and heralding the return of spring. Sam pulled off his sweater, tying it about his waist and walking in his shirtsleeves, leaving the cuffs undone to flap carelessly about his hands. Trotsky trotted along behind them, sniffing the bushes and cocking his leg everywhere because the scent of spring excited him. 'I do love this time of year. The smells are rich, the trees in bud. Just look at that green, it's unreal, isn't it?' he said, pulling a piece of blossom off a tree and smelling it.

'It's beautiful,' she replied, following him up the path that wound its way through the trees.

'I remember when you first moved here,' he said.

'Me too. I nearly died in the lake.'

'Not a very auspicious start,' he chuckled.

'It's got better, though,' she replied. It *had* got better, but now it had all gone wrong.

'Do you miss Chile?' he asked, slowing down for her to catch up as the path widened to allow them both to walk side by side.

'I miss my father,' she said truthfully, swallowing a sob. 'Chile is little more than a faded memory. If I think of Chile I think of my father.'

Sam pulled a sympathetic smile. He was very aware that she never spoke about her father. Nuno had condemned him as heartless, Inigo irresponsible. Only Ingrid took Ramon's side and believed there was more to it than the superficial actuality of a father deserting his family.

When Ramon had left Polperro seven years before, everyone had remained electrified by his sudden visit. Federica had talked

236

proudly about him at every opportunity, clearly expecting him to return every once in a while to see her, perhaps one day coming to stay for good. She had written to him. Long letters in her childish hand, signed with love and sealed with hope. He had written poems for her and a novel which he had dedicated 'to my daughter' about a little girl called Topahuay who lived in Peru but which none of the Applebys understood except for Nuno who had a basic knowledge of Spanish because of his ability to speak Italian. Then the letters had begun to arrive with less frequency until they had almost dried up altogether. There was no surprise visit, no telephone call. Federica kept his letters in the butterfly box, which she hid under her bed. Without knowing why she began to shroud Ramon in secrecy. She stopped talking about him. She showed no one her butterfly box. She possessively protected his memory in the silent halls of her mind where she alone could visit him. The only person she allowed into these halls was Hester. And Hester loyally kept all Federica's secrets. She even managed to keep them from Molly who had attempted to prise them out of her sister with both manipulation and force. But Hester had never given in and took great pride in her loyalty.

As the years passed Federica's shame grew. Everyone else had a father. The other schoolchildren wondered why Federica didn't have one and whispered about it behind her back. Deep in her subconscious she couldn't help but wonder whether she had done something wrong, for he couldn't love her. If he loved her he would want to see her. If he loved her he'd miss her like she missed him. She remembered his words about Señora Baraca because she remembered everything he had ever said to her. 'Sometimes it's better to move on, rather than dwell on the past. One should learn things from the past and then let them go.' He had chosen to stay away, would he prefer them to let him go?

'I liked your father very much,' said Sam carefully. He watched her mouth twist with misery and her eyes glisten again with tears.

'I'm sorry, I shouldn't have brought him up. It must be very painful for you,' he apologised, touching her arm.

'I miss him, that's all,' she sniffed.

'Of course you do,' he agreed, pushing his glasses up the bridge of his nose, a gesture he often did when he felt awkward.

'Sometimes it's fine. Then all of a sudden, for no reason, I think of him and feel sad.'

'That's only natural.'

'I know. Is Mama having a serious boyfriend natural too?' she asked and a large tear wobbled on her upper lip before dropping into the bluebells.

Sam stopped walking and instinctively drew the sobbing child into his arms. 'So this is what it's all about,' he said, hugging her. She nodded but her throat was too strained to speak. 'It was always going to happen, Fede. Look, let's sit down and talk about this,' he suggested, patting her gently on the back before releasing her.

They sat in the sun among the bluebells, Federica cross-legged and Sam with his long legs stretched out in front of him leaning back against the trunk of a tree. Federica couldn't believe that only a moment ago she had been in his arms. To her shame her tears ceased immediately and she blinked across at him, her cheeks aflame.

'She's had boyfriends before, but Arthur wants to marry her,' she said in despair.

'What's this Arthur like?'

'He's all right, I suppose. He's not very interesting. In fact, I think he's very dull. He's quite fat and has no hair, but he laughs at all Mama's jokes and tells her how wonderful she is all the time.'

'What does he do?'

'He's a wine merchant. An old wine merchant. He must be at least fifty. Mama says he's very clever and has a very good job. He's reliable, dependable and nice. Yes, that's the word, nice. Nice, nice, nice.'

'But he's not your father,' said Sam.

'No,' she croaked, 'he's not Papa and he never will be.'

'I thought your parents were still married?'

'They are.'

'Then your mother would have to get a divorce in order to marry this boring Arthur person,' said Sam.

'Yes, she would.'

'Well, that would take ages.'

'Yes.'

'Has your mother agreed to marry him?'

'No, she hasn't yet. I just overheard them talking.'

'What did she say when he asked her?'

'Well, Arthur goes, "You're a delicate flower in need of protecting,"' said Federica in a low voice. Sam laughed at her impersonation. Federica's mouth curled into a small smile. 'Then Mama said, "I wish I were as beautiful as a flower." To which Arthur replied, "With a little watering you'll blossom into one. Marry me, Helena."' Federica grimaced, blinking away tears that now seemed out of place amid the humour of her recital. 'I nearly threw up. Mama might be many things but she is certainly no flower. What would Papa think?'

Sam was chuckling. He had never bothered to talk to Federica before, he had always thought her rather dull and quiet, but he was seeing a side to her that he never knew she had. He didn't blame his sisters at all for liking her.

'It's clear that she's enjoying the attentions of a kind man. You don't know the dynamics of your parents' relationship. As your father was away all the time your mother must have felt neglected. Dull Arthur obviously makes her feel attractive. She's enjoying the attention,' said Sam, believing he had summed up the entire situation in a couple of sentences. He took off his glasses and began to clean them on his shirt.

'But if she marries him we'll have to move away from Polperro,' said Federica in panic.

'Ah, now that is a problem,' he agreed.

Federica's face lengthened again in gloom. 'I couldn't bear to move away. I love it here,' she said huskily.

'I know Molly and Hester wouldn't want you to move away either.'

'What can I do?'

'You can't do anything. But if I were you,' he said loftily, 'I would talk to your mother and ask her what she intends to do.'

'But I can't admit that I was eavesdropping.'

'Why not? I eavesdrop all the time. There's nothing wrong with it. If people don't want to be heard they should make sure no one can hear them. It was their fault. Arthur's not only dull but obviously stupid too,' he said. Sam had little tolerance for stupid people.

'I suppose I could talk to her.'

'Of course you could.'

'But she's only interested in talking about Hal. I don't think I'd make the slightest bit of difference.'

'Oh dear,' said Sam, nodding his head. 'Some mothers adore their sons to the exclusion of the rest of the family.'

'Not in your family.'

'No. Mum has always been far too vague to adore any of us too much. She's not really on the planet, you know. She always looks rather surprised that she had any of us at all. I think if someone told her the stork brought us into the world she'd believe it. She has no memory of childbirth at all. We still manage to amaze her.'

'Your family is the nicest I've ever met. I wish mine was like yours,' she said wistfully.

'One's own problems always seem so much greater than anyone else's because you never see past the veneer of other people's families. Believe me, each family hides skeletons in its cupboards. I'm sure you'd be surprised by some of ours,' he said and laughed.

But Federica didn't believe him. She doubted they even knew what a skeleton looked like.

'I imagine it's only natural that Mama should want to marry again,' said Federica, picking a bluebell and turning it around between her fingers.

'Everyone needs someone,' said Sam.

'Not Papa. He doesn't need anyone at all.'

'You never really talk about your father. Is that because you're ashamed of him?'

Federica wouldn't normally have answered such a personal question but she felt safe with Sam. 'Yes,' she replied, breaking the bluebell into small pieces. 'I wish we were a normal family like everyone else's. Like yours. When I was smaller, in Chile, Papa used to take me down to the beach or into Viña to eat *palta* sandwiches in the sunshine. We'd go and stay with my grandparents in Cachagua. It was lovely then. Although he didn't come home very often, when he did it was like heaven and I always knew when he left that he'd come back. His clothes were in the cupboards, his books in the sitting room. There was evidence of his presence everywhere. Now there's nothing. It's as if he's died — worse, because if he was dead everyone would make an effort to remember him. But no one talks about him at all. You see, in Viña everyone knew of Ramon Campione. He was well-known in Chile. He was a famous writer, a poet, and everyone thought he was very clever and gifted. I was so proud of him. Here no one's ever heard of him. If it weren't for his letters I'd wonder whether I'd made the whole thing up.'

'Oh, Fede,' he sighed. 'I'm so sorry. It's hideous for you. Because you never show your feelings or talk about him we just assumed you were all right. But, how can you be? It's monstrous of him to desert you like that.'

'Is it really that easy to forget?'

'He forgets because he's probably plagued with guilt when he remembers. In that sense it's the easy option, total avoidance.'

'I've always put him on a pedestal,' she exclaimed, pulling a thin smile.

'No one's infallible, Fede. Not even Ramon.'

'But seven years is worse than careless,' she argued.

'Has it really been so long?' Sam asked, feeling very sorry for her. She reminded him of one of his mother's broken animals.

'Yes. He used to write all the time. I haven't had a letter from him for about six months. I still write to him, but not as much as I used to. I'm frightened I'll forget him. I don't want him to turn up one day and not recognise him.' Her voice thinned again as her throat constricted with sadness. She opened her eyes very wide in an attempt to force her tears back. 'I should be angry with him. But I'm not. I just want him to come home.'

'Can't you talk to your mother about this?' he asked, shuffling over to sit beside her so he could place an arm around her.

'I could. But Mama's very fragile. She hates Papa so I can't mention his name in the house. Hal doesn't even remember him. Arthur's become more of a father to Hal than Papa ever was. But he'll never be a father to me, never,' she sobbed and the tears finally rebelled and spilled out over her cheeks.

Sam tried to comfort her by squeezing her around the shoulders and giving her the best advice he could think of. 'Talk to your mother. The most worrying thing is the doubt. You don't know if she's said "yes" to boring Arthur and you don't know what that means for you if she has said "yes". You need to find out. She might have no intention of moving away from Polperro.'

Federica nodded her head and sniffed. 'I'll ask her.'

'Good. You must let me know what she says.'

'I will.'

'You can come and talk to me any time, you know,' he said. 'Hester's all very well, but sometimes a grown-up is better. Especially if you can't talk to your mother. Everyone needs someone to talk to.'

'Who do you talk to?'

'Nuno or Dad. Mostly Nuno, I suppose.'

'Isn't he a bit mad?' said Federica.

Sam smiled at her. 'Eccentric, but not mad. In fact, he's the cleverest man I've ever met. He taught me more than I would have ever learnt at school. He's far too wise for his own good.'

'I wish I were wise.'

'You will be one day. But no one can teach you wisdom, they can teach you knowledge and warn you so that you avoid the mistakes they made. But on the whole you need to live to acquire wisdom. " 'Tis held that sorrow makes us wise" – Lord Alfred Tennyson.'

'Then I must be quite wise by now,' she said and grinned at him with self-pity.

'Don't put your happiness in other people's hands.'

'What do you mean?'

'Don't rely on other people to make you happy or you're sure to be unhappy always. People will inevitably disappoint you,' he said. 'On that positive note, let's head back to the house. I bet Hester's back by now with a whole new wardrobe to show you,' he chuckled, pushing himself up from the ground. 'Feel any better?'

She nodded. 'Thank you,' she said, full of gratitude. Finally Sam had noticed her. She felt a lightness of being in spite of her heaviness of heart.

He patted her between her shoulder blades. 'Come on. And that means you too, Trotsky,' he said to the dog, who had slept through their entire conversation. He got to his feet and stretched before trotting on down the path they had made through the bluebells. The clamour of birds filled the trees, punctuated occasionally by the sharp cough of a pheasant. The sunlight bathed the woods in a resplendent mist and Federica felt she was walking through an earthly paradise. She watched Sam, tall and straight, lead the way and knew that she could never leave Polperro because the Applebys were her family and she simply couldn't be without them.

Chapter Twenty-One

When Helena watched Ramon walk out seven years before she knew she had driven him away. She had admitted regret, opening herself up to be wounded once again by Ramon's indifference. She thought he had changed. But she knew in her heart that he would never, ever change. He had always been far too selfish to think of anyone but himself. So she had swallowed her humiliation and let him go, quietly resolving to get on with her life in Polperro in spite of him.

Helena might have believed she had cleansed herself of her husband's presence, but unknown to her his words had penetrated her subconscious where they had taken root and grown. She began to make some space in her life for herself and her own needs. She relied more on her mother to help her with Hal – Federica didn't need much looking after: she was responsible and self-sufficient. She looked after herself and her mother too. So Helena didn't worry about Federica, she worried about Hal.

Hal was dependent and needy and as self-centred as his mother. He was also extremely moody, up one moment, down the next, floundering in a pool of his own dissatisfaction. Polly was delighted to be needed again and threw herself into the roles of mother and grandmother with relish. Jake just pushed his nose further into his miniature boats and tried to ignore the rest of the household, who moved around in barely contained longing to satisfy the demands of his daughter and grandson.

So, Helena had moved on. She went out on dates. She even slept with a few of the men she dated and almost managed to convince herself that she liked it. But none of them made love to her like Ramon and as much as she knew she was no longer really married and free to see whoever she chose, she was still wracked with guilt afterwards. It wasn't until she met Arthur Cooke that everything changed.

Polly noticed that Arthur was different from the others because Helena cut her hair, painted her nails, bought a new wardrobe and began to take pride in her appearance. A light skip crept into her walk and she held her shoulders back and head up as she had always done as a teenager. Suddenly she began to look her age, thirty-seven, rather than the old woman who had surreptitiously slipped beneath her bitter skin.

Arthur Cooke was forty-nine years old, divorced, with three children who were all in their early twenties. He prided himself in his ability to sustain a good relationship with his wife, who had married again, and children who didn't seem to resent him for the break-up of their family. When Helena had first met him, at an eye-wateringly boring drinks party given by one of her dates, she had thought he looked like an egg. A smiling egg. He wasn't tall, didn't have much hair, didn't dress particularly well and had nothing physically that would have attracted her to him. But Helena was too busy assessing what he didn't have to notice what he did have. She found that out later.

Arthur was kind, witty, energetic, enthusiastic and generous. When she found herself talking to him because there simply wasn't anyone better to talk to, she discovered sharp brown eyes that noticed everything, a smile that reached across the whole of his jovial face and a contagious laugh that bubbled up from his belly. When he touched her hand his was soft and gentle, when he spoke his voice was full of understanding and when he listened she realised that he did so without distraction as if she were the most fascinating woman he had ever met. By the end of the evening she had talked to no one else and had completely ignored the man she had arrived with. Arthur invited her to join him for a drink and she left her floundering date without an explanation, knowing that she wouldn't care if she never saw him again.

They went to a quiet bar that overlooked the bay and sat in candlelight listening to the schmaltzy music that accompanied the soporific rhythm of the tide and talked for hours. By the time Arthur dropped her off at her home he knew everything about Ramon, Federica and Hal. She had allowed him to strip her soul layer by layer with the help of various glasses of wine until she stood naked before him, lonely and unhappy. He had then helped her dress it again with compliments and words of encouragement and compassion. When she awoke the following morning she looked in the mirror and saw a haggard old woman staring back at her in surprise. She had never noticed her before. Shocked, she left her mother to look after the children and disappeared into town for half the day to discard Ramon's wife and emerge as someone different. When Helena returned looking rejuvenated, her mother told her that a man called Arthur had telephoned. She smiled in a way that Polly hadn't seen her smile for a long, long time.

Arthur made her feel good about herself. He seemed to understand her and her needs. He held her hand when it began to shake and taught her how to breathe deeply from the pit of her stomach when she felt nervous. He rang her all the time for no reason at all, simply to hear her voice and to make sure that she was okay. He made her feel protected. He made her laugh with the lack of inhibition that had characterised those first heavenly years with Ramon, with a loose throat and an aching stomach. He made her feel that nothing really mattered and she suddenly realised why Ingrid was always happy, because she dwelt in a vague, carefree world that hovered above the preoccupations of more earthly people. She would never be like Ingrid, but she was now able at least to see her world and aspire towards it.

As much as Arthur had endeared himself to her she was terrified of taking the relationship into a physical dimension. Sex with Ramon had been otherworldly. No one could compete with that. Certainly not Arthur. He wasn't a physical man. He didn't play sport, was flat-footed and unfit. He loved good food, good wine and good company, but she couldn't imagine him in bed and she feared sex would ruin the relationship beyond repair. So she rebuffed his advances when he tried to kiss her. But Arthur's sharp brown eyes had noticed everything. He wasn't the sort of man to dither and brood. If he had something to say he simply said it.

'Helena,' he said one winter evening as they drained their wine glasses beside the boisterous fire in his sitting room.

'Yes, Arthur,' she replied nervously, fearing that he was going to ask her to stay the night.

'Your hand is shaking again. Give me your wine glass,' he said. She handed it to him and smiled hesitantly. 'Close your eyes,' he said, taking her hand in his. 'Now, take a deep breath, right from the bottom of your lungs. That's right. Now let it out. Let out all that fear and all that uncertainty. Well done. Now let's do it again.' He instructed her to repeat the exercise three times. 'Now you should feel better,' he said, but she didn't. 'This time I want you to close your eyes and let me kiss you.'

'No, Arthur . . .' she protested.

'You want me to, but you're afraid. You've slept with men since your husband but none of them managed to satisfy you. You're afraid I will disappoint you. I can assure you I won't,' he said. So Helena reluctantly closed her eyes and hoped the wine would dull her senses. She felt his mouth brush hers, but it could have been the warmth of the flames that flickered in the fireplace. A moment later she felt it again, followed by that familiar tingle in her belly, stirring with the memory of Ramon's touch. She wanted to open her eyes but she kept them firmly shut for fear of seeing Arthur's earnest face close to hers and losing her nerve. Then she felt his lips sink onto her anxious mouth. Surprisingly it felt quite nice. Then his hand was in the small of her back. A firm, supporting hand confidently pulling her towards him as his lips opened and he kissed her with tenderness. In spite of her fears, her senses rebelled against her reasoning and she became aware only of the screaming of her nerves as they cried out for him to caress her and love her.

Arthur took her by the hand upstairs to the bedroom. Then he proceeded to make love to every inch of her body with the enthusiasm and attentiveness of a man whose only purpose is to give pleasure because in so doing does he derive his own pleasure. Helena abandoned herself to his devotion without feeling guilty or undeserving. Then once she was convinced of his prowess he made love to her again with humour until they both rolled about on the bed laughing uncontrollably.

There was no comparing him with Ramon because he was so entirely different. Arthur's sexual proficiency was his trump card. It was so totally unexpected. Once Helena had discovered it, she could not get enough of it. With Arthur she felt feminine again and very much alive. She was no longer getting ready to live but living, and Ramon's sour-tasting memory sweetened into the recesses of her mind until it no longer plagued her or hounded her. Arthur occupied her present and there simply wasn't time to look back on the past.

Until Arthur asked her to marry him and suddenly Ramon reappeared in her thoughts.

She told him that she would think about it. But she had to consider the feelings of her children. She knew Federica didn't like Arthur, in spite of his persistent attempts to befriend her. She answered his questions in monosyllables with a long, scowling face. But the worst was the sad, dejected look in her eyes which Helena was unable to ignore. Hal liked Arthur. But he wanted his mother to himself. As long as she gave Hal enough of her time and attention he would accept Arthur without complaint. If she considered her own happiness she knew that she couldn't do without Arthur. But she was still married to Ramon and something inside her remained reluctant to give him up.

When Federica slipped into her mother's bedroom after having returned from Pickthistle Manor, Helena was getting changed. Arthur was coming for dinner. Federica lay on the bed and watched her mother dry her hair in front of the mirror. She recalled those days in Chile when she didn't bother with her hair and scrunched it up onto the top of her head. Now she spent hours in front of the glass gelling it, teasing it with brushes and combs. She looked radiant again. She looked happy. Federica knew she should be happy too, but she couldn't be. Arthur had made her mother no less selfish, in fact he indulged her on every level allowing her to be the centre of his world. She rarely asked him about himself. She noticed it more when her mother was on the telephone. Me me me, thought Federica gloomily.

'How do I look?' Helena asked, pinching her cheeks.

'Beautiful, Mama,' Federica replied truthfully.

'Try to be nice to Arthur, Fede. He's doing his best to become your friend.'

'He can be my friend,' said Federica, her heart beating with adrenaline in preparation of the next sentence, 'but not my father.' She blinked in surprise at her own courage.

Helena turned around slowly and stared at her daughter, her smile falling off her face, leaving a serious line in the place of her mouth. 'Did you overhear us this afternoon?' she asked.

Federica nodded. She remembered what Sam had told her and tried not to feel guilty.

'You had no right to listen to my conversation,' she said crossly, reaching for the packet of cigarettes.

'I couldn't help it. You were both talking so loudly, I hadn't meant to hear,' Federica explained. Helena placed a cigarette between her pink lips and lit it. Federica winced as she blew the smoke into the room. The smell made her nauseous.

'I hardly need explain to you then what he said,' she snapped sarcastically.

'He asked you to marry him,' said Federica, but her voice was more of a croak.

Helena softened. 'Look, sweetie. He'll never be your father. He doesn't want to be. He has three children of his own already. He just wants to be your friend.'

'He wants to be your husband. But you're still married to Papa.'

'Only in name. A divorce can be arranged very easily,' she said carelessly, for Federica's eyes dimmed with unhappiness. As long as her parents were still married there was hope. 'Your father and I haven't been together now for a long, long time. You can't possibly be hoping for a reconciliation, can you, Fede?'

Federica's lower lip trembled. She shook her head, but in her heart she wanted nothing more than a reconciliation. 'Are you going to say yes?' she asked hoarsely.

'I'm thinking about it.' Helena turned back to the mirror.

'What does Hal think?'

'He wants me to be happy,' she replied in an almost accusing tone as if she were about to add 'unlike you'.

'I want you to be happy too,' said Federica, feeling guilty.

'Then let me do what's best for me. I've sacrificed everything for you children. You're almost thirteen now. Soon you'll be a woman. Aren't I allowed some happiness too?'

Federica nodded her head. 'If you marry him, will we have to leave Polperro?' she asked.

'We might have to,' Helena said, stubbing out her cigarette. 'Arthur's job is in town.'

'Then I don't want you to marry him,' she cried, suddenly overwhelmed by the force of her emotions and unable to control them.

'Now, Fede—' began Helena impatiently.

'No. I won't go. I won't!' she snapped, quite uncharacteristically.

'We won't go far. You can still see the Applebys as much as you want to.'

'I want to stay here with Granny and Grandpa,' she sobbed.

'We'll talk about this later when you're calm,' Helena said, pinching her lips together with forced patience.

'I won't go. I won't go,' she repeated.

Helena was confused by her daughter's outburst. She was usually so quiet and accommodating. 'All right, calm down, sweetie,' she said wearily, sitting down next to her and putting an arm around her. 'I haven't agreed to marry Arthur, and I am still married to your father, so let's not get too overexcited about all of this. Dry your tears and come downstairs, Arthur will be here in a minute and I don't want him to see you upset. He'd be mortified and he's such a kind man.'

Polly and Jake liked Arthur very much because he had lifted their daughter out of her dark pit and made her smile again. They noticed Federica's tear-stained face at the dinner table and the short replies she mumbled to him when he tried to talk to her. They understood her but hoped she would grow to like Arthur because Helena's happiness was their main concern. Federica felt as if she was being swallowed up into a big grey cloud where no one could see her or hear her cries for help.

That night she wrote an urgent letter to her father telling him that her mother wanted to marry a 'horrid, ugly man called Arthur' who was going to take them all away from Polperro to some nasty town. She added that if she was taken away from all she loved she would kill herself. When she sealed the letter she was sure that he would come as quickly as he could to rescue her from the impending doom. Then she lay in bed, the room illuminated by the clear spring moon, and opened the butterfly box. She listened to the clatter of bells and watched the butterfly flutter her wings in the phosphorescent light, giving her a strange, unearthly beauty. She thought of her father and wondered what he was doing and whether he ever thought of her. Falling into the spell of the box she closed her eyes and once more joined him on the familiar beaches of Chile, where the sun was warm and the sand like Lidia's flour between their toes. She concentrated on his stories as if her very life depended on it and slowly she retreated into the secret halls of her mind where no one but her father could reach her.

The following day Helena left Federica alone in the house while she went to church with her mother and the eleven-year-old Hal. 'She needs some time on her own,' she explained to her mother as they wandered up the lane.

'She's having trouble accepting Arthur, isn't she?' said Polly, patting Hal on the head. 'Not like this little monkey.'

Hal looked up at her and grinned smugly. If he had had a tail he would have wagged it.

'I suppose it's understandable, but Ramon and I haven't been together for years, you would have thought she'd be used to it by now,' Helena sighed.

'Well, every child is different and she always had a very close relationship with her father.'

'She's just got to get over it and move on. I had to, Hal had to. I love Arthur and I won't give him up. Not for anyone,' insisted Helena melodramatically.

'I like Arthur,' Hal said, knowing that would make his mother happy.

'I know you do, and Arthur likes you,' said Helena happily.

'Doesn't Arthur like Fede?' he asked.

'He does like her and he's trying very hard to make her like him. But Fede's being very stubborn. Poor Arthur.'

'Poor Arthur,' Hal agreed. 'I hope we see a lot of him. He makes you happy, Mama, and that's all that I care about.'

Helena was touched. 'You're so sweet, Hal. What would I have done without you?' she said.

'Not a lot,' Hal laughed, pushing his thick black hair out of his eyes. 'If you don't mind me saying, Papa's a real moron to have given you up and Arthur's a very lucky man.'

Helena sat through the entire service thinking about Arthur and debating his proposal. She hadn't told her mother about it as she wanted to have time to think about it first before everyone else had their say. She felt cherished and protected with Arthur. He carried all her worries and fears. Ramon had thought only of himself, her needs had always been second to his. With Arthur she came first, in everything. His life now revolved around her happiness and he did whatever was necessary in order to see her content. When the Reverend Boyble spoke about the virtue of unselfishness and putting others before oneself Helena thought of Arthur and smiled with satisfaction, as if she deserved praise for his good qualities. She tried not to think of Ramon. There was no point, he had gone and he wasn't coming back. She had made her choice. He had made his. He didn't want her back. She pictured Arthur's gentle face and persuaded herself that she didn't want Ramon back. But still she doubted and by the end of the service her mind was no clearer than it had been before. She didn't know what to do. Divorce was so final.

Federica met Hester in their cave hidden within the cliffs, where seagulls swooped down and built their nests and where the tide swept in every night to wash away their secrets. They sat in the cool shade of the rock and Federica told her all about Arthur. 'If I have to leave Polperro, I'll die,' Federica said firmly.

'You can't leave Polperro! Does that mean you'll go to a different school?' Hester asked anxiously.

'Everything,' Federica sighed miserably. 'Everything will change. I just don't know what to do.'

'You have to refuse to go. She can't make you. How can she?' suggested Hester naïvely. 'Just dig in your heels and refuse.'

'I don't want to live in a town.'

'I'd hate to live in a town.'

'I don't want to live with Arthur, he's dull. He's fat, sweaty and dull, I can't see what Mama sees in him. Papa's so handsome.'

'Your father is the most handsome man I have ever met. Mummy quite fancied him, you know,' Hester giggled.

'Did she?'

'Yes, so did Molly and I.'

'You all have extremely good taste,' said Federica proudly. 'You know, I wrote to him.'

'Did you?'

'Yes, I told him about Arthur and that Mama wants to marry him. I also said that if they marry and take me away from Polperro, I'll kill myself.'

Hester gasped. 'Oh my God! He'll come over for sure.'

'I think so too. He'll get us all out of this mess, you'll see. He'll never let this happen.'

Federica returned home at lunchtime to find Arthur's car parked outside on the gravel. She rolled her eyes and pinched her mouth into a thin line of resolve before walking into the hall to face him. He was sitting on the sofa in the living room talking to Hal and Jake while Polly prepared the lunch in the kitchen with Helena.

'Ah, Federica,' said Arthur as she walked into the room. 'Just the person. I've got something for you.' He chuckled amiably, pushing himself onto his feet. Federica noticed the sweat collect on his brow and begin to drip down the side of his face. She watched him disappear into the little room that Jake reserved for the drinks cupboard. She looked at her grandfather and raised an eyebrow quizzically, but he just grinned back at her. Arthur then reappeared carrying a large cardboard box, which looked quite heavy for he struggled with it, but he managed to smile as he carefully placed the box on the floor in front of Federica.

'What on earth is it?' she asked, staring at it.

'Open it,' said Arthur.

'Go on, Fede,' said Hal. 'I know what it is,' he added, 'and I know you'll like it.'

Federica opened the box. To her delight and amazement she saw two shiny eyes staring up at her forlornly.

'A dog!' she cried. 'A real dog!' She threw her hands into the box and gathered the fat little puppy into her arms where she covered his white fur with affectionate kisses.

'You have to read the collar,' said Hal, joining her on the sofa and cuddling the puppy too.

'Rasta,' read Federica, holding the silver disc in her fingers. She suddenly felt a rushing sensation in her head as she remembered Señora Baraca's dog and the promise her mother had made her in Cachagua. 'Thank you,' she said sheepishly, feeling slightly guilty that she had been so unkind to Arthur. 'Is he really mine?' she asked.

'He's really yours,' said Arthur, smiling with relief. He caught Jake's eye and nodded. They had all been right, a puppy would do the trick. Rasta wagged his little tail with such excitement he almost took off like a helicopter. But Federica kept him firmly in her arms, letting him lick her face and sniff her skin. She thought of Trotsky and looked forward to introducing them. They were sure to become firm friends. Ingrid would love him too and so would Sam. She decided to take him up to Pickthistle Manor straight after lunch to show him off.

Helena and Polly heard the squeals of delight and rushed into the room to find both Hal and Federica lying on the floor with the dog. 'Ah, he's very sweet,' said Polly, winking at Arthur. 'Aren't you a lucky girl, Fede.'

'He's half Labrador, half something else, but Arthur and I haven't exactly worked out what that something else is,' Helena said. Federica watched her mother join Arthur on the sofa. She noticed he took her hand and squeezed it. He obviously thought he had won her over with his gift, but he was wrong. She grinned deviously to herself. Papa was about to return and change everything.

Chapter Twenty-Two

'Look at the camera, sweetheart. There, you're gorgeous. Gorgeous. That's right, a bit more chest, too much, too much. That's better, now eyes to camera. Simmer, sweetheart, simmer. Good.' Julian clicked the camera in a series of staccato snaps at the laminated young woman who reclined on the divan like a glossy jungle cat. Her eyes were green and swept upwards with heavy lids that fanned her face with long, black lashes. She was beautiful, confident and alluring. So much, so young. She was only eighteen.

Julian had met Lucia Sarafina in a London club and listened to her dreams of becoming a famous singer. 'I have the looks and the body, it's just a question of training the voice,' she had said coolly in a thick Italian accent. Julian, who appreciated the aesthetics of a good-looking woman, had invited her to the cottage he shared with Toby to take her publicity shots. She had agreed immediately, seizing the chance to make use of yet another bedazzled man, seduced by her beauty. She watched him with the steadiness of a preying panther, wearing only a pair of faded denims and sandals, his body firm and tanned. She was sure he was ripe to be converted to the world of the heterosexual.

It was a humid day. A froth of purple clouds advanced slowly in over the horizon promising an afternoon of thunder and rain. But while the light remained in such a tenuous limbo, suspended between sunshine and thunder, Julian hurried to photograph her before it was lost in the impending storm.

Lucia wore a simple white dress that dropped low over the cleavage of her breasts and rose high on the leg to expose her brazen thighs. With every pose she arranged herself to her best advantage and gazed into the camera with the self-confidence of a professional model.

'You can relax now, I'm going to change the film, then perhaps we can take you under the blossom tree or something,' he said, turning around to get a new film out of his bag. 'Do you want a drink?' he asked, ripping open the silver paper that wrapped the film.

'I don't think I can go anywhere dressed like this,' she said and laughed smoothly.

'Why not?' he asked, turning to face her. She smiled at him and raised her eyebrows suggestively, tossing her dress onto the grass with a sly grin.

'What if your boyfriend comes back, I might give him a fright?' she said, running a hand down her naked body. Julian was surprised but not shocked. He had been in the business for long enough to have experienced almost every kind of come-on. In fact, he was tired of fighting them off. Beautiful women found it hard to believe that he didn't desire them in spite of his open homosexuality. They were all sure they could convert him and deeply offended when they discovered that they couldn't. Julian clicked the film into the camera and wound it on as if he hadn't noticed her.

'Right then, sweetheart,' he said in a brisk tone. 'Let's have you somewhere else, that divan's getting tedious.' He cast his eye about the garden. 'A chair under that blossom tree. You'll look like a forest nymph, very alluring,' he said, disappearing into the house. Lucia sighed heavily but not in surrender. She was very sure of her charms.

Julian placed the chair under the pink and white blossom and moved his tripod and camera into position. Lucia glided over naked and turned the chair around so that the back was facing the camera, then she silkily placed herself astride it, resting her head on her folded arms, staring unblinking at Julian.

'Now, sweetheart, I really don't think this is a good idea. You're a singer not a porn star,' he said, focusing.

'This one's for you,' she said and smiled graciously, expecting him to be grateful.

He wasn't. 'I'm afraid it'll go into a file and be forgotten. What

257

did you say your boyfriend was called? Let's do it for him,' said Julian, changing to Polaroid.

'He's called Torquil.'

'Well, this one's for Torquil,' he said, replacing the Polaroid with film.

'He'll be very amused,' she said, sitting up straight and smirking at him. 'We can give him the Polaroid as a present when he comes to pick me up later.'

'If that's what you want,' he replied, tearing open the Polaroid and taking a look at the image. 'Very nice, Lucia. *Playboy* would kill for it. Perhaps you should think of changing your career path – it's less effort and you seem to be a natural.'

'Oh, I couldn't pose like this for just anyone,' she said thickly, looking up at him with doe eyes.

'You could have fooled me,' he replied, clicking again. 'Now sultry, I don't want you smiling. Smoulder, look alluring, cross even. That's better. There, head up a bit, yes, higher, now a little to one side, less, there, eyes to camera, flash them at me. Good.' And he clicked a whole roll.

'Now, how about you put your clothes back on and we do some more publicity shots,' he said, changing the roll.

'I'm bored of posing and anyhow, I like to be naked. Don't you?'

'Sometimes, but not when I'm working.'

'I'm not working now, I'm playing.'

'Well, let's have some tea then.' He began to pack up his equipment. He looked up at the sky and noticed the storm was almost upon them. 'We definitely got the best of the day,' he said, folding up his tripod.

'Oh no, the best of the day is still to come,' she said, getting up from the chair and walking towards him.

Julian sighed wearily. 'Actually, Lucia, it really isn't.'

'Yes, it is,' she said firmly, stopping in front of him and running a long nail down between his pectoral muscles. 'You look after yourself, don't you?'

Julian grabbed her hand with his and removed it from his

body. 'Lucia, I'm gay. I like boys and you're a girl. It's very simple,' he said seriously.

'Come on. Don't tell me you don't think about it occasionally?' she said and pouted.

Julian was repelled. 'Not at all,' he replied.

She then placed a hand on the front of his trousers. 'I can feel you desire me.'

'Then you have less experience than I thought, because I'm far from aroused,' he said brutally.

At least she had the decency to blush. 'You're afraid Torquil might turn up. I can assure you he won't. It's too early. I said I'd be here all afternoon.'

'Let's go in and have some tea,' he suggested again, moving past her.

Suddenly the clouds were upon them and a clap of thunder sent a shuddering vibration across the earth, drenching them both in the rainfall that ensued. Giggling, Lucia ran for cover into the house, followed closely by Julian. Once inside the dark interior she fell upon him, kissing him and undoing his trousers.

'Excuse me, I hope I'm not interrupting anything,' said Toby, standing stiffly in the doorway. He had watched them run in out of the rain and although his stomach lurched, he knew Julian fended off over-enthusiastic girls all the time, it was part of the job.

Lucia pulled herself away and wiped her wet face with the back of her hand. 'You must be Toby,' she said. 'Are you convertible too? We could have a threesome.'

'Sorry, no takers,' said Toby coolly, 'but I'll put the kettle on so you don't catch a chill.'

'I don't have anything to wear. My dress will be soaked,' she said, leaning back against the wall and grinning at Julian. 'Saved by the rain, cameraman.' She giggled.

'I'll lend you a shirt,' he said with a sigh. 'Toby, I'll have a coffee, a strong one please. Come on, Lucia.'

While Julian was upstairs with Lucia, Toby stood by the kettle and tried to suppress the jealousy that sank into his belly, dragging with it the good mood with which he had arrived. He stared at his reflection in the silver surface of the kettle but as much as he despised the expression on his face there was very little he could do to remove it.

Just then the front door opened and in ran Federica, short of breath from cycling and carrying in her arms a fluffy white puppy. 'My God!' he exclaimed. 'Whose is that?'

'It's mine, Uncle Toby,' she cried, placing him carefully on the kitchen tiles.

'He's adorable.'

'Isn't he?'

'What's he called?'

'Rasta,' she said. 'Because I knew a Rasta in Chile. Look, it even says his name on his collar.'

Toby bent down and stroked his soft fur. 'Cuddly little thing,' he mused. 'I suppose you're going to let it sleep in your bed with you.'

'If Mama lets me.'

'That's a difficult one,' he said, knowing how strict Helena could be.

'No it isn't. She wants me to like her boring boyfriend and he gave me the dog. So I suspect she'll let me do anything I want.'

'Ah.' Toby nodded, standing up. 'Arthur.'

'Do you like him?'

'Of course I do,' he replied diplomatically.

'Do you think they should marry?' she asked.

'Do you know something I don't?'

'No. Just, what if?'

'Well, I don't think Helena is ready to marry again,' he replied, taking a few mugs down from the cupboard and pouring the boiled water into the teapot.

'I think she is. They're always together holding hands and kissing. I think he's ugly. Papa is so handsome.'

'Beauty isn't everything, Fede. He's a kind, gentle person and he wants to look after your mother. I think that's much more important than beauty.'

'I don't like him,' she said, sitting on floor and pulling the puppy into her lap.

'That's only natural. If he wasn't in love with your mother you'd probably like him very much.'

'I don't want to leave Polperro,' she said seriously.

'Why on earth would you ever leave Polperro?'

'Because if Mama marries him I'll have to go and live in town with them.'

'Oh. Well, that's another "what if".'

'But I won't go,' she insisted.

'You can live with us instead. I'm never going to leave Polperro,' he said casually, without hearing the turning cogs of her mind or noticing the seed that he had sown there.

'Do you mean that?' she asked in amazement.

'Do I mean what?' he said, spooning out the tea bags from the pot.

'That I can live with you if Mama marries Arthur?'

'Oh that. Yes, darling, you can live with me and Julian. Most certainly.'

When Lucia returned to the kitchen dressed only in a large shirt of Julian's she barely noticed the pale child with luminous skin and long white hair sitting on the floor playing with a puppy. Julian introduced them but Lucia wasn't interested in children and didn't like dogs because they were too hairy and smelt. So she forced a brief smile as she stepped over them on her way to the mug of steaming tea Toby had made for her. She leant against the railing of the Aga to keep warm and sipped her tea.

'Where's that Polaroid, Jules, I want to show Toby,' she giggled, crossing her naked legs to keep warm.

'I don't know where I put it,' said Julian weakly.

'Yes you do. Go on, don't be a spoilsport. I look my best.'

'Beauty's in the eye of the beholder, Lucia, and I've seen you look better,' he replied, digging about in his bag. Finally he pulled out the photograph and handed it to her. She looked at it and smiled proudly.

'Torquil's going to love this. Can you blow one up for me, really big? Then I'll give it to him for his birthday,' she said, showing it to Toby.

Toby smiled to hide his disgust. 'I'm afraid the only pussy I'm interested in is the four-legged variety,' he said cuttingly.

Lucia swallowed her tea to hide her indignation then offered to show the shy little girl who sat quietly on the floor in order 'to teach her a few things'.

Federica blinked up at her uncle in confusion but neither Julian nor Toby thought Lucia's joke very funny and wished her boyfriend would hurry up and come and collect her.

When Torquil finally arrived, the engine of his Porsche sending the nesting pigeons and swallows into the air in panic, he strode confidently into the house without knocking. 'Ah, there you are, Lucia,' he said when he found them in the kitchen. He ignored Julian and Toby, passing them over with a superior grimace and looked his girlfriend up and down suspiciously. 'Where are your clothes?' he asked. She handed him the photograph and watched as his cheeks drained into his neck, turning it red with fury.

'What the hell is this all about? I thought you were doing publicity shots, not porn,' he snapped, pushing his dark hair off his beautiful face.

'This one was a special one for you,' she said, kissing him.

'If the photographer wasn't gay I'd kill you,' he said without smiling.

'Oh, he's gay. Quite gay,' she said. 'Aren't you, Julian?'

Julian recoiled. He wanted them both out of his house at once. 'I'll send you the shots once I've developed them. It'll take a few days,' he said, ignoring her. Ignoring both of them. They were two of the most self-satisfied people he had ever met.

'Right then, let's not hang around. We've got to be in London by seven for the premiere of *Crazy Hearts*, and you, sweetness, take hours to get ready.'

'That very much depends on what she wears, I should imagine,' Toby said, grinning at Julian.

'Come on,' Torquil repeated, deliberately overlooking Toby and ushering Lucia out of the kitchen.

Federica watched them go. He had been quite handsome, she thought, and wondered why men like him fell in love with nasty girls like Lucia. She hadn't even bothered to pat Rasta.

'I'll give you back your shirt sometime, I won't forget,' Lucia called from the hall.

'Don't bother,' Julian shouted, relieved that they were leaving. 'You can keep it.'

Once again the motor sent every bird and animal hurrying for cover. When it had gone the silence was almost audible. Julian and Toby sighed heavily. 'Thank God they're gone,' said Julian, putting his arms around Toby and hugging him. 'That's not what it looked like,' he added apologetically.

'I know,' said Toby. 'And I know you.'

'Good.' He breathed heavily and rested his head on Toby's shoulder. 'Where's that strong coffee?'

'Wouldn't you prefer whisky?'

'You're right. Much better. I need a week off after that. What hideous human beings. I hope they don't breed.'

'They shouldn't be allowed to.'

'The tragedy is that they do,' said Julian.

'Ours is that we don't,' Toby laughed, patting his friend on the back.

'When I come and live here, can I bring Rasta?' asked Federica, who was still sitting quietly on the floor.

Toby and Julian both turned to look at her together.

'Good God, I forgot you were there,' said Toby in surprise.

'Of course you can bring Rasta,' said Julian, then he looked at Toby. 'When's she moving in?'

Chapter Twenty-Three

Just when Helena thought she would never be able to make up her mind whether or not to marry Arthur, she received a telephone call that decided her future for her.

'Helena, it's Ramon, I'm in London.'

Helena's stomach turned over at the sound of his granular voice, a voice that held within it the resonance of too many memories. She floundered, not knowing what to say, wanting to be furious but not having had the time to rouse her fury.

'Helena?' He repeated into the silence.

'What do you want?' she asked coldly, playing for time.

'I want to see my children,' he replied.

'You can't,' she said simply, fumbling for her cigarettes, remembering Arthur's advice to breathe deeply when she was nervous, but it was all she could do to breathe at all. She was not going to allow him to revive Federica's distress; she was just beginning to get over him.

'Helena, you can't prevent me from seeing my own children,' he replied. 'I received a letter from Fede. She needs me.'

'Like a hole in the head, Ramon,' she said sarcastically, placing the cigarette in her mouth and lighting it unsteadily.

'You're angry.'

'Of course I'm angry, Ramon. I haven't seen you for seven years,' she snapped, blowing the smoke out into the mouthpiece. 'Bloody hell, Ramon! Who do you think you are?'

'Calm down,' he said, then inhaled deeply. His tone was irritating.

'For God's sake. You're a useless father. I'm surprised Fede hasn't forgotten about you. She damn well should have. My brother's been more of a father to her than you ever were. You can't come back here after seven years and expect us all to embrace you. You chose to rush off again and you chose not to come back. If you're regretting it, too bad.'

'So, who's Arthur?' he asked.

She dragged heavily on her cigarette. 'My fiancé,' she replied smugly.

'That's what Fede feared.'

'So that's why you've come is it? Fede's knight in shining armour, what a joke.'

'I'm coming down whether you like it or not,' he said.

'Fine, but I won't let you near the children.'

'If you want to deprive your own children of their father, that's up to you, but I'm coming anyway.' He put the telephone down.

Ramon put his bag into the back of the black Mercedes and asked the driver to take him to Polperro. Then he sat in the back and brooded. It had been too easy to let them slip away. How the years had passed without him noticing the relentless passage of time. He had been too happy with Estella and Ramoncito to throw his thoughts across the ocean. Helena and the children had been like nagging stones in his shoe. He was always aware that they were there yet never got around to doing anything about them.

Estella loved him unconditionally like a child, tenderly like a mother and unpossessively like a friend. With her he didn't feel the need to leave all the time, on the contrary, he travelled with speed looking forward to the day when he would be embraced in her warm arms again. Sometimes, when he was far away, alone with his thoughts, he would wake to the smell of roses and believe that she had come to relieve the increasing monotony of his solitary wanderings. Other times he would hear the whisper of the sea or the laughter of a stream and have to pause a moment to recall Estella's honey voice and her joy. As Estella's gentle features supplanted those of Helena, Federica and Hal, he found himself forgetting that they had ever existed. How easy it was to forget.

Mariana wrote to her grandchildren with enforced regularity in order that she didn't forget. Helena sent her photographs when she remembered and Mariana dutifully enlarged them, framed them, and gazed at them with determination, fearful that if she didn't remind herself to look at them at least once a day she might wake up one morning to find that she hadn't thought about them in years. In her mind's eye they were still the little children they had been that last summer in Cachagua, in spite of the photographs that captured their growing up and their growing away. Her other grandchildren visited regularly. She now had twenty-four, making it all the more difficult to remember the two she had loved the most.

Mariana hadn't told Ignacio about her visit to Estella's beach house. She knew his ears would go red with fury. He'd not only be angry but disappointed and she didn't know whether his heart would be able to contain the excess of emotion without breaking. But she was unable to forget about her grandchild. She spent long evenings wandering up and down the beach, gazing out to sea, wondering what to do. She was certain that Estella would dry up with neglect, that Ramon would spend more and more time travelling, leaving his son to grow up fatherless just like Hal and Federica. When she had returned to Cachagua the morning she had visited Estella, she had been so angry with Ramon for his carelessness that she had sent Gertrude home and spent the rest of the day furiously polishing all the floors and furniture in the house. When she was through she had collapsed onto the bed and woken up at lunchtime the following day much to Ignacio's surprise as well as her own, for he had been unable to wake her. Anxious evenings on the beach had ensued where she bit all her nails down to the quick and lost so much weight she had to buy herself a whole new wardrobe when she returned to Santiago. Ignacio believed she was suffering from missing Helena and the children and did his best to comfort her. But she couldn't be comforted.

Finally, at the end of January she had returned to Estella's beach house, pale-faced and grim, not knowing what she was going to say, only that she had to say something. Estella noticed at once Mariana's distress and burst into tears on the veranda.

'Is it Ramon?' she choked impulsively, staggering towards her, her eyes at once welling with despair. 'Is he all right?'

Mariana was so moved by Estella's tears that she embraced her. 'Ramon is fine, Estella. It is you and my grandchild I'm worried about,' she said, releasing her.

Estella stared at her with glassy eyes. 'I'm sorry,' she whispered. 'I forgot myself.'

'I knew already,' Mariana replied kindly.

'You'd better come in then.'

Mariana was no longer curious about the house or surprised by its size. She recognised Ramon's typewriter on the desk and the first pages of a manuscript piled neatly beside it. Ramon had never been tidy, nor had Helena, but Estella kept the place as immaculate as she had kept Mariana's house. Estella showed her into the sitting room, which was light and spacious with pale Venetian blinds drawn half way down the French doors to keep the room cool. She admired the elegance of Estella's taste. The floor was covered with brightly woven rugs from India, she had filled the room with large pots of geraniums and fairy roses and the bookshelf was a library of European writers, philosophers and biographers. Mariana noticed that Ramon had taken the most exquisite pictures of Estella and their son and placed them in silver frames on every surface. Wherever her eye rested she was able to follow her son's travels around the world – a Brazilian balanganda in silver to induce fertility, a Greek icon of Saint Francis from a monk on Mount Athos and an African spear from a tribe he had befriended deep in the African jungle. Together Ramon and Estella had made a warm home for themselves.

Estella sat opposite, staring at Mariana with limpid eyes.

'I'm not here to chastise you, Estella,' she said, following her instincts, feeling her way. 'I worry for you, that's all.'

'How did you find out?' Estella asked boldly.

'At Christmas when I visited you, I left forgetting to give you the gift I had brought, so I turned back.'

'Oh,' said Estella, nodding sadly.

'I heard you call your child Ramoncito, then it all made sense.'

'Yes.'

Mariana got up and walked over to where Estella sat uncomfortably on the edge of the sofa. She sat down next to her and looked at her with understanding. 'I'm a woman too, I know what it is like to love a man. I love Ignacio. He's difficult to say the least. But I love him in spite of his sometimes irksome nature. I know Ramon well enough to realise that it was he who seduced you. I don't blame you. I pity you. I've watched his marriage disintegrate. Helena couldn't cope with his wanderings. Can you?'

Estella's face glowed like a rosy apple and she smiled the smile of a woman contented with her lot. 'I love Ramon. He loves me. That is all that I ask. I don't want to imprison him in the home. I just want his love. I'm happy, Señora. Happier than I've ever been.'

'I believe you,' she said, touching the young woman's arm. 'But, what do your parents think? He's still married to Helena.'

The spring drained away from Estella's face and it acquired an autumnal sadness. 'They have disowned me,' she stated simply, flatly, as if she had built an inner barrier of indifference in order to prevent herself from hurting any more.

'I'm so sorry,' said Mariana. 'If there's anything I can do.'

'No, no,' Estella replied. 'There's nothing anyone can do.'

'Have they seen your child?'

'No.'

'If they were to see him . . .'

'They won't come anywhere near the house.'

'Do they know who the father is?'

'They do, and they don't care. My father wants Ramon to marry me . . .'

'I see.'

'I'm happy. They should be happy that I'm happy, but I bring disgrace on the family,' she said and her eyes glistened against her will.

'Why don't you show them Ramoncito? Their hearts will soften, I promise you. He's so adorable. He's a little angel. Can I see him again?'

Estella showed Mariana into the little room where Ramoncito was quietly sleeping in the cool shadows. She ran a finger down his soft cheek and felt the emotion gather in her throat and in her eyes that stung with tears. 'Take Ramoncito to see them,' she said.

'Shall I tell Ramon that you came?'

'No,' Mariana replied firmly. 'It will be our secret. He will let me know in his own time. But if there is anything I can ever do for you, please don't feel too afraid to call me. You know where I am. I won't impose on you any more.'

Estella touched Mariana's hand and smiled. 'I want you to come. I want Ramoncito to know his grandmother,' she said and her lips trembled.

Mariana was too touched to reply. She nodded her head, swallowed hard and blinked away her gratitude.

The following evening Estella braced herself for the most difficult task of her life. She wrapped Ramoncito in a woollen shawl, packed enough food and clothes for a week and laid him on her parents' doorstep with a note which said, simply, '*I need your love.*' Then she turned and walked away. As she reached the bend in the road she almost repented and ran back to reclaim him, but she remembered Mariana's words and continued up the track with a heart of lead but a mind hardened with resolve. After a suffocating couple of hours, during which time anxiety clawed at her conscience like a crow trying to scratch his way out, she could bear it no longer and hurried back along the coast to where her parents' house nestled against the hillside.

Ramoncito was no longer on the doorstep. Terrified that he

might have been taken by a stray dog or a thief she crept up to the window of the house, holding her breath so as not to give herself away. At first, when she looked through the glass she saw nothing but an empty room. Then just when an inner sob began to choke her, Maria wandered into the room with the baby safely wrapped in her solid arms. She was smiling broadly and the tears were falling over her old cheeks in rivers of joy.

Pablo Rega sat on the grass next to his friend, Osvaldo Garcia Segundo, and began to talk, as he always did, with poetry and candour.

'My old heart has softened, Osvaldo. *Sí*, Señor, it has. Maria returned home to find Estella's bastard on the doorstep. She had just left him there. Just like that. With a note. As if we'd be in any doubt as to who the child belonged to.' He chuckled and shook his head, playing with the Virgin pendant that clung to his chest. 'He's very small, I was frightened to touch him until Maria placed him in my arms – for the love of God, Maria, I said, if I drop him the devil will take him. But she just laughed and cried again. His smile is mine, so Maria tells me, God bless the poor lamb if he resembles me. A lot of good that'll do him! You'd be right to ask what I did. I should have sent him back to his mother. But Maria wouldn't hear of it. There she was with the baby in her arms, loving it as if it were her own, tears of joy running down her face. I'd be a monster to send him back. I'm not a monster, just a tired old man with little to live for but life. Ramoncito is another life, another transient life to suffer and die on this earth. What the devil is it all for? You know, Osvaldo, *sí*, Señor, you do. If you could speak from beyond the grave you'd probably give me a few pointers. Perhaps my old ears are too blocked with earthly concerns to hear you.'

Now Ramon sat in the car and watched the city trail off into verdant English countryside. He thought of Ramoncito, now six years old, almost the age Federica had been when he had waved her goodbye that hot January morning all those years ago. He looked back over the years and recalled how Ramoncito had healed the relationships between him and his mother, Estella and her parents. Pablo Rega was still suspicious of him, though. He had developed a habit of nervously playing with the pendant around his neck in the same way that one would hold up a cross when faced with a vampire, but at least he loved his grandson and embraced his daughter as before. His own father was ignorant of the child who walked around, not more than four miles from his summer house, with his own blood pumping through his veins and his own genes set to father a whole new generation some day. But Mariana had insisted he shouldn't be told. It was their secret, between the three of them.

'The right moment will come,' she had told Ramon, 'but let me tell him in my own good time.' Six years had gone by and she still hadn't told him. Ramon wondered whether she ever would.

Helena sent the children up to Toby's cottage. 'Ramon's appeared. I don't want him to see them,' she told her brother over the telephone.

'What? Ramon's in England?'

'Yes.'

'My God,' Toby exclaimed, sitting down. 'After all this time, what's he suddenly turned up for?'

'To see the children, so he says.'

'Just like that, out of the blue?'

'I don't want him to see the children,' she repeated anxiously.

'Is that wise?' he asked uneasily. 'He is their father, after all.'

'Only biologically. I won't let him come back and upset them. Fede's getting on with things now. She's happy. The last thing she needs is Ramon appearing and promising her the world.'

'Well, you're right about that,' he agreed.

'I know I am.'

'How will you get rid of him?' Toby asked, envisaging Ramon staking out the house until their return.

'Don't worry, I will.'

'I don't think Arthur's much of a match for Ramon.'

'I wasn't thinking of Arthur. I can get rid of him myself. Kill him with kindness,' she said and laughed nervously.

'You've got to be cool, Helena, and strong,' he suggested encouragingly. 'Don't flare up and don't let him walk all over you. You're an independent woman now. You don't need him. You've got on very well without him. Show him how you've changed. You're not the woman he used to know, all right?'

Helena nodded to herself. 'You're right. If I show weakness he'll use it against me.'

'Exactly. You're a force to be reckoned with. Pummel him into submission, he's only human after all.'

Once she'd sent the children up to Toby's house on their bicycles she bathed and dressed, trying to convince herself that the make-up and grooming was simply to show Ramon how she'd changed. But she knew the truth and it angered her that she still felt the need to impress him.

She waited in the garden, on the bench under the cherry tree where Polly usually sat surveying her borders and flowerbeds. As a child Helena had watched her plant that tree. How quickly it had grown. Rather like her children. She, too, marvelled at the rapid passing of time. Chile seemed like another life. A life shrouded in shadow because she had become frightened of looking back on it, frightened of missing it. She had made her choice so she had started another chapter, closing the old one for ever. When she heard the sound of wheels on gravel her heart accelerated, pumping the blood through her veins at an uncomfortable speed. Once again her past surfaced to torment her. She stood up shakily, resisting the urge to smoke and walked with forced calmness towards the garden gate.

Ramon hardly recognised Helena. She had cut her hair short.

It was paler, thicker, and her skin had recovered that lucid quality he had found so enchanting the first time he met her. Her pale eyes shone with health and she smiled serenely. He had expected her to demand that he leave, but she greeted him with the affability of an old friend, catching him off guard and throwing all his plans awry. Helena noticed he was lost for words and growing in confidence she invited him to join her in the garden for a drink.

'You look well,' he said when they were both seated under the cherry tree with glasses of Polly's homemade elderflower juice. Helena thanked him and looked at his lined face and long greying hair. He resembled an ageing lion. He was still awesome and compelling. He was still king of the jungle, just not her jungle any more. His hesitation exposed his weakness and sensing it immediately she grabbed the opportunity to take control. To her amazement she was no longer afraid of him.

'You look well too. Older,' she said with a malicious smile, 'but still handsome.'

'Thank you,' he said and frowned. 'I'm sorry it's been so long.'

'That's an understatement,' she laughed, but she was careful not to reveal undertones of bitterness. 'You're not cut out for fatherhood, Ramon. But don't torment yourself. We've done very nicely without you. In fact, I should thank you. You liberated us from the rut we had dug for ourselves in Chile. We're very happy here,' she said and looked at him steadily.

He noticed she wasn't smoking and her hand wasn't shaking. He felt uncomfortable. 'I've been a hopeless father,' he conceded. 'But I love them.'

'In your own way, I'm sure you do. They love you too. They love the memory of you. But they've survived without you.'

'I see,' he said in a tone that sounded more like a deep groan. He leant forward and rested his elbows on his knees. 'Fede doesn't want you to marry Arthur.'

'I know,' she said. 'She doesn't want anyone to replace you.'

'She wrote asking me to prevent it.'

'How will you do that?' she asked and smiled with confidence, as if she regarded his sudden peacekeeping mission as a source of amusement.

'I don't know. I came to talk to you, that's all,' he said, sitting back and looking at her with solicitous eyes. He drained his glass.

'Look, I'm tremendously fond of Arthur. He's good to me. He's always there for me. You never were, Ramon. But I don't blame you. I chose you and I chose to leave you. It's that simple. Now I want to marry Arthur and Fede will just have to live with it.'

'She doesn't want to leave Polperro,' he said.

'I know but we can't always have what we want.'

'Hasn't she been uprooted enough?'

'You're one to talk,' she retorted curtly, restraining her anger. 'If it wasn't for you we wouldn't have uprooted in the first place.'

'If I remember, I didn't want you to leave.'

'But you refused to change. I had no choice.' Helena's cheeks stung crimson betraying for a moment her inner fury. She turned her face away and poured more juice, aware that if she showed the smallest sign of vulnerability, he would pounce and she'd be lost.

'Do you love this Arthur?' he asked.

'I'm very fond of him,' she replied.

'That's not what I asked.'

'Don't tell me you don't have some poor, neglected woman tucked away somewhere in Chile,' she replied defensively, avoiding answering his question.

He smirked and nodded. 'Yes, I do.'

Helena was stunned by his honest reply in spite of the fact that she knew he would have found someone in the seven years that they had been apart, it was inevitable. She wanted to ask what she was like, whether she was patient and submissive, whether she minded his long absences like she had. But she resisted the temptation.

'Well, you know what it's like then. When you care for someone,' she replied, swallowing her disappointment while outwardly smiling at her husband.

Ramon watched her impenetrable coolness and wondered whether Arthur had given her the confidence to be so self-assured. She had been like that when he had first fallen in love with her. Had he really worn her down like a beautiful rug?

'So, do you want a divorce?' he asked, biting the inside of his cheeks apprehensively.

'Yes,' she replied, ignoring the small voice inside her head, which begged her to hold onto him.

'Then you shall have it.'

She nodded stiffly. 'Thank you.'

'What will you do about Fede?'

'Why do you care?' she snapped in exasperation, suddenly letting slip her carefully cultivated composure. 'You neglect her for seven years then suddenly turn up because of a letter she wrote you? You have no right to even ask how she is, or Hal. They are nothing to you now. They don't belong to you. If you cared you would have been there when Fede fell off her bike, when she was teased at school because she was the only child without a father, or . . . or . . . when Hal awoke with nightmares or the normal doubts that children suffer from. But you weren't. You know you weren't. Why don't you go back to your woman in Chile and forget about us? You've had no problem forgetting us for the last seven years. For God's sake, Ramon,' she exclaimed, raising her voice until it quivered with anger and hurt. 'You've let us all down badly. Very badly. I want you to go.'

Ramon didn't want to leave her. She had changed. Gone was the neurotic, stifling woman who clung to him like ivy, refusing to allow him space to breathe. Helena had grown into a woman who knew her mind and had the strength of character to execute her wishes. He knew Arthur was behind it and he was curious to see for himself the man who had succeeded where he had failed. But Helena looked at him steadily with eyes of stone. Her argument was strong and he knew he was unable to manipulate her like he had always done in the past. She no longer feared him.

Reluctantly he got to his feet. 'So this is it then?'

'This is it,' she confirmed, standing up.

'We'll communicate through our lawyers.'

'Right.'

'I don't think I can go on for ever without seeing my children.'

'Give me time,' she conceded, suddenly feeling saddened by the finality of their decision to divorce. 'I want to marry Arthur. If Fede thinks you're back I'll have one hell of a battle on my hands. You've waited seven years, another year won't make any difference, at least not to Fede.'

Ramon lowered his eyes. 'You really want to marry him?' he asked, wondering why he cared.

'Yes,' she replied, maintaining her composure with a great deal of effort.

'Well, good luck.'

'Thank you.' Ramon leant over and kissed her on the cheek. Helena withdrew quickly, afraid that he might linger there too long, afraid that she might not be able to resist him. Then he turned and left. She sank back onto the bench and waited for the sound of the car to disappear out of the driveway. Then she placed her head in her hands and cried.

Federica cycled down the lane. She had left Hal with Toby and Julian who both agreed that he was too tired to bicycle all the way home after such a heavy tea. They would drive him back later. Federica was delighted – at least on her own she could go as fast as she liked without worrying that a car might appear from around the corner and frighten her brother. She took her feet off the pedals and freewheeled down the road. With the sun on her back and the spring wind raking through her hair she felt exhilarated.

Suddenly a shiny black Mercedes roared around the bend, sending her hands straight onto the brakes in a panicked attempt to control the bike and avoid crashing into the car. With her heart suspended between beats she felt the hot rush of air as it passed dangerously close by, then heard the screech of tyres as it pulled up in the middle of the road behind her. She drew her bike to a shaky stop by dragging her shoes along the tarmac. Then she positioned her unsteady feet on the ground and turned around. The sun was so bright she had to put her hand over her eyes to shield them from the dazzling glare. She watched the car, but no one got out. She squinted her eyes in an effort to make out who was inside, but the reflection on the glass prevented her from seeing in. She remained motionless, wondering what was going through the driver's mind that inhibited him from descending and apologising to her for nearly claiming her life. She was visibly shaken, for her whole body trembled, but still no one appeared. Then to Federica's bewilderment, the car started up again and left just as suddenly as it had come, restoring the lane to its previous tranquillity as if nothing had happened.

Only the black marks on the tarmac betrayed the stranger's indecision.

Chapter Twenty-Four

Autumn 1990

Federica insisted she was too old to be a bridesmaid at her mother's wedding.

'You're fourteen,' said Helena simply, 'and anyway, you're small for your age.' Once again Federica walked out of the room, out of the house and off onto the cliffs, followed loyally by Rasta, who was now a fully grown Labrador with enormous paws and a large black spot on his nose which baffled everyone.

Helena sighed wearily and decided that Hal would have to be a single page – at twelve years old he wasn't very enthusiastic but agreed because of a hidden mechanism in his make-up that made it impossible for him to deny his mother anything.

After Ramon's brief visit Helena had resolved to marry Arthur. It had taken eighteen months for the divorce to come through. Helena had disintegrated into tears at the sight of the physical proof that her marriage to Ramon was over. She had held the piece of paper in her hands and wondered whether marriage to Arthur was really what she wanted after all. But then she had forced herself to remember how unhappy marriage to Ramon had been and how kind Arthur was and she had filed the document away and continued with her plans in her own stubborn way, refusing to listen to her heart that beat inaudibly for Ramon.

During that time Helena had fought almost daily with her daughter who still believed her father would appear to save her from the dreaded Arthur.

'Arthur will never be my father,' she had shouted at her

egation, followed immediately by a gasp. Leading her up
le was none other than Nuno.

od God!' Ingrid exclaimed. 'What's Pa doing?'

o's scowl softened and the corners of his mouth turned up
leasure. 'Now that is splendid. Splendid,' he said, rubbing
ds together.

atever do you mean, darling?' Ingrid replied, nudging him
er elbow.

ll, it's the blind leading the blind.' He chuckled.

ena's not blind.'

must be to marry that turnip,' he said and laughed quietly.

I suppose you're right,' Ingrid agreed. 'Quite a
mise after having been married to the gorgeous Ra-
he added, remembering that handsome Latin who had
em all so much pleasure before leaving as quickly as he
ne.

re's Grandpa?' Federica hissed to her grandmother,
ily emerging out of her dark cave of self-pity. Polly
and glanced over at Toby who blinked helplessly back.
ar,' Polly sighed sadly. 'Jake didn't make it. I am sorry.'

d waited ten minutes outside the church for her father
She had known there was a good chance he wouldn't
she had been prepared to walk down the aisle alone
She wasn't angry, just saddened. If his own daughter's
couldn't soften his prejudice she wondered what on
d. When Reverend Boyble had started playing ner-
h his prayer book and twitching at the corners of his
elena knew she couldn't hold the service up any
n though it was her wedding. Julian, who was taking
aphs, had snapped one last shot of the agitated bride
ping silently into the church. Helena had nodded to
oyble to commence and winked at Hal, who smiled
y in his sailor suit.

denly Nuno's clipped syllables had stopped her at the

mother in one of her many fits of hysterics. 'And I will never
move away from Polperro. Papa's so handsome, what do you see
in Arthur?'

Helena ignored her, hoping that she'd get used to Arthur in
time. She didn't.

Federica had taken to walking high on the cliffs, watching the
surf crash violently against the rocks below and the mesmerising
rise and fall of the cold ocean which, like a beast, seemed to
mirror her own inner fury. Rasta would sit with her, the wind
drawing his ears back against his sandy neck, cowering against her
for warmth, detecting her pain and sympathising in his own
unspoken way.

Federica couldn't understand why her father hadn't written.
She had begged him to help and he had ignored her. She felt
gutted inside. Within her head she was screaming for compassion but no one heard her. Occasionally her despair boiled over
and she fought with her mother, but Helena never bothered to
search beneath the outward expression of a grief that ran much
deeper than she imagined. No one did. Federica confided in
Hester, but Hester was only a child, like she was, and unable to
do more than listen and sympathise. She had a father so how
could she?

Federica would like to have talked to Sam, but Sam wasn't
often at the manor and when he was she found the words dried
up in her mouth and she was unable to communicate with him in
anything other than empty smiles. She knew he saw through her
smiles, he was smart enough to recognise her unhappiness and he
often placed an affectionate arm around her for no apparent
reason, or asked her how she was in a compassionate tone of
voice. Hester told her that she had heard him confess to her
mother that he had a soft spot for her, which only made Federica
more self-conscious and less able to speak to him. But she was
secretly delighted and sensed they shared a special bond, forged
that day in the bluebells. He no longer ignored her. Even though
she was still very much a child, he had noticed her. She felt
herself so in love she was unable to concentrate on anything else.

Only her mother's impending wedding distracted her from her ardour.

The day of Helena's wedding arrived and Federica awoke with the unavoidable sense of doom that had dogged her for the last few months. She looked out onto an October morning. The sky was watery, shimmering through the golden leaves and silky dew that seemed to cling to everything like tears. She cast her eye over the place that had become her home and loved it all the more because she knew she was leaving it.

'Oh, to be a grown up,' she thought miserably, 'then at least I could make my own decisions.' But she was fourteen years old and still had to obey her mother. Moodily she ate her breakfast while her mother paced up and down the house in a pre-wedding panic having lost her shoes, then her mascara and finally the dress itself, which she had forgotten hung in her mother's cupboard because it was less damp. Much to Federica's annoyance she found herself clearing up after her mother, pouring her endless glasses of wine and standing by like an unwilling assistant receiving bouquets of flowers, wedding presents and answering the telephone. Polly sat with her daughter in her bedroom while the stylist did her hair and make-up, trying to prevent her from drinking too much and keeping the atmosphere light.

Hal lay on the bed playing with a computer game oblivious to the chaos that raged around him.

Federica sulked the entire way through her mother's wedding; it was all she could do not to cry. When she thought things simply couldn't get any worse, Sam sauntered into the church with a new girlfriend hanging decoratively on his arm. The girl was tall, with long dark hair and long legs striding confidently out from under a very short pink skirt. Federica wanted to crawl under the nearest tombstone and die.

The ceremony was one of blessing in the village church, given by the excitable Reverend Boyble who'd had his robes dry-cleaned especially for the occasion and his shoes polished with

such enthusiasm that they shone out from und
couple of silver fish.

Jake had refused to attend because Hele
exclude Julian. Polly had told him to 'grow
you're being very childish,' she said as she le
the kitchen among his toy boats. 'This silly fe
on long enough! Honestly, one would think
side in order to give your own daughter awa

Toby was best man and stood apprehensive
aisle with Arthur, whose brow was studded v
and his buttonhole wilted due to the heat ex
body. Toby winked at Federica who mana
smile in spite of her misery. He wasn't sure l
his niece, Arthur was a poor choice of husba
over Arthur's side of the congregation and
were to squint he would see little more than
blur. Federica stared at her scarlet shoes and
them together three times and disappear b

At the moment the bride was due to
silence subdued the chitter-chatter of th
Reverend Boyble strode importantly up
silencing the last of the whispers with the
as he took great care not to slip. Everyone
door. But when it flew open there was n
Molly and Hester who scuttled down th
pressed firmly over their mouths in ar
laughter.

'Shit,' Sam hissed to his girlfriend, r
been at my spliffs again, God damn it.' I
how to roll her own and knew where
Ingrid caught Sam's eye and frowned
side, but he shrugged his shoulde
Hester waved at Federica who looked
was too high to notice her misery.

When Helena finally arrived, dre
dered ivory dress, a sigh of adm

door. 'My dear, who's going to give you away?' he asked, trotting up the path as if he were out on a Sunday stroll.

'Nuno,' she replied, turning around.

'I'm tardy, I'm afraid,' he said, checking the gold watch that hung on a chain about his waist.

'I suppose you're going to tell me that "punctuality is the thief of time",' she laughed.

'No, my dear, age is the thief of time, it steals one's faculties in their entirety, including one's ability to remember important events such as your wedding. I only remembered because I had tied a knot in my handkerchief, but then it took me a good fifteen minutes to work out why I had put the knot there in the first place. You see, dear girl, age steals everything.'

'Well, you had better slip in then,' she suggested, standing aside for him, noticing Reverend Boyble's chubby fingers tapping with impatience on his prayer book.

'God will wait, good man,' Nuno said with a sniff.

The fingers ceased to tap and Reverend Boyble remained for once speechless with his mouth agape.

'Actually, Nuno,' said Helena, with the glint of an idea shining in her eye. 'Would you do me a favour.'

Helena once more suffered doubt as she walked on Nuno's arm towards the man who would in a matter of minutes be her husband. She made a great effort to rid her thoughts of Ramon and pushed aside any uncertainty with a will of iron. She fixed her eyes on Arthur and remembered his kindness and his adoration and her mind cleared. 'I deserve you,' she thought to herself as his clammy hand found hers and he smiled merrily across at her. His eyes told her that she looked beautiful and she returned his smile wholeheartedly.

As Nuno tripped to his seat beside his daughter he heard the muffled squeals of Molly and Hester who jiggled up and down like two clockwork mice in the row behind. 'High on life,' said Ingrid vaguely, shaking her head.

'So that's what they're rolling nowadays, is it?' he replied, sitting down.

'Really, Pa. They're just children,' she replied, opening the order of service.

'No, my dear, they're *your* children and if they continue to screech like a couple of pigs in a farmyard, I would like you to send them out,' he sniffed, lifting his chin up piously and turning his attention to the marriage ceremony.

The service was long due to the over-exuberance of the Reverend Boyble who loved to hear the sound of his own voice, inspired by God, echo about the stone walls of his church. It was better than singing hymns in the bathroom. Every eye was on him, thirsting for his words to inspire them up the narrow path to God. Marriages were his favourite services and he liked to make them last as long as possible not only for himself but for the happy couple and their friends who had gathered together to hear him. So taken was he by the wit and intelligence of his sermon, he failed to notice the eyes of his congregation droop with boredom and the sound of impatient fingers rustle through the order of service, wondering how long it was going to last.

Finally everyone emerged dazed from the church except for Arthur who strode out like a triumphant gladiator.

'My darling wife,' he said, kissing her on her pale cheek. 'My dear, darling wife. Now we belong together for always.'

'Yes,' she replied, swallowing the ugly knot of doubt that had found its way into her throat. 'For ever,' she repeated, not wanting to think too hard about what that meant.

After smiling for Julian they climbed into a horse-drawn carriage and slowly made their way back to the house for the reception. The warm autumnal light set the sky aflame as the evening closed in and the sun began to sink low over the western horizon.

'You are so beautiful, Helena,' Arthur said, taking her hand. 'I am the luckiest man alive.'

Helena squeezed his hand, suddenly overcome by the splendour of the dying day and the affection that blazed in her new husband's eyes. 'I'm lucky to have you,' she replied truthfully, looking into his gentle features that promised her a life of indulgence and love. 'I'm going to give up smoking as a tribute to you and to announce the beginning of a new life. I really am very lucky that you want to take me on.'

'No, my darling. The luck is all mine and something I won't forget even for a moment.' He bent his head and kissed her. She closed her eyes and breathed in the security of his scent. That calmed her nerves and reminded her of all the reasons she had chosen him.

As the guests arrived gasping for sustenance, Polly rushed about the tent they had erected in the garden with trays of scones and sandwiches while Toby saw to it that everyone had a glass of champagne. Hester and Molly found Federica sitting alone in her bedroom.

'We've been looking for you for hours,' said Hester, joining her on her bed.

'Are you all right?' Molly asked. 'You look miserable.'

'I don't want to leave Polperro,' she sniffed unhappily.

'We don't want you to leave Polperro either,' said Hester.

'I don't like Arthur,' she said, crossing her arms in front of her. 'He's now my stepfather. Yuck.'

'He's not that bad,' said Molly helpfully.

'But he's not Papa.'

'No, he certainly isn't Ramon,' Molly agreed, giggling at Hester. 'But no one's as handsome as your father.'

'He didn't come,' said Federica, lowering her eyes. 'I was certain he would.'

'Perhaps he didn't get your letter,' said Hester, putting an arm around her friend.

'Perhaps.'

'I know a way to cheer you up,' said Molly, grinning at her sister and putting her hand in her pocket.

'What a good idea,' Hester gasped, smacking her hand across her mouth and blinking at Federica guiltily.

'What is it?' Federica asked.

'One of Sam's special cigarettes. We didn't finish it.' Hester giggled nervously. 'No one's going to find us here, are they?'

'Hester, it's called a spliff, and no, no one's going to find us here,' said Molly, flicking her lighter. 'I take it this is your first?' she added, nodding at Federica, who nodded back anxiously. 'Okay, so you smoke it like a cigarette,' she said.

'I've never smoked a cigarette.'

'Well then, you'll learn something new today,' said Molly, puffing on the spliff, setting it alight. 'Open the window, Hester.' Hester opened it wide, and the light sound of music wafted up above the low hum of voices.

'They sound like they're having a good time,' Hester laughed.

'Not as good as us,' said Molly, handing Federica the spliff. 'Now, breathe in deeply, hold it in a few seconds then let it out. And for God's sake let's not have any of that silly coughing business, it's so immature.'

Federica was determined not to cough. She put the spliff to her mouth and breathed in as deeply as she could. The two sisters watched in amusement as her face flushed purple while she dutifully held her breath.

'Well done,' said Molly, taking the spliff from her and handing it to Hester.

Federica exhaled frantically and gasped for breath.

'How does it feel?' Molly asked.

'Okay,' said Federica, who didn't feel anything at all.

'Have another go,' said Molly, taking a drag before handing it back to her.

After a few minutes Molly and Hester were laughing like a couple of hyenas while Federica cried without being able to stop.

'I love Sam,' she began. 'I really do. I can't help it. But he'll never look at me. I'm too young and ugly. Not like that model he's brought with him today. I suppose that's his girlfriend?' she asked.

Hester and Molly laughed even louder. 'You can't be in love with Sam, he's such a dork!' said Molly. 'Anyway, he's only interested in one thing. They all are.'

'And that's not poetry,' Hester smirked.

'Hester, that's so clever.'

'Really?'

'Yes, you've just said something very funny.'

'Well, is she his girlfriend?' Federica sobbed.

'For the moment, but of course he'll change her next week. He has a new one every week, you know. Sam's weekly fix,' said Molly. 'I'm not interested in men who only want sex. I want a man with a good mind.'

'Sam has a good mind.'

'Yes, he does, Fede, but it's firmly installed in the end of his willy at the moment,' said Molly, and she and Hester collapsed with laughter.

Federica sobbed even harder.

Finally, Molly realised that the spliff had only made Federica worse and instructed Hester to run off and find Toby or Julian fearing that she might kill herself with despair.

'Don't worry, Fede, you'll go off Sam in the end. You don't want someone that much older than you. Good God, he'll be twenty-nine years old when you're twenty. And anyway, you don't want to be Federica Appleby, do you?'

Federica was just on the point of replying that she wanted nothing more than to be Federica Appleby when the door opened and in walked Toby and Julian, out of breath and anxious.

'Okay, girls. Why don't you leave us alone with Fede and go back to the party,' said Julian, waving his hand to clear the smoke.

'You can chuck away the rest of that spliff,' said Toby crossly, shaking his head. 'You're too young to be experimenting with those.'

Molly and Hester scuttled out of the room. Molly had no intention of throwing away her precious spliff, they were hard to come by, especially as Sam hid them in different places all the time.

★   ★   ★

287

Toby sat beside Federica and drew her into his arms while Julian sat on the chair opposite. 'This is a horrid day for you,' Toby said, kissing her wet face. 'But it'll be over soon . . .'

'And I'll be leaving Polperro.'

'Ah,' said Toby, raising his eyebrows at Julian. 'I quite forgot about that. Julian, will you stay with Fede while I nip down for a second. There's something I need to do.' Julian took his place next to Federica and put an arm around her.

'I'm in love with someone who doesn't love me,' she said, blinking up at Julian in misery.

'How could he not love you?' Julian said gently. 'Who is he and I'll kill him?'

'Sam Appleby.' Federica sniffed.

'Ah, yes, he is very attractive,' he agreed. 'He's clever. I like clever men. He's also a sensualist. You have very good taste.'

'But I'm too young,' she complained.

'Not at all,' said Julian. 'You are at the moment. You're what? Fourteen and he's twenty-two or twenty-three? The sort of women he chooses at the moment are much older than you and prepared to sleep with him. That's what he wants. All men are the same. If I were you, I'd put him on ice like a good champagne and save him up until later.'

'But I can't wait that long,' she protested.

'Of course you can. If you really want someone you'll wait for him for ever. I'd wait for Toby for ever.'

'You're lucky you've got Toby,' she said. 'I've got no one.'

'You've got us and we'll take care of you,' he said, squeezing her.

'I just feel I don't matter. Mama has Arthur and Hal has Mama. Papa no longer writes to me, he might just as well be dead,' she said. 'Arthur will never be a father to me. Never. I'd rather die.'

'He doesn't want to be your father,' said Julian. 'He already has children of his own. He just wants to be a husband to your mother. You can't blame him for that. She's very beautiful and not an easy woman either. Arthur deserves a medal.'

'Perhaps.'

'And she deserves a bit of happiness, don't you think?'

'Yes,' she replied and sighed in resignation.

'It's sad when marriages break up, it's sad for the parents and sad for the children. But you have to move on and make the best of it,' he said. 'You never know, perhaps in time you can go out and see your father yourself. When you're older you won't need permission from anyone. You can just go. So hang in there for now.'

When Toby returned, his face glowing with pleasure, Julian knew he had good news. Federica looked up at him hopefully wondering what his two-minute disappearance had managed to achieve. He sat down opposite her and held her hands. 'I've struck a bargain with your mother. She's in a good mood today, it was the perfect time to approach her.'

'What about?' Federica asked, not daring to imagine.

'Well,' he replied, smiling. 'If you like you can stay on at the same school and live with me and Julian during the week, as long as you return to your mother and Arthur on weekends.'

Federica gasped in disbelief. 'She means it?' she exclaimed, wiping her face with her sleeve.

'She does.'

'And Rasta?'

'And Rasta. I suppose we can cope with the two of you.' He laughed.

'Oh, thank you, Uncle Toby,' she said in excitement, throwing her arms about his neck. 'I can't believe it.'

'It'll be like weekly boarding,' said Julian.

'You can give me photography lessons,' she said happily, 'and I'll bake you cakes and look after you. You won't know what's hit you. I'm very tidy and organised and an extremely good cook. I won't be any trouble,' she added, unable to contain her delight.

'Cakes for photography lessons, that sounds good to me,' said Julian, nodding his approval at Toby.

'Can I move in today?'

'As soon as your mother's safely off on her honeymoon, and on one condition,' said Toby.

'What's that?' she asked apprehensively.

'That you be nice to Arthur.'

'Oh, all right,' she conceded and added mischievously. 'I won't call him an old fart any more.'

Jake sat in his study and smouldered like a freshly stoked piece of coal. He would like to have been at his daughter's wedding, but she had made her choice. She wasn't prepared to sacrifice her brother's lover for her own father. He was deeply hurt. But Helena had always been troublesome. Ever since she was a child she had managed to have everyone running around her. She was stubborn too and always got what she wanted – well, nearly always. He pitied Arthur and wondered whether he had the endurance to satisfy her whims. He knew she still craved Ramon. She never said so, but he could tell. She had brooded over the divorce papers, not wanting to sign them yet knowing she had to, because divorce had been her choice. Like leaving him in the first place. Her choices and she had to live with them. The problem with Helena, he thought, was that she was used to forcing people's hands by pushing them to the edge until they had no choice but to give in to her will. She had probably hoped Ramon would refuse to let her go, then refuse to divorce her. But he was stronger than she was. She had met her match, and lost. Arthur was a safe bet. No match there at all. Maybe after all those battles she wanted a quiet life. Don't we all, he thought miserably, picking up a miniature wooden barrel to stick onto the pirates' boat he was making.

Chapter Twenty-Five

The following year was a happy one for Federica and a miserable one for Jake. While Federica lived in contentment with her Uncle Toby and Julian, baking cakes, learning how to take photographs and cycling up to Pickthistle Manor as she always had done, Jake withdrew further into the bowels of his miniature boats, disgusted that his daughter had allowed Federica to live with homosexuals at such an impressionable age. Polly tried to discuss it with him, but he wouldn't be drawn on the subject.

'It's not right,' he would say at his kindest and 'It's disgusting!' at his most vitriolic.

But it was all part of Helena's plan and typical of her pattern of manipulation. She would force his hand in the end, she was sure of it.

Polly sent Helena photographs of Jake at previous weddings so that she could superimpose him into her album, but Helena only laughed and sent them back.

'Really, Mum, I thought Dad was the eccentric in the family, not you,' she said. But Polly minded much more than she let on. She also missed having her daughter and grandchildren about the house and spent hours devising excuses to drive up the lane to Toby's cottage to see Federica.

'You know, Federica's very happy, Jake,' Polly said, one afternoon after she had watched her return from a boat trip with Toby and Julian in *The Helena*.

Her cheeks were ruddy from the wind and they were all laughing. Toby carried the picnic basket full of empty dishes that Federica had made and Julian had taken photographs. Rasta trotted along behind them, fat from sharing their vegetarian pies and weary from the games on the beach. 'You know, they all looked so well. They could have been any normal family,' she continued, not caring whether or not he was listening. She wanted to share her joy and was damned if his prejudice was going to stop her. He continued gluing the small pieces of wood and sticking them together with total concentration. 'Toby's like a father to Federica. I think it was the best thing Helena ever did sending her to live with them. She's grown up so much, too. She's a young lady now and so capable. She cooks for them and looks after them like a little mother. I'm so proud of her. So proud! Julian has taught her photography. She's got quite an eye, you know. Yes, she really has. He's framed some of them and put them up on the wall. It's done her self-esteem the world of good. That's what she needed, a father. Now she has two.' She eyed her husband warily but he continued to focus on his project as if he hadn't heard her.

When Hester approached her mother with the idea of a six-teenth-birthday party Ingrid immediately called Helena and suggested she share it with Federica. 'Kill two birds with one stone,' she said, knowing she wasn't capable of organising the party by herself.

'What sort of party are you thinking of?' Helena asked, wondering whether Ingrid knew the first thing about sixteen-year-old children and the bedlam they would make of her home.

'Oh, something pretty. A nice tent,' she said vaguely.

Helena smiled at Ingrid's blissful detachment. 'What are they going to eat?'

'Oh, a buffet, I should imagine. I'll get a company to do it,' she said breezily.

'How many people?'

'How many friends do they have?' Ingrid replied distractedly, her mind already focusing on the milky evening sky and the perfection of the lake that had now become home to flocks of nesting birds.

'Why don't we get together with the girls and discuss it,' she said, aware that Ingrid's attention was waning.

'Darling, what a good idea. Why don't you come for tea tomorrow with Federica.' Then as an after-thought she added, 'Do bring Hal, Joey and Lucien will be here and I know they would love to see him. We don't see Hal so much these days.'

Hal was very fond of Arthur. He remembered his father only rarely when the fog in his memory subsided enough for him to see him clearly. A vague impression of a man with the rough, weathered look of a wolf and the imperious nature of a king. As a child Ramon had frightened him but now he was older he only feared him in his dreams. Arthur, however, made him feel special. He took time with him, encouraged him and never belittled him. Arthur's love for Helena was all-consuming, but never too much to come between her and her son. He understood their closeness and was touched by it. He tried to be a good father to Hal and was rewarded with the boy's trust and affection. Helena had expected Hal to be jealous of her relationship with Arthur, it would have been only natural, but to her surprise Hal responded to him in a way he had never responded to his own father.

Only Federica kept a candle lit for Ramon.

Helena watched as Arthur slowly endeared himself to everyone in Polperro. Having started off as a comic figure to be laughed at, he gained the respect of the whole town by the sheer geniality of his nature. He always smiled, always took the time to talk to people and never tired of listening to their problems, offering sound advice with honesty, never gossiping about what they told him. He was a man who could be trusted. Even Ingrid grew fond of him as he won her affection through his surprising knowledge of birds and love of animals. He helped Hester rescue hedgehogs and praised Inigo's flourishing wine cellar. Nuno nicknamed him 'Arturo', which everyone found very amusing and adopted at once. Only Federica continued to call him Arthur out of sheer spite. Helena was infuriated by her daughter's unwillingness to embrace her new stepfather. She felt she was most undeserving of a party.

'"Party-spirit, which at best is but the madness of many for the gain of a few,"' said Nuno, pouring Helena a cup of tea. He raised his thick eyebrows at her, which had aged as he had and resembled two white waves on the sea.

Helena shook her head. 'Sorry, Nuno, beaten again,' she said, smiling at him indulgently.

'Ah, for the sharp wit of young Samuel, were he here he'd get that one in a blink.' He sighed, putting down the pot. 'Alexander Pope, my dear,' he said. '"Woman's at best a contradiction still,"' he added with a smirk, 'that's him too.'

'All right, Pa, enough showing off, my head is spinning,' Ingrid complained, sipping her tea. 'I've noticed you no longer smoke, Helena,' she said, observing that she no longer trembled either. 'Arturo must be doing you the world of good.'

'He is. I'm very happy. Though there are times when I crave just one cigarette,' she replied truthfully. 'He is extremely indulgent, though. I'm very lucky.'

'How nice. I wish Inigo were. The only trace of him I see these days is his black mood seeping under his study door like gravy. I wonder, are all philosophers so miserable?'

'My dear, they are pondering the great mysteries of life which cannot be proven. That must, surely, be demoralising,' said Nuno wisely.

'But really, he should philosophise about himself, there is no greater mystery,' she replied.

'But even more demoralising,' Nuno added.

'Well, let's not get distracted,' said Helena. 'Where are the girls, we should start discussing their party?'

'Of course,' Ingrid replied, lighting a cigarette. 'The party. I can't think of anything nicer than having a jolly bunch of young people to dinner in a tent. How romantic, a tent in the garden! Just like your wedding, Helena. Shame Molly's too young to wed otherwise we could have made more use of it.'

★   ★   ★

The date was set for a Saturday in July, midway between Federica's birthday, which was in June, and Hester's, which fell in August. They planned a large tent on the lawn over-looking the lake because Ingrid wanted the young people to enjoy the magnificent water at sunset. When Helena offered to pay half Ingrid waved her hand dismissively. 'Goodness no,' she replied, flapping her cigarette in the air. 'It's the least Inigo can do and besides, he'll pay not to attend.' She laughed mischievously.

Helena dreaded to think what the whole event was going to cost, the girls had far too many ideas. They wanted a hundred and fifty friends, caterers, disco, dance floor and lots of alcohol. Ingrid had suggested a fruit punch but Nuno insisted that they all drink wine. 'If you treat them like children they'll behave like children,' he said. 'Give them wine and they'll carry themselves with the sophistication of young Parisian aristocrats.'

Helena didn't think it would make the slightest bit of difference: drunk Parisian aristocrats were probably much the same as drunk Cornish schoolchildren. Nuno and Ingrid were in for a nasty surprise.

The evening of the party was typical of English summer weather. It had rained most of the day on and off, flooding Polperro with exuberant sunshine only to withdraw it a moment later and plunge it into shadow. Federica packed her night bag and Toby dropped her off at Pickthistle Manor in the afternoon.

'I can't bear it if it rains the whole way through the party,' she wailed. 'Ingrid's made such an effort making the garden nice.'

'Don't be under any illusions, sweetheart,' Toby said with a smile. 'No one's going to give a monkey about the garden, they're all going to be far too busy looking at each other.'

'Still, not much fun if it rains.'

'I disagree, things go much better when everything's thrown into chaos. If I were you, I'd hope for rain.'

As they approached the house Federica's stomach lurched and

then shuddered. Sam's green and white Deux Chevaux was parked in the driveway.

Since her mother's wedding the year before, Federica had barely seen Sam. He had long since left Cambridge and on Nuno's advice had lived and worked in Rome for a year before returning to a job in finance in London. Nuno was furious that he wasted his 'brilliant mind' on a career that anyone with half a brain cell could do, but Sam reassured him that it would only be temporary; he wanted to see how the City worked. Federica had longed for his car to be parked in the drive, but now it was there, she panicked once again that she wouldn't know what to say when she saw him. She wished she were older, taller, prettier and more confident.

'Toby, Sam's at home,' she said in a thin voice.

'Good. It's about time he saw you blossoming into a beautiful young woman,' he replied, drawing up outside the house.

'I'm scared.'

'Of course you are, and that's what makes it so exciting. If you weren't scared you wouldn't be you, and you're lovely.' He glanced across at her earnest profile and hoped Sam had grown up too.

'But you would think that, you're my uncle.' She laughed.

'I'm also a man,' he said, touching her cheek. 'And I think you're beautiful. So go in there and be you. He won't know what's hit him.'

Federica kissed her uncle fondly before stepping unsteadily out of the car. Toby watched her walk inside and thought she looked like a blushing apple on a tree, she was still green, but with the right nurture she would make a very fine apple indeed.

Federica opened the door just as the sky parted again, pounding the ground with arrows of water. 'Bloody hell!' Hester complained, rushing up to her. 'Thank God you're here. Look at the weather!'

'It'll be lovely, darling,' said Ingrid, floating through the hall with a pot of orchids. 'These will brighten the tent up.'

'Mum thinks we're giving a gala for young debutantes. She hasn't a clue,' hissed Hester, grinning mischievously. 'The bore is Sam and his friend Ben are going to police it tonight.'

'What do you mean?' Federica asked, going pink at the mention of his name.

'Well, check up on us. Make sure nothing naughty is going on in the bushes.' She laughed.

'If this weather continues no one will go anywhere near the bushes,' said Federica, her heart basking in the sunny anticipation of Sam's presence.

When Federica and Hester walked across the sitting room and out through the French doors into the tent, Sam waved at her and then said to Ben, 'She's a dark little horse, that one.'

'What, her?' asked Ben, lying like a spider across the sofa.

'Yes. Fed-er-ica,' he said, clipping each syllable in the name as Nuno did.

'She's jailbait, mate,' Ben laughed.

'She is for now. But mark my words, when she's older she'll be gorgeous. I've been watching her. She's different from everyone else, there's something unfathomable about her and I like it. Give her a few more years and she'll have matured into a beautiful young woman.'

'So why wait?'

'For God's sake, Ben. I'm not into deflowering children.' Sam was appalled.

'Isn't this her sixteenth birthday party?'

'Yes, it is,' he replied.

'Well, she's ripe for the picking then. Better get her before anyone else does. Will you introduce me, I'd like to take a closer look.'

Ben followed Sam across the tent, which Ingrid had filled with large pots of orchids in spite of the florist who was busy decorating it with her own creations. Gazing out onto the garden Hester and Federica stood with their arms crossed gloomily in front of them, watching the downpour while frantic caterers bustled about erecting tables and chairs. Dodging the lighting men and the rehearsing band of musicians, Sam and Ben made their way over to join them.

'Hello Fede.' Federica turned around and felt the heat prickling her neck and chest as Sam sauntered up to her. The more she concentrated on not blushing the hotter her face became. She smiled, trying to act naturally and lowered her eyes. 'This is Ben,' Sam said. Ben extended his hand and studied her face through narrowed eyes.

'The policemen,' she said with a smile.

'The policemen,' said Sam, putting his hands in the pockets of his trousers. 'At least that was the only way we could get ourselves invited.'

'We don't need policemen,' Hester said sulkily.

'That's what you think,' Sam laughed. 'You might be pleased to have me and Ben muscling in when all those drunken boys are fighting over you.'

'I wish,' she replied. 'Look at it,' she said, putting her hand out and feeling the drops.

'I like the rain. It's romantic,' Sam said. Federica avoided making eye contact with him, but in spite of her efforts she could feel his stare on her face like the heat of the sun. She wondered why he was suddenly so interested and wished he'd leave before his proximity suffocated her.

'Well I don't,' Hester complained. 'Of all the days, why does it have to rain today? The place will be a mud bath.'

'You can all get naked and mud wrestle,' chuckled Ben, looking at his friend for approval. Hester giggled. Sam changed the subject.

'How's it going living with your uncle?' he asked Federica. He remembered their conversation in the bluebells and how upset she had been at the prospect of leaving Polperro.

'Fine, thank you,' she replied, managing to look at him briefly before finding the intimacy of his eyes too much to bear and pulling away. She felt foolish, as if her tongue were too big for her mouth. She wished she could find something intelligent to say. 'Julian's giving me photography lessons,' she said, filling the silence that seemed embarrassingly large and vacuous.

'I bet you're quite good now,' he replied. 'You should be with a teacher like Julian.'

'She is. I've seen some of her pictures,' Hester said loyally. Sam raised his eyebrows with interest.

'Not that good,' interjected Federica bashfully. 'Not yet.'

'A career as a photographer would be very appealing,' Sam said, nodding his head ponderously. 'You can take it anywhere, and you'll always be your own boss. There's a lot to be said for freedom, I can tell you.'

'I know. But I've got a long way to go before I get to that stage.'

'It goes very fast,' Sam said, reflecting on how the past year had slipped by almost unnoticed and how much it had changed her.

'I hope so,' Federica replied, noticing to her bewilderment the intense expression on his face as he looked at her. She was thankful when Hester suggested they start getting ready for their party.

'We haven't got time to stand here chatting to a couple of old men,' she said, dragging Federica away by the arm. Federica was only too pleased to go.

'I never wished her a happy birthday,' Sam said, watching them disappear into the sitting room.

'You can do it later when you're pulling her and some groping adolescent out of the bushes.'

'Shut up, Ben,' Sam snapped irritably. 'Sometimes you're more of a child than they are.'

Federica enjoyed a hot bath in the company of Trotsky who took it upon himself to keep vigil as none of the doors in Pickthistle Manor had locks. He lay there in the steam panting with his noble head resting on his paws and his pink tongue hanging out. Once more Federica's mind found Sam within the secrecy of its halls. She closed her eyes and imagined a world where everything she said was witty and clever, where she never blushed or stammered, where she always looked ravishing. Sam loved her in that world. He loved her passionately. He kissed her with tenderness and urgency, barely able to let her out of his sight even for a moment. His affection was all-consuming. In his arms she felt secure and cherished, safe from the doubts and worries that silently plagued her in the real world.

She was dragged out of those pleasant halls by the loud, impatient yawn of Trotsky who had jumped to his feet and was waiting by the door wanting to be let out. Federica found Hester in front of the mirror in her bedroom. She had already dried her hair and Molly was applying mascara with the steady hand of a professional make-up artist. 'I'll do you after Hester,' she said.

Federica shuffled in her towel. 'I don't know. I've never put make-up on before,' she said, screwing up her nose.

'Well, tonight is your birthday party and you're going to look wonderful. Hurry and put your dress on,' she said bossily, standing back from her sister to admire her creation. 'Hester, you look beautiful,' she said, brushing on blusher with brisk strokes.

When Hester and Federica appeared in the tent in their dresses, their hair and make-up gave them the cool sophistication of much older girls. Molly stood proudly behind them like a nanny, pushing them forward so they could be admired. Ingrid clasped her hands together and exclaimed that they both looked like princesses. Helena realised that her daughter was growing up and felt a stab of sadness at her passing childhood. She wore a pale blue strapless dress that matched her aquamarine eyes and Molly had pinned her pale hair up onto the top of her head. She looked innocent yet remote, unlike other children of her age who were either far too knowing for their own good or much too infantile. She had acquired an ethereal quality in the last year, but Helena was certain she wasn't aware of her own allure; she was too insecure.

'You both look lovely,' she said, tucking a stray piece of white air behind Federica's ear. 'Lovely,' she said wistfully. She wished Ramon were there to see her. He'd be so proud. She shook off her regret and pulled a thin smile. 'Toby will pick you up in the morning. You look wonderful, Fede, a young woman now.'

'*Che belle donne!*' Nuno declared, trotting into the tent dressed in white tie.

'Pa, what on earth are you wearing?' Ingrid exclaimed, looking him up and down in puzzlement. 'It's *black* tie.'

'*Cara mia*, I live my own dress code,' he said with a sigh. 'It is my granddaughter's ball and I owe it to her to look my best.'

'Are you sure you want to come to my party, Nuno?' Hester laughed. 'You look like a penguin.'

'I'm flattered, truly,' he said with a bow. 'It's an honour to be in the company of two beautiful princesses. Let us celebrate with a glass of champagne!'

Federica was disappointed Sam hadn't come down. She felt pretty and wanted him to see her. While she drank endless toasts with Ingrid, Nuno and her mother she kept a keen eye on the French doors, her heart quivering in anticipation of his arrival. But he never appeared. Finally she asked Hester, 'Where are the policemen?'

'Watching telly, I suspect,' she said to Federica's disappointment. 'They'll appear when things get going.'

Things got going pretty fast. The guests arrived and proceeded to finish almost the entire supply of alcohol before sitting down to dinner. The buffet was served early to compensate but no one moved towards the food until Trotsky was seen at one of the tables like a canine vacuum cleaner, polishing off the sausages with one inhalation. Once Hester had dragged the dog out into the garden, the guests fell upon the dishes in fear of losing it all to the other animals who wandered in and out as if they owned the place. Federica sat next to two boys she didn't know who talked most of the evening across her about cricket and O levels. Too shy to assert herself she just sat back and listened submissively, watching Molly near by who managed to have the attention of her entire table and smoked a long thin cigarette with great panache. Federica felt conspicuous and foolish by comparison.

Federica danced with a couple of boys, but she was too self-conscious to enjoy it. She noticed they looked over her shoulders, probably hoping for more interesting girls to dance with. She watched one of Molly's friends in a black lace dress move with the lithe sophistication of a professional dancer and wished she had such self-assurance and grace. Finally, when she was about to retreat to a lone chair somewhere in the corner of the tent, preferably underneath a large orchid, her dance partner suddenly swelled green in the face, like mouldy yoghurt, and grabbing Federica by the hand dragged her outside into the night.

'I think I'm going to be sick,' he groaned as the alcohol caused his stomach to heave.

'What do you need *me* for?' she asked in bewilderment, as her heels sunk into Ingrid's sodden lawn.

'I don't want to die alone,' he replied, pulling her into the night.

'I don't think it's that bad, is it?' she asked, hoping he'd make a miraculous recovery and take her back to the party. She shivered with cold as the drizzle dusted her face and shoulders.

'It's very bad,' he replied before throwing his head into a bush and vomiting loudly. Federica winced as he covered Ingrid's beautiful roses with bile and minced sausages. She stepped back in alarm and put her hand over her mouth in disgust. Suddenly the drizzle turned to rain that fell thick and heavy, pounding onto her silk dress and seeping through to her skin. She cowered her head, not knowing whether to leave him in the flowerbed and run for cover or stay with him. When she heard her name echo across the garden she turned her attention away from the grunting bush in relief. It was Sam.

'Federica!' he shouted. Federica strained her eyes to see Sam running towards her through the deluge. 'Federica. Are you all right?' he asked, jogging up to her. His white shirt was so wet it stuck to his skin like paper revealing beneath it the colour of his flesh. His blond hair was dripping over his face, but his smile was broad as if he enjoyed the drama the rain brought with it.

'What?' she stammered, blinking at him in confusion.

'Hester said you'd been dragged away by a drunkard,' he said, catching his breath. Federica pointed into the bush. 'Good God!' he exclaimed, putting a hand over his nose. 'Let's get out of here. He'll sober up by himself,' he declared, taking her by the hand and leading her off in the opposite direction of the tent.

'Where are we going?' she shouted as she hurried to keep up with him in her fragile heels.

'Far away from that dreadful party,' he replied in disgust. 'You haven't been enjoying it, I've been watching you.' Federica's belly shuddered with pleasure at the thought of him watching her, at the thought of him noticing her. She was grateful that the night hid her burning cheeks as well as her running mascara. When he opened the door to the barn they crept into the darkness. She heard him shuffle about with the latch and smelt the scent of warm hay and cut grass. Seconds later he flicked his lighter and lit a candle.

'I've never been in here before,' she said, casting her eyes about her curiously.

'I come in here all the time. Especially at night because there's a family of wild ducks who live here. That's why I don't use the light. It'll scare them away. I keep a candle so I can observe them.'

'A family of ducks. Are you serious?' she said.

'Come,' he whispered, taking her by the hand. 'I'll show you.'

Sam led her slowly over the floor that was covered in golden sticks of straw, which caught the light and glittered. The barn was used for storing grain and hay for the animals and logs for the house fires. The sound of rain rattled on the roof, but inside it was warm and dry. Without making any noise they climbed onto the bales, crouched down and peered over to where the family of ducks sat comfortably in a warm bed of feathers. The ducklings were all asleep, oblivious to the strange creatures who watched them quietly, while the mother, cautious yet fearless, sat unmoving with her black eyes open and alert. Sam grinned at Federica who smiled back in delight. Neither spoke, they just watched without allowing the sound of syllables to ruin the moment.

When Sam leant over and kissed her, Federica was taken completely by surprise. His hand held her by the back of her neck and his lips kissed her stunned lips before drawing away and looking into her face for her reaction. She looked petrified.

'Didn't you like it?' he asked softly. Federica tried to speak but the words didn't form as she had hoped. 'Would you like me to kiss you again?' She nodded mutely, overwhelmed by the closeness of his body. He placed his mouth on hers again, tracing her lips with his, feeling her skin without tasting it. She sat rigidly, too afraid to move, unsure of what to do. As if sensing her discomfort he pulled away and stroked his fingers through her hair that was wet from the rain and hanging over her face.

'Is this the first time?' he asked.

'Yes,' she replied hoarsely.

Sam smiled with tenderness. 'The first time is always a bit frightening. I remember mine,' he said. 'It's worse for a boy because you're supposed to know what you're doing.'

'How did you know what to do?' she asked in an attempt to make conversation but all she could think about was the sensation of his lips on hers and the fearful anticipation of him doing it again.

'Instinct,' he said simply, taking off his glasses. Then he looked at her with an intensity that made her heart lurch and ran his hand down the slope of her neck. 'Look, close your eyes. Don't be shy. Listen to your senses not your mind that's whirring around asking what's going on. Kissing is meant to be pleasurable not uncomfortable. Just relax and concentrate on what your body's feeling. Don't let yourself get distracted by your fears. I'm not judging you, just enjoying you.' Federica giggled nervously. 'Close your eyes, go on,' he insisted. Federica giggled again, then closed her eyes expectantly. Her stomach flinched as she felt his lips on her skin, kissing her jawbone, the muscle below the ear, her temples and her eyes. As much as she tried to detach her mind, she couldn't allow herself to bask in the pleasure of her senses as he had suggested for fear of letting go and looking foolish. She could smell the spice of his aftershave mixed with the natural male scent of his body and she wanted to pinch herself to make sure it was really happening. Then, just when she thought her mind would ruin so magic a moment, his lips fell onto her mouth again, opened and ceased the frenetic racing of her thoughts. She tasted the wine on his tongue and felt his rough chin against hers. Aware only of the sensual aching of her limbs she responded instinctively. He wrapped his arms around her body and drew her against him. There in the flickering candle-light of the barn her whole being stirred with the flowering of spring.

Chapter Twenty-Six

Helena returned home to find a note on the kitchen table from Arthur.

Gone to the cinema with Hal, see you later. Love Arturo.

She opened the fridge, took out a can of Coca Cola and a plate of cold meat and sat down to eat alone. She glanced at the clock on the wall and wondered how Federica was doing at the party. She had been too distracted with her new husband and son to notice the ripening of her daughter. In the past year Federica had quietly begun to metamorphose, emerging from her chrysalis as a lucid young woman, with deep melancholic eyes and the shy smile of a child uncomfortable with the shedding of her girlhood. On one hand she was capable, sensible and independent, yet Helena recognised in her a growing neediness and insecurity because those were the traits she had inherited from her. She ate her meat with little enthusiasm. The resplendent image of Federica in her party dress cast a shadow of regret over her heart that she was unable to shake off. She tried not to think of Ramon, but his image surfaced in her thoughts like a buoy on the sea. There he floated, unwilling to leave. His coal-black eyes bore into her enquiringly and she could almost hear him asking her if she was happy.

She wasn't as happy as she had expected to be. Arthur was good to her and she was deeply fond of him. He was a saint, putting up with her changing moods and impatience with the kindly smile of a doting father. He was everything that Ramon was not. He was unselfish, tolerant, non-judgemental, yet he lacked the charisma, the passion and the drama of Ramon. With Arthur she still yearned for something more. She wished he were better looking, thinner, less clumsy. The jolly bounce in his stride irritated her and she longed for him to hold himself back rather than rushing up to people like an over-enthusiastic Labrador. His ebullience grated. She was afraid to dwell too long on the first few years of her marriage with Ramon because nothing in the world could compete with that all-consuming joy and sense of fulfilment. In Federica she saw the reflection of the girl she had once been. Flawless, like a piece of virgin paper waiting for someone to paint it with love. She thought of her own sheet of paper and what life had imprinted upon it, so many colours, but she didn't have the courage to look deep enough to notice that most of the ugly colours were of her own making.

When Toby arrived at Pickthistle Manor the following morning to collect Federica, he found her radiant face smiling out at him from Hester's bedroom window. She ran down the stairs and threw herself into his arms. 'It was the best party ever!' she enthused, barely able to disguise the smile of a satisfied woman. She had intended to keep her midnight kisses with Sam a secret but once she was alone in the car with her uncle the words came spilling out as if she had no control over them. 'He took me into a barn and kissed me. It was so romantic,' she sighed, fanning her face with the AA manual. 'It was raining outside, but warm inside with the smell of hay. He lit a candle and showed me a nest of sleeping ducks. He was so sweet. We talked all night. He was so understanding and kind, not like those awful oafs I danced with. Sam rescued me like he did that day in the lake. I can't imagine what he sees in me, though.'

Toby smiled a little nervously. He didn't imagine someone of Sam's age would want a long-term relationship with a girl of Federica's, and he knew what she would be hoping for.

'I know what he sees in you, Fede. You're a beautiful young woman. It doesn't surprise me at all that he thinks you're wonderful.'

'What will happen now?' she asked.

Toby sighed and stared ahead of him.

'Don't expect too much, sweetheart,' he said, not wanting to dampen her excitement nor allow it to fly to fanciful heights.

'What do you mean?'

'He's a lot older than you. Just don't expect too much, then if he wants to be with you it will be a bonus.'

'Oh, all right.' She smiled happily, rolling down the window. 'I'll see him up at the manor anyway. Hester's asked me up for tea this afternoon.'

'Good,' said Toby.

'Don't worry, I'll bicycle. The exercise will make me glow.'

'You're glowing already,' Toby chuckled.

Arthur, Helena and Hal came over for a barbeque lunch to hear how the party had gone. The rain had cleansed the sky during the night and it now shone with renewed brightness and clarity. Federica managed to tell her mother and stepfather enough about the party to satisfy their curiosity, without mentioning her tryst with Sam. Toby winked at her and grinned mischievously, silently promising to keep her secret. Arthur, Hal and Julian played croquet on the lawn while Helena sat in the shade drinking Pimms. Federica was too distracted to notice the strain that had become ingrained in her mother's features and skipped off for a walk with Rasta. Toby was never too distracted to notice his sister's moods and joined her at the table. 'Fede's happy,' he said.

'Yes, she is,' Helena replied flatly. 'It's all thanks to you and Julian. I think it's done her good living with a couple of men.'

'She still misses her father though,' he said, pouring himself a cup of coffee. 'I sometimes catch her playing with that butterfly box of hers. You know she keeps all his letters in there.'

'I know. Tragic, isn't it?' said Helena bitterly.

'It's only natural.'

'It's not natural to leave your family for years though, is it?'

'No, it's not.'

'It's not natural for a child to live with her uncle either. Not when her mother is just down the road.'

'Is that why you're depressed?' he asked sympathetically.

'Oh, I don't know.' She sighed. 'I feel I've cocked up. I tore them away from their father, their country, their grandparents. I married again, someone Federica doesn't like. So I let her live somewhere else so that she can be near her friends. Is that natural?'

Toby touched her hand that rested on the table beside her glass. 'Dad ignores Julian and refuses to give his own daughter away at her wedding because he can't face his son's lover. He sacrifices his relationship with his son because of his sexual persuasion – that's not natural either,' he said and smiled with empathy. 'It doesn't matter what's natural and what isn't. It's all a matter of opinion anyway. If Federica's happy with us, it's natural. If Hal is happy with you and Arthur, that's natural too. Fede and Hal see each other enough. They feel like brother and sister. Imagine, some people send their children away to boarding school for years. Is that natural?'

'I suppose you're right,' she conceded gratefully.

'But that's not what's bothering you,' he ventured quietly, glancing across the lawn at Arthur who had just hit his red ball through the hoop and was flapping his arms about in delight, like a fat penguin.

Helena laughed cynically. 'You know me too well,' she said. 'I know.'

'At times like this I wish I hadn't given up smoking.' She sighed, filling her glass. 'I'm content, Toby. Arthur's good to me. He looks after me. Does everything for me. He's the opposite of Ramon who was a selfish shit.'

'But you still love that selfish shit,' said Toby.

'I wouldn't use the word "love",' she interjected quickly, lowering her eyes that burned when she blinked.

'But Arthur doesn't do it for you.'

'Arthur,' she sighed in resignation. 'Arthur isn't enough.' Toby looked at his sister pensively. She shook her head. 'But

I'm stuck. That's it. I've made my choice. Look how much Hal adores him. They've really bonded, it's lovely.'

'Helena, we all have to compromise in life. You're unlikely to get the qualities you like in Ramon and those you like in Arthur rolled into one man. It just won't happen.'

'But I didn't want to leave Ramon in the first place,' she whispered, looking at her brother steadily.

'What do you mean?' he asked slowly, hoping he had misheard her.

'I didn't think he'd let me go.' Her eyes glistened with tears.

'God, Helena,' he gasped, shaking his head.

'Once I'd started I couldn't back out. I had to go the whole way. Then . . .' She hesitated as if barely able to divulge the depravity of her secret.

'Then what?'

'Then, I married Arthur because the idea of it infuriated Ramon. I could see it in his eyes. I was hurting him and it felt good.' She drained her glass. 'Am I evil?'

'Not evil, Helena, but very misguided.'

'Don't tell anyone,' she said firmly.

'I won't,' he promised. 'But by God you've got yourself into one hell of a mess.'

She nodded bleakly. 'And there's no one to tidy it up for me,' she said, and pulled a thin smile.

Federica returned from her walk and went straight to her room where she lay down on the bed and closed her eyes. She mentally replayed the scenes of the night before, rewinding them over and over again, enjoying his kisses and caresses as if for the first time. They had sat in the trembling light of the candle and talked until the music from the party had ceased to reverberate through the rain and the sound of cars and departing guests had faded into the night. Federica had sat in his arms and allowed him into the secret halls of her mind. She had told him about the butterfly box, the story of Topahuay and her father's letters, which she re-read whenever she felt sad. With Sam she had found forgotten memories hidden behind the clutter of her present life, such as the time she had found a dead fish on the beach in Viña and her father had taught her about death. He had picked up a shell and sitting down with her on the sand he had explained that when a creature dies it sheds shells, its fins, its body and floats up into the sky to be with God. He had then made a pendant out of the shell and hung it about her neck. 'You see the shell isn't important, it's the spirit within that matters and cannot be destroyed,' he had said, but it was only later when she was older that she understood what he meant.

Sam listened intently to her, stroking her hair, amused by some of her stories, moved by others. 'You're very special, Fede,' he said wistfully, kissing her temple.

'What do you mean by "special"?'

'Well, you're just different. I think you've lived more than other girls of your age. ' "Experience maketh man",' he quoted, 'and you've experienced more than most women twice your age. I can see it in those big sad eyes of yours.' He laughed, kissing her temple again. 'You need someone to look after you.'

Federica snuggled up against his body and felt for the first time in many years the same sensation of security that she had felt in the arms of her father. 'I wish I was older,' she sighed. 'Independent, not having to go to school.'

'You haven't got long now.'

'You're lucky, you're in London. You'll never have to do anything you don't want to ever again.'

'That's not true. We always have to do things we don't want to do. I'd rather live here in Polperro for a start.'

'Really?'

'Yes, I'm not a Londoner at all. But I'm not ready to "bow out" yet.'

'What's your dream?' she asked curiously.

'A cottage overlooking the sea, dogs, a pig perhaps, a family, an extensive library and a long list of best-sellers behind me.'

She laughed. 'A pig?'

'Absolutely, a cottage isn't complete without a pig.' He chuckled. 'What's yours then?'

'I'd like to take photographs and travel the world,' she declared, then added, 'and I'd like to return some day to Cachagua. I don't know why, but I miss my grandparents' house more than I miss my own.'

'I'm sure one day you will.'

'I'd also like to live in London, be very rich and famous like my father.'

'Well, you'll probably succeed there too,' he said. 'Or you'll achieve your dreams and realise that they were empty vessels all along.'

' "You can teach people knowledge, but wisdom, dear boy, has to be learned through experience," ' said Federica in Nuno's clipped Italian accent.

Sam laughed. 'So you do listen to what old Nuno has to say,' he exclaimed in admiration.

'I can't help it, he repeats everything so many times his sayings get ingrained.'

'And a good thing too. You won't ever meet anyone wiser than him.'

Federica lay on her bed and smiled as she recalled their conversation. She had sat in his arms until her clothes had dried and the gentle light of dawn seeped in through the cracks in the barn, like mist announcing the beginning of day. They had talked like old friends and she had discarded her inhibitions with each caress and her fears with each kiss. When she had crept into Hester's room she had been unable to sleep. All she could do was think of Sam. She had always known in her heart that Sam was meant for her.

Toby and Julian were sitting outside on the terrace reading the papers and commenting on the issues of the day when Federica skipped downstairs, ready to bicycle up to Pickthistle Manor. The house was now quiet as Helena had left with Arthur and Hal to have tea with her parents. Toby put the paper down and scrutinised her.

'Well?' she asked. 'Do I look all right?'

He nodded thoughtfully. 'You look pretty good to me,' he said smiling, removing the square-shaped glasses that gave him the look of a seventies singer-songwriter.

'Well, actually, I'm not so sure you don't look as if you've made too much effort,' said Julian, rubbing his chin.

'Really?' she asked, looking down at her jeans and pumps.

'Darling, she looks wonderful,' Toby insisted.

But Julian shook his head. 'No, no,' he muttered. 'Put on your trainers instead of those pumps, I think that's what it is. You don't want to look like you're trying.'

Federica ran off upstairs, appearing two minutes later in a pair of white gym shoes.

'Darling, you're right,' said Toby, impressed.

'I'm not a photographer for nothing,' Julian replied, tapping his cheekbone with his finger and raising his eyebrows. 'You have to have a good eye.'

'Sweetheart, you look very cool,' said Toby. 'Have fun and behave. Remember, he's much older than you.'

'Be firm and say "no",' Julian added. 'Whatever he asks of you, say "no".' Federica rolled her eyes and laughed.

'It'll make him keener,' said Toby.

'Little bastard, putting his dirty paws on our Federica,' Julian muttered, grinning at her.

'I want to hear you say it, sweetheart,' said Toby. Federica giggled, wandering off.

'Go on!' Julian shouted after her. 'It's the most important word in a woman's vocabulary.'

'NO!' she retorted, turning the corner.

Toby shrugged at Julian. They were both thinking the same thing. They'd be there for her when it all ended badly.

★　★　★

Federica cycled up the winding lanes lined with cow-parsley and buttercups, humming to herself with gusto. When she turned the corner into the drive the first thing she noticed was the space left by the absence of Sam's car. She stopped humming and a frown replaced the smoothness of her brow. She leant the bike against the wall of the house and ran in. During the summer months when the weather was good Ingrid liked all the doors to be open so that the scents of the garden and the roses that covered the walls of the house would fill the rooms with the fertile fragrances of nature. It also allowed the various animals rescued by Hester to come and go freely without having to ask to be let out. The swallows that always nested in the porch year after year dived in through the open windows and the odd brave mouse crept into the kitchen to satisfy his greed in the dog bowls. Federica walked through the rooms to the lawn where the tent was being dismantled by an army of tanned men in baseball caps and khaki shorts. She found Hester and Molly lying on the grass still in their dressing gowns, drinking cups of coffee.

'Hi, Fede,' said Hester wearily, peering at her over her dark glasses.

'We can't be bothered to get dressed,' said Molly. 'We're knackered.'

'It was a wonderful party, though,' Fede said, casting her eye about for Sam.

'Great party,' said Hester. 'Come and join us.' Federica sat down on the grass and played with the daisies distractedly.

'You look sickeningly well for someone who was up all night,' said Molly, looking her up and down.

'Whom did you disappear with for so long? I didn't even hear you come to bed,' said Hester, rubbing her red eyes.

'No one very exciting, I'm afraid,' Federica muttered, doing her best to dissemble.

'Like hell. You're blushing,' Molly said sharply.

'Did he kiss you?'

'No, no. We just talked,' she insisted lamely.

'Talked?' Molly scoffed. 'People don't "talk" at parties, they snog.'

'Well, I'm afraid we talked.'

'What about?' Hester asked, screwing up her nose.

'He talked about himself,' said Federica casually. 'Actually he was sick in the bushes, which wasn't very nice. Then it started to pour with rain so we ran into the barn and sat in there out of the rain. I listened to him until about four in the morning.'

'Poor old you. You missed your own party,' said Hester. 'Was he very boring?'

'Dreadfully,' Federica replied.

Molly looked at her suspiciously. 'Don't be so gullible, Hester,' she said, grinning at Federica. 'I don't believe you for a moment.'

'Molly, she won't have kissed someone just after they were sick.'

'Perhaps he wasn't sick,' said Molly, raising an eyebrow.

'Look, it really doesn't matter,' said Federica. 'What about you?'

Hester giggled. 'I snogged two people,' she said. 'But Nuno caught me the second time and insisted on dancing with me. You know he's a wonderful dancer, you'd be surprised.'

'He hasn't surfaced today, must be hung over,' Molly laughed. 'Mum's on the beach painting, she thought it was a lovely party even though her orchids were all trampled on and Joe Hornish drove his bike across the lawn in the rain leaving marks all over it. Dad's livid and says he'll pay not to have a party next time.'

'And the policemen?' Federica dared to ask, lowering her face to hide her eyes lest they give her away.

'Oh, Sam's gone back to London with Ben,' Hester said.

'Oh,' said Federica, forcing a smile.

'I think he's had enough of drunk sixteen-year-olds to last him a lifetime,' said Molly.

Federica's mind flooded with gloom. Her cheeks flushed with disappointment as she felt once again that clawing sense of rejection. He hadn't even waited to say good-bye. Did the night before mean nothing to him at all? When she had stayed long enough to leave without causing suspicion she rode her bicycle home through copious tears and aching sobs that opened up the old wound her father had made all those years ago. When she arrived back at the cottage she ran up to her room and flung herself on her bed in despair. She had truly believed he loved her, as she had believed her father had loved her too. She opened the butterfly box and recalled with shame how she had allowed him to share her deepest secrets, invited him into her private world, only to discover that he wasn't really very interested. It was a painful awakening.

When Toby arrived back from the sea he saw Federica's bicycle carelessly thrown onto the gravel and sensed that something was wrong. He ran upstairs to find her crying over the letters from her father. Gathering her into his arms he didn't need to ask what had happened. He knew. It was exactly as he had feared.

'Everyone I get close to runs away,' she whispered, wiping her tears on her uncle's jersey.

'That's not true,' he insisted. 'We'll always be here for you.'

'He's just like Papa. Why do they have to leave without a word? I feel so worthless.'

'They don't deserve you, Fede. You're so much better than they are.'

'But I love Sam,' she wailed.

'Darling girl, you're so young and your love is so innocent.'

'No it isn't. I truly love him.'

'He's young too, Fede. What could you expect? He'll want a relationship one day, but right now he's enjoying his freedom. Sweetheart, you're still at school.'

She looked up at him with swollen eyes. 'But I don't want anyone else but him,' she explained. 'There's no one in the world like Sam.'

'I know,' he soothed. 'You just have to be patient. You've

both got a lot of growing up to do. It was highly irresponsible of him to raise your hopes. He must know how you feel.'

'He's so sweet and kind,' she said. 'He would never hurt me on purpose.'

'Of course he wouldn't. You just have different expectations, that's all. I just hate to see you hurt, I'd like to box his ears.'

'I wouldn't let you.' She smiled sadly.

'You're going to be okay, Fede,' he said, and squeezed her affectionately.

But at that moment she didn't think her heart would ever recover.

That evening Federica walked along the cliff-tops with Rasta. Her recollections of the night before had now been soiled. She felt nothing but resentment and self-pity. Everywhere she looked she saw Sam; in the pink clouds that caught the sunset to the waves that washed over the rocks in their eternal battle to wear them down. The familiar feeling of emptiness gnawed at her heart, reminding her of the unhappy times in her life when her love had been thrown back at her. She feared she might never have the courage to love again. Sitting on the grass she pulled Rasta against her and buried her face in his damp fur. Then she threw her wishes into the sea and watched them sink.

Chapter Twenty-Seven

Sam drove up the motorway while Ben snored and dribbled in the passenger seat. He listened to the radio for a while but soon found his mind wandering back through the night until he found himself in the barn with Federica and he was awash with guilt. What had he been thinking of? A few hours of self-indulgence was hardly worth the hurt that was sure to follow. He felt like a monster. That is why he had insisted they leave straight after breakfast. He didn't have the courage to tell her to her face that it had been nice, but that's all it was: a kiss in the hay. He wasn't cruel or callous. He was extremely fond of her. She had grown into a surprisingly beautiful and captivating young woman, but like a peach on the brink of ripening, he had picked her too soon. Her innocence had been too tempting to resist, and he couldn't bear the idea of someone else spoiling her. Any of those oafs at the party could have lured her into a drunken brawl in the bushes, a hurried grope in the dark, a slobbery kiss for no other reason than to boast about it later to his friends. He had seen her run out into the garden with precisely the sort of ruffian he was afraid of and had pursued her with the intention of escorting her back to the tent. His intentions had been good, even if he hadn't had the strength of character to follow them through.

What happened after that was shameful. He was nine years her senior with enough experience to know what a first kiss can do to a girl like Federica. But there in the golden light of the candle, enveloped in the sweet smells of nature, she had looked at him with such adoration and such longing that he had found the seat of his own longing momentarily disturbed. Surprised by his sudden response to a girl he had known since childhood, he was at once disarmed and unprepared. His impulses responded to his instincts and before he had time to listen to the muffled voice of his reasoning he had kissed her. At first she had been awkward and afraid, fighting her own inner battles in an effort to over-come her shyness. But then she had finally surrendered to the new sensations that stirred her loins. Charmed by her innocence he had enjoyed caressing away her fears and watching her conquered by her senses. A kiss is never again so sweet as that first time – that first small awakening and his heart heaved with remorse.

He watched the sun burn away the morning mists and settle into a splendid summer's day, causing the freshly washed coun-tryside to glitter about him. He switched off the radio and glanced across at his friend whose body was recovering in sleep from the alcohol and debauchery of the night before. Sam was happy to be left alone with his thoughts, however much they tormented him. He had listened to Ben's crowing enough. It made him feel even more ashamed; was he no better than him? He firmly reassured himself that he was better than Ben. While Ben was kissing and groping his way around the tent, he had enjoyed a tender moment with a dear friend. Yes, a dear friend. It had been sweet and touching and anyhow, it wasn't just about the kiss. They had talked until dawn, about anything and everything, and were truly fond of each other. But she was too young. It was as simple as that. So why couldn't he do the decent thing and tell her?

Sam struggled with his conscience all the way up to London. Stopping en route for petrol he bought the papers and a packet of chocolate raisins and woke up his friend. He was ready to talk. He needed distracting. 'So,' he said, climbing back into the car and starting it up. 'Are you feeling any better?'

'I'm feeling like shit,' Ben replied, and yawned. 'But it was worth it. Still, I'm looking forward to getting back to the big smoke. I've had enough frigid babes for the time being. There's only so much fun to be had in kindergarten. Know what I mean? I'm ready for the university of life!' He chortled, plunging his hand into the packet of chocolate raisins.

Sam rolled his eyes and switched on the radio. 'Quite,' he agreed flatly. 'The university of life.'

Sam quickly forgot his guilty qualms about Federica as he lost himself in his London life. He travelled to the City every morning by tube, put as little effort into his work as possible, then returned home in the evenings to go out with his friends. Every now and then he would pick up a girl, make love before supper then see her off before bedtime. The thought of waking up to a stray in his bed repelled him. He needed sex like he needed to eat, but once the meal was over the sight of the dirty plate was most unattractive. He never remembered their names and rarely their faces, yet his appetite never waned. Tenderness was an emotion he had left in the barn, along with the family of ducks and the smoking candle. No one managed to stir his heart or unsettle his emotions, which remained cool and aloof and seemingly impenetrable.

In the autumn, when he finally returned home to Polperro, he hid in Nuno's study discussing Balzac's *Cousin Bette*, afraid that Federica might cycle up to see Hester and look at him with those large, sad eyes of hers, and fill him once again with remorse. He wanted to tell Nuno but was too ashamed to mention it. So he skulked about the house filling it with his icy presence.

'Goodness me, Sam,' Molly sighed, 'you're a miserable sight this weekend. What's the matter?'

'Absolutely nothing,' he replied flatly.

'You could have fooled me,' she sniffed, watching him warily. 'Girl trouble, I can tell,' she added with a grin.

'I don't encounter trouble in that department,' he replied loftily.

'Well, why don't you take Trotsky out for a walk or something, you've got that horrid London colour.'

'What's Hester up to?' he asked casually.

'I don't know,' she shrugged, 'but I'm going to watch a video.'

'Which one are you going to see?'

'*An Affair to Remember*,' she said happily, opening the box.

'Not that old chestnut again.' He laughed.

'I adore it. Men just aren't made that way any more.'

'Cary Grant's far too smooth for you, Mol, I thought you preferred them rough.'

'Only as a compromise,' she retorted. 'If a Cary Grant swept me off my feet I'd never look at another bricklayer again!'

Sam chuckled and wandered out of the room whistling for Trotsky.

It was windy up on the cliffs, but it felt good to have the sea breeze on his face. At least out of the house he could avoid bumping into Federica. He swung his arms as he walked, wrapped in Nuno's sheepskin coat, patting the dog every now and then as he rushed back and forth sniffing the dormant earth for sleeping rabbits. He reflected on his work, which he loathed, and the City, which he also loathed, and fantasised about making a home in Polperro one day. London was all very well for a while, but his heart lay in the countryside and his soul belonged to the sea, not to the dusty streets of a sterile town. He looked out over the choppy waves and breathed in the salt, filling up his lungs with memories of his childhood. What he wanted to do more than anything was to write.

Nuno was more than encouraging. He told him firmly that he was wasting his unique creativity in some impersonal bank, doing a job more suited to a halfwit. 'You have imagination, dear boy, and talent, it gives me great pain to see it in restless hibernation.' He was right, of course. But there was something holding him back. Talent was all very well if one knew where to channel it. But Sam didn't know what to write about.

With that gloomy thought, he lifted his eyes. He noticed two small figures in the distance, slowly making their way towards him. Suddenly gripped with panic he was about to turn and walk the other way when one of them waved. She persisted until he responded with an unenthusiastic flap of his hand. It was Hester and Federica and there was no avoiding them.

As they came closer his heart raced with apprehension. He would rather ignore her but that would be unkind. He would have to try to act as if nothing had happened. He hoped she hadn't told Hester.

'Hi, Sam,' his sister shouted through the wind. Rasta bounded up with exuberance and began to frolic about with Trotsky. That enabled Sam to divert his attention to the dogs, calling them and patting them, crouching down on his haunches to cuddle the Labrador.

'Hi, Sam,' said Federica.

He raised his eyes reluctantly and forced a weak smile. Her face was red from exertion and her eyes sparkled from the cold. She was obviously making an effort to dissemble as well. He welcomed her sophistication and his gloom lifted.

'How are you, Federica?' he asked, standing up and looking down at her earnest face.

'Fine thanks,' she replied, putting her hands in her pockets and shuffling her feet to keep warm.

'Cold, isn't it?' he said.

'It's flipping freezing out here,' Hester complained. 'But it's good for the skin,' she added. 'It'll make us glow.'

'You're both glowing rather nicely already.' He chuckled.

'Good,' she enthused. 'Told you, Fede.' Federica smiled shyly but said nothing.

'How's school?' he asked her, but Hester interrupted and answered for her friend.

'We're being made to study so hard my brain's gone on strike.' She giggled.

' "Knowledge is power",' Sam quoted, glancing at Federica who was watching the dogs.

'Knowledge is boring,' Hester moaned. 'Anyway, it's better to keep walking. Do you want to join us?' she asked. Federica looked at him hopefully and he heard himself saying that he'd love to.

'The dogs are happier together,' Hester said. 'I defy you to part them, look they're having such fun!'

They watched Rasta and Trotsky race after a slim hare, who zigzagged across a field as if making a mockery of their stumbling efforts to catch him. They all laughed when the dogs returned with their tongues hanging out and their heavy tails wagging to conceal their embarrassment.

'These two spend far too much time on sofas,' Sam exclaimed.

Federica grinned. 'And too much time with their mouths full of biscuits I should imagine,' she said.

'I don't think they'd know what to do if they managed to catch it,' said Hester, patting Trotsky who nudged his face against her hip. 'Still, he's wanting praise for the effort.'

'They can certainly have that,' Sam laughed, stroking Rasta's sleek back as he passed. It was a fleeting moment when Federica's hand brushed Sam's as she too reached out to touch her dog, but it felt like an age. They both withdrew with speed, each pretending that they hadn't noticed, when in fact their skin burned from the contact.

Federica could barely look at Sam after that, her cheeks stung more from awkwardness than from the cold and she was afraid he might notice. She thrust her scalded hand into her pocket where it tingled with a strange pleasure. She took care not to walk too close in case their bodies jostled together by mistake and kept her eyes fixed in front of her. She was relieved that Hester was talkative because she dominated the conversation, chatting about everything but noticing nothing. Sam tried to include Federica but her words were swallowed up by the enthusiasm of her friend who answered for her, seemingly out of habit. As they reached the house he was beginning to find his sister's dominance tiresome. Federica had barely said a word. He was disappointed. He was surprised to find that he was even more disappointed when she said she had to go.

'But don't you want any tea?' he asked, hovering by the front door while Hester struggled out of her boots in the porch.

Federica shook her head. 'I have to get back to Toby's, Mama's coming to pick me up at four,' she explained.

'Oh, I forgot, you spend weekends with your mother, don't you?'

'Yes,' she replied. 'Most weekends.'

'Well, why don't I drive you back?' he suggested to his own amazement.

'Really, I'm happy to cycle,' she protested.

'It's cold and anyhow, it's getting dark,' he argued, looking out at the evening sky that balanced unsteadily between afternoon and dusk. 'Rasta can sit in the back and I'll put your bike in the boot. Simple!'

'See you at school, Fede,' said Hester to her friend before disappearing into the hall and closing the door behind her.

Federica had no choice. Rasta was already sitting in the back of Sam's Deux Chevaux, steaming up the windows with his hot breath.

Federica climbed into the front seat and waited for Sam to finish securing the bike. She rubbed her hands together nervously. Catching sight of her mottled face and wispy hair in the wing mirror, she did her best to tidy herself up while he wasn't looking. She listened for his footsteps but all she could hear was the rhythmic panting of her dog behind her.

Sam closed the boot as far as it could go then walked around the car to the door. He had no idea what he was going to talk to her about, or why he had suggested he take her in the first place. She seemed to have a knack of undermining his better judgement. He climbed in and closed the door with a slam. 'I bet Rasta doesn't often travel first class,' he joked, lightening the atmosphere.

Federica chuckled. 'He's usually a foot soldier,' she replied. 'I just hope you haven't raised his standards too high or he'll never want to travel any other way.'

'Well, we won't give him any extras then,' he said. 'That's no whisky and no duty free.' They both laughed while Rasta panted in the back.

The car left the drive and bounced down the lane. The evening sky was suddenly transformed into an almost fluorescent flamingo pink as the sun began to set, catching her parting rays on the feathery clouds as she bade farewell to the day. They both looked out on it with wonder.

'It's beautiful,' Federica sighed dreamily.

'It's as if Nature sometimes feels she needs to protest her supremacy and show us all how powerful she can be,' said Sam, slowing down the car.

'It's always so fleeting.'

'I know, a golden moment and then it's gone. But that's what makes it so magical. Sometimes things are more special *because* they're transient.'

'A rare glimpse of Heaven,' she said, unwittingly recalling their stolen kisses in the barn. She lowered her eyes and felt the heat on her face.

'Look how it's washed all the fields with orange,' he exclaimed, drawing the car into the side of the lane. 'I have a sudden desire to walk in it, come on.'

Federica followed him out into the field. Without speaking they strode up the hill to walk in the rare golden light. 'Your face is now orange,' he laughed, looking down at his golden fingers.

'So is yours. Talk about glowing!'

'Let's go to the top. We'll be able to see the effect it has on the sea.' Then he allowed his impulses to once more take control. He took her cold hand in his and led her up to the summit. She felt her heart inflate like a hot air balloon and literally lift her feet off the ground. She was unable to contain the smile which alighted across her entire face. When they arrived at the top they were able to appreciate the full scale of Nature's magnificence. The sea was oddly calm, stretching out to the horizon beneath a canopy of gold.

Neither spoke. They just stood in the tender light and watched the heavenly display take place about them. It was as spellbinding as it was transitory. Once the sun disappeared behind them to entertain another shore they were suddenly plunged into shadow. With the shadow came the drop in temperature. Federica shivered.

'Cold?' he asked, squeezing her hand.

She nodded. 'But it was worth it,' she said, dazed with happiness.

'It certainly was. You don't often get to see a sky like that. I'm glad I shared it with you.' He looked at her with affection.

She caught her breath and gazed at him in bewilderment. His warmth was unexpected. In the aching silence of the last few months she had longed to hear such words. She had dreamed that she would find herself once more alone with him, but as the months had rolled on she had doubted such a moment would ever come again. Now she looked into his face, trying to read his intentions in his features. But he only grinned back at her, giving nothing away.

'Come, you'll be late for your mother and I'll be in terrible trouble,' he said at last, dropping her hand and thrusting his into the pockets of his coat to keep warm. Disappointed she followed him down the hill to the car.

It was only when they got back to the lane that Federica realised they had completely forgotten Rasta. 'I don't believe it!' she wailed. 'Poor darling Rasta. He must have been going out of his mind with frustration watching us up there on the hill.'

'I'm so sorry,' said Sam, shaking his head. 'I was so distracted by the sunset he completely slipped my mind.'

'And mine.'

'Do you think he'll forgive us?' he said and grinned at her.

Federica smiled back. 'I think he will if you promise you won't ever forget him again,' she replied, climbing in. Rasta's tail wagged as much as it was able in such a confined space and he dribbled all the way down the back of the seat in his excitement to see them again.

'I think I'll pay for it,' Sam said, looking at the dog's slobber as it ran in a healthy stream down the leather.

'Oh dear, you're going to wish you had taken him,' she laughed.

'I'm afraid, Rasta, that this was a moment for me and your

mother *only*,' he said, starting the engine. 'You can come next time.'

Federica's spirits lifted at the thought that there might be another time. He may not have kissed her but he had certainly made her feel that she was special. That he cared. When he dropped her off at her uncle's house he leant over and kissed her softly on her cheek. She was sure he lingered there longer than was normal.

'See you soon,' he said, pulling away.

'Thanks, Sam, I really enjoyed that,' she replied seriously. 'So did Rasta,' she added for fear of sounding too sentimental.

'So did I,' he agreed. He helped her with her bicycle while she opened the door for Rasta, who leapt out and immediately cocked his leg on the steaming tyre. They both laughed and Sam rolled his eyes. 'How much longer do I have to go on paying for my negligence?' he joked.

Federica shrugged.

'You take care now,' he said before climbing back into the car.

Federica watched him go and waved until he turned out of the driveway and disappeared down the lane.

PART III

Chapter Twenty-Eight

London, Autumn 1994

'Life would be ever so simple for all of us if robbers walked into the shop in black and white striped prison outfits with sacks of stolen goods slung over their backs,' said Nigel Dalby, the security officer, who sat on the desk with one foot perched up on a chair and two sharp blue eyes skipping eagerly from one face to the other. He spoke with a strong Yorkshire accent and had a head that was too small for the rest of his body, like an urban sloth. Federica noticed that although he spoke to eight new members of staff his eyes kept homing back to her. 'But they don't stand out like that, do they? And they don't have big signs on their foreheads saying "I'm a robber" either.' He laughed at his joke and slapped his thigh. Federica's eyes were drawn to the clearly defined bulge that strained against his tight trousers. Embarrassed that her attention had somehow drifted there she focused on his face and tried to concentrate on the lecture.

'They look like you and me. In a minute I'm going to show you a video of real-life shoplifters so that you can see how clever they are. You all have eyes – I'm asking you to use them. You must always be on guard. In a shop like this thousands of pounds are stolen every year by crafty shoplifters.' He clicked his tongue and pointed two fingers into his eyes. 'Use them. Be vigilant. Now, on the telephones you'll see three buttons: code A, B and C. Code A is only to be pressed if the situation is threatening. Say, for example, a man with a gun walks in and threatens you personally or your customers – this call goes directly to the police station and they can guarantee to be with us in about two minutes. Code B must be pressed if someone looks suspicious, then I'll come down the stairs and subtly follow them about the store. Code C is for assistance, a difficult customer, that sort of thing.' He licked his lips with a dry tongue and looked at Federica. 'Any questions?'

One of the boys put up his hand after a scuffle of encouragement from a friend. 'What does someone suspicious look like?' he asked, trying not to smirk.

Nigel nodded seriously. 'Good question, Simon. I'd say a man looks suspicious if he's wearing a baseball cap, unshaven, sloppily dressed, foreign.'

Federica glanced at her colleagues to see if they were as appalled as she was. They didn't seem to be.

'And in women?' asked Simon, showing off in front of the girls who smiled behind fringes of long shiny hair.

Nigel sniffed impatiently, anxious not to be made a fool of. 'God gave you good brains, that's why we've hired you. Think about it.' He clicked his tongue again and switched on the video.

Federica tried to watch the television but found her eyes drifting back to Nigel Dalby, whose long white fingers fidgeted with the remote control.

After the lecture Federica returned to the gift department on the ground floor and into a dense mist of Tiffany perfume. 'How did it go, m'darling?' asked Harriet, one of the girls who had worked on the shop floor for a couple of years. She was tall and buxom with a penchant for bright clothes and glittering jewellery. 'I'm afraid Nigel tends to love the sound of his own voice, I can see he had you in there for over an hour. Probably fancies you. He's a bit of a ladies' man,' she added and laughed loudly, flicking her chestnut curls over her lime-green shoulders and pearl necklace.

'I can't imagine he has much success with the ladies,' Federica replied. 'He's only compelling because he's so odd to look at.'

'Darling girl, you'd be surprised. Though he's not Torquil Jensen, is he?' she said thickly, pursing together her cherry lips.

'Who's Torquil Jensen?' Federica asked.

'Of course, you wouldn't know who Torquil is.' Harriet's eyes shone with admiration. 'Torquil is the most gorgeous man you're ever likely to meet,' she whispered confidentially. 'He's the nephew of Mr Jensen, the old codger who owns the store, and does a terrific amount of shopping in here.'

'Have I met Mr Jensen?'

'Darling girl, you'd know if you had!' she exclaimed, playing with the pearls about her mottled neck. 'He walks around with a vast entourage of hangers-on and advisers and never talks to anyone. He communicates with his staff through his side-kicks. A little slug of a man, his nephew is a genetic miracle! The old boy rarely comes into the store. I think he sends Torquil in to spy for him. Do watch out, though, the telephones are all bugged. Mr Jensen is a control freak.'

'Really?' Federica gasped, appalled.

'Good God, yes. Don't make any personal calls, m'darling. It's not worth it. They'll sack you immediately. A few months ago Greta had a sweet, sweet girl working as her assistant. Sadly, one personal call and she was out. No explanation given. I think the staff room is bugged too, so no jokes about Mr Jensen, or the Ice Maiden for that matter.'

'The Ice Maiden?'

'Greta.' She sniffed and screwed up her nose.

'What's she like?'

Harriet fumbled with the large silk bow about her neck, pulling it loose and tying it up again.

'A horror, m'darling, an absolute horror,' she stated emphatically.

'Oh.'

'She's from Sweden and if you ask me she's never fully defrosted. But don't worry, she's cold with everyone. She says what she thinks and doesn't bother about the delivery. Torquil once took her out for a few weeks and she swanked about as if she owned the place and started referring to Mr Jensen as William. A definite no-no, believe me. Of course, it didn't last and now Torquil barely acknowledges her. My advice to you is just obey quietly and don't pick a fight with her. Just do what she says and stay out of her way. You're lucky you're so junior. She won't bother with you.' Federica smiled with relief. 'Except you are very pretty. That could be a problem.'

'Is Mr Jensen married?'

'No, bachelor. Shame with all that money. Neither's Torquil. But he always has a girlfriend in tow. You know he drives a Porsche and lives in The Little Boltons. Now, that's a grand address. My father lost all his money in Lloyds. Bloody shame, now I have to look out for a rich hubby. And to think I was once an heiress. Where do you live?'

'In Pimlico with a couple of girlfriends,' Federica replied.

'Pimlico's lovely. Pretty white stucco houses. I like that. They look much grander than they are,' she said.

No sooner had they finished talking when Greta glided down the stairs behind them. She was slim with shiny blonde hair pulled back into a chignon at the nape of her elegant neck. She wore a navy Chanel suit with gold buttons and matching navy shoes. She was much older than Federica had expected, at least forty, and although she was tall and slim she had the thin-lipped, brittle face of a deeply unhappy woman.

She strode up to Federica and looked down at her imperiously with frosty blue eyes. 'I'm sorry I haven't had the chance to meet you yet. Welcome to St John and Smithe.' She smiled only on the surface of her face, a fleeting gesture in order to be polite. 'Rule number one is that you don't stand around talking all day. There are customers to be served and it is very rude to talk to each other and ignore them. Harriet should know better.' She spoke with a slight accent, clipping her words with an icy formality. Harriet began to apologise but Greta cut her off with a snort. 'Ya, ya, she's new so it's okay,' she said briskly. As she walked off through the department to her office Harriet rolled her eyes at Federica and winked.

'Don't look so worried, m'darling, the rest of the group are real muckers,' she said, then looked at her watch. 'Good God, time for a ciggie break, see you in fifteen!'

★　　★　　★

Federica had moved to London at the end of the summer of 1994. She was eighteen years old. Inigo had bought Molly and Hester a flat to share in Belgrave Road, and they had insisted Federica come and live with them for a very low rent, as there was space for another bed in Hester's room. Molly was studying history at London University and Hester was at St Martin's School of Art, following in the footsteps of her mother.

Federica hadn't considered further education. She wanted to be a photographer like Julian and her father, but Helena had shuddered at the thought of her daughter leading the same nomadic life as Ramon and encouraged her to try other avenues.

'You must earn some money first and that can only be done with a proper job,' she had said. 'Once you can support yourself you can do what you like.'

Federica rarely saw Sam except in her dreams. Dreams that punctuated the long days and filled her nights with restlessness and longing. The rare times that they did meet, down at his home in Polperro or occasionally at the flat in London, he smiled at her with fondness and asked her about herself. But the promise of something more than friendship dissolved like that flamingo-pink sky and left her floundering in shadow, wondering why he no longer cared. Living with Molly and Hester only fanned her infatuation and reminded her at every step of the young man who had first won her heart on the iced lake over ten years before. Occasionally he rang to speak to his sisters. If Federica answered the telephone she controlled the tremor in her voice with a will of steel and conversed as friends do, but lived off his every word until the next call as lovers do. As much as she tried to persuade herself that there was no point loving Sam and living off memories which he once shared but had most probably now forgotten, she could not control her heart. There was no one in the world like Sam.

For the first time in her life Federica experienced what it was like to be independent and she relished it. At the end of September she received her first pay cheque; seven hundred pounds. Harriet took her shopping in Knightsbridge and she spent nearly all of it on new clothes, arguing with her friend who wanted her in the same bright colours that she wore. In each shop mirror Federica assessed whether or not Sam would approve of her choice, then found herself wondering whether he ever thought of her at all. But she didn't give up – perhaps she was still too young, perhaps he was waiting for her – perhaps . . . When she appeared at work the following day she looked quite the Londoner in a short grey skirt and high-heeled shoes with her face prettily made up with mascara and face powder that Harriet had insisted she buy.

Greta sniffed jealously at her and told her not to overdo the smiling. 'You're not an advert for toothpaste, Federica, and you look much too keen, you'll frighten the customers away.'

Federica blushed to the roots of her white hair and lowered her eyes in humiliation.

'That's better,' said Greta. Then in a bid to keep her off the shop floor and hidden away she sent her down to the basement to tidy up the stockroom. 'I want it so orderly and clean I could eat my breakfast in there,' she added, stalking back into her office.

In spite of Greta's occasional rudeness Federica loved her job. She enjoyed the security it gave her and the money it paid. She laughed with Harriet and the young people who worked in the other departments swiftly became an almost extended family. The majority of the customers were pleasant and the odd male customer asked her out. But Harriet advised her not to mix business with pleasure and so she declined their offers graciously, flattered that they noticed her. But the number of hopeful men who lingered about the gift department grew as Federica's confidence grew. Exasperated, Greta banished her to the stock-room as much as possible but still they persisted.

One cold November morning Federica and Harriet were standing by the counter when a fat old gypsy shuffled in out of the winter mist, carrying a large number of grubby Tesco bags filled with what looked like more paper bags.

'This is a job for Nigel,' Federica whispered gleefully, pressing the code B button on the telephone.

Harriet giggled, 'He's going to love this one, m'darling.' She snorted. 'This woman lives on the streets and comes in here once in a while to use the bathroom.'

'How disgusting,' said Federica, screwing up her nose in repulsion.

'You think that's disgusting, she washes her bottom in the basin,' she added. 'The secret is not to tell anyone and hope that Greta uses it immediately after her.'

'Damn! Too late now,' Federica hissed, watching Nigel bound down the stairs with a predatory grimace staining his face pink. Nigel blinked three times at Federica who cast her eyes across to the gypsy who was bustling her way down the corridor that led to the Ladies' Room. Nigel deftly dodged a couple of elderly customers but didn't manage to get to the gypsy before she squeezed into the small room and locked the door behind her. Nigel pounded his fists upon the door, exclaiming loudly, 'This is the police, please will you come out of the toilet.'

To which the gypsy replied, 'Fuck off, I'm a lady!' just as Torquil Jensen strode into the store.

Greta immediately sprung out from her office and strode up to Federica. 'I have told you two countless times not to stand and gossip on the shop floor. Federica, go down to the stockroom and sort out the recent delivery of photograph frames,' she ordered.

'But there are hundreds,' Harriet protested on Federica's behalf.

'Do not talk back to me. I am your boss and I am giving Federica an order. If she doesn't have the courage to complain to me herself she might as well find another job, because I have no patience with weak people.' Then turning to Federica, 'The store room. Now.'

Federica hastily departed as Torquil approached the counter. Greta smiled at him, betraying her desperation and her unhappiness in the way her lips paled and her eyes thawed.

337

Torquil smiled back tightly. 'Hello, Greta,' he said, looking at her briefly before turning his attention to Harriet. 'Harriet, you look pretty today.'

Harriet swelled with pleasure. 'Awfully kind of you, Mr Jensen,' she replied buoyantly, enjoying the pain it caused Greta in spite of the fact that she knew she'd have to pay for it later.

'Harriet, I need to start my Christmas shopping. I wonder whether you might be able to help me, when it comes to presents you're a gold medaller.'

'Of course, Mr Jensen, it would be a pleasure,' she replied, sinking into his green eyes and wishing Federica would emerge from the bowels of the store to witness her moment of glory.

'Greta, you're looking a bit pale,' he said, smiling down at her pinched face. 'You must be working too hard.'

'No, no. I am quite well,' she stammered, but her face seemed to melt like an ice cream in summer.

As Torquil and Harriet walked into the crowd of shoppers they parted reverentially, not because of Torquil's status but because of his dazzling beauty.

Greta felt the bile simmer in her stomach and slunk back into the office to lick her wounded pride.

'Fuck off! I'm a lady,' squawked the gypsy in protest.

'You are no lady,' Nigel hissed into the crack in the door, hoping that none of the customers could hear her. 'Now I will warn you only once more, if you don't come out we're going to have to bash the door down and drag you out.'

'Can't a lady piss in peace?' she shouted. 'I have my rights. A piss is a piss, the same for a duchess as for a tramp. I ain't no duchess, but I'm a lady through and through.'

'Right, that's it. We're coming in.'

'All right, all right,' she said, opening the door. Nigel winced at the stench that followed her. 'Not even allowed to piss in peace,' she squawked as she pushed past him.

The customers grimaced as she waddled through the depart-

338

ment, scowling at them angrily. 'I'll bet he lets you piss in peace,' she shrieked to an unsuspecting elderly lady who stood frozen to the ground with disgust. 'This joint smells like the devil's arse!' she added before disappearing into the street. The whole shop seemed to sigh with relief. Only Harriet and Torquil continued to shop oblivious to the commotion.

After a couple of hours of unpacking photograph frames and stacking them in neat piles on the shelves, Federica was pleased to see Harriet's excited face appear in the doorway. 'Darling girl, you're never going to believe it, Torquil Jensen has just been in and spent a whole two hours shopping with me,' she hissed, afraid of being overheard.

'Really!' said Federica, trying to share her excitement.

'He squashed Greta. You should have seen her face. It fell a mile. Silly cow.'

'How wonderful.'

'He is so drop dead handsome. I wish you could have seen him. He's dark and mysterious with the most beautiful green eyes that change to blue depending on what he's wearing and he was wearing a green cashmere sweater today, so they were green, like emeralds. He's so elegant. He exudes wealth and confidence. I can't believe you didn't see him. You simply can't understand.' Federica shrugged her shoulders. 'Anyway, he's bought so many things it's all been taken upstairs and you and I are going to have the honour of wrapping it up.'

'Lucky us!' said Federica sarcastically.

'You'd feel differently if you'd met him,' said Harriet sympathetically, gazing upon the piles of colour-coded frames. 'You know, I wouldn't be at all surprised if Greta sent you down here on purpose because she saw him come into the shop. He'd fancy you, he's got a thing about blondes.'

'I don't think he'd look at me, Harriet. And anyway, I wouldn't want him to. My heart pines for someone else,' she said and sat down on the stool.

'Who?' Harriet asked, leaning back against the doorframe.

'Oh, just someone I've known all my life. It's useless, though, he couldn't be less interested,' she replied and smiled up at her friend in an effort not to reveal the extent of her misery.

'You wouldn't want anyone else if you saw Torquil,' said Harriet, knowing that she would never admire another man as long as she lived. 'If Torquil marries I shall become a nun,' she added with a grin. 'Come on, I think Cinders has suffered enough in the basement.'

Federica didn't have any desire to meet Torquil Jensen. She belonged exclusively to Sam Appleby. As much as she tried to move on and attach her desire to someone else, it ached incessantly for Sam. She loved the mischievous way he grinned, the mop of golden hair that fell over his intelligent eyes, his commanding nature and his confidence. And she missed him all the time.

She spoke to her mother every other day. Helena no longer worried about Federica, who had grown into a sensible young woman, capable of looking after herself. She worried about Hal. He had never been an easy child, not like his sister, but he had always been biddable. Now he was getting into trouble at school, failing exams and acquiring an attitude that questioned everything she did and argued only for the sake of being troublesome. She mourned the loss of the child who used to cling to her and caress her with the adoring eyes of an infatuated lover. Now he scowled at her one moment and loved her the next and she found herself living her life on a permanent roller-coaster without being able to get off. He disappeared with his friends on the weekends and returned sometimes in the early hours of the morning smelling of alcohol and smoke, barely able to drag himself up the stairs and into bed.

Helena despaired. Arthur embraced her with his support and

affection and demanded nothing in return. Selflessly he listened to her as she unburdened her tormented thoughts and he gave his advice wisely in spite of the fact that he knew she wouldn't heed a single word of it. She was too involved to be able to see the situation objectively. 'Ignore him, my darling,' Arthur would advise. 'He's living off your attention like a parasite, if the attention runs dry he'll drop off.'

'My son is not some bloody tick!' she'd retort before freezing her face into the expression of a much-misunderstood martyr. But Arthur understood Hal. He had been indulged all his life because Helena had never stopped feeling guilty for taking him away from his father. In Arthur's opinion a guilty mother was a very dangerous thing. Hal needed a firm hand and until he received one he'd push his boundaries as far as they could go. But Helena wouldn't allow her husband to assert his authority and instead of earning her son's respect with severity she tried to win it with leniency.

Federica also listened to her mother's grievances with the patience of a therapist. At the beginning when Federica had just moved up to London, Helena asked her about her new job and flat, but once she had settled in Helena asked less about her life until her curiosity dried up altogether and she spoke of nothing but Hal. If Federica tried to direct the conversation away from her brother Helena would either wind up the conversation or find some way of bringing it back to her son. Hal was no longer her hobby but her life and his demand for attention was all-consuming.

Federica's life in London was so far removed from Polperro that she was able to detach herself from the tangle of family politics. At first everything was so new she didn't have time to miss home. Then she spoke to Toby and Julian on the telephone and she suddenly felt a yearning for the sea and the cry of gulls and the fresh salty air and silent nights. She also missed Rasta who she had had to leave with her uncle. When she arrived in London she understood why. The city was no place for a dog like Rasta who thrived on his long country walks and games on the beach.

He would decline fast in a place like London, but she missed his company none the less.

At first she found it difficult to sleep in the city for the noise of cars, people and the odd police siren that wailed into the night and turned her blood cold. But after a month she began to find the noise a comfort and the yellow streetlights that flooded into the small bedroom she shared with Hester a trigger of memories long since forgotten. As she familiarised herself with the streets of her new home she began to feel a growing sense of belonging. The city ceased to feel like an overwhelming maze to be feared but a friendly town to be enjoyed. She made new friends and went out almost every night, to the cinema, the theatre or simply to the pub where they'd sit around playing backgammon and talk until closing. But Sam's imaginary presence followed her wherever she went and fought off the men who admired her and longed to have her for themselves.

Then just when she thought that nothing could dilute the ardour she felt for Sam, someone walked into her life to change it for ever.

Chapter Twenty-Nine

'Greta wants us to move all the china to the other side of the department,' Harriet said wearily as Federica entered the department.

'Are you sure? That's a lot of heavy work,' Federica replied, then she noticed the black circles around Harriet's dull eyes. 'Are you all right?'

'I got locked out of my flat last night and ended up walking the streets until dawn.'

'You should have called me,' said Federica.

'I didn't have your number on me, m'darling. I'm fine. Just protect me from Greta, please.' She sighed and smiled weakly. 'Apparently Torquil's coming in today for some more shopping. They delivered all the gifts we wrapped up before the weekend, but he needs a few more. I can't bear it, I look hideous,' she sighed, rubbing her eyes.

'You could never look hideous, Harriet. Greta can look after him,' Federica said, locking her bag under the counter. 'That might put her in a better mood.'

'Some hope,' she moaned.

By mid morning they had moved all the china and were leaning back against the counter exhausted when Mr Jensen entered followed by a group of dark-suited men rubbing their hands together in gestures of deference and answering, 'Yes, Mr Jensen, of course, Mr Jensen', to everything he said. Harriet and Federica at once stood to attention and smiled politely. 'That's Mr Jensen,' Harriet hissed.

'Don't think I didn't notice,' she hissed back. 'You just have to look at the group of sycophants!' The entourage stopped and looked about the room, commenting in hushed voices on the products and the displays. 'Thank God we did the china before he came in,' said Federica.

'Just in the nick of time,' Harriet replied. 'He'd freak out if he saw the department in a mess.'

Mr Jensen's small eyes missed nothing. He scanned the room in one long scrutinising sweep. When his gaze rested on the angelic countenance of Federica he pulled himself up and whispered something into the inclined ear of one of his aides. At that moment Greta stalked out of her office.

'I thought I told you two not to stand together gossiping,' she said in exasperation, her accent shaving the words aggressively.

'Good morning, Greta,' said Mr Jensen, appearing behind her as if out of nowhere. 'I don't believe we have met,' he added, turning to Federica. Greta blinked in surprise and drew herself up with self-importance.

'Federica Campione,' Federica replied, extending her hand. 'It is a pleasure to have you here,' he said with a smile, watching her curiously. 'We need sunny faces like yours in the front of the shop.' He chuckled and narrowed his small black eyes. The aides chuckled too. 'Make sure she's always at the front of the shop, Greta.'

Greta nodded enthusiastically. 'Of course, Mr Jensen, I know an asset when I see one,' she gushed.

'Good.' He sniffed, then his expression darkened as he traced his eyes over the newly moved china. 'Why has the department been changed around?' he asked in indignation. His aides straightened themselves up and folded their arms in front of their pigeon chests in a show of mutual outrage.

'Oh,' gasped Greta, clasping her hands together in horror. 'I can only apologise. Federica is new and did not understand my instructions,' she said without so much as a blink. Federica's cheeks flushed scarlet. Mr Jensen nodded and his aides unfolded their arms.

'Perhaps you'd better make yourself more easily understood next time,' he said firmly. 'I want it all moved back to where it was,' he added, clicking his fingers in the air as if summoning a waiter. Then he turned and led the entourage up the stairs to the furniture department.

'You heard him, do it!' Greta snapped impatiently. 'And, Harriet, if you come into work looking like this again I will send you straight back home – for good. Do you understand?' Harriet nodded. She was too weary to fight. 'Ya! Now hurry, before he comes back.'

Federica watched helplessly as she disappeared into her office. 'I'm speechless,' she breathed.

'You'd better get used to it, m'darling, she does that sort of thing all the time. I've been in trouble so many times because of her shifting the responsibility. She hides behind us. But she takes all the credit when things go well, believe me. Right, back to where we started again. Stupid cow!' she muttered, once again fishing the key to the cabinets out of the drawer.

Federica simmered quietly with fury as she walked about rearranging her department. Harriet was too tired to talk and so Federica wallowed in her own self-pity, wishing she had the strength of character to stand up for herself. When a tall, leather-clad man in a black shiny motorbike helmet stalked into the shop, she pressed the code B button on the telephone in an act of defiance and watched the stairs for Nigel Dalby.

Nigel glided down with as much subtlety as a policeman in a pantomime. Federica caught his eye and nodded towards the man who hovered suspiciously by the door. Nigel approached him, straightened himself up importantly and asked him to remove his helmet. 'I'm afraid we don't permit helmets in the shop,' he explained with self-importance. The man cocked his head to one side in amusement before removing his gloves and then his helmet, shaking out his raven hair and revealing himself to be none other than Torquil Jensen. Nigel spluttered his apologies and visibly shrank.

Federica sighed heavily as the colour drained from her face. Harriet was right, he was quite the most beautiful man she had ever seen. Nigel withdrew backwards, almost bowing as he went, then scuttled up the stairs to hide while his humiliation subsided in the privacy of his office.

Torquil looked at Federica with green eyes and smirked. 'So you're the shop security, are you?' he said, striding over to her and dropping his helmet onto the counter. 'I'm Torquil Jensen.' He extended his hand. He watched her blush as he traced her features with the same scrutinising stare as his uncle had done earlier.

'Federica Campione,' she replied hoarsely.

'Italian?'

'Chilean.'

'What a beautiful country,' he exclaimed. 'I travelled there as a young man.' Then he grinned at her brazenly. 'This may sound crass but I'm so completely stunned by your looks, I've forgotten what I came in for.' Federica frowned in discomfort and felt the wings of a butterfly make her stomach quiver. 'You're very pretty,' he continued. 'You must be new. No one's that keen to assist Nigel Dalby.' He laughed, his face creasing into deep lines around his large mouth and surprisingly pale eyes. 'You did him a favour, he thinks he's much more important than he is, those sort of people need to be taken down a peg or two.'

'It was a mistake. I apologise,' she said, thinking of Nigel Dalby's long knuckled fingers tapping his mortification away alone in his office and felt guilty. 'He was only doing his job,' she added in his defence.

'And you were only doing yours,' he said. 'I've just bought a new bike, you must come for a ride sometime,' he added, caressing her with intense eyes. She smiled awkwardly. He folded his arms and leant on the counter. She stepped back as the spicy scent of his skin and the heat of his body invaded her senses with too much intimacy. 'Oh, I know what I came in for. I need something for a young woman,' he said, then thought a moment, rubbing his stubbly chin with his hand. 'A young woman, about your age. A Christmas present. What sort of thing would she like?'

'How well do you know her?' she asked, trying to sound official in spite of his suffocating proximity.

'Not very well. But I want to give her something,' he said casually, grinning at her.

'How much do you want to spend?'

'Money is no object. If you'd been here longer you'd know that. I never look at prices, they only get in the way. So, what do you think you'd like, for example?'

'Well, if you don't know her too well, I'd go for something pretty but not too intimate. Let me see,' she said, casting her eyes about the shop, feeling the shamelessness of his stare burn her face crimson. She saw Harriet hiding behind the glass cabinets displaying the china they had just moved, and wished she'd come to her aid. But Harriet felt too ugly to show herself and cowered lower until even Federica couldn't see her.

'What about one of those china pots, you could buy a plant and present them together?'

'Would you like a plant?' he asked.

'Of course. All women like plants.'

'I like your ideas, give me another one,' he said, without taking his eyes off her.

'A painting?' she suggested, looking up at the patchwork of pictures on the wall.

'I don't know her taste,' he said thoughtfully. 'What about a silver photograph frame or something pretty that she can use?'

'Oh, I know,' she said, leading him through the shop to a locked glass case that contained exquisite ornate silver frames. 'This one's just come in, it's from China. It's so delicate, isn't it? If you don't know her very well, it's perfect.'

'You're a good salesgirl,' he said, taking the frame from her. 'If a man gave this to you, would you like it?'

'Of course. If anyone gave it to me, I'd like it.'

'Good, wrap it up then. That was easy.'

She began to wrap it up with an unsteady hand for his eyes watched her every move with undisguised fascination. 'Would you like to take it now or shall I have it delivered?'

'I'll take it now,' he replied, disarming her with another wide smile.

'Is there anything else you want?'

'I'm not in the mood any more. I'll come back another time, that will also give me an opportunity to see you again,' he said in a low voice. Federica frantically searched for something to say, but nothing came. She stood mutely staring back at him. When he left the department a large vacuum remained into which Federica stared as if she were seeing something that no one else could see. Then she breathed again and realised that she had hardly dared breathe at all while Torquil had been beside her.

The rest of the day passed in an exquisitely somnambulant haze. When she returned to the flat she couldn't recall a single thing that had happened after Torquil Jensen had left, but she remembered every word of their conversation as if she had learnt it all by heart. As she sat enjoying a glass of wine with Hester and Molly, the doorbell rang. Hester answered it to find a delivery boy with two packages for Federica. When Federica saw the size of the second package she began to tremble. It was a large plant in a blue and white china pot, like the one she had recommended to Torquil that morning.

'Who's this all from?' Hester gasped in amazement.

'This will look divine in the flat,' said Molly, taking it from Federica and placing it in the sitting room where she proceeded to unwrap it. 'What's in the other package?'

'I imagine it's a silver photograph frame,' said Federica in amazement.

'How do you know?' Hester asked.

'I just do.'

'Well, come on,' said Molly impatiently, flicking ash into the gas fire. 'It won't open by you staring at it.'

Federica carefully peeled off the paper and pulled out the delicate frame imported from China. 'It's stunning,' Hester gasped in admiration. 'Look, it's got birds carved into it,' she added, running her hand over it in wonder.

'That would look good in the sitting room too,' said Molly, dragging on her cigarette.

But Federica held it tightly. 'I'll put the photograph of Papa in there,' she said firmly. 'It's going beside my bed.'

'Goodie,' Hester exclaimed. 'I can enjoy it too.'

Federica hurried along the corridor to her bedroom and closed the door behind her. She could hear the whisperings of Molly and Hester who were curious to know who had bought her such expensive gifts. But she ignored them and sat on the bed to carefully exchange her father's frame for the new one. She ran a fond finger over his handsome face and noticed how Torquil's dark looks resembled Ramon's. The same raven hair, the same olive skin and the same generous mouth. But their eyes were very different. Ramon's were black and mysterious like the universe, whereas Torquil's were light and shimmering like a shallow green pool. She set the photograph into the frame and placed it on the side table, then sat back and admired it. That was how Hester found her, gazing transfixed into her father's hidden world.

'I don't want to disturb you,' she said, waking her friend from her trance.

'No, no, that's fine.' Federica pulled her eyes away.

'Who is he?' she asked. 'I imagine he's a "he",' she giggled.

'My God, Hester. You should see him. He's the most beautiful man I've ever laid eyes on,' she said emphatically, lying back against the pillows. 'He's tall and dark with the palest green eyes. When he smiles my stomach turns over. I feel I've been hit by a lorry.'

'More like one of Cupid's arrows.' She chuckled, settling onto her own bed. 'Where did you meet him?'

'He's the nephew of the man who owns St John and Smithe. Thankfully, he's not short and bald like his uncle.'

'So, he just came into the shop?'

'Yes, I thought he was a shoplifter because he wore a biker helmet, so I called Nigel Dalby down to check him out, it was really embarrassing.'

'Well, he obviously didn't take offence.'

'No, he was amused.' She smiled, recalling the moment.

'Very amused, I can see,' said Hester, admiring the frame. 'He's smitten too.'

'I think he's smitten by a lot of women.'

'How old is he?'

'Old,' Federica replied and blushed.

'Okay, how old. Fifty?'

'No, more like late thirties.'

'Hmm, that's old,' Hester agreed, but she couldn't hide her admiration.

'But mature, confident, settled,' Federica breathed and bit her lip anxiously.

'You mean, rich and secure. Someone who will look after you and take away all your troubles with one twinkle of an engagement ring.' She laughed.

'No, just more grown up than the boys I usually meet.'

'God, how exciting. I can't believe it,' Hester enthused, clasping her hands together.

'Neither can I.'

'What are you going to do?'

'I don't know.' Federica sighed and a shudder of excitement momentarily debilitated her whole body. 'I don't think I'll get much sleep tonight.'

'Oh, your fickle heart,' Hester laughed, getting up slowly.

'What do you mean?'

'To think you were in love with Sam,' she said, smiling at her friend. 'I was rather hoping he'd make you into a proper member of our family.'

'Oh, really, Hester,' Federica replied dismissively, shaking her head. 'That childhood crush was over long ago.'

'Well, it's certainly over now, isn't it?' she said. Then she shrugged her shoulders in resignation before leaving Federica alone with her thoughts.

★　　★　　★

The following day Federica arrived at the shop with her cheeks aflame, fearing that everyone would know Torquil had sent her those gifts the night before. But Greta demanded a department meeting and gave them all an angry lecture about how to behave on the shop floor and how not to stand in huddles gossiping when there were customers to be looked after. No one noticed Federica's furtive eyes as they shifted from one face to the next before settling on the carpet where they relaxed their focus and hovered in the space between the floor and the vivid images of Torquil that she caressed secretly in her mind.

When the doors opened at ten Federica received a telephone call. She picked up the receiver with a thumping heart.

'Good morning,' said Torquil in a buoyant voice. 'Did you receive my gifts?'

'Yes,' Federica replied, trying to sound calm. 'You shouldn't have.'

'Of course not. But it gave me pleasure,' he replied, touched by her obvious nervousness.

'Thank you.'

'I know it's a little hasty, but I couldn't help myself. Will you forgive me?'

Federica laughed to cover her embarrassment. 'Of course.'

'I know this is also a bit hasty, but will you allow me to take you out tonight?'

'Oh, I . . .'

'Please don't say no, you'll break my heart,' he pleaded.

'Well . . .'

'It's the only way I can get to know you. I can't keep coming into the shop, can I?'

Federica giggled. 'Okay, that would be lovely,' she agreed, fanning her face with the pad of order forms.

'I'll pick you up at eight at your flat. I've something special planned for you,' he said. 'Wear something warm.'

'Okay,' she replied, curious to know the nature of a surprise that required her to wear 'something warm'.

'I'll see you then,' he added.

Federica put down the telephone and stood staring about her as if the world suddenly looked different. It frightened her.

When Greta summoned Federica into her office, she knew her boss had found out about the call and began to apologise, anxious not to lose her job. But Greta silenced her with a single slice of her cold blue eyes. 'It must not happen again. You know all the telephone calls are monitored in this company. It is for your own good that I tell you.'

'I'm sorry,' said Federica.

'If you want to receive a personal call you must tell them to telephone you at lunchtime in the staff quarters. If it is urgent they can call my office and I will pass on a message. If everyone in the company received personal calls no one would be on the floor. Do I make myself clear?'

'Yes, Greta.'

'Good. I don't want to have this conversation again.'

Federica was too afraid of upsetting Harriet to tell her about Torquil. So she went about her day as normal, hiding the churnings of a stomach turned to liquid and the rapid pumping of her heart that gave her twice as much energy as everyone else. By the afternoon she could barely concentrate on even the simplest task and was relieved when she was finally able to calm her nerves in the scented water of a deep aromatherapy bath.

Molly cancelled the drinks she had planned with a couple of friends from university and hovered with her sister by the window to catch a glimpse of the dark stranger who was courting their friend.

Federica had nothing glamorous to wear. Her wardrobe consisted of sensible work suits. So Molly lent her a cream cashmere polo neck to go with black jeans and Hester offered her the new sheepskin coat she had bought in Harvey Nichols. But when the shiny Porsche drew up outside the flat and the immaculately dressed Torquil stepped out in a pair of black suede trousers, which he wore over boots, Molly knew someone would have to take Federica in hand.

'Christ, he's a knock-out,' Molly exclaimed, her mouth agape.

Hester rushed to her sister's side. 'Wow, Fede, is it really him?' she squealed in amazement. 'You lucky thing.'

Federica stalled by the door, trembling. 'I'm so nervous, I feel sick,' she said hoarsely. 'I won't know what to say.'

'Don't be ridiculous,' said Molly sharply. 'Of course you'll know what to say. Just because he's handsome doesn't mean he's different from everyone else. He's probably just as nervous.'

'Enjoy it, Fede,' said Hester encouragingly. 'Let him entertain you, that's what Mummy always says.'

'He's bloody gorgeous,' Molly sighed, lighting a cigarette and wishing he had seen her first. 'Just don't be innocent. He'll be expecting a sophisticate.'

'Oh, God, Molly,' she wailed. 'You're making me even more nervous.'

'Well, if you don't go out now he'll drive off and that'll be that,' Molly added bossily. 'Go on!'

When Federica descended the steps onto the street, her pale face and anxious eyes were illuminated by the incandescence of the street lamps and Torquil felt as if his stomach was floating inside his belly, lifting him off the ground. She walked up to him with the same shy smile that had made his spirits soar the day before. He greeted her with a kiss and smelt the sweet scent of ylang-ylang that she had put into her bath. 'You look beautiful,' he breathed and noticed the colour sting her cheeks with pleasure. Then he opened the door and watched her settle onto the tanned leather seat. As he closed it and walked around to the other side of the car he cast his eyes up to the window where the faces of Molly and Hester were pressed up against the glass and waved. To his amusement the faces disappeared like a couple of apparitions.

'I'm glad you dressed warmly,' he said, turning the key in the ignition and pulling out into the road.

'Where are we going?' she asked.

'Surprise,' he replied and she watched his profile as he grinned with satisfaction.

'You like surprises, don't you?' she said.

'As long as I'm the one doing the surprising. Don't ever think about surprising me. I won't like it.'

'I'll remember that.'

They drove along the embankment towards Parliament Square. It was a cold, dry night. The sky sparkled above the hazy glow of a city that is never dark and the crescent of the moon floated on the surface of the Thames like the ghost of a sunken ship. Federica could not have hoped for a more romantic night. She opened the window and let the cool air brush away her nervousness. Torquil parked the car and pulled a wicker basket and rug out of the trunk.

'What's that for?' she asked in amusement.

'All part of the surprise,' he said, raising an eyebrow. 'Follow me and you'll find out.' She followed him to a gap in the wall beside the Thames and descended the damp steps towards a pretty red boat that bobbed up and down on the swell. An old skipper waited with the same philosophical patience as the men of the sea that Federica had grown up with in Polperro and she felt a breath of nostalgia. He nodded to her without smiling and extended his rough hand to help her down onto the deck. She accepted his assistance and stepped onto the boat. Torquil climbed up to the front and threw the rug down.

'There, come on up, we're going for a long ride,' he said, watching her smile in delight. He took her hand to steady her. 'It's much more fun over here, we can see where we're going for a start,' he said, moving the picnic basket.

'I can't believe you've organised this for me,' she exclaimed, sitting down.

'I want to impress you,' he replied truthfully. 'Okay, Jack, we're ready to roll,' he shouted to the skipper who tapped his cap and disappeared behind the controls. The engine roared before settling into a gentle rattle and they made their way down the moonlit Thames.

Torquil settled down beside her and opened the basket. 'Let's start with a glass of champagne, shall we?' he said, handing her a crystal glass. 'Have you ever been on the Thames?'

'Only in the car along the Embankment.' She laughed.

'Good. I'm glad this is a first,' he said, pouring the champagne into her glass.

'It's such a stunning night, did you organise that too?'

'I did my best.'

'You did well.'

'I did well finding you,' he said softly, tapping her glass with his. 'Here's to us.'

Federica sipped the champagne and swallowed her reservations. 'I gather you met my uncle,' he said, raising an eyebrow.

'Yes,' she replied carefully, not wishing to comment on the toad-like man who stalked the shop with an inflated self-importance that was both unnecessary and absurd.

'He liked you.'

'Oh?'

'He has very good taste. He's perceptive about people. That quality runs in the family.' Then he looked at her with predatory eyes, admiring her lack of sophistication. 'You're too innocent to have been brought up in London. Were you raised in Chile?'

'Only until I was seven, then I was brought up in Cornwall.'

'From the sublime to the ridiculous,' he chuckled. 'That's why you're different. A bit Latin, a bit Cornish. Something of a mongrel,' he joked. 'I like mongrels,' he added, draining his glass. 'I'm not a mongrel. I hope you like pure-blooded Englishmen.'

'Of course I like Englishmen. I don't know many Latin men. I left when I was young,' she explained.

'And now you're old,' he smirked. 'I'd hazard a guess that you're eighteen,' he said, taking the bottle out of the basket and refilling their glasses.

'You're right,' she replied in surprise. 'Do you know everything?'

'Like I said, I'm a perceptive old devil.' He put on a cockney accent.

Federica laughed. 'Then, I guess you're about thirty-five,' she said and sipped the champagne.

'Wrong, I'm afraid, I'm much older than that. I'm thirty-eight. Far too old for you.'

Federica felt her stomach plummet with disappointment. She wondered what he meant by that and if he really felt he was too old for her, why had he asked her out in the first place?

'Let's have something to eat,' he suggested, pulling out a couple of plates of toast, *foie gras* and caviar.

The boat moved slowly down the Thames, under bridges which cast ominous shadows over the water, past the Tower of London and on into the darkness. They ate the picnic and opened another bottle of champagne. 'I was brought up by my father and stepmother, my natural mother died when I was a little boy,' Torquil said casually.

'I'm so sorry,' said Federica, feeling the full extent of his loss. Although her father hadn't died he had barely shown much sign of life in the last ten years.

'Oh, I was too small to understand and then Cynthia came along. She's been a good mother to me. You see, she was unable to bear children so she adored me to compensate. Being an only child I've been spoilt all my life.' He said this with a chuckle, omitting to mention that Cynthia's love was at times claustrophobic and his father's overbearing.

'I think you probably deserve it. You must have suffered terribly,' she said, and squeezed his arm compassionately.

He frowned at her. 'You've suffered, haven't you?' he said

gently, tilting his head to one side. 'Do you want to talk about it?'

Federica found herself letting him into her life. Her tongue loosened with the alcohol and the beauty of the surroundings, allowing all the pain to slip out uncensored. She hadn't meant to, but there was something in his eyes and his smile that drew her to him. He seemed to see right through her, slicing away her defences with each piercing gaze and understanding what he saw. 'You poor darling thing,' he said, noticing that she had begun to shiver and putting an arm around her shoulders. 'You need someone to look after you. I grew up with too much love, you've grown up with too little.'

'Not at all,' she said, attempting to blink away the light feeling in her head. 'I've been very lucky.'

'Don't fool yourself, sweetness, everyone needs a mother and a father. If you're lucky like me to have a wonderful step-parent, that can make up for the loss of a natural parent in many ways. But Arthur's obviously not a patch on your father.'

'He certainly isn't!' she exclaimed hotly. 'I can't stand him.'

'Well, it's time you had someone to think about *you* for a change. Your mother didn't think about you when she left Chile, did she? Your father didn't put you first either. You need someone to put *you* first.' He pulled out another rug and wrapped it around her. She suddenly felt emotional but didn't know whether it was because she was talking about her father or because he had said that he was too old for her. She wanted to tell him that he wasn't too old for her, but she didn't have the courage. Silently she opened her heart to him and hoped that he might notice.

'Don't be sad,' he whispered, watching her eyes glitter like the water of the Thames.

She shook her head. 'Oh, I'm not sad,' she replied and smiled wistfully. 'I'm very happy. I'm happy to be here sharing this beautiful night with you. You've been sweet listening to me.

Don't get the wrong idea. I've had a magical childhood and I've been very happy. Some people, like you, suffer the death of a parent, sometimes a whole family. I really have nothing to complain about. Papa's not dead, is he?'

'No, he's not dead, just thoughtless,' he said, squeezing her. 'I'm going to make you very happy,' he avowed. He lifted her chin with his hand and wiped away her melancholy with his thumb. 'I've found you now,' he said before kissing her salty lips. She responded with eagerness as his rough face scratched at her skin and his wet lips parted hers to penetrate her innocence and claim it for himself. In those moments of intimacy Federica forgot Sam's tender kisses because she had finally found a man who promised to love her and protect her and erase the scars of abandonment.

Chapter Thirty

'Fede's in love,' Hester said to her mother who stood at the foot of the Christmas tree directing Sam with a vague wave of her hand.

'No, darling, a little more to the left, there,' she said, 'now let's see if Angus will fly in.'

Sam stepped down from the ladder and looked up at the nest that he had secured firmly onto the top branch. 'Who's she in love with?' he asked, folding the steps away.

'He's so handsome you'll faint,' said Hester. 'He's dark with the palest green eyes you ever saw. Sends her presents all the time. Do you know, Mum, he flew her off to Paris just for the day and bought her bags of clothes. You won't recognise her now. She's so sophisticated.'

Sam flopped onto the sofa, stretching his legs out in front of him and placing his hands behind his head.

'To think she was once in love with *you*,' Hester added with a grin.

'No she wasn't,' Sam replied aggressively. 'At least not since she was a child.'

'Where's Angus. ANGUS!' Ingrid shouted, casting her eyes about the room. 'He was in here a moment ago,' she complained, her agitated fingers playing with the monocle that hung between her large bosoms.

'He's probably flown outside,' Sam said irritably.

'In this cold, I doubt it,' she replied, sweeping into the hall with the skirts of her ethnic dress billowing out behind her like the sails of a ship. 'Molly, have you seen Angus?' she said as Molly wandered past her into the sitting room.

'Yes, he's in the library with Nuno. He's trying to teach him to read.' She sighed, rolling her eyes. 'For God's sake, he's a dove, not a parrot!'

'So, Mol, what's Federica's new boyfriend like?' Sam asked, recalling out of the mists of his memory the innocent evening he had shared with her in the barn and the brief walk they had enjoyed on the hill.

'He's nice,' said Molly, sitting down next to her brother. 'Great tree!' she exclaimed. 'But I don't think Angus is going to like it in there, he's happier in Dad's dressing room.'

'Is that all? Nice?' he persisted curiously, wondering why he felt rattled.

'Well,' said Molly, pushing her auburn hair off her face. 'He's handsome and charming . . . but . . .' She paused, trying to put her thoughts into words. 'He's a little too good to be true,' she said decisively. 'Mind you, Fede looks marvellous. I tell you, Sam, you won't recognise her.'

'She really does,' Hester agreed.

Molly loathed talking about Federica and Torquil. Every time she saw them together she felt a nagging jealousy and hated herself for it.

'Is she happy?' Sam asked somewhat grudgingly.

'She's infatuated,' said Molly tightly.

'Yes, she's happy,' Hester replied. 'I've never seen her so happy. He gives her so much attention. Calls her all the time, takes her out. She's blossoming.'

'He looks like her father,' Molly stated.

'Her father?' Sam exclaimed, appalled. 'How old is he, for God's sake?'

'Thirty-eight,' Molly said, raising her eyebrows at her brother, indicating her disapproval.

'What the hell is she doing with someone so old!' Sam retorted crossly. 'He's twenty years older than she is.'

'Age doesn't matter if they love each other,' Hester argued.

'Yes it does,' Sam interjected. 'She's impressionable.'

'What's the difference? She'll be impressionable with whoever she goes out with,' said Hester.

'I don't like the sound of it at all,' Sam sighed, taking off his glasses and rubbing the bridge of his nose between his finger and thumb.

'Well, you can tell her yourself, she's coming over for drinks tonight,' Molly suggested. 'But she's not bringing Torquil,' she added in disappointment.

Sam marched across the cliffs with Trotsky and Amadeus, his mother's new spaniel, watching the waves wrestle with the rocks below, covering them in white foam before retreating to gain momentum for another lashing. He braced himself against the icy wind, pulling his coat around him tightly and hunching his shoulders in an effort to keep warm. Trotsky strode along behind his feet, using him as a shield against the wind, while Amadeus rushed about in a hurry to sniff everything. He thought about Federica crossly, unable to understand why he cared. The kiss in the barn had been a sweet moment of innocent pleasure. It had meant nothing more than that: a kiss on a rainy night. He hadn't planned on kissing her, it had just happened. Afterwards he had felt guilty for taking advantage of her. It was so obvious that she adored him. Then he had impulsively offered to drive her back to her uncle's house one autumn day and they had walked in that heavenly golden light. He had wanted to kiss her up there overlooking the sea. It had been the most romantic moment of his life. That sky, that colour, those smells and Federica looking innocent and ethereal. He couldn't admit his longing, even to himself. She was so much younger than him. He could have anyone he wanted, but Fede had been too young and out of bounds. He thrust his hands into his pockets and sighed heavily. He had felt guilty for desiring her, so he had avoided her again. A cowardly way to go about things, but it was all he could do. He had managed to convince himself that he felt nothing for her whatsoever. But now she was in love with someone else. He wasn't used to not being the focus of her affections. He hoped the relationship wouldn't last. First relationships often didn't.

★ ★ ★

'This Torquil Jensen rings a bell,' Toby said as they drove up the lane to the manor.

'You won't have met him,' Federica replied from the back seat.

'We have met him,' Julian insisted, shaking his head. 'But I can't remember when.'

'He's a bit old for you, Fede.'

'He's older but not too old,' Federica replied happily 'Love strikes regardless of age. And we love each other.'

'Please tell me he hasn't deflowered you yet, sweetheart?' Julian asked anxiously. 'I'll kill him if he's laid a finger on you.'

Federica laughed. 'No, not yet,' she replied in amusement, feeling a shudder of excitement at the thought of making love to Torquil for the first time.

'Thank God for that!' Julian sighed.

'Don't let him push you into doing anything you don't want to do. He's a man of experience but you're a child.'

'Darling Toby, I'm not a child any more,' she said. 'I'm eighteen.'

'*So* grown up,' Toby replied sarcastically.

'Just don't do anything stupid. You'll go through lots of boyfriends before you find Mr Right,' said Julian. 'And we want to vet all of them.'

'Well, you can meet Torquil whenever you like,' she said, leaning forward between the seats. 'You'll love him. He's handsome, funny, sophisticated, worldly . . .'

'He must have some faults,' said Toby. 'We all have faults.'

'Not Torquil.' She sighed dreamily. 'He's perfect.'

Toby and Julian locked eyes, but it wasn't the moment to share their wisdom.

When Federica walked into the sitting room at Pickthistle Manor, where her mother, Arthur and Hal were already celebrating Christmas Eve with glasses of champagne and admiring the pretty white dove that sat at the top of the tree observing them, Sam felt as if someone had just thumped him in the stomach. She looked radiant in a pair of black leather trousers and pale blue cashmere sweater that clung to her slim frame, emphasising the swell of her breasts in the V of the neckline. Her long white hair shone with health and fell about her shoulders, setting off the pale skin of her face and the depth of her tanzanite eyes. She embraced Hester and Molly and remained a while by the door talking with animation. Sam felt his throat constrict and drained his glass of champagne in an effort to loosen it. He watched her without distraction. Molly and Hester were right, she looked different. She looked happy.

Nuno was the first to mention the transformation. '*Cara mia*,' he sighed his approval. 'The duckling has grown into a swan.'

'Pa, she was never a duckling,' said Ingrid in Federica's defence. She brought her cigarette holder up to her scarlet lips and dragged in exasperation, the way she always did when she found her father's comments inappropriate.

'Compared to the swan, my dear, she was a duckling,' he retorted firmly, smiling at Federica.

'Thank you, Nuno,' she laughed. Then her eyes fell on the tortured face of Sam, who still watched her from the sofa. She returned his gaze with a smile, but he didn't smile back. He turned to Toby who was seated beside him as if he were ashamed to have been caught looking.

'It's the new London life,' Helena said. 'Hal's going to go to university, though,' she added, desperately trying to lure her son out of his sulk with compliments. But Hal scowled at his mother. He knew he'd never get into a university and had no desire to go. He had only come to the drinks party because she had begged him to. He didn't like Lucien much, he was too clever, just like his brother Sam, whom he didn't like either. They both made him feel inadequate. He watched his sister in the doorway and resented the attention she was getting; he wasn't used to the spotlight shining on her. But when she sat down next to him his bitterness mollified and he allowed her to coax him out of his mood.

'How's it going at school?' she asked. He shook the black hair that fell over his forehead and looked up at her with their father's dark chocolate eyes.

'All right,' he replied impassively.

'You're frustrated there, aren't you?' she said sympathetically.

'I want to leave as soon as possible.'

'And university is not an option,' she added, noticing the rebellious curl in his mouth when he grinned.

'Right,' he said, glancing across the room at Helena.

'Don't worry. You won't have to go. You can do what you like. Come to London. You'd love London,' she said enthusiastically.

'The minute I leave school I'm out of here. I'm sick of Cornwall.' He scowled. 'I'm sick of living with Mama and Arthur. It's claustrophobic. I need my space. I don't need anyone looking over my shoulder all the time.'

'It's not for much longer,' she said. 'Then you'll be free.'

Once more she raised her eyes to find them unwittingly lock into Sam's. He got up with the excuse of going to get another bottle of champagne from the kitchen and disappeared out of the room. Federica left Hal to wallow in self-pity and followed him.

'Hi, Sam,' she said, finding him alone patting the dogs. He looked up at her in surprise and his face broke into a small smile.

'Hi, Federica,' he replied casually. 'How are you?'

'I'm well. Do you have anything soft?'

'Soft?'

'To drink.'

'Oh, yes,' he replied, feeling stupid. 'Lemonade, Coca-Cola, orange juice?'

'Orange juice would be nice. Thank you.'

He opened the fridge and pulled out a jug of freshly squeezed juice. He poured it unsteadily into a glass and wondered why after having known her for over ten years she suddenly had the power to make him nervous.

'I gather London is treating you well,' he said, endeavouring to extend the conversation in order keep her in the kitchen.

Federica noticed that he was beginning to lose his hair. It was no longer blond but darker and cut very short. He looked older and less glossy than before. He blinked at her from behind his glasses and handed her the drink.

'I really enjoy it,' she replied, leaning back against the work-top.

'I hear from Molly and Hester that you've got a new boyfriend,' he said, trying to look pleased for her, but all he could muster was a tight smile that sat awkwardly on his face.

Federica was barely able to contain her excitement. When she talked about Torquil her eyes sparkled and her skin glowed. Sam felt his stomach churn with resentment.

'Yes. He's lovely,' she said and grinned broadly. 'Molly and Hester have met him.'

'What does he do?'

'He works in property,' she replied. 'He has his own company.'

Sam raised his eyebrows, trying to look impressed. 'Good. I look forward to meeting him,' he lied.

'I never see you these days,' she said, shaking her head regretfully. 'Funny, we all live in the same city and yet, you don't even come around to see your sisters.'

'I know.' He sighed, wishing he had been around more often. 'We move in different worlds.'

'Time goes so fast, doesn't it?' she mused. 'I'll never forget that day you rescued me from the lake.'

'Or the time I kissed you in the barn,' he added and looked at her steadily, silently wondering why on earth he had brought it up.

Federica's cheeks flushed with embarrassment. 'It was nice,' she replied tightly, trying to dissemble. 'It seems eons ago.'

'It was your first kiss,' he said, watching her carefully.

'But not my last,' she retaliated boldly. He lowered his eyes, remembering the dreaded Torquil and stared into the bottom of his glass. 'It was nice of you to initiate me into the world of romance, Sam. I should thank you,' she said coolly, recalling the pain his indifference had caused her and wanting to punish him for it. 'I'd better get back to the sitting room. They'll all wonder what we're doing in here. After all, it wasn't so long ago that I had a crush on you.' She laughed flippantly. 'But we all grow up in the end, don't we?' she said before leaving Sam alone to chew on her words.

But Federica didn't go back into the sitting room. She went into the bathroom and locked the door behind her. She sat on the seat and waited for her heartbeat to slow down and for the colour to drain away from her hot face. She was no longer afraid of Sam, but he had hurt her and she couldn't forgive him for that. He had played with her feelings for amusement and then dropped her once his fun had been had. She was no longer infatuated with him. She felt little more than the sweet afterglow of her first innocent love. But she recognised in his eyes a glimmer of regret, a glint of disappointment. She sensed that her new relationship with Torquil infuriated him and it gave her pleasure. He was too late. She belonged to someone else. He had missed his moment and she hoped he would live to regret it.

Federica soon forgot her brief confrontation with Sam. She returned to London after Christmas and into the all-consuming arms of Torquil. When he told her he was taking her skiing to Switzerland for a long weekend, just the two of them, she knew he was going to make love to her and hastily she booked an appointment with the doctor.

She thought about sex often. When he kissed her she longed for his hands to explore her body and discover it as she had explored it and discovered it as a child. Her limbs ached from wanting him so much, but she needed to be sure that he was going to stay. Her deepest fear was of opening up and giving herself to him only to watch him walk out of her life afterwards, leaving her broken and humiliated. She had to trust him first. But little by little Torquil earned her trust. He was always there for her. He called her when he said he would, he was never late when he arrived to take her out, he was dependable, reliable and most importantly he put her at the centre of his world. When she accepted his invitation to stay in his father's chalet in Switzerland she did so with the intention of letting him in.

Torquil's chalet was nestled into the side of the mountain, surrounded by tall fir trees with a spectacular view down the valley. They stood on the snowy balcony watching the stars glimmer in the clear black sky like cut glass. An incandescent moon lit up the mountains with an almost phosphorescent light, allowing them to see details as if it were day. Torquil took her by the hand and led her into their bedroom where a jubilant fire danced in the grate, fighting off the cold mountain air that entered in through the open window. Then he cupped her face in his hands and kissed her tenderly on the mouth. 'I want you to remember this moment for ever,' he breathed.

'I will.'

'I want it to mean as much to you as it does to me,' he said. Too moved to reply she abandoned herself to her senses, taking pleasure from his caresses and from the warm, wet sensation of his mouth loving hers. She trembled as his hands pulled her shirt out from her trousers and crept up inside, feeling the soft innocence of her skin. He was touched by the knowledge that he was peeling open the petals of an unpicked flower, enabling her to experience physical love for the first time. He traced his fingers over her small breasts, touching her nipples and feeling them swell. He removed her shirt and watched the light of the flickering flames lick her flesh. Then he unbuttoned her trousers and pulled them down so that she stood in her panties, smiling at him shyly.

'You're so beautiful,' he whispered admiringly, tracing with heavy eyes every line and curve of her body. For a moment she floundered with embarrassment, aware of her vulnerability and unsure of what to do. But he seemed to sense her shyness and taking her hands in his he kissed them before leading them to unbutton his shirt and his trousers until he was standing naked and proud before her. He pulled her against him and buried his face in the angle of her neck. Then his fingers ran up the inside of her thigh until they reached the line of her panties. Her legs nearly buckled under her, but he didn't lead her to the bed but insisted she stand as they slid inside to where her longing lay hot and undisguised. She caught her breath as he stroked her with deft fingers, watching the colour rise in her cheeks and her eyelids flutter with pleasure. Then when she had lost herself in his rhythmic touch, riding on the delicious waves of an uncharted sea, he swept her up in his arms and carried her to the bed where she was allowed to give in to the trembling of her legs and lie dazed and brazen for him to cover her body with kisses and the sensuous exploring of his tongue. Finally, gently, he entered her to possess her completely.

Torquil lay back and lit a cigarette. 'I've never seen you smoke,' she said, snuggling up to him.

'Only after sex,' he said, drawing the nicotine into his lungs. 'And only the best.'

'That was lovely, Torquil,' she said and blushed at the recollection of her shamelessness.

He drew her against him with his arm and kissed her damp forehead. '*You* were lovely,' he said emphatically.

'So were you,' she replied and laughed.

'This is only the beginning. I want to take you on a lifetime adventure,' he said, then looked at her steadily with his pale green eyes. 'Once again, I know I'm rushing in. But I know what I want.' Federica blinked at him in bewilderment. 'I want to marry you, Fede.'

Federica sat up in alarm. 'You've only known me a few months,' she protested, wondering what miracle had caused him to love her like he did.

'But you love me?' he asked frowning.

'Yes, I do,' she replied. 'But marriage is for life.'

'And I'm going to love you for life,' he insisted, pulling her down to lie in his arms again. 'Marry me, Fede, and make me the happiest man in the world. I know I'm older than you, but that's just it. I know better what I want and I know what's best for you,' he said, kissing her again. 'You need to be looked after and protected and that's what I'm going to do. Look after you and protect you. You need never worry about anything again. Love cures everything.'

'Yes, it does,' she said, smiling at the intensity of emotion that she felt. 'I love you so much. I'm just scared.' She sighed. 'I watched my parents' marriage disintegrate. I just don't want that to happen to me.'

'It won't, I promise. You won't ever be scared again,' he soothed. 'If you marry me, you'll be happy forever, I promise.'

'If you're sure you want me, then, yes, I'll marry you,' she said and laughed happily. 'Mrs Torquil Jensen. That has a certain ring to it.'

'Nothing like the ring I'm going to buy you,' he said and squeezed her so hard she almost had to fight for air.

Torquil pressed his lips against her forehead before dragging once again on his cigarette. How fortunate he was to have found Federica. Fate had been kind to him. She was perfect in every way. After the choruses of worldly city girls, her innocence enchanted him. Her naïvety empowered him and her beauty and grace bedazzled him. With Federica he felt needed and adored. Aware that she was experiencing love for the first time he was touched and honoured that she had chosen him – an emotion that was new to him. He was her hero. She looked up to him, happy for him to make her decisions for her, content for him to always take the lead. Having sailed through life according to the meticulous coordinates set out by his father he was finally asserting control. His father wouldn't like it. He had always been the dominant presence in his son's life. Like the all-consuming shadow of a powerful oak tree the force of his nature had seemed inescapable. But in the last few years Torquil had been growing up and out of his father's shade. Every small move away he saw as a victory, however minute the step. Now he was taking another, larger pace. Federica was *his* choice. No one could control his heart. It felt good.

When Federica returned to London she rang her mother to tell her the news. 'Mama, I'm getting married,' she said.

Helena sat down. 'You're getting married?' she exclaimed in horror. 'To Torquil?'

'Well, who else would it be?' Federica replied and laughed happily.

'But I haven't even met him,' she protested.

'You will. I'll bring him down this weekend.'

'Sweetie, isn't this all a bit hasty? You've only known him a few months.'

'It's what I want,' she said firmly.

Helena fell silent for a moment. She remembered her own hasty marriage to Ramon and shuddered. 'You're only eighteen. You're a child.'

'No, I'm a woman,' Federica replied with emphasis and smiled to herself.

'Have you told Toby?'

'Not yet,' she explained. 'I wanted to tell you first.'

'Well, call Toby,' she suggested. 'I'm afraid this is all too sudden, I haven't met the man yet so I can't make a comment. Why don't you have a long engagement to give you both time to get to know each other?'

'Torquil wants to marry immediately.'

'Really?'

'Yes. He's so impulsive. Mama, we love each other,' she insisted.

'Your father and I loved each other too.'

'It's got nothing to do with you and Papa. This is me and

Torquil, we're two entirely different people. We both know what we want.'

Helena sighed heavily. As if Federica was old enough to know what she wanted?

When Toby heard the news he was devastated and furious. 'Julian and I are going up to London immediately to talk to her,' he told Helena briskly. 'We'll take the early train tomorrow. I know I've met this Torquil before, so is Julian, and although we can't remember where, he certainly left a bad taste in our mouths.'

'Try to talk some sense into her, Toby, she's out of her mind.'

'She won't marry him, don't worry,' he replied.

'She's determined.'

'I know. But she listens to me.'

'Thank God, because she doesn't listen to me any more,' she replied defensively, remembering with the residue of an old bitterness how she always listened to her father. 'Where are you meeting her? Won't she be at work?'

'No. Torquil's made her give up her job. She's languishing in his house in The Little Boltons.'

'Very nice,' said Helena tightly.

'Very,' Toby agreed. 'We're going straight there.'

News travelled fast. Polly was appalled and accidentally knocked one of Jake's model boats onto the floor where it shattered into hundreds of small pieces. When he returned home from work in the evening to find his treasured creation in bits his mouth twitched with rage until he recognised the pain in his wife's eyes, because they tended to droop like a sad dog when she was unhappy.

'Federica's marrying this man,' she said helplessly.

Jake shook his head, 'There are more model boats but only one Federica. I hope she knows what she's doing,' he said quietly.

'She thinks she's marrying her father,' said Polly. 'According to Ingrid, who hears it all from her girls, the man's forty years old and looks just like Ramon.'

'Handsome devil then,' he said.

'Devil being the operative word, I fear,' Polly replied gravely.

Helena was giving herself a manicure when she heard the newsflash on the radio. She wasn't concentrating, half listening and half dreaming herself out of her mundane existence. But the words focused her thoughts into one small point that sent cold panic slicing through her veins with the violence of freshly sharpened knives.

The train that Toby and Julian had taken to London had crashed.

Chapter Thirty-One

Cachagua

Estella screamed and sat up in bed, staring into the darkness and panting in terror. Ramon was wrenched back from the hot African jungle into the cold fever of his lover's nightmare. He stretched out his hand and switched on the light. He sat up and drew her into his arms, stroking her damp hair and murmuring words of reassurance. '*Mi amor*, it's a bad dream, nothing but a bad dream,' he said, feeling the thumping of her heartbeat vibrate against his body like a terrified creature desperate to break out. 'I'm here, my love, I'm here.'

'I dreamed of death,' she said, still feeling the icy claws of fear scratching at her skin.

'It was just a dream.'

'It's a premonition,' she replied steadily. 'It's the second time I've had it.'

'*Mi amor*, you're frightened of something, that's all.'

'It will happen a third time,' she said, holding him tightly around his shoulders with trembling arms. 'Then it will happen for real.'

Ramon shook his head and kissed her neck. 'So, who died in your dream?' he asked, indulging her.

'I don't know. I didn't see his face,' she replied, blinking away her tears. 'But I fear it was you.'

'It'll take more than a dream to kill me off,' he joked, but Estella didn't smile.

'Perhaps it was Ramoncito,' she choked. 'I don't know.'

'Look at me,' he said, holding her gently away at arm's length. 'Look into my eyes, Estella.' She stared at him with the hollow eyes of the tormented and watched him smile at her with love. 'No one's going to die. At least, you can't predict a death in a dream. You're anxious about something and it's playing with your subconscious. Perhaps you're worried about my trip to Africa.'

She nodded and sighed as the light in the room dispersed the dark horrors of her dream and slowly brought her mind back to reality. 'Perhaps,' she conceded.

'I'm only going for a few weeks,' he said. 'I haven't been away for a long time.'

'I know. You've been a wonderful father to Ramoncito,' she said and smiled.

'And a good lover to you?' he asked, raising his eyebrows and smirking.

'And a good lover to me,' she repeated.

He cocked his head to one side and frowned. 'You know I'll never leave you,' he said. 'You have no reason to be insecure. I'll always love you.'

'I know. And I will always love you, too.'

When Ramon turned out the light and gathered Estella into his arms she was unable to sleep. Not because she was no longer tired, but because she feared that she might dream of death for the third time, thus making it happen in reality. Her mother had once told her that she had predicted her own mother's death in a dream. Three times she dreamed that her mother lay dying in front of a pink house. As she knew of no pink house she didn't worry and forgot all about it. But a few weeks later her mother died of a heart attack tending to the honeysuckle that grew up the side of their white house. It was sunset and the wall glowed a warm, radiant pink. Estella lay fretting until sleep overcame her. When she awoke at dawn she realised to her relief that she hadn't dreamed at all.

When Ramon had finally divorced Helena, Estella had hoped that he would marry her. This hope she guarded secretly, not even telling her parents. But to her dismay he never mentioned marriage. He was contented the way things were. He was free to come and go without the psychological bind of a contract.

Mariana also hoped he would formalise his relationship with Estella. Over the years she and the mother of her grandson had become firm friends. Slowly the divisions imposed upon them by the nature of their places in the world fell away and they were free to live as equals. Estella included Mariana in the life of her son, calling her regularly in Santiago and enjoying her secret visits when she spent the long summer months in Cachagua. At first Mariana had longed to tell Ignacio about Estella and Ramoncito, but little by little she grew accustomed to her secret and it no longer troubled her.

Ramoncito was now eleven years old. He was dark haired and olive skinned like his parents, with the rich, honey eyes of his mother. He was carefree and independent like Ramon and sensitive like his mother, yet his nature was his alone and given to him by God. He was a child who gave only pleasure. He was contented to listen to his father's rambling stories and collect shells on the beach with his mother. He sat talking to the tombstones with his grandfather and indulged both grandmothers with stories of his adventures with his young friends. He hadn't inherited his father's impatient desire to travel nor his selfish need to satisfy his own longings at the expense of those of the people he loved.

Mariana said that he had been blessed with the best of both parents and she was right. She often saw Federica in the honesty of his smile and in the trusting innocence of his eyes, and she wondered whether Ramon saw it, whether he remembered and she consoled herself that she remembered for him. As long as she was alive, Federica and Hal would never be forgotten.

Ramon loved his son with an intensity with which he had once loved Federica. He still loved his daughter and often, when he was inventing stories for Ramoncito, his heart ached with nostalgia, because Federica had loved his stories too. Then he recalled that painful moment when his own negligence had reared up to throttle him with remorse.

He had seen her. Bicycling down the lane on her way home, her face aglow with happiness and exertion combined, ignorant that the man who passed her in the black Mercedes was her father. He had commanded the driver to stop the car at once. Federica, hearing the car screech to a sudden halt, had braked her bicycle and turned around, squinting into the sun. For a few moments, which seemed painfully long in his memory, he had watched her with longing, fighting the impulse to open the car door and run towards her, to sweep her off her feet like he had always done when she had been a child. She was no longer a little girl. She was still small in stature, small for a thirteen-year-old, but her limbs were long and her face that of a young woman; slim, angular, proud. He had suppressed an inner groan that threatened to break out into a desperate cry. Federica was on his lips and he had had to struggle in order to swallow her name. She had shielded her eyes against the sun with her hand, one foot on the pedal, one on the tarmac. Her hair was long and flowing in the wind. She still had the hair of an angel. *La Angelita*. But he had remembered what Helena had told him. Federica was happy without him. If he had embraced her as he had desired, his embrace would have been full of false promises. Promises of commitment, promises of devotion but above all the promise to prevent Helena from marrying Arthur and he knew he couldn't do that. So, faced with promises he could not fulfil, he had sadly asked the chauffeur to drive on. He had owed it to Helena to leave her free to marry Arthur and live in peace with her children.

He had returned to Chile consumed with regret and remorse. If only he had begged her to stay, nothing would have changed. He would still have a relationship with his children. But that wasn't enough of a jolt to open his heart to what he had had and lost, for he had returned into the rose-scented arms of Estella and Ramoncito and once again Federica had retreated into the recesses of his mind where her cries for him could no longer be heard.

Estella told her mother about her nightmares. 'I'm afraid,' she said as her mother lay in the armchair like a fat seal, fanning herself with an Hispanic fan. 'I'm afraid that Ramon's going to die in Africa.'

Maria dabbed her sweating brow with a clean, white *pañuelo* that her mother had made for her and considered her daughter's problem with care. 'You must go and visit Fortuna,' she said after giving the matter some thought.

'To read my future?' Estella replied anxiously. She had often heard people speak about Fortuna for she was the only black person anyone had ever seen. It was said that her father had survived a shipwreck when a cargo carrying slaves had sunk off the coast of Chile. Her mother had been a native Chilean who had taken him in and nursed him back to health. Fortuna lived in a small village up the coast and when she wasn't lying in the sun watching the world pass her by she read people's fortunes for a small fee. How she survived on so little money no one knew, but some said she was supported by an old man whose life she had saved by predicting an earthquake which would have killed him had he not left his house on her instructions.

Estella returned home to sleep on her mother's advice. Ramon was sitting in his study tapping his thoughts into a computer. The evening was calm and melancholic, flooding the coast in a soft, pink light. Estella decided not to tell him about Fortuna, although the books he wrote were filled with mysteries and magic. She feared he might think less of her. Fortune-telling was very much associated with the suspicions of the under-classes. She crept up behind him and wound her arms around his neck. He was pleased to see her and kissed the brown skin on her wrists.

'Let's walk along the beach, I need some air,' he said, leading her out by the hand. They walked through the strange pink light

377

and kissed against the rhythm of the sea. 'I'll miss you when I go tomorrow,' he said.

'I'll miss you too,' she replied and frowned.

'You're not still worrying about your dream, are you?' he asked, kissing her forehead.

'No, no,' she lied. 'I just wish you weren't going.'

'I'll be in Santiago tomorrow night, I have to see my agent in the afternoon. I'll fly out Thursday night. I'll call you from Santiago and I'll call you from the airport.'

'Then I'll just wait,' she sighed.

'Yes. But I'll think of you every minute and if you close your ears to the rest of the world you just might hear me sending you messages of love.' He kissed her again, holding her tightly around her slim waist. Later, when he made love to her in the watery light of the moon that reflected off the sea and shimmered in through the window of their room, he tasted the roses on her skin and smelt the heavy scent of their intimacy and knew he would take them with him across the world and savour them when he was alone.

The following day Estella and Ramoncito waved good-bye to Ramon and watched his car disappear up the hill in a cloud of glittering dust. Ramoncito then skipped off to school with his *mochila* on his back filled with books and a box of sandwiches, which Estella had made him for lunch. He turned to wave at his mother, who stood at the foot of the road, and blew her a kiss. She blew one back and then remained there a while, smiling with tenderness at the unguarded affection of her son which never ceased to amaze her.

She hadn't dreamed about death again. She had floated on the memories of Ramon's lovemaking and had awoken with the radiant complexion of a satisfied woman. But she still felt fearful and because of that icy fear she decided to go with her mother and visit Fortuna.

★   ★   ★

Pablo Rega watched them dig the grave. It was hot and the earth was hard and dry. He leant on the gravestone of Osvaldo Garcia Segundo and chewed on a piece of long grass while they toiled at the other end of the graveyard. 'It's a good position, that,' he told Osvaldo. 'Overlooking the sea, like you. *Sí*, Señor, overlooking the sea is a prime spot. Imagine being stuffed back there without a view. I'd like to be here, where I can see the sea and the horizon. Gives one a feeling of space, of eternity. I like that. I'd like to be part of nature. What does it feel like, Osvaldo?' He breathed in the scent of the dark green pine trees and waited for a reply, but Osvaldo had probably never been a man of words. 'This place is getting pretty full,' he continued. 'Soon there won't be any more room and they'll have to start digging up old graves like yours. There's a good chance I'll be buried on top of you, then we can talk for eternity.' He chuckled. 'I'd like that, *sí*, señor, I would.'

Estella and her mother arrived by bus and walked directly to Fortuna's small house, which stood just off the dusty road. There were no flowers or bushes, just dry sandy ground and rubbish, which Fortuna scattered around the house – not to ward off the evil spirits as people suspected but because she was too lazy to throw things into a bin. Her house smelt of rotting food and sour milk and Estella and her mother found themselves having to disguise their grimaces by smiling in order not to offend the old woman. Fortuna sat outside on a large wicker rocking-chair, watching the odd car pass by, humming old Negro spirituals her father had taught her as a child. When she saw Maria she laughed from her belly and enquired after Pablo Rega.

'Still talking to the dead?' she asked. 'Hasn't someone told him that they can't hear him? They don't hang around you know, they fly off into the world of spirits the moment they leave this godforsaken earth.'

Maria ignored her and explained that her daughter had come to have her future read. Fortuna stopped rocking and sat up, her expression sliding into the serious guise of a wise woman conscious of the responsibility that came with her gift.

She asked Estella to sit down and pull the chair up so that they faced one another with their knees almost touching. Maria flopped into another chair and pulled out her Hispanic fan. Fortuna took Estella's trembling hands in her own soft fleshy hands that had never experienced a day's hard labour and pressed the pads of Estella's palms with her thumbs. She pulled her mouth into various strange shapes and closed her eyes, leaving her lashes to flutter about as if she had no control over them. Estella looked at her mother anxiously, but Maria nodded to her to concentrate and fanned herself in agitation.

'You have never been so happy,' Fortuna said and Estella smiled, for it was true, she had never been so happy. 'You have a son who will be a famous writer one day like his father.' Estella blushed and grinned with pride. 'He will channel his pain into poetry that will be read by millions.' Estella's smile disintegrated as the icy claws of fear once more scratched at her heart. Fortuna's eyelids fluttered with more speed. Maria stopped fanning herself and stared at her with her mouth agape. 'I see death,' she said. Estella began to choke. 'I can't see the face, but it's close. Very close.' Fortuna opened her eyes as Estella pulled her hands away and heaved as her throat constricted, leaving barely any room for the air to reach her lungs. Her mother threw herself out of her chair with the agility of a much slimmer woman and thrust her daughter's face down between her knees.

'Breathe, Estella, breathe,' she said as her daughter gasped and spluttered, fighting the fear that strangled her. Fortuna sat back in her chair and watched as mother and daughter struggled against the inevitability of her prediction. Finally, when Estella began to breathe again, her choking was replaced by deep sobs that wracked her entire being.

'I don't want him to die,' she wailed. 'I don't want to lose him, he's my life.' Maria pulled her daughter into her large arms and attempted to comfort her, but there was nothing she could say. Fortuna had spoken.

'Please tell me it is not Ramon,' she begged, but Fortuna shook her head.

'I cannot tell you because I do not know,' she replied. 'His face was not revealed to me. I can do no more.'

'Is there nothing we can do?' Maria asked in desperation.

'Nothing. Fate is stronger than all of us.'

Estella was determined to change the future. She told her mother that Ramon was leaving for Africa the following day and that if she could prevent him going she might save his life. Maria didn't try to stop her. She knew she wouldn't listen. She was too distressed to stay in Cachagua and wait for disaster to strike. She embraced her daughter at the bus station and reassured her that she would look after Ramoncito while she was away. 'God go with you,' she said. 'May He protect you.'

Estella cried all the way to Santiago. She sat with her head leaning against the window, replaying all her most treasured memories of Ramon as if he had died already. She closed her eyes and prayed until her silent prayers formed words on her tongue that she mumbled deliriously without realising that the other passengers could hear her, but were too polite to ask her to be quiet. When she arrived in Santiago she took a taxi to his apartment. She rang the bell but there was no reply. She stood in the doorway of the apartment block and disintegrated once more into tears. She didn't know what to do or where to go. Perhaps she was too late. What if he was dead in his apartment? She collapsed onto the marble steps and put her head in her hands. When she felt a gentle tap on her shoulders she lifted her eyes expecting to see Ramon, only to be disappointed as the porter stood over her with a sympathetic expression etched onto his smooth brown face.

'Are you all right, Señora?' he asked.

'I'm looking for Ramon Campione,' she muttered.

'Don Ramon?' he said, frowning. 'Who are you?'

'My name is Estella Rega. I am . . .' He cocked his head to one side. 'I am his . . . his . . .'

'His wife?' he said helpfully.

'His . . .'

'If you are his wife I can tell you where he is,' he said kindly, grinning at her crookedly.

'I am his wife,' she said firmly, wiping the tears off her face with a white *pañuelo*.

'He's at a meeting. He left over an hour ago, but I will call you a taxi and he will take you to him.' Estella pulled a grateful smile. 'That's better,' said the porter. 'You're too pretty to be so sad.' Then he watched her climb into the taxi he hailed for her and disappear into the traffic.

Ramon stood up. 'I'm off to Africa tomorrow,' he said. 'I'll be away three weeks.'

'That's a short visit for you,' his agent commented, smiling knowingly.

'Well, I don't have much reason to stay away these days.' He chuckled.

'You mean to say that this woman you've been hiding away all these years has captured your heart?'

'You ask too many questions, Vicente.'

'I know I'm right. I can tell from your writing. There's love all over the pages.'

Ramon laughed and picked up his case. 'Then there's even less reason to go away.'

'But you'll go anyway.'

'I always do.'

'Call me when you get back.'

Ramon closed the door behind him and stepped into the lift. He thought about what Vicente had said to him, 'there's love all over the pages', and he smiled to himself as he thought of Estella and Ramoncito. Then he glanced at his reflection in the mirror. He wasn't getting any younger. He was already greying around the temples and, looking at his physique, he wasn't getting any thinner either. He cocked his head to one side and rubbed his chin ponderously. 'I should make an honest woman out of Estella,' he thought, 'I should have married her years ago.'

When he opened the door into the busy street he stopped a moment, stunned to see a woman who looked exactly like Estella on the other side of the road. She was looking to her left and right in confusion with swollen red eyes that darted about like a terrified animal unused to the traffic. He blinked a few times before he realised that she was in fact Estella and he shouted at her. She heard her name and raised her eyes. She smiled with relief when she saw him and lifted her hand to greet him. 'Ramon!' she cried with happiness, and placing her hand over her mouth she blinked away tears of joy. Then she stepped out into the road.

'Estella, no!' he shouted, but it was too late. The sparks from the truck spat into the air as the wheels screeched to a sudden halt in an attempt to avoid the woman who walked blindly out in front of it. Ramon dropped his case and ran across the road, which shuddered to a halt as drivers leapt out of their cars to see what had happened. When Ramon saw the broken body of Estella lying inert at the foot of the vehicle he threw himself upon her with trembling hands, desperate to find a pulse.

'Talk to me, Estella, talk to me,' he pleaded, pressing his face against hers, whispering into her ear. 'Say something, my love, something. Please don't die.'

But she didn't move. He gazed down at her pale face in shock and noticed that she still had traces of a small smile in the gentle curve of her lips. He placed a finger on them, willing her to breathe. But there was not a breath left in her. There was nothing he could do to bring her back. He lifted her shattered body into his arms and pressed it against his heart, then sobbed loudly from the core of his being as he realised that he had killed her.

'Who was she?' someone asked.

'My wife,' he wailed and rocked back and forth dementedly.

★   ★   ★

Ramon took the woman he had loved as he had loved none other back to her home in Zapallar. Maria had slipped into a deadly fever when she heard the news and lay in a trance, her ears deafened to the desperate pleas of Pablo Rega who held a candlelit vigil by her bed, silently bargaining with God. Mariana went immediately to their house and embraced them both for she had grown to love their daughter as her own. Only Ramoncito remained dry-eyed and composed. Mariana explained to her grandson that his mother had gone to live with Jesus and that she was looking down on him and loving him from Heaven. But Ramoncito just nodded and put his arms around her in order to give comfort. Mariana was confused. His maturity perturbed her. But she didn't hear the breaking of his heart or the crying out of his soul in mute despair.

As Fortuna had predicted, millions would feel his suffering in the words he would write in the future. But for the moment he was unable to comprehend his own grief or know how to express it.

Ramon arrived shrunken and grey with the body of his beloved Estella. He allowed himself to be comforted in the familiar bosom of his mother and then straightened himself up to be strong for his son. When Maria saw Ramon she blinked out of her trance and told them all of Fortuna's prediction. Ramon shook his head. 'She died instead of me,' he said sadly.

'She died because it was her time,' said Maria. 'That's why Fortuna couldn't see her face.'

When Ignacio Campione knocked on the door of Pablo Rega's house the small party of mourners looked at each other in surprise. He walked in with the stride of a man no longer able to play ignorant.

'I'm sorry, son,' he said, pulling Ramon's large frame into his arms. Ramon blinked at his mother in confusion over Ignacio's shoulder. Mariana shrugged and wiped away her tears. 'You don't really believe I'm that stupid,' he said, patting his son on his back. For once Ramon didn't know what to say. He buried his face in his father's neck and sobbed.

Estella was buried on the top of the hill overlooking the sea, in the shade of a tall green pine tree. Pablo Rega later apologised to Osvaldo Garcia Segundo because he would from that moment on speak only to his daughter. Unlike Osvaldo, Estella talked back. He could hear her voice in the rise and fall of the tides and feel her breath in the wind that always smelt of roses.

Ramon looked out over the horizon and reflected on his misguided acts of selfishness that had ruined so many lives. He thought about what he had loved and lost. Then he looked down at his eleven-year-old son. Ramoncito glanced up at him and smiled. In his smile Ramon saw the smile of Federica and the tears of Hal, the frustration of Helena and the unconditional love of Estella and he swallowed his regret as if it were a ball of nails in his throat. He placed his hand on the brave shoulder of his son and vowed that he would make up for his negligence by loving Ramoncito, by being there for him, by changing his ways as Helena had once begged him to.

He threw a single red rose onto the coffin, then walked away a different man.

Chapter Thirty-Two

Polperro

Helena, Jake and Polly sat helplessly watching the television for news of the crash. A number had been given out for worried relatives, but they were still pulling bodies out of the wreckage and had no news of Toby and Julian. Arthur sped over from the office and Hal was picked up from school. Polly's kitchen vibrated with the resonance of their grief. All Jake's model boats lay in scattered abandon, like matchsticks, over the floors and table as he had thrown them all to the ground in a sudden fit of anger and remorse. Polly tried to reach out to him, to give him her hand, as he spiralled into a dark pit where his stubbornness and prejudice laughed at him mockingly, but he didn't take it. He was too ashamed. Too disgusted that he had allowed his intolerance to obscure the value of life.

Sure that Toby was dead and unable to face the rest of the family, Jake stalked out of the house to walk on the cliffs. He strode across the winter grass and allowed tears of self-loathing to sting his face. The bitter wind caused his eyes to burn but he hurried on blindly as if by walking fast he might leave his despair behind him.

He recalled Toby as a little boy. The times he had taken him out on his boat, the times they had sat in silence watching the seagulls and the shoals of fish just beneath the surface. He remembered how he had laughed when Toby had begged him to return to the water a large trout they had just caught. He had teased him, holding the fish in his hands and waving it about in front of the child's tormented face. He winced at the recollection, like so many other recollections. Toby had always known the value of life. He had known it better than anyone.

Then he remembered the times when father and son had been so close they had both believed that nothing could come between them. Toby had helped him glue together his model boats well into the night. They had told each other stories, they had laughed and they had worked together in the familiar silence of the very intimate. There had been a time when Toby had told him everything.

But Julian had arrived and it had all changed.

Jake sat on a cold rock and looked out onto the rough horizon where the waves collided with each other, drawing foam like blood. He searched his tormented soul to find the root of his prejudice. It wasn't just Toby's homosexuality that had set father against son because feelings of resentment had grown up inside him long before he had known of it. There was something else. Something much more primitive. He recalled the first time Toby had introduced him to Julian. He had noticed their closeness immediately. The way they laughed together like old friends, anticipated the other's thoughts like brothers and enjoyed the comfortable silence of father and son. His jealousy had choked him. When he scrutinised his feelings further he realised that he had never really had a problem with Toby's homosexuality, but it had been easier to blame his resentment on that, rather than admit his jealousy, even to himself. He was suddenly consumed with shame.

Jake was not a religious man but he felt the presence of God in Nature and it was there that he prayed. He prayed that God would forgive him and begged him to preserve both Toby's and Julian's lives so that he could make it up to them.

When he returned home Polly noticed that his expression had changed. Somewhere out there in the wind he had slain the dragon that tormented him. Now he was ready to join the rest of the family in hope.

Helena knew she should be strong for her son, but her misery was all-consuming. She sat watching her tears send ripples across the surface of her cup of coffee and allowed the drama to engulf her completely. When Arthur arrived she managed to raise her swollen eyes to indicate that she needed comforting. Arthur put down his briefcase and stood in the centre of the kitchen.

'Right,' he said in a commanding tone, placing his hands on his hips. 'I've spoken to the emergency services on site and so far there's no sign of them. At least we can be thankful that they don't feature among the dead.'

Helena began to wail. Polly clamped her pale lips together in an effort to contain her distress. She had to be strong for the rest of her family.

'Now, there's nothing we can do but wait. I suggest I put a call through every fifteen minutes. Jake, keep the radio on for bulletins. Helena, don't mourn them prematurely, while there's no news there's hope, at least give them that courtesy.'

Helena was stunned. She had never heard her husband speak with such authority. She blinked up at him with admiration.

'We all have to be strong for each other. It's not over until it's over,' he continued and watched his wife straighten up obediently.

'Right, anyone for another cup of tea?' said Polly, filling the kettle.

Federica wished she were in Polperro with the rest of her family. She lay on Torquil's large bed in The Little Boltons and stared unblinking out of the window, willing the telephone to ring with good news. She had called Torquil's office and left a message for him with his secretary. She strained her ears for the key in the lock until her senses were so acute that her heart leapt at the smallest sound.

Helena had telephoned her with the terrible news. But while there was no evidence of their deaths there was still hope that they were alive. She had turned on the television and watched the various reports. The train looked like a toy made out of tin that had been carelessly scrunched up by an overbearing child. She had watched the firemen struggle with the bodies of the dead and searched behind them for those of the living. But she couldn't see Toby or Julian in the blur of unfamiliar faces. When it became too much she had turned it off, lain on the bed and waited for news from her mother.

When the telephone finally did ring she picked up the receiver with a trembling hand and was barely able to hear the voice for the squealing of her nerves in her ears. 'Fede, it's Hester.'

Federica's heart plummeted. 'Oh, Hester, hi,' she replied in disappointment.

'I got your number from your mother. I'm so sorry. We're all thinking about you,' she said. 'Molly and I are sitting in the flat praying they're all right.'

'Thank you, Hester,' she mumbled weakly. 'I'm praying too.'

Hester had heard about Federica's engagement to Torquil but felt it wasn't the time to mention it. 'I'll leave the line free now, but we're here if you need us,' she added sympathetically before hanging up.

When the key finally turned in the lock Federica's hearing was too concentrated on the telephone to notice. Torquil found her curled up on the bed in a tight ball. He walked over to her and drew her into his arms where she sobbed against his chest. 'I thought you'd never come,' she choked, wrapping her arms around his neck. 'They might be dead.'

'You don't know they're dead,' he replied. 'What's the latest news?'

'That's the worst, there is no news.'

'Have you been watching the television?'

'I couldn't bear to look. I'm waiting for Mama to call. They keep ringing that family line they give out.'

'Right, that's all we can do for the moment. That and pray,' he said, stroking her hot forehead. 'They're going to be all right, sweetness, I just know they are.'

But Federica felt nothing but doom.

After a while Torquil stood up and paced the room. 'Moping around isn't going to change anything and it's making me feel claustrophobic. Why don't you have a bath, get dressed and we can go out for lunch to take your mind off it.'

'I can't have lunch at a time like this!' she exclaimed in horror.

'It'll be good for you to get out of the house, have some hot soup, it'll make the time go faster.'

'But the telephone?' she stammered.

'I'll divert it to my mobile. Don't worry, when they know something they'll call us wherever we are,' he reassured her.

News travelled fast in Polperro. Ingrid chain-smoked, unable to paint or rise in her usual vague way above her cares. Inigo closed his philosophy books and sat with his wife in front of the fire, pondering on the meaning of death. Nuno shook his head and knocked back a glass of brandy lamenting that it should have been him. 'My time is nigh,' he sighed. 'Those boys had years ahead of them.'

Sam sat in front of his computer at work, longing to call Federica. Molly had rung up and told him the news. He had immediately turned on the radio and listened to the details of the crash, wishing he could comfort her like he had that day in the bluebells after she had overheard Arthur's marriage proposal. She had been so young and forlorn then, gazing up at him with timid eyes, adoring him unconditionally. He recalled the sweet kisses in the barn and their awkward confrontation in the kitchen at Christmas and felt her drifting away from him. He already loathed Torquil Jensen. 'What sort of a name is that, anyway?' he thought to himself with resentment. In her confusion Molly had forgotten to tell him that Federica was engaged to be married. She had only remembered to give him Federica's new number and ask him to call her. 'She needs our support,' she had explained.

Sam doodled around the number he had written on the corner of the *Evening Standard* and debated whether or not she would be pleased to hear from him. Then he pushed his reservations aside and dialled the number. He leant back in his chair and listened to the tone with an accelerated heart. Finally it ceased and a gravelly male voice responded with urgency, 'Torquil here.'

Sam's gut twisted with irritation. 'It's Sam Appleby for Federica,' he stated coldly.

The man indicated his disappointment with a loud sigh. 'She's in the bath, I'm afraid.'

'Oh,' Sam replied impatiently, taking off his glasses and rubbing the bridge of his nose in agitation.

'Can she call you back later? We'd like to leave the lines free. I don't know whether you know but . . .'

'I do. Just tell her I called,' he interrupted and hung up. Angrily he stabbed his letter opener into the front of the newspaper. He regretted having telephoned at all. 'Torquil Jensen,' he scowled under his breath, 'what an imbecile.'

'Who was that?' Federica shouted from the bathtub. Torquil chewed the inside of his cheek, deliberating whether or not to tell her. He didn't much like the sound of Sam Appleby. His arrogance grated. Anyway, Federica didn't need any male friends now; she had him. 'Nothing, sweetness, just the office,' he replied with a smirk.

Sam Appleby might have hung up on him but he had just had the last word.

Torquil took Federica out to lunch in a small restaurant around the corner from his house. The waiter, who knew Torquil well, gave them a table by the window and Federica sat staring unhappily out onto the grey pavement. 'Uncle Toby has always been like a father to me,' she said, stirring her spoon about the soup bowl. 'My own father never bothered really, but Uncle Toby always had time for us. I have so many memories of him.' She sighed, not bothering to wipe away a heavy tear that balanced on the end of her eyelashes.

'You're talking in the past, sweetness,' said Torquil, stroking her arm with tenderness. 'I'm sure he's alive, you'll see.'

'Oh, he's dead,' she replied sadly. 'If he were alive we would have heard.'

At that moment Torquil's mobile rang with a loud shriek that jolted the entire restaurant.

'Torquil here,' he answered briskly. 'Ah, Mrs Cooke, it's Torquil Jensen. Any news?'

'Is Federica with you?' Helena asked, ignoring the usual pleasantries.

'I'll pass you over.'

'Fede, sweetie, I'm afraid we still don't know for sure. There are thirty-two dead. Toby and Julian aren't among those, but they're not among the survivors either. They still don't know. They're still looking. We're all trying so hard to be strong. Arthur's been wonderful. He's taken over completely. I didn't think he had it in him.'

'Oh Mama, I'm praying so hard,' she whispered.

'So am I. We all are.'

'I never said good-bye,' she choked, casting her eyes into the quiet street. Suddenly she saw Toby and Julian strolling happily up the pavement. Toby was eating a chocolate bar. She paused in astonishment, blinking furiously in case she was mistaken.

'I know, sweetie, neither did I,' Helena said with a sniff. Then after a moment, when Federica failed to respond she added, 'Fede, are you all right?'

'Mama, they're here!' she exclaimed in amazement.

Torquil turned around and looked out of the window.

'Who is?'

'Uncle Toby and Julian!'

'What?'

'They're walking towards me up the road.'

'Are you sure?'

'Yes!' she replied, getting up and running out through the door. 'Toby! Julian!' she shouted.

Toby smiled jovially as his niece ran towards him. She threw herself into his arms. 'You're alive,' she laughed. 'They're alive!' she shouted into the telephone where Helena was anxiously hanging on at the other end.

'Pass me over now!' she ordered crossly. 'They're alive!' she added, looking at her parents, Arthur and Hal in confusion.

'Helena,' said Toby, grinning into the speaker.

'What the hell happened to you?' she demanded.

'What do you mean?'

'The train crash.'

Toby frowned. 'What train crash?' he asked, perplexed.

'For God's sake!' she gasped. 'Don't tell me you weren't even on it?'

'We took an early train, because Julian had a morning appointment in Soho.'

'I don't believe it!' she exclaimed. 'We thought you were dead. You worried us sick.'

'Christ, I'm sorry.'

'You bloody well better be!' she said in fury. 'God, Toby, we thought you were both dead. We've been out of our minds with worry. I'd even planned the speech I was going to give at the funeral. Goddamn it! I love you!' she whimpered before disintegrating into tears.

Jake took the telephone from her. 'Toby.'

'Dad.' There was a brief pause while Jake searched for the words that only a moment ago had balanced impatiently on the end of his tongue.

Toby glanced at Julian in bafflement.

Finally, Jake settled for something less meaningful. 'Come home soon, son, both of you,' he said stiffly. He wanted to say more, but he couldn't do it over the telephone.

Toby's forehead creased in bewilderment. 'Are you all right, Dad?' he asked.

'You're alive. You're *both* alive. I've never felt better in all my life,' he announced triumphantly and Toby recognised his father's old familiar voice, the voice that had resounded with affection before prejudice had throttled it.

Toby was passed to his mother, then Arthur and finally Hal. When he hung up he shook his head in astonishment.

'You'd better come and join us for lunch,' said Torquil, extending his hand. 'I'm Torquil Jensen. You don't know how much of a pleasure it is to meet you both.'

★   ★   ★

When Toby and Julian returned to Polperro they received a welcome neither felt they deserved. Most of the town joined Toby's family and the Applebys on the platform and all clapped heartily when they stepped down from the train. Even Inigo had come out in his shabby cashmere coat and felt hat to show his delight that they had arrived home safely. Polly watched with pride as Jake embraced them both, patting them heartily on the back because his throat was too choked with emotion to speak. Toby's vision misted as he hugged his father, a hug that destroyed the invisible wall that had grown up between them. Their eyes silently communicated all that they felt and their tears demonstrated the love that both considered inappropriate to express verbally. Helena watched happily as her family were finally reunited again, but she couldn't help but wonder how their meeting went with Federica and whether they had managed to stall her marriage plans.

As Toby made his way through the crowd of well-wishers to the exit he was surprised to see Joanna Black, the girl he had once kissed at school, standing awkwardly by the door. She smiled at him. He smiled back, puzzled. 'Hello, Joanna,' he said.

'Hello, Toby,' she replied. 'I didn't think you'd remember me.'

'Oh, I do,' he said and chuckled amicably.

'I just wanted to apologise for cutting you dead that time in the grocery shop.'

'Oh, don't worry, that's fine. It was a long time ago.' He shrugged, watching her shuffle uneasily.

'I know, but it wasn't kind.'

'*I* wasn't kind. That was a long time ago too.'

She lowered her eyes and curled a strand of her mousy brown hair behind her ear. 'Well, that's just it,' she said quietly. 'When you kissed me all those years ago . . .'

'Yes?'

'And I ran off in tears.'

'Yes.'

'I was hurt not because you kissed me. I wanted you to,' she

394

said shyly and laughed with embarrassment. 'I was hurt because of the look of disgust on your face as you did it.'

'Oh, I'm so sorry,' he said, shrugging his shoulders again.

'No, don't be, really,' she replied hesitantly. 'I understand now. You didn't like girls, I didn't know it at the time.'

'Why tell me now?' he asked.

'I thought you were dead,' she replied, simply.

'Oh.'

'I've been meaning to tell you for years, but I had never plucked up the courage.'

'Thank you,' he muttered, watching her slide through the door. He followed her out.

'Well, that's all I wanted to say. I've said it now.' She laughed nervously, shuffling her feet in the cold. Then she embraced him. Toby stood rigidly as she sighed heavily. She had never got over that first girlish crush, or the hurried kiss in the playground. 'See you around,' she added before hurrying off.

Toby watched her go and shook his head. 'You know, death does the strangest things to people,' he said to Julian.

Julian grinned. 'People should die more often,' he mused. 'It brings out the best in everyone.'

Death certainly did bring the best out in everyone. Without realising it each member of Toby's family had changed.

Jake had confronted his jealousy and won. Polly's admiration for her husband had swelled thus uniting them where before his prejudice had divided them. Helena realised more than ever before the value of life and thanked God for Arthur who inflated with joy as she began to hold his hand under the table and smile at him with intimacy, the way she had when they first met. Hal emerged out of himself and began to notice those around him, albeit temporarily.

When Helena finally managed to ask Toby how his meeting had gone with Federica, she realised that it didn't matter if they married. After all, marriage wasn't life threatening.

'I was surprised at how charming he was,' Toby said, tucking into Polly's mushroom risotto. 'He's much older than her, very handsome, clever.'

'Very much the father figure, I think you'll find,' Julian added. 'He couldn't have been nicer.'

'Will he be kind to her?' Polly asked, as Jake filled her glass with wine.

'She's young,' said Jake, 'but she's no fool, Polly.'

'Oh, she knows what she wants, Dad,' Toby reassured him. 'There's no denying that. Anyhow, she's not "little Fede" any more. She's a woman. She's grown up in quite a hurry since she met Torquil. She won't budge on this one, I can tell you.'

'She is vulnerable though, especially with a much older man who can manipulate her,' Arthur interjected.

'Yes, she is vulnerable,' Helena agreed. 'She's impressionable and this is her first love, she should probably play the field a bit.'

'Fede's not up to playing the field,' Hal chuckled, squirting tomato ketchup onto his risotto.

'Well, within reason,' Jake argued.

'Helena's not suggesting she sleep around, Dad, just grow up a bit, gain a little more experience, meet other people. I agree with her. It is a worry her marrying the first man she falls in love with, however charming he may be. After all, marriage is for life,' Toby said.

'It should be,' Helena added wryly.

'It can be.' Arthur grinned, pressing her knee with his. She winked at him coquettishly.

'I think marriage sucks,' Hal interjected. Helena smiled at him and shook her head.

'So, what do we do?' Polly asked, draining her glass. 'Can we really do nothing?'

'Nothing,' said Jake. 'She has to sail her own ship, Polly.'

'Well, when are we going to meet him?' Helena asked.

'They said they might come down this weekend,' said Toby.

'Good,' Jake concluded with a nod. 'Now, no more opinions

until we've given the poor lad a chance. Any more of that risotto, Polly?'

When Molly rang Sam to let him know that Toby and Julian were alive she remembered to tell him that Federica was getting married. He nearly choked on his jealousy. 'Don't be ridiculous, she's only just met him.'

'I know. The whole thing is ludicrous,' Molly agreed. 'But she is.'

'She's Hester's age, for God's sake, what does she know about marriage?'

'Nothing. If she knew more about it I don't think she'd leap into it like this. But Mum says he's a substitute for the father she never had.'

'Well, that's it then. Father-figure syndrome,' he said bitterly and his heart plummeted.

'Quite.'

'When's the wedding?'

'In the spring.'

'What, *this* spring?' he exclaimed, taking his glasses off and rubbing his eyes, which suddenly felt tired and uncomfortable.

'Torquil wants to marry as soon as possible. You know he's stopped her working already?'

'No!'

'Yes, he has. She's moved lots of her things into his house.'

'Where does he live?'

'The Little Boltons,' she replied, her voice heavy with resentment.

'Well, she won't have to work, will she? He's undoubtedly rich.'

'Everyone should do something,' she argued. 'She'll become one of those ghastly women who do nothing but shop all day.'

'Not Fede,' said Sam defensively.

'Yes, Fede,' she insisted. 'He'll make her into whatever he

wants her to be. She hasn't exactly got the strongest character, has she?'

'She's young.'

'Hester's young and she's got more backbone than Fede.'

'She'd have to with a sister like you,' he snapped coldly.

'What do you mean by that?'

'You're just jealous that Fede's been swept up by someone handsome and rich,' he accused, wondering why he was giving her such a hard time.

'Look, I just called to let you know, not to get into a heavy discussion,' she retorted in exasperation.

'Sorry, Mol. It's just been a trying day,' he apologised, sighing deeply. When he put down the telephone he felt nauseous. Unable to focus on his work he pulled on his jacket and left the office early, not caring what his boss thought. He didn't want to work much longer in the City anyway. The sooner he returned to Polperro the better. He certainly didn't want to be in London if Federica and Torquil were married.

He took the tube to Hyde Park Corner and walked around Hyde Park, kicking the leaves and scowling at the squirrels in fury. When it began to rain he stood in the shelter of one of the stone follies, watching miserably as the grey skies opened around him. He couldn't understand why he minded so much that Federica was getting married. After all, he had had his opportunity and let it go. He had kissed her then left her. He consoled himself that he didn't want to be in a relationship, any relationship. He didn't want to be tied down. If Federica were free he still wouldn't make a play for her. He just didn't want anyone else to have her. When he walked through the drizzle back to his flat he felt much better. So Federica was marrying Torquil, what of it? There were many more fish in the sea.

For a while Sam managed to convince himself that he no longer cared for Federica, but the moment he came face to face with Torquil Jensen he was unable to pretend any longer. All his instincts screamed out against the marriage, which, in his opinion, was doomed to fail before it had even started. But no one else seemed to see it like he did.

Torquil and Federica arrived at Toby's house on a Friday night. He had insisted they drive down, stopping on the way at small inns and pubs for the odd break and refreshments. As they weaved along the winding lanes, Torquil felt an odd sense of *déjà vu*.

'I know I've been here before,' he stated, staring out in front of him at the winter hedgerows and bare trees, wondering why it all looked so familiar.

'Probably in a past life,' Federica suggested with a shrug. 'We might have been lovers then too.'

'No,' he insisted seriously, 'I really have been here and it's bugging me.'

Federica shook her head and thought nothing more about it. She was barely able to sit still in her excitement to show her fiancé off to the family. When they pulled up outside Toby and Julian's cottage Torquil tooted the horn. Toby appeared and stood jovially in the doorway while Rasta bounded out to greet them with unrestrained enthusiasm.

'Welcome,' Toby said, smiling warmly. Julian appeared behind him to capture the moment on film. It was then that Torquil remembered why he was so sure that he knew this place. He still had that Polaroid of Lucia which Julian had taken. He took a deep breath and stepped out of the Porsche. He hoped their memory of him had faded with the years; if his recollections were correct it hadn't been a very positive introduction.

Jake and Polly were the first to arrive for dinner. Jake was mistrustful of 'townies' and believed that Federica should marry someone from Polperro. 'She's been uprooted enough in her life, what she needs is stability and to be around the people and place that she's used to. Still, he deserves a chance to prove he's qualified to take care of her,' he conceded as they drove up to the house.

Polly agreed with him, and nodded her head thoughtfully. 'I just wish he wasn't so old,' she sighed. 'It's nice when two people can grow up together. He'll be an old man before she's touched middle age, which is a shame.'

When they entered the sitting room, Torquil jumped to his feet and extended his hand warmly. They were both immediately disarmed by the beauty of his face and the charm of his wide smile.

Polly returned his smile with gusto. 'It's such a pleasure to meet you,' she gushed, not immune to the appeal of a handsome young man. Jake was more reserved, though thrown by the perfection of his features, and watched Torquil through narrowed eyes, endeavouring not to be influenced by his looks.

But even Jake was easily conquered when Torquil placed an affectionate hand on Federica's and looked him straight in the eye, stating earnestly, 'I only have one priority, Mr Trebeka, and that is to make Fede as happy and secure as I can.'

Jake's old heart surrendered and he nodded his submission. 'Well, as you can see, Torquil, she has a close and loving family. Don't let her stray too far from her home, that way she can enjoy her new life with you *and* the security that lies in her roots.' Then he added gruffly, 'And please call me Jake.'

When Arthur, Helena and Hal arrived the sitting room was already vibrating with laughter. Hal had lingered by the Porsche, loving the owner even before he had met him. 'Wow, he must be really cool to have a car like this!' he exclaimed, hurrying in to meet him. Helena noticed immediately the physical similarities between Torquil and Ramon, but also the differences – Torquil's face lacked the rugged character of Ramon's; it was too polished and smooth. However, she couldn't help but relinquish her reservations in the glare of such magnificence. He was not only tall and good-looking but his clothes were immaculate, from his cashmere jacket to his well-polished brown shoes. Taking a seat next to Federica on the club fender she winked her approval. Federica beamed with happiness.

Only Arthur's suspicions simmered beneath the surface of his cheerfulness.

Helena was placed next to Torquil at dinner. Looking into her eager eyes he told her how he wanted, more than anything in the world, to make her daughter happy. 'I can see where she gets her beauty from. You and she could almost be sisters,' he said, watching her cheeks ignite with pleasure.

'She's very vulnerable, Torquil, and really too young to marry,' she replied, sipping her wine. 'But you're older and wiser and I have no doubt you will make her very happy. What she needs is security; something a younger man would be incapable of giving her. I have to admit, when I first heard about you I did worry that you'd be too old for her and that the whole thing was being rushed unnecessarily. But, now I know you I can see exactly why she doesn't want to wait. Why should you both wait when you are so sure of the way you feel? Marriage is a gamble however long you've known each other. But I think I'd put money on you two.'

'Torquil, can you give me a spin in your car after dinner?' Hal asked, shouting across the noisy table.

'You bet,' Torquil replied. Then he took the opportunity to give a small speech. 'I just want to say that when I fell in love with Fede, I never anticipated falling in love with the whole of her family, but I have been pleasantly surprised.' He cast his eyes around the table of hot faces and glistening eyes and paused, gazing down at Federica, apparently unafraid to show his emotion. 'I want to thank you all for making me feel so welcome and for Federica, because I know that each of you have had a large part to play in making her what she is today; the woman I love with all my heart.'

Polly stifled her tears with a gulp of wine while Helena grinned at Toby who nodded back his approval.

'You know, Torquil thinks he's been here before,' Federica declared in amusement.

'No, I got it wrong, sweetness,' he replied quickly, 'I had one of those *déjà vus.*'

Julian looked at him and frowned.

'Actually, didn't I say, Toby, that the name Torquil Jensen rang a bell?'

'You can't forget a name like Torquil, can you?' Federica giggled.

'Well, I know I haven't been here before,' Torquil said carefully, 'because if I had I simply wouldn't have left.'

Toby raised his glass with a chuckle. 'Well said, Torquil,' he applauded. 'Welcome to the family.' They all raised their glasses.

Only Arthur hesitated before he too lifted his to toast their guest with the others. He couldn't put his finger on it, but there was something not quite right about Torquil. He was altogether too perfect.

The following day Torquil and Federica were invited to lunch at Pickthistle Manor to meet the Applebys. Ingrid approved of Federica's choice immediately because he didn't wince at the sight of the wounded stoat which limped nonchalantly across the hall and he patted the dogs with enthusiasm.

Inigo had locked himself in his study asking to be disturbed only under the unlikely circumstances of a house fire, so Ingrid apologised on his behalf and led their guest into the large sitting room where an open fire danced in the chimney beneath a wistful portrait of Violet, Ingrid's mother, and a dusty mantelpiece clustered with curiosities.

Nuno shook the young man's hand and sniffed at him warily while Hester bounded over excitedly and Molly played hard to get, languishing on the sofa, pretending not to notice him. Sam wandered in grimly and kissed Federica on her cheek before nodding to Torquil with an arrogance that ill-suited him. Torquil disguised his aversion behind a friendly smile and nodded back affably before turning away and talking to Hester.

Sam wasn't fooled. He loathed him immediately.

'I don't trust him,' he hissed to Nuno. 'He's too smooth.

There's a portrait of him with all his imperfections hidden away in some attic somewhere, I'm telling you.'

'Ah, a Dorian Grey, perhaps. He's certainly beautiful,' Nuno replied as he watched Ingrid, Hester and Molly turn pink under the brilliance of Torquil's physical perfection.

'God, they're such simpletons,' Sam scorned. 'Why is it that women are so dazzled by looks? It's pathetic.'

Nuno scrutinised his grandson and sniffed knowingly. 'Are you perhaps not a trifle jealous, dear boy?'

Sam shook his head and put his hands in his pockets. 'Certainly not. She's like a sister, I feel protective,' he insisted, smarting at the sight of Federica basking in Torquil's reflected glory.

'Ah,' sighed Nuno with a smile. '"O! beware, my lord, of jealousy, It is the green–ey'd monster which doth mock the meat it feeds on."'

'Shakespeare's *Othello*,' said Sam flatly. 'But I assure you, Nuno, I don't covet Fede for myself. I'm just loath to see her falling into the wrong hands.'

'You can't live people's lives for them, dear boy, they have to suffer their own mistakes and learn. We all do.'

'I know, but it's hard to stand back and watch it happen,' he admitted bleakly.

'Nothing in the world would convince Federica today that Torquil is not all that he seems – if, indeed, he does deceive. Keep your thoughts to yourself. Nothing will come of honesty but bitterness.'

Sam sat through lunch watching Torquil holding forth while the women in the family laughed in admiration at every lame joke he delivered. Once or twice Torquil locked eyes with his aggressor, but it was he who turned away first.

He knows I can see straight through him, Sam thought to himself, *the fool!* Federica noticed Sam's silence and felt her enthusiasm dissipate as if his muted disapproval were sucking her energies dry. After lunch they all decided to go for a walk.

'Are you coming with us, Sam?' Federica asked hopefully.

But Sam shook his head. 'I've got things to do,' he replied. *Better things to do than listen to Torquil's oafish jokes*, he thought sourly, and left the room for Nuno's study.

Nuno's study had the benefit of being situated on a corner of the house. One half looked out onto the garden, the other onto the front. Sam stood by the window watching Torquil play with the dogs, who mobbed around on the grass in front of Molly, Hester and Ingrid.

'I adore dogs, Ingrid,' Torquil was saying, patting their soft heads. 'These two are really special.'

'Dog lovers are good people,' she replied, 'you can always be certain of a person's true nature if he likes dogs.' She wrapped her long cardigan about her body. 'If you're going to walk on the cliffs, I suggest you borrow a coat, Torquil.'

'No thank you, I have one in the car, I'll just go and get it,' he said, leaving the girls to chat among themselves. Sam watched him disappear through the archway and out to where his car was parked on the gravel. He wandered over to the other window. Torquil stalked across the driveway to his Porsche, followed eagerly by Trotsky and Amadeus who sniffed and sprung about his feet. To Sam's surprise Torquil turned on them with impatience.

'Stupid dogs. Piss off,' he growled, shunting Amadeus out of the way with a firm nudge of his shoe. Amadeus shrank momentarily before believing it to be a game and trotted back for some more. 'Bloody animals!' he continued, opening the boot and pulling out his coat. Trotsky lifted his ears in bewilderment and backed away leaving Amadeus to jump up onto Torquil's neatly pressed corduroy trousers with muddy paws. Torquil was furious. He swore again and smacked the spaniel around the face. 'You do that again and I'll eat you for dinner,' he scowled, before marching back through the arch to where the girls eagerly awaited him.

Sam was left floundering by the window, amazed at what he had just witnessed. He wanted to tell Federica immediately, but who would believe him? He sat down in Nuno's leather chair and watched the fire smoulder in the grate. *Over my dead body will he get Federica up the aisle*, he thought to himself, but he didn't have the first idea how he was going to stop him.

Chapter Thirty-Three

Everyone loved Torquil. He had swept into Polperro like a victorious conqueror, winning over everyone he met, slaying them all with his straight white teeth and lucid eyes. Only Sam and Arthur remained suspicious, forming a silent resistance, unwilling to be deceived. But no one else seemed able to see beyond the charm. Nuno was too absorbed in the works of Stendhal to look, the women were all too smitten even to try and Federica's family were so deeply enamoured with Torquil's glamour that they didn't give Arthur the opportunity to state his case. There was only one option open to both of them, but Nuno had warned Sam against speaking to Federica. He fretted away in a fever of irritation feeling powerless as Federica buzzed deliriously about the web of a very shrewd spider. But Arthur had less to lose – his stepdaughter had disliked him right from the start.

He managed to find a suitable moment on Sunday, when Torquil was being shown the Cornish coast in Toby's boat, accompanied by Jake, Hal and Julian. Federica hadn't wanted to go, preferring to spend some time with her grandmother in the kitchen, preparing the lunch in order to impress her fiancé. Helena sat in the rocking-chair beneath a canopy of hanging miniature ships, sipping a Bloody Mary and discussing wedding plans, while her mother and daughter sweated about the Aga with steaming pots of vegetables and treacle tart. After a while Federica wandered into the sitting room to find Arthur alone by the fire reading the papers. She pulled a polite smile.

'How's the cooking going?' Arthur asked, folding the newspaper and placing it on the sofa beside him.

Federica hovered by the door, reluctant to embark on a conversation with her stepfather. 'Fine,' she replied impassively.

'I can't imagine you'll ever have to cook at home once you're married,' he said and watched her carefully.

'Oh, I'll still cook, I've cooked all my life.' Then she looked at him quizzically. 'You don't like Torquil, do you?'

Arthur sighed and sat back against the cushions. He shook his head. 'I'm afraid I don't trust him, Fede,' he replied, fixing her with his sharp brown eyes.

She shuffled uncomfortably, then placed a defiant hand on her hip. 'What is there to mistrust?'

'It's too soon, Fede,' he argued. 'You've known him all of a few months, why do you have to marry him right now? What's wrong with spending time together first? That in itself makes me suspicious.'

'We love each other,' she insisted crossly.

'What do you know of love, Fede? You have no experience. He's the first man who's swept you off your feet. He's handsome, rich, charming, what else do you know about him?'

'I don't need to know anything else about him. You and Mama aren't exactly the epitome of the perfect marriage,' she retorted defensively.

He folded his arms and chuckled. 'We have our problems, of course. Marriage isn't a treacle tart, Fede. I'm concerned because I care about you.'

'No you don't, you care about Hal,' she snapped impulsively, then wished she hadn't said it. Not because it wasn't true, but because it was a childish response and she was trying desperately hard to present herself as an adult. 'Anyway,' she continued defiantly, 'try as hard as you like to find fault with him, I promise you, you won't find it. He's perfect. That's what gets up your nose.'

'That's not true,' Arthur replied patiently. He wanted to ask her what Torquil, a sophisticated, urbane man of thirty-eight, would want with a provincial eighteen-year-old of limited experience, but he knew that would hurt her. He simply added that he was concerned by the speed of the romance. 'If Torquil's got nothing to hide what's the harm in waiting a few more months? I'm troubled by his urgency.'

'It's called *love*, Arthur,' she replied sarcastically and rolled her eyes in exasperation. 'Look, I really don't want to discuss this any more. Mama likes him, in fact, everyone likes him but you. The truth is I don't care what you think,' she said and stalked out.

When she returned to the kitchen she decided not to mention it to her mother or grandmother – she didn't want to dwell on negative things. This was the happiest time of her life and she wasn't going to let her interfering stepfather ruin it for her. He had always disliked her, right from the start.

When the men returned, red-faced from the wind and their laughter, Torquil retreated upstairs to change for lunch. Federica rushed about the kitchen with excitement, putting finishing touches with the same enthusiasm she had once reserved for her father. Toby and Julian stood by the fire telling Jake and Helena about the giant crab that had nearly sent Torquil overboard.

'He didn't like the look of it, but give him his due he's a man who can laugh at himself!' Toby chuckled.

Arthur wandered into the drinks room to pour himself something strong. He rattled a cube of ice about his glass in agitation before filling it with whisky. He looked out of the French doors onto the winter garden and felt a bleak foreboding gnaw at his gut. His talk with his stepdaughter had been worse than disastrous. Lunch would be awkward. With a sinking spirit he opened the door and walked grimly onto the terrace. He breathed in the bitter air and watched his breath rise up on the cold as he exhaled. Then to his astonishment he heard a low voice in the window above him. Creeping back against the wall he listened with deliberation as Torquil continued a private conversation on his mobile telephone, leaning out of the window for better reception. '. . . The wedding will be the last time I find myself in this godforsaken backwater . . . She loves the city, believe me, she's too good for these provincial people . . . I'm rescuing her from a life of dogs and crabs, I've caught her just in time too. Poor girl, imagine growing up here, no wonder she's so grateful I'm marrying her . . . Don't start on that again, babe, I've told you, I love her to distraction . . . So, she's not worldly like you, that's why I like her. She's pure and innocent, untouched. I don't want someone else's cast-off . . . Just wait until you meet her, then you'll understand . . . You don't work in that department, you work in the basement and that's where I like you.' He laughed throatily. 'That's where you like to be . . . Look, I'd better go. The sooner we have lunch the sooner we can leave.'

Arthur held his breath for fear of being heard and waited a moment before he dared open the door and slip back inside. He felt physically sick, but worse than his nausea was his anger because he had nowhere to vent it. No one would listen.

Feigning a headache he sat quietly through lunch while Torquil acted the perfect guest, expressing his love of Polperro and the sea, forging a false bond with the family Arthur knew he despised. Watching Federica was like witnessing a car crash in slow motion. There was nothing he could do to prevent it.

While Arthur and Sam smarted in the wake of Torquil's triumphant visit, Federica moved into his luxurious house in The Little Boltons. It was exquisite, decorated by one of the top London designers with rich fabrics and expensive paintings. 'I can't believe I'm going to live here for ever,' she breathed in excitement, throwing herself onto the bed.

'Not only that, but you're going to have my name and then my children. We'll fill this house with the patter of tiny feet,' he said, lying beside her and kissing her forehead lovingly.

'Oh, Torquil. I've never been so happy,' she said, holding his face in her hands. 'You're everything I've ever hoped for.'

'And you're a dream come true, I've been looking for you all my life,' he said, smiling down at her. 'You're so good, Fede. I'm not worthy of you. You're sweet and sensitive. You're like an angel. Pure like white sugar. I don't know what you see in me. I'm full of imperfections.'

She gazed deliriously into his pale eyes and wondered why Arthur mistrusted him; he had the most trustworthy expression she had ever encountered.

Later when she admired the tidy cupboards full of Chanel suits, Ferragamo shoes, Ralph Lauren casual wear, La Perla underwear and Tiffany jewellery, she noticed that everything had been bought for her by Torquil. When she asked him where all her old clothes had gone he told her that he had given them to Mrs Hughes, the housekeeper.

'Her daughter is your age and they have very little money, sweetness. Besides, you're different now you're with me,' he explained, drawing her into his arms. 'You're shedding your old skin along with your old name. You're going to be Mrs Torquil Jensen and I want you to have the very best of everything.'

Although she would like him to have asked her first, she didn't want to appear ungrateful. She replied simply that he was too generous and that she was undeserving of him. His obvious delight and approval allayed her fears and her spirits rose again. She wanted nothing more than to please him. When she admired her new maturity in the mirror she marvelled at the distance she had come since that morning in Viña, now over ten years ago, when she had gazed upon her childish reflection with distaste. After so many disappointments, she deserved Torquil.

She longed to share her news with her father, but she resented the fact that he hadn't communicated in years. In spite of her joy she felt desperately let down. Now she had Torquil she no longer searched for happiness within the glittering splendour of the butterfly box. She didn't need to. The shadows of the past were exchanged for the brightness of her new life. She didn't need her memories any more; she was going to build new ones with Torquil. So she placed the box at the top of a cupboard and closed the door.

★　　★　　★

Sam had spent the night before Federica's wedding in Nuno's leather chair re-reading Alexandre Dumas' *The Count of Monte Cristo*, the most satisfactory story of revenge ever written. The early birds had awoken him at dawn. He had looked about, bewildered that he had managed to sleep on such a night. He rubbed his weary eyes and gazed out of the window onto a fragile foggy morning. The garden was draped in a tender summer mist like a tent of glittering cobwebs. A frail mist that held in the sheer transience of its nature the promise of a magnificent sunny day.

For Sam it promised nothing but misery.

When Nuno shuffled in at eight he found his grandson staring out of the window in gloom. 'I would like to think it was one of my tomes that has kept you up all night,' he said, glancing down at the heavy book on Sam's knee.

Sam turned around slowly and blinked up at his grandfather. 'I'd like to lock Torquil Jensen in the Chateau d'If,' he groaned.

'Ah!' Nuno sighed knowingly and nodded his head. 'Young Federica's getting married today.'

'Quite,' Sam replied, removing his glasses and cleaning them on his shirt.

' "Love is the wisdom of the fool and the folly of the wise," ' Nuno said and raised a thick eyebrow.

'Nuno, I don't have the patience for this today, but to satisfy the demands of your ego I'll tell you it's William Cook, *Life of Samuel Foote*.'

'*Molto bene, caro*. Even in times of great despair you are able to keep your wits about you and indulge an old man.'

'I'm not in love with Fede, Nuno, I've told you before, I just don't want to see her hurt.' Then he added crossly, 'I don't think I can go to the church, the sight of Torquil Jensen's self-regard might just push me to do something I'll later regret.'

'Dear boy, if you cannot recognise your anger as fuelled by jealousy you're less of a man than I thought you were. If you ask me, you had that gentle creature's admiration for years and you chose to reject it. Now pull yourself together and accept defeat

411

with honour. I suggest a bowl of porridge and a cup of tea, then put on your coat and come along to the church with the rest of us, with good grace. These things are sent to test us and this might be your biggest test yet, I trust you don't want to fail.'

So Sam ate his porridge in silence while the excited chatter of his sisters and mother grated on his nerves and pushed him further into his troubled thoughts. Joey wandered in from the garden with a gigantic toad cupped in his trembling hands, explaining that he had found him drowning in the swimming pool. When Ingrid attempted to take the creature from him the toad leapt into the air with the zeal of an acrobat and proceeded to jump about the kitchen floor, outwitting everyone's efforts to catch him.

'Oh, leave him,' Ingrid sighed wearily, pouring herself another cup of tea. 'He'll find his way back to the pond without our help. I think Mr Toad is quite capable of looking after himself!'

Molly and Hester were to be bridesmaids, or as Molly preferred to put it: 'maids of honour'.

'I wish I were marrying Torquil Jensen instead of walking five steps behind the bride,' Hester sighed enviously. 'I can't believe Fede's luck.'

'Fede of all people!' Molly exclaimed, shaking her head in wonder that a man such as Torquil could fall for someone like Federica, when she was so much more attractive and charismatic. *It should be me*, she thought to herself resentfully.

'Oh wake up!' Sam snapped suddenly, rising from his chair. Molly and Hester both stared at him in confusion. 'Don't either of you have the intelligence to see past his pretty face? It doesn't surprise me that Hester's been fooled, but Mol, I always thought you were more perceptive. Torquil Jensen would be more suited to one of those crass American soap operas. What is it you girls used to watch? *Dallas*? In a language you both understand, he's no Bobby Ewing!' And with that he left the room.

The two sisters blinked at each other in amazement. 'Have I missed something here?' said Molly, putting down her mug.

Hester shrugged her shoulders. 'If you have, Mol, then I

certainly have,' she replied, baffled. 'What has *Dallas* got to do with Fede's wedding?'

'Torquil Jensen might be many things, but he's no JR either.' She sniffed angrily. 'How dare he accuse me of lacking perception. God damn him, he's always believed himself to be cleverer than everyone else.'

'He might be cleverer than Torquil, but Torquil's got all the beauty,' Hester giggled.

'That's obviously what's got under Sam's skin. It's all about hair,' Molly laughed scornfully. 'Sam's losing his and Torquil's got plenty!'

Sam sat stiffly in the pew, ignoring Joey who quietly played with Mr Toad, having finally forced his surrender in the dog bowl. He watched the conceited profile of the groom with silent loathing. Torquil whispered to his best man, their heads inclined together like a couple of conspirators. Unable to bear the torment that sight evoked, he turned his eyes to the vast arrangements of white and yellow flowers and across to the other side of the aisle where Torquil's grand friends sat under ostentatious hats, glancing warily about them at what must have appeared a very parochial scene. Reverend Boyble rushed about importantly, bowing low to the altar every time he passed in front of it. Finally, Torquil's father and stepmother appeared and walked down the aisle with great ceremony. Sam took one look at Mrs Jensen's hat and thought of the Quangle Wangle Quee. He shook his head at the vulgarity of it and caught Nuno's eye. His grandfather smiled wryly and scribbled something down on a bit of paper, then passed it to Lucien, who passed it to Ingrid, who leant across her distracted youngest and handed it to Sam. He opened it and laughed out loud. Nuno had read his thoughts exactly for he had quoted from the same poem by Edward Lear: 'And the Golden Grouse came there, and the Pobble who had no toes and the small Olympian bear, and the Dong with the luminous nose

. . . all came and built on the lovely hat of the Quangle Wangle Quee.'

Buff Jensen sat in the pew behind his son. He was a large man with a wide forehead and thinning black hair combed back and set with wax to give the impression that he had more than he did. His eyes were pale and imperious, set in smooth skin unblemished by the usual lines of humour. Buff rarely smiled. He was too aware of his own importance and the need to show it. Torquil turned around and grinned at his father, a grin that betrayed his triumph as well as his genuine pride. Buff had hoped for a better match for his son and relinquishing control was hard for him to accept. But this small battle Torquil had won. Cynthia only saw the pride in her stepson's smile. He was marrying the girl he loved, there was no doubt about that. She had liked his little bride very much. Had she been a stronger character she might have felt competitive, but Federica would make the perfect daughter-in-law – provided one managed to forget where she came from.

After a short pause Federica's family made their way to their seats with less ceremony than the Jensens. Helena wore a pink suit with a pill-box hat to match and Polly wore red – they obviously hadn't planned their outfits together. When Helena saw the vast expanse of Mrs Jensen's creation she winced with rivalry and wished she had had the courage to wear something bigger. She also caught herself longing for Ramon – Arthur's unimposing presence impressed no one. When Mrs Hammond's hesitant fingers alighted on the keyboard, the idle chat was reduced to an expectant silence as everyone stood up and looked behind them to catch the first glimpse of the bride.

Federica hovered momentarily under the archway at the entrance of the church, before stepping out of the sun into the soft light of the nave. Sam was suddenly gripped with regret. He stood as still as marble, the blood drained from his stunned face, and felt the sharp claws of love tighten about his heart. It was as if the world had frozen around him, only Federica moved slowly towards him with the unearthly countenance of an angel. He barely dared breathe. It was only when Mr Toad escaped Joey's grip and sprung onto the wooden bench behind him before leaping into the aisle that Sam was shaken from his trance and realised to his despair that Federica wasn't walking towards him but away from him. She was walking way beyond his reach and he only had himself to blame. The clouds parted in his memory and he pictured their tender kisses in the barn and her golden face on the hill and he almost choked with misery.

Jake watched with pride as his son led Federica up the aisle and wiped a damp eye at the recollection of his daughter's wedding that he had missed. Helena caught her breath, for Federica floated on the arm of her brother like a princess with diamonds in her hair and a choker of diamonds and pearls about her neck. The ivory dress shimmered in the heavenly light that flooded in through the stained-glass windows and her skin seemed to glow with a translucence not of this world. Helena thought of Ramon until the tears stung her eyes and the memory of him became so strong that she could almost smell him. Arthur squeezed her hand, which wrenched her back to the reality of her dull marriage and the tears flowed more abundantly.

Arthur wanted to cry too – tears of fury and frustration, but he could not, so he sat with grim resignation as his stepdaughter walked past to embrace her destiny.

Ingrid's heart sighed at the beauty of the music and Inigo abandoned himself to the positive vibrations of God's house and took his wife's hand in his as he remembered their own wedding all those years ago.

But Nuno watched Sam. He understood his grandson better than the boy understood himself. He saw the anger in the line of his petulant mouth and the hurt behind his stormy grey eyes and wanted to tell him that everything comes to those who wait.

Sam felt he was watching a public hanging; the sacrifice of the innocent. He watched Torquil with the eyes of a predator, studying his every move, his every blink. There was something sinister in the shine of his shoes, the spotless coat, the starched shirt, the gold watch on the perfect chain, the emerald cufflinks. Not even a strand of hair disobeyed him and strayed over his forehead. Sam watched Federica, tremulous and radiant, in the dress Torquil had chosen for her, the jewels he had given her – only her shy smile was still hers, but Torquil grinned down at her poised to possess that too.

Julian had returned to his place on the end of a pew after having taken the photographs outside the church. He put his camera under the seat and proceeded to watch the ceremony. After a while his attention was caught by a dark-haired woman seated on the other side of the aisle to him. She was sleek and confident in a tight, duck-egg blue suit with her long brown legs crossed, tapping her manicured fingers along to the music. She sensed she was being watched and glanced at him from under her wide-brimmed hat. When she saw it was Julian, she smiled. 'I still have your shirt,' she mouthed. He shuddered as he suddenly remembered where he had seen Torquil before. Those two painfully self-satisfied people he had taken great trouble to forget now surfaced in his thoughts. But it was Federica's wedding day, neither the time nor the place for negative recollections. Perhaps Torquil had grown up since those days, he certainly hoped so. He watched as the ring was slipped onto Federica's finger and Reverend Boyble declared the happy couple man and wife. She belonged to him now. She had left the cove for the wider sea.

Sam lowered his eyes in defeat and noticed Mr Toad staring up at him expectantly from the stone floor. He bent down and gathered the blinking creature into his hands where he held him steadily. 'It's just you and me now,' he said quietly, shaking his head. Then as he watched Torquil's stepmother walk by he changed his mind and placed the sleepy toad onto her hat and grinned.

He hadn't been able to stop the wedding, but this small act of sabotage gave him a shallow sense of pleasure.

Chapter Thirty-Four

Sam returned to his meaningless job in the City and Helena to the dry residue of her marriage, but for Federica, life would never be the same again.

As soon as she returned bronzed and happy from her honeymoon, she rang up Harriet and booked in for lunch. Slipping into the waiting Mercedes in a new Gucci trouser suit she told the driver where to go, then sat back and savoured her new affluence. The seats were leather, the dashboard polished wood. Federica had never learnt to drive. Torquil didn't encourage her. He insisted she have a chauffeur and organised a car for her. 'I want you to have the best of everything,' he had explained. 'Because I love and cherish you.' She rolled the window down and watched the sweltering, dusty city from the cool comfort of her car. She felt sophisticated and glamorous and her spirits floated on the sweet air of her expensive perfume. She fingered the large emerald ring that Torquil had given her and smiled to herself with perfectly painted lips. She was Mrs Torquil Jensen. To Federica the sound of that name had a glorious resonance and she whispered it to herself a few times, Mrs Torquil Jensen, Mrs Torquil Jensen. How far she had come from her uncertain beginnings in Polperro.

The honeymoon had been idyllic. They had spent a week in Africa on safari, a week on the coast and the final two weeks in Thailand. They had stayed in the most prestigious hotels, hired the best guides and travelled first class. Federica had been enchanted by everything she saw and Torquil had enjoyed watching her absorb each new experience after experience like a proud father. But most of all she had savoured their quiet moments together as husband and wife, when he had made love to her in the humid heat of the African jungle and in the jasmine-scented rooms of Thailand. There he had taught her to listen to the calling of her own sensuality and to abandon herself to it. To lose herself in the pleasure of his caresses without inhibition or guilt. When she had found it difficult to discard her shyness he had tied her to the four bedposts so that she had no choice but to give in to her senses and ride unrestrained on the waves of his stroking. At first she had been horrified by the idea, he had never suggested anything like that before. But Torquil had laughed at her inexperience and with gentle persuasion she had agreed to playfully experiment as long as it was done with love. She now blushed at such recollections although she was secretly proud of her new worldliness.

The car drew up outside the doors of St John & Smithe. The doorman hurried down the steps to assist her. 'Ah, Mrs Jensen,' he said in surprise. 'Good morning,' he added reverently, tapping his hat with his hand.

'Thank you, Peter,' she replied as he closed the car door behind her. He didn't comment on her return or make a joke about her sudden rise up in the world. He was too polite. Now she was Mrs Torquil Jensen an invisible wall had grown up between them. Federica Campione belonged to the other side.

When Harriet saw Federica she barely recognised her friend. She was the colour of milk chocolate and her white hair had been bleached further by the sun. She looked so elegant that Harriet had to suppress a pang of jealousy. 'Darling girl, you look fantastic. Marriage obviously suits you,' she enthused, embracing her.

'I love it,' Federica replied with relish, clasping her hands together like a child with a new toy. 'I'm deliriously happy.'

'I can't believe you share a bed every night with Torquil. I hate you,' she laughed. Harriet played with the string of pearls about her neck then shook her head and added more seriously, 'If

I couldn't have him, m'darling, I'm happy he's with someone I know and love.'

'Please don't become a nun!' Federica said, taking her by the hand. 'You really were very fond of him, weren't you?'

Harriet nodded sadly but smiled in spite of her disappointment. 'Yes, I was,' she admitted. 'I always made it out to be a bit of a joke, but . . .'

'Many a true thing is said in jest,' Federica interrupted.

'Spot on.'

'So, are you able to have a quick lunch?' she asked.

Harriet looked around furtively. 'You'll have to ask. Greta's smarting over your wedding,' she hissed, casting her eyes to the closed door of Greta's office. 'I'm going to love watching this confrontation.'

'No one's going to enjoy it more than me,' Federica grinned, pulling herself up in preparation to returning with interest the unkindness her boss had shown her during her short time as salesgirl. 'Go and tell her I'm here,' she said and watched Harriet stalk purposefully across the floor to Greta's office.

Federica looked around at her old workplace, which was now, in effect, her family business. She felt a deep sense of satisfaction and power and resolved to use every ounce of it to humiliate Greta. However, when Greta appeared Federica lost the will to hurt her. It was too easy and besides she had already won. She suddenly remembered one of Nuno's most favourite philosophies, 'What goes around comes around', vengeance was not hers to take.

Greta swallowed hard and smiled with her mouth, leaving her eyes to betray her discomfort. Her face was grey like a bruised apple revealing her unhappiness in every line. She no longer had the power to intimidate.

'Congratulations, Federica,' Greta said tightly.

'Thank you.'

'I hear from Mr Jensen that your wedding was beautiful.'

'It was,' she said, noticing the effort Greta was making to sound enthusiastic, a characteristic that came as unnaturally to her as benevolence. 'I'd like to take Harriet out to lunch, Greta, you don't mind if she takes more than an hour, do you?'

Greta pursed her pale lips together and shook her head. 'Of course not.' Then she laughed uncomfortably and added, 'You're the boss.'

Federica took Harriet to lunch at Oriels in Sloane Square. They laughed at Federica's meeting with Greta and at the absurdity of her sudden change in status.

'I love it,' admitted Federica. 'I feel like a modern-day Cinderella. You know, he's generous to a fault. I can have anything I want. I used to dream of being rich.'

'So what will you do this afternoon?' Harriet asked.

'I don't know. I'm going to have to discuss this with Torquil. I understand that I can't work in the family shop, that would be absurd, but I'd like to be busy. I'd ideally like to do something with my photography. Julian taught me the basics, perhaps I could do a more advanced course and then make a trade of it.'

'That would be wonderful. You've always wanted to be a photographer,' Harriet enthused.

'Mama said I had to earn money before embarking on that sort of career. Well, now I have more money than I dreamed of, I can do anything I like.' She laughed and grinned at her friend who smiled back enviously.

'Darling girl, you are so lucky.' Harriet sighed. 'But no one deserves it more than you.'

That evening, when Torquil returned from work, they had their first serious discussion.

'Now we're back from our honeymoon, Torquil, I'd like to settle into something. I'd like to work,' Federica said, throwing herself onto the sofa in his study.

Torquil wandered over to the drinks table and poured himself a tumbler of whisky. 'Would you like a drink, a glass of wine, perhaps?' he asked. 'They say a glass of red wine a day makes a lady glow. Not that you're not glowing already.'

She laughed. 'A glass of red would be nice, thank you,' she replied.

He handed it to her then sat down in the armchair, putting one foot up on the stool. 'Why do you want to work, sweetness?'

'Well, I have to do something,' she argued, taking a sip of wine. 'Darling, this is delicious.'

'Part of the wedding present from Arthur,' he said. 'He's got very good taste that stepfather of yours.'

'Only in some things,' she replied dryly. 'In others, believe me, he has no taste at all.'

'You're a rich woman now, Fede, you don't need to work,' he said seriously.

'Well, I'll get bored if I don't do something,' she explained. 'It's not for the money. You're more than generous and I really appreciate that. It's to fill my day with, to have a reason to get up every morning.'

'Isn't loving me good enough reason to get up in the morning?' Torquil chuckled.

'You know what I mean,' she insisted jovially.

'You'll be busy soon with babies,' he said and smiled at her tenderly.

'Perhaps,' she replied, hoping God would preserve her from that for at least a few more years. 'But, say I don't get pregnant, surely you don't want me to languish here doing nothing?'

'Sweetness,' he said firmly, 'you have a beautiful house, beautiful clothes, a husband who loves the ground you walk on, what more do you want?' He frowned at her and she immediately felt guilty wanting more.

'Well,' she mumbled, suddenly feeling an uncomfortable sense of uncertainty turn her stomach over. 'Julian gave me photography lessons when I was younger, if you don't want me to work, perhaps I can do a course?'

'If you have to do something,' he conceded reluctantly, 'a course is the only option. No wife of mine is going to work.'

'Thank you,' she replied brightly, relieved the discussion was nearing a conclusive end.

'But not photography,' he added resolutely.

'Why not?' she argued in confusion.

He was no longer joking but looking at her very seriously. 'I'll get a tutor in to teach you whatever you want.' He looked about the room. 'Literature. Yes, you can take a literature course.'

'Literature?' she replied, crestfallen. 'I'm not at all interested in literature.'

'No, I'd like you to do literature,' he insisted, walking over to his bookshelves and pulling one out. 'I've never read any of these. I'd like you to read them.'

'Torquil,' she protested weakly.

'No, I insist,' he said. 'If you want to do a course, literature is the only acceptable one.'

'All right, I'll study literature,' she replied lamely. She'd rather do that than nothing at all.

'Then that's decided,' he said, draining his glass. 'Now, love of my life, come here and give me a kiss, I'd hate to think we've had a disagreement.'

When Federica sank into her bath she reflected on their conversation. She felt uneasy. But rather than trying to get to the bottom of her ill-ease she made excuses for her husband's reluctance to let her choose her own course. 'It's because he loves me and wants what's best for me,' she thought to herself as the bubbles began to dissolve with the soap. 'Photography can wait,' she resolved and decided to broach the subject again another time, when she was feeling more secure in her marriage.

Later, when Torquil wrapped her in a large white towel and made love to her, any remaining doubt melted away and all that was left was unconditional devotion and a strong desire to do anything in order to please him.

That night she dressed up and took her first step into what would become an endless round of cocktail parties and dinners. She met new faces, tried desperately to remember them all by name and quickly learnt how to adopt their social chitchat that said much without saying anything at all. Torquil always made sure she was the best-dressed woman in the room and smiled with pride when she was complimented. But he would become incandescent with rage if he felt she flirted with other men and forbade her to dance with anyone else, explaining that it was a humiliation for him watching another man rub himself up against his wife.

So Federica was careful not to step out of line. Instinctively she knew when he was watching her and modified her behaviour. If she saw his face cloud with jealousy she would move over and link her arm through his and stand by his side like a lovely appendage. When her instincts rebelled against his commands she told herself firmly that he was of another generation and altered her conduct accordingly.

'Everyone loves you, Fede,' said Torquil as they sat in the back of the car on their way home from a party. Federica smiled with pleasure. 'I'm so proud of you,' he added, running a hand down her cheek. 'You're beautiful and serene. I must have been told by at least ten people tonight how lucky I am to have found you.'

'Well, I'm lucky to have found you,' she replied, taking his hand in hers and kissing his fingers.

He then looked into her face for a long moment, as if searching her features for something. 'Are you lucky, sweetness?' he said, shaking his head. 'I don't know that you are.'

Federica frowned and laughed off his strange remark. Torquil noticed her anxiety and her effort to cover up. To his surprise it gave him a strange sense of satisfaction. But he was unable to interpret these new feelings or understand why he felt them. He was too insensitive to notice that he was beginning to resent his wife for all the reasons he married her. Her purity was beginning to grate, her perfection to irritate. She made him feel inadequate. He was unable to help himself put her down as if by pulling her off her marble pedestal he might raise himself up.

★   ★   ★

424

In an effort to exercise more control Torquil announced that he didn't approve of her friendship with Harriet. 'She's not sophisticated enough for you, sweetness. You're too intelligent to waste your affections on some old Sloane. You've moved on in the world, your friends have to change too. Now I've got someone in mind who I know you'll like,' he said happily. 'Lucia Sarafina.'

Lucia was only too happy to be of service. 'I'll befriend your wife if you make time to see me,' she bargained coquettishly when he telephoned her.

Torquil enjoyed the attention. 'She needs to be around women like you,' he said. 'She's too snow white.'

'I know what you mean,' Lucia agreed, delighted by the thought that his devotion might be waning. 'But she's young. She'll grow up.'

'With your help, *maestra*, I hope she will.'

'Leave it to me, darling. Then I want to be thanked in person, *capisci*?'

'*Capisco*.' He laughed. 'You're wicked.' Then he sighed heavily, a sigh that escaped his throat like a deep groan. 'God, I've missed you.'

'You don't have to,' she whispered. 'You know where to find me.'

'I'll hold that thought,' he replied, 'in the meantime you've got a job to do.'

Federica made a great effort to like Lucia. She had to in order to please her husband. Lucia invited her to Harry's Bar where they were given the best table in the far corner of the restaurant. 'Every man in this room will go straight home after lunch and make love to his wife,' Lucia mused in a smooth Italian accent, as Federica sat down. 'You see they're all looking at me. I make them feel lustful.' She sighed and licked her blood-red lips. 'You probably don't remember meeting me at the wedding. You had to be introduced to so many new people.'

'Of course I remember meeting you,' Federica said diplomatically. 'You're Torquil's closest friend.'

'We go back a long way,' she replied wistfully.

'How did you meet?'

'In Italy. I was living in Rome and Torquil came out for the wedding of a mutual friend. We clicked instantly,' she said, smoothing down the manicured cuticles on her nails with a steady hand, recalling their lovemaking in one of the dark halls of the palazzo.

'When did you move to London?'

'Shortly after,' she replied. 'Ah, the menu. Let's choose now then we can get down to some serious gossip. Bloody Mary please and my guest will have . . . ?' She looked at Federica and raised a black eyebrow.

'A Spritzer please,' Federica replied and thanked the waiter graciously.

'You don't know how happy it makes me to see Torquil so full of joy,' Lucia continued.

Federica smiled, 'I'm glad I make him happy,' she replied. 'He's made me happier than I ever thought possible.'

'Oh, he's a unique man,' Lucia agreed. 'I've never met a man so devoted. You're so pure and innocent. That's what he loves about you. Don't ever lose that quality,' she added silkily. 'You are very lucky. He's been in love many times before, but never the way he is with you.'

'How do you mean?'

'Well . . .' She deliberated, playing with a black strand of hair that flopped onto her shoulder like the tail of a fat rat. 'He always wanted to marry an innocent. Someone unspoiled, unworldly. Just like you. He dated sophisticates but he wanted his wife to be untouched by anyone else. That is your strength.'

'I see.' Federica nodded, fighting her unease.

Sensing her discomfort Lucia placed a soft hand on hers. 'I don't mean this as a criticism,' she gushed. 'He worships you, darling. He's never met anyone as perfect as you. He adores you. I'm only giving you advice, woman to woman. You have to be smart in this world to keep your man. You have to know what it is that they love about you and then hold onto it.'

'I can't stay young and innocent for ever,' Federica protested meekly.

'Oh, yes you can.' Lucia nodded and winked. The more 'snow white' Federica was the more Torquil would crave the dark sophistication of his Italian lover. 'You can be anything you want to be.'

Federica shrugged and pulled a thin smile. Lucia had left her feeling uncomfortable. She was becoming sick of being told how angelic and perfect she was. No one could live up to that.

'I'd love to be married to a man like Torquil,' Lucia sighed, pushing the salad around her plate dreamily. 'He's so totally in control. I love that. Unbelievably romantic. And so unusual for an Englishman. Italian men take control and it makes women feel very feminine.'

'Yes, although, sometimes, it's nice to be independent,' Federica argued, remembering their discussion about work and inwardly cringing.

'Don't be a little fool, Fede, you have a gem there, enjoy it,' said Lucia seriously. 'Millions of women would kill to leave their jobs, have their chaotic lives organised by a loving man. You don't know how lucky you are.'

'Oh, I do,' she replied quickly. 'It's just a bit overwhelming.'

'It's his way of showing you he loves you. You'll get used to it and then it will be second nature. Remember he has your interests at heart, always. Every choice he makes for you is for your own good. Goodness, he's, what, twenty years older than you?' Federica nodded. 'Twenty years more experience than you. If I were you I'd put my feet up and enjoy the ride.'

Federica took her advice. She stopped seeing Harriet and avoided going into St John & Smithe in case she bumped into her. She studied literature once a week with an old Cambridge don called Dr Lionel Swanborough, who always wore a three-piece suit with a fedora placed crookedly above his thin face. He was at once impressed with Torquil's library but unimpressed by Federica's lack of knowledge.

'I've barely read anything,' she told him. He gave her *Anna Karenina* and insisted she read the entire book in a week. 'Don't worry, my dear girl, once you've turned the first page the other eight hundred and fifty-two will turn by themselves.' He was right. Once she had analysed *Anna Karenina* she moved on to *Vanity Fair*, *Emma* and *King Lear*. Her eagerness for learning was bred in the boredom of her daily life as Torquil's wife, where she immersed herself in her studies so that she wouldn't notice the world outside her gilded prison and yearn for it.

One grey evening Torquil returned home yet again to his wife's light chatter echoing gaily through the rooms of the house as she attempted to fill the empty hours with long telephone conversations to her mother and Toby. He felt the irritation crawl up his neck in the form of an uncomfortable prickly heat that was becoming as familiar to him as the nagging sense of inadequacy he felt when faced with his wife's natural grace and virtue. His mouth twitched with impatience as he stalked into the sitting room, leaving his briefcase and coat thrown onto a chair in the hall. When Federica saw him standing crossly in the doorway she hastily put down the receiver and swallowed hard as her stomach turned over with anxiety.

'What's wrong?' she asked, hoping it had nothing to do with her. In the brief moment that passed while Torquil chewed on his jealousy Federica frantically cast her mind back to the previous evening in an attempt to remember anything she might have said to anyone that could have roused his anger.

'I'm fed up with coming home to find you on the telephone,' he snapped finally.

Federica breathed out with relief. 'I'm sorry,' she muttered.

But Torquil wasn't satisfied. He walked over to the fire and stood in front of it with his hands on his hips. He shook his head.

'I'm out at work all day, when I come home I want your undivided attention. You have hours to amuse yourself when I'm not here, why do you have to insist on calling your family at the exact moment I walk through the door?'

'I don't do it on purpose,' she protested weakly.

'Perhaps not,' he conceded. Federica stiffened. He often appeared to back down before delivering a harsher blow. 'Sweetness,' he continued carefully, 'I really think you're too old to still be so attached to your mother and uncle. It's about time you devoted your energies to me.'

'What do you mean?' she asked in bewilderment. He sat beside her on the sofa and ran a hand down her hair with tenderness. When she looked into his face his expression had softened and he was smiling at her with affection.

He sighed heavily. 'I'm a jealous old man, my darling,' he explained meekly. 'I'm guilty of loving you too much.'

Federica was disarmed by the sudden change in his tone and felt the colour rise in her cheeks. 'It's okay, Torquil, I understand,' she replied sympathetically.

'I miss you all day, when I come home to find you on the telephone to your mother this anger wells up inside me. I can't control it. I want you all to myself.' Then he chuckled sheepishly. 'Is that so terrible?'

Federica nestled her face against his hand that now stroked her cheek. 'Of course not,' she said and smiled, once more defeated by his charm. 'I won't do it again, I promise.'

He pulled her into his arms and kissed her on her mouth with an intensity that demonstrated his gratitude. 'You're too good to me, little one. No other woman would understand me like you do.'

She laughed and caressed his face with the gentle eyes of an adoring mother. 'No man would understand me like you do, either.'

'We're made for each other,' he breathed. 'You're happy, aren't you, sweetness? I want you to be happy.'

'Of course I am.'

'You enjoy your course?'

'I love it,' she enthused dutifully.

'You see,' he laughed. 'I know what's good for you better than you do.'

Even though Federica did as her husband had asked and made the calls when he was at work, he seemed to know exactly when they were made and for how long they lasted. In his silky manner he managed to persuade her to limit them to once a week. Molly and Hester went the way of Harriet. Although they put up a fiercer fight, Federica let them go in the end. She had to.

'You're too sophisticated now for these provincial people, sweetness,' Torquil said. 'You'll thank me one day.'

At first they journeyed down to Polperro regularly, but little by little their visits became less frequent until they barely went at all.

Federica felt powerless to complain for every time she made plans, Torquil flew her off to Paris or Madrid or Rome.

'Sweetheart, we never see you these days,' Toby lamented one day when Federica managed to call him from the telephone box in Harrods.

'I know, I'm longing to come down to Polperro, and so is Torquil,' she lied, 'he's just travelling so much at the moment, opening new offices abroad, so we spend most weekends out of the country.'

'I know we shouldn't worry, they always say newly-weds disappear into themselves for a while. It obviously means you're happy. You don't need your home like you used to.'

Federica's heart yearned for Polperro. She needed it more than ever, but she was barely able to admit it, even to herself.

'I *am* happy,' she insisted.

'Then we're happy you're happy. If you missed home all the

time that would surely mean there was something wrong with your marriage.'

'There's nothing wrong with that, I can assure you. He's so wonderful; I wake up every day hardly able to believe that I am so blessed to be married to someone so gorgeous. I don't deserve him.' Federica laughed.

'Yes you do, sweetheart.'

'I don't. He does everything for me. I don't have a care in the world. Mrs Hughes looks after the house, in fact she gets cross if I so much as move a photo frame. She's a little too territorial, but then I suppose she's looked after him for so long it's hardly surprising. She knows what he likes better than I do.'

'I doubt that. She's not married to him.'

'That's not what she thinks!' she joked. 'But I shouldn't complain. I live in the most beautiful house. Most men don't buy their wives expensive clothes and jewellery. Torquil indulges my every desire, I'm in great danger of turning into a spoilt princess.'

'Fede, nothing could ever turn you into that. You're a sweet girl and he's bloody lucky to have you. It all sounds so perfect!'

'It is. I do miss you all though,' she said softly and Toby noticed the strain in her voice, as if she were suppressing a cry for help. 'I miss Polperro and the sea, walks along the stormy cliffs with Rasta. Oh, I miss Rasta too, how is he?' she asked, attempting to sound cheerful.

'Missing you. We cuddle him a lot to compensate but he still looks at me with those big sad eyes inquiring where you are.'

'Don't, you'll make me miserable,' she wailed. 'Torquil won't let me have a dog in London because he doesn't want dog hair all over the house. Seeing as he's barely here I'm surprised he'd notice. But he's very proud of his house. He's meticulous about everything.'

'I noticed that. He dresses like a duke,' Toby said enthusiastically but he felt a tingling sensation of discomfort creep up his neck.

'Don't talk to me about his clothes.' She sighed melodramatically. 'He gets enraged if Mrs Hughes leaves creases in his shirts or presses his trousers incorrectly. Thank God he doesn't lose his temper like that with his wife. Well, he does when he's jealous but Lucia tells me that's his way of showing me that he loves me, imagine if he wasn't jealous at all, I'd feel very neglected.'

'Don't you cook any more?' Toby asked, remembering how much pleasure she took from looking after him and Julian during the years they all lived together.

'No, I haven't cooked since I got married. Mrs Hughes cooks or we go out. You see, I'm *very* spoilt.'

Toby didn't dare ask whether she still put flowers in vases, scented the sheets with lavender and filled the house with music because he knew the answer and he couldn't bear to hear it.

'As long as he makes you happy,' he conceded finally. But when he put the telephone down he was besieged by new anxieties, unable to reconcile the Torquil they met before the wedding with the Torquil Federica had just described. Something didn't gel.

But Federica was happy – or at least she believed herself to be happy. She loved her husband to distraction and modified her tastes and her desires to suit him without even realising it. Torquil denied her nothing but her freedom, which, during the occasional moments when his possessiveness threatened to suffocate her, she justified as an expression of his devotion and forgave him. She rarely questioned his motives or his actions. He was her husband, she had chosen him, so she worked through any feelings of frustration because she didn't know any other way. She was determined to make the marriage work. Above all she needed him. He gave her security and love and she willingly sacrificed her freedom for that.

Unable to make the house into a real home, for Mrs Hughes saw to all the domestic needs, Federica began to eat away her boredom. A biscuit here, and piece of cake there, until she was rarely without something in her fingers, making regular trips up to her mouth. Lucia, who believed it impossible to be too rich or too thin, delighted in the swell of her rival's figure and encouraged her with cunning. Torquil, who loathed fat women, watched his wife's changing body with delight; it reflected the gradual surrendering of her independence. Unable to understand it as an outward expression of her inner discontent he felt empowered by it. The ivory goddess was toppling from her pedestal. As her confidence was subtly undermined she grew more needy. Torquil relished his control. She belonged to him. Without intending to be malicious he began to call her 'my Venus' and 'Voluptuosa' while at the same time encouraging her to eat. 'You're not fat, sweetness, you're sensual and I love you like that,' he would say. She believed him because he seemed to desire her more. After all, sex was his way of telling her he loved her.

Within two years Federica had tuned herself to Torquil's pitch without even noticing the gradual relinquishing of her liberty. It was such a steady shift she didn't even realise she was unhappy. In her limited understanding Torquil was the same, sensitive man she had married – just a little harder to please. She didn't buy her own clothes because she knew he liked choosing them for her. She didn't buy him presents because she learned that if he wanted something he would go out and get it himself. She met Lucia for lunch and was soon included in a small circle of women, who, like herself, had nothing else to do all day except lunch, gossip and shop with each other. Yet, Torquil's controlling nature had taught her how to deceive. She learned to splash the soap with water when she was in a hurry after using the bathroom, because she knew Torquil would check it after to make sure she had washed her hands. She learned to ask the chauffeur to wait for her outside Harrods while she sneaked out the other side and wandered up Walton Street just for the sheer pleasure of doing something without being watched. She called her family from public telephones in shops and met Hester once or twice in the ladies' powder room in Harvey Nichols. She managed to justify Torquil's behaviour to her family, using his arguments without realising like a well-trained parrot.

Then Sam rang her up, out of the blue.

'Hi, Fede, it's Sam.'

'Sam!' she exclaimed in surprise. 'My God, I haven't seen you since I got married.'

'I hear you've barely seen any of us since you got married,' he replied. 'I gather that husband of yours is hiding you away.'

'No, not at all,' she replied breezily. 'I've just been so busy. Time has flown.'

'Two years?'

'Is it really that long?' she gasped.

'So, how are you?' he asked.

'Well. Very well. Actually, you'll be impressed, I've been studying literature with an old Cambridge don,' she said proudly.

'I am impressed. What's his name?'

'Dr Lionel—'

'Swanborough,' he interjected in admiration. 'Lucky you, he's a very learned man. What have you read?'

'Oh, I've studied everything from Zola to García Márquez.'

'In Spanish?'

'Don't be ridiculous. I forgot my Spanish years ago.' She laughed.

'Shame.'

'Isn't it.'

'So, he's treating you well, is he?' he asked, conjuring up the silky face of Torquil Jensen with distaste.

'Enough of me, how are you?' she asked.

'Hating the City. In fact, I'm going home.'

'Home?' she asked in surprise.

'Back to Polperro.'

'To do what?'

'To write.'

'How lovely,' she said, suffering a silent pang of nostalgia as she

434

envisaged those windy cliffs and choppy sea. She hadn't been back since the previous Christmas.

'Yes, Nuno's delighted, he says I can use his study to write in.'

'That's an honour.' She sighed, recalling Pickthistle Manor and the golden days she had spent there. Sam detected the wistful tone in her voice and longed to know how she *really* was.

'Oh yes it is. He never lets anyone into that room.'

'How is old Nuno?'

'Old.'

'That's sad. He's a one-off.'

'He certainly is,' he chuckled. 'God broke the mould when he'd made Nuno.'

'Tell me, why didn't you ever call him Grandpa?' she asked curiously.

'*Nonno* is grandpa in Italian, Nuno just stuck.'

'I've always wondered about that.'

'Well, now you know.'

'I don't see so much of your sisters.'

'I know, so they tell me.'

'Things are hectic.' She sighed, glancing around her tidy sitting room and feeling lonelier than ever.

'I'm ringing up to see if you can make lunch. I'd like to see you before I disappear into the depths of Nuno's study.'

'Oh, I'd love to,' she enthused. 'I really would. Can you make it this week?'

'What about tomorrow?'

'Tomorrow's great.'

'I'll pick you up at your house,' he said. 'Remind me of your address?'

When Sam saw Federica waiting for him on the doorstep he immediately noticed the change in her. She was wearing an elegant summer suit in blue with a short skirt and high heels, revealing a larger body and heavier bust. Her hair, scraped back into a ponytail, betrayed a rounder face cloaked in make-up. To anyone else she would have looked sensual and glamorous, but to Sam she looked like a sad clown smiling bleakly through a thick layer of paint. He felt his heart stagger as she walked towards him. He wanted to wrap her in his arms and take her home to where she belonged. But she kissed him warmly, commented on how wonderful it was to see him again and climbed into the waiting cab.

It wasn't until coffee was served that he gently tried to break through her façade. 'You look so different, Fede, I hardly recognised you standing outside your house,' he said, gazing into her blue eyes that failed to disguise her melancholy.

'You haven't changed,' she replied, once again diverting the conversation away from herself. 'You're still wearing holey shirts and worn-out trousers. Torquil should take you shopping!' She laughed and dropped two sugar lumps into her cup of coffee.

But Sam didn't laugh. 'I'm afraid I have better things to do than worry about the state of my clothes,' he said, allowing the bitterness he felt towards her husband to seep into his words. He checked himself, aware that if he angered her he would lose her trust. 'I'm thrilled you decided to do a literature course,' he said. 'I hope you're also continuing your photography, you always had a passion for that.'

Federica lowered her eyes and stared into her cup. 'Oh, I've sort of lost interest in photography,' she replied quietly.

'How could you have lost interest? I don't believe you, Fede,' he exclaimed, feeling the fury rise in his throat.

'I just don't have time.'

'What on earth do you fill your day with?'

'Oh, lots of things.'

'Like?'

'Well, I have a lot of reading to do . . .' Her voice trailed off. Sam moved his hand across the table and took hers impulsively. She looked up at him in alarm before scanning the room in panic to see if anyone was looking.

'Fede, you're worrying me,' he said seriously, his face suddenly grey and anxious. She frowned. Sam shook his head slowly then

436

continued in a very low voice, penetrating her eyes with the intensity of his stare. 'Please tell me, darling, that it was *your* decision not to take a photography course, that it was *your* decision to study literature, that it is *your* decision not to come down to Polperro, to cut us all out of your life, to dress like that and paint your face like that . . .' His voice cracked. 'Because if your husband is imposing his will onto you, you're in danger of being smothered. I won't stand by and watch your spirit harnessed and controlled.'

Federica stared at him in confusion, suddenly having to confront her fears. She bit her lower lip. Sam watched her, attempting to read her thoughts as she so clearly balanced between confiding in him as she had always done in the past, and throwing up her defences and shutting him out.

There followed a weighty silence. Sam squeezed her hand in encouragement. 'I'm only asking because I care,' he said softly and smiled at her reassuringly. To his disappointment she stiffened then withdrew her hand.

'I love Torquil, Sam,' she said eventually. Then she added 'Anyway, you wouldn't understand.'

'I'll try,' he suggested, but she was already looking away. The connection had been broken. Devastated, he had no choice but to ask for the bill and escort her back to her house. When he tried to reach her once more, on the marble steps of her home, he realised to his despair that he had lost her again. He wondered if he'd ever get another chance.

Federica curled up on the sofa with a packet of chocolate biscuits and a glass of cold milk. She snivelled into a piece of kitchen roll and reflected on her lunch with Sam. How could he possibly understand her situation? What he didn't realise was that it was *her* choice to love Torquil and *her* choice to want to be the best wife she could be to him. He needed her and cherished her. If he was possessive and controlling, it was simply because he cared. She needed him too. Besides, she thought crossly, the dynamic of their relationship had nothing whatsoever to do with Sam. But, while she dried her eyes and delved further into the packet of biscuits, the seed of doubt Sam had dropped was slowly settling into fertile ground.

When Torquil arrived home that evening his face was red and harassed.

'Darling, you look exhausted, let me run you a nice hot bath and bring up a glass of whisky,' Federica suggested, embracing him warmly.

'We need to talk,' he said coldly, pushing her away.

She shuddered and immediately felt consumed with guilt. 'What about?'

'You know exactly what about,' he snapped, stalking into his study to help himself to a drink.

She followed him nervously. 'Lunch with Sam.' She sighed in defeat. There was no use trying to hide anything from Torquil because somehow he was as omniscient as the devil.

'Exactly. Lunch with Sam,' he repeated, clicking his tongue impatiently. He poured whisky into a tumbler and drank it straight. 'Were you going to tell me, or were you just going to wait and see whether or not you got away with it?'

'What's the big deal, Torquil, he's an old friend?' she protested.

'That's not what I asked,' he replied angrily.

Federica swallowed hard, his expression was so remote she barely recognised him. 'Of course I was going to tell you, but you didn't give me a chance.'

'You had all of last night to tell me. He called you yesterday,' he shouted suddenly, slamming his glass down on the table in exasperation. Federica flinched at the severity of his tone. 'You didn't tell me,' he continued in a menacingly soft voice, turning around to face her, 'because your intentions weren't honourable.'

Federica's chin wobbled as she fought against the impulse to cry. For the first time in her marriage she felt consumed with fear. 'I didn't tell you, because I knew you wouldn't let me go,' she said hoarsely. 'And I so wanted to go.'

'So you lied to me?' he argued, scrutinising her face with narrowed eyes. 'My own wife lied to me?' He shook his head. 'I can't even trust my own wife.'

'I knew you'd say no,' she explained, unable to swallow the moan that choked up from her chest. 'I haven't seen any of my old friends for years. I miss them.'

'Fede, I'm not your gaoler,' he said in a more gentle tone. 'There's always logic behind my requests. Put yourself in my shoes, how would you feel if I had lunch with an old girlfriend and didn't tell you?'

She gulped. 'I'd probably feel jealous.' Torquil always had a winning argument for everything.

'Look, let me explain with an analogy,' he said, sitting down beside her and taking her hand in his. Torquil loved inventing the perfect analogy to illustrate his case. 'Take a porn video,' he began. She frowned at him. 'No, listen. If there's a porn video sitting on the video player it's all too easy to put it in and have a peek, whereas, if you have to go all the way out to a video shop, risk being seen by someone, face the embarrassment of asking for it, paying for it, then sneaking home to watch it, you're less likely to do it. Do you understand?'

'Are you trying to tell me that by having lunch with Sam, I'm in danger of having an affair?'

'Exactly.'

'But, Torquil,' she insisted. 'That's madness. He's like my brother.'

'But he isn't your brother,' he replied sharply.

'I'm as likely to have an affair with him as have an affair with Hal.'

'It's just logic. I don't want my wife having close male friends. It's dangerous, believe me. I've got more experience than you, you're very naïve, little one,' he said, caressing her cheek. 'I love you. I adore you. I don't want to lose you. In fact, I'll do anything not to lose you. Anything at all.'

Federica shivered and waited apprehensively.

'When I said I'd love you for life, I meant it. All these requests of mine might seem strange to you, but they're implemented to safeguard our marriage. It's for you and me,' he explained. He leant over and kissed her. But Federica didn't feel like being kissed, she felt confused. He took her by the hand. 'Come upstairs, I hate fighting with you. Let's make up.'

'Torquil, please,' she objected in a thin voice that was barely audible.

He seemed not to notice her tears. 'I want to show you why you don't need to have male friends. They can't give you what I give you. Come on, little one, convince me that you're not angry with me.'

Reluctantly she allowed him to unbutton her trousers and pull them off. She lay on the bed in her shirt and panties, trying to control her snivelling. He closed the curtains, took the telephone off the hook and put Pink Floyd in the CD player. Then he dimmed the lights. 'Don't cry, my darling, we're making up now,' he soothed, kissing her forehead. 'I'm going to blindfold you,' he added slowly.

'Oh, Torquil, I . . .'

'Shhh,' he whispered, placing his finger over her mouth. He then put it inside her lips and traced it across her gums. Inwardly she recoiled with revulsion. He pulled a silk scarf out of his bedside drawer and tied it over her eyes. She closed her eyes into the blackness, wondering where he was and what he was doing. Finally, she felt him unbutton her shirt and open it, releasing the catch on her bra. As he traced her skin with a long white feather, slid his tongue between the gaps in her toes and derived a perverse pleasure from making love to her with her panties on she felt nothing and stifled a sob.

She wanted to shout at him to make love to her normally. Then suddenly she realised that he had always made love to her without love and her flesh rippled with an icy chill that debilitated her. But Torquil didn't notice, he liked her to be still. It was then that the seed planted earlier by Sam put out tentative roots and began to grow. For the first time in her marriage she allowed herself to doubt. But once she gave into the first doubt she was unable to control the torrent of uncertainty that invaded her thoughts like wafts of black smoke.

Federica got up and began to rummage around in her cupboard. There at the back, in the very corner where Torquil's pedantic hands had failed to find it to throw away with the rest of her past, was the butterfly box. She sat on the floor, placed it on her knee and opened it. With an unsteady hand she re-read all her father's letters, one by one, reclaiming the past in each tender word until her tears formed another layer of unhappiness on the paper. Then she focused her eyes into the empty distance and drew comfort from the memories she found there.

Chapter Thirty-Five

Autumn 1998

The following two summers passed in a blur of parties, tedious ladies' lunches and endless visits to the gynaecologist because Federica hadn't got pregnant and Torquil was certain there was something wrong with her. As far as the doctor was concerned she was functioning perfectly. 'Give it time, you've only been trying for a few years and you're only twenty-two,' he said kindly. 'Perhaps you're too anxious. Try to relax more.'

Torquil took it as a personal insult to his manhood that Federica hadn't got pregnant immediately. 'A man could scarcely make love to his wife more than I do,' he complained, 'and you're voluptuous enough to be a fertility symbol.'

Federica took offence. Lonely at home in front of the fire, making her way through magazines and Dr Lionel Swanborough's reading lists, she grazed on panettone and chocolate rolls. Torquil took her whenever he had a spare moment, lifting her skirt up and bending her over to inject her with his potency. Each time he withdrew he patted her on her bottom. 'That'll do it, little one,' he'd say confidently as Federica obeyed his instructions and lay on the bed with her feet in the air for half an hour to help the sperm in their struggle against gravity.

Federica desperately wanted a baby, but not for the right reasons. She felt she was too young to be tied down with such a heavy responsibility and yet she longed to please her husband. Each month her bleeding was accompanied by hot tears of frustration and the painful duty of reporting her failure. When she suggested that he go and see a doctor himself he retorted that everything worked perfectly well in that department, the problem lay with her.

As the cold, melancholic winds of October groaned about her Federica sought solace in her books, her chocolate and her memories.

Then Nuno died.

Under such exceptional circumstances Torquil allowed Federica to be chauffeur-driven down to Polperro for the funeral. 'But I want you back by nightfall,' he said. When Federica explained that that just wasn't possible, Polperro was hours away, he grudgingly conceded and allowed her to stay the night.

'I'm going to miss you, little one,' he added, embracing her, 'I need you here with me.'

Federica was devastated that Nuno had died, but her excitement at returning home to Polperro eclipsed her sadness. She longed for that day with such anticipation that she forgot her cautiousness and called her mother and Toby every day from a call box to discuss it. She even managed to avoid sex with Torquil, claiming that she was far too distressed.

The funeral took place in the little church in the village. Those who couldn't fit in spilled out onto the leafy path, pulling their coats and hats about them to keep warm. Ingrid wore a black hat with a heavy veil so no one could see her crying. Inigo helped her down the aisle with a bowed head and red eyes. 'It's you and me now at the top of the pile,' he said gloomily as they sat together in the front pew.

'I don't know about you, darling, but I'm going to reincarnate into a beautiful bird, you'll see,' she replied, placing her monocle into one eye in order to read the service sheet. Inigo pondered on the theories of reincarnation for the rest of the service.

Molly and Hester sat wiping their wet faces while Sam sat staring at the coffin. He thought of his beloved grandfather and his eyes turned to liquid.

Federica arrived late. She had wept tears of frustration as a broken-down lorry had held them in a tight traffic-jam for over half an hour. Sweating, she shuffled down the aisle just as Reverend Boyble took his solemn place in the nave. Federica squashed in beside Toby and Julian who squeezed her arm affectionately, thrilled to see her. Reverend Boyble cleared his throat and waited for Federica to settle.

'No one will ever forget Nuno,' he began. 'He was one of life's originals, a rare ray of light that shone upon us all. We shall miss that light greatly. But now he shines with God. Let us thank God for the life of our dear friend Nuno, who gave each one of us so much.'

Ingrid began to sniff and her shoulders quivered in an effort to control herself. Sam continued to stare at the coffin as if in a trance. Federica turned around and quietly greeted her family who all stared at her as if she were an alien being. How she had changed!

'I know she's unhappy,' Polly whispered to her husband. Jake sighed and nodded. 'She's put on weight. She's not a strongly built girl. It's unhappiness that's done it,' she added, mouthing the same to Helena who sat on Jake's other side. Toby took Federica's hand and she suddenly felt an overwhelming sense of loss. Not just of Nuno but of everyone. She had lost Polperro in the last few years and now she was back she wanted so much to hold onto it. But she knew she couldn't. Torquil wanted her back tomorrow.

Sam walked gravely up to the pulpit to give the address. He had left his cuffs undone and they flapped about his wrists like white doves. Federica watched him. He had lost a lot of hair since she had last seen him. It was now clearly receding at the front and thinning on top. He looked up with a grey face and surveyed the congregation. He didn't need notes because he hadn't prepared what he was going to say. He removed his glasses, took a deep breath as if collecting his emotions and then began in a confident, articulate voice.

'Nuno was my best and most beloved friend,' he began. 'He taught me everything I know and I owe him for everything that I have become.' Then his grey eyes rested on Federica as he quoted from *The Prophet*. '"And let your best be for your friend,"' he said in a slow, almost theatrical voice. '"If he must know the ebb of your tide, let him know its flood also. For what

444

is your friend that you should seek him with hours to kill? Seek him always with hours to live. For it is his to fill your need, but not your emptiness." '

Federica didn't lower her eyes but looked steadily into his. She felt suffocated by a wave of pity and regret. She recalled with nostalgia the moments they had shared in the past. They had been special moments of great tenderness. Then, as she tried to hold onto them they dissolved before her like mist, leaving only the desolation of the present and Sam's grief-stricken face illuminated by the light of God.

'I always sought Nuno with hours to live,' he continued bravely. 'He filled my need for knowledge and my need for wisdom. He also filled my need to understand myself better and taught me not to desire to be understood or admired by others. He was never understood by others and that gave him great freedom, because he was always himself. I shall miss his tedious quoting, his pedantry, his faux Italian accent and his dry, irreverent humour. But most of all I shall miss his wisdom, because without it I am lost. All I have now are the words he taught me in the past, which I shall replay in my memory in my effort to live better.'

Federica listened to his words as they spilled out, without direction, without constraint but from the heart. He spoke at length, holding the sides of the pulpit with his hands, either for effect or for support. He only lifted his eyes from Federica's to gaze down at the coffin as if he were talking to Nuno himself.

When he finished, no one moved or made a sound. All that could be heard was Sam's soft footsteps as he walked slowly back to his seat.

Nuno's coffin was lowered into the ground in the small grave-yard outside the church. The family and close friends stood around in the cold and watched his final journey home. Back into the earth where it had all begun. 'How did he die?' Federica whispered to Julian, who stood solemnly beside her.

'Apparently he knew he was going to go,' he replied, leaning down and speaking quietly into her ear. 'It was Tuesday afternoon and he kissed Ingrid good-bye, then Inigo and went into his study and passed away in his leather chair reading Balzac.' Federica raised her eyebrows. 'Ingrid and Inigo just thought he was going off for a siesta, they didn't realise he really meant "*adieu*".'

'Unpredictable to the last,' she replied, catching Sam's hollow eyes blinking sadly behind his glasses. He watched her but didn't see her. 'Sam's taking it very badly,' she added, smiling at him with sympathy.

But his vision had clouded with grief. He couldn't see anything. Then he turned and walked to the waiting cars with his family and everyone made their way back to Pickthistle Manor.

Federica gave Julian and Hal a lift in her chauffeur-driven car. Hal was impressed. Julian was not. 'Why don't you learn to drive, Fede?' he asked.

'I don't need to.'

'Of course you need to, it's a question of independence.' Federica eyed him nervously and nodded towards the chauffeur. Julian raised his eyebrows. She knew that Paul reported everything back to Torquil.

'I think it's really cool to have a chauffeur,' said Hal. 'Swish car too. You married well, Fede.'

Julian looked at Federica and watched her smile at her brother. But he could feel the unease behind her smile because the light in her eyes had grown opaque. He took her hand and squeezed it, but Federica only squeezed it back jovially as if she didn't want her pain to be recognised by anyone.

The atmosphere at Pickthistle Manor was lighter compared with the heaviness that had hung like an invisible miasma in the church. Everyone unburdened their grief with the effect of the wine and Ingrid asked her guests to celebrate Nuno's life, not to mourn it. The sitting room at once filled with smoke and the vapour of alcohol and body heat as it throbbed with the people Nuno had acquired throughout his life. When Lucien brought in a sodden hedgehog he had found in the driveway Ingrid burst into tears, recalling Nuno's aversion to flea-ridden animals, and knocked back half a glass of vodka.

Helena embraced her daughter and complimented her on her designer suit. Then she launched once again into a soliloquy about Hal. 'We're not doing very well at school at the moment,' she said sanctimoniously. 'We're going to fail our A levels. We've got the brains, we just refuse to use them.' She sighed helplessly. 'We're going through a particularly painful time at present. But our heart's in the right place, we're just a little bit misguided.'

Federica's attention drifted, as it always did when her mother obsessed about Hal. She was relieved when Jake intervened and directed the conversation away from his grandson. 'Hal's fine, Helena, your problem is you won't let go,' he said wisely.

'He needs his mother, Dad,' she replied, offended. 'I don't care what any of you say, I'm not going to leave him to flounder when I can pick him up.'

Molly was too affronted by Federica's fickleness even to greet her. She saw her making her way through the crowd in her perfect black suit, her perfect black shoes, her perfect little black bag and perfect black hat and turned her back and walked in the opposite direction. But Hester remained and embraced her friend with the same loyal affection that she had always shown her throughout their childhood. 'You look well,' she said kindly, noticing her larger frame and pallid skin and wondering what had caused it.

'I am well,' she replied.

'How's Torquil?' Hester, asked wondering if Federica would open up to her like she had always done in their secret cave. But she was disappointed.

'He's a dream,' she replied enthusiastically. 'I only wish he were here today. I hate to be parted from him, even for a minute.'

'How nice,' said Hester flatly. 'It's great that you've found your soul mate. I'm still looking for mine.'

'No one, then?'

'No one. It's a desert out there,' she sighed. 'Molly has a penchant for picking up builders,' she added, trying to lighten the conversation. 'She's happiest on a building site.'

'That sounds like Molly. I was lucky Torquil found me so early on. But you're young, you don't need to find someone yet. Enjoy your freedom while you have it.'

'You're right. I'll keep my eyes peeled for a Torquil. He doesn't have any handsome friends by any chance, does he?' They both laughed, but their laughter was uneasy.

'Sam's miserable,' Federica said, watching him talking gravely to his father.

'Oh, he's devastated,' Hester agreed. 'He gave a good address, didn't he?'

'He's so talented.'

'I know. I'm so proud of him.' She sighed. Then she touched Federica on her arm and looked at her imploringly. 'Go and talk to him. He needs cheering up.'

'Sam, I'm so sorry,' said Federica, when Inigo had moved off to seek the quiet sanctuary of his office.

'Federica.' He kissed her. 'I'm glad you could make it. We'd almost forgotten what you looked like.' Federica smiled awkwardly, recalling their last meeting. 'Let's get out of here, I'm feeling claustrophobic,' he suggested. Sam led her down the corridor to Nuno's study. Once inside he closed the door, blocking out the low drone of voices. 'You can see why Nuno liked it so much in here. It's quiet,' he said, sitting down on his grandfather's worn leather chair. Federica sat on the sofa avoiding the holes that revealed the white foam beneath the leather and crossed her legs neatly under her. 'I can still smell him,' he continued. 'This is the only room in the house that literally vibrates with his presence, even now. I come in here and I still feel that he's alive and about to walk in at any moment and catch me reading in the erotica section.'

'Don't tell me Nuno had an erotica section?' she laughed.

'Oh, yes. Nuno was a big fan of erotica,' he replied. 'But not a big fan of the real thing.'

'He must have done it once to have produced Ingrid.'

'Once. Then he put it away for ever.'

'Really!' she exclaimed, lowering her eyes because Sam's had settled on hers and they made her feel uncomfortable. 'He was a wonderfully colourful person,' she sighed, changing the subject. 'I was fortunate to have known him.'

'You were, we all were.' He stood up and started picking up the papers on Nuno's antique desk. 'So how come Torquil let you come down?'

'He wouldn't want to stop me coming to Nuno's funeral,' she replied coolly, hoping he wasn't going to repeat the speech he gave her at lunch.

'You've barely been back since you got married.'

'I know.'

'Still hectic with that time-consuming literature course, I suppose?'

'I do other courses now,' she retorted. 'They take up all my time.'

'Fede,' he said seriously, flopping into Nuno's desk chair and draining his glass. 'You love Polperro, don't tell me you don't miss it?'

'Of course I do, it's just that Torquil has a different sort of life, we do other things.'

'But not to come and visit your family? Family was once everything to you.'

Federica shuffled awkwardly. She didn't appreciate this sudden attack on the way she had chosen to live her life. 'Family *is* everything to me, Sam, but I'm married now,' she said tightly. 'Things change. I really don't want to go into this again.'

'You're married, but you're not happy,' he said, watching her steadily.

Federica stiffened. So she had put on weight, what of it? 'How do you know I'm not happy? You're judging me by your own

449

standards,' she argued. 'I don't want to be sitting down here writing books.'

'You'd like to be sitting down here taking photographs.'

'Oh, really,' she laughed, 'that was a long time ago, like I told you. I adore London, I wouldn't want to live anywhere else.' She watched Sam's tortured face and wondered why he cared.

'You're living in a beautiful shop window. There's nothing behind it, Fede. If I was worried about you two years ago, I'm even more concerned now.'

'For goodness' sake, Sam, this is ridiculous. Why do you care?'

He stood up again and strode over to the window. 'Because you're an old friend,' he said softly, looking out onto the wet garden.

'Because you kissed me once in the barn.'

'Because I kissed you once in the barn,' he repeated with a bitter chuckle. He wanted to add 'and because I let you go when I should have held on to you'.

'I care, Fede, because I've watched you grow up here. You're part of my family. From the moment I dragged you out of the lake to those times when you came and cried on my shoulder, I've been like an older brother to you. I care about you. For God's sake, Federica, look at yourself.' He turned and stared at her with his grey eyes and grey face twisted in anguish. Federica felt her chest constrict and swallowed back her self-pity. 'Darling, you're not yourself. He's changing you. The Fede I know doesn't wear designer suits with matching handbags. The Fede I know doesn't cross her legs like the Queen. The Fede I know doesn't smile from the nose down. She smiles with her eyes, behind her eyes. She's like a lovely swan on the lake, but this husband of hers is pulling her under.'

They both stared at each other not knowing where to go from there. Sam gazed at her forlornly, fighting the impulse to gather her into her arms and kiss her again. Only this time he wouldn't stop, but would go on kissing her for ever.

Federica's skin prickled with an uncomfortable fervour. She looked at him in confusion while the person she was struggled with the person she had become in an agonising conflict of wills. Finally a fat tear pushed its way through her restraint as she realised that she didn't know who she was any more.

'I'm fine,' she said coldly. 'I'm fine and I'm happy. You're just emotional because your grandfather has died,' she stammered, standing up. 'So am I. I love Torquil and he loves me. I don't think it's right for you to criticise me,' she added defensively before leaving the room.

Sam turned around and stared bleakly out across the lake. The skies were black and dense and a soft drizzle floated on the wind. A few brown leaves swirled about on the paving stones outside the window. Just like Federica, he thought, being tossed about by the will of something far bigger than herself. He remembered the shy, awkward child who had played with Hester in the caves and melted marshmallows on campfires, he hadn't noticed her then. And the inadequate teenager who stammered whenever she spoke to him and blushed with her first tender infatuation, he hadn't noticed her then, either. He couldn't remember exactly when he *had* first noticed her. Perhaps the feeling had crept into his heart without him even noticing, because suddenly his jealousy had been roused, leaving him bewildered at the surprising strength of his emotions.

He had watched helplessly as she had married Torquil. The signs had been there right from the start in large neon letters and yet no one had tried to make her see them. He remembered Nuno's wise words: 'You can teach people knowledge, but wisdom, dear boy, has to be learned through experience.' So far Federica had learned nothing. How much further had she to fall before she gained some self-awareness and inner strength? He sunk into Nuno's leather chair and concentrated on devising a way to help her.

Federica returned to the sitting room and attempted to forget about her strange conversation with Sam. She forced a smile and tried her best to listen to what people were saying. But her ears rung with the echo of his words and as much as she made every effort to ignore them she knew in her heart that he was right. She wasn't happy.

The chauffeur drove her to Toby and Julian's cottage where she had arranged to stay the night. Rasta sat by her chair with his aging white face on her lap, staring up at her with adoring eyes the whole way through dinner. Helena, Arthur and Hal joined them and they talked well into the night. When she slipped beneath the sheets she reflected on the family gathering that had been just like old times. The cottage was the same. The damp scent of the sea that mingled with the smell of rotting autumn had swelled her senses and flooded them with longing for those carefree days of her childhood. They had reminisced, laughing at all the old, well-worn stories that had slipped into family folklore. Even Hal had left his teenage angst back at home and joined in with enthusiasm. Helena was happy because Hal was happy and Federica was happy because she felt herself again.

But no one had failed to notice the change in her and they all worried.

When she left Polperro the following morning she felt a tremendous wave of homesickness. She dreaded returning to London, to the monotonous round of dinners and cocktail parties, ladies' lunches and shopping and shuddered at the thought of Torquil's persistent attempts to impregnate her. She looked down at her crocodile handbag and manicured nails and sighed. What was the point of it all?

Toby watched Federica leave and wondered when he would see her again. As the months rolled into years she was slowly drifting away from them. A small raft barely afloat on the strong undercurrents of a disappointing sea. Her marriage wasn't what she had dreamed of. It wasn't what her family had dreamed for her either. Toby resigned himself to the fact that he was losing her.

'Seeing Fede makes me feel desperately sad,' he said to Helena.

'Oh, she's all right. We all have our ups and downs,' she replied, too concerned with the sorry state of her own marriage to dwell for long on that of her daughter. 'Torquil loves her,' she added, not wanting to sound selfish. 'It'll work itself out.'

'I'm not so sure it will,' he replied bleakly, retreating into the house.

Helena was irritated. All anyone could talk about was Federica. How unhappy she looked. How she had put on weight. How her marriage must be crumbling. From the Applebys to the people who lived in the village, no one had anything else to say. When Arthur decided to add his thoughts to the pile Helena lost her patience. 'For God's sake, Arthur. You don't know what her marriage is like. You never even talk to her. I don't see how you've suddenly managed to penetrate her inner world,' she exclaimed hotly. Arthur's own patience was being slowly ground down by her incessant ill humour. She seemed to thrive on the drama of an argument. If there wasn't a reason to fight she invented one, happier to wallow in misery than try to find a way off her shadowy path of self-destruction.

'Now listen, Helena. Federica might not like me very much for obvious reasons, but I've watched her grow up and I care for her very deeply.'

'So do I,' she retorted. 'She's my daughter, not yours.'

Arthur sighed and narrowed his small brown eyes, resisting the temptation to shout at her. 'I'm only suggesting we do something to help, she's clearly having a hard time. She needs our support,' he said gently.

'What do you want to do? Rush in on a white charger?' she laughed scornfully. 'Fede doesn't want our help. If she did, she would have asked for it. Look, she's top to toe in designer clothes, has more money than King Midas and a husband who clearly worships the ground she walks on. So she looks unhappy; it was Nuno's funeral, if you remember, not exactly a time for celebration.'

'But she never comes down to see us.'

'She doesn't have time.'

'She loves her home, the countryside, the Applebys.'

'She's moved on, Arthur, that's what no one can bear to admit. She's left us all behind. That's fine by me. She's chosen a better life for herself than being stuck down here in bloody obscurity.'

Arthur stared at her in fury. He rarely lost his temper, but this time Helena had gone too far. His face swelled like a ripe tomato. 'Well if you're not happy with your lot, madam, why don't you just leave!' he shouted, throwing his papers onto the floor. Helena gaped at him in surprise. He never raised his voice. 'Go on, put your money where your mouth is, because I'm sick and tired of your hot air!' And with that he left the room.

Chapter Thirty-Six

'What's this?' Lucia asked, pulling Federica's butterfly box out of her bedside table drawer, where she now kept it hidden beneath her books.

'I don't know,' said Torquil, sitting up in bed and lighting a cigarette.

'How sweet,' she said, opening it. '*Adorabile.*'

'Well, what's in it?'

'Letters.'

'Letters?'

'Mmm.' She sighed, pulling one out. '*Che carina.*'

'Who the fuck are they from?' he asked furiously, grabbing it out of her hand. He opened up the first well-handled epistle and turned it over. His shoulders dropped with relief. 'They're from her father.'

'Sweet,' she said in a patronising tone. 'You're so possessive.'

'Like I told you, she's my wife, she belongs to me and I adore her.'

'What about me?'

'You don't belong to anyone.' He smirked.

'Torkie!' she breathed huskily, pretending to be hurt.

'All right,' he conceded. 'You belong to me part-time.'

'I don't sleep with anyone else, you know.'

'I know. I'd kill you if you did,' he said and looked at her steadily with impassive green eyes.

'Give me one of those letters, I want to read it,' she said excitedly. She liked it when he was masterful.

'No you can't,' he replied, folding the letter up and putting it back in the box.

'Torkie, come on, don't be a spoil-sport.'

'I said, no. Drop it.' He enjoyed playing Lucia off against his wife.

'Don't speak to me like that, I've just allowed you to ravage my body.' She laughed.

'And you enjoyed every minute of it. When I'm ready I'll take you again.'

'I might not let you,' she goaded.

'I'm stronger than you are. I'll pin you down and fight my way into you. Don't think you can ever prevent me from getting what I want, when I want it.'

'I like it when you sound rough. Like a gangster.' She smiled and stretched like a glossy cat. 'I wish Federica would spend the night away more often.'

'Absolutely not,' he replied. 'The fewer the better. I like her to be where I can see her.'

'You're a jealous husband.'

'She thrives under my guidance. She needs me. She'd be lost without me.'

'Then why the *diavolo* are you sleeping with me?'

Torquil smiled at her indulgently. 'Because, my angel, you work in an entirely different department. Fede's my wife. You're my lover. I love you both in different ways. I wouldn't want to be without either of you. Besides, you and I go back a long, long way. It's hardly an affair. Rather the continuation of an old friendship.'

'How do you know she's not having an affair?' Lucia asked, fixing him with her wide Italian eyes.

Torquil continued to smoke complacently. 'Because I know her every movement, angel.'

'You little spy,' she said, rolling onto her front and running a long nail down his chest. 'Do you spy on me too?'

'That's none of your business.'

'It's sick that you are reduced to spying on your women.'

'It's not spying. You don't seem to understand. I'm looking out for her. She's young and vulnerable.'

'You're spying on her. If she's smart she's sleeping with your informant. That's what I'd do.' She giggled.

'And I'd kill you,' he replied, fixing her with stony eyes. She flinched with a perverse kind of pleasure as she detected the menace in his expression.

'Your little wife is not so little any more.' Lucia grinned and ran a tongue over her thumbnail.

'She's not fat if that's what you're implying.'

'Not fat, just fatter.'

'She's softer to lie on. I like it,' he said. 'Besides, if she were skinny like you I might muddle you both up in the dark.'

'We both have Italian names, I'm surprised you haven't already put your big foot in it.'

'I never lose control. You of all people should know that.'

'Do you love her?' she asked sulkily.

'Yes,' he replied. 'I love her to distraction.'

'Well, it's one very happy marriage then, isn't it?' she stated with sarcasm. 'But I adore you too.' Then she sat up and pouted at him, allowing her long black hair to fall over her breasts, firm like newly whipped egg whites. 'Why didn't you marry me? I'm more beautiful than she is, more intelligent, more street-wise, I'm independent and worldly and I have no doubt that I'm a better lover. So, why didn't you? *Dimmi, perchè non ci siamo mai sposati?*'

Torquil stubbed his cigarette into the ashtray and rolled out of bed. 'For all those reasons, angel,' he replied. 'For all those reasons.'

When Federica returned home in the early afternoon, Torquil was waiting for her. He embraced her in his duplicitous arms but she felt nothing but a tingling numbness and saw in front of her eyes those black clouds of doubt. 'Are you all right, little one?' he asked, stroking her hair. 'You look exhausted.'

'It was very sad,' she replied, shaking her head, trying not to look into his eyes.

'I missed you,' he said. 'I could hardly sleep without you.'

Federica smiled tightly. 'I need a hot bath,' she mumbled, pulling away from him.

'And a massage,' he suggested.

'No really, just a bath will do.' She sighed, putting her handbag down and slipping out of her shoes.

'I want to rub away your suffering,' he said and followed her up the stairs. 'I know exactly how to cheer you up.'

Federica shuddered.

Torquil ran her a steaming bath scented with lavender essence and sat talking to her while she washed away the memory of Sam and her nostalgia. He told her he was planning to take her away on a long, hot holiday to Mauritius. 'You're anxious, sweetness, it's no wonder you're having trouble conceiving,' he said.

Federica felt a sense of panic creep up to her throat where it tightened its grip and made it difficult to breathe. 'What you need is a relaxing holiday in the sun. We can make love all day.'

'Yes,' she replied hoarsely, although the idea made her skin prickle with repugnance.

When she declined his offer of a massage and began to get dressed, he insisted that she needed it. 'God, you're tense,' he said, rubbing her shoulders. 'You see?'

'I'm fine, really,' she insisted.

'Lie down.'

'I'm fine, Torquil, please.'

'Little one, I know what's best for you, don't I?' he said, pushing her towards the bed. 'Now, do as you're told and let me massage away all that strain.' Reluctantly she lay naked on her front and closed her eyes because if she opened them she feared she might cry. His strong hands kneaded her skin with lavender oil, rubbing away at the muscles that were taut around her shoulders and neck. The room was warm and she was hot from her bath. Soon his hands got the better of her and she felt her body relax against her will. Her mind cleared of thoughts of Nuno, her family and her conversation with Sam and concentrated on the pleasurable feeling of his fingers on her flesh. She was balancing on that tenuous border between meditation and sleep when her senses were alerted to his sudden shift in position.

He spread her legs in one swift movement and fell on her,

probing his way into the centre of her being, jolting her back to consciousness. He rode her hard and selfishly as if he was aware that he was slowly losing control. That little by little she was loving him less. She opened her eyes and fixed them to a point on the wall. Then the strangest thing happened. She mentally withdrew from her body, as if it wasn't happening to her, as if it were someone else lying helpless on the bed. She projected her mind back to Chile, back to Cachagua, to the beach where the sand was warm and soft like Lidia's flour and the sea was hypnotic and soothing, drowning out her discomfort and humiliation.

In the barren months that followed, the butterfly box became her only source of consolation. She opened it to escape her unhappiness, reading her father's letters and floating far away on the memories that were evoked by the magic of the strange, sparkling stones. As Torquil's lovemaking grew more brutal the butterfly box became more vital. It was her lifeline. It was the only thing that sustained her.

It was at her lowest ebb that Federica received an anonymous note, delivered by hand through her letterbox like an epistle from Heaven.

> You shall be free indeed when your days are not without a care nor your nights without a want and a grief, But rather when these things girdle your life and yet you rise above them naked and unbound.

She turned the note over in search of a further note explaining whom it was from. But there was nothing. Just a simple piece of white paper with the verse typed onto it. She sat down and read it again. She didn't recognise it. She read it again slowly, thinking very carefully about each word. Whoever had sent it obviously wanted to help her, but remain anonymous at the same time.

459

There was only one person she knew of who would have reason to hide his identity. Her heartbeat quickened and the adrenaline pumped through her veins awakening senses that had grown sluggish with sorrow.

Ramon Campione. It could only be from her father. How typical of him to send an anonymous note. He had never announced himself. He had always just turned up unexpectedly. It had driven her mother mad, but it was his way. Then the content of the note was also very much his style. She remembered his stories, sometimes mystical, often spiritual. The turn of phrase was reminiscent of his own poetry, but above all it was his philosophy. He had always risen so far above every care and grief, risen so high that they had no longer touched him. He had been unaffected by cares even when his own family's cares and needs had driven them away from him. He had let them go. Once he had cared for her. In fact, there had been a time when she had believed his love to be unconditional and everlasting. But she had been disappointed, bitterly disappointed. Perhaps this was a tentative plea for forgiveness. Maybe he was trying to explain himself and his carelessness. But she hadn't seen him for years. Why was he suddenly thinking about her now? Where was he? How come he knew of her unhappiness? Why did he bother?

Later, when she lay in the darkness next to the distant body of her husband, she pondered on the note that she had hidden at the bottom of the butterfly box. Her father cared. He wouldn't have sent the note if he didn't care. She smiled to herself. He knew she was suffering and he wanted to help. The note was a clear instruction. She had to learn how to rise above her problems. The trick was not to let them get her down, to take control. It was all a state of mind. Her unhappiness was because she allowed life's struggles to burden her. For the first time since her marriage she felt a twinge of excitement as she took the initial cautious step in regaining control. She was tired of being a victim, it was time to take a stand. She was going to go on a diet, enrol in a gym and rise above her cares naked and unbound. But most importantly she wasn't alone. Once more she felt the sun on her face and basked in her father's love.

Ramon sat down at his typewriter and began to write. He hadn't attempted to write a book since the death of Estella which was now over three years ago. He had only written poems. Long poems of tormented verse, venting his pain and his regret in each carefully written line. He hadn't left Chile, preferring to stay with his son and near Estella's grave where he would often go to feel close to her, although his reasoning told him that she wasn't in the ground but in the realm of Spirit. He had watched with pride as his son had begun to write his feelings down in a diary. Sometimes they would sit on the beach and Ramoncito would read to him the lines he had composed about his mother. They were at first faltering, often clumsy, as he seemed impatient to release a grief that saw no other avenue of escape. But little by little he had refined his style, taken more time and begun to produce poems of great clarity and beauty. Ramon was touched. 'Mama will be so proud of you, Ramoncito,' he'd say, ruffling his hair with his hand.

'How will she know?' the boy would ask.

'Because she can see you, my son,' he would reply, confident that she was with them in spirit. 'Because love has no boundaries.'

It hadn't been easy for either of them. But while Ramoncito was distracted by his school friends and his schoolwork, his father was left alone to wallow in self-pity in the house on the beach where everything reminded him of Estella. Sometimes in the summer, the heavy scent of roses would rise up on the air and waft in through the window to hijack his senses. He would awaken from his dreams believing she was there, lying next to him, ready to caress him with her honey eyes and gentle smile. It was in those tormented moments that he felt the urge to sob like a child, clutch her pillow to his face and breathe in the memories that clung to the linen. So he had turned on the light and written his feelings down. Those poems had saved his sanity. They had also changed his life.

Ramon had learnt, through the intense scrutiny of his emotions, why he had run away all his life. First from his parents, then from Helena, then from his children and finally from Estella. He had run away from love. Love had terrified him. As long as he was on his own, far away from the people who cared about him, he was safe from the suffocating intensity of their love. The responsibility had been too heavy for him to carry. So he had enjoyed their love from a distance, returning every now and then to check it was still there before breaking away again before it overwhelmed him. His intentions had always been good. He had suffered regret when he had watched Helena and the children walk out of his life, when he had travelled to England to find Federica crying in the porch of the church because she missed him, when he had seen her that afternoon on the bicycle, squinting into the sun.

He had suffered terribly because he loved them. But he had also been afraid of his own capacity to love. He had run from that too. But Estella had been different. At first he had run from her like he had run from Helena. But Estella had loved him without wanting to possess him. She had loved him enough to give him his freedom. Her love had been pure and unselfish. Without realising it he had learnt from her love. It was because of this lesson that he had decided to write a book, not for publication, but for Helena. An allegory with a hidden message. He wanted her to know why he had run from her. He wanted her to learn too from Estella's undemanding love.

Sam sat on the top of the cliff and gazed out onto a sea that never changed, whatever the season. The winter frosts painted the grass-topped cliffs with icy fingers, froze the rivers and streams, yet the sea stayed the same. It could be rough, it could be calm, but it was never dictated to by the seasons. It belonged to itself.

Nuno had belonged to himself. He had never been influenced by anybody. Sam missed him. The house continued to reverberate with his presence and they all still talked about him as if he were alive, retelling stories of the funny things he had said and the odd things he had done. Inigo had given his study to Sam. Sam had been so touched he had wept. His father had patted him firmly on the back and told him that he could do with it whatever he wanted. But Sam had kept it exactly the same. Ingrid was touched that he wanted to keep her father's memory alive in the one room in the house that had truly been his. Sam had cleared the desk, placing all Nuno's pieces of paper with illegible notes scrawled in his hand across them, into a couple of boxes in order not to throw anything away. Then he had gone through his drawers. It was there that he had come across a yellowing book of Kahlil Gibran's *The Prophet*. It was a book he knew well. Nuno had often quoted from it and had given Sam a copy for his confirmation – indeed he had quoted from it at his funeral. But there was something deeply touching about Nuno's own private copy because he had written down his thoughts and ideas in the margins. However, it was the accompanying letter that inspired him.

It was then that Sam thought of Federica.

The letter was addressed to his wife Violet, Sam's grandmother, and dated 8 May 1935. It was written from Rome. It spoke of his deep love for her and his desire to make her his wife. The marriage was obviously one her parents opposed for she had spiralled into a dark hole of despair from which there seemed no escape. Nuno had seen no other way to console her, being across the waters, so he had sent her his book with notes of encouragement which he had written into the margins alongside the verses he thought would give her strength. Sam was so moved by the letter that he read it more than once. Then he read the verses and Nuno's comments. It had obviously worked for they had married in the end and shared many happy years together.

Sam thought of Federica. If it had helped Violet why not Federica? He sat down at the desk and typed out a verse. He had decided to send it anonymously because he felt there was more chance of her reading it and acting upon it if she didn't know it came from him. After all, he had tried to reach her twice and failed both times. Then he had gone all the way to London on the train to deliver it.

He had stood in wait outside her house under a black umbrella, so that she wouldn't recognise him. Then he had hung around on the pavement for over an hour willing her to return. It had taken him that long to realise that she was already in the house. When he had peered in through the window he had caught a glimpse of her wandering about the rooms in her dressing gown, eating a packet of crisps. It was mid-afternoon. She was most certainly alone. He had resisted the temptation to ring the bell and slipped the letter through the box in the door instead before walking away and returning to Polperro on the late afternoon train.

He had spent the entire journey back to Polperro thinking about her. The image of her wandering through the rooms of her large, elegant house in her dressing gown, eating to assuage her unhappiness, had evoked feelings of both anger and pity. He had wanted to lie in wait for Torquil and hit him over the head, finishing him off for good. But he knew the only way to free her was to teach her how to do it herself. He hoped the letter might inspire her as it had inspired Violet. He dreamed of one day loving her himself, but those dreams were frail clouds on the horizon.

'You know, your wife's going to the gym? She's already lost weight. She only ate a salad last night at the Blights'. Not like her at all,' Lucia said scornfully. '*Poverina*, I'd hate to exercise and diet. Sex is the only pleasant way to stay *in forma*.'

'She's not going to a gym,' Torquil replied loftily. 'She's got a personal trainer. I arranged it for her. It's a good thing too, she needs to lose a bit of weight.'

'Sweet,' she sighed. 'It's all for you, you know.'

'I know. She's been very distracted lately. I can't seem to get through to her. Her silence drives me mad. I don't know what's wrong with her. Perhaps losing some weight will put the smile back onto her face.' He shook his head in order to be rid of his domestic problems and grinned down at his mistress. 'Now how about slipping into that little black ensemble I bought you?'

'Well, you'll have to be quick, I'm meeting Fede for lunch at the Mirabelle.'

'Well, come here then,' he said, holding her against him and running his hand up the backs of her legs.

'Do you still make love to Fede?' she asked as his fingers traced the tops of her lace stockings.

'Of course.'

'No results yet?'

'None.'

'I'm sure *I'm* fertile.'

'I'm sure you are, angel,' he said, spanking her on her naked bottom. 'Ah, you're ready for me.'

'I never wear knickers when you come to visit,' she said and laughed throatily.

But as much as Torquil tried to lose his anxieties in Lucia's succulent flesh, he was unable to stop thinking about his wife. He sensed her detachment and it alarmed him.

Chapter Thirty-Seven

Helena should have recognised her daughter's unhappiness, because she had suffered too and knew marital discontent better than anyone. But Helena had never had the ability to see further than herself and her own needs. She only saw Hal because, unlike Federica, she needed him. He had always been the part of Ramon that she had been able to hold onto. As much as she had tried to convince herself otherwise, she believed she had never stopped loving Ramon.

Arthur was kind and compassionate, doting and generous – everything that a woman should desire in a husband, but she yearned for the magic of those early years with Ramon. They haunted her by night in the form of sensual dreams, which reminded her of that transient paradise, and by day in the form of a constant, nagging regret. The worse she treated Arthur the harder he tried to please her.

At the start of their marriage she had welcomed his affection with gratitude, and she thought she finally had everything she could ever want. But after a while her thoughts had been dragged back across the sea to another life where she believed, at one point, she had truly known happiness. She couldn't help but wish for something else, something more, something better. She seemed always dissatisfied. But Arthur's patience was limitless. He felt he understood his wife. She had been neglected and hurt. She needed attention and understanding not severity. He was sure that given time she would soften and allow herself a piece of happiness. He was certain his love was enough.

The wilder Hal became the tighter Helena held onto him. As a child he had been eager to please, though never as accommodating as his sister. Federica had always been self-sufficient. Like her father, she had been happier in her own company. But Hal had always needed his mother and her unwavering attention and if anything had distracted her from him he had soon found ways of getting her back again. But Helena despaired at his sudden change of character, as if he had been possessed by the spirit of someone else. Someone bent on self-destruction.

Hal was far more complex than his mother believed. Like a clear river Hal's nature was lined with a thick layer of silt accumulated over a long childhood of emotional upheaval. It only needed a bit of agitation for it to churn up and turn the water cloudy. It was his mother's marriage to Arthur and subsequent events that set his heart in turmoil. But the seeds had been sown many years before, as a child, that summer in Cachagua.

At the age of four Hal was painfully aware of his father's obvious affection for Federica. Unable to express his jealousy in anything other than tears and tantrums, Helena had selfishly believed that he sensed the ill ease between his parents and wanted to protect her from Ramon. But Hal longed to be gathered up into the ursine arms of his father and loved like Federica was loved. He felt dejected each time Ramon left the house with his sister and although he had loved his train he had been envious of the attention Federica was given over her butterfly box. When Ramon stayed at the beach house instead of accompanying them to lunch in Zapallar, Hal had taken it, in his own limited way, as a rejection. Ramon barely noticed him and each slight settled into the silt in his character to one day resurface in the form of wretchedness and rebellion. So he had cleaved to his mother like bindweed, suffocating her with his neediness until she could think only of him. Then Helena had failed to tell him that they were leaving Chile for good and promised to give Federica a dog. Hal, unused to being passed over by his mother, took it as a rejection. Desperate not to lose her he clung to her with all his strength, even managing to sleep in her arms at night, exploiting the emptiness Ramon had left and filling it with a need that replenished Helena's longing to be loved.

As he had grown up so had his self-awareness. He felt guilty loving his mother with such intensity and suffered terrible mood swings, adoring her one moment and loathing her the next. He made every effort to hate Arthur because his mother loved him, but he had liked Arthur in spite of himself. Partly because of Arthur's good qualities, but also because his sister hated him and he saw how much her rebellion upset his mother. Hal had always wanted to please Helena so the jealousy bubbled quietly in the pit of his stomach like black tar, to be placated only when he sensed that she didn't love Arthur like she loved him. Her love for her son was as strong as ever. Arthur gave him the attention his father should have given him and Hal found himself responding to his kindness with a thirst that had built up over the years. He embraced him with the same neediness as he embraced his mother. Arthur made time for him, listened to him, bought him gifts, took him out just the two of them – all the things Ramon had done for Federica and what's more, Federica despised him. Arthur belonged exclusively to Hal and his mother. It was Federica's turn to be out in the cold – until Helena had allowed her to live with Toby and Julian.

From that moment on he felt the painful separation from his sister, whom he looked up to and adored. Once more Federica had received special treatment. He suffered silently, unable to communicate his resentment and distress. So he found comfort in the underworld of drink and cigarettes.

At twenty-one Hal was in his final year at Exeter Art school, studying History of Art. But he somehow managed to fall into a group from the university and for the duration of his course, no one knew he wasn't a university undergraduate.

He shared a house with five of his new friends, situated in the middle of a muddy field with no heating and electricity which constantly needed to be activated by slotting money into a meter. There were mice droppings in the kitchen drawers and bags of rubbish by the wall outside which no one could be bothered to move. The house was cold in summer and freezing in winter but they lit the fires and slept in thick jerseys. Hal didn't do any work. He had only agreed to go into further education because he couldn't make up his mind what he wanted to do. As long as he was in education he didn't have to. It gave him three more years to fritter away doing very little.

He smoked because all the other boys smoked and besides, it kept him warm. He drank because it made him forget his worthlessness and his mother, who called him every day to check that he was all right and to dig her clutches in deeper as her husband failed to fulfil her. Alcohol gave him confidence. While the effects lasted he was as charismatic, enigmatic and self-assured as Ramon Campione. During those fleeting hours he even looked like him.

The lows were unbearable. His insecurities would invade the armour the drink had built around him and gnaw at his self-esteem more venomously than before. When the money dried up Helena gave him more, without questioning why he needed it. She didn't ask Arthur, she just gave him what Arthur gave her. When that was no longer enough he seduced Claire Shawton, a mousy girl with a thin, pallid face and long, skinny legs because her father was Shawton Steel and there was no shortage of money in her bank account. Keen to hold on to the dark, impenetrable Hal, Claire gave him money for his drink and his cigarettes, his gambling and his extravagance.

'I'm not an alcoholic,' Hal explained to her when she protested. 'It relaxes me. I'll pay you back, I promise. I'm having trouble getting around the trustees, that's all.' But there were no trustees because there wasn't a trust. Only Helena's blind generosity.

Claire Shawton's uses extended only as far as her bank balance; sexually she couldn't begin to satisfy Hal. He went about his sexual adventures with the same destructiveness with which he confronted everything else in his life. He slept with dozens of girls, promised them devotion and commitment, then dropped them as soon as they wanted a relationship outside the bedroom.

Claire knew of his transgressions but instead of closing her cheque book and walking away she gave him more money and received the kisses that followed with pitiful gratitude.

When Hal returned to Cornwall for the holidays Arthur noticed immediately that he was gaunt and pale, unable to sit still or concentrate for very long. He slept most of the day and stayed up watching videos until the early hours of the morning. When Arthur approached Helena on the subject she excused him by saying that he was overtired, studying too hard and needed the holidays to rest.

'Don't hassle him, Arthur, he's very sensitive about it,' she said proprietorially. 'He's got no confidence as it is. Let me deal with this.'

Once again Arthur rolled his eyes and backed off. Helena had been cold and distant in the last few months. She was prone to moods, adoring one moment, aloof the next, but he was used to that. He wasn't used to the consistent ill humour that now seemed to dominate her personality. Like a diminishing candle, her affection for him seemed to be getting noticeably less and less as each day passed. If he didn't do something the flame would go out altogether. But he didn't know what to do. In despair he wondered whether she was seeing someone else.

Helena was seeing someone else. She was seeing Ramon. When she closed her eyes at night and when her mind drifted off by day and finally when she lay in the rough arms of Diego Miranda, she saw the awesome face of Ramon Campione. The only man she believed she had ever loved. She had cried enough bitter tears of remorse to sink one of Diego's ships. She had looked back on her life and recognised her mistakes. Mariana had been right, you often don't know what you have until it is gone.

She knew where Ramon was. But she hadn't heard from him in years. She hadn't even bothered to find him to tell him about his own daughter's wedding. She now wished she had. It would have been a good excuse. Now there was no reason to call him.

Helena hadn't gone out of her way to have an affair. She hadn't even considered it, or desired it. Her heart was somewhere in the past, barely concentrating on the present at all. She had been in the pub in Polperro with Arthur, one cold summer Sunday, when a strange young man with long black hair and deep black eyes had accidentally knocked into her, pouring her glass of red wine all over her pale cashmere sweater. She had lost the little patience she had, not so much with him, but with life and the misery of it all, flinging her arms in the air and swearing furiously.

'I'm so sorry,' he exclaimed, turning to the barman in desperation. The barman handed him a dishcloth and he proceeded to dab at her chest in his confusion. 'I cannot apologise enough,' he said when Helena stared at him in horror.

'Your accent,' she stammered. 'Where are you from?'

'Spain.' She felt her stomach turn over and her head spin with a strange sense of *déjà vu*. He sounded just like Ramon. When she gazed into his eyes she believed they too resembled Ramon's, until in her state of yearning she believed he was Ramon's shadow, split from him by magic, all the way from Chile.

'Diego Miranda,' he declared, extending his hand.

'Helena Cooke,' she replied. 'I used to live in Chile,' she added, forgetting the wet stain on her sweater.

'Really?' he responded politely. 'You must speak Spanish.'

'Yes, I do,' she enthused, her voice hoarse with excitement. 'But I haven't spoken the language for many years.'

'You never forget a language like Spanish.'

'No, I think you're right,' she agreed, drifting on the music in his voice that seemed to call her from the misty shores of the far-distant past. 'What do you do?'

'Shipping.'

'Ah, the Armada.' She laughed.

'Something like that,' he replied indulgently. 'Please let me give you my address so you can send me the bill.'

'Bill?'

'The bill, for the dry cleaning,' he said, frowning at her in amusement.

'Oh, yes, the bill.' She giggled, watching him smile and feeling her stomach turn all over again. 'Do you live in Polperro?'

'No, just passing through.'

'Oh.' She sighed, trying to hide her disappointment. 'Where are you staying?'

'With friends.'

'Sightseeing?'

'Yes.'

'How strange,' she recalled, shaking her head. 'I met Ramon sightseeing too.'

'Who's Ramon?' he asked.

'Another life,' she said, brushing it off and smiling through the memory. 'I took him around the old caves and smuggling haunts. The places you can't find in guidebooks.'

Diego's eyes twinkled with interest. 'Really?' he said, then grinned at her from under his thick Spanish eyes. 'I'm afraid I'm following the map.'

'You mean, your friends aren't showing you around?'

'They don't have time, they work,' he said, watching her mouth curl up at one corner.

'If you want a guide, I could show you some of the places very few people know about. I grew up here, you see,' she explained.

'I would be honoured,' he replied, kissing her hand and bowing.

She gave him a wide, carefree smile before she was distracted by Arthur's insistent waving from the other end of the pub. 'Oh God!' she sighed irritably. 'I completely forgot about him. Don't worry,' she responded to his inquisitive frown, shaking her head. 'Meet me here tomorrow at eleven.' He nodded in understanding and raised an eyebrow, unable to believe his luck. He had noticed her rings and her husband's concern. He was Latin after all.

★   ★   ★

Diego was surprised by Helena's enthusiasm for an affair and imagined she had had many. She drove him around the coast and allowed him to make love to her on the cliff in the car over-looking the sea. Later she invited him home to her house where she took him to her bed. She enjoyed the firm way he handled her, the confident way he kissed her, the sensual way he caressed her. She closed her eyes and demanded that he speak to her only in Spanish, then she projected her mind across the waters and across the years to a time when Ramon hadn't run off and she hadn't rejected him.

The first time Arthur had trouble turning the tap in the shower he had been surprised. Helena always left it dripping. The second time he was perplexed. The third time his intuition told him that another man had used it. He leant back against the wall to steady himself as his heart plummeted to his feet. In the last few days Helena had been friendlier, happier, she hadn't snapped at him or ignored him. She had embraced him with fondness and quite obviously guilt. He let the hot water pound onto his skin, drowning out the screaming in his head that refused to give him peace to think rationally.

He had believed her detachment to be rooted in her anxiety over her troubled child. Worrying about Hal had become a full-time occupation. He hadn't understood it as a symptom of her waning affection for him. He worshipped her. Sex had never been a problem; they had loved and laughed together in bed even during the difficult times. He was sickened at the thought of her giving herself to another man. He was wounded by her blatant rejection of him in spite of all his efforts to please her.

He wondered who it could possibly be. But Arthur wasn't stupid. He wished he were because it was all too easy and therefore too painful. He had noticed her talking to the dark foreigner in the pub. She had returned to the table crimson-faced and distracted. She had kept looking over at him, watching him, lowering her eyes coyly when he returned her stare. Arthur hadn't liked it, but he had indulged her. There was nothing wrong with a harmless flirt if it made her feel happier, more attractive.

She had left with Arthur in a buoyant mood and talked all the way home in the car. Usually she stared bleakly out of the window responding to his attempts at conversation in monosyllables. But he hadn't suspected anything. He hadn't imagined she could be so devious.

After despair came anger. He thrust the palm of his hand against the wet tiles of the shower room as his lungs filled with fury, causing him to wheeze in torment. He thought of their first kiss, their first touch, their wedding day and their initial marital contentment and felt nothing but hatred and loathing. Then he recalled with precision the many hurtful things she'd said to him, the uncaring manner in which she had treated him and bit his lip with self-loathing. He had taken it all because he loved her. But now he had suffered one humiliation too much.

'I will never forget the face of the Polperro beauty,' Diego said, running his finger down Helena's face, where it lingered on her satisfied lips before following the line of her chin, pulling it towards him and kissing her.

Helena sighed with pleasure. 'When do you leave?' she asked, carelessly revealing the desperate whine in her voice.

'Tomorrow.'

'Tomorrow?' she repeated, the sweat breaking out on her forehead and nose. 'You mean, that's it?'

'You know your problem?' he said, shaking his head at her.

'What?' she replied, pulling away in offence.

'You're too needy.'

'Needy?' she retorted. 'I'm not needy.'

'Yes you are, *mi amor*. You're needy and it's suffocating. You're like an overwhelming octopus. Once in your arms a man feels he can't escape.'

'How dare you,' she snapped, climbing out of the hotel bed.

'Helena, *mi amor*, I'm not criticising you,' he insisted, smiling in amusement at her sudden change in humour. 'You're a beautiful woman. You're fun, too. I'm sure you break hearts all over Cornwall.'

'But not yours.'

'Helena,' he said indulgently. 'Come here.' She walked sulkily back to the bed where she sat down on the edge and allowed him to caress her hair. 'You're like a fallen angel. You found me because you were lonely. You're a discontented woman, any man can see that. But don't worry, there will be others.'

'What do you mean, others?' she exclaimed in disgust.

'Other men. Surely, *mi amor*, I'm not the first man you have betrayed your husband with?'

'Well, of course you are. What do you think I am? A whore?'

'Please, don't misunderstand me,' he said quickly, attempting to correct his error.

'I want you to go,' she said icily, suddenly regretting that she had ever met him. Hearing the echoes of Ramon's indifference resound across the years she wondered why she had only remembered the magic.

'Helena.'

'I do. Now!' she continued, getting up and throwing his clothes at him. 'I wanted you because you remind me of someone. But I've been a fool! You're as much of an illusion as he is. I've been dreaming, but I've now woken up.' Diego squinted at her, trying to understand what she was saying. 'Get out!'

'Come on, Helena. Don't be cross,' he cajoled, reluctantly standing up. 'At least let us part as friends.'

'We were never friends in the first place,' she replied. 'We were lovers, but now that is gone, we are nothing.'

'What happened to this "illusion"?'

'He never really existed,' she snapped. 'Just like you.'

'You're too desperate, Helena. You drive men away.'

'Go!'

'It's true. But we made good love,' he said with a smirk, pulling on his shoes. 'You're a desirable woman, Helena Cooke.'

'I don't want to see you ever again!' she shouted after him. The door slammed and he was gone. 'God, what was I thinking?' she exclaimed to herself, sinking into the chair. All that remained was the unmade bed and a heavy sense of self-disgust. She held her head in her hands and heaved with fury. How dare he think she would betray her husband with just anyone? How could she have been so misguided? She thought of Arthur and was suddenly filled with shame. What had she been reduced to? Arthur was guilty only of adoring her. What was the point of clinging onto the shadow of Ramon when Arthur was real and his love absolute? She had made a terrible mistake.

When she arrived back at the house it was dusk. The late summer sun had sunk behind the town making way for a bright harvest moon. She felt weary and defeated. To her surprise she saw the light on in the bedroom, indicating that Arthur was home. Her spirits rose like bubbles, slowly at first but with increasing speed, until she yearned to run to him like a child and apologise for treating him so badly. The thought of Arthur's familiar smell, his cosy embrace and his encouraging smile filled her with remorse. She longed to curl up against him like they had done when they had been newly wed and feel that sense of security, that sense of intimacy and friendship. She wanted to forget Diego Miranda for ever. She wished she had never gone near the pub that day. How close she had come to losing everything for a pitiful infatuation. Why was it that she was constantly chasing dreams?

She put the key in the lock and wriggled it about in frustration. When it wouldn't turn she rang the bell. When Arthur didn't come down she shouted up at the window. Then to her horror the light extinguished in the bedroom, leaving her alone in the empty street, blinking up in fear at the sudden realisation that he must know. Somehow he knew. Or he had simply had enough. 'Arthur!' she shouted in panic. 'Arthur!' But the house remained silent and impenetrable. 'Arthur, let me in!' she choked. She shouted until her voice was hoarse, until the cold wall of the house echoed her pleas only to mock her. She sank to the ground and crumpled into sobs. Arthur's patience had finally snapped.

Arthur watched through the gap in the curtains as his wife finally retreated to her car and drove off into the night. His throat ached from suppressing his emotions and his heart thumped behind his ribcage because he knew that by shutting her out he risked losing the one woman he had ever loved. But he also knew that he couldn't continue being taken for granted. He had been pushed to the limit. She had gone too far. It was time to win back her respect. She needed space to recognise that what she had with him was something precious, something sacred, something to be nurtured, not worn away out of carelessness and complacency.

He slumped on the side of the bed and dropped his head into his hands. For the first time in many years he sobbed.

Hal had drifted away from Federica. She was married now and her life no longer ran parallel to his. So he was surprised when she called him soon after Nuno's funeral and asked him for lunch in London during the university holidays. 'I need to see you, Hal,' she said and her voice sounded different. Hal was relieved to get out of his mother's house. She was crowding him out with her incessant questions and her unspoken demand to be included in his life. She wanted to know every detail about Exeter, who his friends were, whether he had a girlfriend, what he did in the evenings. He found her attention at once gratifying and invasive. It suffocated him.

Arthur watched him prowl around the house like one of the living dead and decided that at last he was growing up and growing away. But he didn't like his pallor or his disquiet.

Hal met Federica in Le Caprice. He noticed that in the space of a couple of months she had lost considerable weight. She noticed how thin and pale he was. 'You look dreadful, Hal. What on earth is going on?' she asked, ordering a bottle of still water.

'A Bloody Mary for me,' said Hal. 'I'm fine. You look well.'

'Thank you,' she replied. 'I'm getting myself under control,' she added proudly. She had lost almost a whole stone.

'Good for you. This lunch is on you, right?'

'Right.'

'Good, let's order, I'm famished,' he said, opening the menu. 'How's Mama?'

'Fine, I suppose. Annoying as usual,' he muttered.

'Toby and Julian?'

'Why don't you ask them yourself? You never go down and see them.'

'There's been so little time.'

'Sure.'

'Really.'

'I'll have a steak and chips,' he said, closing the menu.

'You don't look as if you eat steak and chips. You look as if you've got an eating disorder.'

'For God's sake, you sound like Mama,' he complained. 'Anyway, what's this lunch for? I can't believe it's just a social.'

'It is a social. I haven't seen you properly in years.'

'Not my fault.'

'No, it's not. But I need your help too.'

'What?' he sighed, rolling his eyes. She had intended to tell him about her father's note, but he was so hostile and aloof she changed her mind.

'I need you to get Abuelita's telephone number from Mama,' she said.

'Why can't you get it yourself?'

'Because I don't want her to know I want it,' she explained. 'All you need to do is look it up in her book, it's sure to be there.'

'Why don't you want her to know? Abuelita is your grandmother.'

'And Papa's mother,' she said. 'Hal, don't be so naïve. Mama hasn't spoken to her in years, literally. She hates Papa. She hated it when he wrote to us.'

'To *you*,' he snapped. 'He never wrote to me.'

'Whatever. It's just better to do it secretly, believe me.'

'It'll cost you.'

'What?'

'Yes, it will,' he said resolutely.

'You're not serious?'

'Of course I am,' he insisted coolly. 'What do I get out of it otherwise?'

'Well, how much then?' she asked.

'One hundred pounds.'

'One hundred pounds?' she gasped. 'You must be joking!'

'I had to take the train, return ticket. Besides, it's a fag. It's the least you can do. It's Torquil's money anyway and he's rolling.'

Federica watched her brother and barely recognised the Hal she had grown up with. She frowned. 'You're strange today. What's the matter with you?' she asked, searching his face for an expression she recognised.

'The money or no telephone number.'

'Address and telephone, Cachagua and Santiago,' she said firmly.

'Okay, done.'

'Good,' she replied, shaking his hand. He dug his knife into the steak.

'I want the money now,' he said, getting up.

'Where are you going?'

'To the men's room. Won't be a minute.' She watched him meander unsteadily through the restaurant and wondered whether their father was keeping an eye on him as well. Then she remembered that Ramon had never written to Hal.

Helena was too ashamed to tell her parents the real reason Arthur had locked her out of the house. She moved back into her old room where she paced the floors in rage.

'Poor Helena,' Polly lamented to her husband. 'She's furious with Arthur.'

'No she's not,' said Jake simply. 'She's furious with herself. She's blown it again.'

Helena wouldn't hear a word said against Arthur. When she called Federica to tell her, she terminated the conversation abruptly by slamming down the telephone because her daughter had immediately blamed her stepfather.

'Oh, Federica,' she sighed impatiently. 'You know nothing about it.'

She had driven round to see Arthur the following morning, beat upon the door and even followed him to work. 'Arthur, I can explain,' she had begged, but he wouldn't listen.

'You've gone too far, Helena,' he had replied flatly. 'You've drained me dry. I don't want you back unless you're willing to change and you can't decide that in a day. Go away and think about it.' Shocked by the apparent stubbing out of his emotions she had limped back home to wail on her mother's shoulder that he no longer loved her.

Only Toby was told the truth. 'I had an affair,' she confessed as they sat on the windy beach, talking over the rush of the surf and the cries of the gulls.

'Oh, Helena,' Toby sighed. 'Who with, for God's sake?'

'A Spaniard.'

'A Spaniard?' he exclaimed, shaking his head at his sister's foolishness.

'A bloody Spaniard,' she retorted, folding her arms in front of her chest and sniffing with self-pity.

'Why?'

'Because he reminded me of Ramon.'

Toby prodded the sand with a stick. 'You're obsessed with a ghost, Helena,' he said gravely.

'I know,' she replied, then more angrily, 'I know *now*, don't I!'

'You always want what you can't have.'

'I don't need you to tell me that,' she snapped defensively. 'I've been an idiot, I'm the first to admit it.'

'Did you ever love Arthur?' he asked. She looked out across

the waves to the grey clouds moving swiftly towards them and recalled her husband's fury. 'Well, did you?' he repeated.

'Of course I did. I just didn't recognise it.' Toby frowned. 'It's not the all-consuming love of Ramon,' she explained. 'It's something quieter. I don't think I heard it. I was too busy listening out for the roar. My love for Arthur is more gentle. It's taken me a while, but I hear it now.'

'The roar always subsides before long, then if you're lucky you're left with something much stronger and more lasting,' Toby chuckled, thinking of Julian. 'Arthur's a good man.'

'I realise that now. I can't believe that it took an empty, meaningless affair to wake up and realise how much Arthur means to me. I've treated him so badly. I've been so off-hand with him. He just sat back and let me behave so appallingly. What other man would be so indulgent? I don't deserve him.' Then she looked at her brother with big, sad eyes. 'I've lost him, haven't I?' she said.

Toby put an arm around her shoulders and kissed her head that smelt of salt. 'I don't know, sweetheart. You never seem to learn from your mistakes.'

Chapter Thirty-Eight

Sam watched the rain rattle against the glass windows of Nuno's study. The flames crackled in the fireplace where Nuno had always stoked the logs with the steel poker when he had needed to gather together his thoughts and Trotsky lay on the rug, breathing heavily in his sleep. But Sam felt the cold in his bones and shuddered. He settled his gaze on the leather sofa where Federica had sat and recalled her eyes, opaque with resignation and her unhappy body that took the brunt of too much comfort food. He felt gutted inside. He had lost Nuno, his beloved grandfather and friend, but he had also lost Federica to another, wholly unsuitable man. He sighed hopelessly; he was fooling himself for he had never had her to lose. When he could have had her he hadn't wanted her.

He stood up and paced the room in order to warm up. He pulled his jersey over his icy hands and hunched his shoulders. He hadn't written a word since he had returned home to write. He had toyed with the idea of buying a cottage like Toby and Julian's, a young man of thirty-one shouldn't live at home with his parents, but he didn't have the energy or the incentive to find one. While he was at Pickthistle Manor he didn't have to go out for company, cook his own food, or pay rent or a mortgage. His father was grateful for his company and talked his theories through with him in front of the sitting room fire where Federica had first roasted marshmallows with Molly and Hester.

Ingrid floated about the rooms like a spectre in her long gowns, leaving a trail of smoke behind her and barely noticing that Sam was there at all. She continued to operate the animal sanctuary which was so overcrowded that when Sam had returned home from London he had opened his sweater drawer to discover a hibernating squirrel curled up in his favourite cashmere V-neck. When he had confronted her about it she had smiled happily and replied, 'So that's where Amos is! You know, darling, I've been looking for him the entire winter. You won't disturb him until the spring, will you?'

So Sam had borrowed his father's sweaters, which all had holes in them, either from moths or mice, for he had never done a day's manual labour in his life and went out so very little they rarely saw the light of day. When Inigo failed to recognise the ragged jersey on Sam's back, he patted him firmly on the shoulder and said, 'Son, if you need money you won't be too proud to ask, will you?' Sam had replied that he was more than comfortable. His two younger brothers came home on weekends. Lucien was at Cambridge and Joey in his last year at school. Molly and Hester came down when they could, as both now had full-time jobs which gave them very little time off.

Molly always managed to find something snide to say about Federica while Hester mourned the loss of her friend. 'We were once so close,' she would sigh. 'We told each other everything.'

'Well, that's what happens when someone lets wealth and society go to their head,' said Molly unkindly. 'If you and I were grander, Hester, you can be sure she wouldn't have dropped us like hot potatoes.'

But Sam knew the truth because he wasn't blinded by jealousy like Molly. He kept his feelings to himself and hid behind the heavy oak door of Nuno's study.

'Sam's just like Dad,' Molly laughed one weekend when he had only emerged for meals, 'he's growing moody too.'

Sam longed to telephone Federica, but he didn't know what to say and he didn't want her to know that he had written the note. After their conversation at Nuno's funeral he doubted she'd be too happy to hear from him. So, out of frustration at not being able to communicate he decided to write another anonymous note. He opened Nuno's book and sat by the fire, shivering with cold, and endeavoured to find a few lines that would be helpful to her. The lines encircled by Nuno were very different from the ones that would be appropriate for Federica, for Violet had needed encouragement to love whereas Federica needed encouragement to live – to live independently and not according to the will of another. He turned the pages, chewing the end of his pencil in concentration. He could use one of the verses on love, but that would be more apt for himself for he was suffering on the 'threshing-floor' of love because Federica tormented his thoughts and burned holes in his heart. He could use one of the verses on sorrow for that would teach her that joy and sorrow are inseparable, for without one it is impossible to know the other.

Then he came across a verse on freedom and realised that none other was more suitable. He tapped the page triumphantly with the damp end of his pencil and thought: it is within Federica's own power to walk away. Torquil treats her according to how she allows him to treat her. She can always say no and she must say no. He read it out loud to Trotsky who opened his saggy eyes, yawned and stretched before cocking his head to one side and pricking his ears up attentively.

'For how can a tyrant rule the free and the proud, but for a tyranny in their own freedom and a shame in their own pride? And if it is a care you would cast off, that care has been chosen by you rather than imposed upon you. And if it is a fear you would dispel, the seat of that fear is in your heart and not in the hand of the feared.'

Sam sat at Nuno's desk in front of his computer and typed it out. Then he spent the next half hour printing it, typing the envelope and sealing it because every action was done with the utmost care as if it were a love letter that contained the secrets of his heart. Excited at the prospect of catching a glimpse of Federica he took the early train the following morning, staring out of the window all the way because he was too distracted to read. He arrived by taxi in time to see her leaving her house and climbing into the awaiting car.

'Follow the Mercedes,' said Sam to the driver, then he sat back and listened to the thumping of his own heart and the cautiously optimistic thoughts that whirred around in his head.

He had been struck immediately by her figure. She had slimmed down a bit and her step had regained that buoyancy it had always had before she married. Her skin was no longer ravaged by strain but glowed with health. He wondered whether his note might have inspired the change. Then his face dropped with gloom; perhaps it was Torquil.

Federica was excited by her new approach to life, though it hadn't been easy. She had had to work hard with her personal trainer to lose the weight and change her diet. It had been demoralising. She hadn't taken a good look at herself in the mirror for months and when her clothes had no longer fit she had simply asked Torquil to buy her more. She was fatter than she had imagined. She had put on a couple of stone and her skin had suffered because of all the junk food. Suddenly she couldn't hide any more, for John Burly arrived on Mondays, Wednesdays and Fridays to weigh her, measure her and work her until the sweat oozed out of every pore like blood, often making her cry out dispiritedly, 'I can't do it. I'm just made to be fat.'

But he would reply, 'All right, if you want to stay fat, that's fine, you don't need me to stay fat,' until she begged him to continue. She had made sure the fridge was stocked with fruit and vegetables and stuck to the rigorous diet only because every time she hankered after a bag of crisps or a bar of chocolate she remembered Torquil's cruel names and chewed on a carrot instead.

Instead of spending Torquil's money on clothes she paid regular visits to the beautician and began to take pride in her appearance again. As the weight fell off, so her confidence grew. She also derived strength from her father's note that she hid at the bottom of the butterfly box and brought out during the day when Torquil was at work and she could be alone with her thoughts. She was certain her father had been in the country, seen her and sent it. She wished he had approached her but understood why he might have been reticent. She wanted him to know that she didn't blame him and that she still loved him. As

485

the days got increasingly colder in the run-up to Christmas Federica waited for Hal to call her with her grandparents' telephone number, but he never did.

Then Federica took her first tentative step at independence. It was small, but highly significant. She took the car to Sloane Street and bought herself new clothes to replace the ones that were now too big for her. They were still the grey and navy trouser suits that Torquil always chose for her, but the fact that she had gone out and bought them herself gave her a satisfying sense of defiance. She had staged her first rebellion.

To her surprise Torquil didn't notice. To her greater surprise she didn't care. He applauded her on her slimmer shape, embracing her in his overpowering arms and kissing her with adulterous lips. 'Aren't you clever, little one, I'm so proud of you,' he said. 'You're almost back to the Federica I married.'

She should have been thrilled; after all she had slimmed for him. Or had she? Little by little Torquil shifted from the centre of her world.

Now Sam followed Federica to St James's where she stepped out of the car and walked up the street. He waited for her to get half way up the pavement and then leapt out to follow her. She was dressed in a long black coat with black suede boots under a pale grey trouser suit and cream silk shirt. She looked elegant and sophisticated, with her long white hair tied into a neat ponytail that fell down the back of her coat. She wasn't the skinny teenager he had known in Polperro, full of uncertainty and doubt. She was fuller and more womanly, reflecting her growing confidence. His emotions caught in his throat because he loved her better like that. He was consumed with the longing to tell her.

She stopped once or twice to look into shop windows or to glance at her own reflection which still succeeded in surprising her. He walked a hundred yards behind her, his head hidden under his father's felt hat, hands buried in the pockets of his coat covered in dog hair, with a hole gnawed into the elbow by an overzealous mouse, no doubt. He hunched his shoulders and watched her through his glasses that kept steaming up due to the cold and drizzle. He felt like a stalker and blushed in shame, causing his glasses to mist up even more until he could barely see through them.

He followed her up Arlington Street towards the Ritz where he was sure she was meeting someone for lunch. But he was surprised when she walked on past the doormen, who all touched their caps with white-gloved hands, and continued on in the direction of Green Park. He walked faster, dodging the people who spilled out of the tube station, and watched her enter the park. He hid behind the gate as she strolled like a homing pigeon along the path to a bench that stood under the bare winter trees. She sat down, placed her handbag on her knees and stared out across the misty park.

Sam walked along the iron fencing until he stood behind her, about one hundred yards away, and gazed upon the solitary figure who was clearly not waiting for anyone, for she didn't look around in anticipation, or glance at her watch, she just stared in front of her, without moving, lost in thought.

Sam took his hands out of his pockets and held on to the wet iron bars that separated him from the woman he loved. He longed to call out her name. The sound of it on his lips would be a luxury for he never spoke of her to anyone. But he didn't dare. He just stood, with his hands frozen onto the railings, wondering what she was thinking about, content just to be near her. He recognised the lonely slope of her shoulders and the wistful tilt of her head because he knew what it was to be lonely and he understood. Once or twice she scratched her nose or curled a piece of stray hair behind her ear, while he waited for her to get up and move on. But after an hour, when she still hadn't made a move to leave, he decided to return to her house to slip the note through the door.

Reluctantly he left her and walked up the street towards St James's. He suddenly shivered with cold and pushed his hands deep into his pockets again. He strode past her car out of curiosity to find the chauffeur asleep with his head buried into the rolls in his chin. He was dribbling out of the side of his mouth and a long web of saliva extended from his jaw down to his lapel.

Sam seized his moment and pushed the note through the gap in the back window, where Federica had left it slightly open. He watched it fall onto the seat, face up, with the name Federica Campione typed onto the envelope with love.

Federica sat and savoured the fact that Torquil didn't know where she was. She enjoyed these private moments alone with her memories. She thought about her inability to conceive and decided that it wouldn't be fair to bring a child into such a troubled marriage. Perhaps it was God's will because He could see the bigger picture. She thought about Christmas and whether Torquil might accompany her down to Polperro to spend it with her family. Every year he had promised, every year he had flown her off to somewhere exotic instead. She had called her mother each time and excused him with such fervour that in the end she had believed her own invented excuses. But inside she had felt desperately let down. She wanted more than anything to go home to Cornwall.

She liked to recall her youth. Her memories comforted her and carried her out of herself and her unhappiness. She remembered the picnics on the beaches when the sand blew into the sandwiches and it was so cold they sat in their Guernsey sweaters shivering in a huddle before Toby would gather them up to hunt for sea urchins and crabs. Julian would collect shells and help them build castles while Helena would sit on the rug talking to her mother, every now and then applauding their efforts absentmindedly. Those had been idyllic days.

She spoke to Toby and Julian, her mother and occasionally Hester, but not as often as in the early days when she had sneaked into Harrods to the payphones. Time and circumstances had come between them like an insurmountable mountain. She made excuses for that too – but if she was honest with herself she knew that it was because Torquil didn't like her family. He thought they were provincial, and he did his best to distance her from them. With determination she could overcome that mountain, but she didn't know whether she had the courage to defy her husband.

Federica was so used to loving Torquil that it had become a habit. At first she had needed him and he had cultivated that need until she had no longer been able to do without him. Then she had lost the ability to think for herself. In the four years of their marriage he had slowly pummelled her into the ground – but from there the only way was up. How auspicious that it had been at the point of utter despair that her father had sent her his secret message, encouraging her to build herself back up again and regain her lost confidence and her lost control. She had been ready to clutch at anything. She couldn't do it alone.

She thought about her father and wondered how she was going to track him down from London. If he had been in the city he would probably have left by now. Ramon never stayed very long in one place. His shadow always caught up with him and urged him on. At one point she felt the heat of someone's eyes burn into the back of her neck. She curled a piece of hair behind her ear self-consciously but didn't dare turn around. She shuffled uneasily on the bench. But there was something familiar about the weight of the stare. Comfortably familiar. She suddenly imagined it might be her father, watching her from the street, not wanting to be seen. With a sudden burst of courage she turned around. With hopeful eyes she searched the crowd of unfamiliar faces through the winter mists, but she didn't recognise a single one. She sighed in disappointment, looked at her watch and decided it was time to make her way back to the car.

She walked down the street, her eyes fixed on the pavement, wondering how she was going to broach the subject of Christmas. When she got back to the car she saw the chauffeur asleep in his own snot and knocked on the window. He jerked back to life, fumbled for the lock and rolled out of his seat to open the door for her. But Federica had already spotted the letter and had opened the door herself. She told him to take her home and with a trembling hand she read the name on the envelope, Federica Campione. It was almost certainly from her father, for he wouldn't know her married name and no one whom she knew would have used Campione. She tore it open and with hungry eyes devoured the words as if they were the word of God. He had been watching her after all.

'For how can a tyrant rule the free and the proud, but for a tyranny in their own freedom and a shame in their own pride? And if it is a care you would cast off, that care has been chosen by you rather than imposed upon you. And if it is a fear you would dispel, the seat of that fear is in your heart and not in the hand of the feared.'

She felt the colour rise in her cheeks until it throbbed with shame. 'Stop the car, I need to get out,' she said suddenly.

'What, now?' exclaimed the chauffeur, glancing at her in the mirror.

'Now,' she repeated.

'Yes, madam,' he replied in bewilderment. Reluctantly he drew into a quiet street and pulled up at the kerb. Federica threw open the door and staggered out onto the wet pavement. She walked hastily up the road until she found a small café. Dashing inside she took the table in the corner, ordered a cup of tea and stared down at the note in horror. Had she really no pride at all? Was her misery really due to her own weakness and lack of character? Was Torquil, the man she believed she loved, really a tyrant, controlling her every move?

She had wallowed so blindly in misery, feeling sorry for herself, she had never dared believe that her salvation was entirely in her own hands. Obedience had come more naturally to her than rebellion. Now she cringed at her own lack of strength. She was pathetic. She read the lines again and it all suddenly seemed so obvious. Staring into her tea she shone an unforgiving light onto the nature of her marriage. What she saw appalled her. She had allowed Torquil to control every aspect of her life, from the clothes she wore to the people she saw. She recalled with regret how he had cleverly prevented her from going home to Polperro. One by one she remembered each gradual move towards total dictatorship. He hadn't been satisfied with her love; he had wanted her freedom too. Sam had been right. She wished she had had the courage to take his hand when he had reached out to her. Even Arthur had warned her, but she hadn't listened.

She finally returned to the house in the late afternoon. Torquil wasn't home. She opened the fridge and pulled out a bottle of grapefruit juice. Then she walked upstairs and ran a bath. Her body trembled with resolution. She was going to spend Christmas in Polperro whether Torquil liked it or not. In fact, she was going to start standing up for herself. She undressed and slipped into a dressing gown, rehearsing what she was going to say to him. It seemed simple, but she feared her throat would seize up when she confronted him face to face.

Then she panicked that he might have organised something else, recalling his threat to whisk her off to Mauritius and she cringed. There's no reason he would have told her. She had always let him plan everything, she didn't even keep a diary. She had to be prepared so that he couldn't manipulate her. She ran downstairs to his study and began to open all the drawers in his desk. Everything had its own place, even the pencils were neatly lined up, sharpened to the same length, barely used. Finding nothing in his desk drawers she continued the search in the cupboards but once again she found nothing. No plane tickets, nothing. She rushed upstairs into his large walk-in wardrobe where polished shoes were displayed in regimental lines, each pair fitted with mahogany shoe-trees.

Suddenly the search ceased to be for a diary but for something else, as if at once she had grown up and was finally able to see the world outside the cocoon her husband had forged for her. Feverishly her hands searched the pockets of his jackets and the pockets of his trousers, all in perfect rows on wooden hangers. Her heart thumped with anxiety for she was aware that he could turn up at any moment. Her curiosity led her to the drawer in his bedside table where her fingers alighted upon a square pocket book. She picked it up and opened it. It was a leather-bound notebook, which contained handwritten lists of things to be done. Stuck onto the front was a Polaroid of a young woman sitting naked on a chair with her legs spread in shameless abandon, smiling with the knowledge of the power of her allure. Federica's heart froze. She recognised the face and she recognised the occasion. How come it had taken her so long to figure it out?

Federica called Hester. Her friend detected the strange tone in her voice and knew that something dramatic had happened. 'What has he done to you?' she asked.

'I need you now,' Federica pleaded and her eyes filled with tears. 'Will you come and pick me up?'

Hester put down the telephone, grabbed her keys and slammed the door behind her, all without a word to Molly who poked her head out of the steaming bathroom and wondered what on earth was going on.

When Hester arrived at Federica's house she was standing in the doorway in her dressing gown, clutching a plain wooden box. She ran down the steps, fearfully looking about her, and dived into the waiting car.

'You're coming like that?' Hester gasped in amazement.

Federica collapsed into sobs. 'Yes, because this is all I took into my marriage. My box and my trust.'

It was only once she was safely in the flat in Pimlico that Federica's sobs turned into hysterical laughter. Molly and Hester looked at each other anxiously, both recalling Helena's wedding when she had sobbed maniacally for Sam. When she had calmed down enough to speak she dried her eyes on her dressing gown sleeve and sniffed.

'Are you all right?' Molly asked anxiously.

'Oh, I'm much better,' she replied, controlling herself with difficulty. 'It's just that I forgot to turn off the bath!'

Chapter Thirty-Nine

Torquil returned home to find water pouring down the stairs. Fearing that Federica might be in trouble, he raced up to the bedroom, his feet slipping on the slimy carpet, the blood flooding to his head with anxiety.

'Federica!' he shouted, 'Federica! Are you all right?' He stumbled into the bathroom where the water was cascading over the edges in a final act of defiance. He turned off the taps and thrust his hand to the bottom and pulled out the plug. It gurgled with satisfaction. 'Shit!' he swore, looking at the expensive carpets which would all have to be replaced.

He cast his eyes about for his wife, but all that remained were her clothes neatly folded on the bed. He noticed only one dressing gown hung on the back of the door. He called her name again and proceeded to check the rest of the house. There was no reply, only the empty echo of his own voice as it bounced off the walls. He sat on the edge of the bed and rubbed his chin with his hand.

He was very worried. She had simply disappeared. But there was no indication of a struggle, or a break in, just the overflowing bath. Finally, he picked up the telephone and called the chauffeur.

'Well, Mr Jensen,' Paul replied thoughtfully, 'she goes shopping in St James's for about an hour, then when I'm driving her back, see, she asks me to stop, all of a sudden. Well, as you can imagine, Mr Jensen, I was a bit worried. She looked upset . . . No, I don't know why, Mr Jensen, she just looked pale like. She runs up the pavement and disappears into a caff for about an hour. When I drop her off, see, she's all right. So I go home, Mr Jensen. She said she didn't need me any more.' A short silence followed. 'Mr Jensen?' asked the chauffeur, afraid that he had perhaps made a mistake. 'Mr Jensen? Mrs Jensen didn't need me after that, did she?'

'It's fine, Paul,' Torquil replied, but his voice cracked mid-sentence. He put down the telephone and scratched his bristled jaw line ponderously. Then something caught his eye. The drawer to the bedside table was open a crack where Federica had failed to close it properly. Torquil always noticed details. He opened it to find his pocket book lying upside down, not as he had left it at all. He picked it up and studied it. With a deep groan he eyed the photograph of Lucia, which he had stuck onto the inside cover. Then it all made sense. She had run off in such a state she had forgotten to turn the taps off.

He unstuck the picture and tore it into small pieces before throwing them in the bin in fury. She had completely misunderstood, that photograph had been taken years before. He'd explain it all to her and she'd forgive him. He cast his eyes fretfully about the room to see if she had packed a bag. She hadn't. She hadn't taken anything, not even her underwear. She must have left in her dressing gown. He relaxed his shoulders. She was obviously planning on coming back. After all, how far could she go in a dressing gown?

Federica told Molly and Hester everything, omitting the part about the anonymous notes of poetry, which would remain her secret until she managed to track down her father.

The three friends sat in front of the gas fire with two bottles of cheap red wine, while Kenny Rogers sang 'It's a fine time to leave me, Lucille'.

Molly was fascinated by Federica's unhappy world. She had failed to see past the designer clothes and crocodile handbags.

Hester listened with deep sympathy. 'I knew you were miserable, Fede, I could tell. What are you going to do now?'

'Go home to Polperro and start again,' she said simply.

'You mean, you're going to leave Torquil?' Molly exclaimed, lighting a cigarette.

'Of course she's going to leave Torquil,' Hester said. 'He's a monster. You deserve so much better,' she added, squeezing Federica's arm affectionately.

'Oh, I don't want to look at another man as long as I live,' Federica sniffed. 'I want to be on my own for a while, make my own decisions. I need to work out who I am. I don't think I'm very sure of anything any more.'

When the telephone rang they all froze. Molly and Hester looked at Federica who stared back with fear. 'You answer it, Molly,' she said and her voice thinned with anxiety. She put her thumb to her mouth and bit the skin around her nail. 'You haven't seen me,' she added gravely.

Molly got up from the floor and the wine flushed from her head to her toes, restoring her swiftly back to sobriety. She took a deep breath before picking up the receiver. The shrill tones ceased leaving the room in a silence that hung heavy with anticipation.

'Hello,' Molly responded, trying her best to sound normal. Her shoulders dropped. 'Sam! What the hell are you doing calling me now? We're in crisis, that's why . . . What, now? Oh God! You'll have to sleep in the sitting room, Federica's in with Hester . . . it's a long story, we'll tell you when you arrive . . . Okay, see you in a minute.' She hung up with a smile on her face. 'One more for the party,' she laughed. 'Let's get out another bottle of wine.'

'Sam's missed his flipping train,' Molly announced, skipping through to the kitchen.

'Well, that's typical,' Hester sighed. 'He's in a world of his own these days, ever since Nuno died.'

'Poor Sam,' said Federica. 'He really loved Nuno, didn't he?'

'More than anyone else. More than Mum and Dad, I think,' Molly said, returning with another Bordeaux. 'You see, Nuno spent most of his time with Sam. He never had a son, and being the chauvinist that he was, he probably wished he had. So Sam was a kind of surrogate son for him. Dad gave him Nuno's study to write in. God knows what he's writing. But he spends all day locked away just like Dad. The only person allowed anywhere near him is Trotsky,' she added, opening the bottle.

'He should find a girlfriend,' said Hester. 'He used to have so many girlfriends.'

'That was when he had hair.' Molly laughed unkindly.

'He's not Samson, Mol,' Hester reproved in his defence. 'I think he looks lovely with less hair. He doesn't look pretty any more. He looks rugged and handsome.'

Molly scrunched up her nose in distaste. 'Each to their own, I suppose,' she sniffed, blowing smoke out of her mouth in rings.

'One thing I've learnt from Torquil,' said Federica sadly, 'looks can be deceptive. No one's as beautiful as Torquil, or as selfish. I'd rather a plain outside and a beautiful inside.'

Molly lowered her eyes, ashamed that she fancied him.

When Sam arrived at the flat Federica was at once struck by the rapid deterioration of the young man who had once been golden-haired and glossy, like a handsome Greek statue. He shuffled in with his shoulders hunched, shivering with cold. His face was as grey as it had been at Nuno's funeral and his eyes betrayed a certain weariness, for his longing had drained him of all enthusiasm and energy. When he saw her he smiled sheepishly, though he wanted to run to her and hold her against him. Federica recalled their awkward conversation at the funeral and smiled back, indicating that she had forgiven and forgotten. She stood up to greet him.

He placed his hands on her upper arms. 'Are you all right?' he asked seriously.

'I'm fine now,' she replied, pulling away and nursing the bruises he had left on her skin. 'I've left Torquil,' she added, sitting down again on the carpet in front of the fire.

'You've left Torquil?' he repeated incredulously, turning away in case she saw the light return to his eyes and the joy curl his lips into a triumphant grin. 'You've left Torquil?' he repeated.

'It's over,' she stated.

'We're celebrating with wine,' Molly added with glee.

'I'd say we were commiserating with wine,' said Hester. 'Poor Fede's really been through it.'

'What happened?' he asked, taking off his coat and sitting on the sofa. He felt very hot. He struggled out of his father's holey jersey and sat in his blue shirt with the cuffs undone and hanging loosely on his wrists.

'Oh, it's a long story,' she said, sipping the Bordeaux and feeling a lot better.

'Mol, hand me a glass,' he said, cheering up. 'Fede, you're so strong. I'm so proud of you. What you've done is the most difficult thing in the world. You've done it all by yourself.'

'Not entirely,' she replied. Sam looked away. 'Let's just say that my eyes have been opened. I suppose I've grown up a bit. I can't believe I've been so blinkered and so weak. I've wasted four years of my life.'

'Nothing is ever wasted, Fede, you've learned a great deal about human nature but above all about yourself,' he said wisely. Then he changed the subject. 'What are you going to do now?'

'I'm going home. Mama and I are going to be a right pair.'

'Yes, we heard about that,' said Hester. 'I'm so sorry.'

'She's a fool,' Federica sighed. They all frowned at her sudden change of attitude, her opinion of her stepfather was well known.

'I thought you despised Arthur?' Molly interjected, flicking ash onto the carpet.

'Let's say I misunderstood him. Everything's much clearer now,' she grinned at Sam. 'I owe him an apology. Someone else I didn't listen to when I should have.'

Sam acknowledged her with a small smile. 'I'll accompany you on the train if you like,' he suggested.

Federica nodded at him gratefully. 'Would you?' She sighed in relief. 'I'd feel so much better. I'm terrified he'll find me and try to drag me back.'

'I'll bloody kill him if he comes anywhere near you,' he said, then chuckled for he didn't want her to know that he really meant it.

That night Federica and Sam barely slept. They sat up drinking and talking long after Hester and Molly had retired to bed. She unburdened her worries and her secrets to him and he listened with sympathy as he had done that day in the bluebells. 'I wish I had had the courage to tell you that time we had lunch,' she said.

'You so nearly did.'

'I know.'

'What frightened you?' he asked gently.

She thought about it for a while, watching the golden flames of the gas fire springing cheerfully in the grate. 'I didn't realise I was unhappy,' she said truthfully and shook her head in disbelief. 'I know it sounds mad, but I couldn't admit it to myself. I believed I loved him.'

'It doesn't sound mad at all.'

'Doesn't it?'

'No,' he said, and took her hand. 'You weren't wrong to love him. He was wrong to abuse your love.'

She grinned at him fondly. 'You understand everything so well.'

'Not everything,' he replied. 'Just you.'

The following morning Federica borrowed clothes from Hester. She was just pulling on a pair of jeans when Molly shrieked from the sitting room. 'Oh God!' she shouted. 'God, God, God.' They all ran to the window. 'No, Fede, not you,' she said, blocking her way. 'He's there! Waiting for you,' she hissed. 'He's seen me looking.'

Federica paced the room. Molly pulled the curtain back and peered out at the handsome man who stood beside his Porsche with his arms crossed miserably in front of him.

'Shit, what am I going to do?' she said nervously, biting her thumb again.

Sam perched on the arm of the sofa. 'I'll book a cab and we'll leave together,' he stated decisively, picking up the telephone. 'It's simple.'

'I don't think I can face him.'

'Of course you can. You had the strength to leave him, didn't you?' he insisted. 'So you can find the strength to tell him it's over.'

'I don't think I can.'

'You can and you will,' he said seriously. 'Or I'll do it for you.'

'You've gone this far, Fede, you can't back out now,' Hester agreed.

'*I* certainly wouldn't want to go home to a sodden carpet and a furious husband,' Molly said. 'However handsome he is.'

Sam rolled his eyes and ordered the cab. 'Just think about what you'd be going back to,' he said carefully. He held his breath as she walked up and down the room, her hands on her hips, deliberating her next move. Then he added simply, 'Fede, do you like the person you are when you're with Torquil?' She looked at him with fearful eyes and shook her head. 'Well, cast her aside then and come with me.' He stood up and took both her hands in his. 'You know you're doing the right thing.'

'But he loves me,' she protested weakly.

Sam squeezed her hands. 'No he doesn't, Fede. He wants to possess you, like his car or his house. If he loved you he'd take pleasure in your freedom, in your growing confidence, in your successes. If he loved you he'd encourage you to make your own path in life. He'd have bought you a camera and paid for you to have lessons rather than buying you ridiculous shoes and handbags, like a doll for him to manipulate. You're not a doll, Fede, you're a person with your own ideas and your own personality. If you go back he'll just sap you dry until you're incapable of a single personal thought. Think about it.'

She stood staring into his eyes knowing that he was right, because she had worked it out herself.

'Okay, let's do it,' she said firmly. 'But when we leave the house I want to talk to him,' she insisted. Then when she noticed Sam's eyebrows rise in objection she added hastily, 'I need to tell him myself. I need to prove to myself that I can do it.'

Twenty minutes later when Sam and Federica descended the steps which led onto the pavement, Torquil ran up to her and threw his arms around her. Sam immediately tried to separate them. 'Leave us alone!' Torquil growled. There followed a brief tussle during which Federica managed to wriggle free.

'Go away, Torquil!' she shouted. 'It's over.' Then she noticed his dejected face, his bloodshot eyes and his shoulders, which stooped pitifully.

'I haven't slept all night. I've been so worried,' he explained, raising his palms to the sky. 'You could have let me know where you were. I thought you'd been abducted.'

Federica turned to Sam. 'Wait for me in the cab,' she instructed. With a suspended heart Sam walked away from her. He stood by the car ready to intercede if she needed him, but he hoped she wouldn't need him. She had to learn not to need anyone, not her father, not her husband, not anyone. Once she had mastered that she'd be ready to love properly. He didn't mind how long it took, he'd wait for her.

'That photograph was taken years ago, little one. Didn't you notice it was old?' Torquil argued, reaching out for her. But Federica stepped back, putting her hands up to keep him at a distance. 'Come on, sweetness, I'm not having an affair. I love you. I'm lost without you. We're good together.'

'It's over, Torquil,' she replied, shaking her head.

'Don't be a fool, Federica. You're angry, I understand. Let's just go home and talk this through sensibly. Don't throw what we have away. It's so special,' he implored, casting his eyes over at Sam who stood by protectively.

'Don't call me "little one". I hate it,' she snapped, suddenly empowered by Torquil's vulnerability. 'I'm not coming home.'

Torquil tried to ignore the defiant tone in her voice. 'It's not what you think, damn it!' he snarled, repressing his frustration with gritted teeth. 'So I made a mistake keeping that photograph, are you going to punish me for a little mistake? What's important is that I love you. Love is about forgiveness, goddammit.'

'Love is about trust,' she replied coldly.

'Then trust me when I tell you I'm not having an affair. Lucia's an old friend, that photograph was a joke.'

'I don't believe you.'

'Do you believe me when I tell you I love you?' he pleaded with her.

'You don't love me, Torquil. You want to possess me, like your car, or your house. I'm like a doll, you dress me, you take me out every now and then to play with me, but you don't love me. If you did you'd let me make my own decisions.' Federica began to feel light in the head with the swelling of her confidence.

Torquil was stunned. She had never spoken like that before. He breathed in through his nose like a seething bull, unable to control his growing anger. 'What are you going to?' he said quietly, narrowing his eyes aggressively. 'A provincial town on the coast? Back to your neurotic mother or your bourgeois grandparents?' Then he nodded in Sam's direction and added cuttingly, 'Or to a family of eccentrics?' Sam suppressed his smile. 'I can give you everything you want.'

Federica straightened herself up boldly. 'What? A few more handbags, a few more pairs of shoes? Please, Torquil, don't patronise me. You're hollow inside and I don't want to be with you any more. We'll communicate through lawyers and don't try to follow me, because, you know what? Sam's family eccentricities are contagious and you wouldn't want to catch them like I have, would you?'

'You'll regret this for the rest of your life. I won't take you back. You'll be sorry,' he shouted as she walked to where Sam waited for her by the open door of the cab. He smiled at her with pride as she climbed in, then he followed her and closed the door behind him. When he looked up at the window to Molly and Hester's flat their happy faces grinned at him from behind the glass. Hester put her thumb up and nodded.

Torquil drove away, the wheels of his Porsche skidding and leaving two black stripes on the tarmac that steamed in fury.

Federica collapsed into the seat, suddenly aware of her trembling hands and legs.

'Any more of those, Gov?' asked the cabbie, who had watched the confrontation with relish. 'That's better than *EastEnders*, that is.'

'To Paddington Station, please,' said Sam, putting his arm around Federica's shoulders.

She allowed him to gather her up as she quietly reflected on the last four years of her life with relief and regret.

Federica returned to much celebrating, because not only was it Christmas, but everyone was delighted to have her back again. Ingrid now admitted that she had thought Torquil a 'ghastly man' while Toby and Julian confessed that they had only remembered where they had seen him when it was too late to do anything about it. 'He was arrogant and self-satisfied then,' they said. 'We really let you down, Fede.'

Helena was delighted that someone else was as miserable as she was and accompanied her daughter on long walks along the cliffs, lamenting Arthur's painful silence. 'I've lost him, Fede. He won't even talk to me,' she whined.

Jake and Polly gathered her up like they had gathered up her mother. Suddenly the family united in the drama. Polly cooked large vegetable lasagnes and bread and butter puddings and all seven of them sat about the table, surrounded by Jake's model boats which now hung suspended from the ceiling so they couldn't be knocked onto the floor by clumsy elbows and hands, drinking large glasses of wine and Polly's elderflower juice, carrying on four conversations at once.

Federica moved straight back in with Toby and Julian and

Rasta, who she'd take out on her long walks with her mother. She helped Toby decorate the rooms for Christmas and Julian took her into town to shop for presents. 'I don't have a bean,' she said, thinking of the mountains of beans she had left in London.

'I do,' said Julian happily, 'and you can have as many as you like.'

She spent as much time at Pickthistle Manor as she did at Toby and Julian's. The squirrel in Sam's sweater drawer had woken up before time, so Ingrid had managed to secure his nest on the top of the Christmas tree, but a family of mice had somehow found their way under Sam's bed so he had to sleep in one of the spare rooms so as not to disturb them. The two families celebrated Christmas with drinks parties and lunch parties that continued long after the festival was over and the New Year had been toasted in with champagne and embraces.

When Sam hugged Federica he kissed her cheek affectionately and said, 'This will be your year, Fede. You'll see.'

She hoped he was right.

Torquil sent her long letters in an attempt to win her back. He wrote about his deep love for her and his regret that he had ever laid eyes on Lucia. 'Everything I did was for you, because I wanted to protect you. I'm only guilty of caring too much,' he wrote. At first Federica read them, then as they got increasingly repetitive and pitiful she simply destroyed them unopened. However, one line lingered in her thoughts: 'I'm only guilty of caring too much.' Said by the deceiving Torquil it was nothing more than an empty sentence; however, applied to Arthur it was given a whole new meaning.

Federica felt desperately sorry for Arthur, so forgotten amid the destruction of her own marriage. She knew her mother was hard to live with, but she also knew that she desperately cared. After all, she had listened to Helena's soliloquies of remorse during their long walks on the cliffs. It was time to intervene.

When Arthur saw Federica at his door he initially felt sick with disappointment. He had thought it was Helena. But then his surprise turned to amazement. 'What are you doing here?' he asked.

'I've come to apologise, Arthur,' she replied. He remained in the frame of the door with his mouth agape. 'Can I come in?' she asked.

'Of course. Of course,' he stammered, standing aside to let her pass. She walked into the kitchen and took her coat off. 'Please sit down, here, let me take this for you,' he said, draping it over the back of one of the chairs. 'Tea?'

'Yes, please, it's freezing,' she said, rubbing her pink hands together.

'How did you get here?'

'By taxi.'

'Does your mother know you're here?' he asked anxiously.

'No.'

'Good.'

He handed her a cup of tea then sat down opposite her. Federica added milk and watched as it disappeared into the brew.

'I've left Torquil,' she stated simply.

'Right,' Arthur replied with care.

'I should have listened to you.'

'No you shouldn't,' he said quickly, disarmed by her sudden change in attitude. 'It was none of my business.'

'Yes, it was,' she insisted. 'You're my stepfather.'

'Was,' he interjected sadly.

She looked into his anguished eyes and realised that she had never really known him. 'You still are,' she said kindly. 'Mama misses you.'

His face flushed with hope. 'She does?'

'She thinks she's lost you.' Federica watched his small eyes glisten.

'I don't know,' he said, shaking his head and pressing his lips together. 'I just don't know.'

'I'm not coming here to negotiate a peace treaty. I came to apologise because I've treated you badly. You've been wonderful to Mama. I know she can be a nightmare,' she chuckled. 'But you handled her really well.' She looked at him steadily. 'You have to take her back, because no one else would know how to cope with her.'

'She is difficult, but never dull.'

'What attracted you to her in the beginning?' she asked out of curiosity, but unwittingly she unlocked the door to the happy memories that he had wilfully subdued.

He sat back in his chair and smiled. 'I could tell she was difficult. She had had a rough time too, so beneath the frost was a little girl desperate to be loved . . .'

Federica sipped her tea and listened while Arthur related the story of their meeting and their marriage, the good and the bad, until he realised that what he had was worth fighting to keep.

It was late when Arthur drove Federica home. He dropped her off at her uncle's house then hesitated at the wheel, debating whether to drive on to Helena's or to return to his own empty home. He still felt the warmth from his conversation with Federica and smiled inwardly at so many tender recollections. Yet he knew that if a reconciliation was to take place, it had to be on Helena's initiative or the balance of power would weigh in her favour and he'd lose her again. What's more, she had to learn from her mistake and be willing to change. He hoped she hadn't given up on him.

Sam accompanied Federica down to the beach where he'd gather wood for the fires he made and insist on roasting marshmallows just like they had done in the old days. He lent her books to read then discussed them late into the evening beside the happy fire in Nuno's study before driving her home in his father's car. He'd sit in his shirtsleeves on the cliffs as much as in the study because he constantly felt warm inside whether or not there was a fire. As long as he was close to Federica he needed little to exist, just the shared air between them and the knowledge that she was there. Little by little he became as comfortable and as familiar to

Federica as Nuno's old chair. She looked forward to their walks and their excursions, to the dinners they had with his parents and the discussions about literature and history. As the weeks tumbled by Federica thought less and less about Torquil and only suffered the occasional nightmare which reminded her in her waking moments of why she had left him.

But she couldn't forget the notes from her father and she knew she wouldn't rest until she found him.

It was a strange telephone call that made up her mind to fly out to Chile. She was just about to leave the house when it rang. She was always reluctant to pick it up in case it was Torquil, but she reassured herself that it couldn't be him, she hadn't heard from him for weeks. Still, her hand trembled when she lifted the receiver. 'Hello,' she said tentatively.

'Hello,' replied a young woman. Federica's shoulders relaxed. 'Am I speaking to Federica Jensen?'

'Federica Campione, yes, I am she,' she answered firmly. 'Whom am I speaking to?'

'My name is Claire Shawton. I'm a friend of Hal's.'

'Oh, hello,' she said in a friendlier tone. 'How can I help you?'

'Well, it's a bit of a delicate subject really,' she began. 'I didn't want to talk to your mother, because I know how Hal feels about his mother.'

'Right,' said Federica, wondering how he did feel about their mother.

'And I couldn't talk to your stepfather either. Hal's funny about him too.'

'Okay.'

'He speaks very highly of you, though,' she said. 'I found your number in his book. No one answered the London number.'

'I see,' she mumbled, trying not to think about Torquil. 'What's up with Hal?'

'He's an alcoholic,' she stated. 'He needs help. He's in a right mess.'

'What?' said Federica, appalled. 'What sort of mess?'

'He misses all his lectures, sleeps all day, drinks all night. He's barely there at all, you know, he's out of it.'

'Are you sure he's an alcoholic?'

'Yes, I am. I know because I've been paying for his drink and his gambling for the last few months.'

'Gambling?'

'You know, fruit machines, poker, horses. I've paid for it all.'

'Why?'

'Because I'm in love with him,' she replied in shame. 'He doesn't have any money and I have lots. But it's got out of hand. He's drinking too much. He's changed.'

'Where is he now?'

'He's here asleep.'

'At this hour?'

'Yes, you see he stays up drinking all night, then he can't get to sleep so he takes sleeping pills, lots of them. Then he can't wake up. It's like he's dead.' She stammered and her voice quivered with emotion. 'I don't know what to do,' she sniffed.

'Oh God!' Federica sighed. 'What can we do?'

'He needs help.'

'I can see that. I'm coming up. But I'll have to bring someone with me,' she said, remembering that she couldn't drive.

Sam was only too happy to drive Federica to Exeter. They talked all the way about the options open to them. But Sam was adamant that the drink was only the symptom of an illness which lay far deeper. 'He drinks to hide from himself,' he said wisely.

'It all leads back to Papa,' Federica sighed. 'I just know it.'

When they found Hal lying asleep on his bed, his face sallow and lifeless, Federica began to shake him violently, fearing that he was dead and not asleep at all. When he woke up his eyes were bloodshot and distant. Not the Hal she knew at all. Sam looked around the room at the squalor he lived in.

Cigarettes were stubbed out on dirty plates which still bore the remains of greasy fry-ups, empty wine glasses and coffee cups lay collecting dust, clothes were strewn around the floor, mildewing from neglect and damp. The room smelt worse than the rabbit hutch that Hester had once had as a child.

'Hal, you're sick,' Federica said kindly.

'Go away and leave me alone!' he cried, thrashing out with his arms. 'I don't need you to come and lecture me.'

'I care about you, Hal. Look at the state you're in. You live like an animal.'

'It's not so bad,' he protested.

'It's terrible. You need help,' she said.

'I'm fine,' he insisted.

'You're an alcoholic,' she stated bluntly.

'I drink occasionally. So does everyone. That hardly qualifies me as an alcoholic,' he said sarcastically.

Then Claire stepped forward out of the shadows. 'I told her everything, Hal,' she said, wiping the tears from her face.

He stared at her a moment, blinking her into focus. Then his face twisted in defeat. 'You bitch,' he spat.

'It's because I love you that I can't stand by and watch you destroy yourself.'

Hal put his head into his hands and wept.

Hal allowed Sam and Federica to take him home. Claire said that she would pack up his things and sort out his room. Federica thanked her gratefully but knew that Hal would probably never want to see her again. He sat in the back of the car shaking with cold and discomfort, his skin an unhealthy pale green colour – he looked as if he already had one foot in the morgue. Federica and Sam decided that they would keep the nature of his illness secret in order not to upset his family. They agreed to say that he had had a nervous breakdown. Federica knew that he needed to get away, start again somewhere else, far from Helena's possessive love and the horror of his own demons.

'I'm going to take Hal to Chile,' she told Sam.

'When?' Sam exclaimed in alarm.

'As soon as possible. He needs to leave the country for a while. There's only one person who can help him through this, because he helped me through my trouble too.'

'Who's that?' Sam asked, feeling an invisible hand wrap itself around his throat.

'My father.'

'Your father?'

'Yes, he's at the root of Hal's problem.'

'How did he help you?' he asked, fixing his eyes on the road in front of him and gripping the steering wheel in an effort to control his impulses.

'I wasn't going to tell you, because I feared you might think it ridiculous. But Papa sent me anonymous notes of such lovely poetry. He must have written them himself, after all, he's a poet as well as a novelist.'

'I see,' said Sam tightly. His heart flooded with disappointment, but he couldn't bring himself to dampen her happiness and tell her that the notes had really come from him.

'He's very spiritual and philosophical. His notes just opened my eyes, I suppose, and helped me to see my situation more clearly. I felt I wasn't alone, that he was there helping me. He gave me the strength to leave Torquil. I want to thank him. But I think he could help Hal too.'

'So, how long will you stay?'

'As long as it takes. I've got nothing to keep me here.'

'No,' he said flatly, swallowing his misery in order to brood on it later when he was alone. 'Nothing.'

Chapter Forty

Hal wanted to get better. Polly said that was the first step and a very brave step indeed. Helena was appalled when she heard, but Federica was firm. 'He needs a new scene,' she said. 'And so do I.'

Helena insisted that she could nurse him back to health. 'You don't need to take him across the world, for goodness' sake!' she exclaimed, hurt that Hal was ready to leave her and humiliated that she hadn't been able to help him herself.

'We're going to find Papa,' Federica admitted finally. 'I know that Hal's problem goes back to when he was a child in Chile. He needs to talk to him.'

Helena went white with indignation, as if Federica was attacking her personally for leaving Ramon. She sat tight-lipped and furious, smouldering with guilt and jealousy because she wasn't included.

Arthur was so relieved that at last someone had taken responsibility for Hal he bought them their tickets to Santiago.

'Don't thank *me*,' he said to Federica, 'this is to thank *you*. You don't know how grateful I am.'

Federica knew he was discreetly thanking her for more than preserving the health of his stepson. She kissed his fleshy face and whispered, 'Don't forget the good times with Mama, will you. There were many more than bad.'

But Arthur was determined to wait. Sadly he had no choice. If she didn't come back of her own accord, he would have to let her go.

Sam was mortified that Federica was leaving Polperro and hurt that she believed there was no reason to stay. He wanted to shake her, tell her he loved her with his whole heart and his whole being, but he knew that if he did he would ruin any chance he had.

She would come to him when she was ready or not at all. He'd just have to be patient. The day before she left he arrived at Toby and Julian's house to say good-bye. He had bought her a gift, hoping that she'd remember him each time she used it.

'Oh, Sam, you really shouldn't have bought me a present,' she said, taking the package from him. He stood with his hands in his pockets, his moth-eaten jersey barely able to keep out the cold that penetrated right through to his bones. She opened the brown paper to find a Pentax camera. 'My God!' she exclaimed. 'This is a proper camera.'

'It's got a proper zoom lens too,' he said, smiling in order to hide his despair.

'You're so sweet, Sam, thank you,' she replied, kissing him on his taut cheek. He breathed in the scent of her skin that invaded his senses whenever she came close and resisted the impulse to pull her against him and kiss her properly like he had done that night in the barn.

'Don't forget your friend, will you?' he said, suppressing his emotion.

She grinned at him with gratitude. 'You've been such a good friend, Sam. I'm so grateful. If it hadn't been for you, I'd never have got through these last weeks.'

'Well, don't forget that you did it all by yourself,' he said. 'You don't need anyone any more, you're strong on your own.'

Federica frowned at him and thought how like her father he sounded.

Mariana had just come in from a walk along the beach when the telephone rang. She picked it up to hear the crackle of a long-distance call and then the thin voice of a young woman. '*Hola, quién es?*' she said, putting her hand over her other ear to muffle the sound of Ramoncito who was playing a competitive game of chess with his grandfather.

'It's Federica.'

Mariana caught her breath. 'Fede? Is that you?' she gasped in English.

'Abuelita, it's really me,' she exclaimed, feeling a wave of nostalgia hit her.

'It's been so long! How are you?'

'I'm coming out to Chile tomorrow with Hal. Can we come and stay?'

'Well, of course you can,' she said in excitement. 'I don't believe it. I thought you'd forgotten about us.'

'I never forgot about you, Abuelita. I have so much to tell you, so much . . .' she said, the joy catching in her throat and making it difficult to speak. 'Is Papa with you?' she asked hoarsely.

'He has a house on the beach, between here and Zapallar.'

'Will he be there?'

'Yes,' she said happily. 'Yes he will. He'll be so happy to see you both! I'll send a car to pick you up and bring you down.' Then she added hopefully, 'How long will you be staying?' And Federica couldn't help but laugh for her grandmother hadn't changed at all.

'I don't know,' she replied and then wondered if she'd ever leave.

When Mariana walked out onto the terrace, her old eyes streaming with joy, Ignacio looked up from his chess game. 'What's happened?' he asked, wondering what kind of miracle had the power to make her face glow like that.

Mariana rubbed her hands together, unable to contain her happiness. 'Ramoncito,' she said. 'You're going to meet your half-brother and sister. They're arriving in two days to stay.'

Ramoncito looked at his grandfather whose face crumpled with delight.

'Woman, you sure know how to distract our concentration,' he said and grinned at her. 'I thought they'd forgotten about us,' he added, taking his glasses off and wiping his eyes.

'No, and what's more they have no plans,' she said hopefully.

'Maybe they're coming home,' he said, looking at his wife with tenderness.

'Maybe.' Then she bustled into the cool interior of the house to prepare their rooms. She wanted to do it personally and Gertrude couldn't be trusted to get it right. Gertrude couldn't be trusted to get anything right, but for some reason Ignacio liked her, so she stayed.

'Abuelito?' said Ramoncito, moving his piece across the board. His grandfather put his glasses back on the bridge of his nose and looked at his grandson over the top of them. 'Will I like Hal and Federica?'

'Yes, you will, you'll like them very much. But you have to remember that they were torn from their father when they were very small. They're coming out with a lot of emotional baggage. Be patient and give them time to sort it out. Your father loves you, Ramoncito, and he loved your mother more than he ever loved anyone. Don't forget that.'

The boy nodded and watched his grandfather turn his attention back to the game.

Ramon typed the last line of his book with great satisfaction. It had been cathartic. Estella had shown him that it was possible to love without possessiveness, to love enough to give the other his freedom. Her life had quite literally changed his. In a way he felt she had unwittingly sacrificed herself for his enlightenment. She had set an example and he had learnt from it. He only wished that he had had the inner ability to learn from her while she had been alive. So he aired his feelings of guilt and failure which had clung to his conscience since he had wilfully abandoned his children, in an allegory about three birds: the peacock who demands love's total commitment, the swallow who flies away from love and the third, the phoenix, who brings her unconditional love without asking for anything in return. When the phoenix disappears into the flames the peacock and the swallow have finally learnt how to love without yearning to possess each other. Ramon was pleased with his work. He entitled it *To Love Enough* and dedicated it 'To those I have loved'.

He thought of Federica and Hal. It was too late to try to make up for his negligence in the past and that greatly saddened him. But he had Ramoncito and poured into him the love he had in his heart for three. He sank into an easy chair and in the half-light of his study he read the manuscript from beginning to end. The shutters were closed against the heat of early afternoon but the gentle surge of the sea filtered through with the scent of honeysuckle and jasmine and caressed his soul that still mourned the loss of Estella.

When Ramoncito found him later he was submerged in his memories, his eyes closed and his breathing heavy. Ramoncito couldn't wait to tell him the news; he knew how happy he'd be. So he shook his shoulder gently. 'Wake up, Papa!' he whispered. 'I have good news for you.'

Ramon opened his eyes and pulled himself out of his warm, rose-scented dreams and blinked up at his son.

'Hal and Federica are arriving in two days from England,' he said and watched his father stare at him in bewilderment. 'It's true. Federica telephoned Abuelita this afternoon. I'm finally going to meet my half-brother and sister,' he said and smiled broadly.

Ramon sat up and rubbed his eyes. 'Tell me again,' he said in confusion. 'Federica and Hal are coming here? Are you sure?'

'Yes,' Ramoncito insisted happily.

'And Helena?'

'No, just Federica and Hal.'

'They're going to stay with my parents, right?'

'Yes.'

'My God, I don't deserve this,' he mumbled, standing up and suffering a terrible head spin.

'Yes, you do, Papa,' said Ramoncito. 'Mama was always telling you to go and see them.'

'And I never listened to her.'

'She'd be happy.'

'I know.'

'Have you finished yet?'

'The book?'

'Yes.'

'Yes, I have.'

'Great, let's open a bottle of wine. We have two things to celebrate now,' said Ramoncito joyfully.

But Ramon was anxious. Federica and Hal knew nothing of Estella and Ramoncito.

Hal and Federica boarded the plane for the long journey across the waters to Chile. Neither knew what to expect, but both hoped that somehow the ghosts of the past would be confronted and exorcised. Hal was pale and visibly shaking with discomfort as his body craved the poison that was destroying it. Federica kept forcing him to drink water to flush it all out, fussing over him like an over-protective nurse. As soon as they boarded the plane he slouched into his chair, closed his fevered eyes and slept.

Federica tried to read but she was unable to concentrate. The events of the last month invaded her thoughts, allowing her no peace. She cast her mind back to Torquil. She had been unhappy right from the start of their marriage, but she had believed she loved him and did everything he asked of her in order to please him. How easy it had been for him to manipulate her and mould her into a submissive pawn. She had taken it all, every humili-ation, until she had grown so accustomed to his controlling nature that she had no longer recognised it or realised that it was within her power to withstand it. She had wanted a father figure to look after her and protect her from the world. It was a miracle that she had grown up at all in the stifling air of their marriage where his overbearing personality had stunted her growth, but somehow she had realised that she no longer wanted someone to live for her, but to live herself in the way she wanted.

It sounded simple with hindsight. She should have left earlier. She was appalled at her own lack of character and vowed to herself silently that she would never let anyone treat her like that again. She thought of her father and the notes of poetry he had sent her. It had been due to his support that she had been able to stand back and look at her marriage with detachment. Then there was Sam who had kept her afloat.

When she thought of Sam she smiled inwardly until the smile rested on her lips, curling them up at the corners. She pictured his dishevelled figure, those shabby sweaters he always wore, the dusty shoes that hadn't ever enjoyed the luxury of a lick of polish, his lofty expression and intelligent eyes. He had been a beautiful boy, she recalled wistfully, remembering their first encounter on the lake. He had had thick blond hair that fell over his eyes, pale pink lips that smirked sardonically, luminous skin that glowed with contentment and the charisma of a young man who knows he is much cleverer than everyone else.

So what had happened? Age had stolen his golden hair, experience had humbled him and Nuno's death had robbed him of his contentment. He was more loveable now, less aloof. But Federica didn't allow herself to dwell on her feelings for Sam; she wasn't ready to confront them yet. She pulled the butterfly box out of her bag and turned the focus of her attention to her father and grandparents, reliving all those glorious moments as a child before her mother had taken her away across the sea.

Hal slept most of the way, waking up to eat and go to the bathroom. It was only when they landed in Santiago airport that he sat up and stared out of the window, the view over the Andes mountains strumming within him a familiar chord that caused his throat to tighten and his eyes to well with tears. He swallowed hard, gripping the arm of his seat as the complex jumble of his emotions churned in his stomach.

'We're home, Fede,' he choked, turning to look at her. She

nodded, for she too was moved and unable to speak. She blinked away her joy and threaded her hand into his.

Mariana had sent the chauffeur to pick them up and drive them down to Cachagua. He introduced himself as Raul Ferro but didn't speak a word of English and Hal and Federica had forgotten the Spanish they had once spoken fluently. So they communicated with gestures and followed him out to the car. The heat in Santiago was stifling and oppressive but Hal and Federica absorbed it with delight along with the long-forgotten memories. At first they sat in the back in silence, watching the scenery pass by the windows, lost in the dusty halls of their past. Then, when the car left the city and sped up the open road that cut through the arid mountains to the coast, they sat back and looked at one another with different eyes. After years of estrangement they were at once reunited by their shared childhood and their shared longing to reclaim it.

'I was only four when we left, but you know, I remember so much,' said Hal wistfully, wiping his sweating brow with his shirtsleeve. 'I feel better already!'

'I thought it would be strange seeing it all again, but it feels as if I never left,' she sighed, watching the heat shimmering above the road ahead like pools of water.

'I never really felt I belonged to Papa,' said Hal suddenly.

Federica looked at his troubled face and pulled a thin smile of sympathy. 'I know. He ignored you didn't he?' she agreed softly.

'It's odd because I was so small, but I've felt his rejection through the years.'

'You were Mama's golden boy, though.'

'That came with a price, believe me.'

'Pretty suffocating, I know.' Federica shook her head as she remembered her mother's overwhelming neediness and constant discontent.

'She's a deeply unhappy woman,' Hal mused. 'I grew up with the responsibility of making her happy where everyone else had failed. You know, Arthur's given up on her too, just like Papa did. I really thought Arthur could make her happy.'

'Oh, don't give up on Arthur,' she chuckled with a smile.

'What do you mean?' He frowned. 'I thought you hated Arthur.'

'I did. But I never gave him a chance. He's a good man and Mama's lucky to have him.' She noticed the perplexed expression on his face and added, 'I went to see him, Hal. They still love each other.'

'Well, that's good.' Hal sighed. 'She's not all bad. Just very misguided.'

'It's taken a while to get over Papa, but I think she learnt the hard way. "In much wisdom is much grief," ' she quoted wisely.

'You sound like Sam Appleby,' he said.

Federica grinned. 'Do I?'

'Yes, his pomposity is catching. You've obviously been spending too much time with him.' Hal gazed out of the window. 'Why do you suppose Papa deserted us?' he asked tentatively, changing the subject. They had never talked about their father like this before. They'd never dared ask those questions.

Federica lowered her eyes. 'I don't know,' she said, allowing thoughts of Sam Appleby to dissolve into her father's shadow. 'But I'm going to ask him. I need to know and so do you.'

'What makes you think he'll be happy to see us?'

'I just know it,' she replied firmly.

'He could always have come to see us in England but he didn't. So why's he going to be pleased to see us now?'

'I know what you're saying, Hal,' she said carefully. 'Just trust me. I know he regrets the past and I know he still cares.'

Hal rested his eyes on the magnificence that surrounded him, so far from the cold cliffs of Cornwall and felt a deep yearning in his soul. He felt as if an invisible force was filling his spirit with something weightless so that his body felt buoyant and bursting with optimism.

$\star$ $\star$ $\star$

Ramon sat on the terrace of his parents' beach house, looking out across the sea that lay still and gleaming in the late morning light. He had barely slept at all for his mind had itched with guilt and anxiety – how was he going to explain himself to the two children he had abandoned long ago and left to mourn him? How was he going to explain Ramoncito to them – and Estella? Would they understand? How was Ramoncito going to feel suddenly finding himself having to share his father's devotion when he had grown up with the exclusive right to it? He looked at his watch; they'd be arriving soon. He felt his stomach churn with nerves. He knew he should have gone to pick them up at the airport, but he needed the moral support of his parents.

Mariana had agreed with him. 'Much better that they see us all together at the house, less pressure all round,' she had said.

'Here, son,' said Ignacio, handing him a tumbler of rum. 'You look as though you need it.'

'I don't know what to expect,' he said sheepishly.

'Don't think about it too much,' said Ignacio simply, sitting down opposite Ramon and pulling his panama hat onto his head to protect him from the sun. 'They're coming out to see you because you're their father, not to torment you. Let bygones be bygones and get to know each other again. That's my advice.'

'So much has happened,' said Ramon, staring into his glass. 'Estella, Ramoncito . . .'

'Life goes on. It has many chapters yet it's one book. There's a common thread that runs through each chapter.'

'What's that, Papa?' said Ramon, sighing heavily.

'Love,' said Ignacio bluntly. Ramon frowned at him, but his father just nodded back. 'I'm old and wise, son, I should be after eighty-four years, and I've picked a few things up in my life. That's one of them. Learn something from an old man.' He chuckled. 'Love will unite you all, you'll see.'

'That and forgiveness,' said Ramon, knocking back his glass. 'A large dose of forgiveness.'

★   ★   ★

As the car drove up the coast Federica and Hal began to reminisce with growing excitement. They recognised the shack where they had always stopped en route to their grandparents' house, where Ramon had always bought them drinks and *empanadas*, where the Chilean children had played football with an empty Coke can under the sycamore trees. They were both struck at how little it had changed in so many years, as if they were driving through a strange void which time was incapable of penetrating.

When they descended the dusty track into Cachagua itself they were both too moved and anxious to speak any more. Hal took Federica's hand, which surprised her for it had always been she who had initiated any demonstrations of affection. She squeezed it, grateful for his support for she was nervous too. The thatched houses were the same, surrounded by verdant trees and bushes, although there were more of them. When the car drew up outside the familiar walls of their grandparents' house they both heard the thumping of their hearts as they beat loudly and in unison.

'I'm scared,' Hal confessed.

'Me too,' Federica replied hoarsely. 'But we're here now, so let's just plunge on in,' she said, trying to make light of their fear.

Ramon heard the engine of the car and then the expectant silence that followed when the ignition was turned off. He heard the doors open and close. He looked across at his parents and Ramoncito, who had all got to their feet and were making their way into the house. Mariana's old legs were slow but she bustled through the sitting room as fast as she could go, her breathing heavy with excitement. Ramoncito didn't understand his father's uneasiness and was caught up in the enthusiasm of his grandparents. He had always wondered what his half-siblings were like, often fantasising that they lived in Chile so that he could enjoy the fun of having a large family like all his school friends, who often had as many as ten brothers and sisters to play with.

Ignacio turned to his son who hesitated on the terrace, pale-faced and apprehensive. 'Son, it's like diving into the sea, the anticipation is uncomfortable but once you're in the water is warm and pleasant.' He smiled at him in understanding. 'You just have to take the plunge and not think about it.'

Ramon nodded at him and followed his unsteady old frame into the dark interior of the house where it was cool and smelt of tuberose. In his mind he still imagined Federica as he had seen her as a thriteen-year-old child on her bicycle in Cornwall. Hal he remembered less well and that made him feel guiltier than ever.

When Federica and Hal saw their grandmother hurry out of the house to greet them their hearts ceased to beat with anxiety but accelerated with joy. She was much greyer and appeared smaller because the last time they had seen her they had been children. But her smile and her tears were the same expressions of her gentle nature that had clung to their memories for almost two decades and they ran to her and embraced her. She wanted to tell them how tall they were, how beautiful Federica was and how handsome Hal was, but her throat ached with emotion and her lips trembled with regret because she was old and had lost countless precious years of their growing up. So she embraced them again, gesticulating with her shaking hands and expressive face all the things she was unable to put into words.

Ignacio appeared next in the doorway because Ramoncito hung back, suddenly overcome with shyness. He hugged his grandchildren, chuckling with happiness because he also was too moved to speak. Hal remembered him for his shoulder-rides but was barely able to reconcile the ursine man of his childhood with the thin, wizened man who now stood before him.

Then Ramon's large body hesitated in the doorway with his son.

Federica detected the anxiety in his eyes and strode up to him and threw herself into his arms as she had always done as a child. Ramon was stunned at her confident display of affection and wrapped his arms around her with gratitude. He was astonished to see in her features echoes of the young Helena he had fallen in love with on the pier in Polperro. Her hair was white and flowing, her skin translucent and her eyes that same clear blue that had disarmed him in her mother. He held her face in his hands and swallowed his regret. 'You're so grown up,' he choked. 'And you've done all this without me?' he said, pulling her into his arms again.

'Without you, no,' she sniffed, breathing in the familiar scent of him that had carried her through the years and prevented her from ever forgetting him. Ramon looked over Federica's shoulders and saw the grey face of his son who stood staring at him with haunted eyes. He gently disentangled himself from his daughter and walked up to him.

'Hal,' he said, extending his hand. Hal tried to say 'Papa' but all that escaped his throat was a dry rasp. He looked into the face of his father, searching for some sign of affection but all he could see was fear and uncertainty. He swallowed hard. Ramon floundered, not knowing what to do next. He lifted his eyes to his father and remembered the advice he had given him. 'Hal, I'm sorry,' he muttered. The boy's eyes softened and the corners of his mouth twitched with emotion. Ramon took the first step, held out his arms and pulled the trembling young man against him. Hal responded with a moan before his decrepit body shook with sobs. 'I'll make it up to you,' said Ramon. 'I promise.'

Ramoncito watched the scenes of reunion from the doorway and felt excluded. The tears and emotion were alien to him for he hadn't even cried at his own mother's funeral. He watched Federica and Hal with curiosity and listened to them speaking a language that he didn't understand. Federica didn't look anything like Ramon but Hal was uncannily similar, except he looked thin and ill. He wanted to go up and introduce himself but he was aware that he played no part in this family gathering because they were all mourning a parting that had happened before he was born.

Suddenly Ramon remembered Ramoncito. He pulled himself

up and turned to face his son who stood anxiously in the shadows. 'Ramoncito,' he said. 'Come and meet your brother and sister.' He said it in Spanish but Hal and Federica understood and blinked at each other in bewilderment. The fifteen-year-old boy emerged into the sunlight. He was tall and athletic with raven-black hair and shiny brown eyes as soft as milk chocolate.

Federica at once recognised Ramon in the languor of his smile and in the poise of his gait, yet his skin was the colour of rich honey and his face was long and gentle, which set him apart from their father.

Hal immediately saw himself reflected in the dark features of Ramoncito and he gathered himself together and strode forward to shake him by the hand. 'I've always wanted a brother,' he said.

When Ramon translated for him, Ramoncito's face broke into a wide smile and he replied in Spanish, 'Me too.'

Federica took him by the hand and kissed him. He blushed to the roots of his glossy hair. Federica smiled at him. Besides their blood, their blushing was something they had in common.

Chapter Forty-One

Both Hal and Federica remembered their grandparents' large terrace, overlooking the wide sea. The scents of gardenia and eucalyptus transported them back to their childhood – but they were very different people now and the past seemed like another life. They all sat in the sunshine, the heat melting away their apprehensions, but still the atmosphere was awkward. There were so many things they wanted to say to each other and yet no one knew how to start.

Gertrude brought out a tray of *pisco sour* and handed them around, wondering why the place vibrated with such intense joy and sadness all at the same time. For once her scowl was replaced with an expression of curiosity as she eyed the two strangers with suspicion. She was more perplexed when Hal asked for a glass of water.

'I can't believe you're here,' said Mariana happily. 'After all this time, what possessed you?'

Federica sipped the alcoholic drink she'd never been allowed to taste as a child and screwed up her nose. 'This is so sour!' she exclaimed.

'All that lemon,' said Mariana. 'You'll get used to it.'

'After one glass you'll be hooked,' said Ignacio.

'So what made you decide to come now?' asked Ramon.

Federica sighed and glanced at Hal, who sat back in his chair and gulped down his water thirstily.

'Things happen in your life that put everything into perspective,' she said, choosing her words carefully. 'I had an unhappy marriage and Hal, well, Hal's been through a tough time too. We needed to get back to our roots. We needed to see you again. It's not natural to be separated from your family for so long.' She lowered her eyes, not wanting to make her father feel guilty for abandoning them. Mariana glanced at her son and felt uneasy. 'It's wonderful to come out and discover another member of the family,' Federica continued, filling the uncomfortable silence. They all looked at Ramoncito who blushed again and smiled bashfully.

'Have you forgotten all your Spanish?' Mariana asked.

'I'm afraid we have,' said Federica. 'I understand bits but mostly I've forgotten it all.'

'Papa, where is your wife?' Hal asked, draining his glass.

Ramon's face twisted with sadness. 'She's dead,' he replied.

Hal stiffened and mumbled an apology. Mariana commented on the weather and then Ignacio got to his feet.

'Son, why don't you take Federica and Hal for a walk up the beach? You have much to talk about. Then you can come back and we can start all over again.'

Ramon looked relieved and translated for his son. Ramoncito nodded and watched his half-brother and sister stand up and walk into the house with his father.

'For the love of God, that was tense,' Mariana sighed once they had gone.

'Be calm, woman, they just need to thrash it all out together,' said Ignacio. 'How about a game of chess, Ramoncito?' he added to his grandson who looked up at him and smiled.

'Beautiful girl, Abuelito!' he said in admiration.

Ramon didn't want to walk up the beach. 'I want to take you somewhere else,' he said, unlocking his car and climbing in.

'I hear you have a beach house of your own,' said Federica, noticing that his hair had turned completely grey at the temples and the diaphanous skin beneath his eyes sagged from too much melancholy. He looked old.

'Yes, I do, but I'm not taking you there either,' he replied, driving off up the sandy track. 'I'm taking you to meet Estella.'

'Who's Estella?' asked Hal.

'Ramoncito's mother.'

'Oh.' Hal coughed away his embarrassment.

'I want to talk to you somewhere we won't be disturbed,' said Ramon.

The cemetery rested in heavenly stillness on top of the cliff overlooking the sea. It was hot and the smells of the flowers and pine trees scented the air with the serenity of nature. Ramon parked the car and they walked across the shadows, taking care not to trample over the graves of sleeping spirits, to where Estella was buried. 'This is Estella's resting place,' said Ramon, rearranging the flowers he had placed against her tombstone that morning.

'She has a nice view,' said Hal, desperate to make up for his faux-pas.

Ramon smiled at him. 'Yes she does.'

'Will you tell us about her, Papa?' Federica asked 'She must have been very beautiful because Ramoncito is tremendously handsome.'

'She was,' he agreed sadly. 'But first I want to start at the beginning. I want to start with you. Federica, Hal and Helena. Let's sit over here,' he suggested, pointing to the grassy slope that led down to the cliffs.

They sat in the sunshine and watched the hypnotic swell of the sea below. Ramon took each child by the hand. 'I ask you both to forgive me,' he said. Hal and Federica didn't know what to say and stared at him in astonishment. 'I ran away from your mother because her love was too intense and I felt claustrophobic. We should have put you both first and tried to work out our problems, but we were both too selfish. I didn't fight for your mother and try to persuade her to stay and she didn't try to change for me. I loved you both but didn't realise what I had lost until it was too late, and then I was too ashamed to face up to it so I just ran away and left you. It was easier to run – after all I had run from love my entire life.' Both Federica and Hal were astounded by his honesty.

He then recounted the moments of their childhood that had touched him and the small details of their characters that he had remembered and taken with him through the years. 'Hal, you used to cling to your mother. I frightened you, I think. You were so sensitive you felt the ill feeling between us and it upset you. You were very small so I used to leave you with Helena and take Federica out with me. I never really knew you. But I'd like to start again and get to know you now,' he said, looking into the troubled eyes of his son and recognising the torment that lay behind them. 'You're my son, Hal, and nothing is more important than blood. I understand that now. It's taken much unhappiness but I now know what is important.'

'That would be good, Papa,' mumbled Hal, whose ability to express himself had been inhibited by the heat and the alcohol that still contaminated his liver.

Ramon told them about the time he had gone to England to see them and how Helena had protected them from him. How he had seen Federica on her bicycle but driven away following Helena's advice. 'But don't ever blame your mother for that. I was insensitive, popping into your lives when it suited me just to make me feel better. She was right, it wouldn't have done you any good.

'Estella's death taught me the value of life,' he continued solemnly. As much as Federica tried to remember the pretty young maid who had floated through the rooms of the beach house, filling it with the gentle scent of roses, she could not. 'I didn't set out to love Estella. She quenched a physical longing, which then grew into something more urgent, something deeper. When I was with her there was nowhere else I wanted to be. I had never experienced that before. I had spent my life running away from people, yearning to be on my own, not wanting to commit to anyone. Estella was different. She made no demands. She didn't suffocate me with neediness. All she wanted was my affection. So I wrote on the beach instead of travelling the world. I didn't need to go anywhere, for she was my inspiration and I wrote my best work with her. Ramoncito is a living expression of our love. When she died in the road I felt as if my whole world had suddenly imploded. I was consumed with regret. I should have married her but it was more convenient for me to remain single. I should have told her more often I loved her. I should have told you both that I loved you too and made more of an effort to be a part of your lives. But now I can. By coming out here you've both given me a second chance. I'll never have another with Estella.'

'Papa, we forgive you,' Federica whispered, taking his hand in both of hers and squeezing it. 'We're together now and we can get to know each other all over again, can't we, Hal?' Hal nodded. 'If it hadn't been for your poetry I would never have had the strength to leave my husband,' she continued.

'Really?' said Ramon in surprise, wondering which ones she meant. Then she told him about her marriage and how the butterfly box, which contained his letters, had sustained her through unhappy times.

'You didn't know it, Papa, but you were ever-present. You were there when I needed you most,' she said.

Ramon smiled at her but he was aware that Hal said very little.

They sat on the cliff top until the sun grew too intense and they had to retreat beneath the pine trees. They talked about the past, bridging the years that had widened the distance between them, until the rumblings of their stomachs distracted them from their emotions and alerted them to the rapid passing of the day. 'Gertrude will be furious that we're late for lunch,' said Ramon and winked at Hal.

Gertrude was indeed more sour than usual. They had lunch out on the terrace and this time the atmosphere was one of celebration. They reminisced about the past and Federica told them about their life in England, the beauty of Cornwall and the eccentricities of the people who lived there. Hal made a valiant effort to resist the flasks of wine that circled the table, quenching his thirst with endless glasses of water. Weary from the heat and the journey he retreated to his room to sleep a siesta.

Ramon took the opportunity to ask Federica about the state of his health. 'He's very unwell, I'm afraid,' she said.

'He looks terrible, *pobrecito*!' Mariana sighed sympathetically, remembering the little boy who used to love eating ice cream, *manjar blanco* and riding on the shoulders of his grandfather.

'Mind you, he ate enough to sustain an army,' said Ignacio.

'He's deeply unhappy,' Federica admitted. 'He's been slowly destroying himself by drinking too much and leading a useless, decadent life. I thought coming here might take him away from his problems.' Then she looked at her father. 'I hoped you might be able to get through to him. After all, you helped me.'

'I'll try,' he replied sincerely.

'How did Ramon help you, Fede?' Mariana asked curiously, longing to discover that he hadn't completely deserted his children as she had supposed.

'He sent me notes of poetry,' she said and smiled at him tenderly. 'You may think it strange that a few lines of verse can change someone's life, but they really did. I had been so blind to my own situation, they opened my eyes. Knowing Papa was thinking of me gave me the courage to leave Torquil. I knew I wasn't alone.'

Ramon smiled back at her awkwardly. Federica understood it as modesty.

'You dark horse, Ramon,' said Mariana proudly. 'After lunch I would like to show you the family photograph albums, Fede. There are lovely ones of you and Hal as children.'

'And I'd like to get my camera and take photos of all of you. This is a reunion I shall never forget.'

After lunch Federica went into her bedroom. She noticed at once the scent of lavender on her sheets and the large stems of tuberose on the dresser. The shutters were closed, keeping the room cool, but she opened them and let the sunlight tumble into her room, illuminating her memories as she remembered the occasional picture on the wall and the furniture. She opened her suitcase and pulled out her camera. She sat on the bed and drew the lens out of its protective covering, remembering how Julian had taught her to hold it. Then she thought of Sam. She wanted to call him up and tell him how it was all going. But she thought she'd take a few photographs first so that she could tell him she had used his gift.

'Fede, can I come in?'

She turned to see her father standing in the doorway. 'Sure,' she replied. 'I'm just putting together this fabulous camera so I can take some photographs to show everyone back in England.'

'Good idea,' he said, sitting down on the other bed. 'About those notes of poetry,' he began.

'They were inspired,' she enthused happily. 'I'm a different person now.'

'I didn't send them,' he declared.

Federica's face drained of excitement. 'You didn't send them?' she repeated in astonishment.

'No,' he said, shaking his head. 'I didn't want to say it in front of everyone else, I didn't want to embarrass you.'

'Of course you sent them,' she replied in confusion. 'There were two notes, one slipped under my door, the other in the car?'

'Were they signed?'

'No,' she said, narrowing her eyes.

'I haven't been to London for years,' he admitted.

'Truthfully?'

'Truthfully. Listen, when Hal wakes up I'm going to take him to my beach house. There's a book I want him to read. Is that okay with you?'

'Of course it is,' she said unsteadily. 'I can't believe you didn't send me those notes.'

'I'm sorry,' he said, getting up. 'I wish I had.'

'It doesn't matter. The result was the same whoever gave them to me,' she said casually as if it was of little importance.

Once Ramon had left the room she stared down at her camera in bewilderment. Then she felt her stomach plummet as she realised that it could only have been Sam who had sent her the notes. Suddenly it all made sense. He had voiced his concern right from the start. He had confronted her at lunch, then at Nuno's funeral. She hadn't listened. Of course he wasn't going to approach her again, certainly not openly. How obvious it was and yet she had wanted to believe so badly that her father was behind them, she had managed to convince herself. How insensitive of her to give all the credit to Ramon. No wonder Sam had looked so crestfallen.

When Mariana showed her the albums of her childhood and the years that she had missed out, Federica had to force herself to concentrate because all she wanted to think about was Sam. Mariana told her a brief anecdote with each picture in the way old people do who have no concept of time. But Federica was agitated and eyed the telephone. Would it be impertinent to ask to make a call to England? While she half listened to her grandmother's stories she weighed up the chances. When Mariana came across a photograph of Estella, Federica's attention was momentarily diverted while she gazed into the serene face of the woman who had stolen her father's heart. She was beautiful and gentle-looking with the same kind expression and long face as Ramoncito's. She knew instinctively that she would have liked her. The tragedy of her death moved her and reminded her of her own mortality. She had been too young and beautiful to die. She immediately thought of Topahuay and imagined that she must have looked just like Estella. In their deaths Federica recognised the transience of life and the importance to live each moment fully because death could come at any time to steal it away.

Ignacio sat on the terrace talking to Ramoncito and finishing their game of chess. The sun was still hot and occasionally

Ignacio would take off his hat and wipe his brow with a white hanky, which he kept in his pocket. Ramoncito would then take the opportunity to let his eyes rest on the beautiful face of his sister when she didn't know that she was being watched. He couldn't wait to tell Pablo and Maria Rega about the sudden arrival of his father's long-lost children. Everything about Ramon fascinated them because he was from another world and yet he had loved their Estella.

When Hal woke up from a long and deep siesta it took him a while to orientate himself. He looked about the room, at the white walls and stark wooden furniture and slowly remembered where he was. His head ached from the heat and his body suffered withdrawals from the alcohol that had nearly destroyed him. He pulled himself up and stumbled into the shower. He let the cool water wash away his exhaustion and any traces of his unhappiness that might have followed him to Chile. When he appeared on the terrace Ramon was waiting to take him to his beach house.

'Is Federica coming?' he asked, when Ramon suggested they go.

'No, just you and me,' Ramon replied. 'I've got something I want you to read.' So Hal followed his father to his car feeling a buoyancy in his step that shamed him, for he was pitifully happy that his father had finally singled him out on his own.

'This was Estella's house,' Ramon explained as they approached. 'I set her up here when she had just had Ramoncito. She loved it by the sea. I love it too.'

'It's charming!' Hal exclaimed, finally finding his voice. 'It's completely charming.' He noticed the abundance of plumbago that crawled up the walls and fell over the roof of the veranda and he noticed the magnificence of the mountains behind. Suddenly he was touched by something that he couldn't understand. 'Does everything here remind you of her?' he asked.

Ramon nodded. 'Everything,' he replied. 'Not a day goes by when I don't think about her at some time or other.'

'I'd like to love like that,' Hal mused wistfully.

'You will one day, I'm sure,' said Ramon. 'You're very young.'

'I know and I have my whole life ahead of me,' he said. 'I've cocked it up so far.'

'There's always time to start again.'

'I want to start again, Papa. And I want to start again here,' he said decisively. 'I can't explain it but I connect with this place.'

'It's in your blood,' Ramon explained.

'Maybe that's what it is,' he agreed. 'In my blood.'

Ramon showed him around the house, grabbed the manuscript he'd written for Helena and a bottle of water and led Hal out onto the beach. They sat down in the waning sunshine and talked, just the two of them, about life and about love. Then Ramon showed him his book. 'I wrote this for your mother and for you and Federica,' he said. Hal took it and flicked through it briefly. 'It's not very long. I'd really like you to read it. No one else has read it yet. I wrote it in English.'

'I'd be honoured,' Hal replied truthfully. 'You really mean that no one's read this yet?'

'No.'

'Why did you write it?'

'Because it was cathartic, because I want Helena to understand where we went wrong.' He hesitated then grinned at Hal. 'Where I went wrong.'

'You've really tortured yourself with this guilt stuff, haven't you?' he said.

Ramon looked at him and laughed. 'Do you think I've overdone it?'

'I don't think you need to flagellate yourself,' he replied and smirked back at him.

'You think I'm flagellating myself, do you?' he said, pushing him playfully on the back.

'A bit. You don't need to feel so ashamed of yourself. Lots of people divorce and leave their children. They survive, don't they? We have, well, just.'

Ramon looked at him with affection and threw his arm around his shoulder. 'You know, for someone who's so unwell you've got quite a mouth on you.'

'I'm glad, I thought I'd lost it.' He chuckled.

'What else did you think you'd lost? Your flippers?'

'You want to swim?' he asked enthusiastically.

'If you'll join me.'

In the magic light of sunset they ran into the golden waters of the icy Pacific. Hal yelped as the cold shot through his body, jolting his senses into focus. Ramon shouted at him to be a man and dive straight in. Following his father's example he dived and felt the water numb his limbs until he was no longer aware of the freezing temperature of the sea. He splashed about, laughing and joking with his father as the gentle waves washed away the turmoil of the last few years. When they finally lay on the sand, drying off in the dying hours of day, Hal knew where he belonged. 'Papa, what if I never go back?' he said, blinking at him with shiny eyes.

'To England?'

'Yes, what if I just don't go back?'

'You'll be where you belong, Hal. Besides, you will have come home,' he said and looked at his son seriously.

'Thank you, Papa,' he breathed, then turned his eyes to the horizon and sighed with contentment. 'I'm home.'

Federica asked Mariana if it would be all right for her to call England. Of course, Mariana was only too happy to lend her the telephone. 'Make as many calls as you like,' she said. 'Your mother will want to know how it's all going.'

But Federica didn't call Helena. She called Sam. The telephone rang for a long while until someone finally picked it up. It was Ingrid. 'Ingrid, it's Federica,' she announced.

'Ah, Fede, darling, how are you?' she asked breezily.

'I'm in Chile,' Federica replied with a suspended heart.

'How lovely.'

'Is Sam about?' she asked.

'No, he's gone,' Ingrid said vaguely.

'Gone?' Federica gasped. 'Gone where?'

'To stay with some old girlfriend, I think.'

'An old girlfriend?'

'Yes, someone he's liked for a very long time. Dear boy, it's about time he started thinking about his future.'

'Yes,' Federica mumbled, but she was barely able to disguise the anxiety in her voice.

'He's not getting any younger,' Ingrid continued, adding to Federica's distress.

'Did he say how long he'd be gone?'

'No, darling, you know Sam! He never lets anyone know his plans.'

'Did he leave a number?'

'No again, darling. Though, I think it's a big house in Scotland if that helps. You know who his friends are better than I. Shall I tell him to call you when he returns?'

'No, it's fine. Just tell him I rang,' she said, swallowing back her disappointment.

Ingrid had just put down the telephone when Sam walked in having taken the dogs out across the cliffs. 'Who was that, Mum?' he asked.

'No one you know, darling,' she said, picking up an orphaned fox cub and stroking its damp fur. 'Someone wanting to know if we had any puppies,' she added, kissing the cub. 'Sadly they're not interested in Little Red, are they, Little Red?' She watched Sam's dejected face and hoped that Federica would realise how much she loved him when she was in danger of losing him. Sam took an apple from the fruit bowl. 'Where are you off to, darling?' she asked, attempting to hide her concern.

'To Nuno's study.'

'You'll lose yourself in there,' she said sympathetically.

'I hope so.'

Federica let Hal do most of the talking during supper and retired early to bed. 'You must be so tired, Fede,' said Mariana kindly. 'You have a good sleep and get up whenever you feel like it. You're home now.' Federica went around the table kissing each member of her family with affection. Ramoncito's face burned scarlet once she had placed her lips on his cheek and continued to smoulder like a rekindled coal for the rest of the meal. Hal and Ramon talked with animation, their faces illuminated by the flickering flames of the hurricane lamps. Ignacio caught Mariana's eye and smiled. They understood each other perfectly. Both instinctively felt that Hal would be staying for good, but Federica was distracted, Mariana noticed – it was a woman thing.

Federica had left the shutters open so that the moonlight spilled into her room along with the nocturnal stirrings of the crickets and the sea. She lay in bed watching the shadows slowly creep across the ceiling and thought about Sam. How ironic, she mused, that when she was in England she longed for her father and now that she was in Chile she longed for Sam. She had felt uneasy ever since her conversation with Ingrid. She wondered whom Sam had gone to stay with and found herself suffering an uncomfortable twinge of jealousy deep in the core of her being. She turned over in frustration and lay on her stomach staring out onto the swaying trees and starry sky. She recalled his unshaven face and tormented eyes and wondered whether his silent intervention in her marriage had been inspired by friendship or love. She didn't dare analyse her own feelings for she was afraid of love.

She remembered the long evenings in front of the fire in Nuno's study, discussing literature and poetry, the chilly barbecues on the beach and the brisk walks along the cliff tops. He had been indispensable to her. If he were to fall in love with someone else she'd lose him, and she couldn't bear to lose him. When sleep finally conquered her, dreams persisted in the place of consciousness to torment her. She dreamed of Sam – he was running down the cliff and she was shouting his name, but he didn't hear her and as fast as she ran she couldn't catch up with him. She awoke in the morning as tired as she had been the night before.

The following day Hal sprung out of bed with an energy he didn't know he had. He couldn't remember the last time he had felt so positive about life. He breathed in the scents of his childhood, drawing the air in right to the bottom of his lungs. He had read his father's book, *To Love Enough*, and discovered a powerful story that explained his own path of self-discovery as well as a philosophy on love that would apply to anyone: brothers and sisters, friends, lovers and husband and wife. He had read it well into the early hours of the morning. But he hadn't felt tired. His eyes had continued to scan the lines of prose until the darkness had been burned away by the tender fire of dawn. As he slept his mind had continued to work on the allegory of life and love so that when he awoke he felt his heart had been touched by something magical. Someone, somewhere had given him another chance at life. This time he resolved to live it wisely.

He almost skipped onto the terrace where the sun was dazzling and the smell of toast and coffee so enticing that he inhaled again and reflected on his own good fortune. 'Good morning, everyone,' he said, bending down to kiss his grandmother. 'Where's Papa?'

'He'll be over shortly,' said Mariana. 'We thought it would be nice to have lunch in Zapallar, where you used to eat *locos* at Cesar's, do you remember?'

'Yes, I do,' Hal replied, rubbing his hands together with happiness. 'Very good idea.' He sat down and poured himself a cup of coffee. 'I'm ravenous,' he exclaimed, buttering himself a croissant. Mariana derived enormous pleasure from watching him eat well. The colour had returned to his cheeks, he looked happy and rested. 'Abuelita, I want to learn Spanish,' he said suddenly.

'That can be organised,' she replied, catching eyes with her husband, who put down the paper and began to take an interest in the conversation.

'I'm not going back to England,' he said casually. 'I want to stay here.'

Mariana was unable to hide her delight. She smiled broadly and clasped her hands together. '*Mi amor*, I'm so happy! You belong here,' she said, touching his arm. 'How lovely for Ramoncito to have a brother. What about Federica?' she added.

Hal grinned. 'No, she won't stay,' he said. 'She's in love with someone in England. She just doesn't know it yet.'

It wasn't until the fifth day, when Ramoncito and Hal were deeply engrossed in a game of chess and Ramon and Ignacio were walking along the beach, that Mariana took the opportunity to talk to Federica on her own.

'You've been very distracted in the last few days, Fede,' she said, sitting beside her on the sofa. 'Is it this young man?' she asked.

Federica looked surprised. 'Which young man?' Federica shrugged defensively.

'The one Hal spoke about.'

'How does Hal know?' she exclaimed.

'Perhaps he's been more alert than you think.' Mariana chuckled. 'He's thriving under the Chilean sun,' she added, watching him on the terrace, laughing with Ramoncito as if they had known each other for ever.

'Oh, Abuelita,' Federica sighed in confusion. 'I want to stay here because I so enjoy being with you and Abuelito and it's just wonderful to see Papa again and to have finally put the past behind us. We're friends now. That was all I ever wanted. But . . .'

'But you've grown up, Fede.'

'I've spent the last twenty years yearning for Papa. I'd read his letters when I was unhappy and remember all the strange tales he told me. I clung onto my childhood. I think Torquil was an attempt to find Papa in someone else. Now there's Sam,' she said softly and dropped her shoulders. 'I think I love him.'

'So what's the problem?'

'I think I've hurt him,' she replied gloomily.

'In what way?'

'Well, I adored him as a child. He's seven years older than me, eccentric and clever – there's no one like him in the world, whereas there are hundreds of Torquils. He used to be beautiful, but he's not any more, he's just adorable and lovely. During my marriage to Torquil he wrote me anonymous notes of poetry, which changed my life. He loved me from afar, helped me leave Torquil and supported me once I returned home. I couldn't have done it without him. But I thought the notes were from Papa. I told him so. Then I said . . .' She paused and blushed.

'What did you tell him?' Mariana asked kindly.

Federica squirmed in her chair. 'I told him that I was leaving for Chile, that I didn't know how long I'd be gone because there was nothing in Polperro to make me stay.'

Mariana patted her knee fondly. 'Oh dear,' she sighed. 'I think you'd better go back and tell him how you feel.'

'The thing is, I didn't know how I felt. I didn't dare feel anything for him. I think I said that on purpose, hoping to force him to declare his feelings. But he didn't. He just looked wounded. I can't bear it. I'm such a monster. I realise now that I do care for him. I care very much. What if I'm too late?'

'Why would you be?'

'Because I called his mother,' she said, lowering her eyes, 'she said he had gone away to stay with an old girlfriend and didn't know when he'd be back.'

'Surely you don't believe he could fall in love with someone else so quickly?'

'I don't know. Could he?' Federica asked, eyeing her grand-mother hopefully.

'My dear, love isn't something you can turn on and off with a tap. It's not possible. If he loves you he'll be waiting for you. If he doesn't, he won't. And Fede, if he hasn't waited he's not worth the lemon in his *pisco*!'

'What shall I do?'

'Go back to England.'

'But I want to be here with you.'

'Dear girl, Chile isn't the moon. You just call me when you want to come back and I'll arrange your ticket, or Ramon will. This isn't twenty years ago. You're only fifteen hours away.' Then she smiled. 'Perhaps you could bring him with you.'

Federica beamed happily. 'Oh, Abuelita, I hope so,' she enthused and embraced her grandmother. 'Thank you,' she added seriously, looking into Mariana's twinkling eyes.

'No, thank *you*!' replied her grandmother, touching her cheek with a gentle sweep of her old hand. 'This is the way it should be.'

Chapter Forty-Two

Polperro

Helena sat on Toby's sofa, sharing a packet of chocolate biscuits with Rasta, smarting after her children's sudden departure to Chile. She munched angrily and imagined their reunion with Ramon and his parents, the beach house in Cachagua and all her memories that lingered there. But by the time she reached the bottom of the packet her thoughts had focused on Arthur and she had barely noticed the digression.

Arthur hadn't made the slightest effort to communicate with her. Not even during the drama with Hal and their subsequent departure. Not a word. She felt desperately isolated and alone. She missed him. She missed his company and his compassion, but what surprised her most was that little by little she began to miss him for the things that she had previously resented: the jolly way he walked, his enthusiasm and brightness, his round girth and his soft doughy hands. Physically he was nothing like Ramon, but her heart yearned for Arthur and she blamed herself entirely for driving him away.

The last few weeks had been painful as she had slowly weaned herself off her delusions. The Ramon in her memory wasn't real. He belonged to a time in the past that had long since dried up and died. She might just as well have been pining for a ghost. All the while she had failed to notice the qualities of the man she had chosen to share her life with, who was real and who needed her. She had been a fool. Like Toby had so wisely said, she never seemed to learn from her mistakes. She was never happy with what she had and only recognised happiness with hindsight. But Arthur had always loved her in spite of her faults. She scrunched up the empty packet and threw it into the fire where it burst into flame and was reduced to ash.

She'd make a new start and this time she'd get it right.

Arthur sat in his office staring out at the blustery street below. It had rained without pause for the last few days, a light drizzle blown about by a vengeful wind. He felt miserable inside, barely able to concentrate on his work, which was unusual as his job had always been an escape from domestic strain. He played about with his pencil, drawing sad faces on his desk notebook. He had told his secretary to take messages; he wasn't in the mood for telephone calls that might require his concentration. All he could think about was Helena. He had hoped she might fight to win him back. Sadly he had misjudged her. He had heard nothing but a screaming silence. Had their marriage really meant so little to her?

He stared at the clock on the wall and watched as the second hand ate its way slowly around the face with methodical regularity. The day had dragged. They had all dragged since the night he had locked Helena out of the house. Her cries still resounded in his ears but he didn't allow himself to feel remorse. He had done the right thing. She hadn't come back so he was now faced with the bleak reality that she wasn't ever going to come back. He had to let her go.

Finally he was able to struggle into his coat and leave the office. He struggled against the wind to his car, then struggled with the traffic to drive home. But most of all he struggled with the impulses that implored him to drop his defences and beg her to come home. Every day was a battle, but so far his determination had won.

It was dark when he arrived home. Gloomily he wondered what he was going to eat that night. He pictured a bowl of cereal or a plate of cheese and biscuits and speculated on the television schedule – there was rarely anything worth watching. Then he noticed the lights on in the house. The cleaner who came twice a week had obviously forgotten to switch them off, which was the least she could do seeing as there was so little work to be done. Helena had needed tidying up after her; Arthur did not. The place was as neat and as dead as a museum. How he longed for his wife's chaos to ruffle the life back into it.

He put his key in the lock and the door. When he stepped inside the aromatic smells from the kitchen reached his nostrils and he recognised at once the familiar whiff of Helena's roast chicken. His breath caught in his throat as his heart accelerated with hope and reserve, in case he should find it a dream and wake disappointed. Without taking his coat off he walked unsteadily up the corridor. He could hear the sound of footsteps and the light clatter of utensils as someone walked about behind the closed door. He dreaded opening it and his trembling fingers hesitated on the handle, aware of the terrible anguish that would follow if he were to discover not his wife but the cleaner, or his daughter or anyone else.

Then he assembled his courage and opened it. When he lifted his eyes he found Helena peering into a steaming saucepan, dressed in a pair of suede trousers and silk shirt protected by her grubby cook's apron. He blinked at her in amazement. She replaced the lid and turned to face him. Her heavily applied mascara could barely conceal her remorse. She smiled at him nervously. But when she recognised the longing in his expression she regained her confidence and walked over to him and drew him into her arms.

Neither spoke. They didn't need to. Arthur pulled her against him and breathed deeply into her softly perfumed neck. They held each other for a long time, appreciating as never before the power of their love. Finally Helena pulled away. She looked into Arthur's shiny eyes and whispered tearfully, 'I'll never behave like that again.'

Arthur stared down at her with intention. 'I know,' he replied gravely, 'because I won't let you.'

★   ★   ★

Ramon waved as the car carrying Federica to Santiago airport disappeared up the sandy track, leaving behind it a cloud of dust and a cheerful sense of accomplishment. He smiled at her until she was long out of sight and recalled that heartbreaking moment twenty years before when she had waved tearfully good-bye not knowing when she would see him again. But now she was a grown woman she would decide when she would return. He was deeply proud of her and grateful, for they had embraced not only as father and daughter but as friends. He had handed her his manuscript to give to Helena and told her she could read it on the plane. She had embraced her grandparents, Ramoncito and finally Hal. But her tears hadn't been of sorrow but of joy because they had all found each other again and as Mariana said, 'Chile isn't the moon' – it was farewell not good-bye.

Then Ramon drove up to the cemetery to talk to Estella. Ramoncito didn't want to go because he was in the middle of a highly competitive chess game with Hal. 'Tell her I'm with my brother,' he said proudly and Ramon smiled at him and nodded. Chess was a language they both understood.

Ramon parked the car in the shade and walked across the long shadows towards Estella's grave. It was early evening and the rich smells of grass and flowers rose up on the air to mingle with the intangible sense of death that haunted the tranquil cliff top. He paused as he often did at the graves to read the inscriptions chiselled into the stone. One day I'll come up here, he thought, and never go back. The certainty of death didn't frighten him, on the contrary, it gave him a feeling of peace. After all, in an uncertain world it was the only thing one could be sure about.

As he approached the tall green pine tree he saw Pablo Rega sleeping against the headstone with his chin tucked into his chest and his black hat pulled low over his eyes. He greeted him cheerfully with the intention of waking him. But Pablo didn't stir. He remained as still and lifeless as a scarecrow. Then Ramon knew that he had made his final journey and crossed himself. He crouched down and felt the old man's pulse just to be sure. There was no movement in his veins, for his spirit had left his decrepit body and joined those of the people who had gone before him, like Osvaldo Garcia Segundo and, of course, Estella. At that thought Ramon felt an acute twinge of envy. He was aged and alone. His sons would no doubt fall in love just like he had, but Ramon was too old to love again. Estella had tamed his fugitive heart and it would always belong to her.

He would spend the rest of his life living on the memory of love.

Federica watched the Andes mountains simmer below her window as the plane soared into the sky with a rumble that shook her to the bones. She yearned to stay. Like Hal she felt she belonged in Chile, it was in her blood. But she longed for Sam and her longing nearly choked her. She compared the childish infatuation of long ago with the mature love she now felt for him and deduced that her marriage to Torquil had been vital. Without it she would have continued to search for her father in the arms of other men, like Torquil, and she would never have realised that she was a victim of her own making and always had been. Sam had liberated her and she hadn't even thanked him.

When the air hostess came up the aisle with the newspaper Federica took one just to have something to look at, even though she didn't understand the Spanish. She flicked it open and glanced at the first page, relieved to be able to concentrate on something other than her tormented thoughts of Sam. When she saw a photograph of the frozen body of a young Inca girl discovered in the Peruvian Andes she caught her breath and sat up in astonishment.

She turned to the man sitting beside her and asked him if he spoke English. When he replied that he did, she asked him if he would be very kind and translate for her. He was only too happy to engage in conversation with his pretty neighbour and began to read it out loud.

Federica bit her thumbnail as she listened. The mummy was that of a young woman, preserved by the cold conditions of the mountains for five hundred years. She wore a fantastically elaborate cloak made out of the most intricate weave, her hair was still studded with crystals and on her head she still had the remnants of a headdress made of white feathers. It was believed that she had been sacrificed to the Gods. When the man handed her back the paper Federica studied the face of the young girl. She relived the horror of her last moments in the words of her father's story.

'Clasping the box to her breast she was dressed in exquisitely woven wools, her hair plaited and beaded with one hundred shining crystals. Upon her head was placed a large fan of white feathers to carry her into the next world and frighten the demons along the way. Wanchuko was unable to save her.'

After a few attempts to make conversation the man realised that she wasn't going to respond and returned to his book, disappointed. Federica sat staring into the face of Topahuay as if she had seen the Resurrection itself. All these years she had believed the legend in spite of her reasoning that had told her it was a myth. She smiled to herself. Perhaps the butterfly box was magic after all.

Sam woke up early due to the restlessness in his soul and walked across the cliffs with the dogs. He could see the first stirring of spring in the emerging buds that endowed the forest with a vibrancy which seemed to waft through the branches like green smoke. But it did little to lift his heavy spirits. He pulled his coat around his body but the cold came from within and he shivered. He hadn't heard from Federica since she had left the week before and he had the terrible premonition that she might never come back. After all, she had said so herself, there was nothing to keep her here. The potency of those words was in no way diminished by the frequency with which he thought of them and they still managed to debilitate him.

He still hadn't thought of anything to write. It had been years, literally, since he had quit his job in London to make use of his creativity, as Nuno had put it. But his creativity was barren. He had tried once or twice to begin a novel but his mind had drifted to Federica, which had only resulted in the most morose poems about unrequited love and death. So he had picked out books from Nuno's library and instead of writing he had sat in the leather chair and read. Anything rather than surrender his thoughts to the rapacious appetite of his anguish.

Alone on the cliffs in the fragile light of dawn he considered his options if Federica was never to come back. He had to face it. He couldn't allow himself to wallow in self-pity indefinitely. After all, wasn't that what he had taught her by way of the notes? Like a doctor he wasn't too keen on his own medicine. He had to pull himself up, decide on something to write, buy a cottage of his own, perhaps a dog and a pig and crawl out of his self-imposed exile.

Federica's journey wouldn't have been as long or arduous if it hadn't been for her feverish impatience that caused her chest to compress with anxiety and her head to ache by the force of her will attempting to change things that it couldn't. The plane was forced to circle Heathrow Airport for twenty minutes before finally landing with a bump. She felt sick from worry as much as from the relentless spiralling of the plane, then hiccuped all the way on the tube to the railway station. It was cold and drizzly, the usual grey skies of London – a cheerless spring. She just managed to catch a train where she sank into a seat by the window and watched the monotonous grey city outside. She closed her eyes for a moment only to open them a few hours later stiff and groggy to find herself passing through the familiar countryside of Cornwall.

As her eyes traced those verdant fields she recalled her long walks with Sam and wondered what she was going to say to him when she saw him. She hoped he'd have returned from Scotland. She knew she'd go out of her mind with frustration if he wasn't at home. Silently she began to rehearse the conversation. 'Sam, there's something I have to tell you . . . no, that's too crass . . . Sam, I love you . . . no, I couldn't, I just couldn't . . . Sam, I realised the notes were from you and came back especially . . .

no, no, horrible . . . Sam, I can't believe it's taken me this long to realise that I love you . . . no, I can't, I just can't be so blunt. Oh God!' She sighed, 'I don't know what I'm going to say.'

As the train cut through the Cornish countryside Federica watched the cows grazing in the fields, the charming white houses and small farms and thought how incredibly beautiful it was in spite of the grey skies and rain. She fantasised about living in a small cottage with Sam, perhaps a dog or two, overlooking the sea and she smiled inside. She didn't care for wealth or Bond Street. She didn't care if she never went shopping again. She had certainly had enough handbags and shoes to know just how empty they could be. She yearned to be wrapped in Sam's arms and nothing else mattered.

When the train finally drew up at the station she dragged her suitcase onto the platform and stood in the drizzle. She debated whether to go home to Toby's house, but her impatience drove her to climb into a taxi and head straight for Pickthistle Manor. As the car turned into the driveway her heart pounded in her chest anticipating the disappointment of finding him not there. She looked about for his car but it wasn't parked in its usual place in front of the house. She gulped back her edginess and jumped out of the taxi, instructing him not to wait. If Sam wasn't there she'd call Toby to come and collect her. Besides, it would be nice to see Ingrid. 'Goddammit,' she murmured, 'I'm fooling myself! If he's not there I just want to be in the house where he's been, sit in Nuno's study where he's sat, feel the echo of his presence in the air and wait.'

She strode into the hall and placed her bag on the marble floor. Then she glanced at herself in the gilt mirror that hung on the wall. She cringed and tried to tidy up her soaking hair and pinch some life into her pale cheeks.

'Sam, is that you?' Ingrid shouted from the landing.

'Ingrid,' said Federica hoarsely. 'It's me, Federica.'

'Fede, darling!' she cried happily, floating down the stairs in a long turquoise dress that reached to the ground. 'We didn't expect you back so soon.'

'Well, I arrived this morning,' she replied, casting her eyes about for Sam.

'You must be exhausted. Poor old you. Do you want a cup of tea or something to warm you up?' she suggested. Then she looked at Federica through her monocle, which enlarged her pale green eye so that it looked like the eye of a monstrous iguana. 'Darling, you're shivering. Really, you don't look very well at all.'

'I'm fine, thank you,' she insisted weakly. 'Is Sam about?' she asked, trying to sound casual.

'He's out with the dogs. He's been out all morning.'

Federica was unable to hide the smile that suddenly opened onto her face like a spring rose. 'Would you mind very much if I went to look for him?'

'You must borrow a coat or you'll die of cold. You won't be any good to Sam if you've died of cold, will you?' she declared, her red lips quivering with delight.

Federica felt the blood rise to her cheeks turning them pink with embarrassment. She followed Ingrid into the cloakroom and took the boots and sheepskin coat she offered her.

'This was Pa's. It's also one of Sam's favourites. If it doesn't keep you warm, Sam will. Try the fox path on the cliff. I imagine he's up there,' she said and watched Federica run outside. In her excitement she forgot to close the door. Ingrid hoped that in her excitement she'd forget to mention Scotland.

Federica ran through the rain not caring how wet she got. The coat made it difficult to run for it was heavy and cumbersome. She searched the cliff top with anxious eyes, scanning the trees and cliffs for any sign of the dogs or their master. 'Sam!' she shouted, but her voice was lost on the wind. 'Saaaam!' She stood helplessly, watching the sea crash against the rocks below and wondered whether he'd be mad enough to venture down to the beach. She recalled her dream and shuddered. Then a movement in the trees made her turn around. She squinted her eyes against the rain and put her hand up to shield her face. First she saw two

549

dogs then the grey figure of Sam in a long coat and hat. He stopped and stared at her. Unsure whether to trust his sight he too squinted and put his hand up to shield his face. 'Sam!' she shouted again.

'Federica?' he replied, and his voice was carried on the wind.

'Sam!' she shouted, walking towards him briskly.

The dogs leapt on her with their tails wagging their entire bodies with enthusiasm and their tongues flopping outside their salivating mouths, breathless and exhausted. She patted their sodden coats, happy that the rain on her face disguised her nervousness.

'Federica!' he called, approaching her. She looked up and blinked at him to clear the rain from her vision. 'When did you get back?' he asked in surprise.

'I—' she began, but the ardour caught in her throat and prevented her from speaking. She looked down at the dogs and patted them again because suddenly she didn't know what to do with herself.

Sam noticed that her hand was shaking. 'Are you all right?' he asked, stepping closer.

She nodded and raised her eyes. She placed her trembling fingers on her lips and swallowed. She wanted to tell him she loved him but all she could do was stare at him mutely while the emotion mounted in her chest.

Sam placed his hand on her arm. 'Did you come back for me?' he asked.

Federica recognised the hope in his voice and she nodded frantically. 'I love you,' she whispered but her voice was swallowed up by the wind. Sam cocked his head. 'I love you,' she repeated, grabbing the lapels of his coat and gazing into his grey eyes with longing. Sam needed no other confirmation of her devotion. He pulled her into his arms and kissed her dripping face. She felt the warmth of his mouth and the rough neglect of his face and closed her eyes so that nothing would distract her from his love.

⋆　　⋆　　⋆

When Sam made love to Federica in the small room in the attic of the house she realised that she was experiencing for the first time in her life the most intense physical expression of true love. He held her with confidence and gazed into her eyes as if unable to believe that she was really there, reciprocating feelings that he had hidden for so long. Every kiss was a demonstration of his affection, every caress delivered with loving hands. They laughed and talked and then when the weight of their feelings overcame them they cried. So many years of pining prevented Sam from falling asleep. All he could do was watch her soft face while she slept and mentally stroke her until the force of his thoughts penetrated her dreams and she smiled.

Federica opened her eyes onto a different world. She heard the barking of the dogs in the driveway below as the postman threw a couple of Bonios out of his window for them to run after, then made a hasty dash for the porch before beating them back to his car and slamming the door behind him. She heard the tyres on the gravel and then a couple of grating gear-changes as he sped out of the driveway. She stretched luxuriously as her eyes adjusted to the bright sunlight that streamed in through the gap in the curtains, illuminating the unfamiliar walls of a room she had only seen once before, when Molly and Hester had first introduced her to Marmaduke the skunk. Then with a blush she brought her hand up to her face and touched the hot afterglow of love that radiated from her cheeks and she smiled with happiness. She recalled his caresses, his kisses and then the joyous feeling afterwards, as she lay in his arms, that she had finally found love.

She turned to discover a small bunch of early bluebells on the pillow where he had slept, together with a worn brown book. She sat up and brought the flowers to her nose where the scent of spring and the taste of dew made her heart inflate with delight. Then she looked at the book. It was dog-eared and shabby. *The Prophet* by Kahlil Gibran. She opened the cover to discover that it was Nuno's own book with verses encircled in his own unsteady hand and comments written into the margins. She recognised the poetry as the source of the notes Sam had sent her. Then she noticed a bookmark and opened it where indicated. A few lines were highlighted in pencil. She read them carefully, then to fully understand their meaning she read them again.

> Beauty is life when life unveils her holy face.
> But you are life and you are the veil.
> Beauty is eternity gazing at itself in a mirror.
> But you are eternity and you are the mirror.

When Sam entered her room with a tray of breakfast Federica was clutching the bluebells to her nose and reading Nuno's book. She looked up and smiled at him, a smile at once tender and flirtatious. He placed the tray on the dresser and climbed onto the bed beside her. They didn't need to speak for their faces shone with feelings that they could never put into words. He drew her into his arms and knew that this time he would never let her go.

It was a few years before Federica Appleby rediscovered the butterfly box in the back of one of the cupboards in their cottage just outside Polperro.

Sam had successfully published his first book, *Nuno, Brought To Book*, and Federica was pregnant with their second child.

She pulled the box out and brushed the dust off the lid. With a sense of nostalgia grown sweet due to her own happiness and the passing of the years, she leant back against the wall and opened it. She was saddened to see the stones that had once lined the interior lying in a pile on the bottom of the box, exposing the raw wooden walls that once glittered with a magical splendour.

Ponderously, she lifted her eyes to reflect upon the past and saw to her delight a red and orange butterfly alight upon the windowsill. It paused a moment, as if in silent communication, then gently opened its wings, fluttered into the air and disappeared out into the sunshine.

If you enjoyed
THE BUTTERFLY BOX,
here's a foretaste of another
compelling Santa Montefiore novel,
THE FORGET-ME-NOT SONATA

Prologue

England, Autumn 1984

The sky was almost too enchanting for a day such as this. An October sky that blessed the countryside below it with a dazzling golden radiance as if the autumn trees and neatly ploughed fields had been set alight by God Himself to mark this great day of passing. Brazen strokes flamingo pink and blood red slashed the heavens in a bid to render them as impressive as possible while the dying sun descended slowly like lava, melting into the evening mists on the horizon. Nature was triumphant, but the humble soul of Cecil Forrester seemed quite undeserving.

Grace was the only one of Cecil Forrester's daughters who didn't cry at his funeral.

Alicia cried. She cried with the same sense of drama that characterised every other aspect of her life, as if she were permanently on a stage, her beautiful face always in the spotlight. She cried glittering tears and sighed long-drawn-out sobs that caused her black-gloved hands to tremble as she dabbed at her cheeks with an embroidered hanky. She was careful enough not to allow her display of grief to contort her features, expressing her emotions in the pretty quiver of her lips and in the gentle tilt of her head, enticingly obscured behind delicate black veiling attached to the brim of her hat. Leonora cried too, quietly. Not for the father she had lost, but for the father she had never had. The man in the coffin might just as well have been a stranger to her, a distant uncle perhaps or an old school teacher. He had never allowed her more intimacy than that. She looked across at her younger sister who watched impassively as the coffin was lowered into the tidy hole in the ground and wondered why she showed no emotions when out of the three of them she had the most cause to grieve.

Grace was more than ten years younger than her twin sisters. Unlike her siblings who had been sent away to be educated in England at the tender age of ten, Grace had grown up in the leafy English suburb of Hurlingham in Buenos Aires. But it wasn't due to the age gap that they felt they barely knew her, the many years of separation that had forged an insurmountable wall between them, but because Grace was different. As elusive as the garden fairies of their childhood, she was not of this world. Alicia said her ethereal nature was due to the fact that their mother had held onto her and spoiled her having suffered so much after they had been sent away, leaving her alone and adrift. But Leonora didn't agree. Grace was just made that way. Their mother had been right not to be parted from her. Grace would have wilted like a wild prairie flower in the cold English schoolrooms where she had sobbed tears of homesickness onto hard pillows.

Grace watched the coffin with little emotion as it was lowered into the ground against the exaggerated sobs and sniffs of her sister who had increased the volume for dramatic effect. It seemed all the more tempting to play the role on such a spectacular evening, beneath such a magnificent sky. Grace didn't judge her. She just watched with serenity knowing that her father wasn't in the coffin as everyone else thought. She knew because she had seen his spirit leave his body at the moment of his death. He had smiled at her, as if to say, 'So you were right all along, Grace.' Then accompanied by his deceased mother and favourite uncle Errol he had floated off into the other dimension leaving nothing behind but a wilted carcass. She was tired of telling them the truth. After all, they'd find out in the end when it was their turn. She shifted her eyes to her mother, who stood beside her with her soft face betraying a mixture of regret and relief and linked her fingers through hers. Audrey squeezed her daughter's hand with gratitude. Although Grace was now a young woman she had a purity and innocence that gave the impression that she was still a child. To Audrey she always would be.

To Audrey Grace was special. From the moment she was born in the hospital of The Little Company of Mary in Buenos Aires, Audrey knew she was different from her other children. Alicia had screamed her way into the world with characteristic impatience and Leonora had followed submissively in her wake, trembling in the face of such uncertainty. But Grace was different. She had slipped out of her mother's small body without any fuss, like a contented angel, and blinked up at her with a knowing smile that played upon her pink lips with a confidence that took the doctor so much by surprise his face flushed before the blood drained away altogether, leaving him ashen with fright. But Audrey wasn't surprised. Grace was celestial and Audrey loved her with an intensity that almost suffocated her. She held the tiny baby against her chest and gazed adoringly into her translucent face; surely the face of an angel.

To Audrey Grace was a blessing bestowed upon her by a compassionate God. Her hair was a wild halo of untameable blond curls and her eyes were like a deep green river that held all the mysteries of the world in their depths. She enchanted people and frightened them at the same time for she seemed to look right through them, as if she knew them better than they knew themselves. But she frightened no one as much as she frightened her own father, who did his best to avoid contact with this creature who was as foreign to him as a being from another universe. She possessed none of his qualities or physical features and was impervious to the force of his will and the might of his temper. She just smiled with amusement as if she understood his nature and the reasons he constantly fought against it. He had never understood her, at least not until the end. After all their differences he had suddenly smiled in the same way that she smiled, knowingly, almost smugly and embraced her with love. Then he had died, leaving an uncharacteristic grin on his face that had never been there in life.

Audrey released her daughter's hand and stepped forward, holding her silver head high with a dignity that had supported her through many tumultuous years, and dropped a single white lily into the grave. She whispered a hasty prayer then raised her eyes to the shrinking sun that descended behind the trees casting long black shadows over the churchyard. It was at that moment that her thoughts lost their focus and drifted nostalgically back to a time when love had blossomed with the jacaranda trees. Now she was old she would never love again – not in the way she had loved in her youth. Age had robbed her of such innocent expectations. Before the dark grave of her husband Audrey finally succumbed to the might of her memories and watched them rise up in her mind like ghosts. They shook themselves free of their bonds and suddenly she was a young girl again and her dreams were all shiny and new and full of promise.

Chapter One

The English Colony of Hurlingham, Buenos Aires 1946

'Audrey, come quick!' Isla hissed, grabbing her sixteen-year-old sister by the arm and tugging her out of her deckchair. 'Aunt Hilda and Aunt Edna are having tea with Mummy. Apparently, Emma Townsend has been discovered in the arms of an Argentine. You have to come and listen. It's a hoot!' Audrey closed her novel and followed her sister up the lawn to the clubhouse.

The December sun blazed ferociously down upon this little corner of England that resisted with all its might integration with those nationalities that had come before and fused into a nation. Like a fragile raft on the Spanish sea the English flew the flag and flaunted their prestige with pride. Yet the heady scents of eucalyptus and gardenia danced on the air with the aromas of tea and cakes in an easy tango and the murmur of clipped English voices and croquet echoed through the park against the thunder of Argentine ponies and the chatter of the gauchos who looked after them. The two cultures rode alongside each other like two horses, barely aware that they were in fact pulling the same carriage.

Audrey and Isla had grown up in this very British corner of Argentina situated in an elegant suburb outside the city of Buenos Aires. Centred around the Hurlingham Club where roast beef and steak and kidney pie were served in the panelled dining room beneath austere portraits of the King and Queen, the Colony was large and influential and life was as good as the cricket. Palatial houses were neatly placed behind tall yew hedges and English country gardens and joined together by dirt roads that led out onto the flat land of the pampa. The sisters would compete in gymkhanas, play tennis and swim and tease the neighbouring ostrich by throwing golf balls into his pen and watching in amusement as he ate them. They would ride out across the vast expanse of pampa and chase the prairie hares through the long grasses. Then as the sun went down and the clicking of the crickets rose above the snorting of ponies to herald the dying of the day, they would picnic with their mother and cousins in the shade of the eucalyptus trees. They were languorous, innocent times untroubled by the pressures of the adult world. Those pressures awaited their coming of age, but until then the intrigues and scandals, passed about the community in hushed voices over scones and cucumber sandwiches, were a great source of amusement, especially for Isla who longed to be old enough to create ripples such as those.

When Audrey and Isla wandered into the Club they became aware at once of the faces that withdrew from their cups of china tea and scones to watch the two sisters weave their way gracefully through the tables. They were used to the attention but while Audrey lowered her eyes shyly Isla held her chin high and surveyed the tables down the pretty slope of her imperious nose. Their mother told them it was because their father was a Chairman of Industry and a very important man, but Isla knew it had more to do with their thick corkscrew hair that reached down to their waists and glistened like sun-dried hay and their crystalline green eyes.

Isla was born fifteen months after Audrey and was the more striking. Wilful and mischievous, she was blessed with skin the colour of pale honey and lips that curled into a witty grin, which never failed to charm people even when she had done little to deserve their affection. She was smaller than her sister but appeared taller due to the joyous bounce in her step and the large overdose of confidence that enabled her to walk with her back straight and her shoulders broad. She relished attention and had adopted a flowing way of moving her hands when she talked, like the Latins, which never failed to catch people's eyes and admiration. Audrey was more classically beautiful. She had a long, sensitive face and pale alabaster skin which blushed easily and eyes that betrayed a wistfulness inspired by the romantic novels she read and the music she listened to. She was a dreamy child, content to sit for hours on the deckchairs in the grounds of the Club imagining the world beyond the insular one she belonged to, where men were passionate and unrestrained and where they danced with their loves beneath the stars amid the thick scent of jasmine in the cobbled streets of Palermo. She longed to fall in love, but her mother told her she was too young to be wasting her thoughts on romance. 'There will be plenty of time for love, my darling, when you come of age.' Then she would laugh at her daughter's dreaming, 'You read too many novels, real life isn't a bit like that.' But Audrey knew instinctively that her mother was wrong. She knew love as if she had already lived it in another life and with an aching nostalgia her spirit yearned for it.

'Ah, my lovely nieces!' Aunt Edna exclaimed when she saw the two girls approach. Then she leant over to her sister and hissed, 'Rose, they get prettier every day, it won't be long before the young men start coming. You'll have to watch that Isla though, she's got a naughty glint in her eye, to be sure.' Aunt Edna was a widow and childless but with typical British stoicism she managed to smother the tragedies in her life with a healthy sense of humour and satisfy her nagging maternal instincts by embracing her nephews and nieces as her own. Aunt Hilda stiffened and watched Audrey and Isla with resentment, for her four daughters were thin and plain with sallow skin and insipid characters. She wished she had had four sons instead, that way the odds on a good marriage would have been more favourable.

'Come and sit down, girls,' Aunt Edna continued, tapping her chair beside her with a fleshy hand made heavy with jewellery. 'We were just saying . . .'

'*Pas devant les enfants*,' Rose interjected warily, pouring herself another cup of tea.

'Oh, do tell, Mummy,' Isla pleaded, pulling a face at Aunt Edna who winked back. If she didn't tell them now she would later.

'There's no harm in relating this tale, Rose,' she said to her sister. 'Don't you agree, Hilda, it's all part of their education?' Hilda pursed her dry lips and fiddled with the string of pearls that hung about her scraggy neck.

'Prevention is better than cure,' she replied in a tight voice, for Aunt Hilda barely opened her mouth when she spoke. 'I don't see the harm in it, Rose.'

'Very well,' Rose conceded, sitting back in her chair with resignation. 'But you tell, Edna, it makes me too distressed to speak of it.'

Aunt Edna's blue eyes twinkled with mischief and she slowly lit a cigarette. Her two nieces waited with impatience as she inhaled deeply for dramatic effect. 'A tragic though utterly romantic tale, my dears,' she began, exhaling the smoke like a friendly dragon. 'All the while poor Emma Townsend has been engaged to Thomas Letton she has been desperately in love with an Argentine boy.'

'The worst is that this boy isn't even from a good Argentine family,' Aunt Hilda interrupted, raising her eyebrows to emphasise her disapproval. 'He's the son of a baker or something.' She burrowed her skeletal fingers into her sister's packet of cigarettes and lit up with indignation.

'The poor parents,' Rose lamented, shaking her head. 'They must be so ashamed.'

'Where did she meet him?' Audrey asked, at once moved by the impossibility of the affair and eager to hear more.

'No one knows. She won't say,' Aunt Edna replied, thrilled by the mysterious nature of the story. 'But if you ask me he's from the neighbourhood. How else would she have bumped into him? It must have been love at first sight. I've been told by a very reliable source that she would creep out of her bedroom window for midnight rendezvous. Imagine, the indecency of it!' Isla wriggled in her chair with excitement Aunt Edna's eyes widened with the fervour of a frog who's just spotted a fat fly. 'Midnight rendezvous! It's the stuff novels are made of!' she gushed, recalling the secret meetings in the pavilion that she had enjoyed in her youth.

'Do tell how they were discovered,' Isla pleaded, ignoring her mother's look of gentle disapproval.

'They were spotted by her grandmother, old Mrs Featherfield, who has trouble sleeping and often wanders around the garden late at night. She saw a young couple kissing beneath the sycamore tree and presumed it was her granddaughter and her fiancé, Thomas Letton. You can imagine her horror when she failed to recognise the strange dark boy who had his arms wrapped around young Emma and was . . .'

'That's enough, Edna,' Rose demanded suddenly, placing her teacup on its saucer with a loud clink.

'Dear Thomas Letton must be devastated,' Aunt Edna went on, tactfully digressing to satisfy her sister. 'There's no chance that he'll marry her now.'

'From what I hear, the silly girl claims she is in love and is begging her poor parents to allow her to marry the baker's son,' Aunt Hilda added tartly, stubbing out her cigarette.

'Good gracious!' Aunt Edna exclaimed, fanning her round face with the menu in agitation, but clearly savouring every detail of the affair.

'Oh dear,' Rose sighed sorrowfully.

'How wonderful!' Isla gasped with glee, wriggling in her chair. 'What a delicious scandal. Do you think they'll elope?'

'Of course not, my darling,' Rose replied, patting her daughter's hand in order to calm her down. Isla always worked herself up into a lather of excitement over the smallest things. 'She wouldn't want to bring shame upon her dear family.'

'How sad,' breathed Audrey, feeling the full force of the lovers' pain as if she were living it herself. 'How desperately sad that they can't be together. What will happen to them now?' She blinked at her mother with her large, dreamy eyes.

'I imagine she'll come to her senses sooner or later and if she's lucky, poor Thomas Letton may agree to marry her still. He's so fond of her, I know.'

'He'd be a saint,' Aunt Hilda commented, dismissing the girl with a swift sweep of her knife as she spread jam onto her scone.

'He truly would be,' Aunt Edna agreed, extending her arm across the table to help herself to a piece of Walkers shortbread. 'And she'd be very fortunate. There's a great shortage of men now due to the war, it'll leave an awful lot of young women without husbands. She should have had the sense to hold onto hers.'

'And the poor boy she's in love with?' Audrey asked in a quiet voice.

'He shouldn't have hoped,' Aunt Hilda replied crisply. 'Now, did you know Moira Philips has finally dismissed her chauffeur? I think they were right to do so considering there was a high chance that he was reporting their conversations to the government,' she continued in a loud hiss. 'One can only imagine the horror of it all.'

Audrey sat in silence while her mother and aunts discussed Mrs Philips' chauffeur. She didn't know Emma Townsend well for she was a good six years her senior, but she had seen her at the Club. A pretty girl with mousy hair and kind features. She wondered what she was doing now and how she was feeling. She imagined she was suffering terribly, as if her whole future was a bleak, loveless hole. She looked across at her sister who was now playing with her sandwich out of boredom; Mrs Philips' chauffeur was extremely dull compared with Emma Townsend's illicit affair. But Audrey knew that their shared interest in the scandal differed greatly. Isla was riveted by the trouble the girl had caused. The romantic, or tragic, elements of the story couldn't have interested her less. She delighted in the fact that no one could talk of anything else, that they all spoke with the same hushed voices that they adopted when talking about death and that they devoured each sordid detail with hungry delight before passing it on to their friends. But most of all the glamour of it enthralled her. How easy it was to rock their orderly lives. Secretly Isla wished it were she and not Emma Townsend who basked in the centre of such a whirlwind. At least she would enjoy the attention.

★   ★   ★

It was a good two weeks before Emma Townsend was seen at the Club. Like a forest fire the scandal spread and grew until she was wrongly accused of being pregnant by the gossiping Hurlingham Ladies. The Hurlingham Ladies consisted of four elderly women, or 'Crocodiles' as Aunt Edna wickedly called them, who organised with great efficiency all the events held at the Club. The polo tournaments, gymkhanas, flower shows, garden parties and dances. They played bridge on Tuesday evenings, golf on Wednesday mornings, painted on Thursday afternoons and sent out invitations to tea parties and prayer nights with tedious regularity. As Aunt Edna pointed out, they were the 'protocol police' and one knew when one had fallen short when the little lilac invitation failed to find its way to one's front door, though it was at times a relief not to have to think of an appropriate excuse to decline.

Audrey and Isla had spent the fortnight looking out for poor Emma Townsend. She hadn't appeared at church on Sunday, which infuriated the Hurlingham Ladies who sat in the pew with their feathered hats locked together in heavy discussion like a gaggle of geese, criticising the girl for not showing her face to the good Lord and begging His forgiveness. When Thomas Letton walked in with his family the entire congregation fell silent and followed his handsome figure as he walked up the aisle with great dignity, his impassive features betraying nothing of the humiliation that Audry was sure burned beneath his skin. The Hurlingham Ladies nodded in sympathy as he passed, but he pretended not to see them and fixed his eyes on the altar in front of him before settling quietly into his seat next to his mother and sister. Emma hadn't been seen at the polo either or at the picnic which followed, organised by Charlo Osborne and Diana Lewis, two of the Crocodiles, who spent the entire afternoon muttering that if she so much as showed her face at their event they would send her home in disgrace while secretly longing for her to appear to give them more to gossip about. Then finally after two long weeks she arrived on Saturday for lunch with her family.

Audrey and Isla sat in the lounge with their brothers and

parents and, of course, the indomitable Aunt Edna, when Emma Townsend crept in with her head bent, staring with determination at the floor in order to avoid catching anyone's eye. Audrey looked about as the chattering ceased and every eye in the room rose to watch the solemn procession file in and take their seats at a small table in the corner. Everyone, that is, except Colonel Blythe, who was too busy with his grey winged moustache buried in the *London Illustrated News*, smoking his Turkish cigarettes, to notice the silent commotion that made a small island out of him. Even Mr Townsend, a large-framed man with silver hair and woolly sideburns, seemed to swallow his indignation, choosing silence over confrontation which would normally have been his response at such a moment. He meekly ordered drinks and then turned his back on the rest of the community who were waiting like jackals to see what he would do next.

'Well,' Aunt Edna exploded in a loud hiss, 'so unlike Arthur not to growl at us all.'

'That's enough, Edna,' Henry chided, picking up a handful of nuts. 'It isn't our place to comment.'

'I suppose not,' she conceded with a smile, 'the Crocodiles do enough of that for all of us.'

'They'll be furious they're missing this.' Isla giggled and nudged her sister with her elbow. But Audrey couldn't join in the merriment. She felt desperately sorry for the family who all suffered so publicly along with their daughter.

Just when the Townsends' shame threatened to suffocate them a gasp of astonishment hissed through the room like a sudden gust of wind. Audrey turned around to see Thomas Letton striding across the floor with his chin jutting out with resolution. Isla sat up with her mouth wide open as if she were about to scream with excitement. Albert, hating to miss an opportunity to pay his sister back for years of teasing, grabbed a peanut and flicked it down her throat. She stared at him in surprise before turning as red as a beet as the nut caught in her windpipe and prevented her from breathing. Pushing her chair out with a loud screech she swept the glasses off the table where they shattered onto the floorboards causing everyone to avert their attention from Thomas Letton and the Townsend family to see what the disturbance was. Isla's bloodshot eyes rolled around in their sockets as she choked and waved her arms about in a frantic attempt to get help. Before Audrey knew what was happening, her father had grabbed Isla from behind, pulling her off the ground and wrapping his strong arms around her stomach, thrusting his wrists into her lungs, again and again. She spluttered and gasped, all the time turning redder and redder until the whole lounge had formed a circle around their table like a herd of curious cows, anxiously willing Henry Garnet to save his daughter from a hideous death. Rose stood petrified with terror as the life seemed to leave her little girl's body in agonizing spasms. Silently she prayed to God. Later she would praise Him for His intervention because with one enormous thrust the peanut was dislodged and the child gulped in a lungful of air. Albert collapsed into tears, throwing his arms around his mother with remorse. Aunt Edna rushed to embrace Isla as she lurched back from the brink of death and began to shake uncontrollably. The crowd of onlookers clapped and cheered. Only Audrey noticed Emma Townsend leave with Thomas Letton. It didn't escape her notice, either, that they were holding hands.

'Great Uncle Charlie died from choking,' Aunt Edna remarked solemnly when the clapping had died down. 'But it wasn't a peanut. It was a piece of cheese, a plain piece of farmhouse cheddar, his favourite. After that we always referred to him as Cheddar Charlie, didn't we, Rose? *Dear* Cheddar Charlie.'